THE IRON JACKAL

A TALE OF THE KETTY JAY

Coming soon from Chris Wooding and Titan Books

The Ace of Skulls: A Tale of the Ketty Jay
(August 2014)

THE IRON JACKAL

A TALE OF THE KETTY JAY

CHRIS WOODING

TITAN BOOKS

The Iron Jackal: A Tale of the Ketty Jay
Print edition ISBN: 9781781167960
E-book edition ISBN: 9781781167984

Published by Titan Books
A division of Titan Publishing Group Ltd
144 Southwark Street, London SE1 0UP

First edition: March 2014

1 3 5 7 9 10 8 6 4 2

A CIP catalogue record for this title is available from the British Library.

Printed and bound in the United States.

ONE

A NEEDLESS GUNFIGHT—ROOFTOPS—
HIS FINAL WORDS—FREY GETS KICKED IN THE
FACE A LOT—A LITTLE MISUNDERSTANDING

'On reflection,' Crake said to Frey, as they huddled behind an upturned table, 'this wasn't one of your better plans.'

'It's hardly the bloody time, Crake!' Frey snapped back. He ducked as a shotgun blast chewed away the edge of the stone-topped table, peppering his face with grit. Blinking and wiping his eyes, he checked on his crew. Malvery and Jez were pressed up against some pillars, which were decorated with an increasingly bullet-ridden snakes-and-lizards motif. Pinn crouched near a small ornamental fountain that trickled with water.

'I'm just saying,' Crake continued, as he reloaded his pistol, 'that maybe walking into a den of drug addicts while brandishing weapons and shouting wasn't the best way to go about things.'

'Tell you what, Crake. If I'm still alive in ten minutes, you can head up the inquiry. How's that?'

'My point is…' Crake replied, then cringed as another volley of bullets chipped along the tiles and turned a nearby cushion into a cloud of feathers. 'My point is, I've noticed a certain lack of healthy cowardice in you recently, Cap'n. And I'm concerned it's going to get someone killed before long. Specifically, me.'

'Well, we can't have that, can we?' said Frey. 'Can we talk about this later, though? I'm trying not to die.'

There was a lull in the gunfire. Frey took the opportunity to snatch a quick look at the room. The den was like a cross between an exotic temple and a whore's bedroom. Pillars and statues gave the place a certain serene gravity that was ruined by the overstuffed settees and gaudy decor. Complex pipes sat in the centre of round stone-topped tables, which had thankfully turned out to be bulletproof. Patterned screens separated off private areas. The air was fogged with sweet smoke, which was making Frey feel a little dizzy and ever so slightly euphoric. Most of the smokers and den attendants had fled when the gunfire started, but there were still some Samarlan addicts huddled in the corners of the room, saucer-eyed and gibbering. Their evening had gone seriously wrong.

Ashua Vode was on the far side of the den, shooting at them from cover and being generally uncooperative. There were four men with her, all Vards. Mercs, Frey reckoned. Two were with Ashua behind the drinks bar, one behind an upturned settee, one behind a pillar.

'We just want to talk, Miss Vode!' he called. 'No one has to get hurt!'

She gave a cynical laugh. 'You can talk to my revolver, if you like.'

'We're not here to kill you!'

'Sure you're not! And I suppose Jakeley Screed didn't send you, either.'

'I don't even know who—' he began, then ducked as the man behind the pillar took a shot at him. Malvery fired his lever-action shotgun and the merc's outstretched hand exploded in a red splash of blood and gristle. He lurched back into cover, screaming at the top of his lungs.

'Real friendly,' called Ashua from her hiding place. 'Quite the pacifist, aren't you?'

'Oh, piss off,' Frey said. 'He shot first.'

'Kedley! You okay? Kedley, mate?' someone was shouting.

The man who had just lost his hand could only howl.

'You rotting bastards!' A merc popped up from behind the bar, a revolver in both hands, firing wildly. Frey kept his head down, waiting for him to run out of bullets. The moment he did, there was a sharp crack from Jez's rifle. Frey peeped out in time to see him stumble back against the shelves behind the bar, a ragged hole just under his nose. He collapsed in a noisy avalanche of smashing bottles.

'You're not doing much to change my mind, here!' Ashua called.

Frey didn't bother to answer. Ashua was on edge, possibly high and, despite her bravado, she was clearly terrified. Why else had she surrounded herself with hired guns? She was expecting someone to come after her. Nothing Frey said would make a difference.

Maybe he should have been a bit more subtle. Getting into a

needless gunfight wasn't the smartest thing he'd done today. He'd just wanted to make an entrance. He'd planned to stride in there at the head of his crew and awe the room. But the mere sight of them had sent Ashua and her men reaching for their guns, and they'd opened fire before Frey could say a word.

He took a moment to size up his opponents, looking for an advantage. He'd only caught a glimpse of Ashua before the gunfight began. Despite having plenty of attitude, she didn't look like much. She was slight and boyish and surprisingly young, with short hair that was a muddy shade of ginger. She wore shabby mechanic's trousers covered in pockets, and a pair of battered boots. There was an elaborate tattoo surrounding her left eye, a swirling, branching pattern that spread along her upper cheek and curled onto her brow. The tattoo and her accent pegged her as a street rat from the bombed-out slums of Rabban. What he couldn't understand was what she was doing here, in the back streets of Shasiith, a city in the Free Trade Zone of Samarla.

Then again, he was beginning to wonder what he was doing here himself.

The mercs were easier to figure out. They hadn't been in Samarla long: they weren't tanned enough to be expatriates. She'd probably found them in a bar, drinking away the profits of their last assignment. The way they fought marked them as enthusiastic rookies, not hardened pros. They were low-lifes. And Frey could deal with low-lifes.

'Hey!' he shouted from behind his table. 'Fellers! One of you is dead, and there's another who'll have to scratch his arse left-handed for the rest of his life. That leaves two of you who can shoot. There's five of us. And we're better with our guns.' He paused for them to digest the situation, and so they could listen to their friend sobbing from behind the pillar. 'You're not gonna be able to spend that girl's money when you're dead.'

'You shut your mouth!' Ashua shouted back, before yelling at the mercs: 'He'll kill us all if he gets the chance!' But nobody was firing any more, and Frey knew he had her companions' attention.

'My name's Captain Darian Frey,' he said. 'You might have heard of me.'

He waited. Just when the silence was becoming embarrassing, a gruff voice spoke up from behind the bar. 'I heard of you. Captain of the *Ketty Jay*. Recognised you from the broadsheets.'

Frey felt a glow as his ego warmed up.

'Don't talk to him!' Ashua snapped. 'He's out to trick you!'

'I heard of 'im too,' said the merc behind the settee. 'He took on the Manes at Sakkan. And that fat one with the walrus moustache is the crazy doctor.'

There was the boom of a shotgun, and the edge of the settee blew off. The merc squeaked and crushed himself into a ball.

'Malvery! Settle down!' Frey barked.

'Sorry, Cap'n,' Malvery said. 'Accident. Must be these fat fingers of mine.'

'Now, everyone be nice!' said Frey. 'Here's the deal, fellers. You can put down your guns and walk out of here. Maybe you'll give up your payday, but ask your friend there without the hand if it's worth it. We just want to talk to Miss Vode.'

'No one's giving up! We'll die first! Right, boys?' said Ashua.

In response, a pair of pistols skidded across the floor from behind the settee. The remaining merc lifted a shotgun into sight and lobbed it over the counter of the bar.

'You bunch of chicken-arse traitors!' Ashua screamed, close to hysteria. Then she sprinted towards a door at the back of the den. Pinn sprang up and aimed his pistol, but Jez lunged over and grabbed his arm.

'We want her alive, remember?' Jez said. 'She can't talk when she's dead.'

'*You* talk and *you're* dead,' Pinn sulked, which, Frey had to concede, was a fair point.

'Cap'n,' said Malvery. 'She's getting awa—'

'I *know*!' he yelled. He'd been torn between chasing after her and the fear of running out into the open, in case the mercs had more guns. Malvery's prompt was the spur he needed. His pride wouldn't let him cower; not after they'd recognised him from the broadsheets.

'Cover me!' he shouted, and came out from behind the table at a run.

Malvery bellowed at the mercs. 'Keep your damn heads down if you don't want 'em blown off your shoulders!'

The mercs obeyed. Not many people argued with Malvery at full volume.

Frey pursued Ashua through the door, and found himself at the bottom of a square stairwell, warm and dim. He could hear Ashua's boots echoing above him as she ascended.

The stairwell was tight, built around a hollow centre. Several storeys above, evening light filtered down from a squat, open-sided tower. Frey caught glimpses of movement above him: a bare arm, a flash of ginger hair. At one point, Ashua stopped, having heard his footsteps. She looked down the stairwell.

'Bugger off and stop following me!' she shouted, and fired a few shots into the gloom. Frey pressed himself against the wall until he heard her boots tapping upwards again.

By the time he got to the top he was out of breath, and the heat had increased noticeably. The tower was little more than a cap for the stairwell, with an arched doorway leading out onto the flat roof of the building. Ashua was already some distance away.

'Hey!' Frey called. 'I need to talk to you!'

She swung around with a sarcastic and slightly desperate chuckle. 'I told you,' she said, 'you can talk to this!' Backing away, she raised her revolver, and squeezed off two more shots. The third time she pulled the trigger, the hammer fell on an empty chamber.

Frey waited a moment in the shelter of the stairwell, suspecting a trick. She pulled the trigger a few more times, more in hope than expectation, then shoved the revolver back into the waistband of her trousers. She looked around for a way to escape. There wasn't one.

Frey stepped slowly out into the open. The sun was low in the foreign sky, painting the horizon in seething shades of red and yellow and purple. A landscape of rooftops spread out around him, a massive, stunning clutter of balconies and spires. Domes shone gold in the evening light. In the distance, a hexagonal stadium reared above its surroundings, rising from a sea of tumbledown apartment buildings. Most of the roofs were flat and strewn with junk: weary chairs, bits of boxes and washing lines. The one he was standing on had a chicken coop built from wood and strips of beaten metal. Long shadows reached through the surly heat, stretching across a scene of grubby magnificence.

The city of Shasiith.

Ashua was backing away towards the edge of the roof. Frey advanced, one hand held out to calm her, the other holding his pistol by his side.

'I'm not going to hurt you,' he said. 'I just need some information.'

'Right,' said Ashua, almost to herself. 'Information.' Then, suddenly, she turned on her heel, ran, and jumped.

'*Damn* it!' he snarled, and sprinted after her. Half of him hoped she'd lobbed herself off the roof to the street below – it would save him a chase – but she didn't seem the sort for suicide. There had been purpose in her jump. She'd landed somewhere out of sight.

As he got closer to the edge the adjacent building came into view, its roof lower than the one he was on. He saw Ashua racing away, and accelerated. He had the bit between his teeth now. He was going to catch her.

The width of the street between the buildings only became apparent at the very last moment. It was narrow by Vardic standards, but it still seemed way too far to jump. Below him, people were crammed into a dirty and colourful market. They seemed very small, and very far away.

In that moment he almost faltered. His instincts howled at him to brake. He ignored them.

For a single horrible second, he was flying and falling at the same time. Then he hit the rooftop, harder than expected. His legs half-buckled, but he stumbled forward and somehow managed to keep his feet.

'Just gonna hurt her a *little* bit,' he promised himself.

There was a sturdy plank bridge linking this rooftop to its neighbour. Ashua scampered across it and stopped at the far end. Frey saw her struggling to prise the planks away. Sensing the opportunity to make up ground, he ran harder, lungs stinging and his scalp wet with perspiration. She wasted precious seconds before giving up and fleeing again.

Frey reached the plank bridge and crossed before he could think better of it. He couldn't help looking down as he did so, and caught another terrifying glimpse of the crooked market lanes, people and animals far below. But it was only a glimpse, and then he was back on safe ground again.

There was a tumbledown shed ahead of him. A goat was poking its head out through a gap, chewing on a thin plant that had taken root in the cracks of the rooftop. Ashua was just vanishing round the corner. He put on a burst of speed and pursued her.

When he turned the corner, she was waiting for him.

He skidded and ducked as she swung a broken length of wood at his head. It crashed into the side of the shed, bounced out of her hands and fell across his back.

It took both of them a moment to realise that she'd missed. She reacted faster than he did, and slipped away just before he could grab her. He followed, close on her heels, as she raced towards another rooftop. This time the building was pressed flush against its neighbour, its edge a metre higher. Ashua sprang up at it and began to scramble over. Frey caught her legs before she could.

'Get off me!' she cried, as Frey tried to drag her back down from the ledge. She thrashed like a cat in a bag. He tried to keep hold of her, but he was only using one hand, since the other was holding a gun. She got a foot free. Frey knew what was coming next. The inevitability of it was disheartening.

'I just—' he began, but was interrupted by a boot being driven into the side of his head.

'— want—'

Kick.

'—to talk!'

The third kick dislodged him, and she was gone in a scrabble. He staggered away, dizzy, blinking to clear the stars from his eyes.

'What is it with women and kicking me in the face?' he asked himself. He wiped his lips with his sleeve and spat blood. 'Oi!' he yelled at Ashua. 'Get back here!'

She gave a little scream of exasperation as she saw him clambering over the ledge. 'I'm not going to talk to you! Haven't you taken the hint yet?'

He stood up, sweaty and soaked and in a considerable amount of pain, but doing his best to look defiant anyway. 'I'm a slow learner,' he said.

Ashua's eyes went wide. 'Amazing,' she said. 'Is that your comeback? You're stupider than I thought.'

'How stupid did you think I was?'

'Slightly less stupid than I do now.'

Frey couldn't think of an adequate response to that. 'Look,' he said, catching his breath, 'how long is it gonna take you to realise that I'm *not trying to hurt you*?'

'But you make such a convincing case, having shot two of my

bodyguards. You're still carrying a pistol, I notice. And there's another pistol and a cutlass in your belt.'

'How about I put them on the floor? Would you stop being so bloody skittish if I did?'

'I might. Try it and see.'

Frey took out his weapons and laid them down. It was all he could do to keep his temper under control. His lip was swelling, and his face was going to bruise. That meant he was going to look ridiculous for the next few days, and Frey was a man who didn't like to look ridiculous. It pricked his vanity. His good looks were the one thing he'd been able to rely on all his life. The thought of having them marred, even temporarily, scared him. And besides, his face was really starting to hurt.

When he was done, Ashua eyed the weapons. 'Now take three steps back,' she said, shooing him away.

He took three steps back. She nodded in satisfaction, turned and bolted.

Frey swore the foulest oath he could think of, started to run after her, then stopped. He wasn't leaving his cutlass behind, that was for damn sure. It was his most precious possession after the *Ketty Jay*: a daemon-thralled blade given to him by Crake, which fought with a mind of its own. He gathered up his weapons as fast as he could, jammed them in his belt, and set off again.

By now Ashua had sprung across to the next rooftop. As he got closer he saw there was a set of zigzagging stone steps cut into the side of the building. Ashua began scampering down them. If she got to street level, he'd lose her in the market.

He reached the edge of the building and jumped.

The moment his feet left the roof, he knew he was going to fall short. Heat and fatigue had robbed his legs of their strength. 'Oh, *shiiiit*!' he wailed. He'd always suspected they would be his final words, but he'd imagined himself delivering them in a slightly more masculine fashion.

He crashed into the edge of the rooftop, bounced off, and plunged towards the street. There was an instant of tumbling, of rushing air and overwhelming terror. Then he collided with something soft which wrapped around him, folding him in bright colours. It only held him for a heartbeat before something snapped and he was dropping again.

He fell onto a second soft barrier, which snapped in turn, and then he hit the ground with an almighty crash, although happily with a lot less force than he'd expected.

He lay where he'd landed, stunned. He was enveloped in a cocoon of tough fabric. Everything hurt. He couldn't quite believe he was still alive to enjoy the pain.

Voices in a foreign tongue were hissing and shouting all around him. Hands reached in, pulling away the fabric. An awning. He'd been caught by a couple of them on the way down. Enough to slow his fall. Enough to save his life.

Lucky, lucky bastard.

People crowded in on him, some angry, some concerned. Dakkadians, with their broad, pale faces, light hair and narrow eyes. Samarlans, with elegant features and skin black as pitch. He tried to untangle himself from the awning. The onlookers helped him up. Some were rougher than others.

Piles of earthenware pots surrounded him. Many of them were smashed. He ran his hand through his hair and looked about in a daze. He'd landed in the middle of a stall. The narrow strip of sky above him was almost closed out by awnings, but despite the shade the market was stiflingly hot. The air was heavy with churned-up dust and the babble of traders and customers.

An old, thin Samarlan – presumably the owner – began to berate him, wagging a finger in his face. Other people started arguing amongst themselves. None of it was in Frey's language, so he didn't pay much attention. He was still getting over the shock of the fall.

Then his gaze found Ashua, and he remembered his purpose.

She was running down the last flight of stairs to the ground, a dozen metres away. As if she sensed that she'd been spotted, she looked over her shoulder, directly at him. His mind sharpened to a hot, angry point. She'd nearly killed him. Her expression turned fearful as she saw the look on his face.

Suddenly the pain didn't matter. The exhaustion and the shock fell away. He was going to *get* her.

The store owner grabbed his arm to stop him escaping. He had his cutlass out in a flash, holding it to the old man's throat.

'I'm not in the mood,' he said.

The old man glared at him hatefully, but Frey's eyes were harder still and the old man let him go. The crowd backed away, seeing he was dangerous. He retreated a few steps to make sure no one was going to come for him, then turned and headed off after Ashua.

He pushed his way through the swelter, shoving people aside when they weren't quick enough to get out of his way. His body twinged and protested with every step as new bruises made themselves known. Roaming chickens scattered at his feet. Robed Dakkadians and finely-clad Samarlans passed by in a lurid blur. He almost tripped over a blind man of the untouchable caste, who raised a gnarled hand and a white-patterned face towards him as he passed.

Ashua was ahead of him, her ginger hair drawing his eye among the black and blond of the locals.

They turned into a lane which had been roofed with rough planks, creating a gloomy tunnel lined with stalls. Sharp sunlight beamed between the gaps in the planks, striping the citizens that bustled along beneath them. The crowd had thinned out here, to make space for a huge beast of burden. It was a leathery desert monster, all tusks and horns and armour, shambling through the dim world of the market. Two robed handlers, Samarlan nomads, walked in front of it, carrying pointed prods.

As Ashua hurried past she snatched a prod from one handler's grip and shoved it hard into the beast's hind leg. It bellowed, rearing and stamping, surprised by the pain. People began to scream and flee, piling over themselves in their efforts to get clear. Frey was almost knocked over in the stampede, but he rallied and fought doggedly through the pack. The nomads tried to calm the beast, which snorted and swiped its head at anyone within reach. Two Daks pulled an unconscious Samarlan out of its way before he could be trampled. Frey pressed himself close to the wall and edged along until the danger was behind him.

She'd gained ground on him again, but she was tiring now. He could see it in the set of her shoulders. When she tried to push through the people in the market they pushed back more often than not. She wasn't as strong or as forceful as he was. The crowd was hampering her more than him.

He found a surge of energy, inspired by fury, and forged on.

Suddenly, the market spat them out into the open, and he found himself on a street that ran alongside a river. The city fell away towards the water in uneven tiers. Temples stood on the banks, their crowded steps descending into the murky flow. People swam among the cows and beasts that waded in the shallows. Women washed their clothes on the shore. Several hulking bridges spanned the river, cluttered with buildings both elaborate and rickety. The sun glittered redly on the wavelets, throwing a dazzling streak across the water.

On another day, Frey might have been impressed with the spectacle. But his whole world had narrowed to a single purpose, a bloody-minded need to catch this damned woman who had caused him so much trouble. Ashua was running along the riverside, with a low wall to her left. She was clutching her ribs, carrying a stitch, and she could barely manage more than a jog. Frey was still riding the adrenaline from his fall, and he renewed his effort, sensing the end was near.

She looked over her shoulder to see how close he was. As she did so, a Samarlan boy wheeling a small cart emerged from the alley ahead of her. She crashed into it, sending fruit and bags of seeds rolling and skidding everywhere. Before she could get back to her feet, Frey was on her. He seized her by the collar, threw her onto her back and pinned her to the ground, his cutlass across her throat. The boy yelped and fled into the alley.

For a long few seconds, they stayed like that, he on top of her, faces inches apart, both of them sweaty and gasping for breath. Frey, still scared and shaken from his brush with death, wanted to exact revenge for what she'd put him through; but now it came to it, he couldn't think how. He was trembling with exhaustion. He was also aware that there was a young female beneath him, which was a good thing more often than not. The feelings that provoked diluted his anger a little.

She gave him a nervous smile. 'Well,' she said. 'This is nice.'

'Can we talk now?' he asked, in carefully measured tones.

'You're really not going to kill me?'

'No.'

'Jakeley Screed didn't send you?'

'Never heard of him.'

'Oh,' she said. 'I feel a bit of an idiot, now.'

'You should.'

'That's, er, one man dead and another man maimed because of that little misunderstanding.'

'Not to mention the fact that I *fell off a building*!' Frey was unable to keep a note of strangled rage out of his voice.

'Yes,' she said. 'You don't look too bad, though, considering.'

'It hurts,' he said. 'A lot.'

'Sorry.' She looked down her nose at the cutlass. 'Could you get off me? I won't run away again.'

'If you do,' said Frey. 'I swear I'll kill you so hard your entire family will die from the shock.'

'You're a little late for that,' she said. 'But I get the point.'

He released her, stood up and stepped back. She got unsteadily to her feet as he put his cutlass away. He pointed meaningfully at the pistols in his belt.

'Yeah, yeah. I see 'em,' she said. She staggered over to the low wall that separated the street from the river bank, and leaned against it. The Samarlan boy, judging that the danger had passed, scampered out of hiding to collect the spilled fruit and seeds. He loaded them quickly into his cart and wheeled it away.

'Right, then,' said Ashua. 'What was it you wanted?'

TWO

ASHUA'S VOCABULARY—FREY IS RECOGNISED— NEGOTIATIONS—OUT ON THE TOWN— PINN MAKES AN ANNOUNCEMENT

Frey pushed his way into the tavern, and let the heat and smell and noise enfold him. The room was crowded with men, mostly Vards, with a few clusters of young Samarlans and Dakkadians brave enough to mix with foreigners. The air was muggy with sweat and the fumes from pipes, cheroots and roll-ups. Shutters had been thrown open, looking out over the street, but the night was thick and still and there was little wind. Conversation was conducted at shouting pitch. Gas lamps lit the corners, fending off the gathering shadows.

He took a deep, contented breath. Taverns weren't the most fragrant of places, but to Frey they meant happiness, good humour and good times. The company of friends. A place where you didn't have to care. Walking into a lively tavern felt like coming home.

The others followed him in. Malvery, who let nothing stand between him and his grog, pushed past Frey and began muscling his way to the bar. Crake and Pinn trailed in his wake.

Jez, who'd stayed by his side, surveyed the place. 'You really do pick 'em, Cap'n,' she said distastefully.

'I used to hang out here all the time when I was sixteen,' Ashua put in.

Frey gave her a curious look. 'When was that? Yesterday? How old are you, anyway?'

'Younger than you,' she replied.

'Well, you certainly don't look a day over thirty.'

'You do. Many, many days.'

He raised an eyebrow at Jez. 'She's a vicious little sprite, isn't she?'

'Kids,' Jez commiserated.

Ashua rolled her eyes. 'Are you done with the condescension? You're boring me, and I'm busy.'

'You're from Rabban, right? Out of the slums?' Frey asked, as they made their way through the tavern. 'Where'd you learn a word like *condescension*?'

'I had a good teacher,' Ashua replied, and something in her tone told Frey not to push it any further.

'Hey! It's Cap'n Frey!'

Frey turned to see a grizzled, wiry-looking man grinning eagerly at him.

'You are, ain't ya?' the man persisted. 'I'd recognise that mug anywhere! Even with all them bruises on it!'

One of his friends had joined him now, and was squinting at Frey like a jeweller studying a suspect diamond. After a moment, his face cleared and he beamed, showing a mouthful of crooked teeth.

'You're right!' he declared. 'Rot my socks, it is 'im! What 'appened to you?'

Frey delayed his response as long as he could, to milk their amazement to its limit. 'Have we met before?' he asked innocently, ignoring the question.

'Naw! I seen your picture!' cackled the first man. 'The hero of Sakkan, that's what they calls you! The man what took on the Manes to save—' He suddenly stopped, and his eyes widened. 'Wait a minute. Is that 'oo you're 'ere for? It is, ain't it?'

Frey gave them his best I-couldn't-possibly-say smile. 'Gentlemen,' he said, touching his forehead in a farewell salute.

'Oh, yes! Don't mind us, Cap'n. You got business, I see,' said his admirer, grinning again as he backed away. 'A treat to meet you. A real treat.'

'You too,' said Frey, with all the appearance of meaning it.

Ashua scoffed to herself, but Frey was too pleased to notice. He didn't think he'd ever tire of the thrill of being recognised. Ever since that reporter from the broadsheets had asked him to pose for a ferrotype, he could scarcely walk into a tavern without being accosted by drunken admirers. Even here, in Samarla. They all wanted to hear the tale of that day over Sakkan, when he'd chased the *Storm Dog* through a hole in the sky and found himself at the North Pole, the home of the terrible Manes. In a short few months he'd gone from a nobody to a minor celebrity. He still hadn't got used to the way people stared at him with awe, hung on his every word, and acted as if they were blessed when he deigned to sit with them.

Still, ridiculous as it all seemed, it was getting to be like a drug. He craved the attention. He liked to feel impressive. And it had other advantages, too. Frey had never been a man who needed much help to get women into bed, but since the whole incident at Sakkan it had become so absurdly easy that he almost felt sorry for them.

Thoughts of other women fled his mind as he rounded the bar and spotted the one he was here to meet. She was sitting in a large private booth, separated from the rest of the room by elaborately carved wooden dividers. Half a dozen burly pirates made sure none of the rabble got anywhere near her. She drank alone at a table, a thin, startling figure dressed in black with her skin and hair white as chalk.

Trinica Dracken, captain of the *Delirium Trigger*.

He recognised Balomon Crund among the guards, the *Delirium Trigger*'s bosun and Trinica's right-hand man. He was a stumpy, ugly fellow with a scarred neck and matted black hair. Frey nodded at him as he approached, and Crund nodded back, though not without a certain reservation. Trinica's crew were intensely protective of her.

'Just you and her,' he said, thrusting his chin at Ashua. 'Your navvie stays out here.'

Frey looked over at the bar, where Malvery was calling for booze with a bellow like a wounded ox. 'You want to wait with the others?'

'I'll stay here,' said Jez. 'Someone's got to keep an eye on you.'

The bodyguards parted to let Frey and Ashua pass. The dividers cut out some of the sound, and the gas lamp had been turned down to minimum, filling the booth with shadows. They sat down opposite Trinica. Frey tried not to wince as he manoeuvred his bruised body into the chair. He was acutely aware that he wasn't looking his best at the moment, but Trinica showed no sign of even noticing.

There were three mugs on the table. Trinica filled the empty ones from the bottle. Frey's eyes flickered to the silver ring she wore. She noted his attention, and regarded him with a black gaze. Contact lenses made her pupils unnaturally large, giving her a frightening aspect. Her hair had been hacked into short clumps. She looked like she'd recently escaped from an asylum.

Frey took a swig of his drink. It was rum. Good stuff, too.

Trinica's gaze switched to Ashua. 'Miss Vode,' she said. 'Rumour has it that you've been gathering men for a job.'

Ashua regarded the other woman for a moment, calculating. 'I was,' she said. 'But now one of them has pulp where his right hand used to be and another has an extra hole in his face. Not sure what happened to the others, but they're probably halfway to Vardia by now.'

Trinica looked at Frey and tutted. Frey tipped his mug at her in a salute. 'Yep. That was me. Can't make an omelette without breaking a few eggs.'

'Captain Frey and his crew will take the job,' Trinica said to Ashua, 'if you're willing to provide the details.'

'Him?' said Ashua skeptically.

'He did dispose of your men and bring you here,' said Trinica. A corner of her painted red mouth curved upward. 'Despite suffering an amusing amount of damage on the way.'

'He is pretty hard to get rid of,' Ashua conceded.

'Oh, I know that very well.'

Frey gave an exasperated snort. 'Ladies, how about we take care of business before you start ganging up on me? I've already had one beating today.'

Ashua sat back in her chair and folded her arms. 'How much do you know?' she asked Trinica.

'I know that you intend to hold up a train which is carrying a valuable Samarlan relic. I have a buyer in Vardia, who heard of the shipment and asked me to obtain that relic by any means necessary.' She sipped her rum. 'What I don't know is when or where the shipment is moving. And I believe that you do.'

'I've got my sources.' Ashua nodded at Frey. 'So what's your deal with him?'

'We go way back,' Frey said wryly. He put his feet up on the table.

'Let's just say he's more capable than he seems,' said Trinica. 'And I don't like to risk my own crew when I don't have to.'

'So you're doing her dirty work for her?' Ashua inquired of Frey.

'And getting paid handsomely for it,' Frey replied with a grin.

Ashua thought for a moment, looking from one to the other. Deciding if she could trust them.

'You know you can't use aircraft, right? It's outside the Free Trade

Zone. You try flying in daylight and the Sammie Navy will catch you and blow you out of the sky.'

'We understand you intend to use *a'rashni*.'

If Ashua was surprised that Trinica could speak Samarlan, she didn't show it. 'Yeah. Rattletraps. That was the plan.' She tapped her toes restlessly. 'I get fifty per cent of the buyer's price. On delivery to you.'

Trinica laughed. 'You get ten per cent, or my men will drag you into a back room and pull out your fingernails until you give up the information for free.'

'Thirty per cent.'

Trinica's face became cold. 'I don't think you heard me, Miss Vode.'

Ashua's nerve broke. 'Alright, ten,' she said with forced airiness. 'But I'll be there every step of the way to make sure I get my share.'

Trinica looked at Frey, who was tipped back with his hands behind his head in a position of easy recline. He groaned. 'Fine. I'll babysit.'

'You can arrange the vehicles?' Trinica asked Ashua.

'If you can front the funds.'

'I think we can manage that. Talk to my purser, Ominda Rilk. He's the Dakkadian over there.'

Ashua was suspicious. 'You sure you want a Dak involved in this? That bunch'll sell you to their masters faster than you can blink.'

'He's a third generation Free Dakkadian. His grandfather bought himself out of slavery. He's loyal to me, not the Samarlans.'

'If you say so,' Ashua replied with a shrug. She got to her feet. 'The shipment moves in four days. I'll be in touch.' With that, she left. Frey watched her depart.

'I like her,' said Trinica.

'You just like her because she booted me repeatedly in the face.'

'It is a point in her favour, I'll admit.'

Frey downed his rum and accepted a refill. He took a swallow and studied her. The woman he'd almost married. They'd been lovers a long time ago, and deadly enemies until recently. Now they were wary allies. Frey could never quite bring himself to trust her – it was in her nature to be treacherous – but he couldn't help wanting to be around her, either. He knew the woman behind the ghostly mask; he was drawn to her in a way he'd never been to anyone else. And he'd come to believe that she, in her own way, still held some of her old feelings for him.

'Your bosun doesn't like me much,' he observed.

'He's suspicious. He wonders why you've been paying so much attention to me lately.'

'He's jealous.'

'A little,' she said. 'He thinks you're a threat.'

'Am I?' he said slyly.

She rolled her eyes. 'Please.'

He leaned forward, his elbows resting on the table. 'You know, one day it'd be nice to meet up without all your chaperones hanging around.'

'I'm afraid that won't happen.'

'Don't trust yourself around me?'

'People would talk.'

'What's wrong with that?'

'You're a man, and I'm a woman,' she said. 'Your reputation would increase. Mine would suffer. I won't allow myself to be weakened because people think you bedded me.' Her eyes narrowed in faint amusement. 'Besides, I doubt your ego needs any more massaging.'

'It wasn't my ego I was hoping you'd massage.'

She gave him a despairing stare. 'I'm beginning to miss the days when we loathed each other.'

'Oh, come on. You still loathe me a *bit*.'

'It's difficult not to.'

He grinned, and there was a rueful acknowledgment in the smile she gave in return. She knew it would never be simple between them. There was too much history there, too much tragedy and regret. But Frey was content just to be near her and, for her part, she seemed content with the same. He knew what she'd been through in the years since he'd run out on their wedding. Those years had turned her from a carefree young woman into a dreaded pirate queen. That couldn't be wiped away in a few months.

But he'd wait. He had all the time in the world for her.

'Any idea what this relic is, or why your buyer wants it so bad?'

'I don't know, and you don't need to either. The relic will be enclosed in a case. You're not to open it under any circumstances. It might well be delicate, and the slightest damage could halve its resale value. Are we understood?'

'Yeah, yeah,' said Frey dismissively. 'What do I care about antiques anyway?'

She poured him more rum, then took some for herself. He picked up his mug and contemplated it idly.

'Who'd have thought that one day we'd end up working as partners?' he wondered aloud.

'It's a strange world indeed,' she replied noncommittally. But he thought, as she said it, that she was secretly glad.

'I prescribe another round!' Malvery declared, as they stumbled out of the bar onto the street. His thick white moustache was damp with grog and his round green glasses sat askew on his bulbous nose. Sweat glistened on his bald pate and trickled into the horseshoe of thinning hair that remained.

'As your cap'n,' Frey said, waving one finger grandly in the air, 'I order you all to take your medicine!' General cheers followed. He beamed foolishly, full to bursting with an expansive love for his fellow man, the consequence of two bottles of some unpronounceable local liquor that he'd shared with the crew after Trinica had left.

The streets of Shasiith were even busier at night, when the crushing heat of the day receded to bearable levels. Here in the heart of the city, the buildings that lined the streets were immense and extravagant in the lamplight. The thoroughfares were a snarl of carts and animals. People spilled across the road, heedless of the wheeled traffic. Merchants haggled loudly by street stalls. The air smelt of strange spices, cooking meat and rank sweat.

Everyone was on the move. Most of them were Dakkadians, but there were Samarlans here too. Some of the Samarlans travelled in motorised carriages of extraordinary design, or were carried in veiled howdahs by slaves. Others were shuffling beggars, their black faces marked with white patterns, the sign of the untouchable caste. Even the Dakkadians kicked the untouchables aside like dogs, or ignored them completely.

Frey and his crew blundered into another drinking den, this one full of locals who eyed them disapprovingly as they entered. The Dakkadian bartender evidently wanted them gone, and pretended not to speak Vardic. This didn't deter Malvery, who kept repeating himself ever louder and more slowly until the bartender gave in and poured from the bottles that the doctor pointed at. After that, they piled around a table in the corner and set to the business of getting properly out of their skulls.

They were in a giddy mood. Success was still a novelty, and every minor triumph was celebrated by a night on the town. Since their misadventures in Sakkan, Frey had been on a roll. Everything he did seemed to work out. Confidence was high. They were looking forward to spending the proceeds of the heist, instead of grumbling about the likelihood of getting shot.

Even Jez, who didn't drink, had picked up the mood and was merry. She'd been making an effort to involve herself more with the crew whenever she could, trying her hardest to fit in. Little Jez, always loyal, always efficient. Jez, her brown hair tied back with a strip of pipe lagging, looking perfectly comfortable in her baggy jumpsuit even though everyone else was sweltering. Jez, who was half-daemon, and who was dead by most people's standards.

Next to her was Crake, who seemed happier these days than Frey had ever known him. He was a handsome fellow, with a close-cut blond beard, aristocratic features and the glimmer of a gold tooth in his smile. In the past he'd always had a haunted look about him, but the shadow had lifted from his brow of late. Frey didn't know why, and he didn't want to know. He was of the opinion that a man's business was his own unless he chose to share it. It was something of an unwritten rule on the *Ketty Jay*. But he was glad that his friend had dealt with whatever was troubling him.

Crake was a smart man, highly educated and eloquent. At the other end of the intellectual spectrum was Pinn, who could be outwitted by a whelk. Pinn was stocky, ugly and stunningly dumb, but he was an incredible pilot and good fun to drink with. Every group needed a scapegoat, a lightning-rod for abuse. Pinn was the best kind of target, because he usually didn't realise they were making fun of him, and even when he did he forgot about it moments later. Right now he was barely coherent, his eyes drifting in and out of focus, swaying in his seat.

Frey felt a sudden, overwhelming surge of affection for all his crew. It was almost two years since Jez had come on board the *Ketty Jay* and completed the group. In that time, his rag-tag bunch of no-hopers had found a balance that had seen them rise from bottom-feeding freebooters to bar-room celebrities. He couldn't imagine what he'd do without them.

'A toast!' he declared suddenly, surging to his feet. 'To all of you! And Harkins and Silo, who can't be with us, on account of how one is scared of his own shadow and the other—'

'Cap'n…' Jez warned, glancing round the room meaningfully.

Frey swept the bar with a disparaging glare, suddenly annoyed by the presence of the locals, who were doing their best to ignore him. Sammies and Daks, any of which would attack Silo on sight. Murthians were considered dangerous animals in Samarla, fit only for back-breaking labour and concentration camps.

'Yeah, well, we know why Silo can't be out with us tonight,' he said, then rallied with a flourish. 'But he's here with us in spirit, or something! So, anyway, I just wanted to say…'

He fought for the words to express the warm feeling of camaraderie that had seized him, his gratitude to them all just for being here with him. But his head was too cloudy, and nothing came. Before he had a chance to recover, Pinn pounded his fist on the table, making them all jump.

'I've made a… a decision!' he slurred. He swept the table with a bleary gaze, for effect, then raised one finger. 'I'm gonna be a famous… a famous inventor.'

There was a pause, a perfect vacuum of incredulous shock, during which everyone stared at Pinn in amazement. Then, as one, they burst out laughing.

Indignation roused him from his stupor. 'I am!' he protested, but nobody could hear him. Malvery was holding his belly, tears rolling down his face. Between his helpless guffaws he pleaded for everyone to stop laughing, because he was going to burst his appendix if they didn't.

It took a full minute for everyone to calm down, by which time Pinn was in a black sulk, with a face like a thunderhead. Crake leaned forward over the table, hands folded under his chin in an attitude of intense interest.

'An inventor, you say?' he inquired. 'This wouldn't have anything to do with your absent sweetheart, would it? Whichever sweetheart it is; I lose track.'

''S only one woman for me,' Pinn said, narrowing his piggy eyes. But, since everyone was paying attention now, he drew something from his pocket and placed it delicately onto the table.

It was a small chrome egg on a pedestal. He tapped it, and it opened out into four quarters. Inside was a tiny clockwork bird in a cage, which began spinning around and making a feeble cheeping noise.

It was a trinket, a gewgaw from one of the local markets. The Samarlans loved their clockwork gadgets.

Pinn was mesmerised by it. 'Look at that,' he said. 'That's amazing.'

'What's amazing is that you paid money for that piece of junk,' said Malvery, still chuckling.

Pinn closed it up and snatched it away resentfully. 'Well, kicking around with you lot isn't getting me rich, is it? Gotta get rich. Can't go back to Lisinda till I do.'

'Emanda,' Crake reminded him.

'Yeah, her,' he waved in the air vaguely. 'Anyway, reckon I'll just invent something. Something… something no one's thought of yet. You lot won't be laughing then.'

'Well,' said Frey, 'since you hijacked my toast, here's to you. Professor Pinn, the inventor!'

And they cheered, and drank, and Frey thought that all was well with the world.

THREE

SIGHTSEEING—THE DUCHESS AND THE DAISY-CHAIN—GHOSTS AT HER SHOULDER—FLOODLIGHTS—A DECEPTION

The *Ketty Jay* groaned and shrieked as she lifted off her struts and began to rise above the landing pad. She was a solid, brutish thing with a humped back, short, downswept wings and a stumpy tail end: a hybrid cargo hauler and combat craft, built tough at the expense of beauty. With her belly lights shining, she ascended into the sultry night, her ballast tanks filling with ultralight aerium gas.

Crake watched from the cockpit as the landing pad fell away beneath them. The aircraft on the ground were all Vard or Yort in design: this was a pad reserved for foreigners. Samarlan Navy craft glided through the sky, blade-sleek predators underlit by the city glow.

Let's hope we don't have to tangle with any of them tonight, he thought.

Jez was in the pilot's seat. The Cap'n sat at the navigator's station, bruised and battered and looking generally dejected. Crake knew how much he hated letting anyone else fly his beloved aircraft.

It had been a few days since Frey's introduction to Ashua's boot, but his face had healed up quickly, although it was still a little lumpy and faintly discoloured. According to Malvery, the rest of him hadn't done so well. His back and ribs were a mass of yellow and purple from the fall he took. He winced whenever he moved.

Harkins hung by the door, pilot's cap scrunched up in nervous hands, his hangdog face animated by some internal distress. No doubt he was feeling lost without his Firecrow. The two fighter craft that normally travelled with the *Ketty Jay* had been left on the landing pad tonight.

Pinn and Harkins had taken some persuading to leave their craft in Shasiith. Pinn entertained the strange belief that he could fly by instinct alone; Harkins was terrified of being separated from his aircraft. The Cap'n had finally convinced them both by making them walk around blindfold and counting how many things they bumped into. Then he reminded them what would happen if they did that at three hundred kloms an hour. They would be travelling over unfamiliar terrain without lights, on a moonless night, in near total darkness. The only member of their crew who could fly like that was Jez, due to her inhumanly sharp vision.

Ashua was here too, leaning against a bulkhead with her arms crossed, keeping an eye on things. Crake found the young woman distasteful. She had a surly arrogance that bothered him. Someone from such an obviously poor background shouldn't carry themselves with that kind of aggressive confidence. It offended his sense of the order of things.

'There's... uh... there's not many aircraft about, are there?' Harkins ventured.

The question was addressed to Jez. He must have been plucking up his courage for several minutes before he dared speak to her. Crake felt rather sorry for Harkins. It was hard to watch him trying to get her attention. Everyone on board knew that he was sweet on Jez, except, apparently, Jez herself.

'There's not much aerium around since the embargo,' Jez replied, to Harkins' evident delight. 'What there is is reserved for the Navy. Everyone else uses road or rail.'

'That's the whole reason they opened the Free Trade Zone in the first place,' Ashua said. 'To make it easy to smuggle aerium in from Vardia.' She eyed the Navy craft in the distance. 'But once you get outside the Zone, they'll take you down hard.'

'Unless they don't see us,' said Frey. 'Which is pretty much the plan.'

'Yeah,' said Jez. 'We really don't want to be messing with the Sammie Navy if we can help it.'

Crake walked over to stand behind Jez, in the pilot's seat, as the *Ketty Jay* ascended and the city spread out beneath them. This was what he'd come to the cockpit to see. Darkness had swallowed the faraway mountains, the plains of yellow grass and the distant herds of unfamiliar animals that he remembered from the day they arrived. Shasiith was a cauldron of light below them, its muddled streets like shining veins. Sun-scorched domes and parapets cooled in the night, darkening to shadow as they rose. Buildings of breathtaking scale and complexity crowded together along the black line of the river. Dozens of bridges spanned the flow. There were buildings on the bridges with lights in their windows, a necklace of dirty stars reaching from one bank to another.

'Isn't that something?' he said, a smile touching the corner of his lips.

Jez murmured in agreement. He knew she'd get it. She was the only other member of the crew who had any appreciation for art and culture. While the rest had been propping up bars and fleecing the locals in gambling dens, Jez and Crake had been taking in the sights, visiting monuments, tasting delicacies and generally soaking in the atmosphere of Samarla. Jez was a guarded and closed-off sort, but she understood beauty and wonder.

Once he'd drunk in enough of the view, Crake headed out of the cockpit and into the passage that ran along the spine of the *Ketty Jay*. After a short way, a ladder ran up one side of the passage to a seat in the autocannon cupola on the *Ketty Jay*'s back. He stopped to look up, saw the bottom of Malvery's boots, and heard a glugging sound.

'Settled in already, Doc?'

Malvery's grinning face appeared, looking down between his legs. 'Cap'n wants me on the watch for any Sammies once we're out of the Free Trade Zone,' he said. He brandished a bottle of grog. 'Reckoned I might as well bring a friend, make a night of it.'

'See anything?'

'Got a fine view of the *Ketty Jay*'s arse end. I'd invite you up for a drink, but it's pretty cosy in here.'

'That's alright. I'm going to see Bess.'

'Give her my regards.'

'Will do.'

His quarters were half a dozen metres down the corridor, behind a sliding metal door that squealed on its rollers as he pulled it aside. The room beyond was cramped and bare, comprising a pair of small bunk-beds, a basin, a chest and a cupboard. It was as clean and tidy as he could make it, but it was still little more than a metal box to sleep in. Since he had these quarters to himself, he'd laid a board across the upper bunk and used it as a bookshelf and luggage rack. He picked a heavy, leather-bound book from the row of several dozen, tucked it under his arm, and went down into the cargo hold.

The belly of the *Ketty Jay* was cavernous in comparison to the upper deck. He was making his way down the steps when he heard a growing roar, and felt the gentle and insistent push of the *Ketty Jay*'s thrusters. He held on to a railing and listened as the lashed-down cargo creaked and shifted in the gloom.

The Rattletraps were secured side-by-side in the centre of the hold. The name was a local Vardic word to describe a Samarlan vehicle that most foreigners found hard to pronounce. Crake thought it perfectly suitable to describe the three armoured sand-buggies that Ashua had rustled up. They were grimy contraptions that looked like they hailed from some distant and uncivilised frontier. They had large, dusty tyres and sat on thickly coiled springs for suspension. Two of them had rotary gatling guns mounted on top of their roll-cages.

He eyed them uncertainly. Ashua would be driving one. Jez had volunteered to drive another. There wasn't much that Jez couldn't drive or fly, when it came to it. Apparently, she'd had experience with similar vehicles while working for Professor Malstrom, back before she was caught by a Mane.

Silo would be taking the third Rattletrap. No one knew *what* he had experience in. His past was unknown to Crake, except that he'd rescued Frey from certain death after Frey had crash-landed in Samarla many years ago. Crake had always supposed there was a story to it but, as far as he knew, no one had asked and Silo wasn't telling.

Crake, for his part, had always wondered where a Murthian slave learned to speak Vardic so well. He hardly ever spoke to anyone on the crew, so it seemed unlikely that he'd learned it on the *Ketty Jay*. Curiously, his phrasing and regional burr came from Draki, the southernmost duchy of Vardia, which bordered onto Samarla. Draki was traditionally regarded as a cultural and literal wasteland, populated by rural people from peasant stock who eked a living from the hard earth, half of it poisoned by the Blackendraft blowing in from the Hookhollow volcanoes to the west. How Silo could have learned Vardic from Draki folk was a mystery.

Well, whatever the truth, Silo was confident he could drive a Rattletrap better than anyone else here. And if Silo said so, then it was true.

He made his way to the back of the hold, where a small area was separated off by a wall of crates and a tarpaulin curtain. Beyond was his makeshift sanctum. It was disappointingly bare, little more than a private area for him to work because his own quarters were too cramped. There was a desk and a chalkboard, a cupboard full of apparatus and equipment and space for a small summoning circle, but that was all. Barely adequate for even a fledgeling daemonist.

For the past few months he'd been increasingly frustrated in his attempts to expand his knowledge of the Art. Frey had given him the space and let him do whatever he wanted – mostly because he didn't understand what Crake was doing – but the simple fact was that he needed a proper sanctum and you couldn't have one on board an aircraft. Anything fragile would eventually break when it was shaken about in flight. His delicately calibrated machines never stayed calibrated for long. The electricity supply wasn't robust enough to risk calling up anything dangerous, since the resonator might fail and let it out. He would drain the *Ketty Jay*'s batteries if he used them while she was grounded, and he'd never dare attempt a summoning while they were in the air.

I need a place to work, he told himself. *A home, with a sanctum. Or I'll never get any better.*

But that would mean stepping off the *Ketty Jay* for good. And there might still be bounty hunters looking for him. He'd seen neither hide nor hair of the Shacklemores for a long while now, but it was dangerous to assume they'd given up.

Bess, who was standing dormant in a shadowy corner, roused herself as he approached and came lumbering over. She was a golem of tarnished metal and chainmail, standing eight feet high and five broad. Her face – if indeed she *had* a face – was set low between enormous shoulders and hidden behind a circular grille. Only two twinkling stars were visible where her eyes might have been, twin glimmers in the abyss.

She hunkered down in front of Crake so he could give her an awkward hug, and bubbled happily in the depths of her chest cavity.

'How are you tonight, Bess? Happy to see me?'

She rocked back and forth. Since she had no neck, it was the closest she got to a nod.

'Good girl,' he said, rubbing his hand over her hump. 'Good girl.'

He found it was easiest to treat her like a pet, though he wasn't exactly sure what she was. Was there still something in there of the eight-year-old she'd once been? Perhaps. But he'd come to terms with the death of his niece as best he could. He'd come to terms with his part in it, too, although that had been much harder. The remorse and regret would never truly end. This golem carried some memory of that beautiful child, but it wasn't her inside that armoured suit. The real Bess was dead. What was left was an echo of her, an imprint.

But that was something.

'Look what I brought you,' he said, holding up the book. The title was printed on the red leather cover: *Stories for Little Girls*. Bess couldn't read, but after a moment she recognised the book. She clapped her hands with a loud crash of metal, tottered backwards on her stumpy legs and plonked herself onto the ground.

Crake sat down cross-legged next to her. She loomed over his shoulder as he opened the book, craning in eagerly to see the colourful illustrations.

'Which one shall we read tonight?' he asked.

Bess made a quizzical noise: an eerie, otherworldly coo. She sensed a question, but she didn't understand what he'd said. He was never quite sure how much she comprehended of speech. She seemed to have good days and bad days. Or perhaps she was just good at guessing his intentions rather than interpreting the actual words.

'I'll pick, shall I?' he said, turning to one that he knew was her favourite.

She hunkered closer, her face-grille pressed close to the page. Maybe it was the pictures she enjoyed, or maybe she just liked to hear him talk, even if she didn't know what he was saying. It didn't matter. While she kept listening, he'd keep reading. He'd brought her into the world, and he had responsibilities. An honourable man had to live up to his responsibilities.

'*The Duchess and the Daisy-Chain*,' he announced, and he began.

The desert was a cold and empty place at night. Sand and stone, from horizon to horizon. Barren outcrops jutted out of the steel-grey dunes like rotten teeth. It was a new moon, only visible as a round absence in the swathes of stars overhead. Their frosty shine, coming from an impossible distance, was barely enough for human eyes to see by.

For Jez, piloting the *Ketty Jay*, it wasn't a problem. The night was as clear to her as the day.

They were a long way outside the Free Trade Zone, deeply into illegal airspace. She flew with the lights out and thrusters running quiet. With only the sky as a background, the *Ketty Jay* was a speck hurtling through an infinity of black. Only her thrusters gave her away, their blazing glow alien to the chill dark. But there was nothing to be done about that, except hope that nobody was sharp enough to spot them.

Jez had dropped into a shallow trance as they flew. Her uncanny vision was something she didn't have to think about, but it was only when she was in a trance that the full range of her Mane senses kicked in. Then she could sense the wind, calculate it, as if its turbulence was something visible and easy to predict. She was aware of Ashua's heartbeat, fast and nervous, betraying her outwardly confident exterior. She could hear the workings of the aircraft, purring with health since it had been overhauled at Trinica's expense. It had been a thank-you for saving the pirate captain from the Manes, the very creatures that had given Jez these gifts. They lurked on the edge of her consciousness these days, no longer calling to her as they used to, quiet presences like ghosts at her shoulder.

She was a half-Mane. Once that knowledge had tormented her, but now she was beginning to settle into the idea. She no longer feared the ones who had made her what she was.

Something tugged at the edge of her senses. A disturbance in the desert winds. She frowned, and tracked its source.

'Malvery!' she called through the doorway. 'Five o'clock high! You see anything?'

The *Ketty Jay* was too bulky for the pilot to see behind the aircraft, which was why they often had a lookout in the cupola. After a few seconds, Malvery called back. 'I see it. Sammie frigate. Bit of a way off.'

'They coming towards us?'

Another pause. 'Reckon so. Reckon they're coming at quite a clip, as well.'

'Might be we're just going across their flight path,' said Ashua from the shadows at the back of the cockpit. 'They might not have seen us.'

'Change course,' said Frey quickly, from the navigator's station.

Jez did so, turning the *Ketty Jay* to a new heading that would force the Samarlans to correct if they wanted to intercept. Minutes ticked by, counted by restless tapping of Harkins' boot as he tried to contain the explosive hysteria building up inside him. When she judged that enough time had passed, she called again.

'Doc?'

'Still coming.'

Jez swore under her breath. 'They've seen the thruster glow.'

'At that distance?' Frey said. 'There's no way they—'

He was interrupted by a flash and a deafening concussion. The *Ketty Jay* rang like a struck bell and slewed to port, sending Ashua and Harkins sprawling to the floor and almost knocking Frey out of his seat. Jez wrestled with the flight stick and brought the *Ketty Jay* back to an even keel.

'Pretty sure they have, Cap'n,' she said.

'They're lobbing artillery at us, the rude sons-of-bitches!' Malvery yelled, outraged. 'And now they're putting out fighters!'

'How many?'

'Four.'

A small frigate, then, if it was only carrying four fighters. But the odds were hopeless even so.

'Better make ourselves scarce,' said Jez. She hit the thrusters and the *Ketty Jay* roared as she surged forward.

'Let me fly,' said Frey anxiously, getting up from his seat. 'I can—'

'Greatest respect, Cap'n, but sit yourself down,' she said with a casual firmness that stopped him in his tracks. 'You'd be blind out there. And you can't fly where I'm going.'

'Where's *thaaaAAAA*—' Frey's question turned to a yell as Jez dumped aerium from the tanks and pushed the *Ketty Jay*'s nose down, sending her into a steep plunge towards the ground.

'Dropping to the deck, Cap'n,' she said. 'Let's see if they dare follow us.'

'Without lights?' Ashua cried. 'Are you insane? You can't fly that low to the ground when you can't *see* it.'

Jez spared a moment to look over her shoulder. 'I've got good eyes,' she said.

Powerful flood beams swung across the landscape as the approaching frigate and its fighters tried to get a light on them.

Harkins let out an involuntary yelp as he saw how close they were to the rocky desert floor.

By going low to the ground, she forced the Samarlans to make a choice. They could either plunge down and match her altitude – a dangerous option in the dark – or they could make shallow dives while firing and then pull up. That meant they couldn't get on the *Ketty Jay*'s tail, and made her much harder to hit.

'Fighters coming in!' called Malvery.

'Deep or shallow?' Jez called back.

'You what?'

'The angle. Deep or… Never mind,' she said. The cockpit was suddenly illuminated from outside as the beams found them.

The fighters were rigged for night-flying, with banks of floodlights along their wings. She could estimate their angle of approach by the slant of the light as it shone past the *Ketty Jay* and cast her shadow on the ground. The fighters had chosen the lowest-risk strategy. Even with lights, flying close to the ground on a moonless night was too dangerous for their tastes. They didn't have the advantages that Jez did.

She trimmed the aerium ballast and levelled out just above ground level, close enough to make Frey give a little squeak in the back of his throat. The desert floor rushed by beneath them. Jez banked hard and swung away from the light as she heard the rattle of machine guns from behind. Tracer fire flitted past the *Ketty Jay*, chewing up the earth below.

'Malvery!' shouted Frey. 'What are you waiting for?'

'Orders?' Malvery suggested.

'Well, consider yourself bloody ordered. Shoot them!'

'Right-o,' said the doctor, and opened up with the autocannon.

Another explosion pounded the *Ketty Jay*, but Jez had sensed the shell whipping through the air and pulled away just in time to avoid being swatted into the ground.

'How in the name of rotting bastardy are they scoring on us at that range?' Frey demanded.

'Lucky shot,' said Jez. 'Next one's going way wide.'

As if to illustrate her point, a bloom of fire lit up the night some distance to starboard. She kept up an evasive pattern. The fighters couldn't draw a bead on her. She could tell when they were lining up on the *Ketty Jay* by the angle of their light beams, and then she would dodge. They swooped, missed, and looped back into the air to try again. They were slender, needle-nosed things, streamlined like flattened darts. Built to look good, like all Samarlan craft.

'Can't keep this up for ever, Cap'n. We need to lose them fast.'

Frey got out of his seat and peered through the windglass of the cockpit. The play of the fighter's lights were showing glimpses of the terrain ahead. A colossal outcrop reared out of the ground a few kloms ahead.

Suddenly his face lit up. 'There,' he said, pointing.

'I don't get it.'

'They're following the glow from our prothane thrusters, right?' he said. 'Well, this aircraft doesn't only run on prothane.'

She grinned as she caught on. 'I'd buckle in if I were you, Cap'n.'

'Harkins!' Frey said. 'Let the crew know. Batten down. It's gonna be choppy.'

Harkins just stared at him, his face blank with fright.

'Move it!' Frey snapped. The shock broke Harkins' paralysis, and he scampered out of the cockpit and up the corridor, calling the alarm. Frey threw himself into the navigator's chair and secured the straps. Ashua slipped her arm through a gap in the bulkhead and braced herself.

The lights from the fighters behind them slipped and swung all around them. Tracer fire chased them through the night. The outcrop loomed ahead, blacking out the background as Jez took them on a course that would skim close to its flank. Another explosion tore through the air. The frigate was getting nearer, and its shelling would become more accurate as it did.

Frey was a bag of nerves by now. Jez could hear it in his heartbeat and smell it on his sweat. 'Malvery!' he yelled. '*Will you get those fighters off our tail*?'

'If you think it's so easy, come up here and do it yourself!' Malvery yelled back. He fired another burst, a dull *thump-thump-thump* of artillery, then guffawed triumphantly. 'There you go! Happy now?'

One of the Samarlan fighters went screaming overhead, close enough to make Jez duck in fright. It corkscrewed through the air, trailing flames from the stump of a wing, and smashed into the side of the outcrop in a smoky cough of fire.

'Here we go,' Jez shouted over the roar of the engine and the sound of distant machine guns. 'Malvery, quit firing when I say!'

'I just got bloody started!' he cried indignantly.

Jez ignored him. 'Everyone hang on to something! Malvery, now!'

The autocannon fell silent. The outcrop was to starboard now, mere metres off their wing-tip. She took it as close as she dared, knowing her pursuers wouldn't match her. They pulled away, intending to catch her on the far side. But instead of flying past it, she banked hard to starboard, swinging around the back of the outcrop. The *Ketty Jay*'s thrusters screamed as she powered through the air. Her frame shook with the stress. Jez heard a string of bumps and crashes from the depths of the aircraft, as everything that wasn't secured went sliding and clattering across the floor. Malvery began spluttering a string of frightened curses as the aircraft tipped to almost ninety degrees, bringing him face-to-face with the sides of the outcrop, only a dome of windglass between him and a thundering wall of rock.

And then the lights disappeared. The outcrop stood between the *Ketty Jay* and her pursuers, and for a few seconds they flew in utter darkness.

Jez did an emergency kill on the thrusters and boosted the aerium engines to maximum, pulling the *Ketty Jay*'s nose up as she did. The aerium engines hummed as electromagnets pulverised liquid aerium into gas, filling the ballast tanks, making the *Ketty Jay* lighter than air. Jez rode the momentum that they already had and took the *Ketty Jay* up into the night, her thrusters now dark, invisible against the background of the sky.

Nobody saw them go.

As the *Ketty Jay* became lighter, the air resistance slowed them down. Jez airbraked until they were stationary and then let them rise like a balloon, straight up into the atmosphere. The frigate glided past like a shark to starboard, dwindling beneath them, its floods trained on the outcrop where its quarry had disappeared. The fighters swooped and banked, searching for the telltale glow of thrusters. But they were all looking in the wrong place.

When they'd gone high enough, Jez vented aerium to equalise the weight and the *Ketty Jay* stopped rising. The Samarlans were still looking fruitlessly for them, a klom below. Jez slumped back in her seat, then turned around and grinned.

'That was a good idea, Cap'n.'

'I'm impressed, anyway,' said Ashua, rubbing her arm where it had been bruised by the bulkhead.

Frey unbuckled himself, rolling his shoulder, and reached over to give Jez a pat on the shoulder. 'Don't know what I'd do without you.'

Jez retied her ponytail to disguise the flush of pleasure she felt at that. Sometimes, she decided, being half-daemon was not so bad at all.

FOUR

THE TRAIN—FREY RALLIES THE CREW— RATTLETRAPS—HARKINS FUMBLES

'There it is.'

Frey wiped sweat from his brow with his shirt sleeve, then took the spyglass from Ashua and put it to his eye. Before him, a scorched and blasted land lurched away towards a broken horizon. Scattered buttes and mesas faded hauntingly into the distance. Shallow hills of scree nursed hardy scrub grass and gnarled bushes. It was a cooked, cracked vista of dusty orange and red, split by narrow, branching fissures.

He followed the curved line of the tracks till he found the train, which was making its steady way towards them. Apart from a few circling birds, it was the only thing moving out there.

'I count twelve carriages,' he said. 'Don't see any guns or escort.'

Ashua shifted next to him. They were lying on their bellies at the crest of a slope, in the meagre shade of an enormous witch-tree that reached twisted wooden claws towards the sky as if in agony. Witch-trees were the only thing that grew to a good size out here in the Samarlan badlands, and they were evil-looking things.

'Might be we got lucky,' Ashua suggested.

Frey snorted to show what he thought of that. He handed the spyglass back to her. She took it and regarded him with narrow green eyes. Her ginger hair was damp with sweat, and a droplet of it trickled down the side of her throat. Frey imagined doing impure and depraved things to her. Fresh sweat on a woman had that effect on him.

'Why don't you go get the crew ready?' she said, in a tone that made him suspect she knew what he was thinking, and wasn't overly impressed by it. 'I'll let you know when it's time to go.'

Frey coughed into his fist. 'Right,' he said. 'I'll do that.' He scrambled down the stony slope, suddenly grateful to be away from her.

You're getting hot for street-rats now? Where are your bloody standards?

He decided it was probably Trinica's fault. While she was around he restrained himself from messing with other women, which meant he'd been celibate for a couple of weeks now, ever since they cooked up this plan together. But just being near Trinica was enough to leave him embarrassingly frisky, and Ashua had begun to seem like an awfully tempting alternative.

No, he told himself sternly. *Behave.*

The crew were waiting with the Rattletraps at the bottom of the slope. Even in the shade it was swelteringly hot, and they were guzzling water when he arrived.

'Train's coming,' he said.

'About time,' Malvery said. 'Reckon Pinn's about to melt.'

Pinn was sitting with his back to one of the buggies, his skin glistening. His little thatch of hair was plastered to the top of his chubby head. 'How does anyone live in this bloody country?' he gasped. 'I feel like I'm a pie.'

Frey prodded him with his boot. 'Come on. Little exercise'll do you good,' he said.

Pinn grumbled sourly as they clambered onto the Rattletraps. Frey had divided up the crew according to who could drive, who could shoot and who was just plain useless. Mentally claiming captain's privilege, he'd chosen the best personnel for his own buggy. Silo was driving and Malvery would operate the gatling gun mounted atop the roll cage. Silo seemed confident in his ability and Malvery, while not the world's best shot, at least had experience manning the *Ketty Jay*'s autocannon.

Ashua would get Pinn on the gatling and Harkins riding shotgun. Usually he'd have left the jittery pilot behind, as he was hopeless with a weapon, but Harkins had insisted on coming, throwing glances at Jez all the while. No one had any doubt who he was trying to impress.

Jez, for her part, was riding with Crake. He was almost as bad as Harkins with a gun, but they needed him to handle Bess. She would go in the back, ready to be unleashed once they'd brought the train to a stop.

'Alright!' he called, when everyone was aboard. 'I didn't see any defences beyond the armour plate, but let's not get sloppy. There'll be men aboard with weapons, at least. I don't want any of my crew getting shot. Doctors are expensive, and Malvery's likely to saw the wrong arm off.'

'Hey!' said Malvery. 'Don't forget I'm gonna be standing right behind you with a gatling gun, smart-arse.'

The crew laughed good-humouredly. They were surprisingly relaxed, considering what was coming. Only Harkins looked in danger of panicking.

'Everyone remember the plan?' Frey cried. He could hear the train approaching now, a distant rumbling, getting louder.

'Yes, Cap'n!'

'Well, I'm sure you won't mind reminding me then.'

Malvery rolled his eyes. 'We'll be heading for the engine carriage at the front, to try and stop the train,' he said, in a dreary sing-song. 'Ashua, Pinn and Harkins are gonna keep the bad guys busy while we do, and—'

'Aren't *we* the bad guys?' Pinn asked suddenly.

They all stared at him. He shrugged. 'Well, I mean, *we're* robbing *them*, right?'

'We're *never* the bad guys!' said Frey, horrified at the suggestion. He was surprised the moral objection had come from Pinn rather than Crake. Pinn didn't have any morals, so he probably just wanted the attention.

He needed to nip this in the bud before they all started arguing, so he gestured towards Silo, the shaven-headed, umber-skinned Murthian, who was sitting next to him.

'Look at this man. Proud example of his race.' Silo gazed at him inscrutably. 'A race that the Sammies have been keeping brutally enslaved for the last five hundred years. And the Daks are no better: they're willing conspirators. Ashua tells me that train will be full of Daks, with maybe a few Sammies in there to keep an eye on things. Does that sound like slavery to you? No. The Daks *run* this country while the Sammies sit back and lick the cream. So don't feel bad about popping one or two of 'em, 'cause frankly, they're all bastards in my book.'

He surveyed his crew to gauge the effect of his words. Nobody seemed much bothered. Pinn just looked confused.

'Plus,' he raised a finger, 'those on that train are gonna be armed guards. They're *paid* to get shot. If people like us didn't try to rob trains, they'd be out of a job.'

'We're providing employment opportunities now?' Crake asked, deadpan.

'Exactly!' said Frey. 'Greasing the wheels of foreign capital, and that.'

'Cap'n,' said Crake. 'I do believe you know as much about economics as Pinn does about hygiene.'

Malvery mopped his pate, which had reddened and begun to peel. 'Look, as long as we stop short of killing women and children, and we ain't shooting adorable little puppy dogs in the face, I'm in. Now can we stop bullshitting and get this done? I want to get out of the sun.'

'You're not *in* the sun.'

'Out of the shade, then. To somewhere shadier. Like the inside of a freezer.'

'Or a bar!' Pinn suggested brightly.

Malvery clicked his fingers and pointed at Pinn. 'Man's got the right idea.'

'Tonight you can get boozed up till your eyeballs float, and I'll pay for every round,' said Frey. 'But we've got work to do first. Now, some of you are carrying dynamite, so if you must get yourselves shot, try not to get hit anywhere explosive.' He looked up the slope and saw Ashua scrambling towards them. 'Seems like that's it for the team talk. Good luck, everyone!'

The din of the train had grown to fill the air now. Ashua was shouting 'Go! Go! Go!' before she'd even reached her Rattletrap. She leaped into the driver's seat, hit the ignition button and floored the accelerator. Her wheels spun against the ground for a few seconds, throwing up a cloud of red dust. When they bit, it threw the Rattletrap forward so suddenly that Pinn almost tipped off the back. Frey, Silo and Malvery raced off just behind her, with Jez, Crake and Bess trailing.

They'd practised with the Rattletraps throughout the morning, to check that they worked properly and to get the drivers used to them, but Frey still found the sense of speed exhilarating. It wasn't the same as being in a cockpit, where there was a brass-and-chrome dash and thick panes of windglass between him and the world outside. Rattletraps were built low to the ground, and their roll cages seemed pitifully inadequate as protection. Though they travelled much slower than an aircraft did, it felt like just the opposite. He was fragile and invincible all at once as he hurtled into the face of the elements.

They sped out of the shadow of the slope and into sight of the tracks an instant before the train appeared. Ashua's timing had been less than perfect: the train was almost past them by the time they'd matched its speed. But the Rattletraps were fast, and they began gaining ground immediately.

The tracks passed through a wide corridor of land flanked by hilly ridges on either side. The land was flat near the tracks, but it became bumpy and rough further away. By hugging close to the train, the Rattletraps ate up the distance.

It was only when they were close that Frey realised what a monstrous machine the train was. A great dirty ogre of iron and grime, filthy with desert dust, charging across the landscape. It was a mobile fortress, built for the rigours of travel across the hellish terrain of the Samarlan interior. Faced with its strength, he suddenly began to have his doubts about whether they could stop it at all.

But it was too late for that now.

There were slatted metal windows in the sides of the train. As they progressed up its length, they saw men running to and fro inside the carriages, alarmed shadows in the gloom.

'Pinn! Malvery!' he yelled. 'Keep 'em busy!'

Pinn whooped and opened up with the gatling gun, stitching bullet-holes along the side of the train. Malvery was a little more accurate, aiming for the windows. The bullets had little effect on the train's armour plating, but it made the men inside duck and scurry, and it kept them from returning fire.

Frey turned to Silo and grinned. 'Some fun, huh? Bet you're glad to be home, getting some of your own back,' he said.

But Silo just looked at him, and his eyes were dark and flat in his narrow face, and Frey was suddenly sorry he'd spoken at all. He opened his mouth to say something else when Silo suddenly shouted a warning.

It was the carriage just ahead of them. One side had opened up, the top half flipping down on to the bottom half with a crash, like a stall at a fairground. Behind it were a row of barricades, with gun-toting Dakkadians hiding behind them. And in the centre of the row, its operator hiding behind a wall of metal shielding, was an autocannon. Pointing right at them.

Frey had time for a wordless yell of abject cowardice before Silo stood on the brakes. The ground in front of them exploded in a geyser of rock and dust. He was blinded for a moment, his face speckled with a thousand tiny impacts. He heard more explosions around him, as the autocannon fought to pin them down. Bullets flew. The Rattletrap jounced left and right, flinging him about in his seat. Malvery was bellowing a string of swearwords in his ear. He blinked furiously, wiping at teary eyes to clear them of grit.

Silo dropped back, away from the autocannon. Frey was still pawing at his face when he heard the sound of gatling guns from behind them. Since Malvery wasn't firing and they only had one other gun, that could only mean trouble. He craned around in his seat, looking down the length of the train, fighting to bring his blurred vision back into focus.

Rattletraps. *Enemy* Rattletraps, coming up behind them.

'Where did *they* come from?' Malvery cried.

Before anyone could venture an opinion, another train carriage opened up in the same way as the first one. This one was close to the rear, but its contents were identical. A bunch of armed men and an autocannon.

An autocannon in front of them, loaded with explosive shells. Another behind. And he counted three Rattletraps with gatlings. No way they could fight those odds.

'Pull away from the train!' he told Silo. He raised himself in his seat and waved at the others. 'Pull away *now*!'

The others didn't need telling. They swerved off to the right, putting distance between themselves and the train, heading for the uneven scrubland at the base of the red hills. It wouldn't get rid of their pursuers, but it would get them out of range of the autocannons.

He fell back into his seat as Silo led the retreat, the Rattletrap skidding and jolting as shells erupted all around them. The confidence his crew had shown earlier seemed desperately misplaced now. What should have been a nice straightforward ambush had just gone horribly, horribly wrong.

* * *

Harkins, as usual, was terrified.

Harkins didn't get scared in the way ordinary people got scared. What they called fear was his standard operating level, the state in which he existed day to day. Most people didn't get really, properly terrified too often. Harkins managed it at least a dozen times a week.

Being so familiar with the sensation, he'd come to experience it in a different way. He still felt the same physical reactions: shortness of breath, sweating, the overwhelming desire to scream, occasional paralysis. But terror had kept him alive many times in the past. It came to him like an old friend. A friend that he loathed and hated unreservedly, but a friend nonetheless.

Amid the explosions, the gunfire and the overwhelming awfulness of the whole situation, Harkins could only think of one thing.

Why didn't I just stay on the Ketty Jay*?*

Hadn't he proved himself useless in a firefight time and time again? Wasn't it well known that his only skill lay in piloting the Firecrow they'd left behind in Shasiith? Nobody thought less of him for opting out of ground missions. In fact, it was assumed that he would. Without his fighter craft, he was like a snail out of his shell.

Jez was the reason, of course. Kind, sweet Jez, the only one who didn't mock or pity him. He was thankful that she couldn't see him now, unmanned by fear yet again. She was too busy fleeing across the scrubland, pursued by one of the enemy. Just as they were.

He looked over his shoulder. The Dakkadians were on their tail, red dust in their blond hair, their faces covered with dirty goggles and leather masks. Their Rattletraps were of similar design to the one Harkins rode, with a driver, a passenger and a gun operator standing at the rear. Bullets cut through the air and pocked the ground to either side of them, but Ashua's driving and the uneven terrain kept them from finding a mark.

'Will somebody shoot at them?' Ashua shouted.

'These damn things don't turn backwards!' said Pinn, struggling to pivot the gatling gun.

'Then use your shotgun, you moron!' she cried.

'Oh, right,' said Pinn. He abandoned the gatling and dropped into a sitting position, facing backwards with his legs braced against the roll cage. Now secured, he pulled out his shotgun and opened up on their pursuers.

'And you!' said Ashua, glaring at Harkins. 'What are you waiting for?'

Harkins jumped at the harsh tone of her voice. He fumbled his revolver out, opened it to check that it was loaded, snapped it shut again. It felt unnatural in his hand, heavy with danger.

He took a steadying breath and then leaned out sideways, pointing his weapon in the general direction of the enemy, bending his wrist backwards to do so. The leather ears of his pilot cap slapped wildly against his unshaven cheeks. He closed his eyes and fired. The noise stunned him; the recoil crashed against his wrist and elbow. The gun shuddered and dropped from his hand to the ground. He drew himself back against his seat, holding his arm against his chest, burning with shame and shock.

'Rot and pus!' Ashua barked in exasperation. 'I thought you were meant to be a freebooter? What kind of jelly-arsed milk-bubble did I get landed with?'

Harkins supposed that was a rhetorical question, so he kept quiet. Ashua didn't say anything further, because at that moment they hit a rise in the ground and took off. They sailed through the air for a few horrible seconds before smashing back to earth with a jolt that made Harkins' teeth clack together.

'I can't hit a damn thing like this!' Pinn complained.

'Then they can't hit us, either,' Ashua snapped, swerving to avoid another volley of gatling fire. She dug into her belt, pulled out a stick of dynamite, and thrust it towards Harkins. 'Light me.'

Harkins stared at the dynamite in horror. She shook it at him impatiently. 'Come on, you quivering gimp! I don't have a hand free!'

He snatched it from her, eager to get this whole business done with so she would stop abusing him. His fingers trembled as he found a matchbook in his pocket. Then he stopped what he was doing and dithered, trying to work out how to strike a match with one hand while holding the dynamite with the other.

'Put the dynamite. Between your knees. And light it,' said Ashua, her jaw tense with barely contained frustration.

Harkins made sure she wasn't looking at him, then gave her what he hoped was a nasty glare. He didn't like her one bit. She wasn't at all like Jez, who was the soul of patience where Harkins was concerned. This one was snappy and mean, and she wasn't even part of the crew.

Resentfully, he stuck the dynamite between his bony knees, struck a match, and touched it to the fuse. The fuse burst into life in a fizz of sparks. Harkins jumped – he couldn't help himself – and the dynamite slipped from between his knees and rolled into the footwell.

'Can't you do *anything*?' Ashua screamed, as he scrabbled around between his feet. Gunfire glanced off the frame of the buggy. Harkins reached for the dynamite, but just then Ashua swerved, and it rolled away from his grasp and under her feet. She began to yelp, pawing around between the pedals, driving with one hand while their pursuers shredded the air with bullets. The Rattletrap swerved crazily left and right.

'What in the name of hammered horseshit are you doing?' Pinn demanded, hanging on to the roll cage for dear life.

Then the Rattletrap swerved again, and the dynamite bounced back to Harkins' side of the footwell. He grabbed it and brandished it triumphantly.

'Ha! Got it!' he grinned.

'*Get rid of it*!' Ashua howled, fighting with the wheel to gain control of the buggy.

Harkins' grin faded as he saw that the fuse had almost entirely burned down. With a jerk of his arm he flung the dynamite over his shoulder. He squeezed his eyes shut and covered his ears, but even so, he couldn't suppress a shudder at the enormous explosion that followed.

Ashua stepped on the brakes, unable to master the careering Rattletrap, and they skidded to a halt in a cloud of rising dust. Harkins waited a few seconds and then opened his eyes.

Something round and heavy dropped out of the sky and caromed off the Rattletrap's hood, causing Harkins to shriek in fright. It bounced in the dust, rolled for a few metres and stopped.

It was a goggled and masked head. It stood on its severed neck, facing Harkins. If he didn't know better, he might have thought its owner was merely buried in the sand.

He slowly turned to look over his shoulder. Behind them, at the centre of a small black crater, were the remains of the Dakkadian Rattletrap. There wasn't much to see.

'Reckon they must've been carrying dynamite, too,' Ashua opined.

Pinn slapped Harkins on the shoulder, making him flinch. 'Nice throw, you gibbering freak,' he said affectionately.

Harkins gave him a weak smile and tried not to be sick.

FIVE

PINN'S JOKE—BESS, ANGRY—THE BELLY OF THE BEAST—FREY ON TOP—JEZ HEARS A VOICE

Crake was having an equally hard time keeping his lunch, but for him the threat came from the other end. His stomach had been grumbling and roiling ever since he'd arrived in Samarla – the food didn't agree with him at all – and it had been making things pretty unpleasant when it came time to visit the bathroom. With all this jolting about, it took all of his concentration to avoid embarrassment. The fact that he might be shot at any moment was a distant second in importance to that fact. He was an aristocrat, even if he didn't look much like one these days. Dishonouring himself in such a manner would be a fate worse than death.

Besides, he wouldn't give Pinn the satisfaction. A few days ago, after one particularly cruel bout of diarrhoea, Crake had found Slag, the *Ketty Jay*'s cat, lying by the door, apparently overcome by the fumes. He'd rushed Slag to the infirmary, where Malvery, between bouts of hysterical laughter, pronounced the cat clear of any kind of toxic poisoning. It turned out to be Pinn's idea of a joke. The pilot had spiked Slag's milk with rum and laid the unconscious animal where Crake would find it.

Maybe it was because they were carrying a highly visible golem on the back, but they'd attracted two of the three enemy buggies. Jez was driving like a maniac to stay ahead of them. If not for Bess, they would all most likely have been shot by now, but she was their shield and most of the bullets that came their way ricocheted harmlessly off her armour. She roared and swiped, making threatening grabs at her tormentors. They were wise enough to stay far out of her reach. Shooting Bess made her very annoyed indeed.

'Can't you keep her still?' Jez yelled, as their vehicle slewed back and forth.

'They're shooting her. With bullets,' Crake replied. 'Would *you* keep still?'

Jez didn't bother to reply to that. 'Where's the Cap'n? Someone needs to take care of these bastards.'

Crake shaded his eyes against the glare of the sun. 'There he is! He must've dropped back. He's coming up behind them.'

'Alright. Let's try not to—'

Jez was interrupted by an explosion to their left, pelting them with tiny stones. The Rattletrap rocked and swerved. Crake looked over at the train, which suddenly seemed a lot closer than before.

'The autocannons!' he said, flapping his hands at her. 'Get away from the train! They're herding us towards the train!'

'They're not herding us anywhere! I've been driving in a straight line!' She twisted the wheel and skidded aside as a gatling gun sent a hail of bullets their way. 'More or less, anyway.'

'Maybe *you've* been going straight, but the tracks haven't.' He pointed suddenly. 'Look there! More help on the way!'

Ashua's Rattletrap was approaching, leaving a column of black smoke behind them, which was all that remained of their opponent. The relief inspired by the thought of imminent reinforcements almost caused Crake to have an accident, and he had to clench tight and concentrate on reciting mathematical tables until the urge passed.

He'd just got himself under control when there was another explosion behind them, which clouded them from their pursuers for a moment. Jez wrenched the wheel around and tore off at right-angles to her original course just as the others arrived.

There was a chorus of gatling fire and a bellow of engines as Frey and Ashua's Rattletraps tangled with the enemy in a dusty knot. They swerved and crisscrossed, and when they emerged from the haze, Ashua was chasing one of the Dakkadian Rattletraps. The other was still following Jez and Crake, but Frey was hot on its tail, harassing it mercilessly.

Crake looked back. The Dakkadians were now forced to concentrate on avoiding Malvery's gatling fire rather than shooting at Bess. The autocannons had fallen silent since they were out of range, but the train powered on relentlessly.

'She alright back there?' Jez asked.

Crake checked on Bess, who was getting more and more agitated. 'She's not what I'd call happy,' he said.

'Let's see if we can do something about getting that son of a bitch off our tail,' Jez said.

She threw the Rattletrap into a skid, carving a quarter-circle in the earth before leaping off a rise. They hit the ground hard and went the other way, making a tight zigzag.

'They're catching up!' Crake said, as he was thrown from one side of his seat to the other.

'That's the idea,' said Jez, turning again. 'They can't slow down with the Cap'n on their back. I want them to pass us.' She slammed the Rattletrap the other way. 'I just don't want them shooting us first.'

Crake saw her method now. Zigzagging made them a hard target, but it slowed them down. With Malvery blasting away behind them, the enemy would be forced to pass by.

It sounded like a good idea. But the Dakkadians didn't play along.

Jez had slipped up. Her zigzags were predictable. She twisted the wheel at regular intervals, instead of varying the turns. It allowed their pursuers to guess where she was going next, to skid in that direction, and to open up with everything they had just as the Rattletrap passed in front of their guns.

Time slowed down as Crake realised what was happening. The enemy was attacking from the passenger side. He stared at the rotating muzzle of the gatling gun, knowing there was nothing between him and it. Knowing, with a cold and dreadful certainty, that he was about to feel a salvo of brutal impacts punching into his body, and after that there would be nothing more.

But suddenly the gatling gun was gone, a wall of metal in the way. Bess. Hanging on to the roll cage with one hand, she lunged across the side of the buggy, making a barrier of her body between Crake and the guns. Bullets sparked and whined as they bounced off her humped back, chipping the metal, ripping through her chainmailed joints to ping around the empty interior of the suit.

The shift in weight tipped the Rattletrap to one side. Two of its wheels lifted off the ground and Crake felt the vehicle about to flip. Jez threw it into a skid, trying to avert disaster, but it was no good. Crake braced himself—

—and then Bess let go.

She tumbled away from the Rattletrap in a crashing ball of metal. The Rattletrap slammed back down onto four wheels, sliding across the scrubland until it came to a jolting halt. Crake was shaken half out of his wits, but he clambered from his seat as soon as the buggy had fully stopped. He staggered dizzily to the ground, looking about. The thought that Bess might have been hurt – *grievously* hurt – made him frantic.

'Bess! Bess!'

But Bess wasn't hurt. Bess was angry. She'd already found her feet, rising from the red dust like some mythical desert beast. And as he watched, she began to run, gathering momentum with every step. The Dakkadian Rattletrap was bearing down on them, seeking to finish them off.

Bess charged it.

It all happened in a second. The Rattletrap was moving so fast that the driver didn't have time to see the golem coming. Bess ran at them from the side, ramming into them with her shoulder. Perhaps she'd meant to catch them square, but her timing was off, and she only caught one of the back wheels. It didn't matter. At that speed even a small shove was enough.

Bess rebounded from the impact and went down in a heap. The Rattletrap slewed sideways and launched into the air, spinning and flipping crazily before it smashed into the earth. It bounced and rolled for another fifty metres until it finally came to a stop. By that time, it was scarcely recognisable as a vehicle, and its occupants had been flung brokenly away, strewn motionless along its path.

Frey pulled up alongside Jez. 'Everyone okay?' he asked.

'Just about, Cap'n,' said Jez, looking Crake over. Crake was leaning against the side of the buggy, breathing steadily, trying to keep his treacherous bowels under control.

Frey nodded and then Silo sped them away. By the time Crake regained himself, the train had passed, rolling away into the distance. Bess seemed none the worse for her experience, though she was still grumpy. She stomped over with an unmistakably apelike slope to her shoulders that said she was ready to tear off someone's limbs.

Jez was watching the departing train. Her eyes narrowed. 'I've got an idea,' she said, suddenly. 'Bess, get on.'

Bess seemed to understand her, for she bounded on to the back of the buggy, making the suspension groan.

'Whoa! Y'know, you could stand to lose a pound or two,' Jez told her. Bess made an angry bubbling noise in response.

Crake got back into his seat, reached around and took one of Bess's massive hands in his.

'Well done,' he said, because he couldn't put into words how much it pained him to see her so battered and bullet-riddled. 'Good girl.'

Jez set off again, chasing the train. The others were far ahead of them now. She put on some speed to catch up.

Crake sat back, relishing a few moments of relative safety when no one was trying to kill them. The baking wind blew his hair around his face. His lips were dry and cracked, and his face felt scoured with grit. The Rattletrap bumped and clattered underneath him as its wheels bounced over the uneven hardpan.

He hated bringing Bess along on missions like these. Even though she'd proved herself all but invulnerable to small-arms fire, he knew it caused her great distress. She was heedless of her own safety, and he was afraid that one day, she would come up against something that really *could* hurt her. What if she took an autocannon shell in the chest? Would the ethereal presence that was Bess survive the destruction of the suit that housed her? He didn't ever want to find out.

'What's this idea you said you had?' he asked Jez. 'Nothing dangerous, I hope?'

She pointed at the train. Crake looked. The back of the rear carriage was lying open. It had flipped downward to form a ramp, which was dragging along the ground between the wide-spaced tracks, scuffing up a cloud of dust. Visible through the dust was the empty interior of the carriage.

'You're joking,' said Crake.

Jez shrugged. 'Reckon that's where the Rattletraps came out. No reason we can't get in that way too.'

'We're supposed to wait for the train to stop. That was the plan.'

'Live a little, huh?'

'That's rich, coming from you. You're not even alive.'

'Touché. We're still going in. I'd cover my eyes, if I were you.'

She swung the Rattletrap to the left, bumping over the rail until they were driving directly behind the train. The cloud of dust that it left in its wake consumed them. Crake held his hand in front of his eyes. He couldn't see a thing. The noise of the train was overwhelming, a torrent of machine sound, clashing and screeching and rumbling.

Then he felt a bump, and a sensation of lifting. The Rattletrap pushed on uncertainly, and then lurched forward. Crake hung on as they raced up the ramp, into the hot gloom of the carriage, and thumped to a clumsy halt.

He wiped his eyes, blinked, and looked around. The carriage was empty but for a few rings set into the walls and floor, hung with restraining straps for the Rattletraps that had been stored here. Bright light shone in through high, slatted windows and from large vents in the roof. The sound of the train was muffled and hollow.

They were in the belly of the beast. Or, more accurately, its colon.

'We need to stop that train!' Frey said over the noise of the engine. 'Any ideas?'

Silo didn't reply. Frey should have known better than to expect a suggestion from him. The Murthian was concentrating on driving, leaning over the wheel. His bald head and beaklike nose made him look like a plucked vulture.

Frey scanned his surroundings, trying to come up with a plan. Having never hijacked a train before, he wasn't sure of the protocol. He'd sort of hoped something would present itself by this point, but it looked like it was going to take a bit more thought than that.

Ashua, Pinn and Harkins were still harassing the last of the Rattletraps: they seemed to have matters well in hand. He'd lost sight of Jez and the others somewhere behind them. Belatedly he wished that he'd issued the daemonically thralled earcuffs they used to communicate with each other in the sky, so that they could keep in contact. He should have known they'd manage to get separated somehow; he just hadn't wanted to listen to Pinn and Harkins sniping at each other the whole time.

He turned his attention to the train. There was still the problem of those damn autocannons, one near the front and one near the back, waiting for anyone to get close enough to shoot at. They couldn't get near the engine carriage with that autocannon in the way, and so they couldn't stop the train. Unless...

'Silo!' he said. 'Get us near to the carriages.'

'Er,' said Malvery. 'Might not be a good idea.'

'Between the guns,' said Frey. 'Close to the side, in the middle. They can't hit us at that angle. We'll be out of their arc of fire.'

'Yeah, but we'll still have to go *through* their arc of—' Malvery began, but Silo had already turned the Rattletrap and was heading at full speed towards the train. Malvery tutted and blew out his moustache. 'Never bloody mind, I'm just the doctor,' he grumbled. 'I'll shoot at them, shall I?'

Malvery laid down fire on one of the autocannons as they approached. The bullets had little effect on the metal shield that protected the gunners, but it was a distraction, at least. Shells started coming their way as soon as they cut closer to the train. Silo dodged between the explosions, the Rattletrap swerving and slithering as geysers of dirt erupted all around them.

A shell landed to their right, and they were shoved sideways by a wall of concussion and pelted by chips of rock. Silo rode the skid until the wheels gripped again, and they powered onward, more shells exploding in their wake.

Frey had to admit, Silo had been as good as his word. However he'd learned to do it, the man could drive.

Then, all at once, the shelling stopped. Frey's ears were ringing and he'd be half-deaf for a day, but they were through. Silo pulled them alongside a carriage that had no windows, right in the centre of the train. A goods carriage, with a ladder bolted onto its side that led up to the roof. Silo had seen his captain's plan.

Malvery looked from the ladder to Frey and back again. 'Cap'n,' he said. 'It's my professional diagnosis that you're liable to get yourself killed doing that.'

Frey couldn't help but agree. Now that the train was close enough to reach out and touch, its brutish power intimidated him. The sheer tonnage of the thing, the speed of it: how could something like this be stopped by one man?

But he'd made his decision, and he couldn't go back. His crew needed him to make decisions and stick to them. That was how it was, these days. The old Frey would have changed his mind about now. But he was the hero of Sakkan. They looked up to him. He felt the weight of their expectation pushing him onward.

'Close as you can, Silo,' he said.

'We get any closer, we gonna be under the wheels,' Silo rumbled.

Frey looked back at Malvery, who touched two fingers to his forehead in a quick salute. 'Rather you than me, Cap'n.'

He braced himself and fixed his eyes on the ladder. Even with Silo's best efforts, the Rattletrap was swaying back and forth.

Well, damn it, I've had a good life. If I fall, I suppose I won't feel much. Unless I get caught under the wheels and dragged for half a klom, screaming all the way until finally I—

He jumped.

It was over in an eyeblink. He felt the push of his legs, and the impact as he tangled with the ladder, but nothing in between. His mind blanked the intervening distance in a white blare of pure terror. He clung to the warm metal rungs, letting relief soak through him.

'Go help Ashua,' he shouted at Silo. 'I'll be alright.'

'You're a mad bastard, Cap'n!' Malvery yelled as they pulled away, but the doctor was grinning as he did so. 'A mad bastard!'

Well, Malvery was probably half right about that, although Frey didn't know for sure. But mad? He wished that were the case. Then he wouldn't have to worry so damn much.

He applied himself to climbing the ladder. Once on the roof, he pulled himself up and shakily got to his feet. The wind and heat pushed at him as he rose. It took him a few moments to find his balance.

Well, here I am, he thought, and a smile crept across his face.

He was on top of the train, the Samarlan desert spread all around him. The sun glared from a cloudless sky, sharp as a jewel, beating on his skin. From up here, he was master of the cracked red earth, the mysterious buttes, the ghostly mountains. He'd tamed the iron beast that had threatened him. He'd earned this moment of triumph.

Silo was peeling away towards Ashua, who was a long way off to the right. Explosions followed him as the autocannons started up again, throwing up plumes of dust which were quickly snatched away as the train thundered onward. Frey saw that the shells were missing Silo by some considerable margin. They'd seemed to be landing much closer when he was in the buggy. He waited until he was sure Silo was out of danger, then turned his attention to his own situation.

His first thought was to get off the roof of the train and drop down into a carriage. His second thought was that they were full of guards, and he didn't much fancy taking dozens of them on single-handed. The only option was the roof, then, all the way to the engine carriage. Nobody seemed to have seen him climb up, but they'd surely hear him running overhead. Once he started, he'd have to move fast.

The carriages all had large vents in the roof. He peered in to the nearest, and saw nothing but darkness. Carefully, he made his way to the front end of the carriage. The distance between this one and the next was an easy jump. Then he looked down. There was a ladder down to a door, and beneath it, the raging clatter of the tracks.

He suddenly recalled what had happened in Shasiith, while he'd been chasing Ashua. His ribs and back still hurt from that.

Don't mess it up.

He backed away. He'd be running into a ferocious wind, so he reckoned he needed to jump as long as he could manage, just to be safe.

He took a breath, let it out, and ran.

It *was* an easy jump, in the end. It was the landing that was the hard part. He cleared the gap by a good two metres, but his ankle turned on the gently curving roof and suddenly he was tumbling and sliding, pulled to the side, towards the edge. He scrabbled frantically for purchase before his hand snapped out and found the lip of a vent. He pulled himself back to safety.

Ahead of him, the train snaked away. He counted the carriages between him and the engine.

Two horribly distressing brushes with death down, six more to go, he thought. *Frey, what were you thinking when you took this job?*

Oh yes. Now he remembered. He was thinking about Trinica.

Bess was too big to fit through the door of the carriage, but that didn't stop her.

The guards who manned the rearmost autocannon were watching Ashua and Silo pursuing the last of the Dakkadian Rattletraps. The first they knew they'd been boarded by a homicidal golem was when a roaring mountain of metal and fury ploughed through the wall. She snatched up the nearest guard and pitched him out into the sunlight, then proceeded to rampage up the carriage, swatting men aside like flies. The men on the autocannon fought to traverse the gun, but Jez had slipped in behind Bess and she took them out with neat rifle shots. Bess ripped the autocannon from its moorings and lobbed it down the carriage, mangling several men who had been unwise enough to stand and fight.

After that, all that was left was the screaming. The Dakkadians crammed through the exit at the far end of the carriage. Some, in their panic, jumped over the side rather than let Bess get her hands on them. The carriage was clear in less than a minute.

Crake skulked in through the hole Bess had left, as she ripped her way through the far side of the carriage in search of more victims. He picked his way among the wreckage and joined Jez.

'She doesn't appear to need much help, does she?' Crake observed.

'She's doing alright on her—' Jez stopped, and the words died in her mouth.

Kill them.

The voice was clear as day, but it came from inside her head.

Do it for the masters (reverence respect awe). Where's your strength? Do it, curse you!

There! She'd heard it again!

Crake was frowning at her. 'Are you alright, Jez?'

But she wasn't alright. The trance was on her, slipping easily across her senses, and she could *see* herself. She was standing with her head cocked as if listening, while Crake peered at her with a look of concern on his face. She'd left her body, watching herself through someone else's eyes; and at the same time she was still in her body. Somehow the division was not disorientating.

The watcher's sight was grey and dim, all colour leached from it. She could feel pain and a dreadful exhaustion, the kind of weariness that could only end in death. But there was no fear of the end. Only a burning, righteous anger.

Raise your weapon! Shoot them!

A pistol hovered shakily into view.

She spun around. She saw herself spin around. She raised her rifle and aimed at the bloodied Dakkadian, lying wounded in a corner of the carriage. She pulled the trigger. Shot him. Shot *herself*. The impact was as hard and real as if it had been her own body, and for an instant she wasn't sure who had killed who.

Then the Dakkadian's mind closed up, draining from the world like water down a plughole, and she was left staring at the corpse. It toppled over sideways and lay still.

Crake gaped. 'Amazing. You heard him move?'

'Yeah,' she said absently. *No.*

Twice before she'd slid into the mind of another living being. Once it had been an animal. Once a man. But that had been almost two years ago. She'd almost come to believe that she'd imagined those incidents. She thought they were hallucinations brought on by her struggle with her Mane nature, which had consumed her in those days.

But this was no hallucination. This was real, and she'd done it.

She snapped out of her trance and gave Crake a quick, tight smile. She didn't want Crake to suspect. He knew she was a half-Mane, but she hadn't told him everything. And now was not the time to consider this strange ability.

'Come on,' she said suddenly. 'Can't let Bess do all the work.'

She hurried off up the carriage, following the wails of dying men.

SIX

FREY UNDER FIRE—A CASUALTY—
ANOTHER SIDE TO SILO—BAYONETS

Frey was just getting the hang of jumping between carriages when the guards started shooting at him.

The first one caught him by surprise. He didn't know anyone was there until he heard a gunshot and felt something whip past him, dragging a searing trail of pain along the side of his neck. He whirled, one hand clutched to the wound. It stung, but the hand came away dry. Just a graze.

There was a Dakkadian at the other end of the carriage, squat, pale and blond, with the narrow eyes and broad features of his kind. He'd climbed on to the roof and was fighting to steady himself against the wind and the rocking of the train. He aimed another shot at Frey, but swayed at the last moment and fired wild. Frey, whose balance was steadier, drew his revolver. He sighted and shot his target in the chest. The guard spun and disappeared beneath the carriages, swallowed by the roaring metal monster beneath their feet.

'Son of a bitch,' Frey muttered sourly to himself, putting his hand to his neck again. The graze was starting to seep. He didn't dare think about how close he'd come to death that time.

He forged on up the train. He wasn't far from the engine carriage now. Ashua and Silo were still chasing down the final enemy Rattletrap in the distance, their wheels kicking up dust. The sharp sound of gunfire drifted over to him.

He still saw no sign of Jez's Rattletrap, but he was no longer worried about it. Through the ceiling vents, he'd heard some kind of commotion aboard the train. Men were fleeing from the rear carriages towards the front, howling. He didn't need to be able to understand them to guess the cause. He recognised the wild fear of someone who'd just come face to face with the impossible.

That meant only one thing. Somehow, Bess was on board.

He took a run-up to jump for the next carriage, his confidence growing. Maybe they *would* take this train down after all. The hot, dry wind opposed him, plucking at his clothes, a hundred faint hands flurrying for a grip.

Just as he reached the gap between the carriages, a head poked up between them. A Sammie, his features handsome and sharp, skin black as oil. Frey saw him far too late to check his stride. He jumped over the Sammie's head, but the man threw up an arm to protect himself, and it caught Frey's foot. Frey flailed in the air and slammed down hard on the roof of the far carriage, his pistol skidding out of his grip and off the side. Pain exploded through him as the mass of bruises on his ribs received sudden reinforcements.

He tried to breathe and found that he couldn't. Winded and gasping, he rolled on to his back, and saw another guard, this one Dakkadian, climbing up on to the roof next to him. Panicking, he fumbled for the second pistol that was stuffed in his belt, yanked it free, and thrust it into the surprised guard's face. He pulled the trigger, and flinched as he was spattered with blood.

His lungs still wouldn't suck in the air he needed. He got his feet under him and began to rise, drawing his cutlass with his offhand as he did so. But he stopped halfway, still in a crouch. He was already too late. The Sammie had a pistol levelled at him, from a distance of no more than a couple of metres. Dead to rights.

A heartbeat passed, and it seemed to last an age. The world sharpened to a point. Frey took in every detail of the man who was about to kill him. The elegant, almost feminine features. Long, black hair, gathered in a queue and decorated with a complex hairpiece of silver filigree. The wonderfully worked blue silk coat, light as air, that hung down to his knees. His brocaded shirt. His beautiful pistol, worked with silver intaglios along its length.

Then the Sammie fired, and Frey's hand moved. It was not by his will; it was pulled by the cutlass, which operated with a mind of its own. There was a spark, and the whine of a ricochet.

The Sammie stared at him, unable to understand why his bullet hadn't found its mark. Frey didn't give him time for a second chance.

He straightened and shot his enemy through the forehead.

It took him a few more moments to get his breath back. He tipped his cutlass and examined it for damage, but he knew there wouldn't be any. He'd barely even felt the jolt of the bullet up his arm. This was a daemon-thralled blade, and it handled itself better than he ever could.

That's another drink I owe Crake.

He checked on Ashua and Silo. They still hadn't managed to take care of the Rattletrap, and now they seemed to be chasing it back towards the train. In the next carriage along was the remaining autocannon, patiently waiting for its targets to stray within range.

Time to do something about that, he thought.

'He's heading for the train!' Malvery called.

Silo swore in Murthian. Malvery didn't understand the meaning, but he heard the disgust and hate in his voice. It surprised him. Silo wasn't one for emotional outbursts, as far as the doctor could tell, but he was plenty mad about something.

The last Dak Rattletrap was proving to be a colossal pain in the arse. The driver was nothing less than incredible. Somehow, he'd managed to keep ahead of his pursuers while they chased him all over, and neither Pinn nor Malvery had been able to take him down with their gatlings.

A lucky shot from Pinn had dealt with the Rattletrap's gunner, at least. He was sprawled across the back of the vehicle, tangled up in the roll cage. But despite Silo and Ashua's best efforts to keep them away from the train, the Daks had given them the slip. A sudden turn, a burst of speed, and now they were on their way back towards their mates with the autocannon.

Malvery and Pinn were doing their best to make sure they didn't get there, but the driver was a slippery bastard. He dodged and weaved, never keeping a straight line long enough to be pinned down, never coming close enough for an easy shot. With all the jolting, the dust and the general inaccuracy of the gatling guns, the best that Malvery could do was catch the Rattletrap with a bullet or two amid the spray.

The Dak on the passenger side was shooting out between the

seats while his companion concentrated on driving. Under the circumstances, his chances of hitting anything were close to zero.

Not close enough, as it turned out.

Malvery only noticed Pinn had been shot when the chubby pilot suddenly stopped firing his gatling. Malvery looked over at the other Rattletrap, which was speeding along to their right. Pinn was swaying slightly, his face grey and slack, wearing a faraway expression. Then he slumped against the side of the roll cage and went down like a sack of potatoes.

Malvery felt something cold clutch at him. Ashua hit the brakes, and suddenly their Rattletrap was falling behind while Silo and Malvery tore on towards the train.

'Silo! Oi, Silo, get us back there! Pinn's hurt!'

Silo didn't reply. He was fixed on the vehicle ahead of him, his jaw set.

'Silo! He's been bloody shot! Get me back there!' Malvery demanded.

'Just shoot your damn gun, Doc!' Silo snapped. 'Ain't nothin' you can do that girl or Harkins can't. We gonna go back after we done this feller.'

His shoulders were tensed and he boiled on the edge of fury. Malvery had only seen him like this once before. Then, they'd been forced to escort a Sammie through a factory full of rioting workers. Silo had ended up throwing the Sammie off a roof.

Malvery tutted and shook his head in resignation. He ought to be back there looking after that lad. Pinn might have the brains of a plank but he was a mate, and he didn't deserve to get shot. The choice was out of his hands, though. Most choices were out of his hands. Had been ever since he started drinking. Best a man could do was go with it, and take what comes.

Silo was right, anyway. There wasn't a lot he could do for Pinn until they got back to the *Ketty Jay*. Harkins had been in the Navy; he knew how to staunch a wound, if he didn't faint first. No sense getting worked up over what you couldn't change. He put his thoughts aside, and set himself to the gatling.

The train loomed closer now, cutting across their path in a dirty slanted line. The autocannon near the rear end wasn't firing any more – in fact, it wasn't even *there* any more – but Malvery didn't have the time or inclination to wonder why. He just wanted to pop that bugger in the Rattletrap so Silo would turn around.

The explosions started up again. Malvery shrank back as dirt showered his face. Damn it all, he was getting sick of being bombarded like this. Now it was twice as hard to shoot. He gritted his teeth and leaned into the shuddering gatling, trying to ignore the blasts and the jerking and the jouncing.

He caught sight of the Cap'n. Frey was up on top of the carriage, above the remaining autocannon. He was crouching by the roof vent, fiddling with something.

What's he up to?

Then Malvery figured it out. He was striking a match. As Malvery watched, the Cap'n lifted something and dropped it through the vent.

Malvery grinned.

The dynamite didn't provide the spectacular explosion he'd imagined, but that didn't matter. The invisible concussion wave was lethal enough. The guards were flung everywhere, broken upon the barricades or pulverised against the walls. The autocannon went silent.

The unexpected loss of covering fire distracted the Dakkadian driver, and he stopped swerving back and forth. It was only for a moment, but it was enough for Malvery, who'd seen it coming, to line up his shot. He pressed down the trigger and a hail of bullets chewed through the buggy. Driver and passenger jerked and spasmed. The buggy swerved to the left and slowly rolled to a halt, its occupants limp in their seats.

Silo pulled up, staring at the dead men. Their faces were mercifully covered by their masks and goggles. The train passed them by and rumbled away. When Silo showed no sign of moving, Malvery laid a hand on his shoulder. He swung around, his eyes full of rage, and half-turned in his seat as if he was about to lunge.

Malvery met his gaze calmly. He didn't know what had got the engineer so worked up, but it didn't matter. He wasn't a man who was easily threatened.

'Mate,' he said. 'We got him. Take me back to Pinn.'

The anger gradually died in Silo's eyes. He gave a quick nod, slid back into his seat, and swung the Rattletrap around.

* * *

Frey climbed down the ladder to the engine carriage. Below him, the rails blurred past beneath the pounding train.

He stepped off the ladder and peered through the doorway behind him, which led into the autocannon carriage. The last threads of smoke were still being chased around the wreckage by the wind. There was a sharp, metallic scent of explosives and blood. Dead men lay scattered about. One was a Sammie, his arm dangling over a barricade, swinging loosely with the rhythm of the train.

Frey surveyed the corpses. A lot of lives lost for the sake of a heist. He wasn't often as messy as this. He usually tried to keep casualties to a minimum, and most of the people he shot were scumbags who pretty much deserved it anyway. Killing dozens of guards just to get some old relic would have caused him a twinge of conscience in Vardia. He probably wouldn't have taken the job on in the first place, unless he could do it without piling up bodies.

But this was Samarla, and these were Daks and Sammies, so he didn't feel anything at all.

Further down the train, he could hear gunshots and the sound of tearing metal. Bess was getting closer now. She'd almost blitzed her way through the entire train.

Frey turned his attention to the engine carriage. The door was thick metal and securely locked, but the handle was just the right shape to wedge a stick of dynamite into. Frey lit the fuse, took cover in the opposite carriage, and blew the door open.

'You in there!' he shouted. 'I'm coming in, and anyone I find in there is gonna get shot. Show yourselves now, and you won't get hurt!'

There was no sign that anyone heard. Instead, a bloodied and confused Dakkadian guard stumbled in through the door behind him, at the far end of the autocannon carriage. He stared dumbly at the carnage until Frey fired a couple of shots, and the guard disappeared back through the door. When he didn't return, Frey guessed he'd jumped off the side. It seemed the option of choice for many guards after they'd had an eyeful of Bess.

The door of the engine carriage was swinging loosely back and forth. With his pistol in his right hand and his cutlass in his left, he stepped across the gap between the carriages and carefully pushed it open with his foot.

The room beyond was cramped, stifling and dim. Sunlight shone in through narrow vents on the walls, but it seemed to cut through the gloom rather than dispersing it. It fell on to a bank of gauges and valves which made up the far wall, limning the chrome in sharp curves of focused brightness. There was no sign of anyone within.

He took a step inside. 'I know you're in here,' he said. 'Don't make me—'

His senses warned him of the man behind the door a moment before it was kicked shut. He wasn't fast enough to get out of the way, but he had time to brace himself. Instead of knocking him back through the doorway to fall between the carriages, the door bounced off his shoulder and sent him staggering sideways into the dim chamber. Before he could recover he heard a high yell, and saw a Dak charging him with a rifle, its end fixed with a double-bladed bayonet aimed at his belly.

His cutlass reacted before he did. It swept up, bringing his hand with it, and knocked the bayonet aside. The rifle discharged with a loud crack, and the Dak cannoned into Frey.

Frey was slammed up against the wall, the Dak's snarling face inches from his. His instincts took over, and he headbutted the guard square in the nose. The Dak stumbled backwards, one hand going to his face. Frey got a fistful of his hair and ran him head-first into the metal wall. He didn't get up after that.

Frey stared at the unconscious man on the ground, panting. As he did so, something welled up within him, like blood from a wound, something hot and ugly and overwhelming. He gave a strangled cry and kicked the guard in the ribs. And then, as if that had opened him up to the flood, he kicked him again and again.

'You *rot*-sucking bastard *son* of a *whore*!' he shouted, punctuating his insults with savage blows. His target didn't flinch. Blood was trickling from his ear. The sight of it dried Frey's anger.

The man was dead. He'd been dead before Frey had even starting kicking him. All this was pointless.

He leaned back against the wall of the chamber, catching his breath, listening to the muffled rattle of the train, the hiss and tick of pipes and gauges. He felt hot, sudden tears of fright coming. His face twisted and almost started to bawl, but he forced the tears back with a grimace and wiped his glistening eyes.

No. Unacceptable. That wasn't what a man of his reputation

was meant to do. So what if he nearly got impaled by a bayonet? Just another lucky escape for Captain Darian Frey. Laugh it off and keep going.

He pulled up his shirt and stared at the jagged brown scars on his abdomen. There'd been another time, years ago, when he hadn't been so lucky. Another bayonet, with another Dak behind it, that one just a stupid kid barely old enough to shave.

He'd had a different crew back then. Kenham and Jodd, an ugly pair of bruisers. Martley, the carrot-topped engineer with way too much energy. Rabby, who always wanted to agree with you no matter what.

He hadn't much liked any of them. They'd only really been passengers on his own personal mission to get himself killed during the Second Aerium War. The Daks hadn't managed to kill him, in the end, but they killed everyone else. His entire crew butchered. All his fault.

But he had a new crew now, and they were not the same. They were his friends.

What if it happens again? he thought. *What if I get them all killed?*

Just the thought of it sapped the strength from him. He slid down the wall and sat staring at the dead guard. He felt like he'd been emptied out.

But he was too close to victory over the iron beast to stay still for long. The urge to end this drove him back to his feet. In the corner, rungs led to a higher level. He took them, and found himself in the control chamber. Slatted windows provided a view of the desert all around. A bank of brass levers and dials faced him. There was nobody here. The Dak he'd just brained must have been the driver.

It didn't take a genius to work out which levers to pull to stop the train. Frey let off speed, hauled the brake, and held on. The massive train began to slow to a stop, and all Frey could hear was the ascending screech of the brakes, louder and louder like madness.

SEVEN

A HIDDEN HONOUR—SILO'S PATH—
FREY IS GOADED—BITTEN

Pinn's wound was not enough to shut him up.

'It's all going grey!' he wailed. 'Doc! Where are you?'

'I'm right here, carrying your fat arse,' Malvery grunted, as he and Crake manhandled Pinn into the *Ketty Jay*'s dingy infirmary.

'Who's that?' Pinn cried, looking about, his eyes unfocused. 'Is that you, Doc? You sound so far away. I can't hear any— *Ow!*' He yelled in protest as they dumped him unceremoniously on the surgical table. 'Hey! Careful!'

'Can we gas him?' panted Crake.

'I'm thinking more like we should put him out of his misery,' Malvery said, running an eye over Pinn's bloodied arm. He took hold of the shirtsleeve and ripped it up to the shoulder.

'Aren't you supposed to have a bedside manner or something?' Pinn complained.

Malvery harumphed and busied himself with assembling his surgical gear. The instruments were hanging up in a dresser that was bolted to the wall and had once been used to keep plates.

Crake could barely suppress a smile as he watched the doctor bustling around. Malvery was in a grump because Pinn had made him worry. Despite everything, Malvery was fond of Pinn. Crake thought him an odious, immoral dimwit with the intelligence of a cough drop, but he was crew, so that was that.

It was sweltering in the tiny infirmary. Since last night, the *Ketty Jay* had been hidden beneath an arch in one of the massive rock formations scattered across the desert. Despite being in the shade, her temperature had slowly risen until it was almost as hot inside as out, and she couldn't get rid of the day's heat without the engine running. Crake couldn't wait for nightfall, when they could get out of here and back to Shasiith.

He could hear the rest of the crew coming back to the ship, bringing the relic they'd found on the train, among other things. Bess was carrying a chest full of assorted salvage. It had seemed a shame to hijack an entire train just for one little Samarlan relic, so they'd scavenged for some extra loot on the side. Apart from the relic, the train had carried an unremarkable cargo, mostly crops and mail. Not worth the effort it would take to haul it away. But Silo and Jez had identified some valuable machine parts and odd Samarlan devices. Frey had found some fine jewellery and a matched pair of exquisite knives on the body of a dead Samarlan. Crake had even discovered a beautifully bound book, which for some reason Frey had quickly appropriated. The Cap'n barely read in his native language, let alone Samarlan.

He'd have to go and check on Bess later. He'd need to ask Silo to help him repair her armour, but generally she seemed none the worse for wear, which was a relief. All in all, the heist was a success. The only casualty was Pinn and, to be honest, if anyone needed shooting, it was him.

'Can you grab me some carbolic, mate?' Malvery asked, as he was laying out the instruments he would use to scare Pinn with before eventually agreeing to gas him unconscious. 'It's in the dresser.'

Crake walked over to it and began opening drawers. 'Where?'

'Third drawer down on the right. No, wait, the second.'

But Crake had already opened the third drawer down on the right. There were no medical supplies in there, but a small collection of keepsakes and personal effects. A ferrotype album and various documents, including an old membership certificate for the Guild of Surgeons. Lying to one side was a small, velvet-covered box.

Ordinarily, he wouldn't have been so rude as to pick it up and open it. But he recognised the size and shape, and he had an idea what was inside. Curiosity got the better of him.

It was a medal, the size of a coin, with its ribbon folded up underneath it. A metal circle surrounding an X. Simple, but carefully detailed with lacquer and filigree.

'The Duke's Cross,' Crake said, his eyes widening.

Malvery looked up from his task. 'Wondered where that got to.

Didn't have space to keep everything in those piddly little quarters we get, so I took to storing bits and bobs in here.'

'Bits and bobs?' Crake said in amazement. He held the medal up. 'This is yours?'

'Aye,' said Malvery. 'Aye, it was. I mean, it is.'

'You've had this all this time and you never told anyone?'

'There's plenty secrets this crew ain't told each other, I reckon,' said Malvery. 'I forgot about it, mostly.'

'How did you get it?'

'First Aerium War, I was a field surgeon on the front line. Saved a few fellers once, pulled 'em out of a firefight. They gave me a medal.'

'So why keep it quiet? Aren't you proud of it?'

'Course I am. Prouder than I ever was about anything. Just seems it belongs to that younger feller who won it, not to me.'

'Hey!' Pinn said indignantly, raising his head. 'Who cares about some stupid medal? I'm dying, here!'

'Exactly,' said Malvery, with a bland look at Crake. 'Who cares? Now can you get me that carbolic, like I asked?'

The *Ketty Jay*'s engine room was like an oven.

Silo was no stranger to this heat. He'd been born in it and had grown up in it. He'd felt it in the cells, in pens and camps, in factories and in the jungle after he'd escaped his captors. It wasn't the same as any summer in Vardia. It was hotter, drier, carrying the smell of baked earth and dust. It drew sweat from the skin and punished the energetic. An oppressive, hateful heat.

Samarla was out there, and it wanted him. He should never have come back here.

He moved through the cramped maze of metal walkways that hugged the *Ketty Jay*'s engine assembly, testing this and that, hovering like a restless wasp at an apple. His adjusted the electromagnets that pulverised refined aerium into ultralight gas. As usual, it was unnecessary. Everything was in order. The whole assembly had only been put in a few months ago, by some of the best engineers in Yortland. Silo had become somewhat redundant after that. Gone were the days when the *Ketty Jay*'s engine just barely held together, and only Silo's frantic industry kept her alive.

He missed those days.

Slag, the *Ketty Jay*'s ancient cat, was lying on the injector pipe, drowsing in the heat. Silo normally liked having Slag around. He approved of the cat's silent company and his independence. Slag wouldn't suffer to be petted. He came and went as he pleased. But the cat's presence irritated him now. The fact that the engine ran so damned well irritated him. Everything irritated him.

Shoulda spoke up, he told himself. He thought in Vardic nowadays, in the same rough border dialect that he spoke. He hadn't heard or spoken Murthian in almost a decade. *Shoulda said somethin' to the Cap'n.*

But what would he have said? Leave me in Vardia, I don't want to go with you? Where would he stay? A Murthian wouldn't last long on his own. If he wasn't lynched by people itching to settle old scores from the Aerium Wars, he'd be kidnapped and returned to Samarla. His former masters offered a reward for returned slaves.

Even in Vardia, he was scarcely more free than he'd been in Samarla. At least in Samarla, he'd been able to see the chains.

Enough o' that, he thought in disgust. *I'm still a man, ain't I? And on this crew, what I say, it got weight. Maybe I don't say much, but that's alright. I chose that path. Chose to keep my silence after what happened.*

But a man gotta raise his voice if he got a 'pinion. Or he can't blame no one but himself when he suffers.

Not long ago he'd met a Samarlan. It was the first time he'd seen one since Frey flew him out of the jungle. That encounter had reminded him of something he'd spent years trying to forget. He was a slave. He'd always be a slave, no matter how far he ran.

He'd killed that Samarlan. Thrown him off the roof of a building. It had felt like liberation, for a while. But one man's death didn't liberate him. He still skulked out of sight, keeping his head down, hiding in the engine room. He still kept his opinions to himself. He still did what he was told.

Anger boiled up inside him. A sudden, uncontrollable fury. He felt it coming, and fought to cap it. He gritted his teeth, screwed his eyes shut, and exerted every ounce of control he had. His fingers tightened around the wrench in his hand. It was like a searing flood inside him, a need to kill everything and everyone, to destroy himself in one glorious rampage and then—

He whacked the wrench against the side of the assembly. Once, twice, three times. The cat took fright and bolted in a scrabble of claws.

That small violence took the edge off his anger. Slowly, it subsided. He was left panting, sweat trickling from his shaven scalp to drip off his nose.

Worse than ever. Damn it. Worse than ever.

Rage had been the bane of his family. It had killed his father and his brother and it had almost killed him. As a young man, he'd made the decision that he'd never let it consume him the way it had them. But sometimes, just sometimes, there was too much to keep inside.

Samarla. Just being here brought back the memories. The beatings. The forced labour. His countrymen, murdered before his eyes. But most of all, most of all, the *humiliation*.

But there were other memories, too. Memories of revenge. Fighting those Daks on the Rattletraps, chasing them down, he'd felt powerful. He hadn't felt that for a long time. But he'd been reminded of it during the battle for the train, how he'd once been more than he was now. It had fired his blood and smashed his calm with an ease that frightened him.

You shouldn't'a come.

He was loyal to the Cap'n, and proud of it. Loyal enough that he'd taken a bullet for him once. But when did loyalty become servitude? And when did servitude become slavery? He didn't blame the Cap'n for not consulting him about going to Samarla. He blamed himself for submitting to the decision without a word of protest.

You chose this path, 'member? After what happened. Never again, you said. Never again.

But Samarla was out there, beyond the *Ketty Jay*. The hated land. And suddenly it felt like everything he'd achieved since he escaped was futile.

He'd never left this place, not really. He'd dreamed of freedom, but a dream was all it had been. He'd exchanged one oppressor for another, and this one he couldn't get away from.

You still a slave, he thought. *And what's worse, you done it to yourself this time.*

* * *

'Well,' said Frey. 'There it is.'

'There it is,' Ashua agreed.

They were standing in the cargo hold, both with their arms crossed.

'So what is it?' Ashua said at length.

'I gather it's a protective case of some kind.'

'So what's it protecting?'

'That, I don't know,' Frey replied.

They regarded the object without much hope of enlightenment. It was a black oblong, a metre and a half in length, twenty centimetres thick and thirty wide. Beyond that, it was utterly featureless. It lay on the flat lid of the chest that contained the rest of the salvage.

The case that enclosed the relic kept its mysteries within.

They were alone in the cargo hold, except for Bess, who had gone dormant and now stood lifeless in the stifling gloom. Crake and Malvery had taken Pinn to the infirmary. Silo was in the engine room, as usual. Jez and Harkins, after helping them secure the Rattletraps, had gone off to run diagnostics in the cockpit. It was only a one-person job, but Harkins was happy to tag along.

Frey briefly wondered if Harkins had thought through the consequences of his obsession with the navigator. Jez's heart didn't beat, and she didn't breathe. If he did manage to consummate his desire, surely it would qualify as necrophilia. Still, he couldn't see Harkins ever making it with a *live* girl, so he supposed it was fair enough to try.

'We ought to look inside,' Ashua said.

'You reckon?'

'Give it a go,' she urged. 'Try to open it.'

'We're not supposed to.'

'Why? Because the ghoul told you? You do everything she says?'

Frey snorted. 'You do it, if you're so keen.'

Ashua made a soft clucking noise, like a chicken. Frey shook his head in despair. 'You're such a child.'

Ashua waited expectantly.

'Although, now I think about it,' Frey continued, 'I don't much like carrying cargo when I don't know what it is.'

'Dangerous for all concerned,' Ashua agreed.

'Your fingers are smaller than mine. You might have better luck.'

'You haven't even tried yet. Might be you do the job just fine.'

They stared at the case for a while.

'Will you just *open* it?' Ashua snapped suddenly.

'Alright!' Frey cried, throwing his hands up in the air. He stalked over to the case and ran his fingers over it, searching for a way in. It had a strange texture, somewhere between stone and metal. There was no seam that he could find. If he hadn't been warned not to open it, he wouldn't have guessed it opened at all.

He should probably just leave it alone, he decided. But he didn't like to look bad in front of a woman. Even if she was a gobby, tattooed street-rat he probably had a decade on.

'Try the other side,' Ashua urged him.

'I was getting to it,' he replied irritably. He turned the case around and felt along the edge, where he encountered a faint row of depressions in the surface. 'There's something here.'

'What?'

'I'm not sure. I—' Then he stopped, because the case was slowly, silently opening with the lazy gape of a crocodile. He stepped back. 'Reckon I did something right.'

The case split open as if hinged on one side, although there were no hinges to be seen. Inside lay a weapon of some kind. It took up the entire length of its container, resting in a delicately wrought cradle of metal. The relic.

It looked like some kind of enormous double-bladed sword. At its centre was a handle of carven bone, big enough to grip with two hands. Projecting from each end of the handle was a long, narrow blade. The blades curved slightly in opposite directions. They were not made of metal, but a stone-like substance which had no lustre. It was beautifully fashioned, but there was an unsettlingly alien quality to the delicate whorls and curves cut into the surface. He saw patterns of circular indentations and tiny clusters of incomprehensible symbols.

On the inside of the lid was a teardrop-shaped emblem wrought in shining grey metal. It looked like a stylised wolf, or some kind of dog. Frey glanced at it for a moment before returning his attention to the infinitely more attractive item beneath it.

'Now that looks like it would fetch a few ducats,' he commented. 'How old do you think it is?'

Ashua crowded close to have a look. She was dusty and filthy and the attractive new-sweat smell of her had been replaced by a stale odour now they were out of the sun. None of which stopped Frey being suddenly very conscious of her proximity.

I need a shower, he thought to himself. *Very long and very cold.*

'Well, the Sammies have been around longer than anyone,' said Ashua. 'First civilisation, and all that. So if this counts as a *relic* to them...' She shook her head slightly. 'Doesn't make sense. It could be thousands of years old, but it looks like it was made yesterday.'

'Maybe they built things to last back then. What do you reckon the blades are made of?'

'Dunno. Touch 'em and see.'

'Hey, I opened it. Your turn.'

'Frey,' she said. He turned to meet her gaze. Then, very slowly, she puffed out her cheeks and began to cluck like a chicken again.

'You,' he said, 'are a bad influence.'

She grinned at him. He put out his hand and laid it on the flat of the blade. It felt completely smooth, almost glasslike.

'I think it's some kind of ceramic,' he said. 'Weird. Never seen a blade like that, in Samarla or anywhere. Not even up in Yortland, and they make weapons out of any old shit up there. Seal bones and bear teeth and whatnot.'

'Try it out,' Ashua suggested.

'What?'

'Go on. Take it out, give it a swing.' When Frey rolled his eyes at her, she cocked her head and raised an eyebrow. 'Don't bother resisting. You know you're going to do it anyway.'

'I really shouldn't,' said Frey, as he gripped the handle and lifted it out. It was startlingly light.

'Careful,' said Ashua. 'Don't—'

Frey yelped as a sharp pain lanced through his hand, and he let go of the weapon. It crashed to the floor with a clatter.

'—drop it,' Ashua finished wearily.

'It bloody *bit* me,' said Frey. The palm of his right hand was aflame with the memory of the pain. A single bead of blood had gathered there. He showed it to her. 'Look!'

'Poor baby,' she said. 'Quite a wound.'

'Oh, piss off.'

She crouched next to the blade, searching it for signs of chips or scratches. 'You'd better not have damaged it.'

'Put it back in the container,' said Frey. 'Damn thing's a menace.'

'You think I'm touching it now? No, thanks. You put it back.'

'*I'm* not touching it!'

'Well, we'll leave it on the floor, then. Makes no odds to me. You shouldn't have taken it out.'

Frey gritted his teeth in frustration. 'You know, I could just kick you out the cargo door and leave you in the desert,' he reminded her. 'We've got the loot now.'

'You won't kick me off,' she said, with infuriating confidence.

'Why not?'

'You're not the type. You're soft on women.'

'I am not!' he said indignantly.

'Oh, you are,' she said with a smile. 'You're a handsome guy under all that dirt. I bet you go through women like socks. That means you're either a self-absorbed narcissist who needs female attention to groom his ego, or you're a bitter closet misogynist who's out to get revenge on women through some weird domination-and-conquest thing.'

Frey was rather pleased that she'd called him handsome. He made a show of considering the question, to disguise the fact that he didn't understand some of the words. 'I like the sound of the first one more,' he ventured.

'That's what I reckoned.'

'Where did you learn to talk like that? You sound like Crake sometimes.'

She shrugged, evading the question. 'You gonna pick up that sword-thing, then?'

Frey didn't much want to, but it was clear that she wasn't going to help him out, and he couldn't just leave it there as evidence of what he'd done. How would he explain it to the crew? Or to Trinica?

'Fine!' he snarled. '*I'll* do it.' He bent down and gingerly lifted the weapon, gripping the blades with his thumbs and fingertips, careful not to touch the edges. He turned it over awkwardly and inspected it. It seemed unharmed. Well, if the buyer noticed any damage, he'd just say it was there already.

'Try not to fumble it this time,' Ashua said.

Frey tensed for a moment, wondering if it was too late to change his mind about kicking her off. He took a breath and decided to be a bigger man than that.

'We never opened the case, right?' he said.

'*You* never opened it,' she corrected.

He put the blade back in its cradle and closed the case. It became a simple black slab again, with no sign of a seam.

'Sooner we're out of this damn country, the better,' he muttered. He stamped off towards the cockpit, flexing his sore hand.

EIGHT

THE SILENT TIDE—TRINICA'S SUGGESTION—
THE TOAST OF THE BARFLIES—A CONFESSION

Frey just couldn't get comfortable. He shifted his weight in the chair, but that didn't seem right either. He didn't know where to put his elbows. He was too hot in the jacket he wore. He plucked at the cuffs and looked about, feeling hunted.

The restaurant was exquisite, with walls and columns of pink marble. Gold chandeliers and sconces spread islands of soft light over the tables. Polished cutlery and glass glittered around small but artfully crafted centrepieces. Dakkadian waiters glided silently past, carrying dishes.

The diners were mostly expat Vards, but there were a smattering of Samarlans among them. Sammies had their own restaurants and clubs, where foreigners weren't allowed, but this restriction didn't apply in reverse. Here, in the Free Trade Zone, the races mixed and mingled in a way they couldn't do anywhere else. Frey had heard on the grapevine that this was the place to go if you were a rich Vard in Shasiith. So that was where he'd gone, even though he was anything but rich.

Frey had one of the best tables. He was sitting right up against the balustrade, on a veranda that extended out over the banks of the river below. The city lights shone from the far bank, multiplied in the slow-moving black water. It was night, and still blood-warm, but a faint and merciful breeze stirred the air.

He was glad he'd insisted on this table when he made the reservation. It meant that he wasn't surrounded. He'd been to society functions before, always unwillingly, and he always hated them. Cultured folk made him deeply uneasy. They had a way of making him feel like an intruder. No matter how well he disguised himself as one of them, they sensed him: an uneducated orphan, without manners or finesse, trying to clamber above his allotted station. One wrong move and they might fall on him like wolves and tear him limb from limb.

He sipped from a glass of water and dearly wished it was something stronger. He fidgeted in his seat and adjusted his clothes. He'd borrowed them from Crake, who was roughly the same size. They were too light against his skin and didn't seem to hang right. He felt unprotected and vulnerable, and despite all Crake's assurances he thought he looked a little stupid.

He picked up the menu and scanned it for the tenth time, to give himself something to do. It was written in both Samarlan and Vardic, not that it made the meals any more comprehensible. He cast his eye over the wine list. His sphincter tightened involuntarily at the prices. How could a few glugs of booze possibly be worth that much?

Don't think about it, Darian. You're in their world now.

Damn, he was nervous.

Then he saw her, as she was led out onto the veranda by a waiter. He raised his hand in tentative greeting, wearing an expression so eager it was almost comical. The waiting was at an end: the tortured awkwardness of the lonely diner was over. He'd wondered whether she'd come at all, or how long he'd be able to stand it if she was late. But now Trinica was here, and everything was alright.

He'd witnessed her transformations before, but they were so rare that they never failed to overwhelm him. Most of the time she looked like she belonged in a straitjacket, but sometimes, just sometimes, she changed for him.

She'd stripped away her white make-up, her red lipstick, her black contact lenses. She'd styled her chopped and tattered hair until, somehow, it flattered her. She'd put on a dark blue dress that clung to her narrow hips. She'd become the woman he'd known before, the woman he'd loved and discarded when he was still just an idiot boy who wasn't ready for marriage or children or any of that.

How he wished he could go back and talk some sense into that boy now. To tell him what he'd be giving up. What ruin he'd bring on both of them, and how he might never be able to make it right again. Maybe then that boy would've thought twice about running out on her on their wedding day.

But, he had to admit, it would probably have made no difference. He wouldn't have listened. And they'd still be where they were tonight, two people on opposite sides of a broken and shattered wasteland, trying to pick a path through the rubble to reach one another.

He got up as she approached and pulled her chair out for her. It made him feel absurd, but Crake had told him to do it, so he did. Trinica must have thought the gesture strange, coming from him, but to her credit she gave no sign, and seated herself as if it happened to her every day. He sat back down, mildly embarrassed but relieved that no disaster had occurred.

She looked over the balustrade at the view. 'I'm impressed,' she said. 'When you coerced me into a private rendezvous, I didn't expect such a lovely venue.'

'*Coerced* is a bit strong,' said Frey. He couldn't keep a grin off his face. 'I'd say *gently encouraged*.'

'I hope that my presence here means the relic will be delivered to me as promised? And there'll be no more talk of running off to fence it yourself?'

'I'll bring it over to the *Delirium Trigger* when I get back,' he said. 'As long as you're nice.'

'Darian,' she said chidingly. 'I'm *always* nice.'

'Oh, I almost forgot. I have a present for you.' He produced a book from beneath the table and passed it to her. She looked down at it and then back up at him with something like amazement in her eyes.

'Hope it's something good,' he said. 'I can't even read the title. Just thought, y'know… you have a lot of those sort of books in your cabin, so I nicked it off the train.'

'It's called *The Silent Tide*,' she said. She stroked the cover lightly. 'It's a beautiful edition. Thank you.'

'What's it about?'

'It's a classic romance.'

'Do they get it together at the end?'

'No. They die. It's a tragedy.'

'Oh.' He wasn't sure if that made it a good gift or a bad one. But she seemed delighted, so he reckoned he'd done well.

The waiter, who had been hovering at a polite distance, approached and asked them if they would like some wine.

Frey bumbled. He'd been so busy gaping in horror at the wine prices that he hadn't actually thought to pick one. He blanked for a moment then said: 'I think the lady should choose?' He looked at Trinica. 'I'm sure you know your wine. Pick any one you like.'

'*Any* one?' she said, in a tone that he didn't like. 'My, my.'

She laid her hand on the wine menu, drawing it towards her. She regarded him for a long moment, a faint smile playing at the edge of her lips. Then she handed the menu to the waiter without opening it, and said something to him in rapid Samarlan. The waiter took the menu, gave a little bow of acknowledgment, and left.

Frey watched her, mesmerised. When he was in the mood, he found her full of little wonders. The effortless way she dealt with the world made him melt in admiration.

She caught his look. 'Darian,' she said, almost as a warning. But he couldn't help himself, he had to stare at her, and after a moment she looked away and blushed. Actually blushed. The sight shocked him. He hadn't seen her blush in more than a decade.

They fell into their old, easy rhythms of conversation. Each time they met, it took them less and less time to relax with one another. The wine came, and they talked. Frey tried to keep the conversation light. He was keen that words shouldn't get in the way. All he wanted was to enjoy this time with her, this being together, and he wanted her to feel that too.

Trinica ordered his dinner for him, because he didn't recognise anything on the menu as food. When it came, it was delicious – she knew his tastes – but he was still none the wiser as to what it actually was. She picked at her dish, eating slowly with tiny, precise bites. Frey usually wolfed his meals down, but tonight he made sure to pace himself according to Crake's instructions, and he talked with such enthusiasm that she finished before he did.

'How was it?' he asked, when the waiter had cleared away their plates and left dessert menus behind.

'Wonderful,' she said, with an earnestness that warmed him. Her eyes shone. It was as if she'd gradually been coming alive throughout the meal, as if every bite restored her more and more.

'I thought you'd like it. All this.' He waved a hand to indicate the restaurant. 'Thought maybe you hadn't been to one in a while.'

An expression of tender gratitude crossed her face, just for a moment, and then she looked away quickly and it was gone. The woman she'd been had enjoyed many meals like this, and in grander places. She was accustomed to finery, and there had been little enough of that as a pirate. This was her normality, but she'd not been normal for a long time.

'I am rather enjoying being anonymous,' she said. 'No one casting sidelong glances at me, no need to worry about where the exits are or who might be out for the bounty on my head.'

'I wish I could do what you do,' said Frey. 'Take off my disguise, stop being a captain for a night.'

'What if *this* is the disguise?'

'No,' he said. 'This is you. That pirate queen get-up might work on your crew, but you can't fool me.'

She seemed pleased. 'Well, disguise or not, I'm still the captain. You never stop being that.' His face must have fallen a little then, because she frowned and said: 'Darian, something's troubling you.'

'Something happened, during the heist,' he said. But he didn't want to tell her about the Dak with the bayonet. He wanted to drop the subject entirely, since they were straying into serious territory, but he couldn't think of a way to deflect her.

'You know what happened to my last crew,' he said, eventually.

It was a statement, not a question, but she answered anyway. 'I know. The Shacklemores told me.'

He grasped for some way to get at what he wanted to say. 'How do you cope?' he asked. 'I mean, your crew worship you. They want you to lead them. But what if you get it wrong? What if you make a mistake, and all those people die?'

'I should think, if that happened, I'd die with them.'

'You would, wouldn't you?' he said. 'You're just the kind to go down with the ship.'

'Not with the ship. With the crew.' She leaned forward. 'Darian, your crew aren't your slaves. They're not even really employees. They choose to do what they do. They share in the risk and they share in the profit. If they're loyal, it's because you earned it from them. And they *are* loyal, though sometimes I'm at a loss as to why. They'd follow you anywhere.'

Frey nodded thoughtfully. 'They'd follow me. That's what I'm afraid of.' Then he hit on a way to the heart of what was bothering him. 'You know what it is? It never mattered if I failed before. Everyone pretty much expected me to screw up. But ever since Sakkan, it's like I have to be right all the time. And every time I *am*, every time I pull off something like this train heist, it only makes it worse.'

Trinica looked sympathetic. 'You never could handle it when things were going well.'

'Reckon you're right at that,' said Frey. He sat back and sipped his wine, his face sour. 'Never really thought I deserved it.'

Trinica cocked her head, her green eyes puzzled, as if that were the oddest thing she'd ever heard. But then her gaze dropped, and she gave a little shake of her head.

'I wish I had something to say that would make it better, but I don't. This is what being a captain is. And you *will* fail, sooner or later. If you keep the course you're on, you *will* lose crew, because the both of us play a dangerous game. If you're not ready for that, then you shouldn't be in command.'

Frey looked downcast. 'You've lost men. And I know you care about them. What do you tell yourself?'

'Some of them I've lost to you,' she reminded him. 'And it hurts, Darian. I won't lie to you. But I tell myself I did my best, and that losses are inevitable in our profession, and all manner of things like that. As long as I don't abuse their loyalty, I can look at myself in the mirror. The day I do is the day I don't deserve to lead them. Same applies to you.'

Frey smiled weakly, tapping his fingers on the table. 'I was kind of hoping you'd find a way to make me feel better, not worse.'

Then she did something that surprised him. She sat forward in her chair, hesitated as if uncertain, then quickly reached across the table and laid her hand over his, stilling his fingers. He felt a flush of warmth at her touch. Just this small contact was a gesture of extraordinary intimacy from her. Damn, how he wanted this woman. He couldn't be near her without feeling the urge to slide his arm around her waist, to kiss her neck, to be close to her. But this was not the woman he left behind, so he never did. He had to let her come to him: each small step needed to be Trinica's, with no sudden moves on his part.

If somebody somewhere gave out medals for restraint, then he reckoned he was due a couple for sure.

'Okay,' he said, breathing out as if he'd just hit the crest of a Shine high. 'That helps.'

She drew her hand away as quickly as she'd put it there, and looked almost bashful for having done it. That was Trinica. One moment she was all elegance, the next she was a child. She could dance and laugh and then she'd cut your tongue out. She would be giddy with happiness and then suddenly drop into a blackness that no one could save her from.

But she turned her anger on him less and less these days. And her dark moods didn't seem to reach her quite so often when he was around.

She looked up suddenly, struck with an idea. 'You need a first mate.'

'Is that an offer?'

She laughed brightly. 'I don't think so. You might be the toast of the barflies but you haven't caught up with me yet. I just think it might help to have someone to share the burden of command.'

'Who would I choose?' he asked. 'Pinn's too thick, Harkins is too scared, Malvery wouldn't want it and Silo's practically mute: he just does what he's told. Crake's smart but he's no leader.'

'Which leaves Jez.'

'Couldn't pick Jez. She's capable enough, but she's a half-Mane. You've seen her flip out.'

'Yes I have. And it saved our lives that day on the *Storm Dog*. Is it so bad?'

'The crew… listen, they all know how great she is at her job, but she'll always make them uneasy. And it doesn't help that she keeps to herself so much.'

'Well,' said Trinica. 'It's your choice, of course.'

But Frey really couldn't think of anyone suitable. 'You don't have a first mate. You've got that ugly feller Crund as your bosun.'

'He deals with the crew, but I don't need someone to discuss command decisions. The slightest hint of uncertainty would undermine me. I'm a woman leading a crew of violent men. I keep my own counsel on the *Delirium Trigger*.'

'Must be lonely.'

'It's what I have to do.'

There was something in her tone that brought the conversation to a halt. Frey became aware of the clink of cutlery, the murmur of the other diners in the restaurant, the steady flow of the river beyond the veranda. It felt like a moment, an empty space that was waiting to be filled, and before he knew it, he said:

'I miss you.'

He was immediately appalled. It was unforgivable to drop his guard like that. He'd been lulled by the night into spilling his feelings in a mess all over the table, and now he'd ruined everything. He waited for her to tell him not to be foolish, to wither him with her scorn.

Instead, she simply said: 'I know.' And there was such regret and sorrow in her eyes that she didn't need to say the rest of it, the part that couldn't be spoken aloud.

I miss you too.

He poured more wine, and they drank and ordered dessert. They talked of other things and didn't mention it again. But from that point on till the end of the meal, Frey had to restrain himself from punching the air for joy.

NINE

CRAKE'S PROBLEM—IMPERATORS, OR OTHERWISE —A DISTURBING REVELATION—THE REVELLERS RETURN—THE BLACK SPOT

The iron ball sat in the centre of the summoning circle, and didn't move.

Crake tapped the gauges on his portable oscilloscope. His fingers moved across the array of brass dials. He checked the wires leading to the tuning poles. Everything was in order. The phantom frequency that had been plaguing him all day was nowhere to be found.

He sat at his desk and let his head sink into his hands. 'I can't work under these conditions,' he complained.

Bess stirred in the corner of his makeshift sanctum. Perhaps she thought he was talking to her. When it became clear that he wasn't, she settled back to dormancy with a creak of leather and a jingle of chainmail.

It had all begun that morning.

Crake had managed a good night's sleep on the flight back to Shasiith – thankfully there were no encounters with the Navy to wake him. He was up early while most of the crew were still in their bunks. After rising he visited the head, where he had his first solid bowel movement in days. Encouraged by such a good start to the day, he decided to be productive. He wanted to try out a new technique he'd read about in a daemonist text he picked up before they left Vardia.

It was nothing dangerous, or even difficult. Just an improved method to identify the properties of minor daemons. It was a procedure that carried little risk, and he felt safe running it in his insecure sanctum.

But there was a problem. His oscilloscope readings, used to detect the presence of the daemons, were being skewed by a faint signal that roamed through the upper frequencies. At first he thought it was a machine fault, but all his tests showed that his equipment was working fine.

He decided it was something on the *Ketty Jay*. A fluctuation in the electrical systems, perhaps, or a vibrating pipe that happened to stray across his field of detection. Just one of the many annoyances that came from having to practise the Art in the back of an aircraft's cargo hold, with only a tarpaulin curtain and some crates for privacy.

By mid-morning the signal was driving him to distraction. He asked Silo to help find the problem, but the engineer seemed distracted. His assistance was half-hearted at best, and came to nothing.

Eventually Crake abandoned his original plan in favour of solving the issue at hand. He set up a small interference field with the tuning poles and wired a resonator to pads attached to a small iron ball, which he placed inside the summoning circle. He intended to thrall a daemon to the ball, and then set it to find the rogue frequency. If all went well, the ball would be attracted to the source of the frequency, and he could follow it. The formulae in his books helped him determine the bandwidth he needed to search to find the kind of daemon he needed. It was a simple task, child's play really.

Simple, but not quick. His target was elusive. It took him several hours of patient searching to drag in a suitable candidate. By bombarding the daemon with sound, he befuddled it for long enough to break its connection with its place of origin. In doing so, he thralled it to the iron ball, trapping it in the world that the uneducated called reality. After that, he doused it in the troublesome signal. This daemon was a seeker, a barely sentient wisp from the aether: it would find the first thing it was set to. The signal was like a rag to a bloodhound, to give it something to track.

When all was done and he was satisfied, he turned off the interference field. It was a weak form of defence, but more than was needed when dealing with such feeble daemons. Then he waited for the ball to roll off in the appropriate direction.

And nothing happened. Because the signal his daemon was supposed to find had gone. After he'd spent all day trying to find it, it had just stopped.

He sat at his desk, his head in his hands, thoroughly depressed. He'd wasted his time. He'd wasted so much of it, these past years. It hadn't seemed to matter when he was sunk in a bottle, grieving over the accident that had taken his niece. But Crake had once been driven in his quest for knowledge. His pursuit of the Art had been headlong and reckless. And he was getting impatient with himself.

Daemonism was what he was. How long could he sit around and do nothing about it?

He heard the hiss and whine of hydraulics as the cargo ramp opened at the far end of the hold, beyond the tarpaulin curtain and the crates. Someone going out, or someone coming back. He didn't care. Bess seemed content enough to sleep, or whatever it was she did when she stopped moving and the lights of her eyes went out. He thought he might go and read a little in his quarters, have an early night.

There was a noise from behind him. A soft rumble. He looked over his shoulder.

Slowly and steadily, the iron ball was rolling out of the circle.

Frey hummed a little ditty as he closed the cargo ramp behind him. He was feeling immensely pleased with himself. His dinner with Trinica had been a complete success. Not only that, but on receiving the bill he discovered that she'd ordered the house wine, the cheapest on the menu. She knew he wouldn't be able to tell the difference, so she'd chosen to have mercy on his wallet. Such a small kindness may not have been remarkable in most women, but from Trinica it was epic.

After their dinner, they took a rickshaw to her hotel. She'd taken a room for the night, but she wouldn't be staying there. It was purely to give her a place to change: to shed her fearsome outer skin after she left the *Delirium Trigger*, and to don it again before returning. Her crew would never know what she'd done for Frey. She was a terrible icon to them, a mistress to be adored, cold and distant as the moon. To show them the woman behind the mask would ruin her. To them, she *was* the mask.

Frey said goodbye at the hotel door. Had it been any other woman Frey would have attempted to charm his way inside, and into her bed. Instead, he kissed her on the cheek and promised to be at the *Delirium Trigger* in an hour with the relic. Every instinct he had demanded more from the encounter, but he mastered himself and walked away, antsy with sexual frustration.

The *Delirium Trigger* was already prepping for take-off when he got to the hangar where the frigate was berthed. They arrived in a pair of rickshaws, with Malvery and Pinn guarding the relic. Ashua took up the fourth seat. She didn't trust Frey to collect her fee for her, and wisely so.

Balomon Crund, Trinica's bosun, took delivery of the relic and paid them. Trinica chose not to make an appearance. Frey didn't mind. He wanted to remember her the way he'd left her.

Ashua seemed surprised that Trinica had paid them off without trying to cheat them. She'd been wired up for an argument that never came. Now that their plan had actually worked out, she became giddy. She even gave Frey a hug, which in his current state of enforced celibacy was all but unbearable.

Malvery and Pinn wanted to go out on the town, and the doctor invited Ashua along in celebration of their victory. Frey didn't feel like it tonight, so he said he'd take the money back to the *Ketty Jay* instead. He planned to take a couple of drops of Shine and lose himself in a blissful private reverie, dreaming of the woman he hoped to win back.

That was the only thing on his mind as the *Ketty Jay*'s cargo ramp shut with a dull thump. But once the echoes had faded, he found himself faced with a hungry and threatening silence. The tune he was humming faltered and stalled. The hollow belly of the *Ketty Jay* seemed cold, despite the stifling air outside. Goosepimples crept across his skin.

Something was very, very wrong.

Imperators.

His mind flew to the conclusion immediately. The Awakeners' most dangerous operatives, beings that could paralyse a man with crushing, primal fear and drag out the secrets of his soul. He drew his revolver. It wouldn't do any good, but it made him feel better.

They've found me.

The seconds ticked by, and nothing happened. His eyes roamed the hold. It was emptier than usual, but that still left plenty of places to hide among the junk that Frey never got round to throwing out. The battered Rattletraps, which Frey had decided to keep hold of until Silo could repair them for resale, were belted down and silent.

He felt alone. His senses told him there was nobody else on board,

CHRIS WOODING

and while he was certain that wasn't true, he didn't dare raise his voice to find out.

Were there Imperators here? Now he wasn't sure. There was no question that the fear he felt was something unnatural, but it wasn't anywhere near the intensity of an Imperator's gaze, which could turn a man's bowels to water. This was the sourceless dread of a bad drug trip, seeping into him like cold blood into a rag. The paranoia, the sense of wrongness and displacement.

Keep it together, Darian.

That was when he heard the sound.

At first he thought it was Slag. It seemed the kind of low, menacing yowl made by a cat at bay. But then the intruder hitched in a breath in a way a cat never would, and he recognised it.

There was a baby crying in the cargo hold.

'You have *got* to be joking,' he muttered to himself.

The crying came from behind a large pile of tarpaulin that had been stuffed in a net and tied down near the port side bulkhead. Frey crept towards it. He'd rather have gone the other way, but there was a certain dreamlike inevitability about this situation. Nothing felt quite real.

He flexed his hand nervously on the grip of his revolver. He wasn't sure whether a crying baby merited a gun in his hand or not, but there was something unspeakably malevolent about that wail. It tugged at him with a sense of awful familiarity. He felt like he should *know* it, somehow.

He rounded the pile. Something was moving there. Something...

Repulsion battled with terror on his face as he saw what was hidden behind the tarpaulin.

His first impression was that it was some kind of giant maggot, a bloated, shapeless thing rolling in a puddle of fluid. It stank: a smell both sweet and rancid that ambushed Frey as it came into sight. The sheer impossibility of its being there, the horror of the thing, stunned him.

But it was no maggot. It was a sac. A grotesque, veined bag, whitish and slimy, with something bulging inside it, pushing against the skin. Something long-limbed, its joints bending unnaturally, turning inside the

womb

and Frey's mind went treacherously to his *own* child, the baby that was never born. The baby that died inside Trinica when she tried to commit suicide as a young woman, broken by a lover's betrayal. *His* betrayal.

The baby was still crying. It wasn't coming from inside the sac. It was coming from everywhere.

This. Is. Not. Happening.

The sac stretched on one side as something long and narrow was pressed against it from within. For an instant it held, then it parted in one quick tear, the lips of the split sliding greasily down the length of the object that poked out.

A bayonet. A double-bladed Dakkadian bayonet, the same kind he'd been skewered by nine years ago, on the day his crew were massacred. The same kind that had almost taken his life yesterday.

He stared as it sliced downward, slitting the stringy tissue of the sac. Sweet-smelling amniotic fluid belched from the rupture and sloshed over the floor. Frey stepped back from it, disgusted. He took his eyes off the squirming sac for an instant, to avoid the wash of liquid. When he looked back he saw that something was forcing its way through the slit in the sac, moist with new birth, and damned if it wasn't a *muzzle*, some kind of *animal*, and—

Something bumped against Frey's boot heel. He swung around with a cry. His arm snapped out straight, revolver in hand.

'Don't shoot! It's me! It's me!'

Me was Crake, who had suddenly found himself with Frey's revolver pressed against his nose. Frey blinked in bewilderment. In an instant, everything had changed. There was no crying baby. The sense of paranoia had lifted, with only his hammering heart as evidence that it had ever existed. He looked over his shoulder at the spot where the squirming thing had been. He knew before he turned that there would be nothing there.

He lowered his pistol. Crake glared at him and rubbed his nose resentfully. There was a small iron ball at Frey's feet, resting against his boot. He shoved it away with the side of his foot.

'Crake,' he said. 'I think I'm going mad.'

Crake watched as the ball rolled away, slowed, and then reversed direction to bump against Frey's boot again.

'What worries me, Cap'n,' he said, 'is that you may not be.'

* * *

'And you're sure you didn't see or hear *anything*?' Frey asked.

'We've been over this. I'm quite sure,' Crake replied. He sipped his coffee and stared off thoughtfully into the distance. In the *Ketty Jay*'s cramped mess, that wasn't very far. It was a grim little room, comprising the fixed table where they sat, a stove and worktop, and some metal cabinets for utensils. Frey had been meaning to pretty it up for ever, but the prospect of the task always defeated him. Interior decorating was not his strong suit.

He frowned in frustration. 'And you don't have any idea what this… *signal* is?'

'All I know is that it's coming from you.'

It wasn't enough. Frey had submitted himself to almost two hours of Crake's tests, wired up to various ticking and humming machines in the sanctum while the daemonist twiddled knobs and scribbled formulae. He trusted Crake to provide him with some answers. But Crake had come up with none.

Crake scratched the back of his neck. 'I've never seen anything like it before.'

'Is it daemonic?'

'Could be. Could be mechanical.'

'A device on me? Something that's transmitting?'

'On you or *in* you.'

Frey was feeling fragile already. He didn't need that.

'The Imperators?' he suggested.

'I doubt it,' said Crake. 'They wouldn't trouble themselves with giving you hallucinations. If they were after you, they'd just kill you.'

Frey found that oddly reassuring. He had special reason to be wary of the Imperators. A few months ago he'd delivered certain documents to a professor named Kraylock. Maurin Grist's research notes, which all but proved that the Imperators were secretly daemonic half-men. Since the Awakeners had ruthlessly persecuted daemonists for over a century, Frey found it somewhat amusing that they'd been caught employing daemons themselves.

The Archduke had been less amused when he saw the notes. He issued a public demand for the Awakeners to hand over all their Imperators to establish the truth of the accusation. The Awakeners refused. Tension across the land was unpleasantly high, and getting higher. Things in Vardia were not looking good, which was half the reason Frey had ducked out to Samarla for a while.

If the Awakeners had discovered Frey's hand in the situation, his life wouldn't be worth crowshit. But Crake was right. This didn't *feel* like them.

'What's going on?' he lamented. There was too much about this situation that was unknown. It scared him when he didn't know who his enemy was.

'I might be able to find out if I could get to a decent sanctum,' Crake said, with a complaining tone to his voice that Frey had heard a lot recently.

'Your friend Plome has one, doesn't he?' Frey suggested quickly, before Crake could start on about the lack of facilities aboard the *Ketty Jay*.

'I think I've abused his friendship quite enough for the time being,' Crake replied. 'Anyway, he won't be at home. It's coming up to election time, and he's running for a seat in the House of Chancellors. He'll be all over the duchy, pressing flesh and kissing babies.'

Frey drummed his fingers on the table. The terror he'd felt in the hold had already receded. The whole incident seemed like a nightmare, and like a nightmare it faded in the face of reality. He was beginning to wonder whether it was just a product of general bad living, or a delayed flashback from some particularly dirty narcotics he'd experimented with in his younger days. But then there was this... *signal*. He didn't really understand Crake's methods, or what frequencies and bandwidths had to do with daemonism, but his friend's manner told him he should be concerned.

There was a clattering from overhead, and raucous voices. Pinn came clambering down the ladder from the passageway above. He missed his grip halfway down and landed heavily on his amply padded arse, making the mugs on the table jump and spill. Apparently he'd forgotten he had one arm in a sling. He looked stunned for a moment, then burst out laughing. Gales of laughter came from overhead. Malvery and Ashua. Both plenty drunk, by the sounds of it.

Frey let his head sink into his arms. He wasn't in the mood for this now.

'You're back early,' Crake commented, as Malvery and Ashua

climbed unsteadily down the ladder and into the mess.

'Spenn all my money,' said Pinn, who had tipped over to lie on his back. 'An' these two won' gimme no more.' He thrust a cupped hand into the air. 'Need an advance, Cap'n!'

Frey raised his head. They'd obviously been going at it hard tonight. 'What's she doing here?' he said, nodding at Ashua. 'I thought we were all done with her.'

Malvery crushed her in a huge embrace. 'She's alright, she is!' he slobbered. 'She's… she's like the daughter I never had!' He swallowed a toxic burp. 'Or wanted.'

Ashua tugged at his bushy white moustache. 'It's like having my own personal walrus!' she beamed.

'Somebody kill me,' Frey murmured in despair. 'Look, if I give Pinn some money, will you all bugger off?'

'What's up with him?' Malvery inquired of Crake.

'He just had a traumatic experience,' Crake replied.

'Oh, I see,' Malvery said gravely. He disengaged himself from Ashua, crouched down next to Frey and put a hefty arm round his shoulders. Then, in a tone more suited to pets and infants, he cooed: 'Did the Cap'n have a twaumatic expewience?' Pinn exploded with laughter.

'Piss off, Doc. It's serious,' Frey snapped, shaking himself free of Malvery's arm.

Malvery looked put out. 'Well,' he said. 'Someone's in a grump.'

'What's wrong with your hand?' Ashua asked. It took Frey a moment to realise that the question was directed at him. He looked down at his hand, and his blood ran cold.

There was a black spot in the centre of his palm, an uneven circle the size of a small coin. Dark tendrils of gangrenous purple spread away from it in an ugly starburst.

All the humour drained out of the room as they stared at it.

'Doc?' Frey asked tremulously.

'What've you done to yourself, Cap'n?' Malvery asked. The way he said it, weak and shocked, struck dread into Frey's heart.

Pinn, sensing the change in the room, got to his feet and staggered over to look. He sucked in his breath over his teeth. Frey expected him to make some dumb crack, but he didn't, and that meant that things were really serious.

'It was the blade,' said Ashua. 'You said it bit you when you picked it up.'

Yes, the blade. The sharp pain, like a pin, that caused him to drop the relic. Frey had barely thought about it. He'd just assumed it had been a tiny, sharp edge that he hadn't seen, a flaw in the hilt that had nipped him.

'Care to tell us all what you're talking about?' Crake prompted.

Ashua filled them in on the details, how Frey had opened the case they'd taken from the train and found the curious weapon inside. Frey noticed that she skipped over her part in the affair, the relentless goading which inspired him to pick it up in the first place, but he was too distressed to care.

His hand. He didn't need the doc to tell him that he was probably going to lose it. The enormity of that thought was too much to handle.

Just a few hours ago, he'd been so happy. Why couldn't he have just left the damned thing alone? Why didn't he do what he was told for once?

'You reckon it was poison?' Pinn suggested. The sight of Frey's hand had sobered him up fast.

'If it was, it's been in there too long to do anything about it,' said Malvery. 'If you'd come to me straight away, Cap'n...'

Frey turned to Crake. 'You think this and the signal might be connected?'

'It would be quite a coincidence if they weren't.'

Frey stared at his hand again. It was so strange. It didn't hurt or feel bad, yet the sight of it was appalling. The angry corruption beneath the skin made him feel sick.

'I was just with Trinica. *She* didn't notice,' he protested, as if he could somehow disprove this thing and make it go away.

'Maybe it just came on in the last few hours. Maybe she wasn't looking,' said Crake. 'Does it matter?'

It didn't matter. None of it mattered, because no one knew what to do. That was the most frightening thing of all.

It was Ashua who shook them out of it. She strode over to Frey and pulled him up out of his seat.

'You need help,' she said firmly. 'Come on.'

'Come on *where*?' Frey asked.

'This is *my* city, remember?' she said. 'Follow me.'

TEN

THE TAIL—JEZ ATTEMPTS—UNTOUCHABLES— SLINKHOUND—TOURISTS

It was the dead of night, which meant little in Shasiith. The place teemed like an ant colony. People swarmed over each other, talking and arguing, shopping and stealing. The air was a stew of heat and sweat and noise. Spiced bread and sizzling meat gave off a muddle of scents as vendors fed the hungry.

Like Jez, this city never slept.

Groups of men sat in the electric light of café fronts, sipping thick dark coffee and watching the chaos. Giant beasts shambled among the crowds, dragging heavy loads, their riders perched behind their heads. They were called rushu in the local tongue. Their tusks and horns had been given decorative tips in a halfhearted attempt to make them slightly less dangerous, but Jez thought they could cause terrible carnage if they had a mind to. Still, that was the way in Samarla. To foreign eyes, life here seemed disordered, frantic and cheap.

Jez had been filled in on the situation with the Cap'n, and she was deeply concerned. She'd come to feel protective towards him during her time on the *Ketty Jay*. He wasn't very good at looking after himself at the best of times: this new, mysterious injury was only confirmation of that. But it was the state of his mind as much as his body that kept her fretting. He was just a boy in many ways. He might have been outwardly handsome and charming, but she saw through all of that, and knew him to be more sensitive and insecure than he admitted to himself.

His relationship with Trinica made her uneasy. Part of her admired him for it, the way he would plough through any and all obstacles in his pursuit of her. She'd never felt that strongly about anything, and she was jealous of his passion. He was not stubborn, or a man possessed of a great amount of willpower, but when it came to Trinica he absolutely refused to quit.

Yet Trinica had betrayed him before, and Jez saw no reason why she wouldn't do so again. Her behaviour was no indication of her intentions; she'd proved that in the past. The last time it had hit Frey hard. The next time, he might not recover.

Oh, Cap'n. I hope you'll be alright.

With the exception of Silo, Bess and Harkins, the whole crew had sallied out into the streets, and they'd gone armed. It was too dangerous for Silo and Bess to leave the *Ketty Jay*, and Harkins was asleep. No one wanted to wake him up. Lately, he'd been keen to include himself in any missions, where he was usually more of a hindrance than a help. She assumed he was trying to ape the Cap'n's recent spate of reckless bravery, though she couldn't imagine why.

Ashua led them on foot through the city for half an hour, through streets that became progressively more narrow and ramshackle. Jez didn't trust her, even if she found her brash and cocky front preferable to Trinica's quiet treachery. But Ashua seemed to know where she was going and, despite being drunk, she went with some urgency.

Where they went, their mysterious tail followed them.

Jez had sensed him before she spotted him. Even among the crowds, he moved with purpose. A Dakkadian, a plain-looking young man wearing a brown embroidered robe and sandals. Jez never caught him looking at them, but she observed him from the corner of her eye when she turned her head to talk to her companions.

At first she hadn't been sure, but he'd stuck with them all the way into the slums. A man dressed so neatly had no business among these reeking lanes with their leaning shacks and steep narrow steps. Here, the air was a fug of petrol fumes from rattling generators, which powered the lights that shone behind tattered fabric curtains. Even the poorest of people in Samarla could lay their hands on petrol: the country welled with it. It was aerium they were starved of.

The slum dwellers were a mix of Dakkadian and Samarlan, all of them wise enough to stay out of the way of the conspicuously armed group passing through. Many of the Samarlans were of the untouchable caste, their black faces mottled with white patterns to signify their low status. Many, however, were not. They were just poor. Jez had visited Samarla briefly as a navvie on other craft, but this was the first time she'd really become aware that most Samarlans didn't live in luxury, as was popularly believed in Vardia. Crake, who had read Politics at Galmury University and knew a thing or two, had been educating her on the finer points of Samarlan society during their sightseeing excursions.

She caught up to Frey. 'Cap'n,' she said in a low tone.

'The feller following us? Yeah, I know. He's not very good.'

'Who do you think he works for?'

'Could be anyone.'

'Think we should do something about him?'

Ashua, who'd overheard the conversation, leaned over. 'Don't bother. He won't follow us where we're going.'

Frey looked at Jez and shrugged. 'What she said, I suppose.'

Jez wasn't satisfied with that. The Cap'n's mind was on other things, but she didn't like the idea of not knowing. She ran through a mental list of possibilities. Awakeners? Yes, they had good reason. The Shacklemores? They didn't usually employ Daks, but the Shacklemores were still after Crake as far as she knew. The man could even be spying for Trinica, although Jez suspected the pirate would have hired someone better.

She decided to try to find out.

The thought gave her a small thrill. She'd never attempted to read somebody's mind before. It had always just happened, as it had on the train the day before yesterday.

Well, she had the ability. There was no denying that. She might as well learn how to use it.

And so, as they walked, she slid into a shallow trance. She could put herself into trances and bring herself out with relative ease nowadays. She no longer feared the Manes waiting for her. They didn't howl and cry for her to join them any more. She'd been given the Invitation, she'd refused it, and they respected that choice. They still waited at the edge of her consciousness, but they never spoke to her.

With the trance came the familiar sharpening of the senses. Minute details became crisp and obvious; everything seemed *closer* somehow. Smells became distinct, so that she could separate out the different scents of her companions. She could hear the murmur of voices in distant shacks. She could never put her finger on the way that a trance made her feel, only that it made her more *here*, more present in the world.

But now that she was in the trance, she had no idea what to do next. She attempted to search with her mind, picturing the man behind them, pushing her thoughts at him. Nothing happened. She tried to remember the sensation she'd experienced when she read the man's mind on the train, but she couldn't duplicate it.

Eventually, she gave up. She came out of her trance, frustrated. There must be a technique to it, but she wouldn't crack it by guessing.

Until recently, she'd been afraid of her Mane side, terrified that it would consume her if she gave in to it. But now that she'd come to terms with herself, now that she accepted she was a half-Mane, she found herself curious about it. What *could* she do, exactly? What were the limits of her abilities? And how could she possibly find out?

It was she who had chosen to refuse the Invitation. She who had turned her back on the Manes and their love. But it was she who felt abandoned now.

Ashua stopped before a door. It was entirely unremarkable, halfway down a lane that teetered with precarious two-storey shacks built from the ruined skeletons of more stable buildings.

'One piece of advice,' Ashua said. 'Nobody draw weapons unless you absolutely have to. Normally they don't mind foreigners, but they've been known to be jumpy.'

Frey was regarding the door without much enthusiasm. 'What exactly is through there?'

'The Underneath,' said Ashua, and opened it.

Beyond the door was a labyrinth of passageways with roughly planked walls like the corridors of a mine. Electric bulbs fizzed, fed by precarious cables. It was close and stuffy, and the taller members of the crew had to duck their heads.

They passed through rooms full of tatty cots and bunk-beds. The occupants were all untouchables: mostly men, some women, and the occasional infant. They were skinny and their clothes were ragged. Sometimes they wore little more than loincloths. Their eyes were dull behind the white patterned masks that identified them, but for all that, their features had a delicate, elfin quality that made them handsome. It seemed strange to Jez to see such beautiful people in poverty, but then, the Samarlans were a beautiful race.

'What've they done to their *faces*?' Pinn asked loudly, with typical lack of tact. Malvery swatted him round the back of his head. 'What?' he demanded. 'They can't understand me.'

'It's a kind of acid,' Crake said. 'It breaks down the pigment in the skin. Like a reverse tattoo, I suppose. And they didn't do it *themselves*. It was done *to* them.'

The untouchables: lowest of the five Samarlan castes. Those whose ancestors had done something so terrible or dishonourable that their family name had been stricken from the records. There was no way back from that, not for the criminal or for their descendants. Newborns were marked by their own parents soon after birth, because it was death for an untouchable to be seen carrying a baby that wasn't of the same caste. And so the stigma carried through the generations, for ever. In Samarla, if you didn't have bloodline, you were nothing.

Jez had found much to admire about Samarla, but she still found it sickening that a culture could be so unforgiving. She had to remind herself that this was the same culture that had subjugated two different races of people and made them into slaves. Samarlan ways were not Vardic ways. She accepted that, but she didn't have to like it.

More corridors, more rooms. They pushed through threadbare curtains and met incurious gazes. Most of the untouchables were sleeping, exhausted by the day's activities. Few spoke, even to each other. They were a worn-out folk, ground down by hopelessness. This 'Underneath' that Ashua had mentioned – presumably a literal translation from Samarlan – appeared to be some kind of haven where they could lay their heads in peace.

Jez couldn't quite work out when they were above ground and when they were below it. She would convince herself that they were deep in the bowels of the earth, and then they would descend a flight of stairs and come across a room with a window looking out over the shallow bowl of the slum. At some point they began to head sharply downwards, and the planked walls closed in around them, with rough black stone visible through the gaps. The air became dense, the temperature dropped a little, and oil lamps replaced electric lights.

Presently they came to a wide corridor lined with shabbily constructed wooden bunks on both sides, like a crowded barracks or a tomb. There were untouchables here, too, but Jez sensed something different about them. They were alert and aware, and they watched the newcomers with interest. As they passed the bunks, some of the untouchables slipped out of bed and followed them. Up ahead, slim dark figures were sliding from their bunks. There were bone knives visible among the folds of their clothes, or hanging from rope belts.

'Miss Vode,' Frey murmured. 'Why do I feel suddenly threatened?'

Ashua stopped moving, and the crew followed suit. 'Nobody draw guns,' she reminded them.

'Pinn, that means you,' Frey added.

Pinn mumbled something obscene and took his hand away from his revolver.

The untouchables surrounded them, though they kept a careful distance. One man stepped forward. He was probably in his forties, but he was so weatherworn that he looked ancient. He spoke slowly to Frey in the moist, hissing Samarlan tongue.

Frey looked helplessly at Ashua, who replied in his place. She and the elderly Samarlan conversed for a time. The elderly man despatched one of the others, who went running down the corridor. Jez tried to follow what was going on by interpreting gestures and expressions, but Samarlans were not an easy people to read.

'What's the deal?' Frey asked, during a break in the conversation.

'They don't want to let us through,' she said. 'Don't worry, though. I've got contacts.'

'Down here?'

'Of course,' she said. 'Your average Sammie or Dak thinks so little of the untouchables that they're practically invisible. If they do notice them, it's just to kick them out of the way. They could plot against the God-Emperor himself with an untouchable in the room and it wouldn't matter, because no Sammie or Dak would ever speak to them to find out what they knew. But foreigners like me, we don't care about caste systems and all that crap. These fellers, they see and hear everything.' She grinned. 'How do you think I knew about that shipment?'

'This lot?' Frey was surprised.

'Invisible people make pretty good spies,' said Ashua. 'Ah, here's my man now.'

There was a commotion up the corridor, and another untouchable arrived. This one was taller than most, and dressed in a patchwork assortment of thin fabrics. He had a small bald head; the white acid-pattern on his black face gave it the appearance of a skull. He moved quickly and furtively, and there was a slyness about him. He looked healthier than most of his fellows.

The newcomer exchanged a few irritable words with the elderly man, gesturing at Ashua. Ashua spoke to them briefly, then turned to Frey. 'Show them your hand,' she said.

Frey did as he was told, and displayed the black corruption on his palm to the crowd. They gasped and shrank back from him.

'Speaking as a doctor,' said Malvery, 'I ain't encouraged by that reaction.'

'It got 'em out the way, didn't it?' Pinn said.

Ashua indicated the untouchable who had just arrived. 'Everyone, this is… well, you probably couldn't pronounce his name, but in Vardic it comes out as Slinkhound.'

Slinkhound grinned, showing crooked teeth.

'That is one rubbish name,' Pinn opined.

'Yeah, it loses something in the translation,' Ashua said. 'They've all got names like that. They get them when they become untouchable. Too much shame attached to their old name, and so on.' She waved in the air. 'Blah, blah, I'm sure none of you give a shit anyway. Let's get on with this, shall we?'

'What about the Dak who was following us?' Jez asked. 'Will they let him through?'

'A Dak on his own? He'd be lucky if he got out alive. We'll take a different way out; he'll never find us.'

Slinkhound beckoned them on impatiently. They followed him down a dark corridor and around several corners before the passage suddenly widened out into a gaping hole in the rock. Daubed around the edge were crude symbols in Samarlan script.

'What does that say?' Jez asked Ashua.

'It says "Welcome to the Underneath",' she replied.

'I thought we were already *in* the Underneath.'

'Nah,' said Ashua, as they passed through the hole. 'That was just one of many routes to get here.' She threw out her arms. '*This* is the Underneath.'

The crew stumbled to a stop. Jez's eyes widened as she looked out and up.

'Bugger me,' said Malvery, quietly.

Ashua shook her head with a smile. 'Tourists.'

ELEVEN

THE UNDERNEATH—NARCISSISM—A SORCERER— CRAKE RECONSIDERS—FREY'S LAST NIGHT

It was an underground town, built of wood and rope, spanning the cavern like a twisted web. The terrain was extremely uneven, plunging and bulging and thrusting up great stalagmites, but the town had conformed as best it could. Huts and shacks crowded into every available niche. Buildings piled up against the walls, the lower ones supporting the ones above. Rope bridges crisscrossed in the air, reaching across terrible drops, linking perch to perch. The cavern roof was lost in a haze of petrol fumes from generators that powered the weak and yellowed floodlights which bathed the town in a queasy glow.

Crake stared. He was amazed that a place as tumbledown and precarious as this had survived long enough to grow to such a size. It was cool and dim, so torches and lamps and oil-drum fires burned everywhere, despite the inflammable nature of the place. The town planners deserved hanging as well. Assuming anyone *had* planned this place, which he doubted. It must have grown like a mould.

He tutted to himself. *Don't be a snob, Grayther.* But he couldn't help it. He was an orderly man, and the chaos of Samarla in general – and this place in particular – offended his sensibilities.

Slinkhound led them down a slope and through a cluster of dwellings. There was activity all around them, though nothing like the free-for-all on the streets above. They passed a stall, little more than a table by the side of the trail, trading in scavenged junk and rags. The owner was haggling with a customer, and ended up swapping a dried strip of unidentifiable meat for some bits of fabric. Men nearby were helping a fellow untouchable put together a clumsy shack. Others sat around a fire, passing round a dirty bottle, smoking and talking.

Crake looked about uneasily at the people of the Underneath, and received suspicious gazes in return. The poverty of this place intimidated him. Especially since these people didn't seem broken and weary like those above, but defiant and possibly hostile. Crake had been brought up an aristocrat, and he'd never been entirely at ease around poor people, who were prone to rough jokes or explosive and bewildering violence.

Nevertheless, he was excited. They were going to see a sorcerer. A real, live Samarlan sorcerer. Crake had only read about them in books. They were the daemonists of the South, who practised the Art without the use of devices and machines. Crake wasn't sure how much of it was superstition and quackery, but the scientist in him was eager to see one at work.

Beyond the cluster of dwellings, they came to a sagging hut which stood on its own. Slinkhound spoke to Ashua and then went inside, pushing through the curtain that hung over the doorway. Ashua turned to the crew and said:

'Now we wait.'

Frey was eyeing the hut uncertainly. 'Are you sure about this? I mean, wouldn't I be better seeing a doctor?'

'A doctor would tell you to chop that bugger off,' Malvery slurred drunkenly. 'Might as well see what this feller can do.'

'There's another reason I brought you here,' said Ashua. 'I didn't want to tell you before, 'cause it sounds... well, unlikely. But that thing on your hand? I've heard of it before.'

'You have?' Frey asked eagerly.

'The black spot. Means you're marked for death. The Sammies say ancient sorcerers used it to deter thieves or something.' She shrugged. 'I mean, it's just a legend. People say all kinds of shit, especially here.'

But Frey had latched on to the idea. 'You reckon it's some kind of curse?'

Ashua looked embarrassed. 'Sounds stupid when you say it like that, right?'

Frey seemed to brighten. 'So it means I won't lose this hand?'

'I'd say it means you'll die horribly instead.'

Frey thought about that, then grinned and gave a little laugh of relief. 'I was worried there for a minute,' he said, looking fondly at his hand.

'Cap'n?' Jez asked with concern in her voice. 'You did hear the bit about dying horribly, didn't you?'

Frey was aware that everyone was looking at him, and became defensive. 'Look, I'd rather be dead than maimed, alright?'

Ashua thumbed at Frey. 'Narcissist,' she said to the crew in general.

'Old news,' Crake replied.

'She keeps calling me that!' Frey complained. 'What does it *mean*?'

'It just means you're exceptionally brave,' Crake lied smoothly.

'Oh,' said Frey. He puffed up a little and glanced at Ashua. 'Thanks.'

Crake gave Ashua a hard look. She rolled her eyes but kept her mouth shut. One day the Cap'n was going to catch on to Crake's habit of mocking his limited vocabulary, but it wouldn't be today.

Slinkhound emerged from the hut and beckoned Frey and Ashua inside. He waved at the rest of the crew, as if to say: *not you*. Crake was alarmed. He wasn't coming all this way only to stand outside.

'Cap'n! Let me come too! I have to see!' It came out sounding rather more desperate than he intended.

Frey looked at Ashua, who said a few words to Slinkhound, who tutted and waved him in.

'*Let me come too*,' Pinn mimicked sourly in a baby voice. 'Why does he get to go? Kiss-arse.'

'Excuse me?' Crake said as he passed. 'I'm sorry, I don't speak Moron.'

It was a cheap rejoinder, but it pleased him nonetheless. He went through the musty curtain and into the hut, leaving Malvery struggling to prevent Pinn drawing his pistol.

The interior of the hut was squalid and cluttered with macabre totems. Skulls and jars of pickled animal foetuses made for a sinister motif, and the air stank of smoke and incense. There was no furniture beyond the mats on the rough plank floor, and a bed of mouldy straw in the corner.

Sitting cross-legged in the centre of the room was the sorcerer. He was an untouchable like the rest of them. His skin was a deep black and his face marked in white but, unlike the people outside, he was obese. Long grey hair, matted into dreadlocks, hung over his face and spilled onto his belly. His filthy beard tangled with the mass of beads and totems hanging around his neck. He wore an animal-skin waistcoat, hanging open to allow his gut to protrude, and a loincloth tied up like a nappy. Despite his size, his leathery skin hung off him in folds, and his face was a maze of fleshy chasms. He was slouched forward and appeared to be asleep, or comatose, or dead.

Crake was less than impressed. He'd been expecting someone fiercely intense, a wild-eyed savage of some kind. Instead he'd found a giant bearded raisin.

Slinkhound motioned for Frey to sit down in front of the sorcerer. Frey did so, though he didn't look keen. Crake wasn't surprised. He could smell the sour-milk reek of the bloated man even over the incense.

The sorcerer stirred, raised his head, and opened his eyes. The sight gave Crake a little fright. They were so bloodshot that they appeared entirely red.

The sorcerer's lips moved, and a small black twig emerged. He rolled it from one side of his mouth to the other, studying Frey with a flat glare. Then it disappeared back into his mouth, and he began to chew it with a horrible crunching sound.

Ah, thought Crake. *Hookroot bark.*

The sorcerers of Samarla had other ways than science to draw daemons from the aether, so it was said. They used secret techniques and rituals, the details jealously guarded. That, and vast quantities of highly potent and dangerous narcotics, like raw hookroot bark.

No wonder the sorcerer looked a mess. He was loaded.

Crake's skepticism deepened. He was beginning to think he was a fool for taking this seriously. Perhaps all the lurid reports from Samarla were just rot after all. He couldn't see how this enormous ruin of a man could possibly command the same kind of power that a Vardic daemonist did, with their careful formulae and advanced machinery.

Eventually the sorcerer spoke. His voice was a shock, so hoarse and deep and croaky that it only barely passed as human. The foreign syllables wheezed and crackled and rumbled from his chest.

'Hold out your hand,' Ashua said. 'The manky one.'

'It's not bloody *manky*, it's *cursed*,' Frey protested, but he held it out towards the sorcerer anyway.

The sorcerer enfolded Frey's hand in his own huge, rubbery paws.

Frey, who didn't like holding hands with men at the best of times, was trying not to squirm away.

The sorcerer closed his eyes, and there was silence until Crake's stomach growled noisily. He reddened and gave Ashua an apologetic look. He'd eaten nothing all day, being busy in his sanctum.

Then the sorcerer shuddered. Frey tensed and tried to pull away, but the sorcerer clamped his hand tight. For a moment, they were frozen like that.

'Er,' said Frey.

The sorcerer's head tipped back, his dreadlocks sliding from his shoulders. He began to tremble. His chewing became frantic. A strange humming noise was coming from his nose, getting higher and louder.

'Er, fellers, I'm not sure I like this...' said Frey, but the sorcerer was strong, and Frey couldn't work his hand free.

Crake scoffed as white foam began to bubble over the sorcerer's lips. He'd seen charlatans like this before. Mediums, pretending to contact the dead. Spit and blood, even the Awakeners were nothing more than a bunch of confidence tricksters, when it came down to it. He wouldn't be fooled so easily.

But despite his doubts, Crake became worried as the sorcerer's fit worsened. A little scared, even. The man's contortions were really quite distressing. He was horrible to look at. Frey was frantically tugging away now, but it was like trying to move a rock. Crake looked over at Ashua and Slinkhound, and he thought he saw them exchange a sly and wicked glance. Some kind of conspiracy? What were they up to?

And then he caught himself. He was becoming paranoid and scared. Of course he was. Everyone did, in the presence of daemons. His subconscious was reacting to the unnatural.

Whatever the sorcerer was doing, it was *working*.

He watched with growing amazement. How could it be? Some kind of trickery? A subtle form of hypnotism, to make his audience feel something that wasn't there? No, that was ridiculous. Crake's senses were finely honed from years of chasing daemons, and this was exactly the feeling he got when he was in the midst of his experiments. The sense of *wrongness*, the involuntary fear reflex. And it was all being done without machines, without devices.

There was only one explanation. It was all as the reports had said. Somehow, between the drugs and their strange techniques, the Samarlans could deal with daemons without using science at all.

The sorcerer's fit subsided to shuddering again, making his flesh wobble. He spoke again, howling words through foam-flecked lips. Frey recoiled in disgust as his face was spattered.

'He says...' said Ashua. 'He says you took something that didn't belong to you.'

'Hey, I didn't steal anything! I just took it from someone *else* who stole it.'

Ashua shushed him as the sorcerer spoke again. 'It's old, he says. Thousands of years. A daemon from before...' She paused, frowning as she worked out the translation. 'Basically, he's not sure what it is. He says... it builds itself from everything you're afraid of, whatever that means. He says...' She shrugged, more and more confused. 'He says to beware the Iron Jackal. Make of that what you will.'

'There was an emblem on the inside of the relic case, you remember? I thought it was a dog or a wolf.'

'Reckon you thought wrong, then.'

'Can he get rid of it? The daemon?' Frey asked. Ashua put the question to the sorcerer, who had fallen quiet and was breathing heavily.

The sorcerer's eyes rolled in his head and he spoke again.

'No,' said Ashua. 'He says no one can.'

'Oh,' said Frey. 'Well, that's just great.'

'No one but you,' she added, as the sorcerer kept speaking. His tone drifted from high to low, raspy to breathy, hoarse to sharp, as if he were a signal being tuned in and out. 'He says you have to take the relic back to the place where it came from.'

'I don't even *have* it,' Frey said.

'Will you shut up?' Ashua snapped. 'I'm listening!' The sorcerer was talking over them both, as if they weren't there. 'Um... restore it to its rightful place... by full dark of the full moon...' Her face cleared and she smiled in understanding. 'That's how you lift the curse! It's like the legends said: it's a curse to protect against thieves. The only way to free yourself is to return whatever you stole.'

'So it *is* a curse?' Frey said.

'Yes.'

'Not just a manky hand, then?' he added, with a certain amount of triumph.

'You are bloody impossible,' Ashua said.

'What happens if he doesn't bring it back in time?' Crake asked.

'Right, good question,' said Ashua. She put it to the sorcerer, whose head was lolling back on his neck, milky saliva drooling from the corner of his mouth. The sorcerer crunched at his hookroot twig again, and his head came up, fixing Frey with bloodshot eyes.

Ashua translated as he spoke. 'He says... the daemon that guards the relic... it will get stronger with every passing day. You've seen it once. It will come for you... three more times. The third time will be at full dark on the night of the full moon. If it hasn't killed you already by then... it will become fully... er... manifest... to reclaim the property of its master.' She paused, and looked at Frey, and Crake saw genuine concern on her face. 'And that night will be your last.'

Frey stared at the sorcerer for a moment. Then he pulled his hand away violently, and this time it came free. The sorcerer cried out and fell back, flopping to the ground where he lay gasping like some vast, blubbery creature of the deep dragged on to dry land. Frey ignored him, getting angrily to his feet.

'Nobody tells *me* which is my last night alive,' he said. He looked at Crake and frowned. 'Wait, which is my last night alive?'

'Full moon's in twelve nights' time, if you don't count tonight.'

'Right!' said Frey. 'Well, I plan to live a lot longer than twelve more nights.' He pulled out a compass from his pocket. Crake recognised it: it used to be his. Months ago, he'd thralled a daemon to it so that it always pointed towards Frey's silver ring, which Frey had since given to Trinica. 'All we need to do is find Trinica and get that relic back.'

'And then we need to find out where it came from in the first place,' said Ashua. 'And then we need to go there and put it back.'

'Yeah, yeah, one thing a time,' said Frey. 'Let's get hold of it first. She's not gonna be pleased when I come asking for it.'

'Hey, I'm not returning my share!' Ashua warned. 'No refunds from *this* girl.'

Frey was gearing up for a retort when the curtain in the door of the hut was pulled aside and Malvery stuck his head in. 'Everyone having fun in here?' he asked. 'Good. We got trouble.'

'You have no idea,' said Crake, and they hurried out to see what else fate could possibly pile on their shoulders tonight.

TWELVE

A MASSACRE—WELL AND TRULY TRAPPED—
SLINKHOUND LEADS THE WAY—PROPERTY
DAMAGE—PARTINGS

'What's up?' Frey asked as he emerged from the sorcerer's hut, with Crake, Ashua and Slinkhound close behind him.

Jez, who was checking her rifle, looked up and nodded back the way they'd come. Frey followed her gaze up the rocky slope to the place where they'd entered the cavern. There was a commotion there. A mob of untouchables was gathering, their voices raised in a hubbub. They sounded angry, defiant, outraged. More and more of them hurrying to join in.

At first Frey couldn't work out what had caused all the excitement. Then the crowd parted, and he caught a glimpse of a uniform and a rifle, a blond-haired man.

A Dakkadian soldier.

'Ashua! Ask your mate if there's another way out of here,' Frey said, drawing his revolver and backing away.

The soldier was holding up his weapon, fending off the grasping hands of an untouchable. The crowd were piling in now, haranguing the intruders, flocking around them like angry birds defending their nest. *Go away, go back, this is ours, we don't want you here!*

Frey knew what was about to happen. The inevitability of it all made his heart sink.

There was the sharp crack of a gunshot and the crowd scattered, their yells turning to screams. Suddenly Frey could see them. Not one soldier but twelve. They were all Dakkadians, clad in white uniforms with gold trim, except for one. He was a Samarlan, taller and more slender than the others. Judging by the beautifully crafted black armour that he wore, he was their leader.

The crowd was running, but the soldiers weren't done. They aimed their rifles at the fleeing untouchables and shot them down. Men and women flailed and pitched to the ground as they were punched in the back by gunfire. They scrambled towards cover, but the soldiers were intent on a show of strength, and they picked off the runners long after it was clear they presented no further threat.

Frey was appalled. He was no stranger to killing, or to killers, but it was their manner that sickened him. The cold, precise way they decimated the beggar folk, as if they were putting down animals; the speed and severity of their response when the crowd began to gather.

'This way!' Ashua said, as Slinkhound pulled on her arm. Just at that moment, the Samarlan general, who hadn't even drawn his weapon during the slaughter, turned his head and saw them. He pointed, gave an order, and the soldiers began hurrying down the slope.

'Time to be elsewhere,' Frey said, and they ran in the opposite direction.

Beyond the sorcerer's hut was a stretch of open ground, with the cavern wall to the left and a steep drop some distance to the right. A scuffed foot-trail led upslope to a flat area that was dense with huts and shacks.

The soldiers opened fire, shooting from the hip. Bullets rang off the stone around Frey and his crew. Only the luckiest shot would hit at that range, but Frey didn't much like the way his luck was running tonight.

His fears were confirmed when Malvery tripped over his own feet after a few dozen metres. They wasted precious seconds hauling the drink-sodden doctor to his feet, while Pinn jigged on the spot, anxious to be away again. Jez provided covering fire, since she had the best eye at long range, but the Daks didn't slow at all. Their leader, the Samarlan, was striding down the hill in their wake, not in the least bit hurried. His arrogant confidence annoyed Frey. He was tempted to chance a bullet just to knock him down a peg.

'I'm okay, I'm okay,' said Malvery, accelerating to an inebriated waddle. Frey loosed a couple of shots over his shoulder, to give the Daks something to think about, but his attempts were as ineffective as Jez's had been.

By the time they were moving again, the Daks had caught up

enough to be dangerous. Frey took a bullet through the sleeve of his coat, close enough to graze his wrist.

Damn it, where's Bess when you need her? She'd make short work of these son of bitches.

They crested the top of the slope and reached the flat ground. Crude buildings of metal and wood were heaped against the wall in a clutter, as if driven there by a bulldozer. Shacks were scattered nearby. The untouchables fled to their houses as Frey and his crew approached. At first he thought it was because they were afraid of him, but he soon saw that the danger came from another direction.

There was another entrance to the cavern beyond the buildings. Sallying through it was a second group of soldiers, also with a Samarlan at their head.

Both groups saw each other at the same time. Frey's crew didn't trouble to wait for an order; they raised their guns and blazed away.

Suddenly everything was scuff and scramble, a rush of hot blood, the firecracker staccato of a gunfight. Frey had replaced the revolver he lost on the train; he held one in each hand as he fired at the newcomers. The soldiers scattered towards cover, taking shelter behind the huts that surrounded the entrance.

Frey and his crew couldn't go forward into the guns, and they couldn't go back, so everyone instinctively began moving in the same direction: sideways. The entrance was in a corner, where the cavern wall curved to the right and continued sloping upwards. They followed the slope, crabstepping as they fired, keeping their enemies' heads down.

'I thought you said not to worry about that guy who was following us,' Frey said to Ashua.

'Turns out I'm not perfect,' said Ashua. 'Who'd have thought?'

'More from upslope!' Jez said.

Frey swore as he spotted a third group of soldiers, blocking their escape. They were well and truly trapped now.

'Oi, Cap'n!' Malvery cried. Frey looked over his shoulder and saw Malvery pointing at a long rope bridge that launched off from a precipice nearby. It reached across the cavern, passing over a dense cluster of dwellings, and ended at a group of huts perched on the lip of a cliff.

Frey didn't much like the look of it, but then he didn't much like taking a bullet in the kidney either. The bridge seemed the lesser of two evils.

They began backing towards it, providing covering fire for each other as they went. They'd seen enough gunfights to keep their cool in this one, except Crake, who would presumably never learn. They timed their reloads to make sure that everyone didn't do it at once. They looked, in fact, surprisingly like a team.

But the soldiers in cover had reorganised themselves and were shooting back. The range was long, but not long enough for Frey's liking. The other soldiers were closing in fast. It was only a matter of time before someone got hit, out in the open like they were.

'Alright, bugger this tactical retreat lark,' said Frey. '*Run for it!*'

They broke into a disorganised mass and fled for the bridge. Bullets whispered and whined through the air, little invisible messengers of death.

Frey had a superstition about bullets: thinking about them attracted them. As long as he never stopped to consider the danger, as long as he never really thought about all the luck and chance that made the difference between surviving a gunfight and getting killed, then everything would be alright.

It helped to get him through.

Frey reached the bridge in the middle of the pack. He wasn't so honourable as to go last; it was every man for himself right now. The ropes were thick and it was surprisingly sturdy, even under Malvery's weight. They raced along the bridge, heads down, horribly exposed. Their only cover was their distance from the enemy's guns.

The soldiers, seeing what they were up to, were scrambling to adapt. The first group reversed direction and began heading back. Instead of trying to cross the bridge, as their companions intended, they were going to skirt the edge of the cavern and come round to the far side of the bridge. But Frey and his crew, who were taking a more direct route, would get there long before them.

The soldiers took pot-shots at the crew as they crossed over. Frey flinched as a bullet puffed off the rope handrail just next to his head, tearing a small chunk from the fibres. The bridge rocked this way and that as they hurried across it. Frey looked down at the dirty roofs of the shacks, the lethal, bone-breaking drop to the hard stone ground fifteen metres below.

Pinn slipped drunkenly and almost fell to his knees, but he was borne up by Malvery, who shoved him onwards. More gunshots. More bullets.

Just a little more luck. Just a little more.

And then he was at the end, running on to solid ground, a rush of relief flooding through him. 'Get into cover!' he called, waving at the shabby collection of huts around them. 'Jez, watch for those bastards coming round the back.'

'On it, Cap'n,' said Jez, hurrying past him.

The cliffside huts were encircled by crude fences made of slabs of metal and wood. A few chickens and scrawny goats scattered as Frey's crew took positions overlooking a rocky slope, pocked with shacks and lean-tos. The first group of soldiers were making their way up it. If they got to the top, they would be able to get around the back of the cluster of huts, and the crew would be trapped between them and the cliff.

They opened fire, shooting down on the soldiers. The Dakkadians ran for the shacks, and shelter. Even their Samarlan captain got a bit of a spring in his step when Malvery nearly took his head off with a shotgun.

Frey turned his attention back to the rope bridge. Dakkadian soldiers had reached it now, and were stepping on with some reluctance, urged by their masters. Frey shoved one of his pistols into his belt and drew his cutlass. He held it up high to show them. They turned and scrambled back towards land. He gave them a few seconds to get clear and then hacked away the ropes. His daemonically thralled cutlass was sharp enough to chop through them in a single blow. The rope bridge slumped and then fell onto the roofs of the huts below.

Frey hurried back and hunkered down next to Jez, who was hiding behind a metal piece of fence, aiming down the length of her rifle at the soldiers below.

'That was surprisingly human of you, Cap'n,' she said. 'Letting them get off the bridge before you cut it.'

'What can I say? Every life is a precious twinkling butterfly.'

'Isn't it just?' said Jez, as she squeezed the trigger and blasted a Dakkadian's brains out of the back his head. 'We need to make a move, Cap'n. If that lot flank us, we're dead.' She looked down at herself, then gave him a rueful smile. 'More dead, in my case.'

Well, at least she's got a sense of humour about being a terrifying half-daemon monstrosity, he thought. He patted her on the shoulder and ran in a crouch over to Ashua.

Ashua was in frantic conversation with Slinkhound as Frey arrived. 'Is there another way out of here?' he demanded.

'That way,' said Ashua, pointing.

Frey couldn't see an exit in that direction, but he had to trust Ashua and her guide. He raised his voice. 'Everyone, we're moving out! On the count of three, hoof it!' Then he made a shooing motion at Slinkhound. 'You lead.'

Slinkhound just looked at him, eyes dark in the sockets of his skull face. He took it as agreement.

'Ready?' he called to his crew. 'One! T—'

Pinn fled past him, yelling.

'Alright, just go!' Frey cried in exasperation. He pulled Slinkhound up, and pushed him off ahead. The Samarlan broke into a sprint, easily outpacing Pinn, who'd just realised that he wasn't at all sure where he was going. The rest of the crew broke cover and followed.

The soldiers saw them fleeing and gave chase, but the crew had a head start, and they ran for their lives. Somehow Pinn and Malvery kept their feet under them, and Ashua appeared almost completely sober by now. Slinkhound led them along a rough trail, with untouchables scattering out of their way, and then suddenly veered off towards the cavern wall. There was a narrow fissure hidden by a fold in the rock. Slinkhound squeezed inside and disappeared. The others followed. Malvery required a hefty boot in the arse to help him through, but Pinn was on hand and he delivered with gusto.

Beyond was a rough stone tunnel, sloping upwards. As they followed it, it split into more tunnels, with oil lamps burning at the junctions. Wooden joists and support frames propped up the ceiling. Frey guessed that these had once been mine tunnels.

He'd never thought he'd be so glad to be surrounded by dark, confining, lamplit passageways of rock. After being out in the open, with all those bullets flying about, this place felt positively safe. But he knew that the Dakkadians weren't far behind, and Slinkhound was already racing off ahead.

'What do you reckon they're after?' Jez asked as they hurried after Slinkhound. 'Us, or the relic?'

'Who cares?' Frey replied. 'How'd they find us, anyway?'

'Descriptions,' said Jez. 'We don't blend in too well, 'specially since you got all famous. I bet they had scouts out looking for us. One of them picked up the trail.'

'Never should've left any bloody survivors on that train,' Frey muttered to himself.

They pressed on at speed, hurrying as fast as the tunnels would allow. Slinkhound led them through the gloom. They came across more and more untouchables as they ascended, but no one tried to stop them. The heat grew as they climbed, and they knew they must be nearing the surface.

They heard shouted voices from behind them, and protests from the untouchables as they were flung out of the way. Frey's group were slowed by Pinn and Malvery, and despite their best efforts, the soldiers were catching them up.

Finally, they reached a narrow set of stairs carved into the rock, which led to a ladder, which led to a trapdoor, which led to a short stone corridor, which led to a heavy door, which opened without warning to the outside.

Frey was taken aback by the sudden sense of space, the electric light that soaked the air, the background clamour of the city and the warm push of night heat. He'd only been underground for an hour or so, but it still felt like he'd stepped into a different world. They emerged onto a quiet, dirty and run-down street. Close by, a rushu was watching them with docile disinterest, tethered to a holding-post.

The door that they'd come from was unmarked and anonymous, hidden beneath a shabby, pillared gallery that overhung it. The whole building looked frankly precarious, with the front portion of the upper floor resting on two wooden pillars. The gallery roof sagged alarmingly.

'They're right behind us, Cap'n!' Malvery panted, as he pulled himself through the trapdoor. He was red-faced and wheezing, and really wasn't going to be able to run much further. Frey's own legs were getting weak, and his chest hurt. Not for the first time, he wished they all got a bit more exercise. But that would cut into their drinking time, so he supposed it was never likely to happen.

Jez saw what he was thinking. 'We could take 'em here, Cap'n,' she said. 'They'd be sitting ducks coming through that trapdoor.'

Frey looked around, and then a sly smile crossed his face. 'I've got a better idea.'

He ran over to the rushu that stood nearby. A tiny eye studied him from a thicket of horns and tusks. Frey moved warily along its leathery flank, careful not to startle it. Its handler was nowhere to be seen. He untied the thick tethers that bound the beast to the holding-post, then hurried over to the doorway where his crew were gathered.

Jez was hunkered down by the doorway, covering the stragglers with her rifle. Malvery was the last to stagger through. He stumbled woozily to one side and threw up. Frey ignored him. He was busy tying the tethers around one of the wooden pillars that barely held up the gallery overhead.

There was a high shout of alarm from nearby. The handler emerged from a nearby alley, still hitching up his trousers.

'Here they come!' Pinn said.

'Get out from under there!' Frey barked at them.

'Now!' They scattered at the urgency in his voice. The driver was running over towards them, shouting curses in Samarlan. Frey stood as close to the rushu's side as he dared, raised his revolver, and fired into the air.

The rushu reared in fright with an enormous bellow, and lunged against its tethers. It only took one pull. The pillar splintered and pulled away with a crunch of wood. Frey scampered back as the gallery above groaned horribly, and then the whole front wall of the upper storey collapsed, crashing down onto the porch in front of the doorway.

The rushu, panicked, lurched off down the street. The handler chased after it, swearing at the top of his voice, although he still took the time to spit at Frey as he passed by.

The doorway to the Underneath was entirely buried now. The floor above was exposed, revealing shabby, barely-furnished rooms. A middle-aged Dakkadian was peering down at them over the edge of his bathtub, with the kind of expression you might expect to see on a man in his situation.

Jez walked up next to Frey, admiring the destruction. 'Nice,' she said.

'It was, wasn't it?' Frey agreed. He surveyed his crew. All present and correct, and nobody hurt, unless you counted Pinn's arm being in a sling. 'Anyone else think we've outstayed our welcome in Samarla?'

Malvery, Pinn and Crake all raised their hands at the same time. After a moment, Jez did as well.

'Yeah. Me, too,' said Frey.

'Think I'll make myself scarce,' said Ashua. 'You lot are dangerous company right now.'

'Thanks,' said Frey. 'For… y'know.' He held up his corrupted hand.

Her gaze flicked from Crake to Malvery, then back to him. 'Right.' She hesitated a moment, then said: 'You need to find me, get a message to the Black Drake Inn. It's a Vard joint. They'll know how to get in touch.'

She ran off without further ado. The doctor watched her go with a melancholy and booze-soaked wistfulness in his eyes, but Frey was glad to see the back of her. Useful as she'd been, she was troublesome, and he didn't need any more trouble right now. He still blamed her in some small way for his predicament. If she hadn't goaded him, he wouldn't have been forced to show off and pick up the relic.

'Alright, everyone,' he said with a sigh. 'I've had enough of Shasiith. Let's go home before someone kills us.'

THIRTEEN

FREY OVERSTEPS HIS MARK—THE AXELBY CLUB— HAWKBY'S OFFER—BACK IN THE SNOW

'What do you mean, you don't have it any more?'

Trinica regarded Frey flatly from the seat behind her desk. 'I can't imagine where you found confusion in my meaning,' she said. 'I don't have the relic. I sold it on.'

'Already?' Frey was aghast.

'Hours after I arrived in Thesk. I told you, the buyer was very keen.'

'Who was it?'

'That's not your business.'

'This is serious, Trinica!' he snapped. 'I need to know!'

Her expression didn't change at all, but somehow the temperature in the room dropped by several degrees anyway.

'You would do well to remember where you are and who you're talking to,' she said, in a voice like a rusty blade.

Frey knew exactly where he was. In the captain's cabin of the *Delirium Trigger*, talking to the ghost of the woman he'd loved. Where was the Trinica he'd dined with two nights ago? Where was the softness of the hand across the table, touching his?

He ran his hand through his hair in frustration, cursing the delay that had cost him the relic. Even following the compass linked to the ring on her finger, it had taken a day to fly to Thesk and another to track her down. The capital was a big place.

Trinica was gazing out of the sloping window next to her, having lost interest in him all of a sudden. She was evidently in one of those moods. The cabin's atmosphere was oppressive, with its heavy brass fittings and dark wood bookcases full of unfamiliar titles. He spotted the book he'd given her over dinner, and felt resentful that her gratitude had been so brief.

Balomon Crund, Trinica's bosun, stood watchfully by the door. After escorting Frey through the passageways of the aircraft, he'd remained in the room instead of leaving.

'What's he still doing here?' Frey asked irritably.

'He's my bosun,' said Trinica, still looking out of the window. He couldn't imagine what was so interesting out there: the *Delirium Trigger* was berthed in a hangar.

Frey composed himself. Peevishness would get him nowhere. 'Might we speak alone, Captain Dracken?' he said with exaggerated politeness.

'I don't think so, Captain Frey. Whatever you have to say, you can say in front of Mr Crund. I assure you, he's very discreet.'

Frey bit back a retort. He didn't need games right now. He was flustered, agitated, on the edge of control. He flexed his corrupted hand, which he'd covered up with a ratty fingerless glove. He wanted to show her, to confide in her and be comforted. He was scared, damn it! But she was evidently determined to make this difficult.

He made an effort to calm himself. 'As a favour to me, in the spirit of our recent alliance,' he said, his voice tight with restrained fury, 'would you tell me who bought that relic, Captain Dracken?' He took a steadying breath and managed a passable smile. '*Please*,' he added venomously.

She turned away from the window and studied him with her black eyes. She was like some terrible bird of prey examining a mouse. 'I sold it to Jid Crickslint,' she said eventually.

Frey gave a small groan and winced. Crickslint was not a name he wanted to hear.

He'd always tried to make it a policy not to rip off anyone who was liable to get their own back on him. In fact, over the years he'd got pretty good at identifying which criminals were on their way up and which were on their way out. The former, he dealt with fairly. The latter he cheated, knowing that they'd likely be dead or ruined before he came back that way again.

But no system was perfect and he'd made the odd mistake. Crickslint was one of them. He was a fence and a moneylender, and a really annoying pain in the arse to boot. Everybody in Thesk hated him, and everybody needed him. By balancing a bewildering mass of debts and favours, he'd ended up a small-scale crimelord.

Frey and his crew had done a few smuggling jobs for him, years ago. Then one day, after receiving the cargo for one of these jobs, they got a bit of news. Someone had finally done what everyone wanted to, and smashed the little weasel's face in.

Frey had sensed an opportunity. With Crickslint's reputation as ruined as his teeth, it was only a matter of time before his rivals overran him. Crickslint would have too much on his plate to worry about one little shipment going missing. So Frey sold the cargo himself, kept the money, and didn't think much more about it.

But Crickslint didn't go under. He found the man who'd embarrassed him and made a bloody example. He ruthlessly crushed the rivals who were jockeying for his spot. Soon he was back and stronger than ever. Frey didn't know whether Crickslint had really noticed his little bit of thievery, but he'd made sure to stay out of his way just in case.

And now Crickslint possessed the only thing capable of saving Frey's life. The world was truly an unjust place.

'I need you to get the relic back,' he said to Trinica.

Her laugh infuriated him. 'Don't be stupid.'

'Return the money. Straight swap. I'll make it up to you.'

Trinica's expression was amazed. 'You actually mean it, don't you? Even if I wanted to do such a thing, he'd smell desperation and double the value. Who'd pay the difference? You?'

'Look, whatever it takes I'll do. Name your price.'

'There *is* no price. I had a job to do and I did it. Tomorrow I'm going back to Shasiith, where I have further business. If you want that relic, get it yourself.'

Her dismissive tone was the final straw. He surged across the room, slammed his hands down on her desk, looming over her. 'This is my *life*, Trinica! Don't you *care*?'

She gazed at him expressionlessly from her chair, not cowed in the slightest. He heard the sinister click of a revolver being cocked, and felt Crund's pistol against the base of his skull.

'Mr Crund, will you remove Captain Frey from my aircraft? I think he may be drunk.'

'You're kicking me off?' Frey said in disbelief.

'Since you helped me get the relic in the first place, I'll extend you the courtesy of leaving with all your limbs intact,' she said. 'Say another word and I may change my mind. Now get out of my sight, before you humiliate yourself further.' She turned away from him and looked out of the window again.

Frey opened his mouth, and then shut it again. She was right. He'd humiliated himself enough for one night.

Crund escorted him out of the cabin. Frey fumed as they walked through the *Delirium Trigger*'s narrow metal corridors, consumed with rage at the way he'd been treated. They climbed up a ladder onto the gun deck and into the cool air of the hangar. Crund saw him to the end of the gangway and stood there, pistol held loosely at his side, barring the way back.

Frey thought about giving him a message to convey to Trinica, something involving a particularly creative orchestra of insults, but he held his tongue. Trinica's crew were fiercely loyal, and Crund might well shoot him in defence of his captain's honour. Having the last laugh wouldn't be much fun with a hole in his lung.

No final rejoinder, then. He simply gathered the shreds of his pride and left.

A combat frigate like the *Delirium Trigger* was too large for a landing pad. It rested amid a cradle of gantries and platforms in a private hangar, its berth obtained with false papers and a hefty bribe. Trinica was still under sentence of death after her ill-advised support of Duke Grephen's failed coup almost two years ago. It was one of the reasons she was keen to spend time out of the country. In Thesk, the capital of the Nine Duchies of Vardia and home of the Archduke, she needed to keep a low profile.

Not that Frey cared whether she lived or died at that particular moment.

He negotiated the levels down to the ground and out into the streets. It was unseasonably cold. Lamp-posts wore haloes of electric light in the faint mist of the autumn night. Windows glowed in the dark. He saw an accountant at work, a family sitting down to dinner, lovers drawing curtains to seal themselves away. Motorised carriages puttered along the roads, and militiamen in blue and grey uniforms patrolled the streets. After the chaos of Samarla, Thesk seemed a sane and orderly place.

He walked fast, with his head down. He felt the beauty in things keenly tonight, and it tormented him. The sudden lack of time had sharpened his attention.

Death was coming. The daemon was coming.

He put some distance between himself and the hangar, letting himself cool off until he could think straight again. He came to a halt by the bank of a canal, one of many brick-lined waterways that cut through the streets of the Financial Quarter. Black water flowed past. The reflected lights of the lamp-posts were dim and stranded suns beneath the surface.

Idiot.

He'd been a fool, going to Trinica like that. Storming on to her craft and demanding her help. He'd overplayed his hand. Whatever existed between them was something private. In public, and especially in front of her crew, he had no right to expect sympathy or favour.

Had he gone to her secretly, met her away from the *Delirium Trigger*, then maybe he could have secured her help. But there hadn't seemed time for all that. The spectre of his impending end raised questions that he didn't dare think about, so he'd acted instead.

Only now did he realise how he'd jeopardised her position. He'd been too familiar, when her authority relied on staying aloof. She should have had him beaten, at the least. The fact that she hadn't was a measure of her affection for him. But even that small mercy would have been noted by her crew, and perhaps counted as a weakness.

Well, he'd blown his chance with Trinica. She couldn't possibly help him now. But she'd done what she could. She gave him a name.

He started walking again. Meeting Jid Crickslint was something he wasn't looking forward to. But he'd better get on with it, regardless.

Time was running out.

The tram rattled and shook as it carried Malvery through streets he'd called home for many years. He sat hunched over, too big for the small hard seat he occupied, peering over the rims of his round green glasses at the buildings sliding by. Metal fittings jittered and jingled as they passed Dicer's Corner, Whisperside, Glassmarket, Glee Row. The names of the tram stops had a kind of mythic poetry to his ears. Once, he'd been a part of this city, and the city had been a part of him. He read the language of a lost life, spelled out in street signs.

He disembarked at Tallowgate and watched the tram rumble away, abandoning him to the lamplit night. Hands thrust in the pockets of his coat, he headed off, breath steaming the air.

Tallowgate was a wide lane flanked by tall buildings belonging to doctors, lawyers and politicians. The houses exuded a polite sense of self-importance, with elaborate porches, wide windows and high ceilings. Malvery had lived in a house like that once. It all seemed a long time ago now.

Halfway down the lane was the Axelby Club, still there and little changed for Malvery's seven-year absence. There was no sign above the door. From a distance, it looked like the rest of the houses on the street. It was formed of two neighbouring houses, three storeys each, that had been knocked through and combined into one. There were a dozen rooms within: parlours with settees and card tables; firelit libraries where a man might read in a creaking leather armchair; dining rooms serving rich red wine and rich red meat.

The sight of the club gladdened him. He'd spent a lot of time within those walls. It was important to him, somehow, that it still existed.

He stood outside and looked in. The ground floor parlours were the only rooms visible from the lane. Panes of steam-dimmed glass separated him from the men with flushed faces who argued and laughed and plotted there, brandy glasses and cigars in hand.

Though he was cold, he remembered the warmth of that place. He remembered nights spent surrounded by the bawdy merriment of the carelessly wealthy. When he was younger, he'd marvelled at their casual arrogance, even admired it. Then he became accustomed to it. Eventually he became as careless as they were.

He'd been at the Axelby Club that night. He'd drunk wine and brandy in that chair – that very same chair by the fire – and returned home long after Eldrea was asleep. Between the surgery and the club – which only allowed men through its doors – he almost never saw his wife any more. It was an arrangement that suited them both.

By then, the marriage had deteriorated to the point where he slept in his armchair rather than share her bed. But he didn't sleep that night. He just kept drinking till the sun came up, for no reason at all. It had become a habit that he indulged more and more often. Drinking had become a pastime in itself.

Then, a knock at the door. A messenger from the surgery. A good friend of Malvery's had been admitted with acute appendicitis. Something had to be done, fast.

Perhaps if things hadn't become so bad between him and Eldrea, he'd have been less drunk when he operated. Perhaps, if they'd been a little more tender with one another, he'd have gone to bed instead of staying up. But these were poor excuses. He was an accident waiting to happen. An alcoholic, so sure of his own infallibility that he refused to let anyone else see to his friend. Drunk or not, he still thought himself the only man for the job.

He was wrong, and it cost a life. Henvid Clack, father of one, a geologist by trade. Henvid didn't deserve the end he got.

'Excuse me.'

Malvery blinked. There was a man leaning out of the doorway of the club, addressing him. He realised that he'd drifted off, his mood cooling to a dank sadness as he reminisced. He might have been gazing through the window for some time, like a hungry beggar drawn by the heat and light within. He was certainly shabby enough to pass as a beggar these days, with his stained coat and frayed jersey. Although, with a belly like his, no one was likely to describe him as hungry anytime soon.

'Sorry, mate,' he said. 'Lost in thought. I'll move along.'

'No, no, that's quite alright,' said the man. 'It's just… aren't you Althazar Malvery?'

Malvery took a closer look at him. He was in his middle thirties, with a broad, handsome face framed by black curly hair and neat muttonchop whiskers. But it was his pleasant, eager manner that triggered Malvery's memory. He'd been a younger man, and clean-shaven, when they used to drink together here.

'Edson Hawkby!' Malvery grinned.

'It *is* you!' Hawkby cried. He came out and shook Malvery's hand vigorously. 'I thought so when I saw you at the window, but it's been such a time. It's freezing out here. Aren't you coming in?'

'Ah. I ain't really a member any more.'

'Pah! You are tonight!' Hawkby declared, steering him into the foyer. Inside was a uniformed doorman. 'This fellow's my guest, alright? Fetch him a jacket, would you?' He looked Malvery up and down as the doorman headed off. 'I'm afraid that outfit would raise some eyebrows in here, stuffy lot that they are.' Then he beamed and patted him on the shoulder. 'Althazar Malvery! Spit and blood! How are you, old fellow?'

Freshly jacketed and carrying a glass of good port, Malvery followed Hawkby to an upstairs den, where they settled themselves in front of a fire. Hawkby chattered excitedly while Malvery listened, content to soak in the atmosphere of the club. Hawkby was an eminent doctor now, the inventor of a pioneering new treatment that used magnetic fields to treat the demented. He had a small asylum of his own in the Chandletown district. Malvery was pleased to hear he was doing well: he'd always been a good, honest sort.

'But enough of me,' Hawkby said. 'You've had quite the life of adventure, I hear!'

'Ha! Is that what they say?'

'We may not move in quite the same circles these days, but I know a thing or two. Surgeon on the *Ketty Jay* under Captain Frey. They say you've been behind the Wrack and gone toe-to-toe with the Manes.'

'It was less toe-to-toe than shotgun-to-face,' said Malvery. 'Look, I ain't gonna say there haven't been high points, but being a freebooter ain't quite as romantic as you've heard.'

'Oh, now you're being modest.'

'Seriously. Most of the time we're just rolling around pissed to fight off the boredom. They're a good bunch, the best bunch, but sometimes...' He accepted a refill of port from Hawkby's bottle, and took a sip. Damn, it was good. 'Sometimes I get to wondering what in buggery I'm doing with myself.'

Hawkby, sensing a story, nestled back into his armchair. 'Whatever do you mean?'

Malvery looked into his glass, studying the way the firelight splintered and shone. Now he'd begun, he wasn't sure if he wanted to be talking about this at all. But he didn't much want to discuss it with any of the crew, and here was someone who'd understand. Lulled by the alcohol and his surroundings, he decided to unburden himself of the thoughts that had been weighing on his mind these last few days.

'Long time after I... well, you know what happened...'

Hawkby nodded gravely. Everyone knew what had happened to Henvid Clack.

Malvery shifted himself awkwardly in his seat, suddenly uncomfortable. 'Anyway, I couldn't bring myself to pick up a scalpel after that. Couldn't do much more than tie on bandages and dish out pills. But I got past it. Our engineer, Silo, got shot pretty bad, and I pulled him through. That was nearly two years ago, I reckon.' He adjusted his glasses and harumphed. 'And since then I ain't done a whole lot of anything, really.'

'Malvery, I'm amazed! If half the stories are true, you've been all over the place! What I wouldn't give for a travelling life like yours!'

'I mean I ain't exactly saved many lives during that time,' said Malvery. 'Reckon I'm well into minus figures as far as that goes.'

Hawkby regarded him thoughtfully, his forefinger resting on his chin. Malvery dug into his pocket and pulled out a small velvet presentation box. He held it out to Hawkby.

'I remember this,' said Hawkby. He opened it and looked at the medal inside. 'First Aerium War, yes? You were a field surgeon then.'

'Aye. Carried some wounded fellers out of a firefight. Didn't think much of it at the time, but they gave me that medal, and it made my name. Brought me to the attention of a bloke named Macklebury.'

'Yes, I recall the Mackleburys. Your patrons.'

'General Gred Macklebury. I met him at the presentation ceremony. I s'pose he liked me. After the war, he asked if I'd be his family's personal physician. Offered me enough money to make your hair fall out. I reckon he liked the idea of having a war hero as a doctor, or some such thing. But I didn't want to be sittin' on my hands when there was surgery to be done, so I cut a deal with him. If he helped me set up my own practice, I'd be at his beck and call whenever I was needed. Whenever I wasn't – which I reckoned would be most of the time – I'd be in my surgery.'

'Eminently sensible,' said Hawkby, closing the box and handing it back. Malvery dropped it into his pocket. He'd been carrying it there ever since Crake had found it in a drawer.

'It worked out well for everyone. Macklebury liked to show me off in the evenings, so I ended up at all sorts of clubs and soirees and such that I'd never have got to otherwise. I wasn't born with much money and never had much growin' up, so you can imagine what I felt like, paradin' around in the parlours of the rich and famous. I thought life couldn't get much better. That was how I met Eldrea, too, and by damn, she was quite a woman back then.'

Hawkby topped up Malvery's glass. 'So far, old fellow, it sounds like the tale of a man justly rewarded for his bravery in the line of fire.'

'You could say that. But then the Second Aerium War kicked off. Lot of folks out there dyin' on the front lines. And I thought: "That's where *I* oughta be. Back in among it." But I had a life in Thesk by then. I was rich and comfy and I didn't much fancy giving up my place by the fire. And I knew Macklebury would make sure I wasn't called up. He wanted my services for himself. So I sat it out. Most of the Second Aerium War I spent in this club, while young doctors like you were sent out to the front.' He hunched forward in his chair, the firelight reflecting from the lenses of his glasses. 'Reckon that was the beginning of the end for me.'

'I think you judge yourself harshly,' Hawkby said. 'There was need of doctors on the home front, too.'

Malvery was unconvinced. 'The old me, he'd have gone regardless. But something changed between the wars. I lost that edge. Too much good living, too much drink. And somewhere along the way the woman I loved became an enemy, whether by my fault or hers, I dunno. Probably both. She thought she was marrying a braver man, I reckon.'

'My dear Malvery!' Hawkby cried, giving him a hearty thump on the shoulder. 'I'm not used to seeing you so maudlin.'

'Sorry,' said Malvery, gathering himself. 'Finding that medal brought it all back, I s'pose. I used to be full of piss and passion, you know? All I wanted to do was save lives. I just wonder what happened to that feller.'

'Well then,' said Hawkby with a shrug. 'If you feel that way, come and work for me.'

Malvery frowned at him. 'You mean it?'

'You can be surgeon-in-chief at my asylum. Rot knows the daft beggars hurt themselves enough to need a man like you in residence. Stay with me for six months, I'll see to your reinstatement in the guild, and after that you can do as you please. No doubt I'd be glad to keep you on, but if you think you'd prefer to work in a hospital or set up on your own, I shan't stop you.'

Simple as that. He'd forgotten how it was in the world of high society, how easily doors were opened.

'I'm sort of out of practice, mate,' he said, but the protest was weak and Hawkby steamrollered it.

'Pish! You were one of the best surgeons I ever saw. You have a gift, and it's going to waste. I'd be honoured to have you on my staff.'

Could I? Malvery thought. *Could I really?*

What would it be like, after all these years, to return to a stable job, a stable world? To save lives again? Wasn't that what he'd always wanted to do? Wasn't it all he *ever* wanted to do?

This time round, he'd be humble. None of this poisonous high society nonsense, and no more marrying above his station. But it'd be good to have a decent waistcoat, to sit in the Axelby Club again, to cut his steak with a silver knife and wash it down with a fine vintage.

But first there was the question of Frey. His Cap'n's life was in danger – his *friend's* – and that was his first duty. It occurred to him that he ought to head back to the *Ketty Jay* soon. The Cap'n would be returning with news from Trinica, and Malvery had better be there for it.

'It's a generous offer, Hawkby,' he said. 'Thank you. But right now I'm in the middle of something that can't wait. Can I have some time to consider?'

'Of course, of course. Take all the time you need. You know where to find me.' They got to their feet and shook hands. 'The offer's there. Think about it.'

'I will,' said Malvery. 'I definitely will.'

Jez hadn't slept in four years. But she was dreaming, all the same. She dreamed the day of her death.

She stood over her corpse, looking down on herself. Her body lay huddled in a hollow in the snow, skin blue and eyes closed. Death had relaxed her features. She was curled up foetally, as if she wanted to reach the end of her life in the same position as she began it.

It was morning, and a heavy lid of grey cloud pressed down, leaching the colour from the world. This was not the same as her memory. In real life, after she'd died, it had kept on snowing. She'd woken in a cocoon, a frosty womb for her rebirth, and had dug her way out to a clear blue sky. But this was a dream, not a memory, and things were different here.

She was not asleep, but she was in a deeper trance than she'd ever managed before. The incident on the train, when she'd heard the dying Dakkadian's thoughts, had inspired her to experiment. Trancing was easy for her these days. It was like breathing out and sinking under water. But she'd always stayed at a safe depth till now, afraid of drowning.

She'd been consumed by the daemon inside her twice before. Then, she'd become something fearsome, something monstrous. She was afraid of what might happen if she lost control again. Perhaps she'd be forced to leave the *Ketty Jay*, for the good of everyone.

But if she ever hoped to find out what it meant to be a half-Mane, a little controlled risk was necessary. So she let herself sink. And she found herself dreaming.

She lifted her head and surveyed her surroundings. She knew this place well, though she'd long since forgotten its name. It was a small settlement near the icy coast of Yortland. She'd come here as the expedition navigator for Professor Malstrom. The Professor was Vardia's foremost authority on the Azryx, a lost civilisation possessing strange and advanced technology which disappeared beneath the northern ice many thousands of years ago. Or so Malstrom believed, at least. There was barely a shred of evidence to support his theory. Even the name came from the Professor himself.

It was a fool's quest, but Jez had been happy to take the money. She wouldn't have been so keen if she'd known what was in store for her.

She followed the winding tracks in the snow, back to the town. Behind the low, domed Yortish buildings, the mountains rose like unsheathed fangs. Up on the glacier were the ice caves, the excavation site where the scientists had searched fruitlessly for a buried city.

An immense silence lay across the frozen wastes. The only sound was the crunching of her boots in the snow.

The bright blood was a shock in this clean white world. Bodies lay torn in hunks and rags, strewn between the close-set domes, their remains flung with great violence. Hide coats soaked red, concealing pieces of their occupants within. She walked past them, curiously unconcerned. They didn't seem like they'd been people.

Her tracks led her to the place where she'd been given the Invitation, in an anonymous spot between the sloped walls of two snow-covered domes. But the Mane who had made her was nowhere to be seen. It had been beheaded before the Invitation was complete, killed by Riss, a colleague who'd felt more for her than she had for him. She hadn't thought of Riss much since that day, even after all he'd tried to do for her. She never found out what became of him. Dead, or taken. Perhaps he deserved more of a tribute than she gave him, but Jez had never been the sentimental kind.

She came to the main street. It was little more than a thoroughfare of packed snow, leading through the buildings towards a tiny landing-pad on the far side, out of sight. A crashed snow-tractor rested against one wall, the windows of its cab cracked and smeared with blood. Bodies lay everywhere.

There was a dreadnought overhead.

She couldn't understand why she hadn't seen it before. But this was a dream, she supposed, and it followed its own logic. It hung there, enormous against the grey ceiling of cloud, all spikes and bolts and filthy iron. Ropes and chains trailed from its gunwales, hanging down onto the thoroughfare. The Manes had swarmed down them when they descended on the town, several years ago. But there were no Manes in sight now.

She stood where she was and looked at the dreadnought. A soft wind blew up the thoroughfare, pushing powdered snow before it. The dangling chains clanked against each other.

Then, through the aching quiet, she heard a sound she knew well. It was coming from the dreadnought. At first it was faint, but soon it grew louder, swelling to a clamour. Feral howls, like mad wolves, mournful, savage and needful.

She listened to her brothers and sisters, and it was like music.

FOURTEEN

CRICKSLINT—A SLAP—TRADING IDENTITIES— A VISITATION

Nine nights left, thought Frey, as he knocked on the door of the curio shop. Next to him, Crake stamped his feet and shivered. The unseasonable cold snap showed no signs of letting up.

'Spit and blood,' Crake muttered. 'If this is autumn, I don't want to be here for winter.'

'Not to worry,' said Frey. 'Chances are I'll be dead by then.'

'That attitude's not going to do you much good, now, is it?'

'Just trying to look on the bright side.'

The curio shop was dark. At this time of night, all the shops were closed. There were only two people visible, a pair of men buried in greatcoats, hats and scarves, muttering to each other as they walked past.

Frey knocked again impatiently. 'Doesn't anyone *hurry* any more?' he griped. He peered through the shop window, and saw a faint light in the back, and movement. 'Finally. Someone's coming.'

'I don't like this plan you've got, Cap'n,' Crake murmured.

'That's because it's barely a plan at all. If I had something better, I'd use it. But we've got no leverage. So we either get the relic out of him this way, or we go to plan B.'

'Plan B? Isn't that just code for "wade in there and shoot anything that moves"?'

'Exactly. And that means bullets flying everywhere. And because I don't like getting shot much, I try to avoid Plan B when I can.'

'Remarkable how often we end up using it, though,' Crake commented.

'That's because Plan A never bloody works.'

The door was opened by a pinch-faced bruiser with hulking shoulders. A little bell tinkled cheerily overhead. 'Mr Frey and Mr Crake, right?'

'*Captain* Frey,' said Frey.

The thug gave him a long and deeply unimpressed stare. Frey returned a cheesy grin.

'*Captain* Frey,' the thug said at length. 'Come in, then.' He let them through, locked the door behind them, and then searched them for weapons. They weren't carrying any, for the same reason that Frey had only brought Crake from his crew. They were going to try and do this the nice way.

The curio shop was an unsettling place. Shelves of glass-eyed dolls stared down at them as they were led towards the back. They passed a stuffed beast that Frey didn't recognise, some kind of hunting cat with a mane of spikes like a porcupine. He was half-convinced it was going to spring to life and snap at him. Ticking toys shifted restlessly in the dark: the kind of clockwork junk Pinn was fond of. He was reminded of the night Pinn had rashly announced his intention to be a famous inventor. The pilot appeared to have forgotten all about it, which was probably for the best.

Mind on the job, Frey. You've got one chance to play this right. Don't mess it up like you did with Trinica.

He shut away that memory. Her scorn had burned him. He'd never even had the chance to tell her about the curse.

Nine nights left. Was it really true? It had been three nights since he'd seen the vision in the cargo hold and spoken to the sorcerer, and there'd been no sign of the daemon in between. Despite Crake's strange readings, despite the sorcerer's words, he still couldn't fully convince himself of the threat. He kept trying to reason his way out of it. A simple hallucination wasn't too much to worry about, really. Maybe Crake's readings were skewed. And the sorcerer was hardly reliable: he might be as much a charlatan as the Awakeners were.

He couldn't quite believe that there was a daemon out there, waiting to get him. That margin of doubt was what kept him going.

Crickslint sat behind a desk in a small area at the back of the shop. There was a single electric lamp hanging from the ceiling above his head. He had a jeweller's glass fixed to his eye, peering at a small golden casket that he was turning over in his hand. Two more bodyguards, inconspicuously armed, stood at the edge of the light. Frey and Crake settled themselves in antique seats that had been placed in front of the desk.

Crickslint ignored them for a while. Darian waited. He was used to these boring displays of importance from people he dealt with.

'Darian Frey,' he said eventually. He put the casket aside, took out the jeweller's glass, steepled his fingers and smiled a chrome-toothed smile. 'We meet again.'

Frey winced inwardly. He'd forgotten how irritatingly theatrical Crickslint was. Every movement, every expression was exaggerated; his conversation was full of dramatic pauses and flamboyant surges in volume. The annoying piece of shit seemed to think he was the Dread Lord of Vardia or some such bollocks, instead of a weasel-faced runt with a voice like a girl.

'Yes,' said Frey, as neutrally as possible. 'Apparently we do.'

'And who is your friend?' asked Crickslint, drawing out the syllables, tapping a finger against his cheek as if pondering deeply. His face lit up. 'Why, it looks like Grayther Crake, the daemonist.'

'How do you do?' Crake said politely, seemingly unfazed by Crickslint's over-the-top delivery. Coming from the aristocracy, he was probably used to odder things.

'Now,' said Crickslint. He adjusted the sleeves of his jacket and made a show of arranging himself. 'What business might you two gentlemen have with me?'

Frey sized up his opponent, trying to spot anything that might give him an angle. Crickslint's teeth were new, since the last lot had been knocked out. He could have had a natural-looking set made up, but he clearly preferred to think of himself as fearsome, so he'd chosen metal. His face was sallow as ever, with small weak eyes. Thin blond hair was slicked back over a long skull.

Frey knew his sort. He was just like the weedy, sickly children at the orphanage where Frey grew up, the ones who got beaten up and pushed about their whole adolescent lives. Frey had to resist the urge to bully him *now*. Something about him made it instinctive.

But Frey would have to tread carefully. Crickslint had grown sly, and he'd gained the power to get revenge on the world for all those humiliations. That made him dangerous.

'Trinica Dracken sold you a relic recently,' Frey said.

'She did.'

'I'd like you to loan it to me.'

Crickslint blinked. 'Excuse me?'

'A loan. You know. Two weeks. I'll pay, of course, and I can leave you a Firecrow as collateral. I just need to borrow it.' He shrugged. 'You lend money to everyone, right? This is the same thing. You can still sell it on at full price after I'm done.'

Crickslint looked faintly amused. 'That's an odd proposition. And what do you intend to do with it?'

'That's my business. But you have my assurance, my absolute assurance, that it'll be returned to you in perfect condition.' It was an easy enough promise to make, since Frey wasn't thinking much further than getting his hands on the relic at this stage.

Crickslint leaned forward across the desk, so that the light from above fell onto his face, calculated to lend him a sinister air. 'Do you even know what it *is*, Captain Frey? The relic, I mean?'

'No,' said Frey. 'Do you?'

'Perhaps.'

Frey narrowed his eyes. 'I reckon you don't. I bet you don't even know where it came from.'

'Oh, I can tell you that quite easily. It was found by an explorer. Ugrik vak Munn kes Oortuk, in fact.'

'Uh-huh. I'm guessing he's not from around here.'

'He's a Yort. He's actually quite famous.'

'Never heard of him. Where'd *he* get it from?'

'That, I'll admit, I don't know.'

'So how'd the Sammies get hold of it?'

'They caught him. Sammies don't like people wandering about outside of the Free Trade Zone. Especially not those who go around stealing their ancient relics.'

'And you heard about it. Through a whispermonger, I'm guessing. And then you sent Trinica Dracken to get it for you.'

Crickslint clapped slowly. 'Very good, Captain Frey. None of which gets you any closer to having it yourself.'

Frey leaned back in his chair. If there was a time to make his move, it was now. 'I like your new teeth,' he said.

Crickslint gave him a sharklike smile. 'Flattery. You must really have *nothing* to bargain with.'

'My friend here's got something similar. Show him your gold tooth, Crake.'

Crake leaned forward and offered a dazzling grin. His tooth glittered in the light from overhead. Crickslint, half-interested, glanced at the tooth. Then a strange expression crossed his face and he peered closer.

'That *is* a nice tooth,' he said.

Frey felt a stirring of hope as he saw Crickslint's eyes glaze over. He'd seen it happen to people before, as they stared into their own reflections in Crake's daemon-thralled tooth. They became mesmerised and suggestible. If he was lucky, the bodyguards wouldn't even notice what was going on.

'It is a nice tooth, isn't it?' he said. 'Listen, Crickslint, we go way back. Why don't you just lend me that relic, and let's not worry about a price. I'll bring it right back to you when I'm done with it. How's that sound?'

'Oh, yes,' said Crickslint, not taking his eyes off Crake's tooth. 'Yes, that sounds *fine*. Whatever you want.'

'Really?' Frey was faintly surprised at how easily he'd agreed.

Crickslint got up in his chair and leaned across his desk to get a closer look. 'Yes, yes, *take* it. Just *one* thing I'd ask, though.'

'What's that?'

Crickslint hit Crake hard across the face, a ringing slap that echoed through the empty curio shop.

'Don't embarrass yourselves by trying any more of that daemonist shit with me!' he hissed, and sat back down. He motioned to one of his thugs. 'Get him out of here.'

Crake was shocked, holding the side of his face. 'He *slapped* me!' he said to Frey in indignation.

'I saw,' said Frey grimly, as the thug descended on Crake and dragged him out of the shop. The bell above the door tinkled happily as Crake was flung out on to the street.

Crickslint had steepled his fingers again, gazing steadily at Frey, having returned to his self-appointed role as pantomime villain. 'Now that... *distraction* is out of the way, perhaps we can negotiate man-to-man?'

'Can't blame a feller for trying,' said Frey. The tooth only worked on people who were weak-willed or stupid. Crickslint was apparently neither.

'I believe you were interrupted in the process of making me a ridiculous offer? You were asking me to entrust to you a valuable Samarlan relic, many thousands of years old, with a *Firecrow* as collateral? You do know the market's been flooded with second-hand Firecrows since the Navy upgraded their fleet?'

'Crickslint,' said Frey. 'It's a classic aircraft. And you could own one, for a limited time.'

Crickslint laughed, a high, hysterical laugh that sawed through the brain and down the spinal column. Frey had to clutch the sides of his chair to resist punching him. He was just so *punchable*. Although it might be pretty hard on the knuckles with those chrome teeth in place.

'You could own one! Very amusing. No, I think we'll forget about the Firecrow.'

Frey was sort of relieved. He didn't fancy explaining to Harkins that he'd have to do without his beloved aircraft, even though it technically belonged to Frey.

'What about I do some jobs for you?' Frey suggested. 'For free, of course. You always need smugglers, right? I'm good at that.'

I really hope he doesn't remember how good I was at stealing from him, too, Frey thought. But if Crickslint did remember, he wasn't showing it.

Crickslint sat upright, one finger pressed against his lips in a classic pose of thought. The very artificiality of it made Frey murderous. He hated having to beg like this. He had half a mind to leave and come back with Plan B – B for 'Bess tears everyone's heads off' – when Crickslint spoke again.

'I have a proposal,' he said. 'I hear you have an exceptional pilot on your crew by the name of Artis Pinn.'

Pinn. Pinn with his arm in a sling.

'What of it?' Frey asked carefully.

'I have a way that you could do me a service. After that, I might consider loaning you the relic you need.'

'Go on.'

'I know a man who owes me a lot. He's also quite the gambler. I have an interest in seeing him lose a large amount of money. Then I'll call in his debt and bankrupt him.'

'Won't that mean that you lose some of your money?'

'Yes. But by bankrupting him I'll be doing a far more valuable service to his rival. It's a game of checks and balances, Captain Frey; you really don't need to worry about it.'

'So what do I have to do?'

'There are races held outside the city. Single-seater craft, racing round a circuit. They're illegal and unregulated, and a lot of money changes hands on them. The man I want is the backer for a pilot named Gidley Sleen. He places big bets on every race. I'm given to understand that Sleen is a virtual certainty to win tomorrow; the competition is feeble. Short odds will mean his backer will place an even bigger bet than usual to get a good return.'

'You want me to enter Pinn in the race?'

'I want you to enter him, and I want him to win. He'll go in as an unknown. I'll back him myself: the odds will be very favourable. When he wins, I'll make a lot, and my target will lose a lot, I'll call in my debt at the right moment and—' He clicked his fingers.

'Then you'll loan me the relic?'

'For two weeks. And if it's not back in my hands by then, I will find you.' He snapped his teeth together. 'You don't want that.'

'Done,' said Frey. 'And don't worry. Pinn's the best damn pilot in Vardia.'

'I'm gonna do *what*?' Harkins shrieked, at the same time as Pinn cried: 'He's gonna do *what*?'

Frey pinched the bridge of his nose and squeezed his eyes shut. To Crake, who was sitting with his feet up on the table of the *Ketty Jay*'s mess, the Cap'n looked tired and harassed. *Good*, he thought pettily. He was still sore at Frey for getting him slapped. His cheek hadn't stopped stinging yet.

'It's pretty simple,' Frey said. 'Harkins, you're gonna pretend to be Pinn tomorrow, and fly the race in his place.'

'Him?' Pinn cried, pointing at Harkins. 'I'm a better pilot even with my arm in a sling!'

Harkins muttered something unintelligible, but probably insulting.

'You can't fly properly with one arm, Pinn,' said Frey. 'You barely managed to land the Skylance in Thesk without crashing it.'

But Pinn was in the midst of a tantrum and wasn't really listening. 'I wanna fly!' he said. 'This is a fringement of my human rights!'

'A *fringement*?' Crake said in weary disgust, rousing from his sulk.

'Fringement!' Pinn snapped. 'Like when someone's in your fringe!'

Crake opened his mouth, and shut it again with a sigh. He couldn't be bothered.

'Is that even a word?' Frey asked Malvery, who was stirring a pot of soup at the stove. Malvery shrugged without turning around. He didn't want to get involved.

Slag watched the conflict with half an eye, having decided to join the crew in the mess. He'd plonked himself down in a languid curve on the table and was surreptitiously lapping at a patch of spilled coffee when he thought nobody was looking.

'Crickslint doesn't know what you look like,' Frey told Pinn. 'As far as he knows, Artis Pinn is skinny and balding and loud noises give him a heart attack.'

'Instead of someone resembling an angry potato with an attitude problem,' Crake added.

'You shut up, you milky little ponce,' said Pinn. 'You just got slapped by a guy with no teeth.'

'Hey, he *had* teeth! Big shiny ones!' Crake protested, but nobody was listening.

'I am *not* pretending to be him!' Harkins declared, thrusting a trembling finger at Pinn.

'He is *not* pretending to be me!' Pinn said.

'Yes. He. Is,' said the Cap'n. 'Because we need that relic back.'

'*You* need that relic back,' Pinn corrected.

'Yes, *I* need it,' said Frey, who was getting to the end of his tether. 'And if I end up dead, what do you think happens to you lot? No more *Ketty Jay*. Are you all going to go and get jobs or something?'

Pinn went pale at that. Before anyone could offer anything else, the cat suddenly sprang up, arched his back and hissed.

'Here comes Jez,' said Malvery, without taking his eyes off the soup.

Sure enough, Jez climbed down the ladder a moment later. Slag bolted, leaping off the table and onto the counter-top, and finally up on top of a cupboard, where he sat crooning malevolently.

'That cat really hates you,' Crake observed.

'He hates everyone,' said Jez dismissively. She turned to the Cap'n. 'Course plotted for the race site. It'll take us two hours, more or less.'

'Fine,' said Frey. 'Early start tomorrow, lads.' There were general groans at the news. 'I know, I know. But we have to get there in plenty of time. We need to tune up the Firecrow. She'll have to be at her best if we're gonna win this race.'

'If *I'm* gonna win it,' said Harkins, puffing out his chest. Thin as he was, it didn't puff too far.

'Oh? I thought you didn't *want* to race?' said Frey wryly.

Harkins glanced at Jez and coughed. 'Well, you know… I changed my mind! If there's flying to be done, I'm the man to do it. Artis Pinn!'

Pinn gave a strangled cry of rage and lunged across the mess at Harkins, who gave a less than manly squeal and hid behind Frey. Jez watched the whole thing in bewilderment.

'If you'll excuse me,' said Crake, getting to his feet. 'I think I'll leave you all to it.'

He slipped through the melee and climbed the ladder to the relative peace of the *Ketty Jay*'s main passageway. From there, he made his way down to the hold to check on Bess.

It was chilly and gloomy in the hold. Crake preferred that to the sweltering heat of Samarla. He was glad to be out of that country, if only because his bowel movements had finally steadied. His stomach really didn't get on with Samarlan fare at all.

In the middle of the hold were the Rattletraps. One of them was halfway disassembled, with Silo's tool box resting on its hood. The man himself was nowhere to be seen. Crake was glad about that. Since they'd held up that train in the desert, Silo had been in a foul mood. Now he spent most of his time in the hold, fixing up buggies with a furious intensity, and if anyone so much as spoke to him they got an irritated glare and no reply. Crake wondered if the engineer had something on his mind, but he knew so little about him that it was hard to tell.

In fact, it wasn't just Silo that was acting oddly. There was a strange atmosphere on the *Ketty Jay* now. Everyone knew that the Cap'n was in trouble, everyone was thinking about it, but no one wanted to talk about it. So they all ran around getting on with whatever they could, or stayed away from the craft altogether.

Nobody wanted to admit it, but the Cap'n's life might be measured in days. And all this, this world aboard the *Ketty Jay* they'd created for themselves, would come to an end then. Without Frey, there was no crew. Nobody really thought they could carry on if the Cap'n was gone. They would each end up going their separate ways. It would be inevitable. They had very little in common, beyond the *Ketty Jay*.

He'd reached the bottom of the stairs and stepped out onto the floor of the cargo hold when he heard a soft clank from the shadows.

His senses prickled. There was a change in the air. The chill he felt wasn't entirely due to the temperature.

'Bess?' he said quietly, although something told him it wasn't her. Dread trickled through him. He stared into the darkness at the edges of the hold.

Something shifted there. Something taller than a man.

Spit and blood. It's here.

He took a step backwards. He was defenceless. There was a daemon here and he was defenceless and it wasn't even meant to be coming for him, it was meant to be *Frey*!

'Bess!' he called, though this time it was more like a shout.

There was a soft growl. It moved to the edge of the light. Somehow it was still impossible to make out a shape, but he saw a claw, a huge iron claw with bayonets for fingers, and then a muzzle like a dog's, wrinkling into a snarl.

'Damn it, Bess! Where are you?' he yelled in panic.

She came thundering from the sanctum, emerging from behind the barrier of crates and tarpaulin at the back of the hold. A mountain of metal and chainmail and leather, boots stamping hard enough to make Silo's tool box slide off the hood of the Rattletrap and crash to the ground.

But by the time she'd arrived, there was only blackness where the thing had been. Crake stared at the emptiness, his heart thumping in his chest. Bess cast about in agitation, searching for whatever had alarmed Crake.

After a moment, Crake patted her on the arm. 'Easy, girl,' he said. 'It's gone now. It's gone.'

Bess allowed herself to be gentled. Crake led her back to the sanctum, glancing over his shoulder at the spot where he'd seen – where he *thought* he saw – the daemon. Already it didn't seem real.

No. I saw it. Just like Frey did.

But what had shaken him, more than the sight of the daemon itself, was the feeling of helplessness he'd experienced in that moment.

He'd never faced a daemon before without his machines, without layers of sonic defences and carefully calculated formulae to hand – without *preparation*. But this one was loose, unconstrained by interference fields or echo chambers.

He was a daemonist. Dealing with daemons was his whole purpose in life. But he realised that he had absolutely no way to fight the thing that had come on board the *Ketty Jay*.

That, he told himself, would have to be remedied.

FIFTEEN

PRE-FLIGHT—USE OF WEAPONS—SILO'S
DIAGNOSIS—THE TUNNEL—HARKINS DISOBEYS

There was something wrong with the Firecrow.

Harkins felt his already unbearable terror slide towards full-blown panic. He tried the switch again, and again, flushing air through the aerium vents. The result was the same. It just didn't sound right.

Was it just his nerves, playing tricks on him? No. Harkins was obsessive about his pre-flight checks. They helped to relax him. He could pass hours checking and re-checking the Firecrow from the sanctuary of his cockpit. Every system on his aircraft had been tested over and over by him personally. He knew the pitch of every squeaking hydraulic pump, the whirr of every actuator.

He looked to his left and right. Beneath a louring grey sky, the other racers were lined up next to him. Eight pilots, including himself. They were parked on a strip of packed earth that had been cleared as a makeshift landing-pad. A hundred metres ahead of them was a cliff, and beyond it, the Rushes: the deadly maze where they would have their race.

There was a cart in front of the aircraft that served as a podium. A man in a badly-fitting suit, who Harkins took to be an announcer of some kind, was climbing on to it.

I can't fly like this. Something's wrong! Something's wrong!

'Cap'n!' he said shrilly. 'I need Silo here now!'

'What's the problem?' came the Cap'n's voice in his ear, transmitted through the silver earcuff he wore.

'There's… I mean… Something's wrong with the Firecrow!' he sputtered.

'You're three minutes from take-off! I thought you checked

everything already? Didn't the officials give all the craft a last-minute inspection for—'

'I did check it! It was alright *then*! It's not alright *now*!' Harkins said, his voice rising to a moderately loud scream.

'Okay, okay. Calm down. Are you sure it's not just your imagi—' He stopped himself wisely before Harkins could explode. 'Never mind. Silo's on his way.'

Harkins jigged and jittered in his seat. Why, why, why had he volunteered for this? Didn't he spend his whole life avoiding situations like these? He'd almost died when he found out that the race would be held in the Rushes, instead of the nice flat plain that he'd imagined. The Rushes were a sprawling network of forested gorges carved from a dozen converging rivers which drained from the Splinters into the sea. Earthquakes and erosion had formed a system of tunnels and arches and fantastically precarious pillars, half a klom deep, with thrashing waterways at the bottom.

He'd done it for her, of course. Jez, kind Jez, who despite being kind *never seemed to notice him*, no matter how heroic he tried to be. Once in a while he managed to admit the truth to himself: it was all beginning to get on his nerves a little bit. But whenever he did, he took it back immediately, not wishing to think bad thoughts about her.

And now he was here, and there were mere minutes to go, and he was desperately hoping that whatever problem the Firecrow had developed would make it impossible to fly.

A small crowd of spectators were gathered along the rim of the gorge ahead of them, where the finish line would be. Nearby was another makeshift landing pad for their aircraft, much bigger than the one Harkins sat on. Among others, he saw the reassuringly ugly shape of the *Ketty Jay* there, and a small single-seater craft which he'd seen Crickslint arrive in.

'Racers!' yelled the announcer. Harkins could only hear faintly through the cockpit hood. Everyone else had their cockpits open, but Harkins had sealed himself in the first chance he got. It felt safer that way. He frowned and tried to concentrate on the muffled words.

'As we're coming up to the start of the race, it's time to remind you of the rules!' he called. He was a stocky man with a shaved head and a roll of fat where his neck should have been, as if he'd been crushed at some point in his life and never quite sprung back into shape. 'You've all been given maps detailing the network of gorges in the race area. You'll also see that there are four markers numbered one to four. You must pass through these gorges, in *order*. We'll have observers watching you, so no cheating. As long as you do that, feel free to pick your own route. There will be *two* laps. Are we clear?'

Harkins glanced down at the map fixed to his dash. He'd done his best to memorise it, but it refused to stick in his head, sliding off the surface of his mind. He was too agitated to retain any new information.

What if I go the wrong way? What if I forget? What if I—

There was a loud rapping on the hood of his cockpit. He jumped violently enough to bang his skull against the headrest of his seat. Readjusting his battered leather pilot's cap, which had fallen over his eyes, he looked for the source of the sound.

Silo. The Murthian's dark, narrow face gazed in at him from the other side of the windglass.

'The aerium tanks!' Harkins cried. 'They don't sound right when I vent air through them!'

Silo's face disappeared. Harkins sat back in his seat, recovering from this new shock. He feverishly hoped that Silo found whatever was wrong. He hoped it was something terminal.

Nervously, he surveyed the other pilots. To his left was an enormously fat man in an Oddsen Blackbird, the craft gleaming silver, its back curved and its wings thin and sharp. He looked like he'd been poured into his cockpit and congealed there. To his right was a brutish-looking Yort in a black Gordinson Airbat. His hair and beard were a tangle of matted locks and braids, his face was tattooed in blue patterns, and there was a curved bone driven through the bridge of his nose. He caught Harkins' eye and Harkins looked away quickly.

Further down the line was the man who was supposed to be his competition. Gidley Sleen. Harkins couldn't see him now, but he could see the nose of the Besterfield Nimbus he flew: sleek, fast, built like a dart. They all had the advantage over him in speed, but the Firecrow was a great all-rounder, and it was far more manoeuvrable than these racer models.

Still, he really didn't think he had a chance of winning.

'Your altimeters should all read five-seven-seven!' the announcer continued. 'Anyone going above six hundred will be disqualified. We have spotters in the air; their decision is final. Stay in the gorges and you won't get penalised.'

Harkins checked his altimeter was right. He didn't want to get disqualified.

Wait a minute. Who cares if you're disqualified? You'll be lucky to survive!

The thought almost made him bolt. He strapped himself in, to make it more difficult to disgrace himself with his cowardice.

'Last rule! Very important!' the announcer said. 'No one is allowed to fire weapons until your *second* lap. Your *second* lap!'

'Weapons?' Harkins shrieked, scrambling for the eject button on his seat belt. 'Nobody said anything about weapons!'

'Weapons?' said Frey in his ear.

'The announcer... I mean... Weapons!... He said we can use weapons on the final lap! What kind of race is this?'

'Weapons are *good*, Harkins. You're the only one flying a combat craft. Those lightweight racers will come apart if you so much as graze 'em with your guns.'

'But... I... did you know about this?' he demanded.

'No. That son of a bitch Crickslint neglected to mention it,' said the Cap'n, angrily. 'Look, you'll just have to do your best. Shoot down anyone faster than you.'

'You want me to kill people just to win a race?'

'Harkins, they're going to try and kill *you*.'

Harkins squeaked. This was getting worse and worse.

Jez's voice cut in. She was wearing an earcuff too. 'He shouldn't have to do this, Cap'n.' Her voice flooded him with gladness.

'It's not *my* fault they're using weapons,' Frey protested.

'Harkins!' She was addressing him now. 'It's too dangerous. We can find another way to get the relic.'

'Hey! Who's in command here?' Frey said indignantly.

'Cap'n, you can't possibly let him take a risk like this on his own.'

There was silence. Harkins listened intently. Finally, a defeated groan from the Cap'n. 'Alright,' he said. 'I s'pose. Harkins?'

'I *want* to, Cap'n,' said Harkins.

Frey's voice was puzzled. He thought he'd misheard. 'You what?'

'I'll do it,' Harkins said.

It was Jez's kindness that made him say it. Jez, always looking out for him, who'd persuaded the Cap'n to let him quit because she wanted to keep him safe. Perversely, it made him all the more determined. He'd *show* her he was brave. He'd *make* her notice him.

The one thing, the *only* thing he was good at was flying. And the Cap'n needed him. The Cap'n was in trouble. The Cap'n who'd let him fly this Firecrow in the first place, who'd rescued him from the misery of a land-bound life after he was discharged from the Navy as a shattered wreck.

'I won't let you down,' he said. He could have been talking to either of them.

'Racers ready!' the announcer yelled.

Silo knocked on the hood again, and this time Harkins didn't jump. 'Try it now,' the Murthian rumbled.

He blasted air through aerium tanks to purge them. The pitch was just right. He grinned a brown-toothed grin. 'Silo, you're… you're a genius! What was it?'

'Somethin' blockin' the vent,' said Silo, his face expressionless.

'Hover!' called the announcer.

'Gotta go, Silo. Thanks!' he called. Silo dropped away and he engaged the aerium engines. The tanks filled with ultralight gas and the Firecrow lifted off. He vented a little to equalise the weight and came to a hover five metres off the ground. The other racers were strung out on a loose line to either side of him, hanging in the air.

'Harkins,' said the Cap'n. 'I want you to know I appreciate this.'

'You come back, alright?' said Jez, worried. Her concern warmed him.

'Good luck,' Pinn chipped in grudgingly on his own earcuff. Then, after a moment, he added: 'You bastard.'

Harkins pulled his flight-goggles down over his eyes and adjusted them. He was scared to death, but then, he was used to that.

Ready as I'll ever be.

'Three… two… one…' the announcer counted.

Harkins experienced a brief moment of sheer horror, when the utter foolishness of what he was about to do suddenly revealed itself in full splendour, and all his noble thoughts of bravery, self-sacrifice and heroism became ridiculous.

'*Go!*'

Then he hit the thrusters, and the moment was forgotten in the thrill of acceleration.

The racers skimmed across the flat earth of the plain, the line breaking up as the faster craft pulled ahead. Around them, in the distance, the grass and rock were broken by gullies and valleys and the grey swathes of streams and rivers, making their way to the softer, broken land to the west, where the Rushes began. Harkins' eyes were fixed on the cliff edge up ahead. That would be their entry into the maze.

They plunged over the precipice in a dizzying tumble. The gorge was deep and wide, its sides shaggy with greenery, descending to a misty torrent at its base. Black and white pennants were hung along its length, with the number '1' printed on each: the first marker. One, in the centre, was larger and bore a pattern of crosses: the start and finish line.

The blood rushed to Harkins' head as he dived, then back out as he banked and levelled, angling himself up the gorge. The other flyers were distressingly close, swooping across his flight path, and for a few seconds everything was chaos as the pilots picked their racing lines.

Through the aircraft in front of him he saw that the gorge split in two, divided by a thin spine of land down its centre. He decided to take whichever side Gidley Sleen took. The group split neatly in half, and Sleen, who was an early leader, pulled left. Harkins followed, along with two others.

The gorge was uncomfortably narrow now, but Harkins had flown in much tighter spots than this, and he concentrated on keeping out of the backwash of the aircraft ahead. They were all pulling away from him at a steady rate. It was obvious he wasn't going to be able to beat them in a straight race. But there were areas where the Firecrow's greater manoeuvrability would be an advantage.

Cold sweat crawled beneath his pilot's cap. Fear swarmed at him with the intensity of a nightmare. He'd *volunteered* for this. He'd actually *volunteered*.

Every firefight he'd been in since the war was the same. A howling torment of primal, animal terror. But still he flew, because if he couldn't fly, he was nothing at all: a joke of a man. And those awful times were the price he paid for the precious hours of peace, the hours when he soared through a clear sky on the wing of the *Ketty Jay*, only him and his aircraft and the endless blue.

The gorge narrowed at the point where the divide ended. It was one thing he remembered from studying the crude map on his dash. As they approached, it suddenly occurred to him that he couldn't see the pilots on the other side of the divide, and that he wouldn't until the very last moment. The pilots in his group had all kept roughly the same altitude, and there wasn't much between them in terms of speed. So that meant...

His eyes widened in realisation. Quickly he dumped some aerium, dropping away from the others. It was going to cost him a little velocity, but it would be worth it if—

The two groups swept together from either side of the divide at the same time, forced together by the narrowing walls. Sleen was out in front, but everyone behind him swerved and swooped as they were shuffled together like a pack of cards, crossing each other's paths. Two craft collided and their wings sheared away with a shriek of metal. Harkins, who was some distance below them, boosted the thrusters and shot past as they came spinning down towards him, trailing smoke. They smashed into the bottom of the gorge and were swept away by the torrent.

Six left, including himself. A slightly hysterical grin split his face. Flying under the pack meant he hadn't had to slow himself down with evasive manoeuvres. Sleed was out in front, but Harkins had grabbed second place back while the others fought to sort out their racing lines again.

The gorge curved hard left, and Harkins swept round to see a short, straight stretch hung with more pennants, this time marked '2'. He swallowed and hunched forward in his seat. Up ahead, the gorge dissolved into a shattered mess of smaller gorges, much tighter than they'd faced so far.

Now things got really dangerous.

I shouldn't have let him go, Frey thought.

He peered over the edge of the crude barrier that had been hammered into place along the lip of the gorge. There was a crowd of several hundred here at the finish line. The racers had disappeared out of sight, and the spectators waited eagerly for them to come back around.

But even if they couldn't see it, they'd heard the crash, and seen the thin line of smoke rising into the overcast sky. They knew that someone had bought it. Frey wanted to say something, to ask if Harkins was alright, how things were going, and so on. But he'd taken his earcuff off, at Jez's suggestion. Talking to Harkins would only distract him. He'd just have to wait, and hope. The rest of the crew, gathered around him, could only do the same.

This whole thing seemed like such a bad idea now. If Harkins died in there, Frey would have no one to blame but himself.

You offered him the chance to pull out, and he didn't take it, he thought, but it didn't convince him. That would have washed with the old Frey, but he was a captain now, and he knew a little more about the responsibility that carried. He hated that Harkins had to take a risk like this, alone. All because Frey was too damn stupid to resist Ashua's goading, or to listen to Trinica. He should have just left the relic alone. His hard-wired instinct to show off in front of a woman had got him cursed, and it might yet get Harkins killed.

Silo slipped his way through the crowd, carrying something wrapped up in a piece of dirty cloth. A Murthian attracted strange and sometimes hostile looks in Vardia, but at least he could move with more freedom than in his home country.

'You fixed the problem?' Frey asked.

Silo stood close to him, shielding the object in his hand from the crowd. He turned back a flap of the cloth. 'Yuh. Found this in the aerium vent. Reckon the maintenance crew put it there when they did that last-minute check.'

Frey's face darkened. He stared at the object, his eyes hard.

Malvery looked over, saw it, and swore under his breath. 'That what I think it is?'

Frey didn't answer. He reached down, adjusted a knob by a fraction, and folded the cloth back over it.

'You know what to do with that, don't you?' he said.

Silo nodded and turned away, making his way out of the crowd. Frey turned his attention to Malvery. 'Don't tell the others,' he said quietly.

The doctor closed his eyes slowly and shook his head, in regret or despair. 'This ain't gonna turn out well,' he said.

Frey was grim. 'Does it ever?'

* * *

Harkins snatched glances at his map as the black and white pennants of the second marker flickered past him like the jerky images from a kinetoscope. He should have studied it harder before he took off. He could have picked the shortest route through the gorges and drawn it in with a pencil. But there was no time now, so it would have to be blind luck.

He felt panic climbing up his ribcage towards his heart. Why didn't he pull up now? Pull up, back out. The Cap'n had said he could. Even *Jez* said he could!

But he didn't. The racers split up as they reached the end of the straight. There, a churning wash of colliding rivers carved new, thin slices through the earth. Walls had collapsed in old earthquakes, slumping into crude new forms that solidified over time, making dark gaps, protrusions and pillars.

Harkins let off the throttle a little. Taking those corners at high speed would be suicide. Here was where his heavier, broader Firecrow would have the advantage over the racing craft, but it would still be a game of reactions in there.

Luckily, Harkins' reactions had been trained by years of living on the knife-edge of fight-or-flight. There were advantages to being afraid of everything.

Occupied with his map, he didn't see which route Sleen took, so he picked one at random and went for it. The walls closed in on him fast, an alley of brutal rock overgrown with green vines. A thin waterfall spewed from the cliffs high above, dropping like a hazy white ribbon towards the floor of the gorge. The wind turned to thunder, blasting against the Firecrow. He concentrated on keeping the wings level, fighting the craft's inclination to roll. The bubble of windglass in the Firecrow's nose gave him a horribly good view of what lay below him.

He glanced over his shoulder and saw that the Yort in the Airbat was on his tail. It caused him a moment's alarm – a fighter pilot's reflex – before he remembered that no weapons were allowed till the last lap of the race.

The alley swung left. He took it wide, in case there was something unexpected on the other side. There was: a sharp kink to the right. He yelped, hit the air brakes and slewed hard, losing speed as he did so. The Airbat, seeing what he'd done, took the corner tight and nosed past him as they came out of the turn into a long, uneven curve. Harkins pushed the thrusters a little harder, and they took the curve neck-and-neck, banking in perfect sync.

A drop of rain hit the windglass. Then another, and another.

'Oh, that's just great,' Harkins complained. 'That's all I bloody needed.'

The Airbat, which was on the outside of the curve, with a better view down the gorge, suddenly pulled up hard. It gave Harkins a fraction of a second's warning before he saw the danger himself: a diagonal arm of rock reaching across his path.

Instinct chose for him. He dived instead of climbing, plunging beneath the arm, where the river had tunnelled through it and left a precarious arch hung with straggling foliage. He blasted past it with a boom of thrusters, close enough to make the vines thrash.

He wasn't allowed even a moment to recover. The gorge fractured again. Three routes to take, no time to decide, so he took the most obvious. He was flying too fast from trying to keep up with the Airbat, and as he climbed and banked out of his dive, he barely missed clipping the wall.

Keep it together! he told himself, as he plunged into a new gorge. He throttled back a little. If he so much as sneezed at this speed, he'd be dead before he opened his eyes again. The walls were even tighter here. The Firecrow rattled and shook, buffeted by the wind. At least the sound of the Airbat's thrusters had faded: the Yort had taken a different route.

Then he saw what was coming, and his heart stopped. A rough, sheer wall, charging towards him. This gorge was a dead end. No wonder the Yort hadn't followed.

No! Impossible! There were no dead ends on the map, he was sure of it!

Pull up now. Pull up, give up, before it's too late!

He looked down through the nose-bubble of the Firecrow. There was a river down there! Where was the river going, if it was a dead end?

Then he saw. The wide, gaping dark. A massive tunnel, a rough and broken maw, swallowing the river.

'Oh, no,' he moaned to himself. 'No, no, no.'

But the momentum of the race had taken over, and he was swept along with it. Before he knew what he was doing, he'd dumped aerium and was diving towards the tunnel. By the time his cowardice caught up, it was too late to climb out of the gorge, and he was committed.

'Harkins, what in rot's name are you *doiiiing*?' he screamed, his high, thin voice lost in the titanic bellow of the river as it rushed up to meet him. He just had the presence of mind to hit the Firecrow's bank of lights before the tunnel consumed him.

There was no space for thought any more. He was lost in the thunderous black. The river was mere metres below him, spray blasting up in great fins behind the Firecrow. The walls and ceiling, illuminated in cruel relief, waited to smash his fragile craft to flaming ruin. His lights lit up the tunnel in an arc, stone upon stone plunging towards and past him, and beyond that was a void. He flew into it, every muscle taut, a thin and constant squeal slipping unnoticed through his clenched teeth.

Then the void was filled with rock.

His reactions saved him again. His instincts knew what he had to do before his conscious mind had worked out what it was seeing. He put the Firecrow into a shallow dive, following the curve of the river as it went over a ridge and sloped down. The tunnel roof sloped down with it for a few dozen metres, then levelled. And there, ahead, was a tight arch of grey light, getting brighter and closer until suddenly Harkins was out, the world expanding around him, and he was in a spacious gorge hung with pennants bearing the number '3'.

He laughed wildly as he turned into the gorge. Behind him, the river burst from the tunnel mouth and plunged a hundred metres to join another river at the floor of the gorge. It was raining in earnest now, splattering across the hood of his cockpit, but Harkins didn't care. He felt invincible. He'd reached a pitch of fear that was indistinguishable from mania.

The span between the third and fourth markers was wide and curved, and a great relief to Harkins. At first he suspected some kind of trick, but then he realised that a long, open stretch would be perfect for the second lap, when the pilots would be using their guns. He also realised, when he saw Sleed coming up behind him in his Nimbus, that he was ahead of the pack. The tunnel had been a considerable shortcut.

He passed a ravine on his left, a narrow slash in the land. Glancing at his map, he saw that it cut across the curve he was flying on, and came out directly at the fourth marker. It was another big shortcut, if anyone was crazy enough to take it, but it was barely ten metres wide.

The chasing pack had caught him up, and Sleed was back in front, by the time they passed the fourth marker. The sky had darkened, and rain slid off the hood of the cockpit, driven away by the Firecrow's speed.

The final stretch was the worst.

The gorge had evidently collapsed at some point in the distant past, then been bored through by the river. The floor rose up by steep, uneven steps in a jumble of stone and waterfalls. Precarious stone bridges soared overhead. Crooked pillars leaned against bulky protrusions of stone. The water found its way through everywhere, joining and dividing, gushing through tiny gaps and leaping off cliffs. Thick foliage hung wherever it could get purchase. It was an upward-sloping obstacle course to the finish, shrouded in a thin water mist.

Harkins airbraked off the straight and took the rise as fast as he dared. The mesh of rock bridges near the top of the gorge made it easier to stay low and cut through the pillars. He weaved left and right, climbing all the time, the Firecrow responding eagerly to every twitch of the flight stick. Huge formations of stone flashed past him with a *whumph* of air. The mist and rain made it impossible to make out detail, but he saw shapes, and that was enough.

Up and over a spidery limb of rock; shooting beneath a ragged arch; rolling his wings to vertical as he screeched past a pillar. Ahead of him, a dirty cough of flame. Another flyer down. Five left, including himself. Harkins scarcely noticed. All he knew was the sound of engines and the sheer panic of the moment.

He burst out on to the straight in third place. Sleen was in front, the fat man in the Blackbird hard on his tail. Harkins was panting and laughing at the same time. It felt like he was losing his mind. The stress of it all was unbearable, and yet somehow he was still flying, and he took a savage joy in that as the starting line approached, and with it the second and final lap. He could see the crowd gathered along the edge of the gorge, hands raised as they cheered.

It seemed impossible that he'd made it this far. And now he had to do it again. This time with guns.

'Harkins!' It was the Cap'n, through the earcuff. 'I can see you. Thank spit you're alright. Listen, Harkins, there's been a development. I reckon Crickslint's gonna stiff us. Pull out. Take the disqualification. Don't risk yourself on my account.'

'Oh, er...' he said. 'I think I'll finish if you don't mind. I think I can win this.' It sounded like someone else's voice coming from his mouth.

'Harkins!' Now it was Jez. 'There's no *point*. He doesn't think Crickslint's going to give us the relic even if you *do* win!'

'Still,' said Harkins.

'Harkins! Pull out! That's an order from your captain, you hear?' Frey barked.

'Yes, Cap'n,' he said. 'I hear you.' And he pulled off the earcuff and threw it in the footwell of the cockpit.

The finish line came flying towards him. He squared his shoulders and hunkered forward. The rain redoubled in fury, and thunder detonated overhead.

'I can win this,' he said to himself. He flashed across the starting line and opened up with his guns.

SIXTEEN

PURSUIT—'LET'S SEE YOU FOLLOW THIS'— FIRECROW DOWN—A STAND-OFF

Harkins abandoned himself to the race. He didn't know what he was thinking – everything was moving too fast to stop and consider it – so he did what he felt. And what he felt was that he wanted to beat these other pilots. He was fiercely, angrily determined to beat them. Every humiliation that had been piled upon him – and he'd had a lifetime's worth – he blamed on each and every one of those men. He was so sick of being pathetic.

Well, no more. Here, for this short time, he wasn't scared any more. Inside the shell of his cockpit, driven beyond fear by the intolerable stress of so many near-misses one after the other, he felt powerful at last. And by damn, he was going to prove he wasn't a loser. He'd prove it to himself. Not the Cap'n, not Jez. Himself.

In some dim and distant recess of his mind, a small cowardly voice wailed and ranted in terror. But it was drowned out in a white blaze of adrenaline, carried away by the roar of engines, the shrieking wind, and the clatter of machine guns.

Through the first marker, and into the second lap. Harkins was in the middle of the pack, third place of five. The pilots broke into evasive swoops as everyone let fly with their weapons. Harkins fired and was fired upon, but the opportunity was brief. The gorge split in two, divided down its length, and the pilots had to choose.

Harkins, conscious that he had two pilots on his tail, feinted to the right, where Sleen and the fat man were heading. At the last moment, he banked hard, cutting under the firing line of his pursuers and down the left-hand route.

Tracer bullets followed him as the walls closed in. He looked hurriedly over his shoulder. He'd lost one of his pursuers, but the Yort in the Airbat was on his tail again. Damn it, why didn't that son of a bitch leave him alone?

The flanks of the gorge seemed to be subtly moving now, thick foliage nodding under the barrage of rain. Harkins dodged and dived as tracer bullets whipped past his cockpit and burned away into the grey gloom. The Airbat was faster, but the pilot wasn't interested in getting in front of him at this point in the race. Harkins hissed a string of curses under his breath as he threw the flight stick left and right.

He could see the end of the divide approaching, where the pilots on either side would come together again. They would be wise to the danger this time, and would vary their altitude. Harkins, occupied with keeping away from the Airbat's guns, pushed the throttle harder. The bellow of the Firecrow's thrusters filled the cockpit. Water crawled past him in branching rivulets along the hood. Lightning flickered and thunder rolled across the sky.

The craft came together in a flurry at the bottleneck, huge, dark shapes swooping in and out of the rainy gloom. Harkins clamped his finger to the trigger and raked a stream of bullets along somebody's tail. The racer's stabiliser fins were shredded in the barrage. It went into an uncontrolled roll, corkscrewing wildly until it smashed into the wall in a bright streak of fire.

Harkins felt nothing about the man's death. All he cared about was that one more competitor had been eliminated. There were four left now, including himself. Sleen in his Nimbus, the Yort in the Airbat, and the fat man in the Blackbird.

The second marker came quickly. This lap, driven by the threat of the guns, seemed so much faster than the first. The Blackbird fired on Sleen, Harkins fired on the Blackbird, and the Airbat fired on Harkins. Mostly they were shooting wild, since they were occupied with dodging and manoeuvring through the tight canyons. But the Yort, with nobody on his tail, was hounding Harkins mercilessly. A few stray bullets hit the Firecrow's fuselage, but the armour turned them away. There were advantages to flying a fighter craft in a race like this.

'Get off my back, you damn Yort sack of shit!' Harkins yelled, spittle flecking his chin. The Airbat seemed to have been chasing him since the race began. He couldn't help feeling persecuted.

After the second marker, the gorge fractured into a maze. Harkins chose the same route he had on the first lap. He had to take risks if he wanted to get ahead of Sleen, and he knew this way was fast. Sleen and the Blackbird took different routes. The Airbat followed Harkins. He might have known it would.

The walls closed in on them. There was barely space to evade the Airbat's guns now, but the hammering wind and the rain meant that the pilot was busy trying to keep stable. He sent a few speculative bursts up the gorge after Harkins, but nothing hit.

The gorge swung to the left. Harkins remembered it from the first time: a steep S-bend. He slowed and hit the corner tight, skimming the edge of the gorge. Hanging vines reached out after him as he passed. The world rolled outside his cockpit as he banked hard to starboard, accelerating out of the S-bend into the curve beyond. He wanted to put distance between him and the Airbat, which would have to slow for the bend. It couldn't turn as sharply as a Firecrow.

But despite his efforts, the Yort was soon close enough to start harrying him again. Harkins vaguely hoped that he would forget about the projection of rock at the end of the curve, but there was no such luck. Both pilots raced past the obstacle with ease, taking the high route over the top.

The route split into three. Harkins had had time to think about his choice this time. The Airbat was going to score some real hits on him sooner or later. He'd been unable to shake him off so far. That left only one real option, if he wanted to win.

He shot down the central route, into the dead end. The Yort had chosen a different path at this point on the last lap. This time, he didn't.

'Alright,' muttered Harkins. 'Let's see you follow *this*.'

He dived hard. The pitch of the engine rose steadily as he plunged towards the river at the bottom of the gorge. The Airbat was slow to follow, perhaps unsure what he was doing, but when he did he came down fast. Harkins levelled out sharply just above the river, blasting a V of spray in his wake as he tore towards the gaping tunnel mouth. The Yort, coming in above him, suddenly found his vision clouded by the heavy mist. Harkins approached the tunnel at reckless speed, forcing the Airbat to keep up. At the last moment he hit the airbrakes hard, turned on his floods, and then he was inside.

The second time was different to the first. Instead of terror there was a steely calm. It was as if he'd been pulled out of the world, into a temporary interlude in reality, thirty dream-seconds of rock and darkness. He travelled in a bubble of electric light, surrounded by an echoing roar of mindless sound, and his only purpose, his only reason to exist, was to fly a steady path through the chaos and not touch the sides.

Distantly, he was aware of the Airbat coming up fast behind him, *too* fast, because the pilot hadn't seen him brake and had been over-eager to stay on his tail. All it would take was one twitch of the trigger finger and Harkins would be done. But taking out Harkins was probably the last thing on the Yort's mind at the moment.

This time, Harkins was ready for the dip in the tunnel, and rode it when it came. The Airbat wasn't. Harkins was on the level stretch, with the end of the tunnel in sight, when he heard an impact: a wing or a stabiliser, clipped by the stone. Then the sound of rending metal, terrifyingly close, as the Airbat ploughed into the wall behind him.

The craft detonated, concussion shoving at his tail. Flame billowed up the tunnel to meet him. Harkins burst out into the open, soaring through a cloud of roiling fire to freedom. An exultant howl escaped his lips as the pennants of the third marker flickered past him.

Gunfire. Harkins' triumph turned to alarm as the rain came alive with blazing tracers. He twisted in his seat, trying to spot his attacker.

Not just one. *Two* of them. The Nimbus and the Blackbird, neck and neck. He'd come out of the tunnel ahead of them.

He remembered thinking the first time round how dangerous the long, wide curve between the third and fourth marker would be when weapons were active. He was about to find out just how dangerous it was.

Harkins dived, banked and swooped, sacrificing speed in favour of making himself a hard target. But his pursuers were laying down a heavy curtain of fire. Glancing bullets pinged and spanged from the flanks of the Firecrow.

He couldn't survive this kind of barrage for long. It would only be a matter of seconds before they took him down. They were already catching up to him fast. He could hit the brakes and let them pass, but that would mean sacrificing first place.

No. He wouldn't do that. It was victory or nothing.

Then he saw it. The ravine, the thin slit in the land that cut off the hump of the curve and went straight to the fourth marker. A ten-metre-wide alley of rock that only an idiot would ever attempt to fly through.

Harkins' mouth twitched into a smile. There was an expression on his face that none of the crew of the *Ketty Jay* would have recognised. The grim assuredness of a man who had survived two wars and countless battles, who had seen death over and over again, and who had gone beyond caring.

He cut left and banked towards the ravine. A storm of gunfire followed him. He felt hard impacts along the fuselage, the sharp punch of bullets on metal. No glancing blows this time: serious hits. But it was too late now, too late to do anything but tip his wings to vertical and hope.

The walls of the ravine were his floor and ceiling. They thundered past, so horrifyingly close that he felt he could reach out and touch them. There was a steadily ascending scream coming from behind the cockpit. Something damaged in the internals. The Firecrow felt like it was going to shake itself apart. It was shivering and juddering so violently that it was all he could do to keep the flight stick straight. His gaze was fixed forward, on the long slice of dull light at the other end of the ravine. He made a tunnel of his will and wouldn't look beyond it. There was nothing in his mind but now. No fear. Just this moment.

He couldn't hold it. Something was wrong with the Firecrow. Something was wrong, wrong, wrong and it was starting to wobble. But there was the end of the ravine, coming at him fast, and he could *make* it, he could make it, just a little further—

There was a loud bang from behind him, the mechanical scream cut out, and the Firecrow's wings tipped from the vertical. But it was a half second too late to stop him bursting out of the ravine, past the fourth marker, and into the final stretch of the race well ahead of the others.

Smoke poured from a hole in the fuselage. He was losing the handling on the Firecrow. Somewhere, a hydraulic leak was increasing the response time to the flight stick, making her lazier as the seconds ticked past.

But he was a creature of pure momentum now. Unstoppable. He was too close to the finish to give up. He'd have seen this through even if his wings were on fire.

Sleen and the fat man were coming up the straight, driving their engines as hard as they'd go. Ahead was the muddy tumble of waterfalls and colossal rocks that rose up steeply to the finish line.

He went for it.

Pillars and bridges and waterfalls, rearing up and flashing past him. The rain and mist blinded him, reducing the world to a blur of green and grey. Harkins was utterly lost to his aircraft. He was in a place he hadn't been since the last war.

His eyes were staring and wild. His lips were skinned back in a horrible rictus, a mad grin of exhilaration. He was the Firecrow, and the Firecrow was him. He sensed the slow death of his aircraft and compensated, taking his turns earlier and earlier, until it seemed that he was guessing which way to turn before he'd even seen the obstacle. He flew like a swallow, slipping through the deadly ruin, up and up while his aircraft became slower and heavier and then—

The Firecrow was hammered with a shocking barrage of gunfire. Bullets stitched it from behind and below, a metallic tattoo on the fuselage and wings. Harkins shuddered and yelled as the cockpit hood exploded, tiny shards slashing his cheek and bouncing off his goggles. Now the howling, tormented wind and the lashing rain were in the cockpit with him, shoving and bullying him, soaking his bloodied face.

He didn't know where his attackers were, and he didn't care. A steep waterfall loomed ahead of him. He pulled back on the stick with all his strength and did an emergency flood of the aerium tanks. But the craft was getting heavier by the instant, and he could tell by the sharp, acrid smell in his nostrils that the tanks had been holed.

The Firecrow's nose came up, too slow, too slow, and the waterfall was rushing towards him too fast. Then something gave, and the craft suddenly lurched upwards and blasted over the lip of the waterfall with inches to spare, and there were no more waterfalls but only the final short straight to the line.

Harkins boosted the thrusters to maximum and didn't let go of the stick. He was still rising as he thundered up the gorge. He looked over his shoulder to see the Nimbus eating up the space between them, but the distance was too great. The Firecrow was getting heavier and heavier as it spewed invisible aerium, but not enough to stop him. He screamed over the finish line a full twenty metres ahead of his nearest opponent, yelling at the top of his lungs, soaring higher and higher, above the lip of the gorge and the cheering crowds.

Until something blew up in the guts of the Firecrow and the thrusters cut out with a clunk.

The silence was terrible. Deeply, disturbingly wrong. As he hung in the air with the wind flapping his clothes and the rain pattering on his face and goggles, he came back to himself. The reckless courage of the race fell away into the quiet. The warrior soul, its job done, departed.

And he was left in mid-air, with no engines and a hole in his aerium tanks.

His thin, fearful wail drifted over the fractured land of the Rushes like the voice of a despairing spirit. Then the nose of the Firecrow began to tip downward.

He clung on to the flight stick for dear life. There was still enough forward momentum to keep him airborne, and the Firecrow had wide enough wings to glide on, but it was too heavy to stay up for long. He banked the craft gently, resisting the urge to wrench the stick. He had to get away from the gorge, to the flat ground where the crowds were.

The Firecrow was agonisingly sluggish in responding. Smoke was billowing from it now, seeping from every vent and several holes. Remembering his Navy training, he hit a sequence of switches and performed an emergency fuel dump to lighten the load and minimise the risk of explosion. The mechanisms still worked. Prothane spewed in a pressurised jet from the bottom of the craft.

Now all he had to do was land.

The gorge disappeared beneath him. The grassy, uneven plain that replaced it was awfully close and coming up awfully fast. Harkins felt like he was having the falling dream he had almost every night, except that this time there would be more than an unpleasant lurch and the sound of Pinn snoring at the end of it.

Gravity sucked him down harder and harder. He struggled to keep the nose of the Firecrow up. If he couldn't land the craft level, he'd be killed for sure.

'*Come on!*' he screamed, and the Firecrow kept falling, faster and faster. The damn aircraft kept trying to tip but he wouldn't let it, he *willed* it level, because he didn't want to die, because death was even scarier than life, and what had he been *thinking*, flying that extra lap when he didn't even have to? This is where bravery got a man! It got him dead!

He screamed again as the ground rushed up at him, and then

the whole world was motion and noise. Metal shrieked and he was thrown about like a doll shaken by a giant, slamming against his seat belt over and again. The craft skidded in a semicircle; he felt it fishtail and turn. Chunks were ripped off it and went bouncing away. Smoke filled his mouth and blackened his goggles. Sparks flew.

Then he was slowing. Slowing. And finally, everything stopped.

Harkins just sat there, breathing. Dazed, he looked himself over. His whole body was a mass of hurt, and yet his fingers and toes wiggled when he wanted them to, and there didn't seem to be any blood except for a few cuts on his face. Satisfied that he wasn't in imminent danger of dying, he slumped back into his seat, took off his goggles, and let the rain fall on his face.

'I won,' he said quietly to himself. Then, louder, a broad grin breaking out. 'I won! I *won*!'

There was a crowd running towards him. He undid his seat belt and clambered unsteadily out of the Firecrow, where he found himself surrounded by people, all of them congratulating him, patting him on the back, asking him if he was alright. He cringed and flinched, frightened by all these enthusiastic strangers. Finally a familiar face broke through. It was Crake, who swept him up in a warm and surprising embrace.

'Spit and blood, you idiot, we thought you were dead out there!' he cried. 'That was damned amazing!'

'Well, you know… Can't keep a good pilot down, I suppose.'

He saw Jez and Pinn, pushing through the cheering spectators. A wry sort of smile on Jez's face, and relief in her eyes. Seized by an impulse, he threw his arms around her, and hugged her to him. She laughed and hugged him back. 'That was really something, Harkins.'

He was actually *touching* her. Her small body was wrapped up in his. It was a moment he'd dreamed of for a long time, but now that it had arrived, all the bravery and recklessness he'd banked with his victory drained out of him. He blushed beetroot red and let her go, tongue thickening in his mouth. He turned away to cover his embarrassment, scratching the back of his neck, and began to examine the Firecrow. Jez, oblivious to his torment, stood next to him and did the same.

'Well, you pretty much thrashed the shit out of it,' she observed with a grin. 'Cap'n's gonna pop a lung.'

The thought of that filled him with dread. Where was the Cap'n, anyway? For that matter, where was Pinn? He could have sworn he saw him a moment ago, and he wanted to rub his success in Pinn's fat, stupid face.

'That was the most brilliant piece of flying I ever saw!' cried a loud voice. Pinn's voice. He'd climbed up on the broken wing of the Firecrow and was addressing the crowd through the rain. 'This feller might be the best pilot in the world!'

The crowd cheered. Harkins could scarcely believe what he was hearing. Pinn's purpose in life was to mock Harkins at every opportunity. To be publicly praised by him... Well, he wondered if the crash hadn't jerked something loose in his head, and he was hallucinating.

'Everyone, I want you to go out and tell all your friends what you witnessed today!' Pinn yelled. 'He didn't just win the race, he landed his craft *with no engines*, and lived to talk about it!'

The crowd cheered again, and Harkins was thumped on the back. He couldn't help a smile. He felt himself swelling with pride. He really had done that, hadn't he?

'Remember his name!' Pinn cried. 'Three cheers for Artis Pinn!'

The blood drained from Harkins' face. The crowd hurrahed.

'Artis Pinn!' Another hurrah.

'No!' Harkins squeaked. 'Wait! That's not my name! I'm Jandrew Har—'

'*Artis Pinn, hero of the skies!*' Pinn roared, arms raised and fists shaking. Thunder boomed in the background, with uncanny timing.

Then Harkins felt himself lifted and borne on the shoulders of the crowd, and his feeble protests were lost in the cheers as he was carried away.

'Where do you think you're going?' said Frey.

Crickslint's bodyguards spun around, saw the weapons hanging loosely in the hands of Frey, Malvery and Silo, and pulled theirs. In an instant, everyone had their guns levelled, three men on either side, fingers hovering over triggers. Rain dripped from pistols and shotgun barrels. Lightning flickered in the distance, and the sky grumbled.

'Let's not get nasty, now,' said Frey. 'It was your boss I was talking to.'

Crickslint peered out from behind his bodyguards. They were standing on the makeshift landing pad, a short distance from Crickslint's single-seater aircraft. He'd been heading for it in quite some hurry before Frey caught him up.

'Captain Frey,' he said. 'My most hearty congratulations on your victory.'

'Yeah, my pilot won, just like I said he would. Aren't you gonna collect your winnings? After all, you put a pretty hefty bet on him, right?' Frey's eyes went cold. 'Unless you didn't.'

The rain had plastered Crickslint's thin blond hair to his skull. He showed his chrome teeth in a grimace. 'No hard feelings, eh? I really didn't think he'd win.'

'Well, he did. And we had a deal, I reckon. Something about loaning me a certain relic.'

'Ah,' said Crickslint. 'The thing about that is, I don't have it.'

'You don't have it,' Frey said, his voice flat.

'Yes, I'd sold it by the time you turned up. Already had a buyer lined up, you see. Bad luck. Did you think I'd forget how you ran off with my shipment when I was at my lowest ebb? Maybe next time you'll think twice about robbing Jid Crickslint.'

Frey took a long, calming breath. If there was one thing worse than being cheated, it was being cheated by someone who referred to themselves in the third person.

He sized up the situation. Too many guns pointed at people for his liking. Three on three: there was no way they'd all survive. 'How about we all lower our weapons?' he suggested. He put out his arm, and gently pushed Malvery's shotgun barrel down towards the ground. Silo followed suit. 'Crickslint?'

'Yes, yes,' he said. 'Lower your weapons, men. No one's getting shot.' He looked at Frey. 'Captain Frey realises that violence is pointless in this situation, I think.'

Frey very much wanted to do violence to Crickslint right then, even the pointless kind. Harkins' frankly extraordinary display of flying had all been for nothing. He'd put one of his crew in mortal danger for no reason at all.

The bodyguards warily lowered their guns, although nobody was putting them away. Still, the tension had been defused a little, and Frey was content with that.

'Tell me who you sold it to,' Frey said. 'You owe me that much.'

'Do I?' Crickslint pondered theatrically. 'Well, it's no skin off my nose, I suppose. I sold it to a man called Grothsen.'

'*Isley* Grothsen?' Malvery asked.

Crickslint pointed at the doctor. 'Your man knows of him, it seems.'

'He's the head of the Archaeologists' Guild in Thesk,' said Malvery. 'The Archduke's personal collector.'

'You sold it to the *Archduke*?' Frey cried.

'I hope you didn't need it *too* badly,' said Crickslint. 'Now, if you'll excuse me, I think our business is done.'

Frey's mind raced. The Archduke. It was in the hands of the damned *Archduke*. What in spit was he going to do now?

Protected by the barrier of bodyguards, Crickslint walked to his aircraft, climbed in and settled himself into the cockpit. Malvery held out his pocket watch to Frey, who glanced at the time and nodded.

'Crickslint!' he called.

'What is it now?' Crickslint called back.

'We found the bomb you put on the Firecrow.'

'Yes, I wondered why that hadn't gone off. Insurance, in case your pilot was as good as you said. You disarmed it, then, I assume.'

'No,' said Frey. 'Just turned the timer back five minutes and put it on *your* craft.'

Crickslint's face fell. Frey winked. 'No hard feelings, eh?'

Frey had to admit, he hadn't expected quite such a big explosion. But Crickslint's bodyguards hadn't expected an explosion at all, so the first thing they did was whirl around to see what had happened. Frey and his men gunned them down while their backs were turned, just in case they were entertaining any thoughts of retaliation. He didn't really hold with the idea that you should wait for a man to face you before you shot them.

Frey considered the flaming wreckage of Crickslint's aircraft. He wiped rain-wet hair away from his forehead. 'Shit,' he said.

Malvery was cleaning his glasses with a corner of his coat. 'Cap'n,' he said. 'Please don't tell me we're gonna try to rob the Archduke.'

'Of course we bloody are,' said Frey.

Malvery sighed heavily and put his glasses back on.

SEVENTEEN

RUM & PIES—PINN'S EXPERIMENT—'DON'T YOU LEAVE ME HERE!'—A CHASE

Archduke Monterick Arken's palace towered over the city of Thesk, set dramatically against the cloud-scattered red dusk. It stood at the peak of a massive ridge of black rock, the plug of an extinct volcano, with sheer grassy cliffs on three sides and a gated slope to the west. Green copper domes and sloping roofs of decorative slate peered over the walls of light beige that surrounded it. Statues of great men and women looked out across the capital in all directions. The roof of an arboretorium could be seen among the towers. What couldn't be seen were the enormous anti-aircraft gun emplacements in the front and rear courtyards.

It was a modern construction, most of it early Third Age, having been knocked down piece by piece and rebuilt after the deposition of the monarchy and the emergence of the Duke of Thesk as the head of the Coalition of Vardic Duchies. The Arkens had all been reformers, and had never let themselves be shackled by history. While other dukes shivered in glowering stone Kingdom Age buildings that were over four hundred years old, the Arkens had demolished their family seat and built a new one with piped heating.

Crake thoroughly approved.

He blew on his pie to cool it and accepted the bottle of rum from Frey. The two of them sat on some steps at the foot of a bronze statue in People's Park, which sprawled around the base of the cliffs. A statue of Osory Crumditch looked over their shoulder: a benevolent, bespectacled old man sitting in a chair and holding a book. Crumditch's daring fictions about love and passion among the peasantry helped wake the aristocracy to the fact that the people who toiled in their fields were human beings too. He never lived to see the serfs freed after the Mad King Andreal was overthrown, but he was more than a little responsible for it.

'You think the relic's in there?' Frey asked, looking up at the palace.

'I dearly hope not,' said Crake.

'Could be in any one of six places I can think of,' Frey mused.

'Well, Crickslint's certainly not going to tell us now, since there's barely enough left of him to fill a jam jar.'

Frey was still looking at the palace, his own pie forgotten on the step next to him. They'd bought them from a shop down the way. The cold snap had come to an end with the rain, and tonight's weather was more typical of autumn in these climes. A little chilly, a little damp, but not altogether unpleasant.

'You suppose it's true about the army of golems he has up there?'

'Could be,' said Crake. 'He's never had much of a problem with daemonists, although politically it wouldn't make much sense to say so, what with half the country believing all that rubbish the Awakeners peddle. I wouldn't be surprised if he used them in secret. Rumour has it some of the gear the Century Knights use is thralled.'

'Really?'

'Some daemonists think so.'

He munched his pie – spiced beef, hearty Vard food, for which he was absurdly grateful after Samarla – and passed the bottle back. The Cap'n was in a strange mood tonight. Crake got the sense he wanted to talk about something, but he hadn't worked up to it yet.

While he waited, Crake watched the traffic in People's Park. A lamplighter was making his way along the paths, leaving lampposts glowing behind him. A pair of young lovers walked arm in arm, wrapped up against the coming night. Three women cooed over a pram by the bandstand. A student, his arms full of books, hurried home from Galmury, the city university, which Crake had himself attended. It was only five years since he'd left, at the age of twenty-six, but it might have been a lifetime ago.

Love. Children. Even the clean, sheltered world of academia. It all seemed so distant from him. Now he was a vagrant, a drifter, moving from place to place and never settling to anything.

But was there even any point in running any more? Were the Shacklemores really still chasing him? Crake had tried to make himself hard to find by joining the crew of the *Ketty Jay*, but the *Ketty Jay*'s crew weren't so anonymous these days. Difficult to believe the Shacklemores couldn't have tracked him down by now, if they'd put their minds to it.

His brother might have called off the bounty hunters months ago. Perhaps his thirst for vengeance had faded. That, or Condred had tired of paying them. But for whatever reason, he'd not seen a Shacklemore for two years now, not since the Winter Ball at Gallian Thade's estate on the Feldspar Isles.

So maybe he didn't need to stay on the move, after all.

Crake dreamed of a library, a house, a sanctum. Somewhere Bess would be out of danger, and he could study the Art. All that, and perhaps a woman to share it with.

Wouldn't that be fine? he thought. But it all seemed so far away.

'Am I a good captain, Crake?' Frey asked, out of nowhere.

'I don't know,' he said. 'You're the only one I ever had.' But the look on Frey's face made him regret his flippancy. 'What's bothering you really?'

'You mean aside from the prospect of getting another visit from that daemon?'

Crake cleared his throat. 'Yes, the daemon. I'm going to see what I can do about that,' he said.

'What does that mean?'

'I'm working on some techniques.'

'Techniques?'

'Yes. You see, most... well, *all* daemonism is done in controlled conditions. They're summoned and contained. But that won't work here. The daemon is already out. So we need a different approach.'

'Like what? Can't you drive it out of me or something?'

'It's not *in* you. That strange signal you're giving off, I think that's more like the way it tracks you.'

'So what do you plan to do?'

'I suppose you'd call it field daemonism. I'm trying to work out ways of dealing with a daemon *outside* the sanctum.'

'You think you can? You can work out a way to fight this thing?'

Not really, he thought, but the edge of desperate hope in Frey's voice revealed just how scared he really was, and Crake had to give him something.

'It can be done,' he said, with more assurance than he felt.

Frey brooded for a while, sucking on the bottle of rum. Crake ate the rest of his pie, glancing at him occasionally.

'Harkins,' he said, then tutted.

'Cap'n, he's alright. Nobody got hurt.'

'He damn near died!' Frey snapped suddenly. 'And for what? For me!' He held up his right hand, encased in a fingerless glove to hide the corruption in his palm. 'All because I couldn't keep my hands off that bloody relic.'

'Cap'n, will you stop trying to be perfect?' Crake cried. 'Spit and blood, it's like you think we've all forgotten how you were when we joined this crew! Might I remind you that, back then, you let someone put a gun to my head, spin the barrel and pull the trigger. *Twice!*'

'You're never gonna let that one go, are you?' Frey muttered.

'My point is, there was a time when you didn't give half a shit about any of us, and none of us gave half a shit about each other. But those days are gone, and most of that's your doing. I wish you'd remember that.'

Frey swigged his rum. He looked like he was taking it on board, at least.

'Nobody expects you to be right all the time,' said Crake. 'Nobody but you, apparently. Stop beating yourself up.'

'I s'pose you've a point,' Frey mumbled, unconvincingly.

'Speaking of Harkins, I note you've taken the destruction of the Firecrow very calmly. If he'd pulled out when you told him to, he'd have come out without a scratch.'

'Heh,' said Frey, and Harkins was surprised to see a smile twitch at the corner of his mouth.

'What did you do?' Crake asked, suspicious.

'I backed him.'

'You what?'

'I stuck a bet on him to win. Pretty big one, as well. Couldn't turn down those kinds of odds.' He scratched at his cheek. 'The winnings more than cover the cost of a new Firecrow.'

Crake laughed in amazement. 'And you still told him to pull out of the race after you found Crickslint's bomb? With all that money riding on him?'

'S'pose I did.'

Crake slapped him on the shoulder. 'Frey,' he said. 'You're a good captain.'

Frey nodded to himself. Then he took a deep breath and sat up, as if to clear away the subject and start on another one. 'I need a favour, Crake.'

'Name it.' Crake swiped the bottle and took a swig.

'I need you to go charm a woman for me.'

The rum caught in his throat and made him cough. 'I thought that was more your department than mine?' he wheezed.

Frey grinned. 'Not this lady,' he said. 'This one's all yours.'

Jez's eyes flickered open.

The trance had been confusing this time. She'd been trying to regain the dream of snow. She wanted to make sense of it. But instead she was left with a muddle of sensations, fading fast in her memory. Her mouth tasted foul, like sour milk with a sharp tang of something else underneath. Her back was hot, much hotter than the rest of her, as if she'd been lying on something warm. But she hadn't. She'd been sitting cross-legged on her bunk.

She tutted to herself. She was never going to get the hang of these trances.

Frustrated, she picked up the book that was lying next to her and flicked through it. No matter how hard she tried, she couldn't read the words. If indeed they were words. The clusters of tiny circles and arcs were arranged in rows, with no breaks that would suggest sentences or paragraphs. Every printed centimetre was full of symbols of identical size, like a wordsearch. It had long ago occurred to her that they might not read left to right at all, as Vardic script did. They could read diagonally, for all she knew. There was no reason to assume it followed the rules of human language, since those who wrote it were something other than human.

But still she persevered. No one was going to help her. As far as she knew, there was no one alive who could read the language of the Manes.

She'd found the book at the tail end of winter, on the savage island of Kurg, in the captain's cabin of a crashed Mane dreadnought. In Vardia, the leaves had grown and reddened and were falling again, and she was no closer to understanding it. But what niggled at her was the feeling that she would understand it, if she could only remember how.

The symbols were familiar to her, though she'd never seen them until the day she found the book. It was as if she'd once known the language and somehow forgotten it. What remained was a riddle she couldn't solve. The answer was there, waiting to reveal itself in a flash of revelation, but it refused to make itself known. She was one step away from making these symbols turn into sense, but it was a step she didn't know how to take.

What did the Manes need the written word for, anyway? They could read each other's thoughts. They'd discarded language and speech as hopelessly clumsy.

Yet here was a book.

She got up. There was no hope of concentrating on anything while the disgusting taste lingered in her mouth. She headed to the mess to get some coffee to wash it away.

Pinn was there, standing on the table, holding a semi-conscious cat at the end of his outstretched arm.

Jez regarded him blandly. 'Should I ask?'

'It's my first experiment,' Pinn said.

'Your... experiment,' Jez replied dubiously. She looked closer at the cat. 'Is that a piece of *toast* strapped to his back?'

'*Buttered* toast,' said Pinn proudly.

Jez folded her arms. 'Huh,' she said.

'I'm gonna be an inventor,' Pinn declared.

'You are?'

He wiggled the arm that was wrapped up in a sling. 'Since I can't be a pilot for a bit, I reckon it's a good time to get started.'

'Are we feeling threatened after Harkins' little display of brilliant flying?' Jez inquired sweetly.

Pinn sniffed. '*I* wouldn't have trashed the aircraft in the process. Now, you wanna see this experiment or not? This cat's heavy, y'know.'

'Alright, I'll bite. What are you trying to do?'

'Well,' said Pinn, eagerly. 'Everyone knows that a cat always lands on its feet, right?'

'Right.'

'And isn't it also true that toast always lands butter side down?'

'Er, I think that's more of a *saying* than a scientific fa—'

'So if the cat has buttered toast on its back, butter side up, then it'll land upside down. Except that's impossible, 'cause cats always land on their feet.'

Jez could feel herself getting stupider by the second. 'So what do you reckon will happen?'

'I reckon they'll sort of hang spinning in the air a couple of inches off the ground.'

'Can you wait there just a minute?' Jez asked. She walked round the table, collecting various jackets from where they'd been left draped over the backs of chairs. When she was done, she made a pile on the floor in front of Pinn.

'Just in case,' she said, and stepped back.

Pinn dropped Slag. Gravity did its job.

'Huh,' said Pinn, looking down at the cat, who was now buried in the pile of jackets. There was a buttery stain on Malvery's favourite overcoat.

'Huh,' Jez agreed. 'I wouldn't want to be you when that cat comes round.'

'Ah, I'm not scared of *him*,' said Pinn, climbing down from the table.

A thought occurred to Jez. 'How did you get him so docile, anyway?'

'Stuck some rum in his milk.'

She ran her tongue around the inside of her mouth. Yes, that was it. That was the taste. Rum and milk. And the hot sensation on her back, as if someone had strapped an enormous piece of toast to her.

'Huh,' she said thoughtfully.

Frey decided not to take the tram back from the park. He needed time on his own to think, and the walk would be some rare and welcome exercise. Crake had gone to gather resources for his new experiments, and Frey was never allowed to come along on daemonist business. They were a secretive bunch, and with good reason. The Awakeners had everyone so riled up against them that they were liable to be hanged if caught practising their craft.

He found himself in a small square, all but empty except for an elderly man crossing it in the opposite direction. It was dominated by a large building with a forecourt and the symbol of the Cipher carved in stone over the archway. Frey stopped in front of it. The symbol of the Awakener's faith, a pattern of circles and interlocking lines that the last king Andreal had drawn obsessively all over his cell in the final days of his madness. His followers believed it to be the key to decoding the language of the Allsoul. Frey thought it looked like something a madman would scrawl on a wall.

The building was boarded up and empty. Obscene graffiti, half-heartedly scrubbed out, were still visible. He couldn't work out whether it was pro- or anti-Awakener in content; just a blare of swear words, a dumb roar of hate.

The House of Chancellors had recently passed down an edict banning the Awakeners from operating in the cities. It was part of the Archduke and Archduchess's long campaign to defang the political threat of the Awakeners' aggressive and profitable religion. But then had come the accusation from the Archduke that the Imperators were daemonically possessed. An accusation based on scientific evidence that Frey had delivered. And that was a provocation too far. Things were turning bloody. Out in the sticks, people were dying.

The broadsheets were full of reports from the countryside, where the Awakeners' influence was greatest. Farming communities rioted. Peasants took up arms when tax collectors came to visit the local hermitage.

Neither the Archduke nor the Awakeners would back down. If the truth were revealed, the Awakeners would be exposed as hypocrites, having persecuted daemonists for a century. And it was just the excuse the Archduke had been waiting for to rid himself of the organisation responsible for the murder of his son Hengar.

Well, technically it had been *Frey* that had murdered his son, but technically didn't cut it as far as Frey was concerned. Hengar's craft had been rigged to explode; it just happened to be Frey shooting at it at the time. It was the Awakeners' fault, pure and simple.

Should I have just let it be?

It was a question he'd been asking himself for some time. He hadn't needed to take those damning research notes from the *Storm Dog*, while they were at the North Pole trying to rescue Trinica from Captain Grist and the Manes. He hadn't needed to tell Crake about them, either, which pretty much committed him to act: Crake had a deep and venomous hatred of the Awakeners, and he would never let Frey sit on that kind of information.

But Frey did both those things, and then he gave the notes to Professor Kraylock at Bestwark University, who passed them on anonymously, because Frey didn't much fancy having the Awakeners and their daemonic enforcers knowing just who had screwed them.

He did it because he wanted to make a difference. Because he wanted to make an impact, a dent in the world. He wanted to run with the big boys, instead of scrabbling about in the dirt, scavenging his way through life. But he was beginning to realise that the big decisions came with big consequences, and he wasn't too keen to be remembered as the man who started a civil war in Vardia. Especially not with the Sammies rumoured to be tooling up for another war. They'd been suspiciously quiet ever since they called a surprise truce to end the last one.

Stop trying to be perfect, Crake had said. But it was easier said than done. He was acutely aware that everything his crew had been through since they held up the train had been for his sake. Not for profit, not even for fun, but to pull him out of the trouble he'd got himself into. And he was pretty sure there'd be a lot more trouble to come.

His friends were risking their lives for him. That was one bastard of a burden to carry.

'*Don't you leave me here!*'

Frey's blood went cold. He couldn't possibly have just heard what he thought he'd heard. A thin, despairing shriek. Words that had been burned on his conscience for nine long years. The voice of his engineer, Rabby, as Frey sealed up the cargo ramp of the *Ketty Jay* and condemned him to be murdered by the Dakkadian soldiers outside.

Yet the words rang out clearly across the square, coming from a narrow alley at the side of the Awakener building.

He looked around quickly. The elderly man was gone. There was no sign of life in the square. The lamp-posts seemed to have dimmed, as if the gas had been turned down. He could hear the distant sounds of the city in neighbouring streets, but he suddenly felt terribly alone.

He walked slowly along the forecourt wall, towards the alley entrance, drawing a pistol as he went. He didn't want to see what was there, but he could hardly ignore it, either. If it turned out to be nothing, at least he might convince himself that it was all his imagination.

He peered down the alley. It was dark in there, and the shadows foiled his eyes.

Well, there was no way he was going in there to look. He wasn't *that* curious.

Then something moved. It was just on the edge of visibility, a suggestion of a shape in the blackness. He fought to make it out. Something large, round, low to the ground.

As he stared, it unfolded long limbs and straightened, and he realised that it had been crouched, curled up, with its back to him. Now it expanded, rising to its feet, dropping one shoulder, turning towards him. And it stepped into the light from the square.

It was seven feet tall to the shoulder, but it would have been nine if it was standing straight. Part human, part animal, part machine. Its short fur was wet and greasy, like something newly born. Its arms were thin and disproportionately long, ending in outsize hands with double-bladed bayonets in place of fingers. The knees of its legs were bent backwards, like a horse or a dog. And a dog was what its face resembled: a snarling hybrid of metal and muzzle.

No, thought a small, clear voice inside that cut through the flapping panic in his mind. He recalled the sorcerer's words. *A jackal. Beware the Iron Jackal.*

One half of its head was metal, as were much of the limbs. Machine parts sewed into and out of muscle and skin; servos and pistons were visible in its legs. Its spine was a spiked chain running up its hunched back, and there were thin plates of black armour scattered haphazardly across its body. Something about the colour and the look of them was uncomfortably familiar, but the connection evaded him for the moment.

One connection didn't, though. One of its eyes was a red mechanical orb. The other stared wildly from its black-muzzled jackal face, without an iris, only a single huge black pupil.

That was Trinica's eye.

He let out an inarticulate cry of fear as he stumbled away from the alley. The Iron Jackal's lips quivered and curled, exposing long teeth. Frey raised his revolver and fired at it: once, twice, three times.

But whether it was his bad aim in the darkness or something else, the bullets hit nothing.

Then he ran, and it came after him.

He fled along the edge of the square, boots pounding on the cobbles. He had too much pride to call for help, but a wordless yell of alarm would serve just as well, if only there was someone to hear it. But the square was eerily deserted, and the shuttered windows that faced it were dark.

The creature bounded out of the alleyway, running on all fours in great leaps, its bayonet fingers shrieking along the stone. Frey heard its hot animal panting, the screech and thump of each leap and landing, getting rapidly louder as it ate up the distance between them.

It's coming it's coming oh shit!

The Iron Jackal bunched and sprang. Frey darted aside, down a lane that ran off the square. A dark pile of muscle and metal and fur swept by, blades skinning the air, missing him by centimetres. Its momentum carried it past the end of the lane and out of sight.

The lane descended in long stepped sections, lit by a few lonely lamps in wall sconces. Frey put his head down and ran hard, driven by utter terror. He had a few seconds to get ahead, and he meant to make them count.

The sight of the thing that meant to kill him, the hard reality of it, had rocked him to his core. Until now, he'd been able to kid himself into thinking that the danger had been exaggerated. He wasn't kidding himself any more.

He looked over his shoulder, and saw that the beast had entered the lane and was coming after him, running on two legs now in a grotesque lope. The light seemed to slide off it, pouring away as it passed beneath the lamps. Its red eye shone in the shadow. In desperation, he fired at it as he ran, emptying his revolver to no effect.

The lane ended in a steep set of steps, which descended to a sunken path by the side of a canal. Frey slipped on them in his haste, heels skidding, and almost ended up in the canal himself. He hit the path with a heavy jolt, but recovered his balance well enough to sprint off without losing too much speed.

There was a high wall to his left and the canal to his right. Boats were moored in quiet rows, bumping gently against one another. Houses loomed above him, black and dank in the chill of the night.

There were lights in the windows, signs of warmth and life. No one there could help him. His lungs were beginning to burn. He wasn't in good enough shape to run this hard, but the fear of what was behind him wouldn't let him slow.

He passed a group of men on the path, who saw him coming and moved out of the way to avoid being knocked aside. As it was, he clipped one of them with his shoulder and sent him staggering into the wall. He ran on with their indignant exclamations ringing in his ears.

More steps, leading up off the path. He took them. The short ascent made his thighs ache. A poky street ran along the top of the canal wall. He staggered across it and into an alley, where he finally rested, heaving air into his aching chest.

He listened, trying to focus past the blood thudding in his ears. Where was the beast? He hadn't seen it since he'd hit the canal path. If it had been following, surely it would have encountered the same men he had?

Perhaps it didn't want to be seen. Or perhaps he'd lost it.

He holstered his revolver. Bullets wouldn't do him any good. He wasn't a crack shot, but he was sure that he'd hit it at least once. The thing hadn't even flinched.

He heard a thump from overhead. He looked up, his breath catching: but all he could see between the buildings was a cloudy sky painted yellow by the city lights.

Something moving up there. Something heavy. The scrape of metal against slate. The sound of an animal breathing.

Frey pressed himself against the wall, eyes fixed on the roof-tops. *You're invisible*, he told himself. *You're not here.*

He glanced at the other end of the alley. There was a street there, well lit. Late night shops were open, and he could see people. People meant safety. It couldn't get him if there were people about, surely? A beast like that wouldn't want to show itself out in the open.

If he could just get to that street…

There was a sinister growl from overhead. The Iron Jackal was craning over the edge of a rooftop, looking down on him. He felt his stomach plunge and his limbs go cold.

He bolted.

He heard the rush of air as it dropped down into the alley, the impact of its landing, the snarl as it came for him. The mouth of the alley seemed a hundred metres away. He put every ounce of his strength into his legs and *willed* himself to make it. Every passing second, the Iron Jackal was closer, and closer, so close that it had to have caught him by now. But not yet, not yet, and then—

His intuition screamed at him, some millennia-old sense that warned him when a predator was about to pounce. Whether he tripped then, or whether he went down on purpose, he wasn't sure. But he went to the ground, rolling and tumbling out of the alley onto the street, and the Iron Jackal passed over him, close enough to make the tail of his greatcoat flap.

Frantic, he got his feet under him and ran up the street, gasping and howling incoherently. Shoppers froze and stared at him. The Iron Jackal picked itself up, surprised at having missed its target. Its head turned, fixed on Frey, and it came bounding after him again.

'Someone bloody help me!' Frey yelled, who'd gone beyond pride and was only thinking about survival now. But the shoppers just goggled, and hurried out of his way. He glanced over his shoulder at the terrifying daemon steaming up the street towards him. It bounded between the shoppers, and none of them took the slightest notice of it. Their eyes didn't follow the creature; they stayed on Frey instead.

They couldn't see it.

A mad thought fled across his mind: was this all in his head, then? What if he stood still and let the thing come at him? Would it prove to be harmless?

It didn't matter. He was far too scared to find out. As if the thing itself wasn't bad enough, the aura of daemonic terror that it put out drove all sense from him.

It was no safer in the open. The Iron Jackal would catch him in moments on the street. He ran for another cross-alley, past lighted windows selling chocolates and toys and clothes. Jolly things for happy people, set in pretty displays. Frey was no longer in the same world. He was alone against the beast, in the midst of an oblivious crowd.

The Iron Jackal saw where he was going and lunged to intercept, but Frey reached the alley first. The beast bounded in after him, back on all fours, charging. The alley was only short, and Frey burst out on to another street, looking behind him as he went. The creature seemed to fill the alley, mismatched eyes glaring above a fanged mouth, a nightmare vision of naked savagery.

A dazzle of light, and a clanging bell. Frey's heart lurched in alarm as he saw something huge bearing down on him. He tripped and fell, rolling onto his side an instant before a tram rumbled past him, and all he could see was a wall of wheels a few centimetres from his nose. He scrambled back, and then suddenly hands were on him and he was being pulled to his feet. He shook them off in a panic, sliding his arms out of his greatcoat to escape, but they grabbed him again.

'Here! Calm down!'

The authority in that voice restored a little sanity. They were militiamen, in the Archduke's blue and grey. Four of them.

'You alright, feller?'

'Here, you nearly got yourself killed!'

He wasn't listening to them. He was looking at his greatcoat, which had fallen to the floor. There were three long parallel slashes across the back of it.

The tram was slowing to a stop, its raucous bell still echoing in the night. It slid out of the way to reveal the mouth of the alley he'd come from.

There, standing in full view of the street, was the Iron Jackal. Frey threw himself back against the militiamen, but they grabbed him and restrained him.

'No! No! It's there! Can't you bloody see it?' he howled.

'Calm down, I said! Don't make us calm you.'

'You ain't gonna like it if we do,' added another.

But the Iron Jackal made no move to attack. It simply watched him, its hunched back rising and falling. It lifted one bayonet-finger to its blunt muzzle.

Sssh.

Then it stepped back into the alley and was gone, leaving Frey to wilt into the arms of the militia as the last of his strength left him.

EIGHTEEN

◆

CRAKE IS TROUBLED—DISTINGUISHED COMPANY —TWO HISTORIES—THE TOOTH

The tavern was called The Wayfarers. It was pleasant enough, nestled on the side of a hill in a quiet district of Thesk, with the palace visible in the distance through windows paned with coloured glass. The bar area was full of niches and sheltered corners, and there were parlours upstairs. It was a place for privacy, away from the raucous press of the dockside taverns. Prices were high, but not exclusive. Guards on the door ensured order within.

All in all, it was Crake's kind of drinking hole. The décor reminded him of his university days, with its cramped feel, the dark wood-panelled walls, the low murmur of conversation and the stuffy warmth of several fires. In other circumstances, he would have taken great comfort in finding himself here, scribbling formulae on a piece of paper with a pint of black ale in a pewter mug. But he was troubled, and he couldn't set himself at ease.

The Cap'n had woken him up in something of a state last night. Crake had listened with growing horror to the story of the attack he'd suffered. Frey showed him the slash-marks along the back of his greatcoat, desperate to prove that he wasn't as mad as he sounded. But Crake needed no convincing. He was already gravely concerned.

Frey had been dragged off to the Militia's district headquarters for causing a disturbance, but once he'd calmed down he managed to convince them to let him go. After that, he came to see Crake, and after that he was going to take a dose of Shine, since it was the only way he'd get any sleep that night. Crake usually disapproved of narcotics, but tonight he couldn't blame the Cap'n.

It will come for you three more times. The third time will be on the night of the full moon. If you're not dead already by then, that night will be your last.

That was the first. And it would only get stronger.

He *had* to find a way to stop it.

He sat in a corner of the tavern, furiously scribbling calculations, pen scratching over paper. He'd consulted what tomes of daemonism he had on the *Ketty Jay*, but they'd offered him nothing. He'd spoken with the daemonists he knew in Thesk, one of whom was an old friend from Galmury who had been responsible for getting him into the Art in the first place. Only one had heard of any daemonist who'd attempted something similar to what Crake was trying: an obscure fellow named Parkwright, who'd published some articles in secret daemonist broadsheets and then went mysteriously silent. Needless to say, those broadsheets wouldn't be easy to get hold of, if it were possible at all.

The problem was that there was so little call for daemonism outside the sanctum. Daemons, when summoned, were capable of escaping a daemonist's protective measures, with terrible consequences – Crake had ample experience of that – but they never lasted long outside of the resonator fields that pinned them to human reality. Their frequency was naturally out of phase with the world that people saw and felt and heard, and they returned to that state unless thralled to an object or, in the case of the Manes and the Imperators, to a body.

The fact was, it was extraordinarily difficult to *find* unthralled daemons outside of the sanctum. Attempting to experiment on them turned an already dangerous pastime into something approaching a suicide attempt. Apart from this Parkwright fellow – who presumably perished during his research – nobody had really tried.

All of which made Crake's task a very tall order indeed. And with no less than the Cap'n's life at stake, the pressure was immense.

Their best chance rested in retrieving the relic and putting it back where it came from. If they could break the curse, the Cap'n would be spared the third, fatal visit on the full moon. But to even begin to do that, first they had to find it. The Cap'n and the rest of the crew were shaking down every low-life and whispermonger in the city, but time was against them.

Crake had his own part to play tonight. It was one he felt deeply conflicted about. But he said he'd do it, for the Cap'n. For his friend.

Lost in his formulae, he didn't see her come in. Didn't see the barman point him out. Didn't see her approach. It was only when she spoke that he jerked out of his state of intense concentration.

'Grayther Crake,' said Samandra Bree. 'As I live and breathe.'

The sight of her gave him a warm flush of pleasure. She was dressed as she usually was, in a weatherbeaten duster, loose trousers and scuffed boots. Black hair spilled in waves from beneath a tricorn hat, framing an appealing and mischievous face that probably shouldn't have belonged to someone who'd shot as many people as she had.

'Samandra Bree! What a surprise!' He was only half faking; he'd been so tied up in his work, he'd almost forgotten the reason he was here in the first place. It had been a while since he'd been so absorbed in the Art.

'Is it?' she asked wryly. She plonked herself down in a chair opposite him with a jingle of buckles and guns, and took a mouthful of grog from the mug in her hand. 'I wondered how long it'd take you to track me down. Gotta say, I wasn't sure you would.'

Crake gaped for a moment. He hadn't expected to have his bluff called quite so quickly. He'd hoped to fence a little before it became blindingly obvious that he fancied the arse off her.

'I'd have come sooner, but I understand you've been occupied of late,' he said, after what seemed like an eternity of embarrassment, but which was probably only a second or two.

'Oh yeah, the Awakeners,' she sighed. She hoisted her feet up on the table. 'Kickin' up a fuss all over.'

Crake stared at her boots with appalled delight. She was so fascinatingly *vulgar*!

She motioned to the small sheaf of notes on the table in front of him. 'You daemonists got brave now the Awakeners have been run out of the cities.'

He was slow to catch her meaning. 'Oh this? Anyone who doesn't know who I am will just think it's mathematics. Anyone who does…' He tidied them away. 'Well, it's not as if anyone ever needed *evidence* to hang daemonists, is it?'

'Reckon more people know of you than you think. You lot got quite a reputation since Sakkan. From the stories, you wouldn't even know the Century Knights were there at all, saving your sorry hides. How's the hand, by the way?'

'It healed up fine, thank you,' he said, showing her. 'You can barely see the tooth-marks any more.'

'Guess you proved you don't turn Mane by getting bit,' she said with a wink.

'I've always said a man should be willing to risk life and limb for science.'

'Is that what you always said? Don't recall you sayin' it to me.'

'That's because our acquaintance has been far too short.'

'That is a shame. I'm always on the move.'

'So am I.'

'Yet here you are.'

'So are you.'

She raised her mug, as if to acknowledge the point, and took another swallow. He sat back in his chair, relaxing a little. The nervousness he felt at the thought of meeting her was fading quickly. Her confidence was infectious.

He motioned to the room. 'They say you come here almost every evening when you're at home in Thesk.'

'They?'

'The Press.'

'The Press,' she said, in a tone that somehow managed to combine fondness and disgust.

'Why here in particular?'

'Good as any other,' she said. 'They know me. They keep the reporters out.' She shrugged. 'S'pose there's better places around, but what can I say? I found it, I liked it, I stayed.' A smile touched the edge of her mouth. 'Guess I ain't very adventurous.'

'Lucky for me. It was easy to find you.'

'Believe it or not, sometimes I *like* to be found,' she said, tipping back her tricorn hat. 'Most of the time it's just me and Colden. Never in the same place for more than a day or two. Colden's a sweetheart, but he ain't the world's greatest conversationalist. Tends to make his points with an autocannon, you know?'

'I understand,' said Crake. 'Civilised conversation is in pretty short supply aboard the *Ketty Jay* too.'

'Now, I didn't say *civilised*,' she grinned. 'Sometimes, Grayther Crake, I think you get me mixed up with a lady.'

'You looked like a lady at Aberham Race's little soirée,' he said.

'Well, I scrub up good for a Draki girl,' she said. 'Can't do much about the accent, though. I'm always gonna sound like a *scuffer*.' She rolled the word round her mouth and released it with a smile. A derogatory term for the simple peasant folk who lived in the poisoned deserts of dust and volcanic ash that made up Vardia's least pleasant duchy.

'I *like* your accent,' he said, without thinking. Then, quickly, to cover up the clumsy compliment: 'Our engineer has a Draki accent too. Thicker than yours, though, from up near the border with the Andusian Highlands.'

'The Murthian? Where'd he pick that up?'

'I've often wondered that myself. I don't know a great deal about him. Nobody does, really.'

She raised her mug in a toast. 'Well, here's to findin' out about people,' she said. She drained the mug, raised it in the air and whistled to the barman. 'Hey, Adrek! Bring a bottle and another mug, huh? I got distinguished company!'

They talked for hours. About politics, daemons, Awakeners and the Samarlan threat. They talked about Thace and Kurg and legendary Peleshar, the Vanishing Isle. They talked about what would happen to New Vardia and Jagos, the distant frontier colonies on the far side of the planet, if the Great Storm Belt kicked up again as the Aviator's Guild feared it would. They talked about the Archduchess's pregnancy and the prospect of a new heir (Crake was careful not to mention how he'd unwittingly had a hand in the demise of the last one). But mostly, they talked about themselves.

She told him about growing up on the blasted flats near the Samarlan border, of an elder brother she'd competed with at everything and who'd died of a scorpion sting. She talked about her father, a militiaman, who brought her up tough and hoped that one day she'd follow him into the profession. So she was enrolled in a militia training school, but she wasn't there a year before the scouts picked her for the Knight's Academy. One of the youngest entrants ever, she said with some pride, and one of the youngest to graduate from the Duke's Guard to a full Knight.

'Course, the Aerium Wars helped with that,' she said, grimly. 'You can only have a hundred Knights, and they gotta die or quit to make spaces. We lost a lot of 'em round then.'

Crake, for his part, talked of a childhood in the aristocracy, as the son of a steel tycoon. He spoke of a father who was overbearing and distant all at once, and an arrogant elder brother who scorned him for his lack of interest in the family business. He recalled his time at Galmury, his disillusionment with the life of politics he was being pushed towards, and his discovery of daemonism there.

There was much that they both left out. Her work and the training methods of the Knight's Academy were secret. Crake couldn't tell her the real reason he joined the *Ketty Jay*, the summoning that went terribly wrong and resulted in the death of his niece and the creation of the golem that bore her name. But she had a plain and straightforward way of speaking that charmed him, and he found himself talking more freely than he had in months. He wanted her to know him. It wasn't something he'd felt for a long time.

There'd been women in his life before, but they'd all been of aristocratic stock. He hadn't mixed with less privileged people in his youth; he found the men frighteningly rough, and the girls were scornful of his airs and graces. It was only his time on the *Ketty Jay* that had brought him into contact with society's more… *fragrant* individuals. He liked to think he was a little more worldly-wise these days, although the truth was, it was not by much.

Samandra was anything but aristocratic. She swaggered. She laughed loud instead of tittering. She said exactly what she thought, and she drank like a trooper. It certainly helped that she was beautiful enough to melt lead, but Crake was not Frey: beauty was not the be-all and end-all when it came to women. He suspected he would have fallen for Samandra Bree even if he'd been blind.

He was having such a wonderful time that he almost forgot he had a job to do. It was late, and they were both quite drunk, when Samandra said:

'How's your captain, anyway? Whatsisface, the cocky son of a bitch…' She slapped the table. 'Frey!'

That name sucked the joy out of Crake. Suddenly, he thought of the daemon, and of what he'd come here to do. Samandra thought he'd come to see her of his own accord, but the truth was, he'd never have had the guts if he hadn't been pushed. He never imagined she'd be so pleased to see him. He hadn't envisioned spending the evening as the sole object of her attention.

But now he was reminded of the real reason he'd come, and the moment was cheapened by deceit. Crake thought of himself as an honourable sort, when it came down to it, but what he intended to do was certainly not honourable. Yet it had to be done, for Frey's sake.

She saw it on his face. 'That bad, huh?'

'He's having some problems,' Crake said awkwardly. When he didn't elaborate, Samandra merely nodded.

Crake looked out of the window, to the Archduke's palace, lit up by electric floods on its perch above the city. 'I'd like to see inside the Archduke's palace one day,' he said.

She went with the change of subject. 'Maybe you will,' she said. 'Mannered feller like yourself.'

'There must be many rare treasures and works of art in there,' he said.

'Sure. All kinds of stuff like that.'

He turned to her, raised an eyebrow, tried to sound casual. 'Has he made any new acquisitions recently?'

'Antiquities ain't really my thing.'

He looked out of the window again, pondering. Damn, how to put this? How to make it seem natural?

'Say if he did,' Crake said. 'Would they go straight to the palace, do you think?'

'Would what go straight to the palace?'

'The antiquities.'

'I expect the head of the Archaeologists' Guild would want to mess around with them first. Why're you so interested?'

'I'm always interested in culture,' he said. Spit and blood, this was clumsy. He could only hope that Samandra was drunk enough not to notice. 'So, hypothetically, if the head of the Archaeologists' Guild acquired a new object, something rare or valuable, say... where would he take it?'

There was a faint flicker of suspicion in her eyes. Crake was surprised by how sharply it wounded him.

'I guess I don't know,' she said slowly. A lie.

I wish you hadn't done that, he thought. Because he saw, at that moment, that she did know, that she must have heard about the acquisition of the relic, and that she'd never tell him where it was. There were no words that could persuade her. She was one of the Archduke's elite, and she'd never help him steal from her liege. A gulf had opened between them.

But Frey's life was on the line.

He grinned. Her gaze flicked to the gold tooth that glinted in his mouth, and stayed there.

'You can tell *me*,' he said.

Crake felt like the lowest person on the planet. He walked through the streets of Thesk, soaked in misery, despising himself. The fact that he'd got what he wanted didn't matter. The fact that it might end up saving the Cap'n was small consolation.

He shouldn't have done that to her.

Employing the tooth required a delicate balance. Push too hard, and the victim would notice, alarm bells ringing in their subconscious as they felt themselves influenced by the daemon thralled to the gold. Even with all the practice he'd had, the tooth wouldn't have worked on Samandra when she was sober. It'd been a terrible risk even when she was drunk. He suspected that it was only her good feeling towards him, and the fact she had her guard down, that let him in.

That made him feel worst of all.

Once she'd explained where the relic was and how to get it, he told her to forget he'd even asked. He meant it literally. But he couldn't forget, and afterwards, he could hardly look at her. It was a harmless act, to make her give up a scrap of information, but he'd taken the choice away from her all the same. It felt like he'd violated her. And even though she didn't remember the conversation they'd just had, she started acting oddly. Not quite so easy in his company as before. As if she sensed something was wrong but didn't know what. Or maybe she just picked up on Crake's torment.

Soon after, he made his excuses and left.

'You come see me again soon, Grayther Crake,' she told him.

'I will,' he said. But he wasn't altogether sure that he would.

He wasn't sure he could, any more.

Damn you, Cap'n, he thought bitterly. The fact that the Cap'n had been responsible for his meeting Samandra in the first place, for the happiness he'd felt in her company, just made him angrier. It wasn't fair that things had worked out this way. Wasn't fair at all.

Using the tooth was exhausting in that state. It leached his vitality, sucked at his will as it sucked at the will of its target. It was only now that he realised how much he'd drunk while they were talking. Too much. He felt weak and depressed and unsteady.

A barque was lifting off from the docks over the rooftops. He headed in that direction, back towards the *Ketty Jay*. At least he could tell the Cap'n what he'd learned. Then he could lay his head down and pretend this whole awful turn of events had never come about.

But he shouldn't have done what he did. Not to her.

NINETEEN

◆❖◆

MADDEUS BRINK—THE NATIONAL GAME— PROMISE IN RETURN

Blood. It was all about blood in Samarla.

The stadium crowd roared in Ashua's ears. Sammies and Daks surged to their feet from tiered benches. Somewhere down on the court, an Urchin had been intercepted by an opposing Juggernaut. Ashua hadn't seen the ensuing tackle – the crowd got in her way – but by the excited comments of her neighbours, the Urchin had very likely been killed, or at least crippled for life.

Blood. They lived and died by it. The blood of their athletes, drooling out onto dusty *a'shi-shi* courts. Blood torn from the flayed backs of the Murthians that had built this enormous hexagonal stadium. Blood curling lazily into the barrel of a syringe, just before the plunger was pressed. Blood was who they were.

The average Samarlan could trace their family back twenty generations or more. The custodians in the Black Archives kept records that went back much further than that. The Sammies had the finest chemists and doctors in the world, and they knew techniques that could identify a person's lineage with extraordinary accuracy. From a single drop of blood, they could match an unknown child to its parents, and from there to the rest of the family through their exhaustive genealogical records.

It was a necessary process in a culture where family was everything. Individual reputations paled in comparison to the legacy of their ancestors. Every Samarlan was born with the weight of previous generations on their shoulders, for better or worse. To be otherwise was to be without family, an untouchable.

Ashua supposed that she was an untouchable herself. Maybe that was why she had such an affinity with their kind. She had no blood relatives to speak of; at least, none that she knew. But she had family, of a sort.

She spotted him approaching, sliding his way between the spectators. His eyes were on the game: he was craning over the standing crowd to see the damage done to the Urchin, just like the rest of them.

She studied him while his attention was elsewhere. He looked worse than ever. Flesh melting off his bones, eyes sunken and dark, his long blond hair limp and straggly in the punishing heat. He was dressed expensively, as always, and he had the effortless poise of the aristocracy. But there was no hiding the ravages of his condition. Not any more.

Maddeus Brink sat down next to her, looked her up and down, and said:

'Pensive.'

'Thoughtful,' she replied.

'Asperity.'

'Harshness.'

'Mordant.'

She stared at him blankly. 'Dead?' she guessed.

He tutted. 'I expect you to put it in a sentence next time we meet. Have you been keeping up with your reading?'

'I've been busy.'

'So I hear. Jakeley Screed is very keen on having a chat with you.'

'I'm not worried about Screed,' she lied.

'You should be, my darling. You should also be worried about the Sammie soldiers who are asking for you all around the city. Something about a stolen relic that they're *extremely* keen on getting back.' He tossed his hair and sighed, bony shoulders rising and falling. 'It may be prudent for you to get out of Shasiith for a while. In fact, it might be best to get out of Samarla altogether.'

Ashua felt something twist inside her at the suggestion. 'I'm not leaving you,' she said, her voice kept carefully flat.

'I rather suspect *I* shall be leaving *you*, and sooner than either of us would like,' he said. 'And I'd very much prefer it if you didn't get yourself murdered before I made my exit.'

She didn't reply. It hurt her that he should think of sending her away, especially at a time like this. Hadn't she stayed by his side all these years, ever since he'd come across her as a child begging on the street and offered her work in an act of drunken charity? Hadn't she carried the narcotics he peddled all over Rabban, even while the Sammies were busy bombing it to rubble? Hadn't she followed him to Shasiith, because he'd got bored of Rabban and it just wasn't 'fun' any more?

Silly girl. She'd let herself believe that he needed her, but of course he needed nobody, and never had.

He saw the look on her face and steered on to a lighter subject. It was his way. Maddeus didn't like things that made him unhappy.

'Who's winning?' he asked, even though he could look at the scoreboard for himself, if he troubled to.

'I haven't been paying attention,' she said, sullenly.

'Oh, my Ashua. You're hopeless. You'll never understand Samarla if you don't understand their national game. At once chaotic, precise and vicious, it has no respect whatsoever for human life. It's a perfect metaphor for their society. They're so delightfully *cruel*.'

She had to agree with that. *A'shi-shi* was an obsession for the Sammies, and the Daks, who aped their masters in all things. Played on a sunken stone court in the shape of a hexagon, the object was simple: get the ball in the scoring-hole of an opponent's wall. But the process of achieving it was considerably more complex.

The game was played with three teams of seven. Each team had two heavily armoured Juggernauts, named for the mythological monsters from Samarlan legend. With them were two Warriors with club-ended staves for tripping and bludgeoning, and two Urchins, chosen for speed and agility. The final member was the Hero: only he was allowed to score.

As much as she could make out, the Juggernauts were supposed to protect the Hero, the Warriors to clear a path for him, and the Urchins to run the ball into passing positions so the Hero could receive it and score. Each team was up against two others, and the in-game alliances shifted moment to moment.

But Ashua had never troubled herself with the finer points of the game. The nature of it offended her.

Most Vards still thought that all Samarlans were idle rich, but that was because they'd only ever seen the upper castes: the nobles and the Divine Family, who could claim lineage to the God-Emperor. They were the ambassadors, politicians and powerful businessmen who had been frequent visitors to Vardia before the Aerium Wars. But many Samarlans were poor, or came from bad families whose reputation they couldn't overcome. Men who didn't own slaves were low in status and usually spurned by women. For them, becoming an athlete was often the only way to distinguish themselves. Except that most athletes didn't last long, and all but the very best ended up maimed or dead on the bloody hexagonal battlefields of the *a'shi-shi* stadiums.

Ashua had grown up in the slums of Rabban. She'd seen what desperate people would do. She knew how they'd clutch at anything to get them out of the hole they were in. This game exploited their misery, made them into objects of entertainment for people rich enough not to care. It didn't sit right with her.

She wondered what she might have been forced to do to survive, if she hadn't met the man sitting next to her. If he hadn't taken her in, looked after her, treated her like a daughter after his own curious fashion. She'd been seven years old and alone when he found her, desperate for love like any child. He gave her that, and his was all she ever needed.

And now he was leaving her.

She stole another glance at him as he watched the game. She couldn't look for long. It would have made her want to cry, if she could remember how.

This was what happened when your blood turned against you. He'd been poisoned by a lifetime of needles, having stuffed his veins full of that filth he loved so much. It had to happen, but it never seemed like it would happen to him. He was so damned *blithe*, swanning through life with a quip and a careless flick of the wrist, a dissolute aristocrat who'd found his place among the wasted and the dead.

'I can hear you feeling sorry for me,' said Maddeus. 'I won't have it, you know.'

'I have to ask you a favour,' she said.

'I see. And I thought you just enjoyed my company.'

'That's not fair,' she said miserably. 'You're the one who keeps me away. I'd live with you if you let me.'

'To look after me? Feed me pap while I slobber out my last? I think not.' He gave her a wry look. 'Where's your sense of humour these days, my darling?'

'Some things aren't especially funny.'

The crowd cheered and surged to their feet at something playing out in the court below, but Maddeus stayed where he was. He huffed. 'You are a sad sort today,' he shouted over the noise. 'Ask your favour; I shan't say no, I imagine, since I never do.'

'You've heard of Ugrik vak Munn kes Oortuk, right?'

'Of course. Famous explorer. Fourth son of the High Clan Chief of Yortland.'

She produced a letter from one of the many pockets of her mechanic's trousers. 'I got this from the feller I was working with to get that relic. He sent it from Vardia. Turns out it was Ugrik that found the relic, before the Samarlans caught him somewhere down south. Which is how it ended up on the train we robbed.'

'And you need…?'

'I need to know where Ugrik is. If he's alive, we need to find him. Ugrik can tell us where the relic came from, and we have to put it back.'

'We? What's your interest in this?'

'Money. He'll pay for the information. I'll split it with you, of course.'

'Oh, don't bother. I won't have time to spend it.' He studied her, and there was a knowing look on his face that she didn't like. 'It's the crew of the *Ketty Jay*, isn't it?'

There wasn't much that got past Maddeus Brink. 'So?' she said, sounding like a sulky teen again. She hated how she got that way around him.

'How have they been, so far?'

She scowled. 'The doc's nice, I suppose. They're a decent bunch. They look out for each other, which is more that I can say for most.'

'And the captain?'

'Apart from the fact that he clearly wants to jump me, he's a good sort. What of it?'

The crowd roared again, but she'd tuned them out by now. They were in their own small world, locked together in the muggy heat, surrounded by a wall of foreigners who surged and bellowed like a storm tide. Shasiith was a place where everyone lived on top of each other. It was hard to find space here. You got used to being hemmed in, or you left.

'I'll help you, naturally,' he said, She could see he was calculating something. 'But I want a promise in return.'

She waited, knowing what would come, willing him not to say it.

'I want you to leave Shasiith for a while.'

She felt her jaw tighten. It wasn't fair. It wasn't fair!

'You want me to leave you to die.'

'I want you to live,' he said, taking her hands in his. 'That's my price, and I won't change my mind. Promise me.'

She sat there for a moment on the bench, and it seemed that she was terribly, awfully alone. Then she pulled her hands out of his, suddenly infuriated by his weak, papery grip, and stood up.

'Just get it done,' she snapped, and then she pushed past him and away down the row, towards the steps that would lead her out. She wanted to be away from the crowds, from the heat, from this dirty, seething place that had killed the only person she ever felt love for. She wanted to smash everything she'd ever known to pieces, and start from scratch. She wanted to die, and be reborn; or maybe just die.

She was glad she couldn't remember how to cry.

TWENTY

THE MENTENFORTH INSTITUTE—
LITTLE BRIGHT STAR—CHLOROFORMED—
HISTORICAL ARTEFACTS

'Hurry up, hurry up!' Frey muttered.

Crake ignored him and concentrated on the skeleton key in the lock. The thralled daemon was singing faintly in his hand at a pitch that he could sense rather than hear. Using the tooth last night, followed by an insidious day-long hangover, had worn him down. It was harder than usual to make the key do its job.

The Cap'n glanced around uncomfortably. 'Someone's gonna come.'

'Will you please shut up?' Crake asked. No one needed to tell *him* to worry about getting caught. Crake had an ingrained terror of authority born from a lifetime of strict social rules and regulations.

Frey cursed to himself and flapped around, beating off the autumn chill. The slashes along the back of his greatcoat were letting in the cold air. Silo watched him without obvious emotion.

Towering above them in the darkness were the imposing walls of the Mentenforth Institute building. Its pillared front entrance looked out onto one of the most expensive streets in Thesk, but they weren't at the front entrance. They were round the back, in a small yard that was uncomfortably well lit. Not suitable for criminal activity at all. They were out of sight of the road, but well in sight of the buildings that overlooked the yard.

The key slipped and slid around the inside of the lock, seeking the right configuration. Crake frowned and tried again, harder. His hand was going cold. He couldn't stop thinking about last night. About Samandra.

Come on, come on. Get on with it.

'Jez? Are you up there?' Frey whispered, his hand to his ear where the earcuff sat. They were all wearing them. When someone spoke, the earcuffs repeated it a fraction of a second later. It was slightly disorientating, and the Cap'n had complained about it, but Crake had insisted in case they got separated.

'I'm here, Cap'n,' came Jez's voice in Crake's ear.

'Can you see us?'

'I can see the Mentenforth building but I... oh, wait, there you are. Hi!'

Frey waved up in the air. Crake glanced up briefly. The *Ketty Jay* was hanging up there in the dark somewhere, a klom above them, but all that was visible over the city lights were a few stars.

'Be ready. We might need a quick evacuation.'

'You told me that half a dozen times, Cap'n. What do you think I'm doing up here?'

Frey didn't reply, but turned his attention to Crake instead. 'What's taking so long?' he demanded irritably.

Crake didn't take offence. He understood the Cap'n's impatience. Everyone knew that time was ticking down for him, and every new delay was harder on his nerves.

They hadn't been able to move immediately, even after they found out where the relic was. They needed to scout the location, they needed to talk to their shady underworld contacts about what was inside and, more importantly, Crake needed to sober up. They would require the use of his daemonist talents if they hoped to penetrate the Mentenforth.

They barely had a plan at all by nightfall, and Crake was still far short of his best. But the Iron Jackal wouldn't wait.

Six nights left until the full moon. Where had the time gone?

Crake felt the key turn in his hand with a *thump*. 'We're in,' he said, with no small amount of relief.

Frey pushed the door open carefully. It whined on its hinges, making Crake's shoulders tense up. Frey looked inside, then darted through and beckoned them.

Silo went after him. Crake took a deep breath and followed. It wasn't as if he hadn't done enough criminal things during his tenure as a crewman on the *Ketty Jay*, but he was usually doing them to other criminals, or foreigners, or Awakeners, so that was alright in his book. But breaking in to a highly respected institute of learning, *stealing* from it, went against pretty much everything he stood for. He didn't think he could take the disgrace if he was found out. The only thing keeping him going was the fact that they'd stolen the relic in the first place, so technically it belonged to them. Sort of.

Give it up, Grayther, he told himself. *Admit it. You're not quite the noble fellow you pretend to be. In fact, you probably never were.*

The Mentenforth Institute. A private museum and place of study and learning, founded by members of various guilds, including the Archaeologists and the Explorers. If Samandra's information was accurate, the relic was inside.

In retrospect, this was the most obvious place for Isley Grothsen, the head of the Archaeologists' Guild, to bring it after Crickslint sold it to him. A Samarlan relic so ancient and valuable would presumably require some time to study and authenticate, and this place had all the necessary equipment, as well as being highly secure.

But they hadn't had time to guess. It might have gone straight to the palace for the Archduke, or to Galmury for the professors to pore over, or to the official Archaeologists' Guild headquarters. The transaction had been kept under wraps; none of Frey's contacts knew anything about it. And Frey couldn't rob *all* those places.

So Crake did what he had to do. He used the tooth on Samandra. The memory of it caused his guts to knot. He'd used the tooth on all kinds of people before without the slightest compunction, but never on someone he cared about. It made him feel dirty. Part of him blamed the Cap'n for that, but mostly he just blamed himself.

Well, if he didn't have nobility and decency, at least he had loyalty. At least there was that. Even if it did end up thoroughly ruining what was left of his life.

The back door let on to a plain corridor. Electric lamps sat in wall recesses, running very low, providing a steady twilight. They closed the door behind them and slipped up the corridor until it ended in another, smaller door. Frey listened, then opened it, lifting it on its hinges to cut out the squeak.

Beyond was a display room, cool and full of shadows. The walls were stone, with narrow windows set high, and the floor was polished marble. Several rows of glass cases, set closely together, stood dark. At both ends, archways led into brightly lit corridors. The only light in the room was that which spilled through the arches.

They listened. Slow footsteps were faintly audible. Guards walking the corridors somewhere. Crake tried to guess where they were, but the place had an institutional hollowness to it, and sounds echoed.

'Alright, fellers,' Frey whispered. The earcuffs allowed them to talk at a barely audible level. 'In and out without being seen. I don't want anyone getting shot. Not you, and not any guards either.'

'I thought you said guards were paid to get shot. What happened to "providing employment opportunities"?' Crake replied sarcastically.

'Oh, bollocks to all that,' he said, waving it away. 'I just don't want to add murder to the list of things we'll get hung for if they catch us.'

Crake didn't feel like adding another retort after that.

'Relax,' said Frey, seeing his face fall. He pulled a small bottle from inside his greatcoat, wrapped in a dirty rag, and showed it to him. 'The doc's given me a little something to take care of any troublemakers, nice and quiet.'

Chloroform. Crake was hardly reassured.

Frey picked a direction, and they crept along the aisles between the cases. Crake couldn't help looking in as he passed. Usually, only guild members got to see the treasures housed in the Institute, and he wasn't going to let the prospect of getting executed stop him taking advantage of the opportunity.

There was so much to see. The first case held a stuffed bird from parts unknown, fearsome and unsettlingly strange. There was a petrified gargant egg, bigger than his head, a remnant of a bygone time when monsters preyed on men. Next was a stretched animal-skin parchment, painted with the indecipherable characters. The accompanying plaque declared it to be Old Isilian, the forgotten tongue that had been the predecessor of all other languages on the Pandracan continent.

Further on was an old wind-map, used by suicidally brave balloonists to explore the world beyond Pandraca, before the First Age of Aviation ushered in powered flight and the wind-maps got replaced by storm charts. Next to it was a blurred ferrotype, taken from the prow of a ship in the midst of a hurricane. Amid the black-and-white spume and the rearing waves was the shadow of something huge, something coiled and spiked and unmistakably animal.

Crake moved slowly down the aisle like a mesmerised child in a sweet shop, gazing rapturously at everything. His mind was filled with the immensity of the past, of great men and women at the frontiers of new discovery. Just where he'd wanted to be, once, before he overstepped himself and his niece died because of it. But the tragedy had only stunned his ambition, not killed it. He *was* an explorer, a pioneer of unseen worlds. And by damn, he was going to distinguish himself, one way or another.

He wished there was more light. He wanted to see everything.

Someone was coming back down the aisle towards him. The Cap'n, an expression of exasperation on his face. Crake realised he'd been dawdling.

'Will you move yourself?' he whispered angrily. 'This isn't a family bloody outing!'

'Yes, right,' Crake murmured. 'Sorry.' But suddenly Silo came hurrying down the aisle, waving at them urgently. They didn't need words to know what he meant.

Guard coming.

The three of them slipped into cover behind pedestals and display cases. The wonder and excitement of a moment ago was blasted away by the cold fear of being caught doing something wrong. Crake had never grown out of that feeling. He'd lived through multiple gunfights and commanded unworldly creatures from the aether, but trespassing was another matter entirely. He dreaded the moment that guard laid eyes on him, the shame of discovery, more than he dreaded the hanging that would probably follow.

The guard had come in through one of the archways, and was idly walking through the room, humming to himself. A lullaby: 'Little Bright Star'. Did he have a child, then? Crake didn't want to think about that, in case the guard ended up getting shot. He pressed himself further into hiding. He could see the Cap'n across the aisle from him, gun drawn, a serious expression on his face.

No telling which aisle the guard was going to take through the display cases. If he came too close, he couldn't fail to notice the men crouched in the shadows.

Crake didn't dare to peek out, in case he was spotted. The footsteps were approaching. He tried to listen, to work out which aisle the guard was coming up. He looked at Frey, who was hiding across the aisle to his right. Frey gave him a shrug and a helpless face: *search me!*

Best they could do was stay still. Best they could do was—

No. Suddenly, he was sure. The guard was coming to his left. He moved, slipping around the pedestal into the aisle that lay between him and the Cap'n. By some miracle he did it without so much as a rustle. An instant later the guard passed by, inches from the spot where he'd been hiding. He went off up the aisle, a dark figure in the gloom, walking with a jaunty swing.

Crake didn't move a muscle until the guard had left the room, through the archway at the other end, humming the lullaby as he went. He let out the breath he'd been holding.

Frey went to the opposite arch and looked out into the corridor beyond. He beckoned the other two to join him.

'Right,' he said quietly. 'Here's the plan. This place isn't that big, but we can cover it faster if we split up. Use the earcuffs to keep in touch and—'

'No,' said Silo.

Frey and Crake both looked at him in surprise.

'It's a dumb plan, Cap'n. We don't know the layout of this place. One of us find the thing, we gonna be tryin' to direct the others to where we are, not knowin' where they are neither, an' all of us runnin' round like headless chickens. Place is full of guards. Three times the chance o' getting caught.'

'Er,' said Frey, who seemed rather taken aback by the whole thing. He wasn't used to defiance from the quiet Murthian. 'I suppose you've got a point. Let's *not* split up, then.'

'Right,' said Silo, and slipped through the archway, taking the lead from Frey.

Frey and Crake exchanged a look of bewilderment. 'Something's got into him lately,' said Crake. 'He's not been the same since Samarla.'

They followed him into the lighted corridor. Paintings of famous explorers and scientists adorned the walls. Jeddius Clard, the first man to circumnavigate the planet; Cruwen and Skale, discoverers of New Vardia; Gradmund Jagos, who found a fog-shrouded land on the far side of Atalon and named it modestly after himself.

Footsteps, shuffling sounds, distant coughs. More guards, somewhere nearby. They hurried along the corridor for a distance, before Silo paused and listened. The footsteps were getting louder. He pulled open an oak door to his left, glanced inside, and ushered them through.

Inside was another darkened room, illuminated by the city lights seeping through the windows. This time it was a study chamber, with rows of heavy desks and bookshelves lining the walls. Crake went in first. He'd barely taken a step into the chamber when he felt the floor sink by a fraction, and heard a soft *click* from beneath him.

He went cold and still, warned by instinct not to move. 'What is it?' Frey hissed.

'I think I stepped on something,' he whispered.

They listened and waited. Nothing happened.

'Shift it!' said Frey, nudging him. Crake stepped off the sinking tile, expecting something terrible to result; but it simply resumed its position with another click. Frey and Silo slid into the room and closed the door behind them, shutting out the light from the corridor, and the footsteps of the nearby guard.

'Pressure plate,' Silo murmured, kneeling down next to it. 'Prob'ly linked to an alarm.'

'I don't hear an alarm,' Crake said hopefully.

'Guards around here. These ain't armed, case the guards set 'em off.' He stood up, and his eyes glittered in the gloom. 'When you don't see no guards, then you worry 'bout the traps.'

Crake nodded, an uncertain look on his face. There was something faintly menacing about Silo these days. An edge to him that hadn't been there before. Crake had always rather liked the Murthian, and had never minded his tendency towards silence. But lately his quietness seemed more like dangerous brooding.

They crossed the study area to another corridor. On the far side, across the marble floor, they could see a wide, curving stairway. Silo made a quick check and they crossed to the stairs.

The stairs bent back on themselves as they climbed, ending in a small landing at the top and a carved door inlaid with swirling motifs. Overlooking the landing was a huge portrait of the Archducal Family: Archduke Monterick Arken, his wife Eloithe, and their son Hengar. Monterick tall and athletic, wearing a high-collared uniform, his hair and neatly trimmed beard a dark, rich red. Eloithe small and dark-haired, but with a fierceness in her eye that had made her beloved by some of her people and loathed by others.

And then Hengar. Earl Hengar, who'd inherited his father's fiery hair and bright blue eyes. He was a handsome man, but he wore an enigmatic smile that made him look cruel. At least until Frey had accidentally blown him up aboard the *Ace of Skulls*, almost two years ago.

Crake glanced at Frey, who was looking at the painting. 'I always thought he had brown hair,' he whispered.

Crake frowned. 'Why?'

'Ferrotypes don't come in colour, do they? Never seen a *painting* of him.'

Silo, who had no interest in the painting whatsoever, had quietly moved to the door at the top of the landing. It opened inwards, towards him. He peered out through the gap he'd made, then turned back to his companions and put an urgent finger to his lips.

They crept over to see what Silo had spotted. As soon as Crake peeked out, he saw the problem. The door was set halfway along another corridor. There was a shaven-headed guard sitting on a chair a half-dozen metres away, leaning up against the wall. His eyes were closed, but his hands were behind his head, and his foot was swinging lazily. There was a gun in a holster strapped to his thigh. He didn't look asleep, just bored.

There was no way they were getting past him unseen. Crake pointed back down the stairs.

Silo cupped a hand to his ear. They heard a humming from down below, the simple stepped melody of 'Little Bright Star'.

Crake began to feel a growing sense of alarm. They were trapped on this staircase. Maybe the humming guard would just walk on past, but maybe he wouldn't. Maybe he'd come up the stairs, rounding the curve until they came into sight. And then the shooting would start.

Silo was hurriedly yanking off his boots and socks. That done, he motioned at Frey, who didn't understand him until Silo reached into the inside pocket of Frey's coat and took out the bottle of chloroform. He pulled off the rag that it was wrapped in, wadded and soaked it, then gave the bottle back to Frey.

He'll see you, Crake mouthed, well aware that the guard was only a few metres away through a door that was ajar.

Silo took off his earcuff and showed it to Crake meaningfully, although Crake wasn't sure what the meaning actually *was*. He followed at Silo's shoulder as the Murthian went barefoot to the doorway, aimed the earcuff, and tossed it down the corridor.

It flew silently past the guard, hit the floor on the far side of him, tapped and skittered. The guard's eyes flew open at the sudden noise and he leaped to his feet, hand going to his holster. In doing so, he turned his back to the door. Silo broke cover, running silently on the pads of his feet. The guard heard him at the last moment, but wasn't quick enough. Silo seized him from behind, clamping the chloroform-soaked rag hard to his mouth, using the other hand to stop him drawing his revolver. He struggled and jerked, making muffled cries, but Silo was surprisingly powerful for someone so lean. The strength leaked out of the guard in seconds, and his eyes fluttered closed, having never even seen his assailant.

Crake and Frey slipped through the door into the corridor. Frey was carrying Silo's footwear at arm's length, his nose wrinkled. Crake closed the door quietly behind them. Silo propped the man up in the chair, so that it looked for all the world like he was asleep.

'You know,' Frey whispered to Crake. 'It occurs to me that I don't know shit all about that feller.'

'He is surprisingly, um, I believe the term is *bad-arse*, for someone who's spent their whole life as a slave,' Crake observed. 'He can handle a shotgun as well, and he sure didn't learn that from any of us.'

'It's all *veeeeery mysterious*!!!' said Jez in a spooky voice, making them jump.

Frey and Crake exchanged a weary glance. 'Sometimes I hate these bloody earcuffs,' Frey said, as Jez cackled at them from the cockpit of the *Ketty Jay*.

Silo had retrieved his own earcuff by now. He returned to his companions and put his socks and boots back on. Then he looked at them both as if to say: *Well?*

'That way,' said Frey, pointing in a direction which Crake assumed was random.

The next door took them into a small, barrel-vaulted chamber with bronze busts in alcoves to either side. At the far end was a metal door, set deeply into the wall beneath a great stone lintel. Its surface was decorated with several sturdy guild crests in bronze and gold and copper.

'Now that looks like the kind of door a feller might keep something behind,' said Frey.

Silo put his palm on Frey's chest as the Cap'n stepped forward. 'No guards,' he said.

Crake listened. They couldn't hear any footsteps anywhere.

'Right,' said Frey, catching on. 'Everyone, stay sharp. And watch where you're stepping.'

'Edge of the room,' said Silo. 'Any pressure pads, they'll be in the middle.'

Crake took the engineer's word for it. They stayed close to the wall. Crake let the others go first, and trod where they stepped. He didn't want to be the one to bring everything down on their heads.

They reached the door without incident. Frey tried it, but it wouldn't budge. A large keyhole sat within a flower of moulded metal. Silo tapped Frey's arm and pointed up. Crake looked. No wonder the door was set so deep. There was a gap in the lintel overhead, and the bottom of a gate could be seen within it.

'Ah,' said Frey.

'Best guess, they got triggers inside,' said Silo. 'Trip one, gate come down. Traps you inside 'n' the guards come.'

'Let's not trip any, then,' said Frey. 'Mr Crake, if you please?' He swept his arm theatrically towards the door.

'My,' said Crake. 'Manners. Whatever next?'

'My toe in your arse, if you don't get on with it.'

'Ah, that's more like the Cap'n I know,' said Crake, drawing out his skeleton key. He still didn't feel right after last night, and breaking into the Mentenforth hadn't helped. His fingers felt slightly numb, his grip weak and his forearm was a block of ice. There was a price to pay for using thralled daemons, even the weak, senseless ones in their earcuffs. He'd improved the earcuffs so that the effect was negligible, but the tooth and the skeleton key were hungrier entities. They fed on the user's strength, and he needed time to recover. He vaguely wondered if he might be doing permanent damage to himself.

Well, once more won't hurt, he said to himself, although he was pretty sure it would.

The lock was a complex one, made for a specialised key, intended to defeat thieves. Crake's key didn't even touch the sides, but that didn't matter. The daemon's invisible influence expanded to fill the space, feeling out the interior, pushing and twisting and testing until it understood the lock and defeated it. But it was a clever lock, with many parts, and Crake's arm was trembling and numb to the shoulder by the time the key turned.

'There,' he said weakly. He wanted to be sick.

'You alright?' Frey asked him, concerned. 'You don't look alright.'

'Let's just get that relic,' he muttered. He wanted this over with. He wanted to forget that today and yesterday ever happened. He wanted to sleep, and be miserable, and be left alone.

Silo pushed the door open. The chamber beyond was circular with a domed roof. Arranged in a semicircle were a half-dozen glass display cases on veined marble plinths. Crake's eyes widened. The most precious treasures that the various guilds possessed, gathered in this room. But he didn't see the relic on display.

A worm of uncertainty crawled into his gut. He glanced at Frey, and knew that he felt it too.

Spit and blood, please don't let me be wrong about this.

Silo crouched down and examined the floor inside the doorway. 'Wait,' he said, then pointed to a pair of slabs and added 'Don't step there.'

They watched as Silo did a cursory check of the room. Crake examined the slabs so he didn't have to think about what he'd say to the Cap'n if it turned out Samandra's information had been inaccurate. It was actually quite easy to see the seams of the pressure pads, when you knew what to look for.

Silo returned. 'Room looks clean,' he said. Then he pointed at one of the display cases. 'Relic's in that one.'

Crake felt a wonderful moment of relief at those words. They stepped over the pressure pads and into the chamber, and went where he'd indicated. The relic case was inside, closed and lying flat on the bottom, which was why they hadn't seen it from the doorway. Frey had told Crake about the double-bladed object inside, but at the moment it just looked like a black, featureless oblong. It wasn't arranged for display like the other objects. It had simply been put there.

Frey's eyes lit up as he saw it, but only for a moment. 'There's something not right,' he muttered.

'They've only had it a few days,' said Crake. 'That's not enough time to study it, really. No point putting it on display till they know what it is.'

'So, what, they're just *keeping* it here?'

'In the vault? Why not?' Crake said absently. He'd already strayed to the other exhibits in the chamber. An enormous and beautiful vase from pre-republic Thace. And there… Spit and blood, could that suit of armour have come from the War of Three? And look! An engraving from ancient Samarla, showing men and women worshipping at the feet of the God-Emperor. There was a plaque next to it, dating it to PU 1400 or thereabouts, long before the unification of Vardia under Wilven the Successor. He did a quick calculation and marvelled. Four thousand eight hundred and fifty years old, or near enough.

Silo came up to stand beside Frey. 'Problem, Cap'n,' he grunted.

'Don't tell me,' Frey said. 'Pressure pads underneath the exhibits.'

'Yuh,' said Silo. 'My guess is, we lift one of 'em off, that gate by the door slams down.'

Frey blew out his cheeks. 'How in damnation are we gonna get that relic out of that case, then?'

'Boys, I'd say that's the least of your worries right now.'

Frey and Silo swivelled at the sound of the voice, guns flashing into their hands. But they froze when they saw who it was.

Crake didn't need to see. He knew, and it caused a crawling nausea in his stomach. But he turned and looked anyway, because there was nothing else to do.

Standing in the doorway of the chamber, guns trained on them, were Samandra Bree and Colden Grudge.

TWENTY-ONE

'YOU AIN'T MUCH MORE THAN THIEVES'—
A THOUSAND WAYS TO DIE—PLAN B—
FREY HOLDS ON

Bree and Grudge, of the Century Knights. Sometimes they'd been allies to Frey, sometimes enemies. Tonight, they were definitely the latter.

Colden Grudge towered over his companion, shaggy-haired and bearded, clad in dirty plates of armour, carrying an autocannon cradled under his arm that could put a hole in a man the size of... well, pretty much the size of a man. Bree looked positively delicate next to him, her twin lever-action shotguns puny in comparison. They stood just outside the doorway to the circular chamber, covering the room. Three guns for three targets.

This wasn't going to go well.

'Samandra...' Crake began limply.

'You shut your meat-hole,' she snapped, raising the shotgun in her left hand, aiming at his head. 'I don't mind admittin' to a certain amount of disappointment, Grayther Crake. Thought you were better than this.'

Crake looked crushed. 'I'm sorry,' he said. 'You weren't supposed to remember.'

'You think that makes it *better*?' she cried, and Frey saw with some surprise that she was genuinely angry. 'You got in my head, you bastard! I oughta gun you down like a dog!'

'Hey,' said Frey quickly. 'Let's nobody shoot anybody. Crake here had a good reason to do what he did.'

'Yeah, I know the reason,' she sneered. 'Grothsen's new acquisition.' She spat on the floor. 'Damn daemonist trickery. For all the tales told about you, you ain't much more than thieves.'

'I *need* that relic,' Frey said. 'This isn't about stealing. See, there's a thing called the Iron Jackal, it's a daemon of some kind, and I've got a curse on me that—'

'Don't,' said Crake, holding up his hand. He looked at Frey sadly. 'Don't bother. Even *I* wouldn't believe you if you told me.'

'Well, then,' said Samandra. 'If you're quite done bullshittin', gentlemen, I suggest you lower them guns.'

Frey's eyes flickered around the room, skipping over the exhibits. His mind raced. *A plan, a plan.* Fighting was out of the question. Apart from being crack shots, the Century Knights had the advantage of cover. Frey and his companions were out in the open; the Knights only had to duck behind the doorway. He didn't much rate his chances of making it behind one of those marble plinths with all his organs still functional.

'I ain't gonna ask twice,' Samandra warned.

But Frey knew that the moment he lowered his pistol, he was as good as dead. He wouldn't even make it to the gallows. It wouldn't be the Knights that killed him, though. They'd find him in a dark cell, a scream of terror frozen on his face, torn to ribbons by bayonets. The metal claws of the Iron Jackal.

There were a thousand ways he might die. But it wouldn't be helpless in a cage.

'You really gonna start a gunfight in here?' he asked, his mouth running to buy time. 'With all these valuable artefacts?'

'Won't be much of a fight, way I see it,' said Samandra. 'In case you hadn't noticed, we don't miss much.'

'That feller's got an autocannon,' Frey pointed out.

'Colden here's touched by your concern for our heritage, Captain Frey,' said Samandra. 'He'll be real careful not to hit anything else while he's killin' you.' She steadied her aim. 'Don't make me count to three.'

'Alright,' said Frey. 'Guns down, fellers. Nice and easy, so the lady doesn't get nervous.'

Silo laid his shotgun on the ground and slid it away from him with his feet. Crake, who hadn't even drawn his pistol – and couldn't hit a barn door with it anyway – did the same.

'Can't help noticin' that one of you still has a weapon trained,' said Samandra. She switched her aim so that both guns were on Frey.

That's right, he thought. *Focus on me. The others aren't part of this.*

'You thinkin' of makin' somethin' of this, Frey?' said Samandra. 'Wouldn't be the smartest thing you ever did. Sure would be the last, though.'

Frey gave a slight smile. 'I'm not stupid, Miss Bree.' Slowly, he swung his aim away from her, until he was holding his arm out to his side, level with his shoulder. As if he was about to drop it.

But he didn't. He pulled the trigger instead.

He was throwing himself down even as he fired, slamming flat to the marble floor. Samandra, faster than her companion, pulled her triggers reflexively at the sound of the pistol. But she hadn't been expecting the shot, and that split-second of hesitation saved Frey's life. Even so, she blasted the tail of his greatcoat to rags as it followed him to the floor. If he'd dropped into a shooting crouch, it would have been his face she hit.

Glass exploded, shards pattering across his cheek. The huge Thacian vase inside the display case exploded with it, shattering like an eggshell.

Samandra switched her aim, pointing her shotguns right at Frey where he lay helpless on the floor...

And suddenly she was gone, obscured by a thundering wall of metal that slammed down from above, inches in front of her gun barrels. The gate, triggered by the pressure pad beneath the vase. Trapping them inside the chamber.

'Heh,' said Silo appreciatively, as the clamour of alarm bells began in the distance.

'You... you...' Crake gaped. 'That was a *priceless antique*!' he shrieked. '*Over two thousand years old!*'

'Smashed pretty good though, didn't it?' said Frey, getting quickly to his feet. He struggled out of his greatcoat and flung it to the ground: it was tattered to the point of uselessness. 'Jez! We need out of here, right now!'

'Plan B, Cap'n?' said Jez in his ear.

'Plan B,' he agreed.

'Oh no,' groaned Crake. 'There's a plan B?' Then he flinched as Silo put the butt of his shotgun through another glass case, and snatched up the relic.

'On my way. Where are you?' Jez asked.

Frey looked around the chamber, then up to the roof. 'Top floor. There's a dome above us.'

'I see it. Be right there.'

Something pounded against the gate. 'Frey!' came Samandra's voice, barely audible over the alarms. 'You come out of there now! You and that son of a bitch daemonist of yours!'

'Ain't gonna be long before someone opens that gate for 'em,' Silo muttered, handing Frey the black oblong case.

'I don't intend to be here when it happens,' said Frey. He dropped to his knees, brushed aside shattered glass from the floor and laid it down. He began to feel over its surface, trying to locate the row of small depressions he'd found before.

'What are you doing?' Crake asked, pacing the room helplessly.

'Reckon I've got about thirty seconds to kill. I'm gonna make sure that... ah!'

A seam appeared in the oblong and it slowly opened. There was the double-bladed weapon suspended in the delicate metal cradle. And there was the teardrop-shaped emblem of a jackal, wrought in shining grey metal on the inside of the lid. He stared at it for a moment.

What are you?

Then he closed the case, got to his feet and handed it back to Silo. 'I'd feel a bit of a fool if I nicked off with an empty box, now, wouldn't I?' he said to Crake.

There were shouting voices outside the gate. Guards. Frey wasn't sure how the alarm system was deactivated, or how the gate was opened once it slammed shut, but he was betting it wouldn't take long. And the Century Knights were going to be pretty mad when that gate came up.

'Folks,' said Jez. 'I'd get under cover if I were you.'

'Up against the wall!' Frey yelled at the others.

'What? What's going to—' Crake began, but he was cut off by the sound of the *Ketty Jay*'s autocannon smashing through the roof of the dome overhead. They ran for the walls, arms covering their heads, as chunks of rubble rained down from the ceiling, spinning end over end to smash into the remaining display cases. Crake cried out in horror as a suit of elaborate armour was crushed and scattered. The rest of the exhibits were obliterated in a cacophony of tumbling stone and tinkling glass.

When it was all over, Frey took his hands from his head. The alarm still rang, and he could hear the hiss of stabilising gas-jets as the *Ketty*

Jay manoeuvred overhead. He appeared to be undamaged, which was more than he could say for the chamber.

'Frey, you bastard!' Crake howled, surveying the wreckage.

'You're alive, aren't you?' said Frey, who was getting a bit sick of his ungratefulness. 'I'd like to see you appreciate the historical value of all this worthless junk when you're swinging from a bloody gallows.'

'*Worthless junk?*' Crake spluttered.

A rope snaked down through the hole in the dome, slumping in heavy coils on the rubble-strewn marble floor.

'Get up there,' he ordered everybody, while running for the rope himself. He wasn't about to be the last one up, especially not with the Century Knights on the other side of that gate. Despite his enthusiasm, however, Silo was quicker off the mark than he was. It was with some surprise that he saw the Murthian race ahead of him and grab the rope. He gripped the relic between his knees and climbed, using only his arms.

Damn, that feller's strong, he said to himself. He had to admit that he was more than a little perturbed that Silo hadn't let him go first. He wouldn't have expected it of anyone else, but he'd become used to Silo deferring to him over the years.

The alarm stopped suddenly. Frey had a dreadful feeling about what would happen next.

'Bess!' he yelled, as he grabbed on to the rope. 'Pull!'

Somehow, she heard him over the gas-jets, and he was hauled off the ground, up and up in clumsy jerks. Crake, slowest of all, ran across the chamber and grabbed on to the rope a few feet below Frey. He was pulled into the air with an uncertain yelp.

'Jez! Vertical ascent! Keep her steady!' Frey barked. The hole in the dome overhead was getting closer, but not fast enough. He concentrated on hanging on to the rope and fought the swarming vertigo as the chamber floor receded beneath them.

'Cap'n!' Crake cried, and there was something in his voice that flooded Frey's veins with ice. He looked down. Crake had a desperate, horrified, helpless expression on his face.

'Cap'n... my arm... it's too numb to...'

And suddenly he lost his grip, slipped a few inches, grabbed on again with a frantic clutch. His legs flailed above a fatal drop as they were pulled upwards ever faster by the combined efforts of the golem and the *Ketty Jay*'s aerium tanks.

There was no time for Frey to think. No time to do anything but prevent what he saw was about to happen.

Crake was several feet below him, beneath his feet on the rope. Frey swung his legs out, shifting them out of the way, and climbed downwards with his arms. He wasn't strong enough to do it for more than a few seconds, but a few seconds was all it took to get his arse down to a few inches above Crake's hands. In other circumstances he'd have found it all childishly comical, but now things were deadly serious and he moved with a grim efficiency. He twisted the rope round one wrist to anchor himself, and reached down with the other one.

'Frey, I can't—'

He slipped again. Frey lunged and caught him by the wrist. The jerk almost took his shoulder out of its socket. Pain blazed across his back; the rope cut into his wrist. Bess pulled again, and they were yanked upwards, almost at the roof of the chamber now. Crake swung in the air, reaching with his other hand, grabbing on to Frey's wrist as Frey had his. His eyes were wild with terror, but Frey was calm. There was nothing else in this moment but holding on. All he had to do was hold on.

Below him, there was a clanking sound as the gate to the chamber was winched up. Bree and Grudge came running into the room. They looked around, and then up, and Samandra raised her guns; but suddenly they were gone, blocked out by the green dome of the Mentenforth Institute as Frey and Crake were pulled through the hole and out into the night sky.

'*Don't let go of me!*' Crake screamed, and for an instant he thought he heard Rabby's voice instead, the voice of his dead engineer. '*Don't you leave me here!*'

'I'm not letting go,' said Frey, steadily. He didn't take his eyes off Crake's. He didn't want to see the city spreading out beneath him, the carpet of lights, the immensity of death waiting to meet him on the ground. Bess pulled them in, hand over hand, her inexorable power drawing them closer to the great black shape of the *Ketty Jay* above them.

One more second. And when that had passed, one more. And then another. The pain was meaningless. His strength was infinite. They'd have to pry his fingers open with a crowbar before he'd let go of Crake's wrist.

After an eternity that seemed to pass in no time at all, there were hands on him, reaching over the lip of the cargo ramp, pulling him aboard. Silo was lying on the edge, and he grabbed Crake's other wrist. Malvery had raced down from the autocannon cupola to help out. Harkins was babbling frantically as he grabbed at them, and even Pinn was there to lend his good arm. Behind them all, the anchor at the end of the rope, was Bess, a massive presence in the gloom.

He didn't release Crake until he was sprawled on the cargo ramp next to him. Harkins scurried over to a nearby lever and threw it. Hydraulics kicked in, and the metal floor that they lay on began to rise as the ramp came up. Silo and Pinn dragged them both away from the steadily closing gap, and they were finally deposited on the floor of the cargo hold, panting and breathless.

'Jez,' said Frey. 'We're in. Cane it.'

The *Ketty Jay*'s thrusters boomed in response, and she thundered away across the city. The cargo ramp slid shut, sealing them in, the protective metal cocoon of home.

Crake was lying on his back, panting, halfway to sobbing with relief. Bess lumbered over and crouched next to him. She made a concerned bubbling noise and poked him in the arm. He shook his head in disbelief, staring at the ceiling. 'Spit and blood. We are in *so* much trouble,' he gasped.

Frey got slowly and painfully to his feet, brushed sweaty hair away from his forehead, and straightened. 'Anyone else think we've outstayed our welcome in Thesk?'

Pinn, Malvery, Silo and Harkins all put their hands up. Crake did the same, from where he lay on the floor. Bess looked around in confusion, turning this way and that, and then tentatively raised her hand, because everyone else was doing it and she wanted to join in the game.

'Yeah, me too,' said Frey, tiredly. 'Let's go back to Samarla.'

TWENTY-TWO

ASHUA TAKES THE FLOOR—IMPOSSIBLE ODDS— PINN COMBUSTS—A CONVERSATION IN THE ENGINE ROOM

Five nights left.

Everyone was in a hurry at the moment, thought Harkins. They'd hurried out of Thesk as fast as the *Ketty Jay* would take them. They'd hurried across Vardia, flying non-stop all day, with tireless Jez taking the controls when the Cap'n had to sleep. They hurried over Silver Bay, red and gold in the last light of dusk, into the Free Trade Zone, back to Shasiith by midnight. There they dropped the Cap'n off, with Malvery for a bodyguard, and then hurried back out of the city again, because they didn't want to stay in dock for too long. They were afraid of being caught by the Sammie soldiers, still out for their blood after that whole messy business with the hijacked train.

They'd returned to the city a few hours later, to a different landing pad, for the rendezvous. No one had turned up, so they took off again, hanging in the dark of the night sky, floating weightless on aerium ballast until it was time to head to the second rendezvous at a different landing pad. By now it was past dawn, but this time the Cap'n was waiting, with Malvery and Ashua. He'd had some trouble tracking her down, despite the fact she'd left word for him, and he was fretting about the wasted hours. He called a crew meeting immediately, and everyone hurried to get it over with so they could get back in the sky.

Hurry, hurry, and it didn't really feel like they were getting anywhere. The more they hurried, the faster time seemed to slip away.

If the Cap'n died, the *Ketty Jay* died. They all knew it. None of them were capable of taking command. Their little world would fall apart. They assembled in the mess with a grim sense of purpose.

Ashua stood at the head of the room with Frey. Harkins couldn't say he was exactly glad to see that ginger-haired young woman back on board. Her stupid tattooed face annoyed him. He hadn't forgotten her unkind words while he was fumbling with a lit stick of dynamite in the Rattletrap.

The rest of the crew were arranged around the table in varying positions of recline. Crake was yawning in his pyjamas and robe, looking hollow-eyed and exhausted. He'd been working in his sanctum all day and night, and had somehow roped Silo in to help him with the strange mechanical bits and bobs he'd picked up in Thesk. He'd just gone to bed when they woke him up again for the meeting.

Next to Crake, Malvery was sucking down coffee and looking dour. Silo smoked one of his vile roll-ups, which made Harkins' eyes sting and his throat tickle. Pinn sat eagerly to attention, instead of his usual slouch.

He was up to something. Harkins could tell.

Pinn had been in a sulk last night, because they had to leave his Skylance in dock at Thesk. During the day, he'd disappeared into the quarters he shared with Harkins and banned anyone from entering. When he emerged, he was fairly bouncing with excitement. It was all very suspicious.

Harkins hated that hamster-cheeked dunce more than ever since his little stunt at the race. Bad enough that Harkins had no aircraft any more, nowhere to escape to. He felt like half a man without it, and he'd gone a bit hysterical until the Cap'n assured him he'd get a new one. But to have his moment of glory stolen from him… that was the worst thing yet! It was enough to make a man mad with rage, enough to make him… well… stamp his feet, or something.

Jez had seen it, though. Jez, leaning against the wall in her jumpsuit with her arms folded, hair tied back with a rubber strip. Jez, who stubbornly refused to swoon at his feet. His display of extraordinary bravery – doubly impressive since it came from an abject coward – had produced no discernible effect on her at all.

What was a man supposed to do to stir her heart, for rot's sake? How much heroism would it take? Harkins was seriously beginning to think that he wouldn't survive much more of it.

He glanced at the cupboards above the stove. Slag, not to be left out of a crew meeting, had installed himself up there, and was listening with one ear while noisily devouring a rat. A thin trail of blood had been smeared across the counter and up the cupboard door, which surely couldn't be hygienic. But at least the cat didn't bother him these days. He took some satisfaction in that.

'Alright, listen up!' said Frey. 'Let's make this quick, before the Sammies get wind we're here. Try not to interrupt for a minute, if you can manage that, and we'll get on our way. Miss Vode has a couple of things to tell us.'

All eyes moved to Ashua. She leaned forward over the table, hands on the back of a chair.

'Here's the situation,' she said. 'The man you want is being kept by the Sammies a long way south of here, outside the Free Trade Zone. Usually they'd have executed him without a second thought, but Ugrik is the fourth son of the High Chief of Yortland, and I suppose they're not keen on starting an international incident. That said, they're not keen on letting him go, either. I reckon they don't want him telling anyone where he got that relic from, in case more go looking.'

'So, what? We're breaking him out?' Crake snapped his fingers in the air. 'Easy! Why not? Maybe we can smash a few more national treasures on the way.'

Ashua looked at Frey uncertainly. He rolled his eyes and waved at her to continue.

'Er... well, anyway, there's a problem,' she said. 'We know where he's being kept, but we don't know exactly where it is. It's located somewhere in the *Chi-a'ti* sulphur basin – otherwise known as the Choke Bowl – an area covered with toxic geysers which is more or less permanently clouded by fumes.'

Silo moved in his seat and spat a word. Harkins didn't know what it meant, but it came loaded with a frightening quantity of hate, and it sounded like he was naming the place. *Gagriisk.*

'You know it?' Frey asked him.

Silo glared at the table. 'Allium mine. Murthian work camp. Place is a death-hole.'

'It's also well fortified,' said Ashua, 'with a standing defence force of a single small frigate and ten fighters.'

'Oh, that's just bloody fantastic!' said Crake, who was evidently in a snarky mood this morning. 'And I suppose we're just going to waltz in there, guns blazing, yes?'

'Waltzing in with guns blazing is pretty much the only way you're gonna get your man out,' said Ashua. 'None of you lot would pass for Sammies or Daks, so chances of infiltrating it are pretty slim. You'd all be mordant before long.'

'That means dead,' said Frey proudly.

Crake looked at Ashua with a puzzled frown. Harkins saw her give him a quick wink, and he cracked a small, private smile. Harkins wasn't sure what had passed between them – a shared joke about the Cap'n, perhaps? – but he wished people would just say what they meant and stop using words like 'mordant' altogether.

Jez spoke up then. 'So, what you're saying is, the only way to get Ugrik out is a frontal assault on a fortified camp?'

'Yeah,' said Frey. 'That, and we don't know how to find it.'

'The Choke Bowl covers hundreds of square kloms,' said Ashua. 'And the mine's location is secret.'

'Cap'n,' said Jez, with the tone of someone struggling to understand why she was even having this conversation. 'There's seven of us. Nine if you count Bess and the cat. Ten if she's coming.' She nodded at Ashua, then looked at Frey. '*Is* she coming, by the way?'

'Yeah,' said Frey and Ashua at the same time, though neither of them looked at all happy about it. 'Temporarily,' Frey added. 'We can always use another gun.'

Harkins wondered if that was the real reason, or if Ashua had demanded to come in return for the information. It seemed like the kind of weaselly trick she might pull. Apparently, the reason the Cap'n hadn't been able to find her last night was because she'd had a close shave with some Sammie soldiers, and gone into hiding. Shasiith must have been *really* dangerous for her now, if she thought she was safer on the *Ketty Jay*.

'So,' Jez continued, 'let's be generous and say Bess counts for three. That makes twelve of us, assuming we put the cat in some armour and strap an autocannon to its arse.'

'Which isn't actually a bad idea...' Malvery mused, studying Slag. Slag looked up from his rat, sensing that he'd become the centre of attention, and hissed at them.

'How many guards in this camp?' Jez asked Ashua.

Ashua shrugged. 'I'd say at least a hundred.'

Malvery coughed and spat half his mug of coffee into Crake's ear. 'A *hundred*?' he cried.

Crake sighed and dabbed at his face with the sleeve of his robe.

Harkins had some sympathy for him. It seemed like you couldn't get through a day round here without someone spitting something over somebody.

'That does sound rather a lot,' the daemonist pointed out.

Malvery sat back in his chair, folded his arms over his belly and blew out his moustache with a huff. 'Well, Cap'n, allow me to be the first to say that this frontal assault plan is bollocks.'

'Seconded,' said Crake instantly.

'Thirded,' said Frey, which threw everybody off. 'Look, nobody's frontally assaulting anything with those odds. But right now we've got no other leads to where the relic came from, and unless we get it back there pretty damn fast, I'm gonna die horribly.'

'Least you won't lose your hand, though,' Malvery pointed out.

'Yeah, there is that,' Frey admitted, looking fondly at his hand in its fingerless glove. 'Anyway, we're gonna get moving, get out of Shasiith and head to the border of the Free Trade Zone. Soon as the sun goes down we're heading south. And between now and the Choke Bowl, someone needs to come up with a plan better than the one we got.'

He surveyed the room. The atmosphere was gloomy.

'I'm telling you all so you know just how shit out of luck we are on this one. Seriously, I don't have a clue how we're gonna do this. I want to offer you the chance, if you want, to step off now.'

Harkins felt a shiver of horror. He looked at the faces of the people in the mess, and was appalled to find that nobody was protesting.

'You serious, Cap'n?' Malvery's tone was grave.

'Yep,' said Frey, with forced lightheartedness. 'Take a week, do whatever you need to do. Catch up on family, see the sights. Pinn, you could go see that girl you hardly ever mention any more.'

'Hey!' said Pinn distractedly. He was fiddling with something under the table. 'True love is never in a hurry.'

Crake snorted and muttered something sarcastic that Harkins didn't quite catch.

'Anyway,' said Frey, 'the point is, nobody has to do this. This is my problem. None of you have any stake in it, so this is your chance to get out if you want, and no hard feelings. Reckon it's only gonna get worse from here on in.'

Harkins was agape. No! Nobody was allowed to *leave*! He'd already lost his wings. He was damned if he'd lose the only people in the world he wasn't mortally afraid of.

'We don't… I mean… you think we don't have any *stake* in this?' he demanded, his voice more shrill than he would have liked. 'I haven't forgotten why I'm here today! You… Cap'n, you gave me the chance to *fly* again.' He swept the room with what he hoped was a fierce glare. 'And I'm betting everyone else here owes you just as much.' He stuck out his unshaven chin. '*I'm* with you!'

Jez was gazing at him with an expression of naked surprise on her face. He felt a touch of bitter satisfaction. *See?* he thought. *You don't know me like you think.*

Malvery was nodding. 'Aye,' he said. 'Reckon you're right. Don't believe any of us'd be much right now if it weren't for the Cap'n.'

Frey waved his hands. 'No, no, you don't get it!' he protested. 'I don't want anyone coming out of a sense of obligation.'

'Cap'n,' said Crake. 'Nobody *wants* to do this. Even you don't *want* to do this.'

'Still goin' to, though,' Silo rumbled.

'Right,' said Jez.

'Right,' said Harkins firmly.

'*AiieeeaAAAAARRRGHHH!!!*' said Pinn, whose arm was on fire.

The whole room watched, stunned, as Pinn scrambled away from the table, flailing. His coat was aflame up to the elbow, a bright burning wing flapping in the air. But before anyone could gather their wits and react, something even more disturbing happened.

Pinn started to laugh.

'Suckers!' he crowed.

'Um,' said Crake. 'But your arm *is* on fire, though, right?'

Pinn was holding the blazing arm out straight, away from his body. 'I don't feel a thing!' he declared, a big grin on his chubby face. 'And you know why? Because my sleeve is coated in Professor Pinn's Incredible Flame-Slime!'

A few seconds passed, during which the only sound was the restless grumbling of the flames.

'Er... what?' Malvery said at length.

'Professor Pinn's Incredible Flame-Slime!' Pinn enthused. 'See, I was mixing all this stuff together that I found down in the hold, trying out some new *experiments*.' He paused to gauge how impressed everybody was with his scientific prowess. 'And I came up with this! I only worked out what it could do when I accidentally set my finger on fire.'

Crake had shaken off his drowsiness and was sitting up, fascinated. 'So it's highly flammable and yet it insulates you from the heat,' he said. 'That's actually quite astounding, Pinn. How did you make it?'

'Ah!' said Pinn, preening. 'That'd be telling.'

Malvery studied him for a moment and then said confidently, 'He doesn't know.'

'I do!' Pinn protested.

Malvery scoffed. 'Aye. I bet you were keeping met-*ic*-ulous records all the way through.'

'Well, what kind of inventor bothers with all that boring stuff when there's inventions to be... er... invented?' Pinn protested. He looked slightly worried now. No doubt it was the first time it had occurred to him that he might not be able to make it again.

'You mean you've invented this Incredible Flame-Slime and you've no idea how you did it?' Crake asked in astonishment.

'I made a whole pot of the stuff,' Pinn said lamely, with a helpless shrug. 'I mean, I...' An expression of alarm crossed his face and he stared at his burning arm. 'Wait a minute. This is getting pretty ho*aaaaaaaAAAARRRGH!!!!*'

'Oh, come on. You pulled that trick once already,' Harkins sniffed, as Pinn flapped at himself, screaming.

'Don't think he's faking this time,' said Malvery, surging to his feet and pulling his coat from the back of his chair. He bundled into Pinn, knocking him to the floor and smothering his arm. Pinn rolled around shrieking beneath the doctor's not inconsiderable weight, but finally came to rest, panting, his face white and sweaty.

'It's out?' Malvery asked.

Pinn nodded weakly.

'Come on, then. Let's get you to the—'

Malvery never finished, because at that moment Slag, sensing vulnerable prey, leapt from his perch atop the cupboard and launched himself at Pinn's head. Pinn howled and twisted as the cat savaged his scalp. Malvery swore and tried to beat Slag away, but the cat hung on tight, and Pinn's thrashing meant that Malvery hit him more often than not.

'Somebody get that cat off him!' Frey cried in exasperation.

'Right you are, Cap'n,' said Jez. She went down to one knee and held out her arms. Slag disengaged from his bloodied foe and bolted across the mess towards her. She picked him up and held him protectively against her chest, while he groomed himself in satisfaction.

'I thought that cat hated you!' Harkins accused, feeling somewhat betrayed at the sight of his old enemy showing such affection towards the object of his desire.

Jez ignored him, which hurt. She looked at Pinn instead, who was being helped to his feet by Malvery. 'I think he had a grudge about the whole rum and toast thing.'

'Infirmary. Now,' said Malvery to Pinn, who was amusingly close to tears.

'I can't get up the ladder,' Pinn whined, holding up his arms: one mildly burned beneath the tatters of his coat sleeve, the other still in a sling.

Ashua was shaking her head in despair. 'How you lot managed to hijack a train, I'll never know.'

Frey clapped his hands together. 'Well, then,' he said brightly. 'That was fun. Now if Pinn's done being an idiot, let's get airborne, shall we?'

Jez liked the engine room of the *Ketty Jay*. It reminded her in some way of her father's workshop: the smell of grease and oil, the heavy presence of machinery, the sticky warmth in the air. And it was certainly warm now. The *Ketty Jay* had only recently put down near the edge of the Free Trade Zone, and the residual heat from the prothane engine, combined with the baking afternoon sun, had driven the temperature to sweltering.

She picked her way through the tight mesh of walkways and steps that surrounded the engine assembly, following the sounds of movement, the occasional clank of a spanner. Silo was around here somewhere, as usual. In fact, she'd been counting on it. She needed to talk to someone, and there was only one man on the crew she thought would understand.

She found him kneeling in front of a panel, tinkering with the engine. Slag was there, too, lying on top of a warm pipe. The cat gave her a steady gaze as she approached.

'Hey,' she said to Silo.

He didn't reply. Beads of sweat were trickling from his shaven head as he worked.

'Can I talk to you?'

'You talkin', ain'tcha?' he replied.

Jez hunkered down next to him, undeterred. He'd been in a dark mood for several days now, and she didn't reckon he'd come out of it soon. She briefly considered asking him what he was doing, but Silo wasn't much for smalltalk. Besides, she could see that he wasn't really doing anything. There wasn't much to be done: the new engine needed very little maintenance. Not that it stopped Silo constantly looking for something to fix.

'I had this dream,' she said. 'Well, more like a vision, I suppose you'd say.' And she told him about it, how she'd gone back to the day she died, and looked down on her body in the snow, and how she'd stood beneath the dreadnought and listened to the cries of the Manes.

'And I was *drawn* to them, you know?' she said. 'Damn, it was like… Well, I suppose you've not heard anyone speaking Murthian for a long time now, but I bet it'd be music to your ears if you did.'

Silo glanced at her, and then away. He'd stopped messing with the engine and was paying attention now. 'Reckon it would.'

'I mean it felt familiar, like I *missed* it or something. And there were chains and ropes and things hanging off the side of the dreadnought, and I thought… I felt this compulsion to climb up there and join them.'

'But you didn't, huh?'

'No,' she said. 'At first… When I first got caught by the Manes, for a long time after I was scared that I was turning into one of them. That nothing could stop it, and it wasn't my choice.' She picked at the toe of her boot awkwardly. 'But then I faced up to them, right? You helped me with that.'

'I recall,' he said.

'And they let me go. They stopped calling to me, they accepted my decision. I didn't want to be with them; I wanted to be with you lot.' She sat back against the rail of the gangway. 'But ever since then, all I've done is wonder what I was missing out on. I mean, they can *do* things. *I* can do things.'

Silo looked at the cat. 'Noticed that,' he said.

She caught herself, fearing that she'd said too much. The crew could tolerate or ignore the fact that she was half-Mane because her daemonic side rarely ever got loose. But she couldn't let anyone suspect she might be able to hear their thoughts, even if it was in an uncontrolled and random fashion. On a craft full of secrets, it would be the final straw.

'I want to know who they are,' she said. That, at least, was something she could admit. 'But I can't get close to them. I know they're out there. I can hear their voices. But I can't be a part of their conversation.'

The Manes were bonded by mutual understanding. Each was connected to the others in a thousand subtle ways through the daemon that united them, yet each was an individual, capable of privacy of thought. It had to be that way, or else why would the book in her quarters exist? Manes read, for enjoyment or education. It all seemed a far cry from the feral ghouls of legend.

But she'd chosen not to be a part of that, and they, in turn, had withdrawn from her. She didn't know the plans and mysteries of the Manes. She wouldn't be allowed to know, unless she was one of them. Humans were enemies to the Manes, and she was half-human. Until she wasn't, until she was indisputably, entirely, a Mane, she would always be a foreigner to them.

But she'd never go that far.

'I'm not scared of being turned into a Mane against my will any more,' she said. 'I'm scared that I'll *want* it. I'm scared that the more I learn about them, the more I'll learn to *be* like them.' She looked into his dark eyes. 'And the less I'll be like me.'

'You gonna be you no matter what,' he said. 'It's just that time makes a *different* you. Seems stupid that people try 'n' improve 'emselves the whole time, yet they don't never want to change.' He studied her, and there was an intensity to his gaze that unsettled her. 'Like it or not, they your *people* now. Ain't easy to turn your back on your people. You don't never stop wantin' to be with 'em, no matter what it might cost.'

He began tinkering with the panel again, as if the conversation was over. Jez chewed over what he'd said. She might have told him more, but his face suddenly took on an expression of disgust and he threw down his spanner, making her jump.

'This damn engine!' he said. 'It don't need fixin'. There ain't no call for me to be here no more. Man ain't nothin' if he ain't useful.'

He got up, rising to his full height, and strode off down the walkway towards some steps.

'Where are you going?' Jez asked, bewildered.

'I'm goin' to tell the Cap'n how he can find what he's lookin' for,' Silo threw over his shoulder.

Jez sat there for a moment, frowning. The cat regarded her with feline inscrutability. Then she scrambled to her feet.

'Hey!' she called as she chased after him. 'How do *you* know?'

TWENTY-THREE

THE SOUND OF LIVING—TRINICA AND DEATH—
SILO TELLS HIS TALE—DISCOVERED

The noise, the damned *noise*.

Frey remembered that sound. He remembered hearing it as he lay dying on the tilted floor of the *Ketty Jay*'s cockpit. Through the cracked windglass, through the metal hull, he'd heard it, endless, dipping and swelling but never, ever stopping.

That day, he'd lain for hours in the punishing heat, while his life leaked slowly through the bandage around his waist. The blazing Samarlan sun was made green by the foliage pressed up against the windglass. He sweated, and breathed, and the tiredness in every muscle seemed to multiply with every breath until it felt like he was being smothered with heavy blankets. His eyes wouldn't stay focused, and the edges of his vision had gone dark.

He'd listened to the insects. The nameless, invisible monsters, who existed in their millions but could never be seen. They sawed and creaked and chirped and whirred and chattered in a maddening cacophony.

That's the sound of living, he thought that day. *One big, confused and messy blare, nothing matching or making sense, and nothing of it meaning shit all. Just everyone trying to yell louder than everyone else. I'm better off out of it.*

It was a rare philosophical moment, but he'd reckoned he was due one, since he considered himself dead meat at that point. He'd crash-landed his aircraft in the trackless mountain jungles of northern Samarla with a bayonet wound in his guts. The rest of the crew was gone, butchered by the Daks in an ambush when they set down to deliver supplies for Vard infantrymen. When he finally blacked out, he never expected to wake up again.

But Silo found him, having crawled in through the cargo ramp, which had fallen ajar during the crash. The Murthian nursed him back to health, using the medical supplies and food that had never been delivered. In return, Frey flew him out of Samarla.

Nine years since that day, give or take a few months. And now they were back. Back to the same sweltering jungle. Back to the same spot where he'd crashed, more or less. It was just inside the Free Trade Zone now, which had been set up after the last war, but its new status hadn't changed it a bit.

Nine years, and those bloody insects still hadn't shut up.

Frey pushed through the undergrowth, his trousers damp and his shirt sticking to his back. Silo was ahead of him, clambering up a slope, picking his way through the trees. The jungle was menacingly foreign to Frey's eyes. The trees that grew here were not like the trees of home. Their strange forms, scaly bark and towering size made him uneasy. Almost as uneasy as the stranger he followed.

Nine years, and he'd never asked who Silo really was.

It seemed ridiculous, when he put it like that. He'd always just assumed that he was naturally incurious. He respected a man's privacy, and it wasn't his business what Silo's life had been like before they met. But after nine years in each other's company, well, there had to be more to it than simple idleness, on both their parts. Silo didn't want to tell him. Frey didn't want to know.

Or was it that he didn't want to *care*?

And it wasn't only Silo, either. He found himself actively switching off on the rare occasions when the less close-mouthed members of his group started talking about their past lives. Usually they were drunk at that point, so he had an excuse to forget it, but still... strange behaviour, really.

He supposed it was because their past lives didn't involve him, and anything that didn't involve him was by definition unimportant. Each of them existed only from the moment he met them, as far as he was concerned. Past experience suggested that they'd fade just as quickly after they were gone, although that wouldn't make the parting hurt any the less. He didn't feel bad about that; he thought it an honest appraisal of his character. He'd been that way since he could remember. Growing up in an orphanage meant a lot of goodbyes and a lot of new faces. Impermanence was the defining quality of Frey's life.

But it bothered him that Silo knew how to find the place where Ugrik was being held, and he'd waited almost a half a day to tell him. And it bothered him that he still didn't know where they were going.

Not for the first time, he wondered if he should have come at all. Silo hadn't wanted him to, saying it was far too dangerous. But Frey had insisted. He was buggered if he'd sit back and let another member of his crew risk their lives in his stead. The least he could do was get himself killed alongside them.

In the end, Silo relented. 'Just you,' he said. 'Not no one else. And you gonna regret it.'

Frey was already regretting it. The heat, the exhausting climb, the bloody *noise*!

And the memories. Because somewhere not far from here was an old ruined village where his last crew had died. Where he'd closed the *Ketty Jay*'s cargo ramp in the face of his hapless navigator, Rabby, trapping him outside to be carved up by the enemy.

'*Don't you leave me here!*'

He'd heard that same cry in Thesk, when the Iron Jackal had lured him into an alleyway. A cry from the past, the sound of all his guilt and shame. He'd been trying to secure his own extinction, but he hadn't been brave enough in the end, and he'd only ended up securing everyone else's. They might have been a worthless bunch, that crew, but they didn't have to die for it.

Yet the daemon that haunted him *knew* about that day.

There were other things it knew about him, too. When he first saw it, it had been fighting its way free of an amniotic sac, and he'd been powerfully reminded of the unborn child that had died in Trinica's womb. The bayonets that it had as fingers were the same kind that almost took his life, that day when his crew were killed. One of its eyes was Trinica's, or rather the eye of the pirate queen she disguised herself as: a pupil black and huge in its orbit.

And the armour plating that sewed itself in and out of its skin. He'd thought there was something familiar about it. It had come to him suddenly during the night. It was the same colour and texture as the hull of the *Delirium Trigger*.

It builds itself from everything you're most afraid of. That's what the sorcerer had said, back in the Underneath. The daemon came from him. He'd constructed it with his own fears and flaws.

Great, he thought mordantly.

Death and Trinica. Trinica and death. The two were inseparable. It frightened him that she should figure so large in the dark churn of his subconscious. Almost as large as the day Rabby died.

And all of that wrapped up in the shape of an enormous man-jackal. He'd only ever seen jackals a few times in his life, during the last war, when delivering emergency supplies to the site of a recent battle. They would be picking their way among the dead: sneaky, thieving things, feeding off the scraps of what the big boys left behind. Opportunistic skulkers with a vicious bite.

Oh, wait, thought Frey. *That sounds like me.*

Failure, failure, failure. He'd failed Rabby and his crew. He'd failed Trinica in spectacular style. He'd failed the child he never had. And he'd failed himself.

A sobering thing, to have a mirror held up to you like that. To have your inadequacies made flesh. He'd been fooling himself into thinking he was a hero. He'd believed his own hype. And look at him now. Desperate, sweaty, chasing the slimmest of hopes because he knew that the Iron Jackal would come for him twice more, and the next visit couldn't be far off.

Time was short. Time to get a few things straight, then.

'Hey!' he called. Silo stopped and watched expressionlessly as Frey struggled up the slope towards him. When Frey had caught him up, he stood with his hands on his burning thighs, panting.

'Reckon we're far enough from the rest that you can speak up now,' Frey said.

Silo just looked at him. His silence made the racket all around seem louder. Frey straightened and wiped sweaty hair from his forehead.

'Come on, Silo,' he said. 'You're a Murthian; that means you were a slave here. Crake told me one time that you used to work on aircraft in factories, which is how come you're so good with a spanner. He also said you escaped, and that's when you found me.'

'That's what I told him,' Silo replied. 'Might be I left some out.'

'Uh-huh. So at what point between escaping the factory and finding me did you learn how to speak Vardic and drive a Rattletrap and handle a shotgun?'

Silo turned his head and looked away into the undergrowth, scanning the trees, as if concerned that someone might be watching and listening. 'Didn't want you to come with me, Cap'n,' he said.

'I didn't much want to come. But we're here now. And I'd really appreciate knowing where we're going.'

Silo's eyes fell on something. He walked over to a tree and ran his fingers down the bark, where the wood had been chipped. Then he squatted down and turned over a stone that lay at the base of the tree. He held it up to Frey. There were marks in an unfamiliar language scratched on the bottom.

'There's signs all round, if you know what to look for,' Silo said. 'Pointin' the way. When I left, there was a settlement near here, hid deep in the jungle where no one gonna see it. Might be it's gone, but I reckon not. Markers have been kept up.' He put the stone back.

'A settlement?'

Silo rolled his shoulders beneath his shirt, pulled out a pinch of herbs and began expertly constructing a roll-up. 'You fought in the wars, yuh?'

'I wouldn't say *fought*,' said Frey. 'I was *there*, put it that way. Only the second time around, though. First war, I never left Vardia.'

'Well, you prob'ly heard they had Murthians fightin' alongside the Daks. Usually they din't want us out of our pens. Said we was hard to control. But they needed cannon fodder and they didn't much like wasting the Daks. Sammies need the Daks for their smarts, and they ain't big on doin' their own dirty work. We was expendable, so they broke us out on the front lines.'

'They gave you weapons?' said Frey. 'That was a bit dumb, wasn't it?'

Silo gave a bitter little smirk, licked the rolling paper and stuck the roll-up in his mouth. 'They kept the women and children back. Said they'd kill one for every man who deserted or rebelled.'

'But you did it anyway?' Frey guessed.

'Nuh. Maybe I would've, given the chance. Didn't have no women nor children of my own, and freedom's a powerful incentive, I reckon. But I wasn't there. They had me in the factories, buildin' aircraft, on account of I had a talent with machines.' He struck a match and lit up, then motioned to Frey. 'Keep movin', huh? Not far.'

They set off again, labouring through the foliage. The air was hot and steamy and thick, and the sunlight filtered through the canopy in hazy beams, as if they were under water.

Frey felt a certain trepidation about where he was being taken. Not just for what was waiting up ahead, but for what he would hear as Silo continued his story. He didn't want to know anything that might change his opinion of the man. He didn't need any moral dilemmas. If Silo hadn't told him about his past, there was probably a good reason for it.

But it was too late to take it back now. Silo was talking, and that in itself was a rare thing.

'They lost a lot of Murthians durin' the wars,' Silo said. 'And I mean *lost*. Plenty o' folk jus' took their guns and ran when the fightin' started. Scattered into the mountains or the deserts or whatever. Most died, I s'pose. But some didn't, and more often than not they found a place to hole up together. More an' more who escaped heard about 'em and joined 'em.' He took a drag and let the smoke seep out between his lips. 'Pretty soon we all heard about 'em, even us in the pens. Free Murthians, livin' off the land, hid where the Sammies weren't never gonna find 'em.'

'So you... what, you broke out and went looking for them?'

'Couldn't stand bein' kept, thinkin' there was something better outside. Didn't never have that hope before. So I did it, me 'n' a couple others. Escaped from the factory. They hunted us up into the mountains, but we scattered and they din't follow me after that. Dunno what happened to the others, but I got lucky. Weren't far off starving when they found me.'

He went quiet for a time, but Frey was used to that, and didn't prompt him. Eventually he spoke again.

'You know that some o' your folks came to Samarla to help out the Murthians after the First Aerium War?'

Frey dredged his memory. 'Rings a bell,' he said.

'Young men, too much heat in their blood, needin' a cause to fight for. They heard about the Murthian deserters. Started comin' over in secret with weapons, intent on findin' Murthians and trainin' 'em how to fight back. Them that found me, they were a group like that. Bunch of Vards in there fightin' alongside us.'

'And that's how you learned Vardic,' said Frey.

Silo blew out a cloud of smoke and chuckled. 'Had to in the early days, if you wanted to talk to 'em. Them Vard fellers were good sorts, but their Murthian... Pains a man's ears to hear his mother tongue spoken like that.'

'Yeah,' said Frey. 'Scuffers might be tough as cured shit, but they're not the smartest, as a rule.'

Silo looked over his shoulder and frowned. 'How'd you know they were from Draki?'

'You talk like one of 'em,' Frey said, shrugging.

'Huh,' said Silo, considering that. 'Never noticed.'

'So you lot were resistance fighters?'

'S'pose you'd say we were,' Silo spat into his hand and crushed out the dog-end in his palm. Then he dropped it in his pocket. 'Didn't really hold out much hope of liberatin' our people or any such thing, but we could liberate a few. And we could make the Sammies' lives miserable. Blowin' up supply lines. Ambushin' convoys. The Vard fellers taught us tactics that we din't have, growin' up in pens like we did.'

'And these people, this group you fought with... These are the people we're going to see?'

'Yuh,' said Silo. 'They got maps. I know they know where the mine is, 'cause I remember we had a plan to hit it once. In the end it was too far to be worth it. It's way down south, and we din't have the fuel to burn to get us there.'

Frey felt a small ember of hope begin to glow inside him. 'But I thought you said it was dangerous?'

'Yuh.'

Frey was puzzled. 'Why?'

Silo stopped and turned around. 'When you woke up on the *Ketty Jay*, and I was there, I was half-starved. You remember?'

Frey nodded.

'Been lost. Been on the run for days. Got lucky, when I saw your craft come down.'

'I suppose so. What's your point?'

'Point is, Cap'n, who d'you think I was runnin' *from*?'

Frey looked over his shoulder and pointed. 'I'm guessing it was them.'

TWENTY-FOUR

STORIES FROM THE DREAMING-HOUSE— OLD FRIENDS—AKKAD'S JUDGEMENT— FREY INQUIRES—A WARREN, NO RABBITS

His past was still here, lying in wait.

The sight of the camp disoriented Silo. How many times had he come up this trail at the end of a day's hunt, emerging from the rich green undergrowth to find this same clutter of huts waiting for him in the swelter of a late afternoon? It had been nine years since he fled this place, but those years were like the loop of a slipknot, vanishing to nothing with one sharp tug.

The camp had no name. They'd always just called it the camp. To name something was to give it permanence, and they'd always known they must be ready to abandon it at a moment's notice, to drop their possessions and flee if the Sammies should ever discover them. No one thought they'd be here long.

Yet here they were.

Their three captors were young men, scouts, twitchy with pent-up aggression and eager to pull their triggers. They were new: Silo didn't remember them. But the mere sight of his own people, even hostile ones, gave him a rush of pleasure that made his head light. And to hear them talk! The rapid, silken flow of syllables, washing over his senses, achingly beautiful in contrast to the ugly surrogate he'd been speaking so long that it had even invaded his thoughts.

But the men weren't interested in conversation. They had their orders, and followed them rigidly. Strangers were to be taken captive and brought back to the camp. One of them seemed curious about how Silo and Frey had come to be travelling together, but his companion shut him up, and told the prisoners not to speak. Their leader would decide what was to be done with them.

But who's your leader these days? That's the question, ain't it?

It was a question on which their lives might depend. Silo didn't bother to ask. Knowing or not knowing, it wouldn't change a thing, so it didn't matter a shit's worth. He kept his silence. The Cap'n did the same.

The trail wound up a slope beneath the dense canopy, heading into the heart of the camp. The buildings were made of wood and leaf thatch, arranged haphazardly wherever the massive trees would allow, nestled in the dim, blood-warm world of the deep jungle. Most of them were obscured, hidden by trunks and leaves, but even at this familiar edge, Silo saw new dwellings. The camp had grown.

Some things hadn't changed, though. There was the pen for the domesticated *ari'shu*, Samarlan jungle-hogs, who rooted and snuffled in the earth among the fat black chickens. There was the eating-round, a circular, open-sided hut where meals were taken. The men would sit on their mats in a strictly arranged hierarchy, with the most important closest to the centre, while the women sat wherever they pleased.

Further up, half-hidden by the trees, was the flank of the infirmary, where the witch-sisters treated the sick and the wounded. Next to it was the dreaming-house, where the children went to hear the tales of the old country, and to be taught of the grace of Mother. Silo had spent many a night there himself, listening to the witch-sisters tell of the time before the fall, before the Samarlans swept through Murthia and enslaved its people. Stories of Makkad, who led his armies to the walls of grand Ail and brought them down; stories of Elos and Kaf, whose journey of love and hate was the subject of hundreds of songs and cost thousands of lives; stories of Odadj, who'd slain the Bengist by plunging a spear into each of its three throats. An age of legends and greatness. It had swelled Silo's heart to hear those stories when they were told to him as a child in the pens and work camps. They were scarcely less powerful as an adult.

Those stories were what bound his people together. Many things had been lost. Many arts and crafts had faded because there was no opportunity to practise them in slavery. The Samarlans had done their best to stamp out the old way of life, but they hadn't succeeded. Not entirely. The Dakkadians had folded under the yoke and assimilated into their masters' world. They had no language of their own any more, no culture left that hadn't been copied from the

Samarlans. But the Murthians had held on, over five centuries. It was death for a slave to be heard speaking Murthian, but they spoke it anyway, in secret. They had their own tongue, and their stories, and the promise from Mother that each of them would one day see the end to their bondage. Whether in this life or the next, or the next, or the next.

They kept the flame alive.

As the captives passed through the camp, people began to emerge from their huts, drawn by the news. They were mostly Murthians, a few Vard men, and even a pair of scrawny half-breed children, their skin a warm yellow-brown and their hair blond. Some of them looked in bad shape, walking with the support of their relatives. They seemed malnourished or sick. Even the healthiest were tired and haggard, and they watched the newcomers with a fearful curiosity.

He searched for people he knew. There were many strangers, but there were still plenty of people he recognised, and who recognised him in return with astonished expressions. Jaraz, who'd been a headstrong young firebrand, still here despite his reckless nature. Bahd, that sulky crank, pooching out his lips in disapproval. Ehri and Fal: the broad-shouldered huntress and the slender, thoughtful man who was her constant companion. She cried out his name as she saw him, and hurried to meet him, with Fal only a step behind her.

~ Stand off, Ehri, warned one of the young scouts. ~ We're taking him to—

~ Quiet your voice, she said, dismissing him scornfully. She clasped Silo's upper arms and looked him up and down, a grin of amazement spreading across her face. Then she embraced him.

~ You live, she said. ~ I don't believe the thing I see before me.

~ I live, he said, and he couldn't stop a grin of his own at the sound of Murthian words rolling off his lips. He stepped back and lifted up her hand: there was an intricate shape tattooed on her left palm, as he'd known there would be. He looked up at Fal, who was crowding in, offering heartfelt greetings over the protests of the scouts.

~ My deepest congratulations, he said.

Fal slid an arm round Ehri and held up his own palm, which bore an identical symbol to Ehri's. Their own personal sign, unique to their love. Silo was gladdened at the sight. At least some good had come out of the tragedy, then.

~ You should not have returned, Fal said, his words in direct contrast to the look on his face.

~ Akkad?

~ He still leads us, said Ehri, her grin fading slightly. ~ He hasn't forgotten.

Silo had expected no less, but the news was a blow all the same. ~ I must see him.

~ Wait, Ehri, who is this man? demanded one of the scouts.

Ehri and Fal exchanged a glance, then she shook her head. ~ You know your orders, she said. ~ Take them to Akkad.

The scouts nudged them into motion again. As they did, Silo asked ~ The others?

~ The warrens, Ehri replied, her face grim. That was no surprise, either, but the confirmation of what he'd always known came unexpectedly sharp.

Frey glanced at him as they walked up the trail. No one else came near. They hung back, staring.

'Old friends?' he asked.

'Hope so,' said Silo, looking over his shoulder. 'Tell you the truth, I ain't sure. But if they is, they the only ones we likely to meet.'

Akkad's hut was new, larger, befitting a leader of men. It stood on a slope overlooking the camp. At its front, a covered semicircular balcony jutted out into the air, supported by tree-trunk pillars. It was an impressively elaborate construction, given their tools and circumstances. Not the kind of thing that suggested a temporary stay.

Akkad met Silo on the balcony. He sat in a heavy, crudely carved chair softened with hide throws, his back to the jungle. The sides of the balcony were open, and provided a hundred-and-eighty degree view of the shadowed greenery all around. To Akkad's right stood his wife Menlil, and to his left were three children, a boy and two girls, ranging from eleven to seven years old. A half-dozen others stood at the edge of the room: three bodyguards, a witch-sister, a hard-faced Vard that Silo didn't recognise and a Murthian that he did. Babbad, who had once been a rival of his. No doubt he and the Vard were Akkad's right-hand men.

Silo would have stood in their place, once. Now he stood alone in the gathering, without even the Cap'n for an ally. Frey was being guarded outside. Even Silo had only been allowed in after a thorough check for weapons.

Akkad had become careful. And he was very wary of Silo, it seemed.

~ We all thought you were dead, said Akkad.

Silo spread his hands. ~ Evidently not.

~ You should have stayed away.

~ So I'm told, he replied. ~ But this is my homeland. How could I?

Akkad's penetrating stare never wavered. A gambler's stare. Calculating him.

He seemed more careworn than Silo remembered, but he was still a powerful man. His jungle-stained hogskin jacket was sleeveless and left open for ventilation, showing a lean, muscled torso and big arms dense with tattoos. His tightly curled black hair shone with oil, thick despite his forty-something years. He had a sharp, beaklike nose and a short beard that tapered to a point. A handsome man, often fierce, but capable of great charisma when the occasion called for it.

~ Why have you come? Akkad asked. ~ To see to unfinished business?

~ I have no quarrel with you, Akkad. All that was long ago.

Akkad studied him closely. Working him out. He didn't know what to make of Silo. Didn't believe him. Couldn't understand why he'd come walking in to the camp unprotected, after all that had gone before. He suspected a trick or a trap. Perhaps there was an army waiting in the jungle? Perhaps Silo had sold them out to the Samarlans?

That was Akkad. Always suspicious. Silo thought it best to keep him guessing for now. It wouldn't be long before Akkad realised that he had no cards in his hand. His best hope had been that Akkad had left, or died, or been usurped in his absence. But Akkad was still here.

Silo had no fear for himself. Death didn't worry him. But he wished the Cap'n hadn't come along. He should have fought harder to keep Frey away from this place, forbidden him, even. But he'd decided long ago that his days of ordering people around were done. Nowadays, he only took orders, like a good little slave. He'd given up the right to tell people what to do.

He'd warned Frey. Frey hadn't listened. So it was on the Cap'n what happened to him.

~ I saw many sick people outside, Silo said.

~ The days are cruel, said Akkad.

An old Murthian saying. He was giving nothing away.

~ Yet your numbers have become greater.

~ They have.

~ And have you given your home a name, yet?

Akkad's eyes tightened a fraction. ~ We have.

Silo nodded to himself. It was as he suspected. This was no longer a hideout, a place for dangerous men, plotting war on their oppressors; this was a village.

Akkad took his silence as a judgement. ~ Things have changed since you left us, he said, a hint of anger in his voice. ~ We plan for the future now.

The Vard looked down at his feet, then away. A tiny movement, but Silo spotted it. *Seems at least one of you ain't too keen on your plan for the future. Reckon there were a lot that weren't keen on it back when I was here, neither.*

If Akkad wasn't going to give away any information, he'd have to divine it himself. He decided to push a little.

~ I recognise many faces I knew in the past, he said. ~ It's a credit to your leadership that so many have lived so long in these violent times.

The Vard's gaze flickered up to meet his, just for a moment. The man didn't know Silo, except perhaps by reputation, but he suspected what Silo was implying.

Akkad did, too, and now the anger in his voice was more than a hint. ~ They are alive because I kept them *safe*, he said. ~ Alive to enjoy their freedom, instead of living out their next lives back in the slave pens and work camps. You would have driven them to their deaths.

Silo said nothing. He didn't need to. Akkad had been too quick to defend himself, and he noticed the minute flickers of uncertainty on the faces of the people in the room. All except Babbad, whose face remained rigid.

~ Where have you been, Silopethkai? Akkad asked at length.

Akkad used his full name. Formal. Distancing himself from the friendship they'd once had.

~ Vardia, Silo replied.

~ I had understood that our people were not welcome in Vardia.

~ I did not say I was welcome there.

It felt strange to talk like this. Fencing was a part of Murthian conversation, and he was out of practice. The language was precise and elegant compared to Vardic, which was constantly rearranging itself, buried in slang that changed like the seasons. Murthian was an old and static tongue, rigid and dignified.

~ And now you have returned, said Akkad. ~ Walking from the jungle as if nothing has happened. All those deaths on your head, Silopethkai. Do you imagine they have been forgotten?

~ I did not kill them, Silo said.

~ Yes, said Akkad. ~ You did.

~ You had the choice.

~ I had *no* choice! he said, his voice rising as his fist came down on the arm of his chair. The men and women in the room looked uneasy.

Akkad's gaze locked with Silo. Silo saw no remorse in the eyes of the man who had once been his friend. No regret at all. And so Silo looked away first. Because if Akkad felt no responsibility for what had happened, then Silo carried enough for two.

There were things that weighed on a man's soul. He'd hit a woman he loved, once, while in the grip of one of the wild rages he used to get. He'd never stop being ashamed of that. But that didn't even come close to the events that led to him fleeing this place nine years ago. Fifteen lives, friends and companions, all lost that day. And while he didn't actually kill any one of them, he might as well have done, the way it turned out.

~ Do you remember Gagriisk? he asked eventually.

~ Of course I do, said Akkad. ~ It is a name burned on the heart of every Murthian. Those who did not escape and leave their people's conflict behind them.

That was a provocation too far. ~ I see little evidence of conflict here, said Silo, looking around. ~ There are many ways to escape, Akkad.

But Akkad didn't rise to it this time. ~ You lost that argument, Silopethkai, he said. ~ Good men and women died for it. Now speak your piece, and then I will decide what to do with you.

~ Gagriisk is one of the most notorious murder-camps in Samarla, said Silo, for the benefit of the Vard in the room. ~ Hidden in the poisonous mists of the Choke Bowl. Many years ago, we talked of an assault on that place.

~ You talked of an assault. A bloody and suicidal one. As was your habit.

Silo let it pass. Akkad's churlishness only hurt himself in the eyes of his followers. He didn't remember him being so prickly and easy to rattle. His eyes went to the children standing alongside him. Perhaps eleven years of fatherhood did that to a man. Or perhaps it was the sight of his old friend and old enemy, back from the grave.

~ We obtained a map, said Silo. ~ A map that showed the location of the target in amid the vast, shrouded wastes of the Choke Bowl.

~ I recall.

~ I have come to ask you for that map.

Akkad looked at him for a long time. Silo could see the gears in his mind working, trying to figure out the trick.

~ And what if I refuse? said Akkad, when he'd finally tired of trying to outguess his opponent.

Silo had entered the camp with no answer to that, but an answer came to him now. ~ If you refuse, you won't receive the medical supplies that I offer you in exchange.

The witch-sister raised her head sharply. Akkad glanced at her and scowled. His brow darkened as he turned back to Silo. ~ You presume to offer us *help*?

~ I offer you a trade. You appear to be in need of supplies. Food, too. I can get them for you.

Murthians kept their feelings off their faces, as a rule, although Akkad had always been too passionate to learn it well. Silo's expression was rigid. He let nobody see that the gift he offered was something he'd just thought up, and that he had no idea how he would actually deliver it. But it wouldn't be a difficult thing to fly back to Vardia and buy or rob what they needed. It would cost them two days, perhaps, but without that map they might lose two weeks trying to search for Gagriisk.

Murthians were good at hiding their emotions, which made them seem inscrutable to foreigners, but they were also adept at detecting them. He looked around the people assembled on the balcony. Tiny shifts in expression, unguarded instants, told him what he needed to know. His offer had caught their interest keenly. The sickness must have been worse than he imagined. Only Babbad seemed unswayed, but that was hardly surprising. He'd always been unfailingly loyal to his leader, and would never forgive Silo for what had passed.

But the only opinion that mattered now was Akkad's. He got slowly to his feet, rising out of his chair. He looked to his wife, who was pleading him with her eyes. Then he gave his answer.

Quite a crowd had gathered on the path that led up to their leader's hut while Silo was inside. Frey had watched them trickle up from the camp below, faces anxious, as if they thought something of great importance was going on inside. He was being guarded by two of the young Murthians who'd captured them earlier. His pistols and cutlass had been taken from him. No one spoke to him or answered his questions. All he could do was wait, and trust that Silo knew what he was doing.

The sight of the engineer being led from the hut at gunpoint was not encouraging.

A fierce-looking Murthian emerged from the hut after him, and addressed the crowd. There was general consternation at his words, and many glances thrown sideways at Frey. Then one of the scouts gave him a rough shove, and he was pushed along in Silo's wake. He thought about calling out to his friend, but decided it would only get him a rifle butt in the kidneys.

So they were being taken somewhere. Great. He was as much in the dark as ever. Being a leader was hard enough for him, but it certainly beat being the feller who didn't get to know shit.

It seemed like most of the camp was following as he and Silo were led along a barely visible trail through the jungle. Silo was the object of everyone's interest: Frey was an unimportant afterthought. It pricked his pride a little, even in their current predicament.

He soon lost track of which direction they were going. For a time, there was only the maddening sound of the insects, the distant hoots and growls of things he'd rather not meet, the heat in the air and the damp clothes sticking to his body, the steady trudge of his boots on the red earth.

Then he saw a face he recognised. The Murthian woman who had greeted Silo so enthusiastically in the camp. She'd fallen into step alongside him. She was a striking woman, with the body of an athlete and broad shoulders. Her face wasn't exactly the kind of beautiful that Frey went for, but it had a statuesque quality about it that was hard to ignore. She had the same umber skin as Silo, and thick black hair in coiled ringlets, held back from her face with a beaded band.

'You speak Vardic?' he asked. He remembered how she'd cowed the scouts before, and hoped he wouldn't get hit for speaking.

She looked him up and down, her eyes cold. 'Yuh. Name's Ehri.'

'Frey. Can you tell me what's happening?' he asked, when his escorts didn't seem inclined to interfere.

'We goin' to the warrens,' she said.

'The warrens? Like rabbit warrens?' Frey asked hopefully, envisioning fields and daisies.

'What down in them warrens, it ain't rabbits,' she replied.

Frey cursed. 'I bloody *knew* it wouldn't be rabbits.'

She studied him, apparently unimpressed. 'What're you to Silo?'

'I'm his capt—' he began, then corrected. 'His friend.'

'You the reason he came back here?'

'Reckon he was trying to help me out. I'm in a certain amount of trouble, see. Long story.'

'He must think a lot o' you, to set foot in this place again.'

'What *is* this place?' Frey asked. 'What happened here?' He motioned towards Silo, a bald, lean figure just visible through the trees and the crowd. 'Who *is* that feller?'

'You don't know? Thought you were his friend?'

'Hey!' Frey said, offended. 'I'm friend enough to respect his privacy.'

She considered that for a time, then turned to his escorts. 'You idiots don't speak a word of Vardic, do you?' she asked. One of them sneered and said something in the fluid, musical tongue of the Murthians. She ignored him and spoke to Frey again.

'Who was he?' she said quietly, her eyes on the captive walking ahead of them. 'He was a hero.'

Frey did a double take. '*Him?*'

'I was still young when he turned up in camp,' she said. 'Right away, we knew he was dangerous. I mean, people were afraid of him. He had that madness in him. Like when someone's so angry they can't stand it, so they bury it under a whole pile o' calm.'

Frey thought about that for a moment. '*Him?*' he asked again.

'I guess you don't know him that way.'

'You bloody guess right!' said Frey. 'The Silo I know wouldn't get angry if you cut his feet off and hung 'em round his ears.'

But is that really true? Didn't he chuck a Sammie off a roof once? Hasn't he been stewing ever since you hijacked that train? Shouldn't you really have paid a bit more attention?

'So what *did* he do?' he asked, when it became clear that Ehri wasn't in a hurry to speak again.

'What he did was kill Sammies and Daks,' she said. 'You didn't never see nobody wanted revenge as bad as he did. For what they did to our people, what they did to his family, to him. He wanted blood off 'em, and he got it. Akkad, he was the leader back then. At first, he was worried about Silo, but he saw how the camp got inspired by him. Other people, they worried about gettin' enough to eat, about hidin', about all kinds o' things. Silo, he just wanted to get even. That kind o' single-mindedness, you gotta respect it.'

She was looking ahead as she said it, and there was something in her voice, a hint of wistful fondness. Frey thought she'd felt more than respect for Silo at one time. He might not have been the most perceptive of individuals, but he reckoned he knew enough about women. Well, all except Trinica, anyway.

'So what then?' he urged. He was amazed to hear of this side of Silo's character. He wondered what other secrets he might unearth about the rest of his crew, if only he could be bothered to dig.

'Akkad felt which way the wind was blowin', I guess,' said Ehri. 'Took Silo under his wing. Eventually he got to be second in command, and by then they was great friends. Silo was always there with some new plan, some way to sabotage this or blow up that. Awful good at solvin' problems, he was: he could overcome anythin' if it meant he got to kill some Sammies or free some of our kin at the end of it.'

Frey put the pieces together. 'This Akkad feller, he's still your leader?'

'Yuh.'

'So I'm guessing he and Silo had a falling out?'

'You could say. See, Akkad was always puttin' the brakes on Silo. He saw himself as the sensible one, lookin' out for the good of the settlement, makin' sure we didn't risk too much, makin' sure most of us came home alive. And that was fine by us, don't get me wrong.

The two of them, they were some combination.'

She motioned towards the fierce-looking man Frey had seen before, whom he assumed to be Akkad. A woman and three children were walking near him, picking their way through the undergrowth.

'Then Akkad had a son,' she said. 'I guess that was what did it for him. Suddenly he had something to protect, something to *really* protect, and he wouldn't take *no* risks no more. I mean, he put the brakes on *everythin'* Silo tried.' She wiped her nose with the back of her hand and sniffed. 'Pretty soon it became obvious what he was about. He wanted to stop hittin' the Sammies. Called it a pointless waste of life, that we couldn't do no good that way. It was like a fly bitin' a rushu, goin' up against the Sammie Empire.'

'And Silo didn't like that,' Frey guessed.

'Lotta people didn't. Split the camp. Some reckoned we'd do better to build a new life here in the jungle, try 'n' make the most of what freedom we had. Some of us, it didn't sit well that we should be hidin' while our kin were out there bein' worked to death. One of them was Silo.'

'Reckon I see where this is going,' said Frey. He squinted as a spear of sunlight found its way though the canopy and dazzled him.

'Yuh,' Ehri replied. 'So did Akkad. Silo, he never wanted to kill Akkad. Just wanted to knock him off his perch. But Akkad din't see it that way. A bunch of 'em, they tried to take over the camp, but Akkad outsmarted 'em. Some got away, but they was all caught or killed in the end. 'Cept Silo. The rest that were still alive, Akkad made an example of 'em. Took 'em to the warrens.'

'The warrens without the rabbits?'

'The same.'

Frey steeled himself. He had the unpleasant looming sensation that usually accompanied imminent bad news. 'And what happens in the warrens?' he asked, wincing.

'What you think happens?' She frowned at him. 'You get eaten.'

Frey sighed wearily. 'Bollocks.'

TWENTY-FIVE

THE MURTHIAN WORD FOR IRONY—MOTHER— DYING IN THE DARK—SHOOTING FISH

The entrance to the warren was a circular shaft, a jagged throat of red stone in the jungle floor, some distance from the camp. There was a wooden pulley off to one side, and a worn rope dangling from it, which split at the end into a pair of stirrups. Frey was put next to Silo, and they stood together at the edge while flies sucked at their sweat. He looked down. It wasn't so deep that he couldn't see the bottom, only a dozen metres or so. But that was plenty deep enough.

Akkad gathered everyone around, and he gave a short speech in Murthian. Frey didn't need a translation. He could tell by the tone that it was some self-justifying horse-arse declaration as to why he felt it necessary to lob his prisoners into a pit full of hungry whatevers. Some of the audience – mothers with sickly children, or the elderly who looked sick themselves – groaned and murmured at one point. Most of them didn't seem too happy about what was going on. He wondered what kind of deal Silo had tried to cut with the big man, but whatever it was, it hadn't been enough to wipe away the memory of that failed coup. The engineer was stone-faced as the judgement was rendered.

After that, they were made to put their feet into the stirrups, one foot each, and they clutched onto the rope as they were swung out over the pit and lowered down. Frey caught sight of Ehri in the crowd, standing with the smaller man he'd seen her with earlier. He had an arm round her. Her face was full of anger; his of sorrow.

Then the rock of the shaft obscured them from view. The insects became muted and everything was uncannily quiet. His world narrowed to a circle of dusk overhead. He and Silo held on to the softly creaking rope, so close they were practically hugging, and they sank through the air, which cooled quickly as they descended.

At the bottom of the shaft was an uneven chamber, with several openings at its edges that led into shadow. The light from above, weak though it was, seemed fierce and warm in contrast to the chill darkness that lurked at its edge. Frey looked around without enthusiasm.

'How do I get into these situations?' he moaned to no one in particular. He felt like he should be scared, but he hadn't seen anything to be scared of yet. Vague threats of danger weren't enough to bother him. Not when he'd seen so much of the real stuff.

He was still looking around when something dropped through the air and hit the ground next to him, making him jump. It was a hemp sack. He could see the hilt of his cutlass within, and the grip of a pistol.

'We get our weapons?' he asked Silo.

'Yuh,' said Silo, pulling open the sack. He handed Frey his pistols and cutlass, and took his shotgun and dagger. Frey checked the pistols, found they were empty, and then saw Silo counting through a handful of bullets and shells.

'Any particular reason why they didn't just shoot us?'

'Gunshots make noise. They tryin' to hide.'

Frey rolled his eyes. Silo was feeling obtuse, apparently. 'Chop our heads off, then! You know what I mean.'

Silo handed him bullets for his pistol. 'Ten there. I got five shells.' He started loading them in to his shotgun. 'Old law. Murthians ain't s'posed to kill each other. We got enough people doin' that already.'

'But they can be abandoned in a…' Frey looked around. 'What *is* this place, anyway?'

'Ghall warren.'

'Ghall?'

He shrugged. 'Don't know a word for 'em in Vardic. You'll meet 'em soon enough. They hunt the river banks at dusk, come back to the warren when the sun goes down. We got till then to get out of here.' He chambered a round with a loud *crunch* and gazed steadily at Frey. 'Best way for a Murthian to die is to die fightin'. Most in the pens don't get that chance. Free Murthians…' he trailed off. 'It's the way it is. Gotta respect your own.'

The remaining objects in the sack were a pair of flintstones and a pair of wooden torches, their ends wrapped in fabric and covered in viscous pitch.

Frey looked up at the mouth of the shaft. The rope was being winched back. 'You put a lot of people down here?'

Silo knelt and began chipping the flintstones together. 'There was hard justice in the early days. Some people, they din't take to the bigger picture too well after all the desperation they was used to in the pens.' He struck a spark, and a torch ignited. 'People stole. Hoarded food. Men fought over women, sometimes killin' one another. We din't have no courts out here like in Vardia, nor no time for 'em either. Needed a deterrent for the bad folk.' He straightened. 'Later it got used on good folk too.'

'Your friends?' Frey asked, as he put his cutlass and one of his pistols into his belt.

Silo's shoulders tensed for a moment. Then he relaxed, lit the other torch and handed it to Frey. 'Let's get movin'.'

Silo led the way, with an urgency and purpose to his movements that Frey wasn't used to seeing. He headed for one of the exits from the chamber, thrust his torch inside. A fissure too narrow to pass through. He tried another, and seemed to like the look of it better. Then he picked up a stone and scratched a mark on the wall.

That's a good idea. Marking our route so we don't go round in circles. I should've thought of that.

Frey followed Silo into a cramped tunnel. As the light from the shaft faded behind them, the reality of their predicament closed in on Frey, tight and hard as the rock that surrounded him. Away from the jungle heat, he suddenly felt very far from safety. Whatever was down here, Silo clearly felt it was something to be reckoned with. That was all Frey needed to know. That, and the implication that no one had ever come out of here alive.

They emerged in another chamber, kidney-shaped and more cramped than the first. The only illumination came from their torches now, and shadows jumped in the crevices. Frey began to feel claustrophobic. He couldn't stop thinking about the tonnage of stone all around him, the sheer immovability of their surroundings. Everything around them was dead and tomblike. The scruff and scrape of their boots was an invasion of the silence.

'Your mate Akkad's a nasty bastard, to think up something like this,' he muttered.

'Weren't him,' said Silo. 'Was me.'

'You what?'

Silo looked over his shoulder. 'My idea,' he said. 'Din't have much tolerance back then for them that didn't subscribe to the cause.'

Frey sucked his breath in over his teeth. 'What's the Murthian word for "irony"?' he asked.

'Ain't one,' Silo replied. ''Sides, I'm here 'cause I put myself here. Man's just a great big sum of the choices he made on the way, and what he did with what Mother gave him. Ain't no irony to it, or otherwise.'

'Mother?' Frey asked. The word jarred; it seemed excessively formal, coming from Silo. Scuffers used 'mama' and 'papa.'

Silo's dark eyes glittered in the torchlight. Then he turned away, and didn't say anything else.

Frey watched as Silo made his way around the edge of the chamber, thrusting his torch into various gaps and fissures.

'What are you looking for?' he asked, when it became apparent they weren't moving.

'Brcczc. Ain't none.'

'Then that way's good as any,' he said, pointing at the largest exit he could see.

Silo grunted, made another mark, and headed into the fissure he'd indicated. Frey followed. It was narrow enough to pass through if they hunched their shoulders. After a dozen metres it was blocked by a fall of rubble. Silo lifted his torch and said 'Reckon we can climb up.' So they did.

The upward shaft was even narrower than the fissure, and more uneven. Frey had to squeeze his way through gaps that were barely big enough for his hips. His cutlass scratched the rock and caught on corners as he struggled after Silo.

He was beginning to sweat again, and this time it wasn't the heat. The smoke of the torches was thickening the air and making him cough. The sour taste of suppressed panic gathered in his mouth. He had visions of all that weight of stone coming down on him. Damn, he didn't want to go out that way.

He needed to talk, to take his mind from the oppressive gravity of his surroundings. Silo had made it pretty clear that he wasn't interested in talking about 'Mother,' but the way he said it made Frey think she was something more than a parent. He made a rare intuitive leap.

'You a religious man, Silo?' he asked.

'Show me a Murthian that ain't,' came the reply from up ahead.

'Mother?'

Silo stopped and looked back down the shaft they were climbing. 'Don't, Cap'n,' he said. 'You ain't gonna understand.'

But Frey wouldn't be deterred. He'd suddenly developed a keen interest in anything that stopped him thinking about where he was. 'Just saying,' he continued. 'If you got any prayers up your sleeve, we could use 'em right now.'

'Don't work that way,' said Silo, who had resumed his clumsy ascent. 'She ain't into interventions. She bring a man into the world, and she watch 'n' weep at his troubles, but every one o' her children gotta make their own way. Just like a real mama.'

'Not like mine,' said Frey. 'Bitch dumped me on the doorstep of an orphanage.'

'You reckon that's why you spent the rest of your life tryin' to get attention from women?' Silo asked.

'Probably,' Frey admitted. 'Couldn't give a flying cowshit about the reasons, to tell you the truth. Shagging's fun.'

Silo gave a deep chuckle and shook his head. 'You some sort o' feller, Cap'n. Don't think I never met anyone like you.'

Frey grinned. Absurdly, in the midst of all this, he was enjoying himself, albeit in a slightly hysterical kind of way. He'd learned more about Silo in the last nine minutes than he had in the previous nine years. He felt closer to his engineer than he ever had before, and that wasn't only because he was practically crawling up the man's arse.

The shaft opened out halfway up the wall of a new chamber. Frey heard running water as Silo passed him back the torch and climbed down. He made his way to the edge of the opening, handed down both torches, and climbed down after.

The flames beat back the dark, and showed them part of a low-ceilinged cavern, with the far side still lost in shadow. Before them was black water, slapping and sloshing through a winding channel. That small, restless noise was loud in the silence.

'The water's gotta go somewhere, right?' Frey suggested. Desperate hope ignited inside him at the idea.

'Yuh,' said Silo. 'But water's where they gather. They eat fish when they can't get nothin' bigger.'

'How long you think the light's gonna last, Silo?' Frey asked, waving his torch about to illustrate his point.

A distant cry echoed through the cavern, a sound somewhere between a croak and a shriek. Both of them turned to look in the same direction: the way the water was flowing.

'Still think it's a good idea, Cap'n?'

'I'm not dying in the dark, Silo,' he said, and it was only as he said it that he realised how absolutely, utterly serious he was about that. 'I'd rather meet whatever made that sound than wander till our torches go out.'

It wasn't bravado. Hearing that shriek, an unmistakably inhuman noise, had made the danger he'd been ignoring seem suddenly present and real. But he still feared the lonely, empty dark more than any violent end. Dying unnoticed and unseen, lost and helpless: that was the worst thing he could imagine.

Silo gave an approving grunt. They followed the water along its course, with Silo making occasional marks, until it disappeared into a cleft in the cavern wall. Frey kept a nervous eye on the shadows at the edge of the torchlight as Silo climbed into the water. It came up to his thighs. Frey did the same, and found that the water was surprisingly warm.

They waded into the cleft. Frey was careful to ensure his pistols stayed dry as he went. His cutlass blade stuck into the water, tugging at him like a wayward rudder, but that wasn't much of a concern. It was a daemonically thralled blade that moved of its own accord and was capable of deflecting bullets. Given all that, he assumed it was rustproof too.

'What do you reckon happens when you die, Silo?' he said quietly.

'You really think this is the time, Cap'n?'

'Well, since I'm likely to find out pretty soon, yes.'

Silo looked over his shoulder, saw that Frey meant it, and forged on through the water. 'Me, I'll go back to Mother 'n' get born again,' he said. 'Back in the pens, most likely. But the stuff I learned this time round, it'll all be down there, hidden off in the back o' my mind. And I'll be better next time.'

'You're not scared of dying?'

'Nuh,' he said. 'Ain't keen on losing my liberty, though. S'pose I won't remember. But I reckon I'll remember the sense of it, and I'll want to have it again.'

Frey thought about that. 'What about me?' he asked.

'You ain't Murthian. You're screwed.'

Frey rolled his eyes. 'Yeah, that sounds about right. Members only.'

'Ain't too late to convert to the Awakeners,' said Silo. Frey saw a flash of white teeth as Silo turned his head, and realised he was smiling. 'Mebbe the Allsoul will take care o' you.'

A joke? From Silo? Frey wondered if he'd already died. But it was such an unexpected thing that he couldn't help smiling along.

'Crake would kill me faster than these ghalls would,' he said.

'He'd have to find you first,' Silo pointed out.

Frey looked at his hand. Once, he'd worn a silver ring. A ring that was daemonically connected to a compass, which always pointed towards it. Crake had fashioned it to keep track of his wayward captain when he disappeared on a three-day drunk. He might have used it to find Frey now, but Frey had given it to Trinica.

'I knew that woman would be the death of me,' he murmured, because a bit of black humour was the only way he could deal with the thought of her right now.

'Worse things to die for,' said Silo, and they didn't speak any more for a while.

Trinica. If it all finished here, then it would have finished badly with her, and he couldn't face the idea of that. Despite the ignominious way she'd kicked him off her aircraft, he'd only thought of it as a temporary setback. Something to deal with after he'd got the Iron Jackal off his case. But if that really had been their last meeting, it was a damned pathetic way to be remembered.

The cleft ended in a slope of rubble, where the water splashed down over the rocks into the shadows of a long cavern beyond.

They splashed out of the cleft and made their unsteady way down the slippery rocks. Frey's legs were soaked, and his socks squished in his boots. Once on steady ground, they tried to get an idea of the cavern they'd found themselves in. It was dank and chilly, kinked and narrow, cluttered by protrusions that bulged from all angles. The stream ran through it in a trough of its own making, carved over centuries through the relentless indifference of nature.

There were no obvious exits in sight, but the cavern extended far beyond the reach of their torches, which showed them little except for the tips of the stalactites that hung menacingly overhead.

There was another shriek from a ghall, this one much closer, loud enough to make Frey jump. He turned on his heel, holding his torch high. There, just on the edge of the light, high up on the wall: *eyes*! He cried out and raised his pistol, but suddenly he had nothing to aim at. He could have sworn he saw a glitter of light, reflected from the wet orbs of something monstrous. But when he moved closer and thrust out his torch, there was nothing there. Only an angular hole, a patch of darkness in the red rock.

'There was something there,' he said, breathlessly. He was frightened by how much it had frightened him.

'Calm down, Cap'n,' Silo rumbled. 'Ain't *one* of 'em you got to worry about. It's when you got *ten* of 'em you should be scared.'

'Well, I'm getting an early bloody run-up on it, alright?' Frey snapped. Then something splashed in the water right by his boot heel, and he spun around and fired.

The report of his pistol was dreadful in the silence. Frey listened to the echoes bounce off up the tunnel, his nerves jangling, a wince frozen on his face. He sucked in air over his gritted teeth.

'That was a fish, wasn't it?' he said.

'Yuh,' said Silo.

There was a quiet hissing coming from the edges of the cavern now. An unmistakably sinister sound. The ghalls, out there in the dark.

'Stream goes that way, Cap'n,' said Silo.

'Right,' he said, and they followed it.

TWENTY-SIX

POINT BLANK—THE LAIR—GHALLS— THE LAST STAND

What are they waiting for?

Frey had no idea how long the torment had gone on. Minutes? An hour? More? Perhaps it was his imagination, but the torches seemed to be burning with less vigour than before. And all that time, the ghalls had stayed out of sight.

He could hear them. He heard their soft hisses, from behind, to his left and right, *overhead.* He heard their quiet, hoarse croaks, an occasional distant screech. He caught glimpses of quick scuttling movements, and dusty falls of pebbles that tapped and skittered down the cavern walls. But he never got a look at them.

The dark, he told himself. *They're waiting for the dark.*

Progress through the cavern had been slow. The stream had deepened too much to wade through, and the tunnel walls crowded up to the banks so that sometimes they had to edge around protrusions which threatened to push them in. Every metre gained was made with careful treads, in expectation of an attack at any moment. They dared not let their guard down. But the torches were burning low, and the dark was growing stronger. The massive dark that lived underground.

'Problem,' said Silo, up ahead. Frey moved closer to the Murthian to see what new obstacle had been put in their path, his pistol ready and eyes scanning the blackness.

He saw the trouble immediately. They'd reached the end of the cavern. The stream they'd been following ran right into the stone and disappeared.

'Goes under,' said Silo.

'Can we swim under with it?' Frey asked.

Silo pointed meaningfully at his torch.

Frey shook his head at himself. 'Right, yes. Water puts out fire. I remember.' He was so jumpy, he wasn't even thinking straight any more.

Silo moved the torch around, and found a hole in the wall, a metre off the ground. 'Way through, maybe,' he said.

Frey stuck his torch in the hole. Beyond was a tunnel that looked even narrower than the shaft they'd climbed up earlier. He'd barely be able to fit his body into that space.

'I am *not* crawling through there,' Frey said.

There was a chorus of shrieks from the darkness behind him.

'Although,' he added hastily, 'a little light wriggling would probably be okay.'

He pushed himself into the tunnel, moving awkwardly on elbows and knees, his torch and pistol held before him. Belatedly he realised how terrible it would be if this was a dead end, or if something was waiting for them at the end of it, but by then he was in. Silo made a mark on the wall and came cramming in after him.

Real claustrophobia attacked him now. He couldn't move in any direction but forward. If he'd been certain of a way out at the other end, he might have been able to bear it more easily. But it was just as likely that this narrow passage would pinch closed or bend in a way his body couldn't follow.

'You can do it, Cap'n,' said Silo. 'Ain't no worse than what we already climbed through.'

He realised that he'd stopped, paralysed by the thought of being trapped. He took a shuddering breath and got moving again.

He should never have clambered in to this tunnel. He should never have insisted on going with Silo to the settlement, when Silo was clearly trying to save him from the danger. He should never have picked up that bloody relic and got himself cursed. They were just the latest in a long, long line of bad decisions that he could trace all the way back to one moment, the mother of every calamity that had befallen him since.

Running out on Trinica on their wedding day.

I should've made up with her. Shouldn't have left it like I did.

Too late. Far too late. But at least he had Silo here with him. At least there was that.

The tunnel widened out by a fraction. Frey gave heartfelt thanks to Silo's goddess. He reckoned it was worth currying a bit of divine favour at this point, whether he was Murthian or not.

Eyes and throat burning from the smoke of his torch, he made progress. The tunnel curved to the left, but not tightly enough to jam him. His cutlass caught on the rock for one heart-stopping instant, but it came loose with a tug, and he was off again.

Keep going forward. Keep going forward. He repeated it over and over in his head. It was the only thing stopping him from falling to pieces, and he focused on it furiously.

Then, a sight more wonderful than a hundred chests full of ducats: the end of the tunnel! The cold, black opening would have seemed forbidding in other circumstances, but now it promised freedom, and Frey squirmed towards it as fast as he was able.

He was almost there when a face out of his worst nightmares appeared in the gap. Something that seemed to be all mouth, with double rows of long, thin, transparent teeth gaping wide. It had night-black skin, shiny and wet as a seal's, and bulbous eyes, like a deep-sea fish he'd seen preserved in a museum once, when he'd been dragged there by Amalicia Thade once upon a time. It was a monster out of prehistory, brutally hammered on evolution's forge and then tossed aside for more elegant things.

Its jaws gaped as it shrieked at him. Frey yelled in response, panic-fired and put a bullet point blank through its tonsils. It fell away with a puzzled squawk.

'Cap'n!' Silo snapped at him, as he began to back up frantically. 'They're comin' in behind us, too!'

It was that, and the realisation that Silo had a flaming torch in his hand, that pushed Frey forward again. He thrust his own torch out before him and poked his head out of the end of the tunnel. It emerged close to the floor, so he scrambled through and then pressed himself against the wall, waving his torch about and aiming every which way.

Silo came hot on his heels. As soon as the Murthian found his feet, he shoved his shotgun one-handed into the tunnel mouth and fired with a deafening boom. A fine spray of blood coughed out of the hole and settled on his cheeks and nose.

'Should hold 'em for a while,' he said.

Frey stepped over the ghall that he'd shot, which was lying on its side in a loose tangle of limbs. It was a scrawny thing, its narrow ribcage visible, and it had long, thin arms and legs that ended in webbed digits. It was the size of a child, and its skinny body made its huge jaws seem larger still. Its pupils were enormous and froglike, dilated and blinded by death.

'I never even heard of anything like this,' he said to himself.

'What you don't know about Samarla could fill a library, Cap'n,' said Silo.

'What I don't know about *libraries* could fill a library,' Frey replied. His nose wrinkled in disgust. There was a terrible stench here, too strong to be coming from one small body. 'Let's get a look at this place.' He raised his torch, and Silo did the same, adding his light to Frey's.

The cavern was strewn with bones. Fish bones, animal bones, and that was definitely a human skull right there. Most of them had rotting bits of flesh still attached, and there were chunks of fur and bits of rodents and monkey tails scattered among the carnage. They could see the edge of a black pool, and as their light fell across it, they saw a half-dozen ghalls there, crouched threateningly, with several more slinking out of the water.

'Well,' said Frey. 'This is bollocks.'

More of the creatures were gathering now, emerging from the depths of the cavern where the light didn't reach. They slunk closer with terrible purpose, hissing quietly. No longer afraid, not in these numbers. Frey and Silo had climbed right into their lair.

'Don't shoot 'less they come at you,' Silo murmured, glancing about. He swung his torch one way and then the other. Shadows lunged as he illuminated the nearby folds and cracks in the rock, but Frey saw nothing that might have been a way out. Croaks and shrieks were coming from the blood-splashed hole they'd entered through. As he watched, a ruined tangle of bodies was pushed out of the hole to slop nauseatingly on to the floor, and more ghalls crawled through.

A grim feeling settled on him, dampening his fear, stifling regret and remorse. The kind of feeling he got when all his choices disappeared, and there was only do or die. Or, in this case, do *and* die. But under the influence of this morbid sense of the inevitable, death didn't mean anything. It was just a word to him now.

Time to fight, until he couldn't.

There was a splash as a ghall broke out of the water, and a rapid slapping of wet feet. He swung his torch towards the sound. The creature came fast, but not fast enough. He straightened his arm and shot it through the chest. Its charge became a tumble and it fetched up in a heap near his feet. Frey booted its corpse in the chops for good measure.

The others didn't seem fazed by the death of their companion, or startled by the noise. They circled like careful predators around a wounded beast, probing warily and then pulling away. Frey and Silo retreated before them, stepping backwards over cracked bones and rancid flesh.

His arse bumped against the wall of the cavern, and he realised he could retreat no further. They were hemmed in. The ghalls at the edge of the torchlight seemed to have multiplied, an audience of savage, lipless faces with masses of backward-slanting teeth for catching and ripping. There had to be two dozen at least, slipping from the water or clambering over the rocks like grotesque salamanders.

'Silo,' he said. 'Reckon we're surrounded.'

Silo made a tutting noise. He jammed his torch into a gap in the rock behind them, freeing his other hand, then chambered a new round into his lever-action shotgun.

Frey took stock. Two bullets left in his first revolver. A full one in his belt, and the cutlass too. The need to hold the torch was a handicap, but he wouldn't relinquish the light. Not for anything.

He spat on the ground. 'I'd love to see the Iron Jackal's face when he finds out I'm already dead,' he said with half a grin. 'Now *that's* irony.'

'No it ain't, Cap'n. It's just some shit that happened.'

'That there is the best description of my life I ever heard,' Frey said. 'You do have a way of getting to the heart of things, old mate.'

Silo looked at him, as if surprised by such an expression of affection. Frey was surprised himself, but he didn't think it mattered much now.

'Good knowin' you, Frey.'

Frey gave him a rueful smile. 'Kinda wish we'd done it sooner, huh?'

Silo shrugged. 'It's how it is.' He nodded at Frey's pistol. 'You savin' a bullet for yourself?'

'Nah.'

'Me, either.'

One of the ghalls opened its jaws and made a long, low croak, which was taken up by the others. It rose and gathered until it became an unearthly screech, a primal battle-cry that rang through the cavern and pounded at their ears with its hideous discord.

Frey raised his revolver and shot the two ghalls nearest to him, just to shut them up.

As if that were a signal, the ghalls attacked. Silo's shotgun boomed. Three of the creatures were caught in the blast, pulverised into a soggy mass of wrecked flesh. Frey dropped his pistol and reached for the other, but somehow his hand found the hilt of his cutlass instead, which had jumped of its own accord into his grip. It was a better idea than the pistol anyway, he reckoned, so he pulled it free. It swung out in a vicious arc towards a ghall that was springing through the air towards him, and halved the creature diagonally from collar to hip. One of the chunks thumped into Frey's shoulder and spun off, but he was already into his next swing by then. The sword led his arm, and he could only do his best to go with it.

Silo's shotgun roared again and again, cutting swathes through the ghalls. They were soft-skinned and easily shredded, but they were fast and nimble and came from everywhere. Frey dodged and sliced and thrust, fending off the ghalls with his torch while his sword hand was busy. They feared the flames, but only enough to make them hop back a little and find a new place to strike.

Fresh corpses were sprawled among the old, bleeding over the bones. But more appeared, attacking randomly and without coordination, and more after that.

To Frey's right, Silo fired again, and something clicked in his head. *Five shells. He's out.*

'Take my pistol!' he snapped, sidestepping so Silo could reach it. Silo didn't need telling twice. He dropped his shotgun and snatched the pistol from Frey's belt, bringing it up in time to shoot another ghall that came springing out of the dark.

'Come on then, you toothy little bastards!' Frey yelled. He was suddenly angry. Rage was flooding in to fill the void that was left in the absence of fear. He was angry that he should die down here, angry that his life would be left so unfinished, angry at the bullshit set of circumstances that had condemned him to finish things in the dark.

And by damn, he was gonna take it out on somebody.

Perhaps, in some dim way, they understood the challenge in his voice, because they came at him in numbers then, and Frey was glad of it. *Let's have this over with.* Teeth gritted, he let the blade take him, hacking left and right as they scrabbled and sprang. He felt webbed hands scratching at his body, clawing his clothes, but he threw them aside and stabbed them, or shoved his torch in their faces. Everywhere he glimpsed movement, horrors swarming from the flickering shadows. But his cutlass knew its business, and drenched itself in the thin, salty blood of the ghalls.

Some automatic part of his mind had been counting the shots from his revolver, and he heard the last one ring out with a solemn finality. Something heavy knocked into Frey's off-hand and sent the torch tipping from his grip. He reached after it, but in doing so he exposed his arm from behind the protection of his blade. One of the creatures appeared from nowhere, snatching at him with eager hands, jaws snapping. He pulled his arm hard out of the way, but not entirely: teeth slashed down his bicep in a sharp flood of pain before he flung the damned thing off and beheaded it.

He looked for his torch, but it had rolled away along the wet cavern floor. Its last light underlit a trio of fang-stuffed faces, like daemons out of some macabre children's tale. Then the flame died, and he couldn't see them any more.

Silo pulled down the torch that he'd jammed into the rock, and backed up against Frey. He had only a dagger in his other hand now. It was a pitiful defence against these monsters, but it was the only one they had left.

The ghalls drew back, perhaps sensing that their prey was weakening, perhaps fearing Frey's blade. Silo and Frey, breathing hard, stood in their diminished island of torchlight, their faces and chests spattered with gore.

The battle was suspended for a few moments, but it was a few moments only. The ghalls still surrounded them. It was a temporary reprieve, and the end was inevitable as it ever was.

But then—

'Is that *light*?' Frey said.

It *was* light! Torchlight, illuminating the mouth of a tunnel on another wall of the cavern, that had been hidden in the blackness till now. Torchlight, and the sound of running feet, and—

'Hey!' Frey yelled, with a volume he didn't know he possessed. 'In here! In *here!*'

The ghalls turned their faces towards the new intruders. Voices were calling out in Murthian. The torchlight brightened and flared as they came into view, four, five, six of them, running into the cavern, weapons in their hands.

At their head was Ehri. She barked a command in Murthian and the newcomers opened fire. Rifles cracked and shotguns boomed. Someone threw out a phosphorous flare and furious white light swelled to fill the cavern.

Frey was horrified at what it revealed. The place was aswarm, infested with ghalls, racing about like cockroaches caught in the sudden glow of an electric bulb. It was a scene from one of the hells of the old pre-Awakener religions: prancing grotesques threw shadow-shapes against the walls of some terrible subterranean pit.

But despite the ghalls' superior numbers, they were in disarray. The newcomers stormed into them and they fled, slipping through holes in the rock or sliding into the great black pool in the centre of the cavern. Frey hacked at the occasional ghall who strayed too close to him, but they were too busy trying to get away to pay him much mind now. They were just animals in the end, and the panic spread fast. In minutes, only dead ghalls remained within the range of the flare.

Frey let the tip of his bloody cutlass sink to the ground. He was unable to believe that he was still breathing. Dazedly he gathered up his pistols and put them in his belt, but the effort of standing up and the plummeting adrenaline in his body made his legs give way, and he would have fallen over if Silo hadn't caught him and helped him up.

Once the ghalls were gone, Ehri hurried across the chamber, accompanied by the man Frey had seen her with before, who he assumed was her lover. They both embraced Silo with quick and rough hugs.

~ I wasn't sure you would show, Silo said in Murthian.

~ I wasn't sure you would be here when we did, Ehri replied.

~ Akkad will kill you all.

~ He won't get the chance, said Ehri, her eyes hard. ~ Tonight we will finish what you started. Tonight we will end him.

TWENTY-SEVEN

INSURGENTS—THE PACT—A LACK OF INSPIRATION—ASHUA'S PRICE

Silo listened to the night sounds of the jungle as he watched the last of his rescuers step off the pulley. The warm, wet air brought back a flood of memories and feelings from a time long ago, when he'd been a more passionate man, when the world had been so simple. Black and white. Sammie and Murthian.

He'd slipped through this dark with a knife in his teeth. He'd prowled past guards beneath its cover. He'd seen it lit up with muzzle flashes, the chaos of a firefight. It had been a time of violence, a time of freedom. A time of certainties.

Ehri and Fal stood with him, Fal making roll-ups with his nimble fingers. Ehri was already smoking one. They were older now, but this was the same. This silent togetherness.

He looked over at the Cap'n. Frey was sitting up against a tree, his head bent forward and one hand on his neck. He'd had a rough time of it down there, Silo reckoned. He'd given up hope and got ready for death. Getting pulled back from the brink like that, it wasn't easy to take. But he was stronger than he thought he was, Silo knew that much.

~ You were lucky, Ehri was saying. ~ We lost track of the marks you left in the dark. We had to follow the gunfire. That place is a maze.

~ You found us by a different way, said Silo. ~ But you came none too soon, and I am grateful.

Nearby, three young Murthians sat on the grass dejectedly, tied up and gagged. The scouts that had captured Silo and Frey on the outskirts of the camp, left as guards by Akkad. They'd always left guards in the past, in case friends or relatives attempted a rescue. But

Ehri had brought many friends, and the guards had submitted without a fight.

Fal passed Silo a roll-up, and began working on one for himself. Silo lit it and motioned towards the prisoners.

~ What will you do with them?

~ Let them go, said Ehri. ~ After.

He looked at her in the leaf-choked moonlight.

~ We can either run or finish this, she said. ~ I will not run.

~ All this because of me?

She shook her head. ~ It was happening anyway. Tomorrow, next week, next month. We were ready. But your arrival has forced our hand.

Fal explained, his eyes on the tube of herbs and paper in his hands. ~ There are many who feel as we do, that Akkad has forgotten the plight of our fellow Murthians. He is no longer interested in freeing our imprisoned brothers and sisters. He wants only to hold what he has.

~ He has become paranoid, said Ehri. ~ Every day he tightens his grip.

Silo drew on his roll-up, his thoughts dark. Akkad had been obsessed with disloyalty even before the failed revolt. Afterwards, he must have been many times worse.

~ This is not the same place you left, said Fal. ~ People are afraid. The ghalls have been fed too often. He sees traitors among the innocent, and so makes traitors of their relatives.

~ He'll do anything to protect us, said Ehri bitterly. ~ Whether we want it or not.

She was harder than he remembered, and she was tough even then. But they were different times, when he and Fal had competed for her attention, and she'd been unable to choose between them.

The day he tried to usurp Akkad, Ehri had fallen ill, bitten by a snake. Fal had refused to leave her side. Silo had refused to wait for her to recover. There were too many pieces in place for that. Each of them decided in that moment what or who was most important to them. Ehri had come second best for Silo, but not for Fal. He hadn't been surprised to find them married when he returned, each wearing the band of the other.

They'd made a pact, while planning their coup. If any of them were put into the warrens as traitors, the others would get them out. But in the end there were no 'others'. The only able-bodied one of them was Fal, and he could scarcely save them all on his own. He and Ehri escaped retribution because they'd played no part in the coup, and their names were never mentioned. Silo himself was long gone, having fled for his life.

He hadn't been sure Ehri and Fal would remember the pact. Hadn't even been sure if they'd been the ones who tipped off Akkad to the plan. The snakebite had been a suspiciously convenient get-out for both of them. But that was an unworthy thought, and he'd never truly believed it. The Ehri he knew would have been torn with guilt at not being there when it counted, and she would have done anything to make it up. As for Fal, he went where she did, as always.

He watched the others checking their weapons and making ready. They were well-drilled and purposeful. Among them was the Vard that Silo had seen standing at Akkad's side in his hut. His name was Griffden. The rot in Akkad's world had gone deep, it seemed.

~ How will you do it? he asked.

Fal lit his own roll-up. His fingers were finally still as he breathed in the smoke. ~ Last time we were betrayed. This time we won't be. He suspects nothing. He only has four guards on his hut, and two of them are ours.

~ And you? asked Ehri, dropping her roll-up to the ground and grinding it out.

He caught the tension in her tone, and guessed at its cause. She was the driving force behind this uprising. He should have seen it immediately; it could only be her. She might have been glad to have him back, but his unexpected return threatened her. This was *her* rebellion.

~ I need a map, he said.

~ We heard. You're looking for Gagriisk.

~ And when you have it? Fal prompted.

~ Cap'n needs me.

~ *We* need you! Fal protested, aghast. ~ You're a legend in this camp. You're everything Akkad isn't. He won't even let us raid Sammie camps for the medical supplies we need! But you, you're *ruthless*.

~ He's right, said Ehri, though her voice was tight and her eyes flinty. ~ After we're done with Akkad, if you were with us, they'd unite behind you. People remember what you tried to do.

~ I'm no leader, said Silo.

~ No, said Ehri. ~ But I am. And I would have you on my side in this. They'll follow you.

Silo sucked on the last of his roll-up, hard enough to make his throat burn, then spat in his hand, docked it out and put it in his pocket. An old habit. Leaving smoking dog-ends around the jungle was a sure way to let an enemy know you were near. ~ They followed me once. I won't bear that burden again.

Ehri had taken a step away from him. Something was dawning on her face. Something ugly behind her eyes.

~ You didn't come back for us, did you?

~ No, said Silo. He indicated Frey. ~ I came back for him.

~ A Vard? she sneered.

~ A friend. An old friend.

~ Older than *us*? Fal said in disbelief.

Ehri had turned her face away from Silo. She radiated disappointment. He hadn't come back to reclaim his place. Hadn't come to inspire anyone. He'd come for a map, and then he was going to leave. Turn his back on his people for the second time. Turn his back on the *cause*.

~ Why are you looking for Gagriisk? she said, her voice distant and unfriendly in the warm murk of the night.

~ To free a prisoner.

~ A Murthian?

~ A Yort.

Ehri spat on the ground. ~ What happened to you, Silo?

~ I tried and failed.

~ You tried and *gave up*, she said venomously. She could scarcely disguise her scorn now.

~ Ehri... said Fal, ever the peacemaker. He reached out to touch her, but she shrugged him off angrily.

~ You promised Akkad medical supplies and food, she told Silo. ~ Deliver them, and you'll have your map.

~ That's fair, said Silo.

She crossed her arms. ~ You have transport? For fifty?

~ They'll fit.

~ Ehri! said Fal. ~ Gagriisk? You can't be serious.

~ That place has been a byword for the murder of Murthians since we were born, she snapped, rounding on her husband. ~ There are hundreds of our brothers and sisters being worked to death there right now!

Fal was hurt, his delicate features drawing together into hard lines. ~ And you want to attack it?

~ Yes! And every free Murthian will hear of it. It's exactly what we need to get the young men behind us. To show them that things will be different after Akkad.

Fal shook his head. ~ It's suicide.

She glared at Silo. ~ It's what Silo would have done.

Silo looked down at the ground and nodded to himself. He deserved all the ire she directed at him.

~ We don't need you, she told him. ~ Take your captain. Go back to your craft. By dawn, this will all be over.

~ What about Akkad? he asked. ~ What will you do with him?

~ That's not your concern. You're no part of this.

Silo turned away. ~ Time is a factor. I hope to be back tomorrow, or the next day at the latest. Be ready.

He walked over to Frey. Behind him, he could hear Ehri organising her people. They would sneak back to the camp, and do what had to be done. Silo's path led in another direction.

Frey looked up as he approached, then past him, noticing the activity. 'What's going on?' he asked.

It took Silo a moment to switch his brain back to Vardic. 'Tell you on the way back,' he said.

'We're not going with them?'

'Nuh,' he said.

Frey reached out an arm and Silo helped him up. Frey frowned. 'You alright?'

'I'm good, Cap'n,' he said.

Frey let it drop, and Silo was grateful for that. He wondered then if the reason he'd stayed with this man for so long was not because he had nowhere else to go, or because he feared to come home, but because deep down he believed Frey would *understand* him if his past ever came to light. Maybe Frey was the only man who could.

The day he'd found Frey dying in the crashed *Ketty Jay*, he'd also found the body of a young Dak boy in the hold, shot dead, with a rifle nearby and a bloody bayonet affixed. Since there were no other crew on board, it didn't take a genius to work out what had happened.

They'd both failed as leaders, and they both knew it now, even if neither had ever spoken of it. Their reactions to tragedy had been different, though. Silo chose never to lead again, thinking himself unworthy to decide anything for anyone. Frey carried on being a captain, on the condition that he didn't have to care.

But time had *made* him care. Time, and the things they'd been through since Retribution Falls. And now the weight of expectation was crushing him. Silo saw how it killed the Cap'n to be dragging them through his problems, making them atone for his mistake. It would shatter him if one of them died for his sake.

He wished he had the words to convince the Cap'n that his crew were behind him. That it didn't matter whether it was his problem or everyone's: they were in it together. But he didn't think he could. He didn't have the right to give advice about leadership. Not any more.

Nine years passive. Nine years a slave of his own making. And now here he was, full circle, a lesser man than when he started.

That didn't sit right with him. Didn't sit right at all.

Pinn was frustrated.

He sat on the dirty metal floor of the quarters he shared with Harkins. His little Samarlan gewgaw lay in front of him, on top of several sheets of paper covered in crude diagrams. The damned thing had broken two days after he bought it, and now the clockwork bird sat motionless in its cage, its cheeping forever quieted. But it was still a thing of beauty, a mysterious masterpiece forged by craftsmen who possessed a skill just short of sorcery. And it was most definitely not, as Malvery had repeatedly claimed, 'just a knackered old rip-off piece of junk.'

Harkins was asleep in the lower bunk, twitching violently, as if he dreamed of being mauled by something horrible. Pinn was glad of the peace. Harkins hated him working in the room, and he'd complained about everything: about the light being on, about the noise of Pinn's pen scratching, about Pinn's loud and noxious farts which caused him to gag and which made his vision go dim. But this was Pinn's inventing space, so Harkins had been forced to put up with it, until he was finally overpowered by the meaty fumes from Pinn's arse and slipped into unconsciousness.

Pinn knew he had it in him to be a great inventor. He knew it because he reckoned himself great at everything he turned his hand to. Maybe he didn't know how to make those fiddly little trinkets that the Sammies did, but that was okay. He was an ideas man.

It was just that he wasn't having any ideas.

The toast-and-cat theory he'd put on hold until he could get some more cats. He'd never seen Slag fall off anything and land on his feet. It was completely possible that Slag was a defective cat. He was certainly mentally defective, so it followed that he was weird in other ways, too. Wasn't he about a thousand years old or something? Very unusual. Plus, he was violent, as evidenced by the dozens of plasters all over Pinn's face and head. The scratches still stung.

Slag. Definitely not a good subject for his experiments.

He tried to remember how he made his batch of Professor Pinn's Incredible Flame-Slime, but he found himself at a loss. His experiments at remixing it just ended up with goop. Besides, despite his obvious brilliance in coming up with it – even that pansy Crake was impressed! – he was having a hard time working out what it would actually be useful for.

He'd taken to carrying a small pot of it around with him, searching for some practical application for his invention. The best idea he'd had so far was to put some on the end of a cigarette to make it last longer, but smoking it made him hallucinate. He'd seen something lurking in the shadows of the cargo hold, some awful half-dog half-man half-metal thing – fractions weren't Pinn's strong suit. After that he decided that maybe his Flame-Slime was a bit poisonous.

He'd sat up all night in his quarters trying to come up with a new idea while Silo and the Cap'n were away, but he was short on inspiration. He'd managed a few messy scrawls, and a lot of arrows pointing to different things, but an hour later he wasn't sure what he'd actually been trying to design. It didn't help that both his arms were in slings now, which made it damned hard to draw anything at all. He felt like a man in a straitjacket, or a plucked turkey waiting for the oven.

He dug into his pocket with some difficulty and pulled out a folded-up ferrotype. It was one of two he had of his sweetheart Emanda. The other was in a little frame that hung off the dash of his Skylance. He vaguely remembered some other girl who used to occupy that place –

Larinda? Lisandra? – but whoever that was, she was gone now.

White creases divided Emanda's portrait into quarters. She was in her late forties, almost twice his age, and wearing a low-cut, frilly dress that revealed an expansive bosom. A broad grin was on her face, her front teeth adorably crooked. She had a thick head of curls, probably red, but they might have been brown. He wasn't sure. Ferrotypes only came in black and white, and it had been a few months since he'd seen her.

Usually her picture made him sigh, but this time he thought he detected a judging look in her eyes. *When are you going to be rich, Artis? When are you going to give me all the things I deserve?*

'I'm trying, Emanda,' he muttered. He wiggled his wounded arms to show her. 'It's not my fault.'

None of the crew understood him. Everybody thought they knew about love, but none of them really did. Look at Harkins, mooning after Jez while she ignored him. Look at Frey, chasing that corpse-skinned bitch, when any fool could see she'd put a knife in his back just for giggles. Look at Crake, who thought he was so much better than Pinn, but got all flustered whenever anyone mentioned Samandra Bree. Talk about pipe dreams! She was so far out of his league that... that... Well, he couldn't think of a decent comparison, but it was pretty damn far.

All of them were jealous of him. Because he *had* a woman. A woman who loved him. She'd told him so, or near enough, during that heady few days of drinking and gambling in Kingspire. That was when he decided that a penniless vagrant like him wasn't good enough for a lady like that. Once he got rich and famous, he'd go back to her. Once he could afford to treat her right.

He wondered if she'd heard of his exploits in the Rushes yet. Pinn's grip on reality was always a bit slippery, and in his mind, the rumour had become the literal truth. It really *had* been him that flew that day. *He* had won that race, *he* had landed his aircraft with no engines. Artis Pinn. What a pilot he was. She must have heard by now; it would be all over Vardia. She'd be proud. Proud that she loved a hero.

But his amazing exploits still weren't getting him rich.

With an annoyed huff, he folded up the ferrotype, put it back in his pocket and left his quarters. It wasn't an easy task to open the sliding metal door with both his arms restrained. He wondered why Malvery had bothered to put his burned arm in a sling, instead of simply wrapping it up. It didn't seem to need any support. It occurred to him, as he finally got the door open, that the Doc might just have done it for a laugh.

He encountered Slag out in the corridor, who eyed him menacingly, a rat hanging from his jaws. Deciding if he was disabled enough to be worth savaging again. Pinn aimed a kick at him, but Slag just turned around and padded off with an insulting lack of fear.

Sounds from the cargo bay drew him downstairs: voices, and the whine of the ramp hydraulics. When he got there, he found that the Cap'n and Silo had returned. Grey dawn light filtered in from outside. Ashua and Crake were there too, and Jez followed Pinn in, all of them alerted by the sound of the ramp. It was unusual to see people up at dawn, but the crew of the *Ketty Jay* kept odd hours. Jez didn't sleep, and Crake barely did these days: he'd been looking more and more worn out lately. He was inventing something of his own, apparently. Pinn took it as further evidence of his jealousy.

'Good trip, Cap'n?' Crake asked, yawning into his fist.

'Could have been worse,' he said. 'Why's everyone awake?'

'Inventing!' Pinn declared loudly.

Crake gave him a look. 'I think I might have something to help with your daemon problem, Cap'n, when you've got a minute.'

'Fix that daemon, and you can have my firstborn,' said Frey.

Ashua scoffed. 'As if *you'll* ever have kids.'

'As if I'd want one of *his*,' Crake added.

Frey didn't seem in the mood for a jolly retort. 'Look, we have a problem. There's a camp full of people back there that need general medical supplies and food. Food's easy; meds, not so easy. I don't need to tell you the clock's running on this one.'

'Taking time out for charity, Cap'n?' asked Jez, puzzled.

'It's a trade. They get help. We get our assault force.'

Crake looked questioningly at Silo, who gave him a blank gaze in return. Crake sighed. 'Spit and blood, you really *are* going to waltz in there with guns blazing, aren't you?'

Frey ignored him and appealed to his audience. 'Any ideas about where we find a lot of medical supplies at very short notice? Or does someone want to wake up Malvery?'

'I've got it covered,' said Ashua.

Everyone turned to look at her. 'Sorry?' Frey said.

'Medical supplies. Take me to Shasiith, I'll get you what you need.'

Frey blinked. 'Really?' he asked at length, as if he couldn't believe it would be that easy.

'Yes!' she snapped, exasperated.

Frey became suspicious. 'How much will it cost me?'

'The man I know, he doesn't need money. There's only one thing I can think of that would persuade him to part with that amount of drugs that fast.' She tapped her foot in agitation, took an irritable breath and looked up at the ceiling. Pinn was surprised to see that her eyes shone with moisture. 'The price is that I get to join your crew. Permanently. Until I say otherwise.'

'No!' Pinn cried, horrified.

'No!' Jez protested.

'No!' Crake blurted.

'Done,' said Frey.

TWENTY-EIGHT

HOMECOMING—LEGITIMATE BUSINESS—CRAKE SEES AN OPPORTUNITY—JEZ & THE CAT

The door was opened by a gangly Samarlan girl with hostile brown eyes. She was maybe twelve years old, maybe thirteen, with the elegant features and pitch-black skin of her race. She radiated suspicion and scorn, and a casual, predatory confidence beyond her years.

Ashua wasn't fooled for an instant. She'd been the same way at that age. Despite the superficial differences, she recognised her replacement.

((Let me guess)) she said in Samarlan. ((He found you on the street and he's been improving you ever since. How's your vocabulary?))

'Exquisite,' the girl sneered in Vardic. 'He said you'd be coming.'

'He was right,' Ashua replied.

The girl looked her up and down for long enough to let Ashua know she wasn't impressed, that Ashua wasn't shit to her. Then she stepped back and let her in off the alley.

Maddeus had lived in many places, but they all ended up the same. The fine settees in the hall were frayed and stained. The huge mirror was smeared and bleary. Paint peeled off the walls. Tiny windows let in the dusk light through a screen of grime. Maddeus moved to each new dwelling in a flurry of fresh finery, but his very presence rotted his surroundings. In the three months since he'd moved into this latest hideaway, it had already fallen into neglect.

The girl went ahead of her up the corridor. It was dim and stifling hot. They passed beneath electric fans, which were still.

In the rooms off the corridor, she saw strangers. There were always strangers in Maddeus' home. He surrounded himself with them: strung-out philosophers and decadent artists, stragglers and strays, people who'd wandered into his web and never made it out. The days were short to them, passing by in a muddle of stoned conversation, punctuated by hits of their drug of choice. Once, she'd thought them marvellous creatures, godlike in their refusal to submit to the realities of the world. But they all came to nothing in the end, and she despised them now.

She recognised nobody. She hadn't visited him here, out of respect for his wishes, and it seemed he'd had a reshuffle. Out with the old, in with the new. Another handful of junkies to tickle his interest.

But there was one man Maddeus would never abandon. She spotted him in a study off the corridor, sitting at a desk and sipping mint tea. The decay that afflicted this place had been held off here, but he couldn't keep away the fug in the air and the sickly-sweet smell of sweat and excess.

He looked up over his glasses as Ashua passed the doorway. Osbrey Fole, a taut, narrow man, grey before his time. Osbrey was Maddeus' accountant, among other things. The man who ran his business.

She'd always liked Osbrey, and he, in his way, had liked her. They were a conspiracy of two: the only sober heads in a flock of the deluded. He gave her a curt nod, which was as much emotion as she'd expect from him, and went back to work.

At the end of the corridor was a grand set of double doors. The girl opened them and let Ashua inside.

The room beyond was warm and close. The windows were covered over with thin curtains of green and red. Pungent smoke hung in slowly coiling layers in the gloom. It was full of expensive furniture, yet it felt shabby and dispiriting, and beneath the smell of narcotic fumes there was the hospital scent of the dying.

Maddeus lay reclined on a gilded chaise longue, eyes half-lidded. Next to him was a lacquered tray table, on which lay a silver syringe, a tourniquet and a skooch pipe, among other paraphernalia. A forgotten cigarette, little more than a bent column of ash, smouldered between his fingers.

The girl made to follow Ashua inside, but Ashua blocked her way. 'The cigarette!' she protested.

'I've got it,' said Ashua, and shut the door in her face.

The haze in the air made her feel like she was walking through a dream. She'd forgotten the sense of unreality that pervaded the places where Maddeus lived. As if time and sense had become derailed. She'd been away long enough to get used to clarity.

Maybe that was why he'd told her she couldn't stay with him any more. That she'd have to make her own way in Shasiith. After an adolescence spent at his side, midway between a daughter, an employee and a pet, she'd been cast out.

It had hurt her, but she'd taken to independence with a vengeance. She'd been in Shasiith long enough to know the language and the ways of the underworld, and living on her wits was something she'd been doing ever since she could remember. She cut deals, made allies and enemies, stole when she had to, cheated when she could. She wanted to show him how capable she was. How she didn't need him. And then, the lesson learned well, he'd take her back.

She'd never seriously thought it was more than a temporary thing.

She sat down on the chaise longue next to him, took the cigarette from his fingers and crushed it into an ashtray. He stirred and his eyes opened a little more. A stupefied grin spread across his face.

'Ashua. My darling,' he slurred.

'Hello, Maddeus.'

He reached weakly towards the tray table. 'I don't suppose you'd like to…?' he said.

She stopped his hand by taking it in hers. 'Ah,' he said. 'You never did, did you?'

His skin was dry. The bones of his hand felt hollow and brittle, like a bird's. He looked sallow and wasted. She felt something gather in her throat, and she didn't want to let him go.

He kept smiling that idiot smile. 'I remember the day I met you…' he said, but the sentence was crushed beneath the weight of the colossal lethargy that lay on him.

She was glad. She didn't want to reminisce. She patted his hand. *It's alright. Whatever it is, it's all alright.*

Maddeus coughed and reached feebly for a cigarette. Without thinking, Ashua took one from his gold cigarette case, lit it for him, and put it in his mouth. She'd done it so many times while he was in this state that it was like a reflex.

He took a drag and settled back into the chaise longue with a sigh. She saw him drifting, and squeezed his hand before she lost him completely.

'Maddeus!' she said sharply.

He surfaced from his daze, and he looked at her as if it was the first time he'd noticed she was in the room. His face became concerned. 'What are you *doing* here, my darling? Don't you know it's dangerous?'

She tried a frail smile, but it died on her lips. 'I'm leaving,' she said.

'Hmmm,' said Maddeus, whose attention had already gone elsewhere. She brushed his lank hair back from his face, made him focus on her again.

'I'm leaving,' she said, more firmly this time. 'Leaving Shasiith for good. I'm joining the crew of the *Ketty Jay*.'

He became grave. 'Oh.'

'That's what you wanted for me, isn't it?'

'Yes, yes,' he said, with the vague tone of someone who couldn't remember.

'There's a price. I'm pretty sure you won't mind. Medical supplies. I've got a list from Malvery.'

'He's the doctor, isn't he?' Maddeus smiled broadly, but his eyes shimmered with tears. She felt something surge up inside her chest, something that made her breath shudder, a feeling of such terrible enormity that it would burst her. She turned her face away from him quickly. How much of that sorrow was him, and how much was the drugs? Was there any difference any more?

'I'll give the list to Osbrey, shall I?' she said, her voice a hoarse whisper.

'That'd be best. He'll take care of it.' His eyes fluttered closed, and she thought for a moment that he'd fallen asleep. Then he spoke again, barely forming his words. 'This captain, what's he like?'

'Mordant.'

He snorted. 'That's not a sentence, darling, but I'll forgive you this once.' He stirred and groped across the tray. His fingers brushed past the tourniquet and found the silver syringe. He sighed with pleasure. 'Will you… call the girl for me?'

Her eyes prickled as she picked up the syringe and the length of rubber tubing. 'There's no need,' she said softly. 'I'm here.'

* * *

'He's late,' said Crake, holding up his pocket watch.

Malvery peered over his round, green-lensed glasses at the daemonist.

'Well, he is!' Crake protested.

'He's a wholesaler. We're buying food. This is the least dodgy thing we've done for months. Calm down, eh?'

Malvery looked over the balcony of the café and down into the street. Below them, donkeys and rushu brayed and lowed, carts creaked, people jostled and called to one another. On the far side of the dusty river of traffic was a warehouse, its worn wooden gates thrown open. Fair-haired Dakkadians sauntered in and out of the baking gloom within.

'Takes time to load up that much food,' he assured Crake. He fanned himself with one beefy hand. 'And they don't do anything fast in this country.'

Crake put away his pocket watch, picked up a Vardic broadsheet that he'd bought from a boy on the street, and snapped it open. It was yesterday's paper. The front page bore the headline which had put him on edge: *Mentenforth Vandals still at Large.* Beneath it was a ferrotype of the domed ceiling of the Mentenforth Institute vault, which Malvery had autocannoned a great big hole in.

There was no mention of them. That meant Bree and Grudge hadn't told the Press, which meant… well, he wasn't sure *what* that meant. But it was too hot to get concerned about things.

He sat with his feet up on a chair, sweating in the shade of a parasol. The parasol was held up by a circular wrought-iron table, upon which was a pot of spiced tea and a carafe of sweet local liquor. Malvery had been steadily working his way through the carafe for the last hour, and he had a lazy buzz on. Crake, who was drinking the tea, was altogether more jumpy. He didn't like being back in Shasiith. He was afraid the Sammie soldiers would catch up with them.

Malvery, for his part, was reassured by the chaos and complexity of the mad sprawl that surrounded them. Hard to imagine anyone finding anyone in a place like this. They'd taken precautions, registered their craft under a false name, and Jez kept the *Ketty Jay* moving from dock to dock around the city. It had taken a bit of time to sort everything out – another night wasted that they could scarcely afford – but everything was on track now. He and Crake would get the food. Ashua was handling the medical stuff.

The Cap'n, for his part, had gone to see Trinica Dracken, who was in the city somewhere. With that compass of his, he could find her anywhere, and she obviously didn't mind being found, since she still wore the ring. Whatever was going on between them, Malvery didn't want to know; but the Cap'n said he had a plan for attacking Gagriisk, and it involved her, and that was that.

'Look at this,' Crake said, looking up from his broadsheet. 'There's a town in Aulenfay that's publicly declared they'll fight the Archduke if he tries to outlaw the Awakeners.'

'Bad stuff going down,' he murmured.

'Peasants! They must know the Archduke won't stand for that!'

Malvery took a sip of liquor. He didn't like discussing religion with Crake. Crake's loathing of the Awakeners meant that he tended to rant. Malvery didn't believe in the Allsoul — it was all too obviously made up by disappointed royalists trying to make their last king into a messiah – but he didn't much mind if anyone else did. Problem was, the Archduke didn't share that view. He'd been dying for a chance to get rid of them. And that meant things were going to get ugly.

They'd fought two wars to keep Vardia free, and word had it the Sammies were getting ready for a third. But instead of sticking together, they were squabbling amongst themselves. He didn't dare think what might happen if someone didn't back down. Vardia hadn't seen a civil war since the Dukes deposed the monarchy. The idea of his countrymen fighting each other made him angry. It was their *country*, damn it! They were Vards first and everything else second. When did people forget that?

It was the Cap'n who gave the Archduke the ammunition he needed, when they came back from the Wrack a few months ago. Malvery should have stopped him. But he just let it slide, the way he always did.

His thoughts turned grim, and his buzz faded. He drained his cup and filled it again in the hopes of getting it back. It didn't work.

Suddenly uncomfortable, he stretched, slapped at a fly on his neck and looked around the café balcony. A lone waiter drifted about. Sammies and Vards sheltered from the fierce sun beneath the parasols, sometimes at the same table. The scene had become sinister to his eyes, the air humming with plots and the secret mutterings of spies. How much longer would this go on, this tentative peace?

Were the Sammies even now eyeing up their neighbours, jealous of their abundant aerium? Would there come a time when the smuggled supply through the Free Trade Zone wasn't enough to match their dreams of greater empires?

Things were changing. He could feel it. And he didn't reckon they'd change for the better.

His mind went to his encounter at the Axelby Club. He'd been turning Hawkby's offer over and over these past few days. A steady job in an asylum, treating the demented. And maybe after that, a surgery of his own. It had sounded wonderful at the time, but now he wasn't so sure. The thought scared him slightly. Or, to be more accurate, the *drink* scared him slightly.

He remembered what it was like before. The routine. The same places, over and over. Home, surgery, club. He feared that rhythm. Where there was a rhythm, he found places where he could fit a drink, and soon those drinks became the beats of his day. He'd become regular as clockwork in his old life: a quick drink to get him going in the morning, another before his morning consultations, one between each consultation while he was writing up his notes, one at lunch to relax him for the afternoon surgeries. He'd stay off the booze while he was operating, but he'd be gasping at the end of the day, so he'd have another to get him to the club. Then he'd start to *really* drink.

On the *Ketty Jay*, he spent a fair amount of time bored, but he was hardly ever in the same place for more than a few days. Sure, he got drunk, but he was usually sharp enough when the crew needed him. You never knew when you were going to get into something when the Cap'n was around. That random element actually served to keep him relatively sober for most of the day, or at least to stop him getting hammered. He didn't want to let his mates down by being a big fat comatose whale while they were off risking their necks.

But scared or not, he was still tempted by Hawkby's offer. He wanted to feel like he was *worth* something again. He wanted to feel like that young surgeon who'd earned a medal by rescuing soldiers from a battlefield.

'You thought about what you'll do if... y'know?' Crake put down his broadsheet. 'If what?'

'If the Cap'n don't make it.'

'Malvery!' He was shocked.

'Oh, come on. Don't pretend it ain't crossed your mind.'

'The Cap'n is *not* going to die!'

'Oh, aye? Got some way of stoppin' it that we don't know about?'

Crake became shifty. 'Maybe I do,' he said.

Malvery waited. Crake sipped his tea.

'Well?' Malvery demanded. 'Do you or not?'

'I don't know!' Crake cried. 'I've got some ideas, that's all. It's all theoretical!'

'The Cap'n was carrying something around with him today. A metal ball with a couple of wires coming out of it. Wouldn't say what it was. Was that one of your theoretical ideas?'

'Yes.'

'What does it theoretically do?'

'Theoretically? It means the Iron Jackal won't be able to find him.'

'The Iron Jackal? That's what he's calling it?'

'That's what the sorcerer called it in the Underneath.'

'Oh.' He sat back, interested now. 'How's it work?'

Crake put down his tea, eager for the distraction. The tiredness fell away from his face. 'It's like this,' he said, steepling his fingers on the table. 'This curse, if you can call it that, I think it's actually a very advanced form of daemonism. There'd always been evidence of primitive daemonism before we applied the sciences to it, though it was hard to distinguish from superstition. The Samarlan sorcerers have done it for centuries, it seems. But *this*! This is daemonism decades ahead of our time, and it's thousands of years old. To bond a daemon of such intelligence and sophistication to an object, to give it such complex instructions… You know, it may be that the daemonism we know today is simply the remnants of something we knew how to do long ago, and forgot, which we've been painstakingly relearning ever since! And if that's the case, it'd turn everything we know about daemonism on its head! I'd be *fascinated* to know where and when that relic came from.'

Malvery chuckled at his friend's evident excitement. 'Blimey, it's obvious what fires *your* engine.'

Crake grinned. 'Yes, well. One of the things they somehow did, and I've no idea how, is they've made the Cap'n into some kind of… some kind of *beacon*. He's putting out a signal, and I think that's what the Iron Jackal uses to find its target. There's no question of him getting away. It always knows where he is.'

'And you think you can block it?'

Crake snapped his fingers. 'Exactly. Competing frequencies interfere and cancel each other out. That device I gave the Cap'n is a modified resonator, which should – *theoretically* – cut out that signal.'

'I'm sensing a *but*,' Malvery said.

'But, the problem is power. My portable batteries are so big you have to cart them around in a backpack, and even they only last a short while. Unless the Cap'n wants to stand by a plug socket the rest of his life, I can't cut out that signal for long.'

Malvery frowned. 'So what use is it, then?'

'With a small battery pack, he can cut it out for a few minutes. Now I don't know how the daemon hunts, but maybe it'll give the Cap'n a chance next time it comes for him. And what I *do* know is that there's only three nights left before the full moon, and the Iron Jackal still hasn't put in its second appearance.' He tapped the table nervously. 'I've got some other ideas too, but they're not ready yet. I've been going as fast as I can.'

Malvery could believe it. Crake looked about ten years older than he was. 'Sounds like you're doing a bloody good job, mate.'

Crake gave him a half-smile to acknowledge the compliment. He looked the doctor over uncertainly, then said: 'You know, not so long ago I was thinking about leaving the *Ketty Jay*.'

'You were?' Malvery was surprised to hear that Crake's feelings had been running so close to his own.

'Yes. I decided that... Well, I'd gone as far as I could go.' He fidgeted awkwardly and lowered his voice. 'I'm a daemonist, Malvery. That's who I am. And while I stay on the *Ketty Jay* I'll never have access to the proper equipment. I'll always be limited by that.'

'You've got a talent and it's going to waste,' said Malvery, smoothing his moustache with a knuckle. 'I get that.'

'But this business with the Cap'n, it's given me a bit of a jolt. Forced me to think on my feet. I don't have state-of-the-art gear, so I'm having to make do with what I have. What's happening here, it's a unique opportunity.'

'An opportunity, you say?' Malvery's tone indicated what he thought of Crake's choice of words.

'You know what I mean. I'm doing my damnedest to be ready in case the curse isn't lifted when – *if* – we return the relic to its rightful place. But I'm not blind to the scientific value of all of this. As far as I know, no one's ever reliably documented the methods that I'm trying out.'

Malvery felt slightly uncomfortable about the idea of the Cap'n being anyone's guinea-pig, but he reckoned it would be churlish to make a thing of it. After all, Crake was doing a lot more about the situation than *he* was.

He flexed his hand back and forth into a fist, frustrated. 'I wish I could, I dunno, be more useful. I mean, I can help out with relics and all that, but a daemon? A daemon that you can't bloody *see* and you never know when it's coming? I get to thinkin', what if that was me in the Cap'n's shoes? Waitin' for that thing to come and get me when I was alone.' He took a drink. 'I'd be scared to buggery.'

'He *is* scared to… er… buggery,' Crake replied. 'Look, we don't know when it's coming next, but we know when it's coming last. On the full moon. And he won't be alone that time, I promise you that.'

Malvery coughed on the liquor. 'Let me get this straight: you're gonna *take on* that thing?'

Crake looked down at the table. 'I'm going to try,' he said. Then he gave a terrified little smile. 'Let's hope it doesn't come to that, eh? We'll put that relic back, and all will be well.'

'Blimey,' said Malvery, with genuine admiration. 'You're a braver man than me.'

'I doubt that,' said Crake.

They sat back in their chairs and listened to the hubbub of the street below, sharing a companionable silence for a time.

'You know what does scare me, though?' Crake said suddenly. 'The thought that I might have missed out on this.'

'This?'

He waved a hand across to indicate the café and the scorched, grubby city around them. 'This. Here. Now. I was really thinking about leaving, you know. I was so fixed on the idea that I *needed* to do this thing, that I needed a sanctum of my own. I was going to leave my friends behind and go live in some stuffy, safe world of my own. A nice little existence with no hard choices and no nasty shocks. And there'd be no more visiting strange new places, no more saving whole cities like we did at Sakkan—'

'No more dating Century Knights,' Malvery said.

Crake flushed and looked downcast. 'Yes, either way there'll be no more of that. I'm quite sure she'd shoot me if she saw me again, and I'd deserve it too.'

Malvery chuckled. 'Still. Samandra Bree. Even the Cap'n can't say *that*.'

'I can't deny, being on the *Ketty Jay* does put you in the thick of it.'

'That,' said Malvery, 'is bloody true.'

Crake looked uncomfortable, and Malvery realised that he was more upset about Samandra Bree than he'd been letting on. He probably shouldn't have laughed, in hindsight, but it was a bit late now.

'So have *you* thought about it?' Crake asked.

'About what?'

'What you'd do if the Cap'n was gone?'

Malvery sipped his liquor. 'Aye,' he said. Down by the warehouse gate, a thickset Dakkadian was waving up at him. Malvery raised a hand in response. 'Breaktime's over. Let's get to it.'

'You know,' said Crake, as they got to their feet. 'I rather like being an honest trader. It's quite relaxing. Makes a change from getting shot at all the time.'

'Don't get used to it,' said Malvery, and they left.

Fang and flurry and hot blood bursting in her mouth, the salty victory of the kill. The musty stench of the rat, her hated enemy, filled her nostrils as it struggled in her pinning grip. She marvelled at how the flesh gave way before the points of her teeth and claws. Such a soft sheath for a life, so easy to penetrate.

It was a small rat, no contest at all. Not like the bigger ones down in the depths of the craft, monstrous foes almost as big as she was. But big as they were, she didn't fear them. Some were more dangerous than others, but they all died the same in the end. She'd never been beaten in a fight by anything.

Except once. One of the warm tall beings that clomped and stank in the wide spaces of her world, the corridors and cargo bays. The gangly, nervous one, who'd trapped her and flown her into the endless terror of the sky and then...

She wasn't sure. It was a smear of feelings rather than an ordered sequence of events, like all her memories. All she knew was that the gangly one was not to be trifled with.

She devoured the rat, tearing open its belly and gobbling the innards. She was mistress of the kill. This was rightness.

Slag ate, and Jez ate with him.

It was hard to know where the cat ended and the person began. She was sewn into the fabric of him, her instincts muddled by his. Her body sat in the pilot's seat of the *Ketty Jay*, but her mind was divided. One part was with her body, still aware, ready to lift off from the landing pad at the first sign of trouble. The other was a passenger in Slag's brain, down in the warm vents and crawlways of the *Ketty Jay*.

Slag, for his part, didn't understand what was happening. He was aware of her, she knew, but he had no concept of the implications. Once, he'd feared her, sensing the Mane in her; but now she was a familiar presence, and he was as comfortable with her as if she were his litter-sister. She'd soaked into him, and it was like he'd known her for ever.

She ate her fill with him and then groomed herself, finding comfort in the ritual of cleaning, the rough scratch of tongue on fur. Sated, she felt the need to sleep. It would be good to find a spot to curl up. She looked up and down the narrow vent. Everything was in black and white, like a ferrotype, and the vents were bright and sharp as a full moon.

That way.

She took off in that direction, padding down a vent towards a junction. Faint light filtered through a fan overhead; more than she needed.

That way.

And that was the way she went. Except suddenly she wasn't sure whose thought it was that had directed her. It had seemed too clear to be the cat's, too focused and decisive. But she was only a passenger here, along for the ride. Wasn't she?

Was it a coincidence that Slag had twice gone in the direction she picked?

Stop.

She came to a halt and began to idly lick her paw.

The other paw.

She put that paw down, and started on the other one.

Slag didn't seem in the least distressed by this. He thought the idea to lick the paw was his own. But it wasn't. Jez was sure of that now.

Stretch.

And she did, a luxuriant lengthening of the spine.

Well, now, she thought to herself. *Isn't this something?*

TWENTY-NINE

A NOVEL USE OF TECHNOLOGY—AN INVISIBLE ENEMY—THE SLAUGHTER-YARD—DEAD MEAT

Frey pressed himself up against the wooden wall of the corridor, his eyes wide and his heart pounding.

Couldn't have been.

He leaned out and looked round the corner. Down a short half-flight of rickety steps was a doorway to the street. Beyond was light and bright fabrics, dust and noise and chaos. A thoroughfare like a thousand others in Shasiith, hammered by the afternoon sun, hot as a kiln. And off the street were more doorways and alleys and passages: shadowy tributaries to the blinding river of humanity that ran between them.

Couldn't have been.

Maybe he hadn't seen what he thought he saw. Damn, the sun in this country was enough to give any man a touch of the strange. And no one could blame him for being jumpy.

Last night, he'd sent a message to the Trinica on the *Delirium Trigger*, to ask for a rendezvous in secret. When the time came, he decided to walk instead of going by rickshaw. He needed to rehearse his apology. And after that, he needed to work out how the spit he was going to persuade her to help him. Assuming, of course, that she turned up at all.

Wrapped up in his thoughts, nervous at the prospect of their meeting, he'd hardly been paying attention to the people around him as he walked. Hardly noticed his surroundings. It was only chance that he looked up when he did, and noticed the crumbling stone alleyway, and the Iron Jackal lurking in its shadow.

He'd thought himself safe in the day. Night was the time for horrors. Night was when he couldn't sleep for fear that the Iron Jackal would come when his eyes were closed, when he couldn't even have a drop of Shine to take the edge off because he needed to be alert in case… in case…

Couldn't have been.

He clutched Crake's device in his left hand. A chrome ball, the size of a large apple. It was featureless except for a single press-stud. Two slender wires ran from it to a battery pack that hung at his hip. The pack was heavy and clumsy and had been bashing against his leg all day, but Frey had gladly endured it. He'd take any chance he could get right now, and Crake's invention was the only one offered to him.

You'll only get a minute or two out of this, Crake had said, as he was strapping the pack to Frey. *Don't waste it. Find a hiding place and hold down the stud. It won't work if the daemon can see or hear you, but it might stop it finding you by other means.*

Agitated, he retreated from the corner, further up the corridor. Where was he, anyway? It was a dim wooden back-alley, a raised passageway that ran parallel to the street, with several doors leading off it, all closed. At one end was a rectangle of light, and a hubbub of voices and activity. He was protected from the sun here, but not from its heat, and the warm, soupy air drew sweat from his skin.

Halfway along the corridor, he stopped. *Had* he seen it? It was nothing more than a glimpse, really, and given how wound up and exhausted he was, the odd hallucination here and there was nothing to be surprised at. As the seconds ticked by, he became more and more certain that it hadn't been anything at all.

Until he heard footsteps on the stairs.

His heart bucked in his chest. He drew a revolver with his free hand – an unthinking response to danger – and his body tensed, ready to run or fight. But probably run.

The panic only lasted a moment. The footsteps were too light, too fast to be made by the thing he feared. A middle-aged Dakkadian woman in dusty hemp robes came into view, carrying an armload of white sheets. She froze as she saw him, sucking in a shocked breath. Her narrow eyes widened at the sight of his revolver.

He shoved it quickly back in his belt and held up the empty hand to show her he meant no harm. 'Sorry,' he said. 'Sorry. My fault. Thought you were a horrible daemonic monster.'

She frowned at him, evidently decided he wasn't a threat, and hissed something in Samarlan that sounded insulting. Then she hustled past him, still muttering. He slumped back against the wall, letting out a sigh of relief.

A long, rattling snarl made his blood run cold. He turned his head slowly.

It came up the steps into the gloom, a hulking, blade-fingered shape that filled the passageway. It brought the darkness with it, shrouding itself in shadow. It twisted towards him, muzzled head cocked at an angle. The red gleam of its mechanical eye shone keenly against the blackness.

Frey backed up, tripped on his heel, turned and fled.

The Dakkadian woman hadn't yet reached the end of the passageway. She spun around as she heard him running, and shrieked in alarm, thinking he was about to attack her. He shoved past her instead, knocking her against the wall, too scared to care about chivalry. She fell over in a bundle of sheets, and he raced past her and out into the light.

The passageway came out onto a raised plank walkway running through the middle of an enclosed square. Grubby apartments were stacked up on all sides, their balconies rusted and plaster walls cracked. To either side of the walkway were dye-pits, lurid circles of purple and yellow and red. Dozens of Dakkadians worked around the pits. Men stirred the thick dye with poles; women spread dripping fabrics onto racks, their arms stained to the elbows. Prowling along the walkway were three Samarlan overseers, keeping an eye on the slaves below.

Frey looked back over his shoulder. Maybe the Iron Jackal was confined to the darkness. Maybe sunlight would protect him. That hope died as the saw the Iron Jackal come lunging up the passage on all fours. It sprang over the fallen woman and landed in a predatory crouch on the walkway. In full view of everyone. Except that nobody was looking at it. They were all looking at *him*, wondering at the crazed foreigner who had come sprinting into their midst.

The nearest Samarlan, seeing Frey approach at pace, stepped back uncertainly. Then, reaching a decision, he dropped into a low stance, ready to tackle the intruder.

'What are you doing, you moron?' Frey screamed at him in disbelief. 'Get out of the way!'

But the Samarlan wasn't getting out of the way. He lunged when Frey was close enough. Frey clubbed him round the head with the chrome ball he was holding. The Samarlan pitched limply off the side of the walkway and plunged into a pit of purple dye. Frey scampered down a short set of steps that took him to ground level, and ran off between the dye-pits while workers were still trying to fish their unconscious overseer out with their poles.

The Iron Jackal didn't need steps. It leaped off the walkway, over the heads of the oblivious workers, and landed in Frey's path. He skidded to a halt and then dashed off in another direction, running along the line of the vats, colours burning in the sunlight as he passed.

The workers scattered out of his way. Others clapped and jeered, enjoying themselves at a madman's expense. None of them saw the towering hybrid of animal, machine and man that ran through the dye-pits in the madman's wake, outpacing him easily, bearing down on him.

Frey spotted an open door at the base of the apartments that surrounded the dye-pits. He put his head down and sprinted for it. He didn't dare look behind. The Iron Jackal was upon him, surely. In an instant he'd feel those bayonets in his back, the way he'd felt one in his guts long ago. The sickening, precise, impossible pain as blades punched through skin and muscle. Now? Now?

Now?

He threw himself through the door, spun and slammed it shut. He caught the briefest glimpse of the Iron Jackal, bearing down on him like a steam train, and then the door met the jamb. He backed away, one step, two, three, waiting for the door to shatter into splinters, the beast to crash through.

Four steps. Five.

Six.

He stopped. The door was still there.

The Iron Jackal wasn't coming through.

Somehow, that was worse.

He was in another corridor, this one made of plastered stone. It led between half a dozen identical doors with numbers on them. Apartments, he presumed. He ran past, his armpits, thighs and back soaking with sweat now. At the end was another door: heavy, wooden and slightly rotted.

He pushed it open and found himself in a narrow lane crushed between tall buildings on either side. Other alleys crisscrossed it: a back-street maze. A thin stream of filthy waste-water trickled past his feet. Bits of litter were half-submerged in the mud, absorbed by the ground, made part of it. The air stank of too many people and something worse, some vile reek that he couldn't place.

To his right, the lane came out onto the busy street where he'd first spotted the Iron Jackal. No point going that way: crowds didn't deter the daemon, and they'd only hinder him. So he turned left, and went into the maze.

Off the main thoroughfares, Shasiith was a haphazard muddle of lanes and passages that curved and plunged and rose with the landscape. Makeshift steps – stones buried in red mud – had been put where they could fit. Alleys that were barely wide enough for two abreast stood between leaning buildings of three or four storeys, reducing the sunlight to a distant glow. It was possible to hear people talking and children playing, the sounds of washing-up, a dog barking; but Frey didn't see anyone at all, and the city felt eerily deserted.

Frey ran for a minute, enough to get himself thoroughly lost, and then pulled up to catch his breath. He was at the bottom of a shaft in the middle of several buildings, an atrium to allow light in for the interior windows, which were covered with dirty shutters. Foul water dripped from an outpipe with a streak of green mould beneath it.

He judged that he'd put some distance between himself and his pursuer now. Once, he might have felt safe, but he knew the Iron Jackal would find him again, just like it had last time. He lifted up Crake's chrome ball and put his thumb over the stud.

'This better work, Crake,' he said, and pressed the stud.

Nothing happened. Absolutely nothing. Crake had told him that its effect was invisible, but when he'd been demonstrating it to Frey, it had hummed in his hand and vibrated. It hadn't been much, but it was enough for Frey to be able to tell it was on. Now, it was just an inert piece of metal.

Horror crumpled his guts. He turned the sphere round in his hand and saw a small dent on one side, where he'd whacked that overseer round the head.

'Oh, right,' he said quietly to himself.

There was a clattering growl from above.

He didn't need to look. He bolted.

The Iron Jackal dropped into the atrium, landing with a thump and a sharp hiss of hydraulics. Frey was already plunging down an arched stone passageway, searching frantically for an escape. Tight corners and narrow spaces were the only way he'd stay ahead of the creature: it would beat him in a straight race.

At the end of the alley was a T-junction. He was approaching too fast to see which way was best, so he picked one and went for it. He sprinted into a new alley and saw a corroded metal gate standing open ahead of him, on his right. He heard the sounds of animals, and smelt the source of the stench he'd detected earlier.

None of that deterred him. There were no other exits along the length of the alley, and he could hear the Iron Jackal pounding up behind him. Whatever was beyond the gate, it wasn't worse than getting caught. He pelted through, his lungs burning in his chest, the daemon hot on his heels.

It looked like the site of a massacre. Everywhere, red and glistening flesh, freshly stripped of its skin. Headless, limbless carcasses hanging from hooks. Piles of guts and organs spilling off tables. Moving between the carnage were men in gore-smeared aprons, wielding long knives and machetes. The hot air buzzed with flies and reeked of new death.

A slaughter-yard.

The area was fenced off into various pens. Dakkadians lined the fences, shouting orders to the butchers, who killed the beasts in front of them and began carving them up on the spot. Chickens squawked and cows lowed, instinctively distressed. A bull, secured by handlers in metal stocks, was having its throat cut as Frey came racing in. Blood splashed into buckets while the bull's hooves skidded in the mud as it pissed and shat itself.

The sordid efficiency of the scene might have nauseated Frey in other circumstances. But he was too busy running for his life to care.

He sprinted through the yard, between the pens. A Dakkadian butcher stared at him as he passed, a freshly beheaded chicken still twitching in his hand. Customers exclaimed in surprise and made way. He glanced over his shoulder, just in time to see the Iron Jackal leaping through the gates, its teeth bared in a snarl, its mismatched eyes fixed on him.

But twisting his neck while running at full speed caused him to wobble, and his foot went out from underneath him in the churned mud. He tumbled, crashing shoulder-first into a stack of small cages full of rabbits. The cages toppled onto him, bouncing painfully off his back, and some of them broke open, freeing the animals inside.

He heard cries of alarm and anger as he scrambled desperately to his feet, driven on by fear of the daemon. The butcher in the pen emerged from behind hanging rows of rabbit skins and stormed over, a bloody knife in his grip. But Frey saw that it wasn't only his accident that had disturbed the people in the slaughter-yard. The animals had gone berserk. Chickens threw themselves against their cages; cows thundered about, eyes rolling; geese honked and flapped. Frightened customers backed away while butchers fought to control their animals. A herd of pigs broke through a fence with sheer weight of numbers, squealing as they climbed over each other. The yard was suddenly in chaos.

I'm not crazy! Frey thought as he ran for the far end of the pen. *The animals sense it too!*

He pushed his way through people who were fighting to get out. Pigs and rabbits darted about, zigzagging past butchers trying to recapture them. Jostled and shoved, he lost sight of his pursuer. He spotted a small gate on the edge of the pens, leading into the surrounding buildings, and went for it, barging panicked Daks this way and that. When he reached the gate, he paused, scanning the yard for a sign of his adversary.

It was there, between the pens, standing upright on its hind legs. The only still figure in the chaos. Daks and animals ran this way and that around it, but none touched the invisible thing in their midst: the horror with its hunched back and spiked-chain spine, machine parts sewing in and out of its moist fur, half its muzzled face made of black metal.

It was watching him. Like it had all the time in the world. Like it knew he couldn't get away.

It's playing with me, Frey though. *It's damned well playing with me!*

Then it came for him, bounding through the crowd.

Just inside the gate was an anteroom, with empty racks and grubby, bloodied tables pushed against the walls. The only exits Frey could see were a narrow set of stairs leading up and a heavy metal door on the far wall. He didn't want to go up, so he took the door instead. The handle was heavy and cold to the touch as he turned it. When he hauled the door open, he saw why.

Rows of carcasses stretched away from him, swinging gently on hooks, receding into an icy fog that stirred in the breeze from the door.

The meat locker.

He turned away, thinking he could make it to the stairs instead. He was just in time to see the Iron Jackal loom through the gateway to the slaughter yard. That black eye of Trinica's fixed on him. He let out an involuntary shriek of fright as it lunged towards him, then he slipped inside the meat locker and pulled the door shut.

Not fast enough. The door was inches from the jamb when a hand bristling with bayonets clamped around the edge. The door hit the Iron Jackal's fingers with a clang. But it didn't close.

He let go of the door and fled into the depths of the meat locker. He pushed his way through sides of beef, racks of ribs, a forest of hard-frozen flesh. The cold enfolded him, chilling his skin with frightening speed. He was only wearing his lightest clothes, and even they had been too much in the heat of the Samarlan afternoon. Here, they were no protection at all.

The far wall appeared out of the fog. No way out. *Course there's no way out, it's a damned meat locker!* But he *needed* a way out, so he went towards the corner, slipping in between the rows, pulse thumping in his ears.

Stop moving. Think.

He stopped. Listened.

Somewhere out there, he could hear the heavy breathing of a large animal.

He ducked down to look beneath the hanging carcasses, hoping to get an idea of where the Iron Jackal was. The white fog foiled him, suggesting phantom movements everywhere.

He tried to make a plan, but his thoughts were tumbling over themselves. He couldn't see the daemon, but the daemon knew where he was. Maybe it couldn't pinpoint him exactly, but it knew enough to track him down. He peered between the obscuring slabs of meat. It could come from anywhere.

The chrome ball was still clutched in his hand. If only that overseer hadn't had such a thick skull.

Then he noticed something. There were two wires coming from within the ball, running to the battery pack at his waist. One was more slack than the other, hanging loose. He pulled up his shirt and checked the pack where it was strapped to his waist, and as he did so, the end that was supposed to be attached to the pack fell free.

He'd yanked out the wire when he swung it at the Sammie, and it had come loose of its clip. The bloody thing wasn't broken at all!

He raised his head. A huge silhouette crossed the row ahead of him; but then it was gone, without seeing him. Quickly, he ducked away, and slipped off in the other direction, moving as silently as he could.

Just give me a few seconds, you son of a bitch.

He tucked the ball under his armpit and snatched up the loose end of the wire. With both hands free, he coiled the wire around the battery terminal and secured the clip.

Now we're in business!

The thump of the daemon's clawed feet warned him an instant before it attacked. He threw himself back as a handful of blades slashed through the air towards him. They ripped into a frozen carcass and tore it in two. Frey tripped and crashed into a side of beef, hard as a wall. He fell to the ground, the chrome ball dropping with him. Somewhere in amid all the fog and flesh was a monster, close enough to grab him and tear him to pieces. He scrambled away on his hands and knees, snatching up the ball as he went. The beast snarled, hacking through carcasses to get at its prey, setting them all to swinging on their hooks. Frey found space to stand, got to his feet and ran for all he was worth in whichever direction he was facing.

Ahead of him, a blank wall. *No, no, no. Wrong way!*

He looked to his left, along the rows. And there it was: the door. He heard the thump of clawed feet again: the Iron Jackal, racing along the rows. Done playing now. Intent on the kill.

He burst through the open doorway, out of the meat locker, back into the anteroom. His one and only thought as he crossed the boundary was to close the door behind him, to trap the thing, shut it inside. But two of the butchers were just coming in from the slaughter-yard with cleavers in their hands. They saw him coming out of the locker, recognised him, and charged.

His revolver was out in a moment. He fired at the ground in front of them, and they faltered. They backed away, hands held up. Frey looked past them into the yard, and saw more of their fellows coming, drawn by the gunshot.

'Shit,' he muttered. He didn't have time for this. He ran for the only quick exit he had: the stairs.

The stairs turned back on themselves and let out onto a short corridor with doors to either side. At the end was a large window. There was no glass in it – few windows had glass in Shasiith – but it was shuttered against the sunlight.

Frey heard someone or some*thing* crashing up the stairs behind him. He sprinted the length of the corridor and threw himself at the shutters. They were flimsy, and splintered before him, sending him tumbling out onto a sloping roof. His legs went from under him and he bounced and rolled before plunging off the edge and into the alley beyond.

The drop was only a couple of metres, a single storey, and the floor was packed mud rather than stone. It was still enough to knock the wind out of him, and it was only because he landed well that he didn't break a bone. Gasping for breath, his vision blurred with pain, he raised his head. Right in front of him was a cart full of hay.

Why couldn't I have bloody landed on that?

The owner was nowhere to be seen, having left the donkey that drew the cart tethered up in the deserted alleyway. Frey scrambled under the cart. He only had seconds to act before the Iron Jackal appeared. In the hot shade under the cart, he fumbled the chrome ball into his hands, and pressed his thumb down on the stud.

It vibrated in his hands.

There was a loud impact above him as something heavy landed on the cart, and the bottom suddenly dropped towards Frey. He cringed and squeezed his eyes shut: it took a second before he realised he hadn't been squashed. One of the wheels had snapped, and the floor of the cart was now tipped at an angle, mere centimetres above him. But he was still here, and still holding down the stud for all he was worth.

The donkey was braying frantically and pulling against its tether, making the cart wheels scrape back and forth. Frey was caught between trying to catch his breath and trying not to breathe. He gasped silently like a landed fish and did his best not to move.

The cart creaked above him as the Iron Jackal shifted its weight.

He heard a long, low snarl. Angry. Suspicious. Suddenly, a flurry of savage movement: hay went flying everywhere, landing in clumps to either side of the cart.

You can't find me, you bastard, he thought, terror making him defiant. *You can't find me.*

Then the cart lurched again. Another impact, this one lighter. The Iron Jackal, launching off.

He listened, not daring to move. The donkey gradually stopped bucking and braying.

He kept holding down the stud until long after the ball had stopped vibrating, and the battery pack had died.

After the donkey had been calm for several minutes, he crawled out into the light. He still half-expected the Iron Jackal to be hiding on top of the cart, waiting to stab him in the back from above. But there was no sign of it, and something told him it had gone.

He'd survived the second visit. That only left the last. If the sorcerer was to be believed, the Iron Jackal wouldn't give up a third time.

He coughed and spat. Aching everywhere, he made his painful way up the alley. He still had a rendezvous with Trinica to get to. And he was pretty sure the damned daemon had made him late.

THIRTY

THE NAMELESS—JUGGERNAUTS—FREY IS PARANOID—THE WATER GARDEN

'What happened to *you*?' Trinica asked, laughing. Then she saw the look on his face, and the laughter drained out of her. 'What happened?' she asked again, serious this time.

Frey sat down next to her on the broad stone steps that led from the shrine behind them to the river below. He was muddy and tattered, his hair was everywhere, and he stank of sweat and dead animals.

'I've had a bit of a bad day,' he said.

She reached towards him, hesitated, then brushed the hair away from his forehead with quick and uncertain movements. The concern in her eyes forced him to turn his head away as tears threatened. Exhaustion and fright had made him overemotional. He took a few breaths to get himself under control.

'You want to see inside the shrine?' she asked, out of nowhere.

He didn't want to see inside the shrine. He couldn't have cared less about it. But she sensed the state he was in. She sensed it, and pretended she didn't, and she was giving him something to distract himself until he was ready to talk.

Damn, this woman was so *right* for him. Nobody understood him like she did.

'Yeah.' He nodded and managed a smile. 'That'd be nice.'

She got to her feet, bringing her parasol with her, and held out a hand. He took it, glad of the excuse to touch her. The effort of standing up made him wince.

It was the old Trinica who had appeared today, the one he'd almost married. She was wearing short trousers, sandals and a shirt, exposing slender, marble-white limbs that glistened with an unguent for protection against sunburn. Frey hadn't seen her wearing so little for more than a decade. Even beat up and filthy as he was, he suddenly found himself very interested in all that unclothed skin.

Her chopped-off white-blonde hair had been fixed into a style that she carried off well. While she still hacked her hair, these days she never did it so much that she couldn't make something out of it when she wanted to.

She saw him staring at her. 'What?' she asked with a smile.

'You know what.'

She rolled her eyes. 'Darian,' she said, and it could have meant anything. But he thought she was pleased.

She was in a lighthearted, girlish mood today. Their sour parting had been forgotten, and there would be no apology necessary from either side. He was glad of that. He was rubbish at apologies at the best of times.

She chatted about nothing as she led him up the stairs towards the shrine at the top. Her manner was such a contrast to the horror he'd experienced on the way to meet her that his spirits began to return. So what if he looked a mess? Trinica had forgiven him. That was a result.

The shrine was a simple semicircle of white and weathered columns beneath a flat roof. It was plain in comparison to the grand and elaborate buildings he could see crowding the far bank of the river and clinging to the bridges that spanned it. Dakkadians and Samarlans passed by, going unhurriedly about their business, or loafed on the steps, watching the boats on the river, but none came inside.

It was a relief to be out of the sun. The shrine seemed dim in comparison, even though it was open on all sides to the light. Inside the shrine, nine huge alabaster figures stood against the flat rear wall. None of them had a face. They were blank and smooth. There were six identical males and three identical females, the difference being the height, the shape of the body and the length of the hair. Other than that, there was no decoration at all. It was a white, quiet, empty place.

Frey looked from one statue to another, and back again. 'Their gods are really boring, huh? Who are this lot?'

'The Nameless,' said Trinica, with a wry glance.

Frey snorted. 'Should've known, really. Honestly, folks worship all kinds of shit. You know, I just found out that Silo believes he'll be born again in another body after he dies.'

'Of course he does. He's a Murthian.'

'How comes everyone knows about that except me?'

She patted him on the arm. 'Books, Darian. You know, if you open one, you'll find it full of words.'

'Words, eh?' Frey said. 'Tell me more.'

'Well, for instance, in books there are stories about the old gods of Samarla, and how they once lived on Atalon among their people. It was a paradise, and nobody wanted for anything. But the people became corrupt and decadent, and they stopped worshipping their gods. Evil grew in them—'

'*Now* it's getting interesting,' Frey interjected.

She gave him a look. 'Evil grew in them, and this evil became manifest. A plague – the translation is literally soul-plague – swept through the land, killing the good. Many people died, but only the most pious, the most faithful. And then the gods began to die too. One by one they fell, killed by the ungratefulness of their subjects. And the evil people saw them die, and thought that they might not be gods after all, and made war on them. The gods departed the world in despair, rising up into the sky on a pillar of fire.'

'Right,' said Frey. 'Pillar of fire.'

'A little open-mindedness wouldn't hurt you, Darian.'

'I dunno,' he said. 'Every time I open my mind, things fall out.'

'That explains a lot,' she replied. 'Anyway, listen, you'll like this bit. As punishment for the soul-plague, the gods unleashed seven great beasts of unstoppable power to destroy the paradise they'd created. They were called the Juggernauts. They roamed the land, destroying settlements, eradicating crops, slaughtering anything that moved. The people hid, and starved, and prayed to the gods for mercy. It took a hundred years of suffering before the Juggernauts stopped, disappearing as mysteriously as they came.'

'So what's up with the no-face thing?' Frey asked, gesturing at the statues.

'I'm getting to that. For hundreds of years after the Juggernauts, the gods were silent, and the scattered tribes reunited. In that time, a man called Nezzuath appeared, and he—'

'Wait,' said Frey. 'Let me guess. He claimed he could speak to the gods.'

'Oh, Darian. So cynical. You think you're so wise in the ways of the world.'

'Hey, I *know* the ways of the world. Let's not forget, I wasn't the one born with a silver spoon in my arse.'

'No,' she said. 'Just a colossal chip on your shoulder.'

'Touché.'

'Do you want to know about the Nameless Ones or not?'

'Not really,' he said. Then he grinned. 'But I do love to hear you talk.'

'Well, shut up and be educated, then.'

'Yes, ma'am,' he said, falsely contrite.

She composed herself again. 'Nezzuath,' she said, 'claimed he could speak with the gods.'

Frey cracked up. She swatted him, but he couldn't stop, so eventually she had to hustle him out for fear of offending the locals.

'You're a terrible student, you know,' she said, as they walked down the steps towards a street that ran along the river bank. The parasol rested against her shoulder, casting her into the shade. She couldn't stop smiling, and that made him smile too.

'I've been told,' he replied. Then he stopped and frowned, looking off into the distance.

'What is it?' she asked, catching the change in him.

'Nothing, I…' he said, still staring. Then he shook his head. 'Sorry. There was a woman over there, a moment ago. I thought…'

He thought it was Samandra Bree.

No, it couldn't have been. He'd only seen her from the back, for an instant, as she disappeared round a corner. It could have been anyone. She'd been wearing light travel clothes instead of a greatcoat, and she'd been bareheaded, with thick dark hair spilling down her back. She was a Vard, but there were plenty of Vards in Shasiith.

But still, something about the way she moved had caught his eye.

'Darian? I'm still here,' said Trinica.

He shook himself. *Getting paranoid, Darian. No way Bree could have found you here.* 'Sorry. Nezzwozz-whatever could speak to the gods, yes. Then what?'

She gave him a look to check he was taking it seriously. He put on his best serious face. She closed her eyes and shook her head in mock despair.

'Well, *he* claimed that the gods were still angry with the people for their ancestors' faithlessness. He said they weren't worthy to speak the names of the gods or look upon their faces, and they certainly weren't worthy to worship them. The gods' names would be stricken from the records and forgotten, their images erased. But there was hope: the gods had told him that they would choose one representative on Atalon to be their voice, and when they died the mantle would be passed on to their first son or daughter. Nezzuath, and his descendants. The people were meant to obey and worship him in their stead. And one day, when they were judged obedient and contrite enough, the gods would return and bring paradise again.'

'But in the meantime, they had to do everything he said.'

'Exactly. That was the first of the God-Emperors. The line's remained unbroken for thousands of years since.'

Frey stopped at the bottom of the steps and looked back up at the shrine. 'So that place isn't really a shrine at all, then? It's a reminder.'

'Yes. It's forbidden to worship there.'

'Huh,' said Frey. He sniffed. 'I know I should find this culturally fascinating and all, but actually, it's just a bit weird.'

'You're hopeless. I give up. Someone else will have to civilise you.'

'Good luck to 'em.'

Standing there, the river flowing before them and the sun blazing in an azure sky, she put her arm around his waist and laid her head against his shoulder. It was done so casually, and felt so natural, that it took him a few seconds before his mind caught up with the implications. His heart began to pump hard. He looked down at the top of her head, nestled against his collar. Her eyes were closed.

She's holding me, he thought in disbelief.

She gave a little sigh. 'Darian?'

'Yes?'

'You really stink.'

He burst out laughing, and the tension of the moment was gone. 'You always did know just the right thing to say.'

She let him go. He was surprised at how sharp his disappointment was. She danced a few steps away from him, then gave him a childish frown. 'I have a question.'

'Which is?'

'You are aware that it's hot enough to fry a fish out here, aren't you?'

'I'd noticed, yeah.'

'So why are you wearing a glove?'

Frey looked down at his hand, and the fingerless glove that covered it. His good mood faltered. 'Ah,' he said. 'About that…'

He wouldn't show her in public, so they went into a nearby water garden where there would be privacy. On the way, he explained everything that had happened to him. The moment when he'd handled the relic and been bitten by it. The Samarlan sorcerer's prophecy. His meeting with Crickslint and how they'd robbed the Mentenforth Institute. Silo's homecoming.

He told her about the Iron Jackal, too, how it had appeared to him three times now. But he left out any mention of how the daemon was a patchwork of his subconscious; and how it had one of her eyes, the black eye of the pirate queen, and it was plated in pieces of the *Delirium Trigger*'s hull.

He told her all that, but he didn't think it hit home until he took off his glove and showed her his hand.

She sucked in her breath sharply. 'Oh, Darian,' she murmured.

The corruption was no worse than it had been the first day he saw it, but it never got any easier to look at. The black spot still sat in the centre of his palm, gangrenous tendrils radiating out from it. It didn't hurt, and it didn't restrict the movement of his hand, but he could feel its presence in his flesh. The daemonic mark, condemning him to death.

Unless he returned the relic to its rightful place. Unless he gave back what was stolen.

They sat on a bench in a stone arbour, beneath a ceiling of vines. Water trickled over rocky miniature waterfalls nearby. A lily pond spread out before them, and trees rose up beyond. Dragonflies darted through the air in jerks, and birds flitted from branch to branch. The water garden was a many-tiered maze of hideaways: a place of calm in the chaos of the city. Frey needed a bit of calm right now.

Trinica held his hand in hers, her gaze flickering anxiously over the mark, as if searching for a way to prove it a fake.

'How long?' she asked.

'Three nights.'

'And you have the relic?'

'Back on the *Ketty Jay*. Still have no idea where it came from, though.'

'What will you do?' She sounded helpless.

'There's a place down south. A facility, like a work camp or a mine or something, hidden in the Choke Bowl.'

'Gagriisk. I know of it.'

'That's where they're keeping him.'

'Who?'

'The Yort explorer feller. The one who found the relic. Reckon he can tell us where it came from.'

'So you have to get him out?'

'Right. Basically, we're gonna plough in there, shoot everyone, and rescue his arse so he can rescue mine.'

She let his hand go, and sat forward, staring out over the lily pond, her elbows on her knees. Her fingers twisted and knotted themselves. He wasn't used to seeing her so agitated.

'It's a fortified target, Darian,' she said. 'Have you thought it through?'

'We'll have help,' he said. 'Fifty-odd Murthians. Revolutionaries or whatever.' He shrugged. 'They sound like they can fight better than my lot, anyway.'

'You don't have any more subtle way of doing it?'

'I don't have time for subtle.'

She looked down at the ground between her pale forearms.

'Three nights,' she said quietly.

'Hey.' He touched her shoulder, and she met his gaze. 'I'm not dead yet, you know.'

She held his eyes for a moment, then turned away and nodded. 'What can I do?'

'I need the *Delirium Trigger*.'

Her brow creased. 'You need… Why?'

'The compound keeps a few aircraft on hand. A few fighters and a small frigate. Not much, but it's too much for the *Ketty Jay* to handle, and both my outflyers are out of action. Fact is, if we launch a ground assault on that place, they'll take to the sky and decimate us. But if the *Delirium Tr*—'

'No,' she said.

He was taken aback by her bluntness. 'No?'

'I'll go with you if you want. I'll fight with you if you need me to. Ask anything you like of me. But not my crew.'

'You're their captain,' he said. 'They'll do what you say.'

'Exactly. I'm their captain. And this isn't their fight. They don't know you, Darian. Most of them don't even like you. What am I to tell them? That I'm leading them into battle for no reward? Risking their lives for no purpose that they care about?'

Frey felt suddenly exasperated. Her qualms didn't seem all that important in the wake of the terror he'd recently experienced. 'Don't tell them anything!' he said. 'Last I heard, the *Delirium Trigger* wasn't a democracy. If you say fight, they'll fight.'

'Yes,' she said. 'And that's why I can't ask them. Don't you understand, Darian? Being a leader is a position of *trust*.'

'I get that, Trinica!' he said. He was getting frustrated and angry. 'I'm taking my *own* crew into the firefight, remember? You don't think I feel guilty enough as it is?'

'But they're your friends. They're willing to stay at your side. They have a reason that my men don't.'

'Trinica, look at my hand,' he said, holding it up.

'I've seen it.'

'Look again!' he snapped.

She glared at him sharply, then did as he asked. She couldn't do it for long.

'There's no other way,' he said slowly. 'If you say no, I'm gonna die. It's that simple.'

She didn't say anything. Her jaw was clenched, the muscles of her neck tight.

'It's only a few aircraft,' he said, softening his tone. 'Your men won't even have to break a sweat. Shoot 'em down. Drive 'em off. Whatever. We'll be doing the dirty work on the ground.'

'Don't ask me to do this, Darian,' she said. 'Don't make me choose between my crew and you.'

He closed his hand. 'I don't want to die, Trinica,' he said. 'The question is, do *you* want me to?'

THIRTY-ONE

THE CHOKE BOWL—OBSERVERS—A CAREFULLY TIMED APPROACH—THE CHARGE— SILO INTERROGATES

The fouled air stirred and turned in slow coils. Overhead was a dirty yellow murk, thickening as it descended until it lay leaden on the ground in a soupy mist. The earth was poisoned and dead. Sulphurous vents were open wounds, seeping fumes; geysers and craters were smoking pustules. There were sad marshes, their waters streaked with metallic greens and greys. The silence was huge, broken only by dull and distant booming sounds.

The Choke Bowl.

Frey lay on the lip of a desolate ridge, squinting through the spyglass. It was hard to see through his goggles, but taking them off would only make his eyes itch and tear. His breather mask was sweaty and uncomfortable, rubbing at the bridge of his nose and rasping against the stubble on his chin. Everything reeked of rotten eggs.

'They couldn't have built it somewhere a bit less horrible, then?' he asked.

Ehri was lying next to him on the ridge. 'Sulphurous lowlands. Only place for mining allium. Rare and expensive. They use it for jewellery.' The sneer in her voice was detectable even through her mask.

Beyond her was Fal, and on Frey's other side was Silo. The Rattletrap that had brought them here was parked downslope. A klom away, on a flat and desolate plain, was Gagriisk.

The compound encompassed dozens of buildings and a small quarry, surrounded by a high wall dotted with guard-posts. It was roughly divided into three sections. The first looked like administrative buildings and guards' quarters and so on. The second was the pens, a compound within the compound. There he could see rows of long buildings: sleeping quarters for the slaves. The third section was the quarry, which was almost invisible at this distance, a kidney-shaped smear that took up three-quarters of the space inside the wall. Standing amidst the buildings was a tall metal tower, a gas derrick, surrounded at its base by a complex apparatus of pipes and enormous tanks.

A frigate hovered at anchor on the far side of the compound, a hulking shadow at the limit of his vision. There was a landing pad outside the walls with a cargo freighter sitting there, but no sign of the fighters Ashua had mentioned. Presumably they were stashed in the belly of the frigate, ready to deploy.

It was hard to make out detail, even with a spyglass. The drifting yellow vapours turned everything to a haze. But as he scanned the compound there was something that caught his eye and made him frown. He passed to the spyglass to Silo.

'Left side, just inside the wall,' he said. 'What d'you reckon?'

Silo took a look. 'Anti-aircraft gun,' he said at length.

'That's what I thought.' Frey swore under his breath. 'What the spit do they need an anti-aircraft gun for? Apart from, y'know, shooting down aircraft.'

'This place ain't just a work camp,' said Ehri. 'It's a prison. Always the chance someone'll try 'n' rescue whoever.'

'I thought the Sammies just executed anyone they didn't like.'

Fal raised his head. 'There's always exceptions, for one reason or another. People they don't want to be found, people too valuable to kill, people they just wanna punish slowly, interrogate, torture. They get sent here.'

'Course, they don't send 'em out to work down in the quarry with the Murthian slaves,' said Ehri, bitterly. 'That'd be too shameful, even for a criminal.'

Frey still couldn't get used to the way that Ehri and Fal spoke Vardic with the same Draki accent as Silo did. He checked his pocket watch.

'What time do you have, Silo?'

Silo checked his own pocket watch and called the time, which matched with Frey's exactly. It was late afternoon, although it was difficult to tell in the unsettling gloom of the Choke Bowl. The sun was a dim disc, and most of its scorching heat had been swallowed, leaving the air tepid and cloying.

A series of low booms sounded in the fog.

'What *is* that?' he asked.

Fal said a word he didn't recognise. 'They live in the marshes,' Ehri added.

'There's something out there that can *breathe* this shit?' Frey asked in amazement.

Ehri shrugged. 'They don't give the slaves masks. Too expensive to keep replacin' the filters.'

'And what happens?'

'They last a year. Fifteen months at most, before they're too broken down to work. Then they get shot.'

Her tone was matter-of-fact, but Frey could hear the thrumming anger underneath. She took the spyglass from Silo and trained it on the camp.

'The pens,' she said. 'The gates gonna be guarded, but if we can get through them, we can let out the slaves. That's the priority.'

'That's *your* priority,' Frey said.

'We let the prisoners out, they overrun the camp,' Fal reasoned. 'Gotta be three times as many slaves as guards.'

'And while you're doing that, we'll be looking for Ugrik.'

'While we're drawin' their fire, you mean,' said Ehri.

Frey was unmoved. 'We've both got our reasons for doing this.'

Ehri snorted and looked off into the distance. 'Your woman better show up,' she said.

'She'll be here.'

'On time?' Fal asked. 'They'll hear us approach. If she's not on time…'

'She'll *be* here,' said Frey irritably. He was annoyed at the implied doubt, doubly so because it touched his own. He wasn't at all sure of her.

In the water garden in Shasiith, she told him she'd be there. But the way she said it, it felt like a goodbye. Things had been going so well between them – barring his minor lapse of judgement in her cabin on the *Delirium Trigger* – but it occurred to him now that he was placing an awful lot of trust in her. It had only been a few months since she'd been merrily betraying him left, right and centre. Wasn't it naïve to expect her to change now? The same kind of naïvety he scoffed at when pretty girls gave themselves up in the hope that they could change him?

No. He'd seen it in her eyes, when he showed her the black spot on his palm. She was afraid for him. She wouldn't let him die.

He was certain.

Kind of.

He brought out the compass from his pocket. Over the last few months it had become a habit to stare at it while he was blissed out on Shine. It was a connection to her, always pointing to where she was. It made him feel closer to her, knowing she was wearing the ring he gave her.

It was pointing north, which told him nothing. He had no idea how far away she was. Shasiith was north: she might never have left. Or she might have left, and she might never have found the coordinates he'd left at the rendezvous, even though he'd daubed the chest in ghostlight paint, which was invisible to the naked eye but showed up brightly through polarised goggles.

He'd been forced to do things in an infuriatingly roundabout way. Ehri wouldn't give up the coordinates of Gagriisk until she had the medical supplies, but without them he couldn't tell Trinica where to go. Trinica couldn't come with him to Ehri's camp because the *Delirium Trigger* was too big to conceal anywhere nearby. And there was no time to go back to Shasiith. So he'd been forced to give Trinica a rendezvous point just north of the Choke Bowl, where she could pick up the exact location of Gagriisk.

Except that a dozen things could have gone wrong. She had to fly overnight from Shasiith, find the stash in the dark, and then hide in the Choke Zone until morning, when it would be bright enough for the attack. That was, if she was coming at all.

If all had gone to plan, she was on her way even now, approaching from the north. If it hadn't, she was probably back in Shasiith. Either way, the compass afforded no answers.

'She'll be here,' he muttered to himself. He really hoped he was right.

He was still worrying about it as he sat in the pilot's seat of the *Ketty Jay*, an hour later. The yellow murk writhed lazily past the windglass of the cockpit. Jez kept casting concerned glances at him, which he ignored. She was wearing a breather mask for appearance's sake, so as not to alarm the Murthians, but she hadn't bothered with goggles.

He checked his compass again. It hadn't moved. But then, if Trinica was heading towards him, it wouldn't.

Still, though. Shouldn't it maybe move a *bit*?

'Time, Cap'n,' said Jez.

Frey busied himself immediately, glad of the distraction. He fed aerium gas into the ballast tanks and warmed up the thrusters. Footsteps sounded from the corridor behind him, and he turned in his seat to see Silo in the doorway.

'Your people ready?' Frey asked.

'Yuh. More than ready. Some o' them kids ready to shoot each other if they don't get at the Daks.'

'We'll be coming in pretty rough, I reckon,' said Frey. 'You're my man down in the hold. We need to do this right.'

Silo nodded and headed back up the passageway, boots clanking.

'Heading oh-five, Cap'n,' said Jez. 'Keep it straight, an even two hundred, you'll be on the button. Thrusters quiet as you can make 'em.'

'Right,' said Frey, and opened up the throttle. The *Ketty Jay* rumbled as she began to pick up speed. They'd been forced to set down thirty kloms from the compound, for fear of alerting the guards with the sound of their engines. In between was nothing but blasted ground, oozing marshes and the disconcerting booms from the creatures that somehow contrived to live in this stinking miasma.

The timing had to be perfect. Trinica was going to attack from the north, intending to draw off the fighters while the *Ketty Jay* slipped in from the south amid the confusion. Since they couldn't get too near without warning the enemy, it was necessary to synchronise their attacks. If they waited till they heard the sound of Trinica opening fire, the men on the ground would be forewarned and forearmed by the time the *Ketty Jay* closed in.

Of course, Frey wouldn't like to be in Trinica's presence when she found out about the anti-aircraft gun. But even taking that little surprise into account, the *Delirium Trigger* was well capable of dealing with a small frigate and a few fighter craft.

If she was coming. Because if she wasn't, they were in a whole pile of trouble. The *Ketty Jay* wouldn't stand a chance by herself.

The yellow blankness swallowed him. The murk curtailed his vision on all sides. He passed a foetid lake, and thought he saw something shadowy, four-legged and huge go lumbering along its shores.

He replayed his last conversation with Trinica, mining it for nuance. Had there been a message in her tone, in her expression, that he hadn't picked up? Why had she seemed so sad and resigned when she agreed to save his life? Was it because she knew she wasn't going to?

'Twenty kloms,' said Jez. 'Reckon they'll be hearing our engines soon.'

'No going back, eh?' said Frey. Nervous dread filled him.

Jez was quiet for a moment. Then she said: 'You'll be alright, Cap'n. We'll get you out of this.'

He smiled at her weakly, but then realised she couldn't see it behind his mask and goggles. They lapsed back into silence.

'Ten kloms,' she said.

He checked his watch. 'Shouldn't we be hearing gunfire or something?'

'Probably,' she replied. 'Throttle back a bit. Let's give her time to get there.'

He did so, but a miserable certainty was beginning to grow in him now. Damn it, how many times did he have to let her kick him in the pods before he learned not to trust her?

He was still stewing when Jez said: 'Five kloms. She's not coming, Cap'n.'

'She'll be here,' he said.

'Cap'n, maybe you ought to pull away before it's too late.'

But the camp was approaching fast, a dark smear resolving out of the mist, and he wouldn't pull away. It would be a defeat too hard to take. An admission that all his hopes had been based on smoke, that he'd been gulled, that he'd condemned himself to death.

Don't make me choose between my crew and you, she'd said.

Well, it seemed she'd made her choice, in the end.

He still believed she would appear right up until the first explosion shook the *Ketty Jay*. A bloom of fire lit the cockpit and concussion hammered the craft. The shock of it jolted him into action; he wrenched the flight stick and banked. The anti-aircraft gun kept up a steady thumping. Another explosion shoved the *Ketty Jay* from below, tipping her steeply. Frey felt the weight on the flight stick as fifty men and women went sliding to one side of the hold.

Damn you, Trinica.

He swung the *Ketty Jay* level again and dived. Guards were swarming from the grim buildings beneath him, out into the packed-earth training squares and thoroughfares that lay between. The *Ketty Jay* screamed in low over the rooftops, to give the anti-aircraft gunners something to think about. They wouldn't want to shoot into their own camp.

The frigate took on shape and clarity: a sleek Samarlan design, smooth and insectile. The Sammies built their aircraft fast and beautiful, at the expense of little details like armour. It was all about aesthetics with them. If you had to die, die pretty.

The frigate's anchor came loose of its mooring, whipping through the air as it was drawn into the body of the craft. Already the frigate was scrambling the first of its fighters, shooting them into the sky like darts.

How'd they get them out so quick? They must be on permanent standby.

Frey had spent enough time at card tables to know when he was holding a losing hand. The trick was to know when to fold it. If those fighters got on his tail, they'd shoot him down. Time to run, while he still had the mist on his side, and he could lose them.

He was glad of the mask that covered his face. No one could see the bitter set of his mouth as he—

Light flared, and a series of bellowing explosions ripped along the flank of the frigate. Looming from the yellow fog came the slow black hulk of the *Delirium Trigger*, its outflyers streaking past it to engage the Samarlan fighters.

'Yeah! You beautiful bitch!' Frey cheered wildly, swept up in the hot rush of vindication. Hope surged back, just when it had been slinking off to die. She was here! She came for him!

She cared.

His blood was fired now, and he felt himself overwhelmed by the giddy madness of conflict. He was no longer plain old Darian Frey. He was Captain Frey, of the *Ketty Jay*: a legend, not a man. And it was time to do what he did.

He raced past the camp and then banked hard to bring her about again. The anti-aircraft gunners had lost all interest in him the moment the *Delirium Trigger* appeared. He lined up on the camp and headed back, coming in on the east side, where he'd spotted a likely landing spot.

The guards on the wall took pot-shots at him as he approached, but their bullets were useless against the *Ketty Jay*'s armour. He flew over the top of the wall, decelerating hard, then swung the *Ketty Jay*'s arse end around one hundred and eighty degrees and opened fire with her underslung machine guns. Puffs of stone dust clouded the air as the wall guards fled for cover. He didn't really hope to hit anyone, just to keep them from putting a shot into the cockpit while he landed.

Below him was a small square, perhaps a drill ground or an exercise yard, bordered on all sides by buildings and the compound wall. Defensible and out of the way. Hydraulics whined as the *Ketty Jay* extended her landing skids.

He killed the thrusters, dumped aerium from the tanks and was already opening the cargo ramp when the *Ketty Jay* hit the ground with a teeth-rattling crash. Then he slumped back in his seat and grinned.

'There,' he said.

The force of the landing made the assembled Murthians stagger and stumble. They hung on to bulkheads, cargo netting, whatever they could. The ramp at the back of the hold was gaping slowly open: the Cap'n had timed it perfectly. Its lip hit the ground a couple of seconds after the *Ketty Jay* did. There was a dazed moment, as if no one could quite believe that they were down, and then Ehri's voice rang out: 'Go! Go! Go!'

Axes swung, severing the straps that had kept the Rattletraps in place. There was a growl of engines, deafening in the enclosed hold, and two of the buggies skidded forward and down the ramp with their gatlings blazing. With them went Bess, roaring as she thundered into the fray. And after them came everyone else.

They were like an undammed tide. After a long night of anxiety and anticipation, the Murthians were desperate to be unleashed. They were mostly young men, who had chafed under Akkad's rule and were sick of restraint. Years of anger had brought them to this point. They screamed behind their masks, and flooded out of the *Ketty Jay* with guns in their hands.

There was no subtlety to it. The object was surprise. If they allowed themselves to be hemmed in, pinned inside the *Ketty Jay* by gunfire, they'd all end up dead. The Dak guards had barely realised the enemy had landed amongst them before the Murthians were out with their weapons blazing. Gatlings strafed the surrounding buildings: guards danced and jerked in the windows as they were mown down. Some of them had been caught in the open, and tried to flee from the square to the wider compound beyond. None of them got far. The Murthians flooded into the buildings, faceless warriors in their goggles and masks, mercilessly slaughtering anyone in a uniform. Bess caught up with one unfortunate Dak, pounded him into the earth and tossed his corpse clear over the rooftops.

Ehri was shouting orders amid the chaos, trying to keep the overenthusiastic youngbloods under control. Silo found himself doing the same. He couldn't help it. Surrounded by his own language, he felt like the person he'd once been, instead of the impostor he'd become who thought and spoke in Vardic. He felt the savage joy of vengeance, the fury of uncounted generations of slavery and suffering.

It was just like old times.

The Murthians were disorganised, chasing off without thought for cover or tactics. They hadn't learned much of battle under Akkad. But the wiser heads remembered, and he saw signs of order emerging as the veterans began to rein in their wilder companions.

He grabbed someone nearby – he didn't recognise them behind the mask – and pointed up at the wall. The guards were reorganising up there. He didn't want them capable of firing on the square until everyone had a chance to clear out of it.

~ Get three more men. Kill those guards if you can, keep their heads down otherwise. Can you do that?

The young man nodded firmly, glad to be given purpose among the madness. He yelled at someone nearby and pointed up at the wall. Silo left him to it and ran across the square, using the body of the *Ketty Jay* as shelter from the guards.

The Daks had been mostly cleared from the square now, and many had fled the surrounding buildings. The Murthians had been warned not to scatter far, but some needed reminding. Griffden – the Vard who'd been Akkad's lieutenant – sprinted here and there bellowing, bringing back those who threatened to chase off after the enemy. Silo spotted a few who had thrown themselves into cover, their body language fearful, shocked by their first taste of combat. Overhead, the sky boomed with explosions as the Sammie frigate engaged the *Delirium Trigger* in earnest. Fighters weaved through the poisonous sky with their guns rattling.

It took Silo a few moments to find what he was looking for. A gutshot Dak, his breather mask torn off, gulping in air and coughing back blood. Silo grabbed him by the scruff of his collar and dragged him into the shelter of a doorway.

By now the Cap'n had made his way out of the *Ketty Jay* and was sealing up the cargo hold behind him, locking it with the external keypad located on one of the rear landing struts. The rest of the crew were clustered around him, except for Ashua, who had seen what Silo was up to and was hurrying over towards him.

Silo made a quick check of the room – bullet holes, bodies and wrecked office equipment – then returned his attention to his prisoner. He tore off the man's goggles so he could look him in the eyes. Just the sight of a Dakkadian face close up ignited a killing hate. The Samarlans were the authors of Murthian misery, but they were distant and remote, glimpsed occasionally as overseers in the pens. It was the Daks who were the guards, who doled out the brutality, who killed with impunity. It was the Daks who were the ever-present danger, and he'd learned to despise and fear their pale skin, their blond hair, their narrow eyes and broad faces.

The Sammies had beaten the Murthians long ago. But the Daks were slaves, who'd never bested anyone. Slaves killing other slaves to assert their superiority, in a sick little tangle engineered by their masters.

He didn't feel anything for the suffering of the dying man in front of him. They had been the unquestioned enemy for so long that empathy was impossible.

((Where is the Yort?)) he demanded. He hadn't spoken Samarlan for a very long time. It brought ugly memories.

The Dak just gazed at him, wide-eyed. Ashua scampered up and crouched next to him. He ignored her and slapped the Dak around the side of the head to focus him.

((The Yort. He is here. You know where. The prison?))

The dying man coughed fresh blood onto his chin, bright and glittering against the whiteness of his skin. ((Solitary)) he said, and began to cough again. ((No one…. sees…))

((Where?))

((The quarry. In the quarry. Away from the others.))

Silo looked at Ashua, who nodded to indicate that she'd understood. Then, abruptly, he stood up, lifted his shotgun and fired it into the prisoner's chest. Ashua got to her feet, unconcerned, turning away as if the Dak had never existed. Death was nothing new to her, it seemed. It didn't appal her in the least.

Frey joined them. He looked over Ashua's shoulder at the body on the floor, glanced at Silo, and then said 'Find anything?'

'He in solitary. Down in the quarry.'

'The quarry. Right.'

Ehri came running up behind him, and looked in at Silo. Fal was hastily organising people in the background.

~ The pens! she snapped. Then she gave him a hard stare. ~ Are you coming, or not?

He met her eyes steadily. For all the new distance between them, there was something in her look that spoke of past days. The savage certainty of purpose that they'd once shared. A solidarity forged in the heat of terrible risk. They were people who'd known slavery, and who'd needed to prove again and again that nobody shackled them anymore. Silo, perhaps, had forgotten that of late. But he remembered it now. He was nobody's slave.

He turned to Frey. 'I gotta go, Cap'n. The pens.'

'Reckoned you would,' said Frey. 'Good luck.'

Silo grunted. For a long moment, he studied the man who'd pulled him out of Samarla, who'd sheltered him for nine years, who'd been his leader and, in a way, his friend all that time. He reckoned he could have picked a worse man to throw his lot in with.

Then Ehri hissed at him to get moving, and he followed her out into the square, where his people were waiting.

THIRTY-TWO

FREY PLANS A BETRAYAL—MORTIFICATION— THE MURK—AN AMBUSH—STALEMATE

Frey cast one last look at the *Ketty Jay* as his crew hurried past him, down a passageway between the buildings. It pained him to leave her there sitting in the middle of the square, even sealed tight as she was. But then, he supposed, unless they pulled this off he wouldn't be alive to come back to her anyway.

That was a heartening thought.

He'd memorised the layout of the compound as best he could from a distance, but the quarry wouldn't be hard to find. Compared to the camp itself, it was massive. They slipped from building to building, shooting at any guard that came near, heading in the direction of their target. The drifting murk turned distant men into shadows and helped to conceal them.

The Murthians had driven most of the resistance back towards the centre of the camp, pushing the Daks before them. The guards hadn't been ready for a ground assault of these proportions. Still, it was only a matter of time before they regrouped and realised they had twice the numbers the Murthians did. Frey hoped the Murthians would get to the pens before that. And he hoped the slaves were up for a fight when they were freed.

Well, it would play out however it played. No time to worry. He had his own agenda.

Bess clunked along ahead of them, terrifying – and occasionally maiming – anyone who crossed their path. The rest of his crew, except Silo, were with him. That was unusual. He almost never managed a full muster, and he wished his engineer had been there to complete it. He missed Silo's taciturn presence by his side, and belatedly realised he should have given him an earcuff to stay in touch. But he'd had to let him go. He knew well enough how a man sometimes had to do a thing, regardless of anybody else. He'd seen that need in Silo ever since they went back to his old camp.

Malvery had taken Pinn's burned arm from its sling after confessing that he'd only bound it up to piss him off, so Pinn could manage a revolver again. Harkins had come too, although he was jumping at every loud noise. Well, if he wanted to get himself killed to impress a woman, Frey could hardly turn him down. Frey had done similarly stupid things in his time.

Then there was Ashua. She was a problem he'd have to deal with later. He'd said she could be part of his crew, but he'd have agreed to anything at that point, if it meant saving his neck. She'd find out soon enough that a man's word wasn't worth shit if his life was in the balance. As soon as this was all over, he fully intended to kick her off.

The crew would thank him, in the end. Especially the more long-standing members, who would recall the disastrous tenures of previous females on board. Granted, Frey had tended to favour attractiveness over competence in those days, but even the competent ones were kicked off or left behind in the end. It was only a matter of time before Frey got drunk and made a move on them, and whether it was successful or not, life would be unbearable for everyone until she was gone. The *Ketty Jay* was far too small for sexual tension, but Frey was simply incapable of restraining himself.

It was alright having Jez aboard, because he didn't fancy her, and she was dead. A live, warm woman, and one that made him unaccountably frisky, was a complication he didn't need.

Ah, spit on it. You can give her the boot when the time comes. Let's just try and survive the next few days, eh?

The buildings came to an end near the lip of the quarry. Frey checked the coast was clear and then waved his companions down, indicating that they should stay put. Then he hurried across the open ground to the edge, where he crouched to scout the lie of the land below.

After a few moments, the crew followed him in a flock, crouching all around him. Bess settled herself with a creak of leather and a clash of metal.

Frey sighed. 'I told you to wait by the buildings.'

'Was that what that was?' Malvery asked, waving his hand in the air in a poor imitation of Frey. 'Sorry, Cap'n.'

'Maybe next time you could use words, instead of interpretive dance?' Crake suggested.

Pinn spluttered a laugh. 'Interpretive,' he leered, as if it was something lewd. What Pinn found funny about it was a mystery.

'Can't see bugger all down there,' Malvery commented, squinting.

Frey had come to the same conclusion. The toxic fog that hazed the upper atmosphere thickened near the ground, and the quarry was like an enormous collecting bowl. Tiers were cut out of the rock, with ramps and ladders between them, but he could only see the uppermost shelf, and a hint of the next. After that, they disappeared entirely. All he could see of the bottom was a yellow bleary blankness, with a few smudges of light.

Frey sighed. Another handicap. 'Alright,' he said. 'Everyone stick together down there. We don't want anybody shooting anybody by accident. That means you, Pinn.'

'Hey! Is that 'cause I shot that feller in the rainforest that time? He didn't even die!' Pinn was indignant. 'That's victiming!'

Crake turned his head slowly towards Pinn. 'That's *what*?' he said, his voice dripping scorn.

'Uh… Victiming?' Pinn said, as if talking to a child. 'Like when someone's picking on you? Ring any bells, Mr Education?'

Crake gave a weary sigh. 'One day I'm going to buy you a dictionary,' he said.

'He can share it with Frey!' Ashua beamed.

'Why do *I* need a dictionary?' Frey complained.

'No reason,' said Ashua. 'Now let's get down there and mortify some guards.'

Frey was caught in one of those moments when he didn't know what somebody meant and couldn't decide whether to pretend he did or not.

Pinn groaned, as if explaining things to Frey was extraordinarily tiresome. 'Mordant means dead, don't it? So mortify means kill, obviously. They even sound the same. Right?' He looked at Ashua, who nodded encouragingly.

'Oh,' said Frey. '*Oh*! Let's *mortify* some guards. I'm with you now. Didn't hear you right the first time, that's all.'

Crake and Ashua exchanged a glance, though it was hard to tell its meaning behind their goggles. Malvery tutted to himself. Frey had the distinct impression that a joke was being had at his expense, but he couldn't for the life of him figure out what it was.

Something exploded just overhead, making them all duck. One of the *Delirium Trigger*'s Equalisers shrieked through the air.

'Probably shouldn't be hanging around in the open like this,' Jez pointed out.

'That's why I told you to stay in cover,' said Frey. 'Don't want to see anyone get mortified.'

He suspected that was Crake stifling a laugh as they headed along the lip of the quarry, but the daemonist might have been just coughing behind his mask.

They caught sight of several guards running away from them, towards the almighty firefight in the middle of the camp, but they managed to reach the nearest ramp unnoticed. The stony slope was wide and built for vehicles. They made their way down it, and on to the first tier. The quarry wall hid them from sight from the rest of the camp, making Frey feel marginally safer. There were no guards in sight, and they followed the shelf to another ramp, which took them further down into the quarry.

The fog closed in around them, stifling the sounds of conflict. The sound of machine guns faded to a distant rapping. Explosions became dulled and lost their threat. Little noises were amplified by this new quiet: Frey could hear the rustle of clothes, the creak of Bess's joints, Harkins trying not to hyperventilate. They could hear faint cries down in the quarry. Guards were calling to one another in Samarlan.

'They're down there somewhere,' said Malvery. 'Could be they don't know we're here. But I reckon some of them'll be heading up to the camp to find out what all the commotion is.'

'Right. Eyes peeled, everyone,' said Frey.

'For all the good *that'll* do,' Ashua muttered.

Frey took her point. They really couldn't see a great deal. Anything more than ten metres away was only a shadow, and anything past twenty was invisible. 'Well, y'know. Do what you can.'

They made their way down to the next tier. On the way, they passed sinister, hulking shapes, sitting motionless and silent. Earth-moving vehicles, with drills and scoops and tracked wheels as tall as a man.

There was something about the brute scale of industrial machinery that intimidated Frey. He felt very small in comparison.

'Footsteps,' whispered Jez. She held up her hand to halt everyone – for some reason they understood when *she* did it – and then slid through the fog to the edge of the tier. Frey went with her. They squatted, and she pointed.

On the next tier, fifteen metres below, a dozen shadowy figures hustled through the murk. Frey could just about make out the rifles in their hands, the Dak bayonets fixed to the barrels. He felt a chill, and waited till they passed by.

'I reckon, if they're going that way, we should go the other,' Frey opined.

'Sounds like a good plan, Cap'n.'

They returned to the others and moved off in the opposite direction to the guards. This quarry was so big that there had to be more than one ramp between each shelf. Shortly afterwards, and with a smug glow of self-congratulation, it turned out he was right. They slipped down to the level below, evading the guards on the way.

The lights on the quarry floor were much closer now, but they still had no idea how far they had to go. It was hard to know where anything was in this ghostly netherworld. The sounds of the battle above were a fuzzy percussion, coming to them as if in a dream.

They were moving along the shelf, searching for the next ramp down, when Jez suddenly put her hand on his chest to stop him. The rest of the group halted with him, some more silently than others.

'What is it?' he whispered.

She narrowed her eyes in concentration. 'Not sure. Hard to tell where the sounds are coming from.' She listened. 'I think they're trying to be quiet.'

'They?' He peered into the gloom. He could just about make out the looming shape of another bulky vehicle ahead.

Pinn joined them. 'Why've we stopped?'

Jez shushed him. 'They're above us,' she whispered, looking up at the ridge. 'I think they know where we—'

The silence was destroyed by the bellow of an engine, and the fog filled with dazzling light. The vehicle ahead had come to life. Powerful headlamps and floods beamed through the haze. In their glare, Frey saw the outline of some kind of enormous bulldozer, a monster of black iron, seeping smoke. There was a shout, and suddenly rifles were firing, sharp flashes in the gloom.

Caught out in the open, the crew scattered in panic. Frey's first instinct was to run back in the direction they'd come, but then he caught sight of figures running along the ridge overhead, setting themselves in position to fire down on their targets. They'd be cut to pieces, unless—

'Up against the wall! Take cover against the wall!' he yelled.

The crew, thankfully, listened. The wall to their left was roughly carved and deeply rucked, and there was an overhang at the top, which meant that the guards above wouldn't be able to hit them without leaning out over the edge. Bullets pinged and sparked around them as they crammed themselves into whatever niches they could find. Most of the shots were aimed at Bess, who was counted as the biggest threat, but they had no effect on her other than to make her angry.

'Bess! You need to shield us!' Crake called to her. She squatted down with them, putting her metal body between the crew and the bulldozer.

Frey leaned out of the fold of rock where he'd stashed himself and fired off a few shots in the general direction of the enemy. The lights made it impossible to see his targets, but it lit the crew up nicely for the guards.

Crake and Harkins were panicking, fumbling with their guns and covering their heads whenever a bullet came their way. The rest of the crew were calmer in returning fire, but their situation wasn't good. The enemy had the high ground, which meant they couldn't move. And there was nothing stopping the Daks coming down the ramp and round the back of them. If that happened, their cover would mean bugger all: they'd be sitting ducks.

Then, just when he thought things had got quite bad enough for the moment, the bulldozer started to move forward.

Frey's heart sank. The tier was only a dozen metres wide. Getting past the enemy would mean running onto their guns – onto their *bayonets* – down the narrow space to either side of the bulldozer. A choice between a wall or a steep drop. But if the vehicle got too close, the enemy would get an angle on them, and they would have to flee their cover. Which meant the soldiers above could pick them off with ease.

He muttered a string of swear words under his breath. He took a shot at where he thought the cab might be, to see if he could get the driver, but he only heard the long whine of a ricochet.

'Cap'n? Any ideas?' Jez asked.

'Nope,' he said. And that meant they were in deep, deep trouble.

Pushing on, out from the cluster of buildings that surrounded the *Ketty Jay*, across the open spaces of the camp. Silo's boots pounded the packed earth as he ran, his shotgun cradled in his arms. The metal tower of the gas derrick rose high above him. Huge storage tanks rested at its base, inside a tangle of pipes and distillation apparatus.

Bullets picked at the ground, sending up scuffs of poisoned dirt. Men were running around him, forging through the foetid air and the stench of rotten eggs. Someone to his right was hit in the chest and went down in a tumble, rolling to a stop. His companions jumped over him and carried on.

On the far side of the open ground were the barracks and more administrative buildings, and beyond them, the gates to the pens. The Daks still hadn't got themselves organised. Most retreated before the attack. Others took cover and attempted to resist, but without the coordination of their fellows, they were soon overwhelmed. The Murthians were not well drilled, but they had a clear purpose and the advantage of surprise. Bodies fell on both sides, but many more Daks than Murthians.

Silo pressed himself up against the side of a long narrow building, grateful to be out of the firing line for a moment. The buildings in Gagriisk were low, ugly and practical, with a temporary feel about them. Their windows were sealed with bubbles of windglass and their doors were stout and metal.

He heard a hiss. The door of the building opposite popped ajar with a rush of air that stirred the surrounding fog. Silo crossed over and hid behind it as it came open. He heard muffled voices, the scuff of booted feet. Two of them.

He kicked the door closed and fired twice.

They were Samarlan officers in uniform, wearing masks that covered their whole head instead of just goggles and a breather. It made them faceless and machine-like. Still, they died like everyone else when you shot them.

Silo stepped past their bodies and looked into the doorway. There was another sealed door beyond the open one. An airlock, to keep the atmosphere clean inside. So that was how they endured this toxic place. There'd be no such luxuries for the slaves.

Two Murthians ran past him, sparing him barely a glance as they headed towards the pens. Silo hurried after them. There was the sound of machine gun fire ahead, audible over the booming of the anti-aircraft gun and the scream of engines in the sky.

The two Murthians ran out of the cover of the buildings, into the open, carried on by the momentum of vengeance. A machine gun rattled; bullets chipped and puffed at the ground and walls. One of them jerked like a badly-handled marionette and went down; the other skidded to a halt and fled back into cover. Silo caught up with him at the edge of the building. He was breathing hard and whimpering, staring at his dead companion, eyes shocked behind his goggles.

Silo had no words of comfort for him. He'd learn, just as Silo had. Or he'd die.

Around the corner of the building was an area of clear ground in front of the gates to the slave pens. The Daks were dug in deep here. There were machine gun emplacements on the walls, and bunkers surrounded by stone barriers at ground level. A pair of tracked flatbed vehicles were parked near the gates, for transporting the slaves from pen to quarry. Plenty of cover for the thirty or forty guards that defended the gates, but almost none for the Murthians if they tried a frontal assault.

This is where the Daks were going, he realised. This was their emergency plan. They knew that if anyone invaded the camp, they were either coming to free the men in the prison, or the slaves from the pens. Since the invaders were Murthians, it was obvious which they'd go for. The Daks had been caught offguard by the Cap'n's plan, but they'd regrouped here, and Silo couldn't see any way to winkle them out that didn't end in a shitload of dead Murthians.

His gaze roamed the surrounding area, and then settled.

Unless...

He caught sight of Ehri and Fal, hiding close by. He made his way back through the buildings towards them, avoiding the open ground. There were still Murthians and Daks battling here and there, but he avoided the gunfights and soon reached Ehri's side. She looked back at him, her expression unreadable.

~ We cannot attack with those guns there, she said.

~ We have to get through somehow, said Fal urgently. ~ Listen to them.

Silo could hear something between the sporadic rattle of gunfire and the explosions from overhead. A distant hubbub of shouted voices. The slaves on the other side of the gate. They sensed the chance at freedom, and they'd roused.

He felt a surge of fierce pride at the sound. The Murthians weren't like the Daks; they would never lie down and submit to slavery under the Sammies. So many generations they'd been under the yoke, yet they were still angry, still eager for the fight. Once, he'd thought a more subtle approach might have been more sensible, that their mule-like resistance to being ruled would be the very thing that kept them in chains for ever. But, hearing those voices, he knew he'd been wrong. The smallest compromise would have been the first step to giving up. And his people never gave up.

He surveyed the ground in front of the gates. Several bodies lay there, Daks and Murthians, blood seeping into the dirt. Too many had fallen on the Murthian side already, some of them barely adults, killed in the first battle they ever saw. All of them here on his account, because of his plan to attack Gagriisk.

He thought he should feel something, but he didn't. Where was the crushing weight of responsibility? Where was the guilt he'd been so terrified of all these years? He'd never wanted to be a leader again after his failed coup against Akkad. He'd become a follower instead, for fear of repeating the same mistake and inviting another tragedy. But now here they were. People were dying because of him. And he looked on their bodies, and nothing happened.

He was a violent man who led a violent life. That was the way of it. Handing off responsibility was just a chickenshit evasion. How many people had he killed on the Cap'n's behalf? A fair few, he reckoned. The Daks brutalised his people all their lives, but in the end they were slaves too, and only following orders. Did that make them innocent? Not in his eyes. So how did being a follower excuse him from responsibility, just because he let someone else make the choices?

Lead or follow, it didn't matter half a damn. People lived and died, regardless. If those kids didn't die because of him, they'd likely die some other way pretty soon. In the end, all a man was responsible for was himself. And that went for everyone.

Well then, he thought. *Raise your voice, or don't.*

~ I have an idea, he said.

~ Tell us, said Fal.

Silo pointed. Beyond the open ground there were a few more small buildings, and visible behind them was the anti-aircraft gun emplacement, set atop a shallow rise.

~ I think that gun could be more usefully employed.

Ehri and Fal exchanged a glance. Silo saw the grin in Fal's eyes.

~ Lead on, old friend, he said. ~ We're with you.

THIRTY-THREE

THE LAW OF AVERAGES—DESPERATE MEASURES—JEZ IS LOST—PANIC— A COSTLY ASSAULT

Time was running out.

Jez's eyes were better than anyone's, but even she couldn't see through the dazzle of the bulldozer's lights as it came grinding towards them. She'd managed to shoot out two of the floods, but it was a waste of time and bullets. The lights all merged into the glare, making them indistinct and hard to hit. The bulldozer would be on top of them before she could take them all out.

She couldn't see any way to get past it, either. Guards hid behind it, using its metal body as a shield, the way their targets were using Bess. The crew would be butchered if they tried an assault. Even if Bess led the way, that vehicle was big enough to crush her under its plough, and the instant they broke cover the bastards crouching overhead would shoot them.

She could smell the fear-sweat on her companions. This wasn't the kind of scrape they could skip out of with a daring plan and a bit of luck. They were out of options, and genuinely scared. Pinn was the only exception. He laughed at death for the same reason he laughed at complex mathematics: it was all a bit too much for his brain to handle.

She popped up and aimed a shot over Bess's hump. No good. The mist foiled her again, and she had to duck away from a volley of return fire.

Bess was virtually impervious to small-gauge rifles like the Daks had, but she moaned in distress all the same as she was peppered with gunfire. Crake muttered soothing things to her and occasionally yelped as a bullet came too close. It was a miracle no one had been hit yet.

CHRIS WOODING

But the bulldozer was getting nearer, and the folds of the quarry wall would be scant protection once the enemy got an angle on them.

She racked her brains for an answer. A sharp smell filled her nostrils, derailing her train of thought. She looked over her shoulder, and saw that Pinn was crouched down, holding a tin full of some kind of transparent jelly in the hand of his wounded arm. With his free hand, he was dipping bullets into it. When he was done, he struggled to put the tin back in his pocket, and then began loading the drum of his revolver.

'Pinn?'

'Flame-Slime!' he cried over the gunfire. He snapped the drum closed and spun it for effect.

'What?'

'Professor Pinn's Incredible Flame-Slime! Don't you remember?'

'Yes, but what are you *doing* with it?'

'Fire-bullets!' he said.

'You're making incendiary bullets? What's the point?'

Pinn shrugged. 'It's gotta be useful for *something*.' Then he stood up and aimed. 'Watch.'

'Wait, Pinn, don't!'

But she was too late. He fired the gun. A flaming bullet, like a tracer round, shot away into the murk.

'Ha-*ha*!' Pinn cried triumphantly, after he'd pulled himself back into hiding. 'Told you it'd work!'

Jez pointed at his revolver. Flames were licking out of the drum, where the other bullets had caught fire. Pinn yelled and lobbed the blazing revolver away. It skittered to the edge of the rock shelf and came to a halt with its barrel facing towards them. A moment later it went off as the bullet in the firing chamber ignited, sending it skipping over the edge and away.

Pinn looked down at his bound arm, resting in its sling. Blood was seeping into the white fabric. His chubby face was grey. Lodged in the wall behind him, the bullet was still on fire.

'Bollocks,' he said. 'Right in the same damn place.' Then he fainted.

'Doc!' Harkins cried.

'I saw,' said Malvery, who was busy firing off shotgun rounds. 'Ain't got time to deal with that shit-wit right now. Even if he has just invented self-cauterising bullets.'

'You did warn him not to shoot anyone by accident,' Ashua said to Frey. 'You should take up prophecy.'

'Just playing the law of averages,' Frey replied.

'S'pose it wasn't victiming after all,' Malvery commented.

Jez crammed herself back into cover. Bullets pinged and scuffed around her. The crew's casual quips didn't fool her; it was cheap bravado. She felt the beginnings of panic taking hold. The breather mask felt suddenly confining – a remembered response from the days when she used to breathe – and she tore it off and threw it away. Damn it, there had to be a way out. Half-Mane or not, if they shot her in the right place, she'd be dead for real.

The Manes.

She realised she could hear them.

She closed her eyes and tried to concentrate. They weren't here, not physically. Their howls were phantom echoes on the edge of her consciousness. But they were distressed. They sensed her fear and shared it. All this time they'd stayed away, respecting her wish to be left alone, but now they couldn't help themselves. Like a mother unable to resist the cries of her child, they flocked to her, offering her their support and solidarity, lamenting their inability to help.

Why didn't I want to be one of them? She couldn't remember now. There was a feral simplicity to their love, the call of the pack. They were intelligent, they were *people*, but the daemon in them had made them primal. Like animals.

Like *animals*.

Her eyes flew open. Once, when she hadn't been long on the *Ketty Jay*'s crew, she'd found herself in a situation like this. Pinned down on a landing pad in Rabban, defending the craft with Silo and Harkins, surrounded by twenty of Trinica Dracken's men. She'd heard a man's thoughts that night, sensed where he was, and shot him through the head at forty metres in the dark. While he was running.

She could jump in and out of the cat's head. Why not these guards? She'd tried and failed before to force herself into a human's thoughts, but she'd had more practice now. If she could *feel* where they were, she could shoot them.

If she could do it. But any chance was better than no chance at all.

The chaos all around her was no obstacle. These days, she could slip into and out of a shallow trance easily, even while doing something else. But she needed to go deeper now. She'd been tentative while trying out her new abilities, afraid of what might happen. But there was no time to be careful any more. She needed to *plunge*.

It was as if she was falling into a deep well, dropping like a stone towards her own core. Her head went light and then she couldn't feel her skin any more. Suddenly, she wasn't there, no longer in the body of Jez but limbless and loose in the void. She fought to find the path she'd learned to take when she rode inside Slag's skull, the route her instincts had carved. She knew how to do it; she just didn't know how it was done.

She felt herself slipping, felt a change in her mind that sent it flowering open, thrown wide to the world. And she could hear voices, a dozen voices, then ten times that, the babble of a crowd. Frantic snatches of thought invaded her head, cramming in, a bewildering muddle. She heard three languages and understood them all. She felt the screams of the dying as if they came from her own throat. She was all the people everywhere in Gagriisk, she was inside their skins: her friends, the Daks, the Murthians, all at once.

And suddenly it was too much, this overwhelming tide, but it kept on coming, relentless. Terror surged within her as she realised she was out of control, losing her grip. She fought against the pandemonium and madness but she was no longer sure who she was or if *she* was a *she* at all.

She was a Murthian, shot and killed; she was the triumphant Dak marksman. She was the Cap'n, frightened; she was the guards overhead, grim, predatory, waiting for the moment when their targets would break cover. She was a slave in the pens, watching the fighters battling in the sky, daring to wonder if long-dreamed freedom had finally come. She was—

She was—

She was lost.

Harkins, as a veteran of being afraid, could identify the fine distinctions between different states of terror in a way that non-cowards couldn't. The stock phrases that people used to express how scared they were seemed woefully imprecise to him. He may not have had the smarts to put his wisdom into words, but he knew what he knew.

The creepy silence of the fogbound quarry had been a slow,

constant kind of fear, like a child waiting for a monster to push open the wardrobe door in a darkened bedroom. The sharp alarm of the gunfight was different to that, a barrage of shocks that unmanned him and made him want to cringe and gibber. But the thought of Jez's scorn pushed him to courage. He'd recovered himself enough to send a few wild shots in the direction of the enemy. Maybe it was his imagination, but he fancied he was getting a bit braver lately.

Fear came in many forms for Harkins. But nothing came close to this moment. The moment he heard an unearthly blood-freezing screech, from right by his ear, as he crouched behind the metal bulk of Bess. A sound that issued from the blackest hell of his subconscious. And even that came a distant second to the moment which followed, when he looked over his shoulder and saw what had made the sound. It was Jez.

Jez, and yet not Jez.

She'd changed. Not physically, but in some other way that Harkins couldn't understand. Where there had once been a woman he adored was a creature of inexplicable horror, something that wore Jez's shape but which radiated the cold dread of a nightmare. There was a senseless savagery in her eyes that he'd never seen before; her teeth were bared in a crooked snarl; she was coiled in the tight hunch of a hunting cat.

Her face was inches from his.

Harkins' throat closed up. His heart stopped. His eyes bulged. Then she leaped past him in a blur, the wind making the ears of his pilot cap flap against his head.

He stared at the empty space where she'd been. Then something unjammed inside him and he screamed, because it was impossible not to.

'*GaaaaaAAAAAAAH!*'

Wet heat spread down his inside leg. He'd pissed himself. He didn't care.

'*GAAAAAHHAAHHHHHH!!!*'

She was a *daemon* and she'd been *right there in his face!*

'*GAAHHAARRRGHHAHAHAHHHH—*'

He was interrupted by a brutal impact that knocked his head sideways.

'Better?' asked Malvery, raising a meaty hand to give him another slap.

Harkins whimpered and nodded, holding his cheek.

'S'pose you weren't there the last couple of times she flipped out, eh?'

Harkins shook his head, still making wounded eyes at the doctor.

'Well, she's sure as spit flipped out now,' said the Cap'n, who was peeking out over Bess's shoulder.

The screams of the guards were terrible to hear, but Harkins couldn't help looking, if only to make sure that *thing* didn't come back towards them.

The bulldozer was very close now, and he could see silhouettes in the backwash of its lights. Guards flailed about, frantic, aiming their weapons every which way. Darting among them, almost too fast to follow, was the small figure of Jez. If not for her ponytail, he wouldn't have known it was her. She leaped and sprung and seemed to flicker, although that could have been a trick of the fog. Where she landed, the guards crumpled, or were flung away. Frey ducked as a forearm, torn off at the elbow, went wheeling past him, end over end. A Dak staggered out of the gloom, tripped, and went under the bulldozer's plough with a wail.

As Harkins watched agape, Jez jumped up on to the side of the bulldozer and was lost in the glare. There was a desperate shriek – whether from the daemon or her victim, he couldn't tell – and a cracking sound like an ogre chewing bones. The bulldozer turned, its headlight sweeping away from them, and then tipped alarmingly as its tracks found the drop at the lip of the ledge. Metal groaned, tracks sped into empty air, and the massive machine slid over the side of the tier and crashed to the ground twenty metres below.

'Get those bastards above us!' Frey yelled. He backed out of cover, aiming upward at the guards crouched overhead. The others did as he did, unleashing a volley of gunfire. Harkins stayed where he was. Two bodies fell through the air and landed in broken heaps in front of him. He covered his ears and shut his eyes and yelled.

When he took his hands away, the shooting had stopped. Malvery hauled him roughly to his feet.

'Come on, you. Ain't no time for lying about.'

'What about him?' Harkins whined, pointing accusingly at the unconscious Pinn.

'Never mind about him,' said Malvery. 'Go help the Cap'n.' He knelt down and began to examine the fallen pilot.

Harkins backed away awkwardly. His wet trousers were chafing his leg. He looked around for signs of the daemon-Jez-thing, but he couldn't hear it. All he could hear were distant explosions and gunfire from the frigates fighting in the world outside, somewhere beyond the oppressive poison haze that enshrouded them.

Not knowing what else to do, he went over to the Cap'n. Frey was standing among the scattered remains of Jez's victims. He was looking over the edge at the wreckage of the bulldozer, dimly illuminated by its own lights.

'Er,' said Harkins.

The daemon shrieked from somewhere down below. Rifles fired. Frey raised his head and looked at Harkins. 'Reckon we'll leave her to it for a while. Let her burn off some energy.'

Harkins swallowed. 'Right.'

'Can someone get Bess over here?' Malvery called. 'Pinn's alright, but he ain't looking like waking up anytime soon. And I'm buggered if I'm hauling this lard-arse all the way down the quarry.'

Ehri left Griffden in charge of the battle around the slave pen gates. She instructed him to dig in tight, to clear out the surrounding areas of stray Daks, and to keep the guards on the gate pinned down. On no account were they to try and charge it. Griffden, an infantry veteran of the Second Aerium War, didn't need telling.

That done, Silo, Ehri and Fal slipped away from the gate, retreating to a safe distance from the machine guns. They skirted the open ground, sticking to the paths between the buildings, making their way closer to the gun. Silo led the way, and the others fell in behind him, just like old times. It felt like the natural thing to do.

There were still Daks about, who hadn't managed to fall back to the gate before the Murthians got there. Some were hiding and trying to wait out the firefight. Others did their best to ambush the attackers when they could. Silo only saw two, who emerged from behind a building. He fired on them, along with Ehri and Fal, but they fled back the way they came. Silo crept up to the corner, listened, and eventually peeped round. The Daks were gone.

Just like Daks, he thought scornfully. *Ain't never been the types to stand and fight.*

The buildings ended at the base of the rise where the anti-aircraft gun emplacement was positioned. It was surrounded by a wall of sandbags. Within were five guards. Two of them were operating the gun. The other three were crouched behind the sandbags, watching for attackers.

Silo scanned the area, careful to keep himself hidden.

~ We cannot get up the slope without being shot, said Fal, at his shoulder.

Ehri was huddled behind him, her rifle held upright like a staff. ~ I could hit them from here.

~ You may hit one, said Fal. ~ But once they know where we are, they will focus their fire on us. You will not have another chance to aim.

Silo frowned for a moment, then his brow cleared. ~ That is exactly what we must do, he said. ~ Draw their fire. There are only three of them to defend the emplacement.

~ I don't understand, said Fal.

~ You have a pocket watch?

Neither of them did. Silo gave his to Fal. ~ Wait five minutes. Then start shooting. Stay in cover. Kill them if you can.

~ And you? asked Ehri. There was still suspicion in her voice. She didn't trust him yet. She probably never would.

~ While they are looking at you, they will not see me, he said. He tapped the face of the watch. ~ Five minutes.

Then he was moving, heading back among the buildings, circling the rise in the land to get around the other side of the anti-aircraft emplacement. He could see the outer wall of Gagriisk ahead of him. Many of the guards in the watchtowers had abandoned their posts, having moved to different positions that allowed them to fire down on the enemy. Beyond the wall, he could see the Samarlan frigate in the distance, barely visible in the murk. It was listing heavily in the air, belching smoke and flame from its flank. As he watched, it was hit by another volley from the *Delirium Trigger*, and began to sink out of the sky. Dracken had demolished her opponent; now there were only the fighters left to mop up.

He was looking up when a Dak ran out from the doorway of a building just in front of him. Neither of them saw or heard the other until a split second before collision, and by then it was too late to react. They went down, tangled together, struggling instinctively even before they'd realised what had happened. The Dak rolled on top of him and punched wildly at his shoulders and head. Silo's hands found a forearm and used it as leverage to shove the guard off him. There was an instant of scrabbling and thrashing as they fought on the ground, before Silo got the advantage. Still gripping the forearm, he brought it hard up the enemy's back, making him yell, driving him face-down into the earth. The Dak scrabbled for his weapon with his free hand; the gun lay a metre away. Silo got onto his back and reached an arm round his throat, making a vice of the crook of his elbow. He gritted his teeth, braced himself, and with one quick jerk he broke the guard's neck.

He rolled off and knelt in the dirt for a moment, panting. Been a while since he'd killed a man with his bare hands. It was a whole different sort of killing than shooting somebody.

No time to stop. Time was ticking. He got back to his feet, picked up his shotgun, and ran again. On his way, he heard a distant sound like a slow avalanche of metal, followed by an explosion that shook the earth and rattled the windglass seals of the buildings around him. Out in the poisoned wasteland, the frigate had crashed.

He stopped when he came up against the outer wall of the compound, and followed it till he came to the bare rise surrounding the anti-aircraft gun. Hidden by the angle of a wall, he watched the guards behind the sandbags. They'd positioned themselves to have a good view all around. He wasn't exactly on the far side of it from Ehri and Fal – he reckoned a hundred and twenty degrees rather than a hundred and eighty – but it would have to do. The expanse of open ground seemed daunting, now that he came to it, but it was too late to back out now.

He'd lost track of the time. Hadn't it been five minutes yet? He checked his shotgun was fully loaded. Perhaps he'd been quicker getting here than he thought. Perhaps Ehri and Fal had decided not to go ahead with it. Perhaps Ehri believed he was trying to pull some kind of trick, that his loyalty to the cause of freedom had been forever compromised by living among the foreigners.

Then there was the sharp bark of a rifle, and one of the guards in the emplacement flew back from the sandbags and fell in a heap.

More shots came. The other two guards found their source and returned fire, moving around the sandbags until they were facing away from Silo. The men operating the anti-aircraft gun seemed oblivious, focused on the Equalisers that were chasing the last of the Samarlan fighters through the yellow sky.

Silo broke cover and ran up the rise towards the emplacement. A copper adrenaline tang on his tongue. If they saw him, they would shoot him, and there was nowhere to hide as he sprinted up the slope.

But they didn't see him. It was as if the world had turned its eyes away and made him invisible. The gunners were attending to their gun; the guards were occupied with Ehri and Fal. Unobserved, he clambered over the sandbags and into the emplacement.

The first they knew of him was when he shot the first of the guards in the back at a distance of a couple of metres. He cocked his lever-action shotgun and blasted the second Dak as he turned in alarm. Hard to miss at that range. Then he went for the men on the gun.

The gunner's assistant was still fumbling with his sidearm when Silo shot him. He went staggering back against the control assembly and slumped bonelessly to the ground, holding his guts. The gunner himself was still in the control seat. He raised his hands.

((Get out of the seat)) said Silo.

The gunner did as he was told.

((Over there.))

He stepped away from the gun, arms raised high. The barrel of Silo's shotgun followed him. But then something in Silo's expression, or lack of it, must have warned him what was coming, because his eyes filled with horror and his face crumpled.

((No! Please, I have children!))

Silo pulled the trigger and silenced him. He didn't want to hear about a Dak's children. They didn't think children so precious when they were Murthian boys and girls, growing up bent from working in mines or with lost fingers from the cotton mills.

When he was a younger man, revenge had made him feel better. It had dampened the rage inside. Now it didn't make him feel at all. A dead Dak was only a drop in the ocean. It didn't change a thing.

Ehri and Fal came climbing over the sandbags and into the emplacement. Fal's eyes were twinkling behind his goggles.

~ We did it! he said. ~ That was amazing!

~ Just like old times, said Silo.

~ Just like old times, Ehri agreed, her voice softer than he was used to hearing it.

A gunshot close at hand made them jump. Fal grunted. Silo pushed him out of the way, and saw one of the Daks dazedly trying to sit up, a revolver in his hand, a deep gash across his temple. Ehri hadn't killed the one she hit, just winged him. Silo put him back down, and this time there was no mistake.

~ *Fal!*

He didn't want to turn around. Didn't want to see what he knew would be there. Everything had happened so quickly, it had simply been a reaction to kill the Dak when he heard the shot. But now he put it all together. The shot, Fal's grunt, Ehri's cry.

Damn it, he thought to himself. *Damn it all to rot and shit.*

Fal was on the ground. Ehri was cradling his head with one hand, and pressing the other on his chest. Blood welled out between her fingers in pulses, spreading across Fal's clothes.

Silo had seen enough bullet wounds in his time. The volume and colour of blood, the location of the hole, told him that this one was fatal.

~ Fal! Fal! Stay with me!

Fal coughed inside his mask. His eyes were roving, confused. ~ I don't... I—

Silo bent down to lay a hand on his shoulder, to offer some comfort, but Ehri screamed at him to get away. He stepped back. Fal was hers, not his. He'd left and hadn't returned for nine years. He didn't deserve any claim on his friend.

Fal focused on Ehri's face, which was bent down close to his. The masks and goggles seemed cruel barriers to their final moments together.

~ Mother's coming, he said.

~ No. She shook her head. ~ No.

He spluttered and gasped. ~ Maybe... maybe I'll be reborn... outside the pens.

~ You're not going to die, Fal, she told him solemnly, through gathering tears.

~ Maybe one day you'll break me out.

Silo saw Ehri's throat clench, and whatever words she'd meant to say were lost. She held up her hand in front of him, to show the tattoo on her palm. His eyes creased in a smile. He tried to lift his own hand to show his matching design, but he didn't have the strength. Ehri did it for him and pressed it to her own.

~ It's cold, said Fal. Then he gave a short and humourless laugh. ~ Why am I scared?

He didn't say anything else. Silo looked away and began reloading his shotgun. He could see over the tops of the buildings to the gate of the slave pens. The battle was still going on around them, the rip and crackle of gunfire, but neither side had moved an inch. The fighters overhead still dodged and weaved, but it seemed like they were almost all Equalisers now.

When he was done reloading, Ehri was still leaning over the body of her husband.

~ Ehri.

~ Don't, she said. ~ Don't speak to me.

She raised her head and stared at him hatefully. Then she stabbed a finger at the enormous gun looming over them. ~ Get on with it! she spat.

He got into the seat, his eyes running over the controls. His brain wouldn't make sense of it at first. Fal, dead, because of him. He'd thought he wouldn't feel responsible for other people's deaths any more, but he realised he was wrong. It was just people he didn't know that he didn't care about.

He seized the firing handles. Move forward. It was all a man could do. Keep moving forward, and forget what got wrecked in your wake.

The controls, once he applied himself, were easy enough for an engineer to figure out. He lowered the barrel. When it was horizontal, it wouldn't go any lower, but he reckoned that the shells would dip over distance, so it would be enough for his purposes. He swung the gun around until it was facing the gate to the slave pens.

This is for you, Fal, he thought, and pressed down on the trigger.

The report of the gun pounded at his ears, a slow and steady *whump-whump-whump* as it spat blazing tracer shells over the rooftops. As he'd hoped, gravity sucked them down, and they hit the gates of the pen squarely, smashing them to pieces in a series of detonations. But Silo wasn't done yet. He altered the angle, sending shells into the walls to either side of the gates, raining rubble down on the men hidden at their feet. The machine-gunners on the walls were swallowed in a cascade of brick and dust and flame. Daks fled from cover, trying to escape the destruction, and were mown down as they did so.

When Silo let off the trigger, the gate had been swallowed by a dirty, malevolent cloud, swelling outward. But as it swelled, it cleared. He heard the sound of raised voices. A charge had begun. Whether it was the slaves, or the free Murthians, or both, he couldn't see.

But the day was won, he knew that.

He waited for a sense of triumph, and felt none. All he could think of was Fal. He got out of the gunner's seat, and saw that Ehri was standing, her rifle in her hand, and her eyes were hard and dry.

~ Are you coming? she asked.

He looked down at Fal. There was no ceremony for the dead in Murthian culture. The dead were just meat, their spirits gone back to Mother.

'Reckon I'll stay here a while,' he said, and the words came out in Vardic. 'Lost my appetite for killin'.'

Ehri looked away with a snort of bitter disdain. 'Reckon you have,' she said. Then she was away, over the sandbags and running down the slope towards the battle.

Silo watched her go, then knelt down next to Fal. He took off the mask and the goggles. Fal's eyes were closed. Silo sighed.

'Reckon I have,' he muttered.

THIRTY-FOUR

REPARTEE—BESS THE LIBERATOR—A HUMBLING MOMENT—THE PRISONER

It was mayhem on the quarry floor.

Visibility was down to ten metres in the fog. Everyone was shooting at shadows. Bullets whizzed randomly out of the gloom. Jez was out there somewhere, still on a rampage, her screeches like the cry of some prehistoric animal. As if one of the gargants that lived on Atalon long ago had been resurrected and set loose among them.

Frey and his crew sheltered behind a massive tracked vehicle with a drill-tipped hydraulic arm that was parked near to the quarry wall. Harkins was a total mess: every new shriek from Jez made him flail and splutter. Ashua was jigging on her haunches, a bundle of nervous energy. Crake was fussing over Bess, checking her for damage and cooing reassuring words. Pinn was groggy but alive, muttering deliriously to himself about how he won some race or another, and how he was a hero of the skies. Malvery had patched him up and declared that he'd be fine, but he wouldn't be flying for another few weeks.

They weren't in great shape, but they were alive, and they were close to their goal. Frey allowed himself a bit of hope.

He peered out from behind the vehicle. He could see a blurred patch of light, which he could only assume was the solitary confinement building. There were altogether too many bullets flying about in the space between him and it.

A figure came running out of the murk, across his field of vision. He raised his revolver, not sure whether it was worth taking a shot or not. The decision was taken out of his hands. A silhouette – small, ponytailed, feral – pounced into view and landed on the newcomer from behind. Frey was glad he couldn't see what happened next.

Crouched over the remains, Jez looked left and right, searching for new victims. He ducked back into cover with a thrill of fright. A short while later, he heard screaming on the far side of the quarry, and felt safe enough to move again.

He became aware of a chorus of yells from nearby. They weren't cries of distress. They were meant to attract attention.

'It's the Murthians,' said Ashua, catching his thought. 'The ones on the mining shift.'

'What are they saying?'

'Dunno. It's in Murthian.' She ruffled the hair on the back of her head. 'But I'd guess it's along the lines of "Get us out of here".'

'Reckon we ought to oblige 'em,' said Frey. 'A few dozen people running all over would help soak up some bullets, I reckon.'

'You're all heart, Frey.'

'Hey! It's *Cap'n* to you now. And I'll have you know that beneath this tough exterior I'm actually fascinatingly sensitive and complex.'

'Yeah, I'll just bet you are. A fascinating narcissist.'

'Thanks. I *am* pretty brave, aren't I?'

Ashua swore under her breath. 'Forgot about your amazing skill with words. I must get you that dictionary.'

'Will you two stop flirting and bugger off?' Malvery said. 'Go free those slaves, if you're going to.'

'We are *not* flirting!' Ashua snapped.

'Aren't we?' Frey asked.

'No.'

He raised an eyebrow. 'Aren't we?'

'No. Literally, actually no.'

Frey's eyebrow cranked a few notches higher. 'Aren't w—'

'*Is this really the time or place, Cap'n?*' Harkins screamed, making them all jump.

'Blimey,' said Malvery. 'Someone's wound up.'

'Reckon he's a mite distressed at seeing Jez's morning face,' Frey said.

'That was not her *morning face*!' Harkins was on the edge of an apoplectic fit. 'That was her bloody hideous awful daemon face!'

'Relationship troubles,' said Malvery sagely. 'I prescribe booze.'

'Always worked for me,' said Frey.

'*Pissoffthelotofyou!*' Harkins squawked, sounding like a strangled crow.

Frey grinned. 'I like him angry,' he said. 'Right then. Harkins, stay here, take a breather. Doc, you look after that idiot.' He pointed at Pinn. 'The rest of you, with me.'

He moved, and they followed. They skirted the wall of the quarry, staying out of the crossfire and away from trouble. Without Silo, Jez and Malvery, Frey wasn't confident about their chances in a stand-up fight. Crake was an appalling shot, and wouldn't be much use, but he and Bess were a pair. Ashua could handle a gun, but she needed practice judging by her performance so far.

He kept an eye out for Jez. Where was she? Should he be worried about her as much as the Daks? He couldn't deny that she'd saved everyone's lives a short while ago, but she still scared him. When she was out of control like this, there was no knowing what she'd do. She was probably the most competent member of his crew, but she was the biggest liability as well.

He was still thinking about it when he became aware of a low whine, getting louder and louder. He frowned. Hard to tell what it was.

Louder.

Engines. That was it.

Louder.

He looked up and saw a flaming spear come plunging through the mist. Lit by fire, he caught a glimpse of one of Trinica's Equalisers a moment before it hit the ground. It scored a blazing trench along the valley floor and crashed into the far wall with a noise that made him shudder.

He let out a breath. 'Trinica's gonna kill me,' he murmured.

He hurried on heading towards the voices, Bess clanking alongside him. Soon they found the Murthians. They were shackled in a row near the cliff face, dressed in shabby and battered clothes. Each man and boy wore an ankle shackle and an iron collar. Long chains linked them, passing through metal loops in the shackles and collars. The chains stretched between stout posts that were used as anchors.

The Murthians were holding pickaxes, and waved frantically as they saw Frey. Then they saw Bess, and they shied back in panic, and some began frantically trying to pull themselves free.

Ashua called out in Samarlan, and said something which Frey

assumed was meant to calm them. It worked, at any rate. The panic subsided, but they stayed wary.

There were no guards to be seen, so Frey pointed at the metal posts that secured the slaves. 'See about those posts, will you, Bess?' he said. 'Gently, though, huh? There's people attached.'

Bess lumbered over and pulled up one of the posts, yanking a dozen slaves off their feet as she did so.

'Bit gentler,' Frey advised.

Crake showed her how to snap the chains that secured the slaves without hurting anyone. Once the main chains were broken, the slaves could work themselves free by passing the chains through the loops of their shackles and collars. Bess passed down the line, pulling up posts, breaking chains.

There were fifty or so, all told, coughing and cheering and shouting. Some helped their fellows free. Some ran immediately into the fog, desperate for any kind of escape. Some, enraged, hefted their pickaxes and headed off with a purpose, looking for their former captors.

The blazing streak of fire left by the crashed Equaliser was a hazy, restless glow on the valley floor. Shadows ran across it, howling. There were Daks, Murthians, and Jez somewhere in the middle of all that. Gunshots and screams became more frequent as the slaves dispersed.

'Think there's quite enough chaos yet, Cap'n?' Crake asked nervously, evidently hoping there wouldn't be any more.

'It'll do,' said Frey. 'Let's go.'

They headed away from the quarry wall, towards the white smudge of electric light that Frey had decided was the solitary confinement building. Bullets still cut through the air, but now they were just a few silhouettes among many, and nobody targeted them.

Somebody ran out of the murk, startling them. Bess reacted fastest, lunging out, snatching them up by the arm and lifting them into the air.

'No! Bess, no!' Crake cried in alarm.

A Murthian slave dangled from her grip, face slack with terror.

'Blond!' said Crake, pointing at his own hair and his neatly cropped beard. 'Like this! Don't squash the other ones.'

Bess made an echoing noise deep in her chest, a sound that rose and fell and sounded distressingly like the 'Ohhh!' of an infant who'd just grasped a particularly tricky concept. Frey shivered. Sometimes that golem creeped him out as much as Jez did.

She let the Murthian drop. He backed away a few steps, holding his arm – which looked a bit dislocated, if Frey was honest – and then fled.

'We're still the good guys, right?' Crake asked sarcastically.

'Hey, we freed him, didn't we?'

They reached the building without seeing anyone else. It was a low, bleak box of a place, with a fringe of floods around its roof that blasted out light. A generator rumbled somewhere nearby. By chance, they'd approached it on a side which had an entrance: a stout-looking metal door, firmly sealed.

'They must *really* want these people solitary, to keep them all the way down here,' said Ashua.

'Bess, get the door, would you?' Frey asked.

Bess made a gleeful bubbling noise and punched her fist through the door, then pulled it off its hinges.

'She's very direct, isn't she?' said Ashua to Crake.

'She just likes smashing things,' said Crake, with a hint of apology in his voice. 'It doesn't help that the Cap'n encourages her.'

'You should see her when she's *really* mad,' said Frey eagerly.

Gunfire sounded from within the building. Bullets sparked from Bess's armoured skin. Frey ducked as a ricochet almost parted his hair.

Bess shook the door off her arm and thundered in through the doorway with a roar. The sounds of crashing and rending followed, and agonised screams.

Ashua tilted her head, listening to the carnage. 'I suppose this makes me the third most psychotically lethal female on the *Ketty Jay*, then,' she observed.

'Must be a humbling moment for you,' commiserated Crake.

'I feel practically harmless,' she complained.

'You're not *that* harmless,' said Frey. 'My back teeth are still loose from when you kicked my face in.'

'Oh yeah,' she said, smiling. 'The day we met.' She sighed wistfully. 'Good times.'

'I think Bess is done,' said Crake, now that the screams had stopped. He leaned in through the doorway and came back looking nauseous. 'Yes, she's done.'

Frey went inside. All but one of the overhead lights had been smashed. Bess hulked in the shadows, her eyes twinkling in the black depths of her face-grille, with a long chain of someone's bloody spine hanging from her fist and a very surprised-looking face at the end of it.

Frey stepped inside, his boot squishing into something he'd rather not think about. Fog seeped through the doorway in his wake, lazily invading, fouling the clean air. There wasn't much left of the furniture in the room, but it seemed like a foyer of some kind, where paperwork might have been processed. To his right was a wooden door; to his left, a metal one. The kind for keeping prisoners behind.

Bess obligingly wrenched it open.

He followed the corridor beyond. Bess trudged along behind him, swinging the head as she walked. Crake and Ashua trailed after.

There was a row of cell doors to his right. Each door was solid metal, with a riveted porthole for viewing the cell, and a sealed slot.

'Ugrik!' he yelled. 'I'm looking for Ugrik! Anyone seen him?'

There was no reply. He peered into the first cell. It was plain and bare, with a bunk, a chamberpot and little else. There was a Sammie in there, dressed in a plain hemp shirt and trousers. He was pacing the room, and as he saw Frey he ran to the porthole and began frantically saying something. His words were muted by the soundproofed door. The Sammie indicated the slot below the porthole, miming that Frey should open it. Frey didn't bother. Then Bess leaned in behind him, and the Sammie silently screamed and retreated to the back of the cell.

He looked in on the other prisoners, and their reaction was much the same. There were Sammies and Daks in here. None of them looked particularly dangerous. Frey wondered what was so terrible about them, or what knowledge they possessed, that would merit putting them here.

Each of them reacted in the same way as the first. They'd heard the explosions outside, and thought they might be rescued. He seemed like salvation, until they saw the gore-spattered metal monster he'd brought with him. Then they were less keen to leave the protection of their cells.

In the last cell on the corridor there was a Yort.

He was sitting on his bunk, picking at his fingernails. A short man, but broad-shouldered and stocky, wearing the same prison uniform as the others. His hair was a deep red, matted and dirty. It hung in three thick braids down his back, and his long beard was braided too. There were bones and beads and little ornaments tangled in amongst it all.

Frey unbolted and opened the slot in the door. The Yort looked up. He was in his mid-forties, his face lined and weathered. There were blue stripes inked on his cheeks, above the line of his beard, and a ring through his nose like a bull.

'Ugrik?'

He got up and stood there grinning, exposing wide-set teeth. He had odd-coloured eyes: one green and one blue. Frey wondered what he was grinning at.

'You Ugrik?' he said again.

'That I am,' Ugrik replied.

'Remember that relic you had when the Sammies caught you?'

'That I do.'

'Can you take me to where you found it?'

Ugrik was still grinning. 'Maybe I can, maybe I can't.'

Frey wondered if he was a moron. He pinched the bridge of his nose. 'And maybe I'll leave your bearded arse to rot in this cell. How's that?'

Ugrik came up to the porthole, and pressed his face to the glass. He rolled his eyes to take in Frey's companions. The sight of Bess didn't seem to perturb him in the least.

His eyes rolled back and fixed on Frey. 'You messed with it, didn't you?'

Frey pulled off his glove and slapped his corrupted hand up against the glass, right against Ugrik's face. Ugrik didn't move back, but regarded the hand from the distance of a few centimetres. Far too close to actually see anything.

'How long?' Ugrik asked.

'Tomorrow night, at full dark.'

Ugrik paced away from the porthole. Frey put his glove on again. His patience was wearing thin. Maybe they'd tortured him, or addled him with drugs. 'Look, do you want out of here or not?'

'Here's the deal, stranger,' said Ugrik, with his back turned. 'I'll let you break me out of here on one condition.'

'You'll *let* us break you out?'

344

'Aye.'

'What's the condition?'

'That you take me straight back to where that relic came from.'

Frey blinked. If he'd been prone to migraines, he'd be getting one about now. He looked to Crake, but the daemonist was equally bewildered.

'Ugrik,' said Frey. 'Am I right in thinking you're mad as a bag of otters?'

The Yort looked over his shoulder and grinned. 'I'm not the one with the black spot on my hand,' he replied.

Frey opened his mouth, then shut it again. He'd just roused a small army, organised air support, and fought his way through a fortified compound to get to this man. After going through all that, a little gratitude and cooperation wasn't too much to ask. It was all getting on top of him a bit.

He took a long, calming breath and walked away up the corridor. 'I really, *really* don't have time for this,' he said. He thumbed over his shoulder. 'Bess, get the door. That feller's coming with us.'

THIRTY-FIVE

THE INFIRMARY—CONSEQUENCES— A BITTER PARTING

Jez lay on the operating table in the *Ketty Jay*'s infirmary. If he ignored the fact that she was covered head to foot in other people's blood, Frey would never have guessed that she'd been tearing people's throats out an hour ago.

She lay serenely, unmoving. Her chest didn't rise or fall. She wasn't dead, as far as he could tell. Well, no more dead than normal. It was just that she wouldn't wake up.

'What's wrong with her?' he asked Malvery.

'Dunno,' said the doctor. 'She passed out the first time she did this. Was out for a while, as I recall. Second time she didn't, but I reckon she had it a bit more under control then. This time...' He shrugged. 'Can't do much but wait and see.'

It was lucky they'd found her at all. One of the Murthian slaves had rescued her, in fact. He'd tripped over her, lying unconscious on the quarry floor. Seeing that she wasn't a Dak or Sammie, he figured her for an ally and helped her. Nobody equated her with the shrieking horror that had terrorised the enemy; most of them had only seen her in shadowy glimpses, if at all.

Frey felt bad that he hadn't thought to search for her. He'd just assumed she'd be alright once it passed, that she'd take care of herself. It only now occurred to him that maybe, in this state, she couldn't.

'What is she?' asked Ashua, who was the only other person in Malvery's cramped, squalid infirmary.

Frey reckoned there was no percentage in keeping the secret. Ashua had seen her flip, after all. In fact, she'd been remarkably calm about it. He liked that. A level head was a rarity on the *Ketty Jay*. It was almost a shame he had to boot her off.

'Jez is a half-Mane,' he said. 'Long story.'

'A Mane?' she asked. 'I thought they were just stories.'

'Maybe in the south,' said Frey. 'Up north, they're pretty bloody real.' He gave her a sharp look. 'Mention this to anyone and Bess will punt you into the sea.'

'No one would believe me anyway,' she said.

Frey was satisfied enough with that. He turned to Malvery again, who was stroking his moustache and examining Jez, as if the key to her recovery might be visible somewhere on her body.

'What about Pinn?'

'He's okay. I slipped him something to knock him out. Give us all some peace. Where's the Yort?'

'Eating out the pantry in the mess. That feller can put it away. He was making a fuss about how he couldn't eat "unblessed meat" or some such rubbish, so I left him to it.'

'Oh, that's a Yort thing,' said Malvery. 'They only eat wild meat, and it's gotta have some ritual done over it right after the kill.'

Frey shrugged. 'More meat for us.'

'What's the plan now, Cap'n?' said Ashua. It still sounded faintly like she was taking the piss when she called him Cap'n, but it was hard to tell through the mask.

'Soon as it gets dark, we get out of this fog. Ugrik's given me coordinates. He reckons he can navigate if Jez can't.'

'You trust him?'

'Not a great deal of choice,' said Frey. 'Besides, if he's messing us around, I'll only have a day or so to regret it.'

Crake appeared in the door of the infirmary. 'Visitor for you, Cap'n,' he said. 'She's in the cockpit.'

Frey's shoulders tensed. He'd been hoping to put off this moment as long as possible. 'Ah,' he said. 'Thanks.'

The door between the cockpit and the *Ketty Jay*'s main passageway was closed, which was unusual. He opened the door with some foreboding.

Trinica was sitting in the pilot's seat, looking out through the windglass. Outside, the day was rapidly dimming. The *Delirium Trigger* hung malevolently at anchor in the yellow murk. Shuttles flew back and forth, ferrying the Murthian slaves from the ground.

'Shut the door,' she said. He did so. That was when he noticed that the air in here was clear, and that she didn't appear to be wearing a mask. There was a whirring sound. He looked about for its source.

'It's an air filtration system,' she said. 'It removes the smoke in case of a cockpit fire.'

Frey was bewildered. He took off his mask and inhaled. 'How long's *that* been there?'

'Since I had the *Ketty Jay* overhauled for you in Iktak.'

He knew that voice. The words came out slow and tired, as if the act of speaking them was an effort. It was the voice that came from the blackest depths of her darkest moods.

'Trinica...' he began.

'Five men,' she said. 'Two went down in Equalisers. The rest were killed on board, when the frigate got a shot past our armour.'

Frey had that inadequate, paralysed feeling he got when he had nothing to say that would make things better. He tried anyway.

'We got our man,' he said. 'We couldn't have done that without you. I've got a chance, now. You gave me that.'

'Five men died to give you a *chance*?' Her voice had sharpened.

Frey listened to his instincts this time, and stayed quiet.

She got up and turned away from the windglass, but she still didn't look at him. She was wearing a grey cloak over her black outfit, a deep cowl gathered around her shoulders. A breather mask hung from her hand, the kind that covered the whole face, with lenses for eyes. Her own eyes were that awful, empty black of the pirate queen that had stolen the woman he'd once loved. The black of the Iron Jackal's eye.

'You shouldn't have asked me,' she said.

'You'd rather I died?'

'Those were my men. Men who trusted me.'

'Men who knew the risks,' Frey pointed out.

She shook her head. 'I see it in them, Darian. The doubt. Even Balomon. Even my bosun.'

'You've led them all this time. They'll forgive you.'

'It's not about *forgiveness*,' she hissed. A flash of anger, quickly gone. 'They're not stupid. They know why I did it.' Her eyes tightened. 'You made me weak.'

Frey bridled at the accusation. He couldn't help it. Diplomacy went out the window when he argued with Trinica.

'Hey, I did *exactly* the same for you, back in Sakkan!' he snapped. 'I put my crew at risk to save *your* neck, and at considerably greater bloody odds.'

He was surprised to see her flinch at his tone. It took the sting out of him.

'They owe me,' he added, more gently. 'Don't they get it?'

'You don't understand,' said Trinica. He hated when she did that.

'So explain better,' he said, the edge creeping back into his tone.

'They see what's going on between us!' she cried. 'And now people have died for it! People who they respected, people who were friends and companions!' She caught herself before her anger could get out of control, and suddenly she was tired and mournful again, the fire doused. 'I'm in charge of fifty cut-throat men. Men like that don't take orders from women. But they take orders from me. You know why? Because I don't let them think of me that way. They want me ruthless, Darian. They want me cruel.'

She met his gaze, and he saw tears glittering in her black eyes. 'You're taking that away from me,' she whispered.

Something terrible was coming. He sensed it. Suddenly it was hard to breathe.

'I know you, Trinica. That isn't how you are.'

'No,' she said, and she held out a gloved hand to him. 'You *knew* me.'

Lying in her palm was a silver ring. A ring he'd given her once, in place of the one he should have given her all those years ago. The ring that linked them together.

'Take it,' she said, her voice cracking.

'No,' he said. The words sounded distant. Blood was beating in his ears. 'It's yours.'

Then she tipped her hand, and the ring slid from her palm and fell to the floor of the cockpit. 'I don't want it.'

He felt suddenly weak, and sat against the edge of the metal desk at the navigator's station. He couldn't take his gaze from the ring on the floor. It felt as if something dark was thundering towards him. He was shocked that anything would unbalance him so much.

When he looked up at Trinica, she was wearing the breather mask, and pulling the cowl over her head. She turned her face towards him, and he couldn't see anything of her any more.

'I'll deliver the slaves to the camp, as we agreed,' she said. 'You have more pressing issues to deal with.'

She walked to the door and slid it open. There she stopped, her head bowed slightly.

'Consider us even for Sakkan, Captain Frey. I doubt we'll meet again.'

And then she was gone, walking up the passageway.

Frey crouched down slowly. He was suddenly unsure whether his legs would support him. His stomach felt like it wanted to cramp, to pull him into a ball. He reached out, picked up the ring, and stood up again.

I don't want it.

He turned it over in his hand. His corrupted hand. Then he slipped it on to his little finger, where he'd worn it before he gave it to her.

Footsteps were coming up the corridor. He swallowed down the nameless feeling that was swelling in his gut, crushing it back. He pulled on his breather mask, stared hard into the middle distance. Control, control. Be the captain. No time for this.

It was Silo. He stuck his head in through the open door of the cockpit. 'Cap'n?' he said.

Frey nodded at him.

'Last shuttle up to the *Delirium Trigger*'s about to leave.'

'Trinica's gone,' he said. The double meaning almost broke him, but he firmed his mouth behind his mask.

'Yuh,' he said. 'Passed her. Just thought you'd want to know.'

'You're…' he began, then stopped. Did he really want to ask the question? 'You're not going with them?'

Silo's face showed nothing. 'Man can't go back, I reckon,' he said. 'It's Ehri's show now.'

Frey walked over to stand behind the pilot's seat and looked out through the windglass at the *Delirium Trigger* and the fog-shrouded buildings of Gagriisk.

'We did some good here, right?' he said.

'Some,' said Silo.

Frey let out a breath, with only the slightest of trembles in it. 'Being a hero really bites shit, huh?' he said.

'Wouldn't know, Cap'n,' said Silo.

'No,' said Frey. 'Me, neither.'

THIRTY-SIX

❖

'WHERE ARE YOU, JEZ?'—AN UNEXPECTED MEETING—GOOD NEWS, BAD NEWS— TURBULENCE

Silo sat amid the tight maze of metal walkways that surrounded the *Ketty Jay*'s engine assembly. He was staring into space, one arm dangling over his knee and a wrench held loosely in his hand, listening to the engine with half an ear. Everything was smooth. Not even the hint of a fault.

Sweat ran insidiously across his shaven scalp. It was night outside, but the engine kept things hot in here. There was a wet chewing sound from nearby: Slag, devouring a rat somewhere out of sight.

Silo felt restless. His mind wouldn't settle to any kind of peace. He'd tried to distract himself with duties, but as usual there was nothing for him to do.

He should go see if he could help patch up Bess, perhaps. But Crake was feverishly working at something for the Cap'n, and wouldn't welcome the disturbance. She'd only taken a few holes; it could wait. Besides, it was painfully obvious make-work, and it smacked of desperation.

He downed tools and headed out of the engine room. He couldn't stop seeing Fal's dead face, or Ehri's hateful eyes. She'd blamed him. In time, perhaps she wouldn't, but he wouldn't be there to receive her forgiveness if she did.

And what about Akkad? Akkad, a man who'd been his friend. What had they done with him? Did he go to the Warrens? Did they put Babbad and his other allies in there with him? What about his wife Menlil and their children? Surely not them. Surely Ehri wouldn't do that.

He'd never asked, not after that first time. He hadn't dared to. And now he never would.

The door to the engine room was at the end of the main passageway that ran up the spine of the *Ketty Jay*. The first doorway on his right was the infirmary. It was open. Jez lay on the operating table. Malvery had his feet up on a chair and was sipping from a mug, idly reading a broadsheet.

'How is she?' he asked.

Malvery looked up. 'Same.'

'Mind if I sit with her awhile?'

Malvery swung his legs off the chair and got up. 'Could you? I've been waiting for someone to keep an eye on her. I've got one hulking colossus of a turd to unload. Feels like I'm about to give birth to my own leg.' He rolled up his broadsheet and strolled off towards the head, whistling.

When he was gone, Silo slid the door shut and took a seat. Jez lay motionless. Malvery had sponged off the blood from her face and hair and hands, but her clothes were still covered with dried gore. There was nothing about her to indicate that she was alive. They were just going on faith that everything would be alright.

Ain't we always?

He sat there a long while, listening to the rumble of the thrusters. Outside was the desert and the night. They were headed on a course plotted by the Yort explorer, flying to who knew where. By this time tomorrow night, that damned relic would have to be put back wherever it came from.

But what if it wasn't?

'I lost my place, Jez,' he said. He surprised himself by speaking aloud. There was a hollow ring from the empty walls of the infirmary as each word faded.

He looked at Jez. She didn't move. After a moment he sighed to himself, and settled, and spoke again.

'Time was, there weren't no choices and there weren't no questions. I got born a slave. There weren't no other way to be. In the end I broke out, but things were just as straight-up then as before. Black 'n' white, us 'n' them. And I had a lot of anger to work off.'

He rolled his shoulders, then fished in the pocket of his trousers and drew out a pouch.

'World ain't that simple no more,' he said.

He built himself a roll-up full of Murthian herbs. The process was relaxing. He enjoyed the comforting rhythm of spreading the dried herbs, rolling the paper, licking and sealing it. He let his mind wander while his fingers worked, allowing his thoughts to percolate. He lit a match, took a drag, sat back and waited for what he wanted to say to come out of his mouth. He wasn't in any hurry, and nor was Jez.

'When I was back there, back with my people...' he said at length. 'Y'know, for a while it felt like things was right again. Like the last nine years din't happen, like I won instead o' losin' when I went up against Akkad, and the world just rolled on without no break.' He dragged and exhaled, filling the infirmary with the pungent, acrid smell of the herb. 'But I ain't that young man no more, Jez. Got old enough to feel my losses. And bein' back among my people, killin' Daks... It makes me someone I don't wanna be. If I'd stayed, they'd suck me right back in. That's what your people do. They suck you in. Happens whether you like it or not.'

He examined the roll-up, held between his long fingers. He'd smoked them ever since he escaped. Seemed like the sort of thing a free man should do.

'I thought lettin' another man make my choices for me was the best way to go about things. Turns out it ain't. Might be the Cap'n gonna be dead this time tomorrow. Might be we all be goin' our separate ways then.'

He shook his head. 'Reckon you can't never go back to what you were,' he said. 'But I done bein' quiet now, I know that.'

He took another drag, drawing the smoke into his lungs. He held it there till it started to burn, then he let it seep out from between his lips.

Jez still hadn't moved. He wondered if she ever would.

'Where are you, Jez?' he asked quietly. 'Where you gone?'

Snow flurried around Jez's face, driven by a chill wind. Loose strands of hair fluttered against her cheek. She stood over her own dead body, looking down.

The Yortish coast. The bleak settlement where the Manes had caught her. White flakes sifted from the grey clouds.

Her corpse lay on its side in a foetal position, half-buried. The snow had gathered in the hollows of her body and face, obscuring her.

Had she been here before? She couldn't quite remember. Had it been different then? She couldn't remember that, either.

She followed her own tracks back to the town. Between the domed buildings, she saw hints of more corpses – a frozen hand, a blue face in a drift – but the carnage had been mostly erased beneath the whiteness, and it was possible to ignore it as she wandered.

She found the main thoroughfare. A snow-tractor lay in a deep drift, with only the corner of its cab visible. She had a vague recollection of cracked windows and smeared blood, but there was nothing visible now. The street had a quiet, abandoned feel. The only sound was the restless whistle of the wind.

A dreadnought hung in the air above the thoroughfare. Ropes and chains hung from its flanks, trailing down to the ground. The chains clanked softly as they were stirred by the wind. She regarded it curiously, running an eye over its spiked gunwales and dirty iron keel.

She was waiting. Listening. And soon she heard it: the slowly swelling sound, the baying of the pack, their screeching. They were up there, on the dreadnought. She couldn't see them, but she knew they were there. They didn't call to her as they had in the past. They keened and howled to each other instead. But their voices provoked in her a desire to be with them, to join them in the feral simplicity of the hunt. To be a sister to them, and be enfolded in the warmth of their community. She was always in between, not quite human and nowhere near Mane. She felt the lonely ache of separation.

A hand touched her shoulder, and she turned. Standing there, dressed in thick furs, was someone she'd never thought to see again. The man who'd been with her that day when the Manes came, who'd tried to protect her when her own courage had failed. Who'd saved her from the Invitation by killing the Mane that caught her.

His hood had been thrown back and his mask hung on a strap round his neck. Thick black hair framed a plain and honest face.

Rinn.

She hugged him, surprising herself. He was the last person she saw before she died. It was important to her that he was here.

His arms folded around her with uncertain reverence, then he clutched her tightly. There was longing in his touch. The pilot had always felt something for her that she never had for him.

'I thought you were dead,' she said.

'No more dead than you are.'

She let him go. 'They took you?'

'Yes,' he said.

'What happened?'

'After you ran into the snow, I tried to follow. But I was alone, and two of them caught me. There was no one to help me.' He smiled. 'Now I'm glad of it.'

Jez searched his face. He seemed like the same old Rinn: solid, reliable, relentlessly normal.

'What's it like?' she asked.

He shook his head slightly, as if to say: *you wouldn't understand*. He held out a gloved hand to her.

'Come with me,' he said.

And then, in the way of dreams, they were elsewhere.

They stood inside a huge cave of ice. At their feet, the ground fell away in sharp steps, cut out in great squares and rectangles that descended towards a narrow shaft in the centre. Excavation machinery, brutal claws and drills, sat among the ladders and scaffolding, their surfaces rimed with frost. The wind blew outside, but within the cavern was a vast quiet, and the air was still. It felt like an abandoned temple.

'Remember this?' Rinn asked.

'I hardly ever came up here,' she said. 'I didn't know they'd dug down so far.'

'The Professor was warned. He knew it was coming up to blizzard season, and that was when the Manes went raiding along the coast of the Poleward Sea. But he was obsessed. He was convinced there was an Azryx city buried under this spot, and he couldn't wait.'

She studied the excavation. 'I knew it too,' she said. 'I just didn't really believe the stories. But all that talk about the Azryx's wonderful advanced technology, this utopian civilisation lost beneath the ice…' She discovered that she was wearing a fur-and-hide coat, the same one she'd been wearing the day she died, and she drew it close about her even though she wasn't cold. 'Sort of romantic,' she said. 'Making history. I wanted to be part of it.'

'But there was nothing down there in the end,' he said.

'What happened to the Professor?'

'He was killed,' said Rinn. 'When we came for him, he surrounded himself with men with guns. We don't like that.'

Something in his voice had changed. Jez turned to look at him. He was gazing back at her with sunken, blood-coloured eyes. His teeth had sharpened to points. His face was gaunt and hollow. None of it disturbed her in the least.

'Why are you here?' she asked.

'To warn you. You've been testing your abilities, Jez. Pushing your boundaries. But you don't know the cost involved. The more you use them, the more you unlock, the more you'll become like us.'

'I thought the Manes had agreed to let me be.'

'We have done. The Manes don't want the unwilling. That's why I'm telling you now. It's *you* who's doing this.'

'Ah,' she said. 'Curiosity killed the cat.'

'You could say that.'

'What can I do?'

'Do nothing. You're a half-Mane. Be content with that.'

She nodded to herself. Suddenly, she was tired of the sight of the excavation, and a moment later they were outside the ice caves, on the glacier, looking down over the town and the dreadnought hanging over it. She could see its decks now. They were empty, but she could still hear the singing of her brethren, and it tugged at her.

'What if I'm *not* content with that?' she asked.

'Then you'll be welcome among us, beloved,' said Rinn, now wearing rags, his skin like parchment, his voice breathy and hoarse. His thick hair had become a greasy straggle, and his lips had peeled back to show yellowed and daggerlike fangs. 'But if you choose that way, you'll walk a fine line. We can think because we used to be human. The daemon you have inside you, it doesn't think in any way you can comprehend. It'll change you if you let it. It can't help itself. Bit by bit, you'll become more like us and less like them.'

'Is this how it works, for those who refuse the Invitation?' she asked. 'You let them go, so they can make their own way back? Because you want them willing?'

'We're not so devious. The choice is yours.'

'But I bet they all come back in the end, don't they?'

'Most do. Some don't. The others…'

'They kill themselves,' said Jez.

'Yes.'

Jez could understand. She'd never contemplated it herself, but the terror of the Manes and the temptation of their call could have easily driven her to madness in those early days. A more delicate soul might have ended themselves rather than risk succumbing to that.

She surveyed the scene. The snow was falling more heavily now, and the far side of the town was becoming obscured. 'When do I wake up?' she asked.

'That's up to you.'

She thought about that. Then she walked over to a hillock of ice and sat down. 'I reckon I'd like to stay a while yet. Chew things over. Will you stay with me?'

Rinn was Rinn again, pink-cheeked and healthy, clad in furs and hide. The man she'd known when she was alive. He sat down next to her.

'I'd like that,' he said.

Crake stood in his makeshift sanctum at the back of the *Ketty Jay*'s cargo hold, his hand on his bearded chin, and regarded the relic with deep suspicion. It sat on the floor inside a protective summoning circle, amid a jumble of cables and detecting devices. The black case was open, showing the jackal emblem inside the lid. The double-bladed weapon lay in its finely-wrought cradle. He hadn't dared to touch it.

But then, as it turned out, he hadn't needed to.

He checked the readings on the oscilloscope again. There was no question.

Something was very wrong here.

He frowned. The damned thing was so *alien*. The long, narrow blades at either end of the handle were made of some material he'd never seen before. They had a crisp, dry ceramic quality, and gave off no reflection. The way they curved in opposite directions resembled no ancient weapon he'd ever seen. Admittedly he was no authority, but he knew his way around a museum.

Then there were the symbols, cut with exquisite precision into the handle and blades. Faintly suggestive of language, but if so it was a long way from any he recognised. And there was the question of its age. They had only Crickslint's word that it was ancient. It might have been fashioned yesterday, judging by its lack of wear.

But most puzzling of all was the daemonism. It simply defied his analysis. He couldn't hope to penetrate its complexities with the equipment he had. All he'd gleaned were clues, and they would have to be enough.

If this relic was indeed thousands of years old, then it was the find of the century. It proved that daemonism was alive and thriving long before most civilisations and religions got to their feet. It hinted at untold possibilities for today's practitioners, if only they could overcome the prejudice fostered by the Awakeners. And as long as nobody mentioned that the Manes were created by the hubris of the early daemonists.

But what if it *wasn't* thousands of years old? He was beginning to wonder. Because he'd decoded part of the orchestra of chords that had been thralled into the relic. And what he found was a very modern technique indeed.

There were sheets of formulae and diagrams all over the room. One side of the sanctum looked more like an engineer's workshop, where he'd been experimenting with all the devices and parts he'd bought in Thesk. Bess was slumped in the corner of the sanctum, a blanket draped over her shoulders, stumpy legs sticking out. Her glittering eyes had disappeared; there was only darkness behind her face-grille. Her favourite storybook lay loosely in her hand.

The sight of her caused a sudden, plunging sadness. There were new bullet-holes in her soft leather parts that would need repairing. New chips and dents in her armour. She was in a sorry state. He didn't take care of her as well as he wished he could, and he'd been distracted of late with his mission to protect the Cap'n.

What if he failed? What if they couldn't get the relic back in time, and Crake's untested methods came to nothing? Crake would survive without the *Ketty Jay*, but where would Bess go? He could hardly walk around with her in public: she was evidence that he was a daemonist. It struck him then that he'd been so obsessed with his own needs, and later with the Cap'n's, that he'd barely thought about her at all since this whole affair began.

You're a despicable person, Grayther Crake, he told himself. *No wonder you did what you did to Miss Bree.*

Grim-faced, he marched out of the sanctum, through the tarpaulin flap that led into the hold.

It was more of a mess than usual down here, after hauling fifty Murthians to Gagriisk and Frey's hefty landing, which knocked everything around. It was a miracle that most of the equipment in his sanctum survived a jolt like that. Only his harmoniser had broken, but luckily he could do without that for the moment.

The Rattletraps had been retrieved after the battle. They'd only used two of the three – the ones with mounted gatlings – but those had made it back in surprisingly good condition. They may have looked like pieces of junk, but Ashua evidently knew what she was doing when she bought them.

Reminded by that thought, he stopped at the bottom of the stairs and peered round the side, into the darkness that gathered against the bulkhead. He could hear breathing in there. Not the Iron Jackal, thankfully. The heavy breathing of sleep.

He could just about make her out among the pipes, curled up in a nook in the bulkhead that had been padded out with tarp. She was lying on her side, swallowed by a dusty and voluminous sleeping bag. The shiver and shudder of the wind against the *Ketty Jay* didn't seem to bother her at all.

The Cap'n had made noises about shuffling people around to give her a bed – Crake had feared he was going to have to swap quarters with Jez, and lose the upper bunk he used for books and storage – but she preferred to be down here. She said she'd grown up sleeping rough, and couldn't sleep in a bed anyway. Plus there was lots of space in the hold. It was a little odd, but nobody complained.

He still wasn't sure how he felt about having her on board. His initial reaction had been horror. He hadn't wanted anyone or anything to upset the delicate balance that they'd managed to maintain all this time. But he wondered now if he'd been overly harsh. She appeared to have a brain, which was something that Crake generally approved of. Her sass was never directed at him, which was a point in her favour. In fact, she seemed to have chosen him as her co-conspirator when mocking someone else. That was a nice feeling. Malvery seemed quite taken with her, too, and he respected the doctor's opinion in most things.

So maybe it wouldn't be so bad, if the Cap'n could keep his hands off her.

The Cap'n, he thought. Yes. He had news to deliver.

He made his way up to the cockpit. Frey was flying them low over a sea of dunes. The moon was dead ahead, only a slim black fingernail away from a perfect circle. It was a bright night. Crake tried not to think about the risks of being spotted by a Samarlan patrol. Maybe that was why they were flying so distressingly low.

Ugrik was in the navigator's seat, amid an untidy mass of charts. He turned in his seat as Crake entered, and cackled at him.

'The mysterious Mr Crake emerges from his den!' Ugrik declared. 'What've you been up to down there, eh? Stirring up the infinite?'

'Something like that,' said Crake stiffly. He found the bluntness of Yorts rather rude, and he hadn't thought he was being especially mysterious anyway.

'Something like that,' Ugrik muttered to himself, sotto voce. 'Aye, something very like that, I'll bet.'

Crake couldn't work out what he meant by that. It sounded disconcertingly like a threat. Ugrik went back to his maps. Crake gave him a doubtful glance and then turned his attention to the Cap'n.

Frey was staring ahead with the fixed concentration of a man determined to think about nothing. Crake had heard that Trinica had been on board. It wasn't hard to guess who was responsible for the Cap'n's present mood.

'Any word on our destination, Cap'n?'

Ugrik cackled again, not looking up from his charts. 'You'll see! You'll see!'

Frey thumbed at Ugrik, as if to say: *there's your answer.*

Crake cleared his throat. 'Would you like the good news or the bad news first?'

'Bad news first is traditional, isn't it?'

'I believe so.'

'Gimme the good news.'

'The bad news is... er, right. The *good* news is, I've made a certain amount of progress on the question of the daemon. I've been working on some things based on your rather brave field test of my concealment device, and I've developed a few techniques that might prove effective. If the worst should come to the worst, that is.'

Frey nodded, without much enthusiasm. 'Did I ever thank you, Crake?'

'For what?'

'That thing, that device. Saved my life.'

'Oh, yes,' he thought for a moment. 'No, you didn't.'

'Thank you,' he said. 'I know you've been working flat out on my behalf all this time. I want you to know I appreciate it.'

It was delivered in an oddly emotionless monotone. Crake began to worry about the Cap'n's state of mind. Perhaps he was just exhausted. They were all exhausted. It seemed like they hadn't had a chance to catch their breath since they first found the black spot on Frey's hand.

'You're welcome.'

'Bad news now,' Frey said.

'Bad news.' Crake paused for a moment, wondering how best to approach this. 'I don't suppose you've heard of a harmonic resonance bounce?'

Frey gave him a withering look over his shoulder. Crake decided it was not the look of a person who was likely to have heard of a harmonic resonance bounce.

'Silly question, I suppose. Let me put it simply. You remember that ring I gave you a while ago, that was linked to a compass?'

'This ring?' Frey asked, raising his hand.

Crake suddenly understood. 'Oh,' he said. 'Cap'n, I'm very sor—'

'Buy me a drink if I'm not dead by tomorrow night. You were saying?'

Crake had been knocked off his stride. 'Er... anyway. The way the ring and compass works is that you thrall two daemons which oscillate at the same frequency to both objects, allowing one to always find the other, rather like a magnetic pull. The earcuffs run on the same principle of matched oscillation, though they're a sight more complex. When a daemon is thralled to something in this way, it forms a unique chord which is out of phase with the rest of the object, setting up an invisible wave which travels between the objects, which is what we call a harmonic reson—'

'Layman's terms, Crake,' said Frey, getting ever so slightly annoyed.

'Someone's tracking the relic.'

'There, now, that wasn't so hard.'

Crake wondered if he did have a tendency to over-explain. He ought to work on that. 'It's just like the ring and compass, although,

I reluctantly admit, more skilful and precise. But somebody, somewhere, has a device that tells them exactly where the relic is at all times.'

'And only a daemonist could do this?'

'Yes.'

'Know any?'

'None that have been anywhere near that relic.'

'Can you block it?'

'Should be easy enough. But it'll take time.'

Frey tutted. 'Time's exactly what we *don't*—'

A heavy shudder ran through the *Ketty Jay*, violent enough to make Crake stumble.

'—have…' Frey finished, in a tone of apprehension.

They waited, eyes roaming their surroundings as if they might see what had caused the disturbance.

'Turbulence, I reckon,' said Frey.

The *Ketty Jay* shivered again. Then suddenly it was shaken hard, and Crake wheeled across the cockpit to crash into the bulkhead on the far side.

He shook his head to clear it, only to find that the sickening slant to the cockpit was not a result of his disorientation. The *Ketty Jay*'s thrusters puffed and boomed, dying and relighting again. She was listing hard to starboard, and there was a horrible ascending drone that Crake had learned to associate with plummeting aircraft. His stomach plummeted in sympathy.

'Cap'n!' he cried. 'What's happeni—'

'Shut it! I'm busy!' Frey barked at him. The Cap'n was struggling with the flight stick, frantically pulling levers, turning valves, kicking pedals. 'Everything's gone haywire!'

Crake clambered to his feet with the help of the back of the pilot's seat. Over Frey's shoulder, he could see all kinds of brass dials and meters on the dash. They were flicking crazily this way and that. The steel-coloured waves of desert sand outside were tilted at a frightening angle.

'One of the aerium tanks is jammed half open!' Frey cried, thrashing at a nearby lever. They lurched forward, throwing Crake hard against the back of the chair. 'And the damn thrusters are—' He swore and punched a button. The thrusters boomed once more and died.

The quiet was sudden and awful. The *Ketty Jay*'s nose tipped steadily downwards. Frey wrestled with the stick to stop her rolling to starboard.

'*What did you do to the thrusters?*' Crake screamed.

Ugrik chuckled. 'This is just like this time in Marduk. So cold, it were, the engine froze, and we—'

'You can shut your trap as well!' Frey yelled at him. He began frantically strapping himself in with one hand, while trying to hold the course with the other. He craned round in the seat and shouted down the corridor. 'Everyone hang on!'

'Hang on to what?' Crake howled, casting around the cockpit for something to attach himself to. In the end, he stayed clinging to the back of the chair. He felt the *Ketty Jay* getting heavier and heavier as she lost aerium. She glided with terrible silent grace through the moonlit night.

'Do something!' Crake flapped.

'Suggestions would be good!'

'Hit some buttons!'

The Cap'n suddenly lit up. 'Hey, I never tried that button before.' He stabbed it with his finger.

The silence was filled by the steady whirring of fans as the air filtration system kicked in.

'Oh, *that's* where it was,' said Frey, and then Crake felt a terrific shove from behind, he struck his head against something hard, and the world went black.

THIRTY-SEVEN

MAROONED—FREY DESPAIRS—SHINE— THE THING ABOUT UNDERDOGS

The moon hung bloated and malevolent against a dense backdrop of stars. In all directions, to the horizon and beyond, was the deep desert. Endless dunes, utterly still. Not a breath of wind stirred the silver sand. It might have been the landscape of a dead planet.

The *Ketty Jay* lay at the end of a massive furrow, a scar in the pristine vista. Her nose was buried where the sand had braked her. Her tail end was tilted up into the air at a shallow angle. She'd come in on her belly, her armoured undercarriage taking the brunt of the impact, and it was only as she'd come near to a halt that her front end had ploughed into the sand. There was enough aerium still in her tanks to make her much lighter than her size suggested, and Frey had managed to take a lot of speed out of her in the seconds before they crashed. The *Ketty Jay* had taken a battering, but she'd held together.

All things considered, it was a damned fine landing. Not that that made Frey feel much better about things.

'Ain't no reason for it, Cap'n,' said Silo, who was peering into a panel underneath the dash. He had an electric torch, attached by wires to a nearby battery pack, and he was shining it around inside. 'Can't see none, anyways.'

Frey crouched next to him in the semi-darkness with an oil lantern from the stores. The cockpit windglass was almost entirely covered by the tide of sand. Only a sliver of moonlight was left, and the *Ketty Jay*'s internal lights weren't working. Not even the emergency backups.

'How did this happen?' Frey asked. 'She just got overhauled.'

'Ain't nothing to do with the aircraft,' said Silo, emerging.

'Systems that ain't even connected all went down at the same time.'

'So it's something from outside?'

The Murthian's face was sinister, underlit by the torch. 'Couldn't say, Cap'n.' He thought for a moment. 'You got your pocket watch? Left mine with a friend.'

Frey brought it out. Silo shone a light on it. 'Still working,' said Frey.

'Watch is pretty simple. Clockwork. So maybe it's just the delicate stuff got muddled.'

'Can't you, I don't know, reset the systems or something?'

'Cap'n, there ain't no reason why some o' them systems ain't working. But they ain't. I reckon whatever did this to the *Ketty Jay*, it's still doin' it. We ain't even gonna get the lights up till we sort that out.'

Frey was grim. 'Do what you can, then,' he said, and then carried his lantern to his quarters and shut himself inside.

He laid his lantern on top of the cabinet, after making sure it wouldn't slide off due to the *Ketty Jay*'s uncomfortable tilt. The weak light made the small, grimy room even smaller and grimier. The flame flickered in uneasy streaks on the metal walls. He washed his face in the tiny sink – the water was running, but it didn't heat – and regarded himself in the mirror.

He looked haggard. There were dark bags under his eyes and he hadn't shaved recently. How long had it been since he slept properly? Seemed like for ever.

He returned to the cabinet and unlocked the drawer where he kept his Shine. It was a small clear bottle with a screw-top pipette. He went over to his bunk and sat on the edge, tipping the bottle this way and that, studying the liquid inside.

Probably enough to kill him in there, he reckoned.

He snorted. *Stop being dramatic.* He'd never had the temperament for suicide. But a couple of drops of Shine seemed like a good idea right about then. Forget everything for a few hours. Dream the blissful, feathery dreams of the Shine-stoned.

No more scrabbling about in the gutter, he'd told himself. Time to make the big moves, he'd said. After all, that was the kind of thing the hero of Sakkan ought to do. The kind of thing that was expected of him.

And look where he'd ended up. Cursed by some rat-damned ancient blade that he couldn't keep his hands off. Jez in a coma.

Pinn shot for a second time. The Firecrow wrecked. The *Ketty Jay* crashed in the trackless desert a thousand kloms from anywhere. Very possibly his crew would all die of starvation if the ship didn't get fixed, but he had a messy evisceration at the hands of the Iron Jackal to look forward to instead. He'd probably helped to kick off a civil war back in Vardia, and he was on the Century Knights' hit-list after his little stunt at the Mentenforth Institute. On top of that, he'd ruined things with Trinica, and he didn't know if he could ever make it right, even if he did manage to survive long enough to try.

When you stacked it all up, he'd done a pretty shabby job of things.

Maybe he just wasn't cut from the right cloth. It seemed like there were people who carried the burden of the big decisions lightly. People born to a life of command: aristocrats and officers and leaders. Their choices saved lives and cost them, too. Those weren't the kind of decisions that should be left in the hands of a shiftless orphan boy.

His whole command was a sham. Unwittingly, he'd tricked his crew into trusting him. By pretending to be a captain, he'd somehow become one, and for a time he believed he deserved it. But he didn't. The evidence was pretty clear on that.

At least Trinica had the sense to turn her back on him before he destroyed her life a second time.

He dug into his pocket and brought out the compass that Crake had given him once upon a time. The silver ring was on his finger. The compass pointed at him now, accusingly. He tossed it onto his bunk and unscrewed the cap on the Shine bottle.

Damn it, what was the point? He'd tried to do everything right by Trinica and it still hadn't worked. The first time, at least, had been his choice and his fault. When he ran out on their wedding, the overwhelming emotion was relief. Relief that he'd escaped her, and the child she carried. Relief that he was out of the trap. Regret had come later, and slowly. By the time he changed his mind it was too late.

But this time was like nothing he'd ever felt before. There was a tight point of pain just below his breastbone. He was taken by a sense of enormous absence and dumb bewilderment.

Everything around him had faded since she left him. The crew slid in and out of his world like ghosts. He barely listened to them and replied on automatic. Only when the *Ketty Jay* had been going down did he sharpen up, threat pulling him from torpor. But mostly he was mired in an exquisite misery, complex, layered and pervasive.

He looked at the bottle of Shine in his hands. A drop in each eye, and the cloudy joy of a drugged sleep. It was as good a way out as any. Was it really worth clinging to the faint hope that the *Ketty Jay* would come to life again in time to get them to where they were going? It all seemed pretty futile, in the end.

You've been losing since the day you were born, he told himself. *You'll never be a hero. You'll always be an underdog. So take the drug. Stop fighting. Stop trying to be something you're not.*

He nodded to himself. He was right. All this time, he'd been trying to be something he wasn't.

He flung the bottle of Shine against the wall. It smashed with a tinkle and a splatter of clear liquid.

Time to stop pretending, then.

'Ugrik!' he snapped as he slid down the ladder into the mess.

The Yort coughed through a faceful of cake, spraying crumbs across the table. It was one of Malvery's sugar-laden creations that had been sitting in the pantry since the dawn of civilisation. Ugrik quickly slobbered down some coffee straight from the pot, as if fearing it would be snatched away from him.

Frey regarded him with mild disgust. Ugrik was still dressed in the plain beige prison uniform they'd found him in, except now it was covered in coffee stains. He wiped his bearded chops with his sleeve and burped. The oil lantern in front of him flared briefly.

'We had a deal,' Ugrik said. 'You were meant to take me back to where that relic came from. Wouldn't have let you break me out otherwise.'

'What do you think I'm *trying* to do, arse-for-brains?' said Frey, who was frankly in no mood for any bullshit. He stamped over – an awkward process on the slanted floor – and stood across the table from the Yort. 'Now I need some answers, and I need them now, and if I hear one cryptic comment out of you I swear I'm gonna take every piece of cutlery in this room and shove it up your arse!'

He slammed his hands down on the table, making Ugrik jump. 'This place we're going. How far?'

'Fifty kloms or so,' said Ugrik.

Now they were getting somewhere. Fifty kloms, though. Too far to get there before tomorrow night on foot.

'You've been there before, right?' he asked Ugrik. 'Course you have, that's where you got the relic. So how'd you get there the first time?'

Ugrik rolled his eyes as if it was a stupid question. 'Ridin' on a *ka'riish*. Out here with some Sammie nomads.'

'A ka-what? That an animal?'

'Aye.'

'And how did you find it? Where *did* you get that relic, anyhow?'

'I had an idea where it was,' he said, answering the first question but ignoring the second. 'Found some tracks and followed 'em.'

'Tracks?'

'Aye. I got lucky. It was a still day, no wind. The sand hadn't covered 'em up yet.'

'What kind of tracks?'

'Tyre tracks.'

Frey slammed his hands down on the table again, this time in triumph. Ugrik jumped a second time.

'Wish you'd stop doin' that,' he mumbled.

'Can you find it again? This place?'

'Aye. Due east. Can't miss it. Well, actually you *can*, but I—'

'Right,' said Frey sharply. 'Get up. We're going.'

'Can I finish me cake first?'

'No!' Frey snapped.

Ugrik gave a resigned sigh. He pushed out his chair, as if he was about to get to his feet. Then, suddenly, he lunged across the table and snatched up the cake, stuffing as much of it as he could into his mouth before Frey wrestled it off him. Ugrik glared at him resentfully, chewing.

'Baftard,' he said.

Frey filled a bag with supplies from the mess and then bullied Ugrik down into the cargo hold. He encountered nobody on the way. Crake was in his quarters, being nursed by Malvery for a mild concussion. Pinn and Jez were out of it. Harkins was hiding, Silo was working, and he had no idea where Ashua was.

Nobody to stop him, then.

He slung the bag in the back of one of the Rattletraps parked in the middle of the hold, then walked over to the lever that controlled the cargo ramp and threw it. The cargo ramp whined and screeched as it opened, letting in moonlight and the chilly desert breeze. It bumped to a stop several feet off the ground, due to the fact that the *Ketty Jay*'s tail was tilted in the air.

'Get the straps,' he told Ugrik. He pointed to a corner of the hold. 'And grab some fuel from over there.' Ugrik got to work on the restraining straps that stopped the Rattletrap from sliding about. Frey stalked purposefully towards Crake's sanctum at the back of the hold. He threw aside the tarp and walked in.

The relic was lying in a tangle of wires and cables, where it had been thrown in the crash. The blade still sat in its cradle inside its smooth black case. Frey walked over, snapped the case shut and picked it up.

A curious cooing noise from behind him made him turn. It was Bess, hunched in the shadows. She stirred and the chips of light behind her face-grille glinted into life.

'Only me, Bess,' he whispered. 'Go back to sleep.'

Bess sagged again, and the lights of her eyes went out.

When he returned, he found Ugrik putting canisters of fuel in the back of the Rattletrap, along with a bundle of tarp and some twine. He didn't bother to ask why they needed tarp. He was just keen to be out of here before any of his crew happened along.

'You reckon this thing'll run?' Ugrik asked, as they climbed in.

'You said you saw wheel tracks. Silo says it's only the delicate stuff on the *Ketty Jay* that's gotten messed up. And these Rattletraps are about as basic as you get.' He fired the ignition, and the Rattletrap growled into life. 'Like I said.'

Ugrik looked around the empty hold. 'Ain't nobody else comin'?'

'Reckon they've done more than enough on my behalf already,' said Frey. 'This is just you and me.'

'Well, alright,' said Ugrik with a grin. 'I like a man who goes down swingin'.'

'That's the thing about underdogs,' Frey replied. 'We never know when we're beaten.'

He stamped on the accelerator. The Rattletrap raced across the hold, down the cargo ramp, and leaped off the edge into the night.

THIRTY-EIGHT

DESERTERS—THE VANISHING ISLE—THE REAL STORY—TARPAULIN—A MIRAGE, POSSIBLY

The sun, the relentless sun.

Frey had briefly wondered why Ugrik had bothered to pack a sheet of tarpaulin while they were loading up the Rattletrap. He'd assumed it was another facet of the Yort's general oddness. It wasn't until dawn, when they stopped to fix the tarp to the roll cage with twine, that he saw the sense in it. Frey had brought water, but he hadn't thought about shade. He never was much of a forward planner.

He drove stripped to the waist, his back running with sweat. The sand was bright enough to blind. The morning had been the worst, when they were driving into the sun. Now it was overhead, and the tarp was doing its work, but his eyes still hurt from the light and the sand thrown up by the Rattletrap's wheels.

He took a swig of warm water from a canteen and passed it to Ugrik in the passenger seat. Ugrik was also half-naked, revealing a scarred torso covered in tattoos. He had a bit of a gut on him, but he was built like a bulldog.

Ugrik had been muttering for an hour now. The conversation he was conducting with himself veered from argument to agreement and back again. Frey could only imagine what was being said. He couldn't understand a word of the yawling, snarling Yortish tongue.

Eventually, Frey couldn't bear it any more. He had to talk. He needed something to distract him from the monotony of the journey and of other, darker thoughts. And besides, he was beginning to feel left out.

'So what's your story, Ugrik?' he asked.

'Eh?' Ugrik seemed confused by the interruption.

'You're an explorer, right?'

'Aye,' came the suspicious reply.

'Explore anything good?'

'Oh, plenty,' he said. 'I was on the first craft out after they found New Vardia. Spent years out there, I did. Trailblazin' and so forth.'

'Yeah?' Frey was interested. He'd always thought of New Vardia as a possible bolt-hole if he managed to screw things up too badly in the country of his birth. 'What's it like?'

'Wild out there. Every man for himself.' He ran a clenched hand down the red braid of his beard and tugged at the end absently. 'My kind of place.'

'The broadsheets reckon that whole towns full of people disappear out there. Without a trace. That true?'

'Aye,' said Ugrik. 'Gone. Hard to tell if they upped and left or if something did for 'em. Some head into the wilderness 'cause they don't want to pay the Archduke's taxes. They say there's a whole lot of people all banded together in secret under a man named Red Arcus, who don't answer to no Archdukes or Chiefs or God-Emperors, nor no Speaker for the Republic like they got in Thace.'

Frey steered the Rattletrap along the flank of a dune, careful not to skid on the loose sand. 'You ever seen any of 'em?'

'Not a sign,' he said. 'Lot of stuff goes missin' out there, but it's the frontier.' He cackled. 'Course, that's only one story. Lot of worse tales they tell. Some say New Vardia weren't as deserted as we thought when we set down, and them that were there don't take kindly to sharin' their land.' He scratched his cheek and snorted. 'But I got nothin' to say about that.'

'Ever been to Jagos?' Frey asked, keen to keep him talking. He was better entertainment than the silence.

'Aye. I was one o' the first.'

'What's there?'

Ugrik's face darkened. 'Fog 'n' shadows. Seems like the Wrack reaches right down into that land. A barren place, I saw, and damn if there's not somethin' fearful unnatural about it.'

'Didn't reckon on a famous explorer being superstitious,' Frey said, with a sidelong glance.

'I know what I know. Strange things happen there. They're settlin' New Vardia as fast as they're able, but only madmen go to Jagos.'

Frey opened his mouth to point out the irony in that statement, then decided not to bother. 'Anywhere you *haven't* been?'

'Peleshar,' he grunted. 'That's next on the list. It's a big 'un.'

'You haven't heard? It's disappeared, or some such bollocks.'

'Oh, aye? Your broadsheets tell you that, did they?'

'Maybe,' he said. He'd seen headlines in some of the more lurid publications. PELESHAR: THE VANISHING ISLE! Crake had sniffed at it and dismissed it as rubbish.

'Well, this time they're right. Sammies lost it.' He chuckled. 'Don't mean I can't find it again.'

Frey raised an eyebrow. 'Seriously? You actually believe there was a whole country that disappeared?'

'Lot of things we don't know about Peleshar,' Ugrik said. 'Only one aircraft came back from the Sammie's first expedition out there, and the pilot had some tales to tell, but not many that made much sense. Then the stupid bastards sent a war fleet, 'cause that's how Sammies are. Invade, invade, invade. Those fellers didn't ever come back either.'

'You don't know that,' Frey scoffed. 'You're making it up.'

'Believe what you like,' Ugrik huffed. 'Only one of us is the son of the High Chief of Yortland, y'know. We got spies just like everyone else.'

Frey drove on for a while. He wasn't sure whether Ugrik was taking him for a ride, or the other way round. The sun beat down, and the Rattletrap growled and sputtered.

'Really?' he asked at length, unable to resist. 'I mean, the Sammies had a war fleet? And they lost them?'

'Aye.'

'Why didn't anyone hear about it? I mean, it's bad enough that they have a war fleet at all, but—'

Ugrik muttered something to himself, then waved a calloused hand at Frey. 'Most people don't know a thing about what goes on down here. Anyway, that was more than twenty years ago. A few years before the First Aerium War. They had plenty o' aircraft then.'

'You're joking. They've known about Peleshar for that long? That's...' he worked it out, 'That's before Crewen and Skale discovered New Vardia.'

'Crewen and Skale were lookin' for Peleshar,' said Ugrik.

'Bullshit!' Frey said. 'You're having me on.'

'Course they were! Your lot heard about what happened in Samarla, with your spies and whatnot, and you sent your fellers out to look. Only the Great Storm Belt was kicking up again, and with aircraft not being so good back in those days, lot of men got lost and some got blew off course. New Vardia was an accident.'

'Bullshit!' he said again, although he wanted to believe it. It fitted with his sense of the world, that it was a random and ridiculous place.

'You don't have a bloody clue, do you? Half the reason they had the First Aerium War was 'cause Samarla felt threatened by having Peleshar over there – that 'n' wounded pride – and they needed the aerium to tool up an even bigger fleet!'

'Bullshit!' Frey cried.

Ugrik roared with laughter. 'It's true! Then the Storm Belt really kicked up, and for the next fifteen years or so you couldn't even get across the Ordic Abyssal from Pandraca, and meantime we were all at bloody war and no one much fancied goin' the other way round the planet to try 'n' find it again. After the storms cleared and everyone had stopped killin' each other, they all headed out west again. But Peleshar wasn't there no more.'

'It's been seven years or so since they've been heading west to settle!' said Frey.

'Aye. Seven years since the Sammies knew Peleshar had gone. Seven years since your Archduke knew, and my father, and everyone else wi' spies in the right places. Took your broadsheets a sight longer to catch up.'

Frey shook his head. 'That is quite a tale,' he said. 'I could dine out on that one for a while.'

'Heh,' said Ugrik. He took a swig from the canteen.

They drove on into the late afternoon. Ugrik drowsed in the heat. Frey steered the Rattletrap across the dunes, always heading east by the compass.

He found himself unexpectedly light of heart. He'd cast himself out into the wilderness, alone but for his guide, and there was liberation in that. He wasn't intimidated by the endless emptiness of the desert or the punishing sun. He welcomed the threat of it all.

For the first time in years, he only had himself to worry about. His crew were behind him. Their fates were beyond his ability to influence. Trinica was gone, a remnant of an old life. He put her out of his mind as best he could. He'd grieve tomorrow, if he ever got there.

All he needed to think about was tonight.

His life had been compressed to a handful of hours, and the proximity of death unburdened him. If he survived, if he somehow evaded the doom that awaited, the years would stretch out before him again, unfolding like a concertina into the future. Then he would have to return to the *Ketty Jay* and deal with his broken aircraft, his marooned crew. But for now, just for this one day, he was free. It was only now he realised how heavily his responsibilities had laid on him.

'It's gonna be alright, Darian,' he muttered to himself. 'Gonna be alright.'

The Rattletrap's engine sputtered, clunked and juddered before coughing its last in a wheeze of noxious black smoke. The buggy rolled gently to a halt.

Ugrik opened his eyes to find Frey thumping his forehead against the steering wheel. He blinked, rubbed his eyes and looked around.

'Why've we stopped?' he asked.

Frey had never thought of himself as a man prone to homesickness. After all, he'd never had a real home. Patriotism was an affliction for people like Malvery and Harkins. To Frey, his country was just the place he happened to be born.

Not today, though. Today he dreamed of familiar shores. He'd have given anything for one honest Vardic raincloud. Or better still, a nice slate-grey sky, like you got in the North most days in autumn. He'd always found them depressing in the past, but he promised never to bad-mouth the weather at home again, if only someone would relieve this endless bloody heat.

The sand gave easily beneath his boots, making every step a struggle. Ugrik trudged alongside him. Each of them wore one half of the black sheet of tarp, which Frey had split down the middle with his cutlass. They'd put it across their backs and tied it with twine to their wrists and shoulders. It overhung their heads like crude cowls, it flapped in their eyes, and it caught around their calves and ankles. Ugrik assured him that exposed skin would burn quickly in the desert heat, but Frey would almost rather that than this. The tarp was ungainly, uncomfortably hot, and worst of all, he felt ridiculous. They looked like lost manta rays, or a pair of particularly rubbish kites.

They laboured up the flank of a massive dune that cut across their path. Ugrik was muttering to himself, as was his habit. Frey wasn't sure if he was insane or just eccentric, but either way he didn't trust the explorer's competence. The sense of liberation and freedom he'd enjoyed had faded quickly once the discomfort of the march set in, and he began to wonder, far too late, if Ugrik was leading him on a wild goose chase.

Frey stopped just before the ridge of the dune and turned around with some difficulty, the tarp tangling around him like a sail. He rested his hands on his aching thighs and caught his breath.

It was getting towards evening, and the sun was lowering towards the horizon in the west, reddening the sky. The sight filled him with dread. Soon the night would come. He was suddenly seized with the horrible notion that he might have wasted the last day of his life slogging pointlessly through a desert with a cackling Yort nutbag for company.

Ugrik was lumbering up the slope in Frey's wake, the relic clutched to his chest. Each step caused a miniature landslide. Frey was happy to let him carry the burden. He wanted to touch it as little as possible.

'How much further?' Frey asked.

'Not far now, not far at all,' Ugrik said blithely. He didn't seem the least bit concerned by their predicament.

'That's what I thought you'd say,' Frey murmured. He straightened and took a swig from his canteen. It was almost empty.

Ugrik climbed past him and up to the ridge of the dune. Frey screwed the top back on to the canteen, sighed, and followed.

'Don't you worry,' Ugrik threw over his shoulder. 'According to my calculations, we'll be there well before nightfall.'

Frey joined him atop the crest of the rise. What he saw there took the last of the strength from his legs, and he dropped to his knees.

The desert stretched out before him, all the way to the horizon. As far as the eye could see, there were only dunes, shimmering in the heat-haze. It had to be fifteen, twenty kloms to the limits of his vision, and in all that distance, there was nothing but sand.

'According...' he muttered, and swallowed. 'According to your *calculations*?' He felt rage boiling up within him.

'Allowin' for a small margin of error, o' course,' Ugrik said cheerily.

Frey got to his feet and flung out one arm towards the empty horizon. 'That's what you call a *small margin of error*?' he demanded in a strangled voice.

'Here, now, there's no need for losin' your rag,' said Ugrik.

'You crazy son of a bitch!' he screamed. 'This is my last day alive! Don't you get that? I could've been drunk, or stoned, or at the very least trying to get a sympathy shag out of Ashua! But instead I'm going to die here in the desert, in the dark, and there won't be a single person here who ever gave a shit about me! You've killed me, you dumb Yort bastard! You've killed me, and what's worse, I'm still wearing this stupid bloody tarpaulin!'

He flailed ineffectually, trying to dislodge the tarp from his back, then launched himself at Ugrik and clamped his hands round the explorer's throat. All his pent-up fear had turned to fury, directed at this grinning idiot who'd cheated him out of the final precious moments of his existence. He was going to die in the same absurd manner as he'd lived, and it was too much to bear.

His fault, he thought, as Ugrik's eyes bulged. *His fault.*

Then Ugrik rammed the relic into his belly. Frey's foot slipped in the sand, and then the two of them were tipping, rolling, bouncing uncontrollably down the far slope of the dune. This flank was steeper than the one they'd climbed up, and there was no stopping themselves as they fell. They tumbled end over end, black tarp flapping around them. By the time they came to a halt at the base of the dune, they were thoroughly battered.

Frey pulled his face from the sand and pushed the tarp out of his eyes. He blinked.

He didn't believe what he saw.

Swimming in the heat-haze, less than a klom away, there was an enormous oasis. Tall trees were densely packed together, thick with deep green leaves. Above the trees he could see the tips of strange structures, their details obscured by the haze. Thin towers, and arched constructions that curved like ribs.

He wiped his crusted lips and coughed. 'Ugrik!' he said, looking around.

The Yort emerged from beneath the desert like some mythical horror, sloughing off sand as he rose. He was still clutching the relic. 'A-ha!' he cried.

'Tell me that's not a mirage,' said Frey.

Ugrik cackled. 'What are you, mad?'

Frey stumbled to his feet and finally fought his way clear of the tarp. He threw it aside and glared at it. 'How come we couldn't see this place till we got close?'

'Same reason your craft went down, I reckon,' said Ugrik. 'Same reason Peleshar's gone missin'. Same reason you got that manky hand. They made it happen.'

Frey wasn't so amazed that he couldn't summon up a bit of indignation. 'My hand is *not* manky. I'm *cursed*, alright?'

'Whatever you say, Frey,' he said, then chuckled. 'Frey, say. Say, Frey, whaddya say?'

Frey ignored him. He'd be entertaining himself with that rhyme for hours if he got any encouragement.

'I reckon,' he mused, studying the oasis, 'those ancient Samarlans were actually pretty bloody clever.'

Ugrik gaped at him. 'You think the ancient Samarlans did this?' He bellowed with laughter and lifted up the relic in his hands. 'This thing is more than ten thousand years old! The Sammies could barely scratch their own arses back in those days!'

'So who built *them*, then?' Frey asked, pointing at the structures beyond the oasis.

Ugrik grinned his infuriating grin.

'Azryx,' he said.

And he walked off towards the oasis, leaving Frey staring after him.

THIRTY-NINE

THE OASIS—AN EYE—BRASS AND BONE—
'SOMEONE'S FOLLOWIN' US'—THE DROP

Frey pushed through the undergrowth. It was sweltering hot beneath the leaf canopy, but there was shade, and the trunks were dappled in the red light of the evening sun. Bats flitted, hunting insects. Unseen birds called to one another. The air was not so oven-dry among the trees, and Frey thought he smelt water.

Only an hour ago he'd been in the trackless depths of an endless desert, and this oasis hadn't been here at all. But here he was, and it was real.

Ugrik led the way, red braids swinging, his broad back a mass of tattoos. Frey didn't quite know what to make of him now. He might have a couple of screws loose, but if he'd been to half the places he said he had, he must be someone to be reckoned with. And after what Frey had just witnessed, he was ready to believe anything the Yort told him.

Then they emerged from the trees into a small clearing scattered with bright flowers, and Frey saw it.

It was a city.

Frey wasn't someone to be awed by history. He didn't share Jez and Crake's fascination with crumbling buildings and pointless art. But even he couldn't suppress a shiver of wonder at the occasion. A lost city! A lost *Azryx* city! And he might be the first Vard ever to lay eyes on it.

The oasis was situated in a huge, shallow depression, at the bottom of which was an unevenly shaped lake. The city began at its edge and radiated away up the slopes. For the most part, they were so consumed by the undergrowth that it was hard to see the shape of them, but what he could see was amazingly well preserved. The burrowing plants had toppled some towers and collapsed some walls, but if this place really was as old as Ugrik said, then it had withstood the millennia with miraculous endurance. He glimpsed buildings in snatches, visible through a thick covering of strangling creepers or crowded by ancient trees that grew up against their flanks.

It was an alien place. There was a fundamental strangeness to it. It was not made of brick and mortar. Its curves were too smooth, and it had swooping lines that were beyond the ability of the best architects in Vardia or elsewhere. Whatever material they'd used must have been incredibly strong. Spidery pillars supported structures that seemed impossibly heavy. He saw a building with a vast elliptical space in its side, like a mouth, and realised that it was probably a window once. No Vardic window had ever been built so large.

Not stone, then. Some kind of ceramic, like the material they fashioned the blades of the relic from. Something the colour of yellowed bone, peeping from the trees. Perhaps this had once been a place of bright hues, or perhaps not. Either way, the colours had gone now, and left only the skeleton of a dead city.

But alien as it was, it was built for people. He saw stairs and the remnants of boulevards. There were doorways and walkways and even a ridiculously thin bridge, now a rail for a ragged curtain of vines and moss and flowers. The lake was surrounded by a wall, built one-third of the way up the slope. He traced its outline as it sewed in and out of visibility. There were oval gateways there, but the gates were long gone.

He only had a moment to take it all in before Ugrik grabbed him and pulled him down into a crouch. 'Don't get yourself seen,' he warned.

'Seen by who?' Frey asked, faintly alarmed. It hadn't occurred to him that there might be someone else here.

Ugrik moved to the edge of the clearing, back into the undergrowth. Frey followed. Ugrik held aside a spray of leaves, allowing a view down the near slope.

'Sammies,' he said.

Some way below them, a large section of the city had been exposed. Vines had been cleared, trees uprooted, soil dug away. The earth-moving machines were still at work down there, carefully quarrying out the extraordinary buildings, reclaiming them from the earth. Around them moved the Sammies, dozens of them, heading in and out of doorways, coordinating the loading of items with small cranes. Some were gathered around tables where they pored over plans, while others milled or loafed in a busy campsite that had been set up in a plaza. Many of them had guns.

With the foliage gone, Frey could see the true strangeness of the city. Low, flat buildings that were little more than boxes sat next to humped, segmented constructions that looked like a row of crouched beetles. Nearby was a colossal ball, flattened at the bottom where it touched the ground, with no apparent windows and only a doorway at its base. He saw a landing pad on the edge of the bared streets, built atop a pillar that branched out like a tree to support it.

But all that paled in comparison to the centrepiece of the excavation.

It looked as if two giant hourglasses of brass and bone had been stood next to each other. They were linked across their lower halves by a complicated building of many curves and angles, but it was the hourglasses that drew the attention. Within their frames were bizarre assemblies made up of twisted rods of metal and squat stacks of discs. Orbiting each half of the hourglass was a brass arm, like a blade, that swept around the interior edge. The upper and lower arms rotated in different directions. Occasionally a section of machinery shifted, moving to a new position as if under its own command. The whole edifice gave an impression of whirling movement contained inside a rigid structure.

There was something inside those hourglasses. A coloured gas, the consistency of cloud, full of pale colours that made Frey's eyes hurt. Within the gas he saw a hundred storms, miniature flickers of lightning, striking in flurries.

He had no idea what it did, but one thing he did know: it was active. And the Sammies had it.

'How long have they been here?' he asked.

'My guess? Since the end of the Second Aerium War.'

Frey squeezed his eyes shut. He couldn't look at those hourglasses any more. 'This is why they called the truce? We thought they'd somehow found their own aerium source or something. Maybe on Peleshar.'

'Reckon they found this,' Ugrik grunted. 'And they worked out what it was.'

'But what good does it do them?'

Ugrik pointed down through the leaves to where a group of Sammies were using a crane to lift a massive metal device of coiled pipes and tubes on to the back of a tractor-trailer. 'Know what that is?' he asked.

'No,' said Frey.

'Nor do they,' he said. 'But you can bet they're gonna find out.'

'Salvage? That's what they're after?'

'Technology,' he said. 'There's things in this city like you can't imagine. And the Sammies want it all. They want to know how to do what the Azryx did.'

Frey was only just beginning to appreciate the enormity of the situation. 'If they manage to reverse engineer Azryx technology...'

'They'd be well nigh invincible, I reckon,' said Ugrik. 'And they'll be in your back yard before your next shit.'

'And then in yours.'

'Aye.'

Frey whistled quietly. 'Anyone else know about this?'

'Outside of the Sammies? You and me.' He cackled. 'That's why they slung me in solitary. Didn't want me talkin'. I don't s'pose they reckoned anyone would come lookin', either.'

'I wouldn't have, if I hadn't managed to get stuck with that damn thing,' Frey complained, pointing at the relic that Ugrik still held in his brawny arms.

'Funny how things work out, eh?' said Ugrik.

'Hilarious,' Frey agreed, his eyes narrowing.

'At least you got cursed by the best,' said Ugrik, scratching at his cheek.

'That's a good point, actually.' Frey brightened as he looked at his gloved hand. 'This is an *Azryx* curse,' he said with some pride.

'There you go, then,' Ugrik said.

Frey returned his attention to the scene below them. 'You know what this information would be worth to the right people?'

'You got optimistic all of a sudden,' Ugrik observed with some surprise. 'How about we concentrate on sorting out the mess you're in, first? Sun's going down.'

He *was* feeling optimistic. He'd found the place where the relic had come from. Everything seemed possible now. He began to believe there might be a dawn.

Ugrik waved a hand. 'Down there, by the lakeside. That's where I found it. We'll have to skirt round the Sammies, but there's patrols all over, so be careful.'

Frey couldn't see the exact building, but he didn't need to. It didn't seem all that far. All they had to do was get past the Sammies and put the relic back.

Easy.

Later, they found the eye.

By then they'd made their way downslope, and were nearing the outermost limits of the city. Ugrik had taken to muttering under his breath in Yortish again. They'd both put their shirts back on, warned by the purr and whine of insects that exposed flesh would end up bitten. The foliage rustled with birds and small wildlife. Frey was wondering if there was any danger of encountering *big* wildlife when he suddenly pulled up short next to a cliff that rose up on their left.

'Is that an *eye*?' he asked.

'Aye.'

'That's what I said. An eye.'

'And I said aye.'

'Yes! An eye!'

'Aye! Aye meaning yes! Aye, it's an eye!'

'Oh.'

It was as big as Frey, smooth and white, staring emptily from within a mass of vines. It was set high off the ground, tilted at an angle, without brow or lid. In fact, it was hard to know how he recognised it as an eye at all. Perhaps he'd sensed the proportions of the surrounding face, which he'd mistaken for a cliff at first, masked as it was by trees and creepers. Or perhaps it was because it felt uncomfortably like it was watching him.

Now he had the eye, it was possible to estimate the rest of it. It was the same bone colour as the buildings in the city. He made out the outline of a heavy jaw, sunk into the earth. There seemed to be no nose, whether by design or by the ravages of time, and there was a muzzle of some kind. No human face, then. The head lay askance, half-buried, and it was truly colossal.

'That,' he said, 'is one big statue.'

Ugrik gave a noncommittal grunt. Frey tried to see if the head was attached to a body, but he was foiled by the undergrowth. 'They had some ugly-arse gods, huh?' he commented.

When he looked back, Ugrik was holding up a pocket watch and pointing at it impatiently.

'Oh, right! My imminent death!' said Frey, slapping his forehead in mock-astonishment. 'Totally slipped my mind.'

'I don't plan on gettin' caught by the Sammies a second time,' Ugrik growled. 'Someone needs to fly me out o' here when we're done. And I doubt your crew'd be all that welcomin' if I came back without you.'

Frey looked him over. 'You're not half as crazy as you pretend, are you?'

'I'm not crazy, nor pretendin' to be,' he said. 'If I was crazy, I'd have told you where we were goin' when you asked. You'd have booted me off your craft right then, curse or no curse.'

Frey had to give him that. Until a short while ago, he'd been certain the Azryx were entirely made up. 'Come on, then,' he said.

They left the statue behind and headed further down the slope.

'What's your interest in this, anyway?' he asked, keeping his voice low. 'Shouldn't you have gone to tell your father about this place? Why'd you want to come back?'

'Need the relic so they believe me,' he said. 'You weren't gonna give it back to me, I reckon. So I'm helpin' you, until you've got that black spot off your hand.'

'You want the relic?'

'Aye,' said Ugrik. 'Soon as we put it back, and that curse o' yours is lifted…' He stopped and grinned. 'I'm gonna nick it again.' Then suddenly his face turned grave. 'That's the price, by the way, Cap'n Frey. When we're done here, I get the relic.'

Frey was taken aback. 'You're negotiating this *now*?'

'Think you've got time to find where it came from before the moon's up?' Ugrik countered.

Frey had to respect his enterprising nature. 'You're welcome to it,' he said. 'Might be worth a fortune, but I'm damned if I'm keeping hold of that thing. It's given me nothing but trouble.'

'Shouldn't mess with what you don't understand,' Ugrik advised.

'Thanks for the advice,' Frey said sarcastically. 'Just in time. I almost did something stupid.'

Ugrik gave him a flat look and started walking again.

'How did *you* know not to touch it, anyway?' Frey asked, keeping pace. He swatted at a dragonfly that seemed intent on landing on his nose.

'I didn't,' said Ugrik. 'The curse is written on the blade.'

'You can read Azryx?'

'No. But I can read Old Isilian.'

They forged on through the foliage for a while.

'Okay, you're gonna have to tell me what that is,' said Frey eventually.

'All the languages we know – Yortish, Vardic, Samarlan and the rest – they all have their roots in one dead language from way back. Old Isilian. Couldn't read much of what was on that relic, but there's enough similarities so I got the gist. Don't touch. The thing was in its case when I found it, so I never took it out.'

'Strikes me that was probably the sensible thing to do,' Frey said.

'Aye, well, we can't all be sensible, can we?'

Frey looked glumly at his hand. 'Apparently not.'

They'd picked their way down to the edge of the city. The undergrowth was broken by glimpses of walls and doorways, and it was almost possible to make out nearby thoroughfares. They were staying well away from the excavated area that was swarming with Sammies, but Ugrik was cautious anyway, and Frey took his cue from that.

He was feeling more confident now he had a grasp on the situation. At last he knew what had happened to him, and why, and what he could do about it. All he had to do was sneak past the Sammies and put the relic back where Ugrik had found it. It sounded easy when he said it to himself. Time was short, but he'd had closer shaves. There was still a good hour till sunset, and no sign of the moon.

Ugrik held out a hand to stop him. 'Ssh,' he said.

'I wasn't making any n—'

'*Ssh!*'

Frey shut his mouth, peeved. Ugrik was listening attentively. Frey did, too. He heard nothing but the repetitive cry of some exotic bird.

'I reckon someone's followin' us,' said Ugrik.

Frey belatedly remembered what Crake had told him just before the crash. That someone was tracking the relic. It had gone right out of his head when the *Ketty Jay* went down, and Crake had been concussed and in no state to elaborate. Ugrik had been there too. Frey wondered if the Yort had forgotten, if he hadn't been paying attention, or if he just didn't think it mattered.

Suddenly, it came to him. He knew who'd planted that signal. He should have figured it out straight away. And if he was right, then there really wasn't much point running at this stage.

They waited till they were passing through a particularly thick patch of foliage, and then ducked aside, hiding around the corner of a low building that had been half-consumed by soil, its walls dense with dangling tree roots. Anyone behind them would have to walk by, and they could jump out and confront them.

Frey waited, ears straining, sweat trickling from his temples. Ugrik, who was carrying a rifle from the *Ketty Jay*'s armoury, drummed his fingers silently on the barrel.

Nothing happened. After a time, Frey leaned over to Ugrik and whispered 'You sure you heard—?'

'*Ssh!*'

'Right.'

They listened. A wild pig lumbered through the undergrowth nearby, snorting. Birds and insects rustled and peeped. Frey couldn't imagine how Ugrik could have possibly detected anyone in amid all that noise.

Behind him, he heard the snap of a twig breaking under a boot.

He looked over his shoulder. Standing there were two uniformed Sammies, rifles trained on him.

That was mildly surprising. They weren't who he was expecting at all.

Ugrik had noticed them too. He turned around slowly, his hands in the air. They said something in their own language.

'Reckon they want us to—' he began.

'Drop the guns, yeah, I know,' Frey said. He held up his pistol and threw it down, then tossed away the other one from his belt. Lastly he surrendered his cutlass. Ugrik laid down his rifle. The Sammies watched them carefully through narrowed eyes.

'So I suppose these were the fellers you heard following us, then?' Frey asked Ugrik from the corner of his mouth.

'No,' he grunted, pointing with his chin. 'It was them.'

There was the unmistakable crunch of lever-action shotguns being primed, and Samandra Bree stepped out of the undergrowth behind the Sammies. Colden Grudge came with her, his autocannon ready.

'Hello, Frey,' said Samandra.

'Hey, Samandra,' he said cheerily. Now the world made sense again.

The Sammies, seeing that the Century Knights had them cold, tossed their rifles to the ground and raised their hands.

'These friends o' yours?' Ugrik asked Frey.

'Oh, we're all *best* of friends,' said Samandra. 'Ain't we, Frey?'

Ugrik frowned. 'She don't sound too sincere.'

'You noticed that, huh?' Frey asked, hands still in the air.

Grudge moved over to the Sammies and herded them up against the wall of the building, covering them with his fearsome cannon. Samandra never took her twin shotguns off Frey and Ugrik as she came closer.

Frey raised an eyebrow at Samandra. 'You must've been pretty extraordinarily pissed, to follow me all the way here.'

'You could say. Ever since your snake of a daemonist tried to mess with my head, you ain't been my favourite people. But we got daemonists too, in the Century Knights. Bet you didn't know that.'

'Actually, pretty much everyone's guessed by now,' Frey told her with a shrug. 'Sorry. By the way, I spotted you in Shasiith when you were following me around. Gotta be more subtle than that.'

'You really shouldn't tick me off any more than you already have, Frey,' she warned.

'Can't help it,' he said. 'I'm just in one of those moods. So, what, you got your daemonist to tag the relic after you twigged that Crake was after it?' Realisation dawned on him. 'You were gonna let us escape, weren't you?'

'First we were gonna see if you talked. Then if you didn't, we'd let you slip away with the relic. Just you. So you thought it was an accident.'

'And then you'd follow me and find out who put me up to the theft.'

'Exactly.'

'But you *shot* at me,' said Frey.

'You shot first,' she replied.

'Not at you, though.'

She shrugged.

'Anyway,' he said. 'As you can probably see, no one put me up to it.' He put on a mock-pitiful face. 'Although I'm hurt that you'd underestimate me like that.'

'Well, regardless,' she said. 'You led us a merry damn chase all the same.' She smiled. 'But I got the drop on you in the end.'

There was a noisy clatter of weapons being cocked and loaded all around them. Malvery, Pinn and Crake stepped into view on the roof of the building, weapons pointed at Grudge. Silo and Ashua emerged from the trees behind Samandra, their guns trained on her back.

'What's up, Cap'n?' Malvery asked. 'Got some trouble?'

Samandra stared at Frey in amazement. 'How do you *do* that?' she asked.

Frey held up his hand with the ring on it and grinned. 'I've got good people,' he said.

FORTY

ADARIK—HARKINS IN THE DARK—FREY PLAYS MATCHMAKER—AN ALLIANCE—FIRST MATE

It was snowing hard now. Not the blizzard conditions Jez had experienced the day she died, but a heavy, downy snow that drifted from the sky and laid a blanket over everything.

She'd gone to find her body, but it had been lost. Beyond the settlement was a clean white expanse, and no tracks to be seen. If her corpse was out there, she'd never find it. It didn't seem very important anyway.

Rinn had disappeared at some point. Jez hadn't noticed him leave, but that was how dreams worked, she supposed. Dreams, or trances, or whatever this was.

She made her way back through the domed Yort buildings. The drifts had built themselves high. There was no trace of what had happened here.

What *had* happened here? She was finding it hard to remember.

When she looked back, she saw that her tracks were filling up as fast as she left them.

She'd been here too long. It was time to leave. Time to will herself awake.

Where was Rinn? She'd enjoyed talking with him. She wished she could recall what they'd talked about.

Listlessly, she drifted through the settlement. It seemed like she was the only person in the world now. Just her and the cold and the turning, tumbling flakes of snow.

Adarik. That's what it's called. This tiny little town where I died. Adarik.

Why had it taken her so long to remember a thing like that?

She came out onto the main thoroughfare, and there was the dreadnought. The ropes and chains that hung from it dragged softly against the snow as they were brushed by the wind.

They were singing up there. The baying, discordant animal howls touched chords inside her. She found herself wanting to howl with them. There was freedom in it, and release. There was no self-consciousness among the Manes. Each knew its fellows intimately. Each was connected on a level that was at once primitive and near-divine. She listened, and swayed to the sound.

She'd been here too long. There were things she needed to do. Her people needed her.

She walked over to one of the dangling chains. It swayed before her.

She'd been here too long. It was time to wake up.

She grabbed hold of the chain and began to climb, up towards her brethren at the top.

Harkins was scared.

This was nothing new, of course. But today it was a different flavour of fear, and one he hadn't tasted for a long while. Tonight, he was scared because he was alone.

Well, alone except for *her*.

He stood in the passageway, just out of sight of the infirmary door, jigging from foot to foot. A lantern dangled from each hand. The spare was necessary, because if he only carried one it might suddenly go out, and then he would probably die of a heart attack.

The *Ketty Jay* was eerily quiet, and a terrifying dark lurked beyond the lamplight. The sunset was a meagre glow, filtered through sand banked up against the windglass of the cockpit, which lay at the end of the passageway. Hardly enough to see by. Without engines or power, the *Ketty Jay* was just a lump of metal, still baking from the heat of the departing day. The floor underfoot seemed foreign and unfamiliar: the decks slanted forward because her nose was buried in the desert.

He wasn't used to being here when it was empty. There was always *someone* around, even if it was only Bess. He'd have even taken the cat for company right now, that hateful bag of mange, but Slag had buggered off into the depths of the *Ketty Jay*'s circulation system and wasn't coming out.

He should have gone with the others. Maybe they could have squeezed him on to a Rattletrap. After all, he was only skinny.

When they heard him volunteer to stay behind, he could tell what they were thinking. *Same old Harkins.* As if all his recent bravery had just been a phase, and they knew he'd return to type in the end.

But they were wrong about him. Staying here *was* being brave. Staying here alone with *her*. That was braver than chasing off after the Cap'n with a gang of gun-toting companions.

There was something he needed to do. And he needed to do it alone.

He checked on the knife in his belt. Good and sharp. He might only get one chance at this.

He took a deep breath, let it out shakily, and then peered through the doorway to the infirmary.

She was still there, on the operating table. Lying still as death.

That was a relief. If she hadn't been there, it would have been worse. He didn't think his sphincter had the sheer clench-force to handle an event like that.

He crept into the infirmary, fighting the awkward slope of the floor, and laid the lanterns on the top of the cabinets. Their flickering light reflected from the glass doors of a dresser, behind which hung Malvery's surgical instruments. They gleamed in the light. They were the only clean thing in here.

The smell of blood made his stomach roil. Jez's clothes were soaked in it, and it had long dried and begun to reek. Flies hummed around the room. The *Ketty Jay* ticked and creaked as she cooled.

He licked his lips.

'Jez?' he whispered hoarsely. Then, realising that even the cat would have been hard-pressed to hear him, he coughed lightly and said 'Jez?' with a fraction more volume.

She didn't stir. He took a step towards her, extended one trembling finger, and gave her a sharp poke before springing back across the room in anticipation of violent reprisals.

There was no reaction, so finally, he drew out the knife.

'I'm sorry, Jez,' he said. 'I mean... I really am. I didn't want to have to do this. Not... not to you.'

He crept closer again, his coward's instincts fearing some trick.

Had she heard him, and was waiting to spring when he got close enough? Did she sense what he intended?

He swallowed. *Be a man*, he told himself. *Finish this.*

'I never knew,' he said, his voice giving him the confidence to take another step. 'They said you were a Mane, but... Spit, I didn't realise... I mean, I only saw *you*, the *nice* Jez, the one who was always... always kind to me when everyone else laughed.' His eyes went from the blade to her. 'I never knew how it'd be... to see what you really are, underneath.'

Still she didn't move. Not so much as a muscle. *Maybe she's already dead. That'd make things easier.*

He couldn't allow himself any excuses. He crept closer, the lanterns throwing his shadow across her. He brought up the knife. It was shaking in his hand.

'This... it's really for the best,' he said.

The edge of the knife came closer to her throat.

'I'm doing this for us.'

He firmed his will, and made ready to do what had to be done.

'You see...' he said. He took another breath, and then the words all came out in a tumble. 'The thing is, I just don't fancy you any more.'

With one hasty movement, he grabbed up a lock of her hair and sheared it off. He put it to his face and sniffed it. He was appalled to find it stank of old blood. He retched and stuffed it in his pocket.

It was while he was wiping his mouth with his sleeve that he saw her eyes were open. His heart kicked in his chest and dread flooded him. She was staring at him, like she'd heard him, like she *knew what he'd done!*

'It's a memento!' he shrieked.

She looked around blearily. 'Harkins?'

'I just wanted something to remind me of the romance!' he gabbled.

Jez was deeply confused. 'What... er... what romance?'

She lifted herself up on her elbows, and that was the final straw. Harkins' attempt at explanation degenerated into a gibbering wail and he took to his heels at full speed.

He didn't get far. In his panic, he'd miscalculated where the doorway was. He caught his shoulder on the edge of it, caromed into the corridor, and charged head-first into the wall. The impact was a shower of stars, and then he was being dragged down into the dark.

The last thing he heard was Jez calling his name in a tone of utter and complete bewilderment.

'Harkins?'

Then nothing.

Frey took off the fingerless glove and showed his palm to Samandra Bree.

'Ew,' she said. 'That is one manky hand.'

'Shows what you know. This is one of the finest curses you're ever likely to come across,' Frey said, prodding at it. 'Straight from the Azryx! Ten thousand years old!'

'Looks like gangrene to me,' said Samandra, unimpressed.

Frey snatched his hand away and put the glove back on. 'Anyway, *now* do you believe him?'

They both looked at Crake, who was standing a short way away, gazing at Samandra with the plaintive eyes of a recently whipped dog.

'There wasn't any other way,' he said quietly. 'The Cap'n was going to die otherwise. I'm so very, very sorr—'

'Save it,' said Samandra, crushing him. 'I ain't interested in your apologies. What I'm interested in is what *those* fellers have to tell us.'

She nodded towards the Samarlan guards, who were trussed up against a tree. One had been gagged with a sock. The other was talking rapidly to Silo and Ashua, no doubt encouraged by Silo's knife resting just beneath his kneecap. Frey vaguely wondered if he should send Malvery over there to make sure Silo didn't get out of hand – he tended to, when Sammies were concerned – but the Murthian seemed surprisingly calm.

Once everyone had stopped pointing guns at each other and decided that they were on the same side for the moment, the Century Knights and the crew of the *Ketty Jay* had led their prisoners back into the depths of the undergrowth. They needed to get off the patrol route for a quick and dirty interrogation. Frey chafed at the small delay, but he went with it. He reckoned he had a much better chance of getting to where he needed to be with the Century Knights on board, and they might come with him once they'd satisfied themselves here. Besides, their encounter with the patrol had made him wary. He wasn't so sure that getting the relic back to its rightful place would be as simple as he'd hoped.

'The way I see it,' he said to Samandra, 'I've led you to the most important find since they discovered New Vardia. Wanna know why the Sammies pulled out of the war? Wanna know what they've *really* been up to for the last eight years or so? Look down there.' He waved vaguely in the direction of the excavation, then folded his arms. 'I reckon that more than cancels out a few smashed-up museum pieces and some petty theft.'

'Oh, you do, do you?' Samandra said.

He was stoic in the face of her scorn. 'Yep.'

Her expression showed him nothing. She flicked her gaze to Crake, and her eyes hardened. He cringed. Then she stalked over to the prisoners. Grudge followed her, glaring at Frey as he passed.

Crake sidled up. 'She hates me,' he lamented.

'What? Samandra? No! Didn't you see that look?'

'You mean that look of pure loathing she just gave me?'

'You joking? That wasn't *real* loathing. That was *I'm not ready to forgive you yet* loathing.'

'I had no idea there were such subtle variations,' said Crake. 'Well, I know women, and take it from me, there are,' Frey assured him confidently. 'And it means she *is* gonna forgive you eventually. You might have to jump through a few hoops first though.'

'You really think so?' The hope in Crake's eyes bordered on pathetic.

Frey squeezed his shoulder. Cajoling his mates through heartbreak was comfortable territory. 'You had honourable intentions, right? You were trying to save my life. She knows that now. You just gotta give her time to get over being angry.'

Crake watched her uncertainly.

'Of course, she might be a while torturing you before she does,' Frey added.

'I deserve it,' said Crake unhappily.

'That's the spirit! They love it when you come out with that kind of stuff.'

'But I do!' he protested.

'Keep it up,' said Frey with a wink.

Crake gave up trying to persuade him and mooched off to the other side of the clearing, where Malvery and Pinn were loafing against a tree. There was a pile of backpacks there: Crake's portable equipment, which he'd insisted they bring. Bess lurked nearby, doing her best to be quiet. Every so often she made to lunge after a passing butterfly, before remembering her instructions and withdrawing, chastened. They'd kept her at a distance once Silo picked up the trail of the Century Knights, otherwise they'd never have got close enough to spring the ambush. Bess was incapable of being stealthy.

Frey watched the four of them. There was such a feeling of unbearable warmth glowing in his chest that he feared he might disgrace himself and well up. They'd never stop taking the piss then.

They'd come after him. He left them behind, and they followed him anyway. Even after he'd absolved them of all responsibility for his life. Even after all the screw-ups and disasters he'd put them through. They'd found the daemon-thralled compass in his quarters, jumped in the remaining two Rattletraps and chased off after him. They could only fit six in all, so Harkins had stayed behind, to keep an eye on Jez, who still hadn't recovered.

'Is anybody *not* tracking me?' he'd asked when they told him, but secretly he was overjoyed. Being everyone's centre of attention was never a bad thing. He wondered if he'd subconsciously left the compass behind on purpose.

The loss of Trinica was an ache that nothing could soothe, but it seemed a separate thing to the love he felt for his crew right then. Strange that he could be so happy and sad at the same time. Maybe, given time, his feelings might sort themselves out; but there was no time to be had right now. He had a job to do, and his men were relying on him.

He was their captain, after all.

He strode over to the prisoners, pushing aside leaves and creepers as he went. 'What's the story?' he asked Silo.

'Ain't much they can tell us that the Yort hasn't already figured out,' said Silo. 'Couple things, though. That big buildin' makin' lightnin'? They reckon that's what powers this place. It was workin' when the Sammies got here.'

'Do they know why our craft went down?' Samandra asked.

'Yours too?' said Frey.

'Happens to everyone,' said Ashua. 'It's some kind of invisible force that scrambles anything more complex than a basic engine. Even the Sammies can only come in and out by ground vehicles.

Apparently there's one or two Sammie aircraft that come in and out – that's why they cleared the landing pad – but they've no idea why they're immune to the force and others aren't.' She shrugged. 'Anyway, that's probably why the place went undetected so long. That, and the fact that you can't see it till you're right on top of it.'

'If we wanna get out of here, we're gonna have to shut off whatever's scramblin' our engines,' said Samandra. She motioned towards the prisoners. 'Do they know what generates it?'

'Nuh,' said Silo. 'But I'll bet whatever it is, it won't work so good without power.'

Samandra thought about that for a minute. 'Can I talk to you for a minute, Frey?'

They moved away from the group, out of earshot. Samandra leaned in close, talking low. Frey would ordinarily have committed murder for that chance to be this close to a woman as beautiful as Samandra Bree, but Trinica's rejection had temporarily crippled his libido.

'Here's the deal,' she said. 'You've been a son of a bitch, Frey, but this is bigger than both of us. The Sammies are pullin' up Azryx tech. Spit knows what they could do with it. That's why, in the national interest, I'm gonna forget what you got up to in Thesk, and you're gonna help me shut down that power plant so our craft can get airborne. Someone needs to get back to the Archduke and tell him what's up.'

'Hmm,' said Frey. 'See, the national interest doesn't do me much good if I'm dead, and I'm really short on time for lifting this curse. I got my own priorities.' He lifted up his gloved hand.

'Damn it, Frey! Then lend me some of your men and go do what you have to do. It's only a matter of time before they notice their patrol is missin'. We have to strike now!'

He shook his head. 'My men wouldn't follow you, and I wouldn't trust 'em to you anyway.' He thought for a minute, and then it all suddenly became clear. 'But I've got a way. One condition, though.'

'What?'

'Be nice to Crake. That poor idiot's halfway in love with you, and he did what he did on my account. You can bet it tore him up to do it. I shouldn't have made him choose between me and where his heart was.' He gave her a rueful look. 'It's a bad habit of mine.'

Samandra softened for an instant, surprised he'd spoken so plainly. Then she turned away with a snort.

He didn't wait for anything else from her. There'd be no easy forgiveness for Crake. But maybe he'd gone a little way to righting the wrong.

'Gather up, everyone!' he said. They got to their feet and came over: Malvery, Pinn, Ashua, Crake and Silo. Ugrik came after, and Bess, who was making a clumsy attempt at sneaking to minimise the creak and squeak of her joints. The two Century Knights remained at a distance.

Frey looked over Silo's shoulder as the Murthian approached. The prisoner he'd been interrogating had been gagged now. He hadn't been harmed. Silo could have cut the Sammies' throats and no one would have stopped him, but there didn't seem to be any of that in his eyes when he looked at Frey. The last shreds of doubt at what he was about to do fluttered away then.

'Here's the plan,' he said. He looked up at the red sky: the sun was no longer visible through the trees. 'And we don't have time for argument. Ugrik's gonna lead me to the place where he found the relic. We can move quicker and quieter with just a few. Crake, you come with us. In case of daemonic emergency.'

'What about the rest of us?' asked Pinn.

'You go with Bree and Grudge. You guys are gonna take out that power plant.'

There was the expected chorus of protests, led by Pinn. 'Hey, there's no way I'm taking orders from a Century Knight!'

Frey held up his hands. 'I know, I know. And you won't be.' He clapped his hand on Silo's shoulder. 'You'll be taking orders from the first mate of the *Ketty Jay*.'

There was a puzzled beat while everyone caught up with the implications of that. Malvery and Crake looked at each other.

'Fair enough with me,' said Malvery.

'And me,' said Crake.

Pinn shrugged. 'Yeah, I suppose,' he said, without enthusiasm.

'I thought he already *was* the first mate,' said Ashua, puzzled. Silo hadn't taken his gaze from Frey's. As if he was trying to divine his captain's intention, searching for some ulterior motive that wasn't there.

'You sure about this?' he asked.

'Should've done it years ago,' said Frey.

Then, shockingly, Silo grinned. Frey could count on one hand the amount of times he'd seen the Murthian smile big enough to show his teeth.

'Alright, Cap'n,' he said. 'First mate it is.'

Frey was glad at that. The decision, once made, seemed right and obvious, but he hadn't been sure Silo would accept.

'If I don't make it…' he said. He frowned, wondering if he should take this final step. But it seemed there would be no other time to say it, and it had to be said. 'If I don't make it, the *Ketty Jay*'s yours,' he said. 'Jez knows the ignition code; she can fly it when she wakes. You… well…' He was embarrassed to find a lump gathering in his throat. 'You make sure this lot stick together, if I'm not around to do it.'

His crew stared at him. A long, awkward string of seconds followed, such as men often experience when something of emotional importance occurs. Then Silo gave a small nod.

'I will, Cap'n.'

Frey breathed out, relieved to be released from the moment. Suddenly, he was all business. 'Ugrik, Crake, let's go.'

'We'll need to bring my gear,' Crake said.

So the three of them picked up a pack. They weighed a lot more than their size would suggest, but Frey didn't care at this point. Crake's tricks were the last line of defence, if things went wrong. And Frey was planning on scrapping every inch of the way. He was damned if he was dying tonight.

That done, they distributed the earcuffs to stay in contact, and Crake gave the compass to Silo so he could find the Cap'n again if necessary.

Ugrik, Crake and Frey headed off into the undergrowth. As they were leaving, Frey stopped and looked over his shoulder.

'Keep 'em safe for me, Silo,' he said. 'I'll be back.'

FORTY-ONE

DYNAMITE—THE LAKE—TOMBS—ASHUA MAKES AN ENTRANCE—'YOU GOTTA SEE THIS!'

The power station towered over the surrounding buildings, flashing with miniature storms in the gathering dark.

Silo watched it distrustfully from the foliage. The enormous hourglass structures to either side were lit up by flurries of lightning. The gas within glowed with pale colours, stirred by the rotating arms that orbited each half of the hourglasses.

It seemed somehow malevolent to his eyes.

The power station stood on the topmost of three great platforms, each offset from the other to form irregular steps. The platforms were linked by wide ramps, and stood on perilously slender pillars. Several of the pillars rose from an ornamental pool at the base of the platforms. Once it might have been picturesque, but the water was turgid now, muddied with soil washed down from the slopes.

They were gathered at the fringe of the excavated part of the city, where the undergrowth suddenly stopped and the streets and buildings of the Azryx were revealed in all their strangeness. Beyond, there would be few places to hide.

Electric lights had been set up in the streets, running off petrol generators that rattled and fumed. Presumably the Sammies hadn't worked out how to tap the energy from the city yet. Clumsy cables and scuffed metal seemed out of place here: the smudged fingerprint of industry on a place of serenity, clean lines and silence.

The approaching night had put an end to the excavation work, and there were diggers and tractors and earth-moving machines parked up in the avenues. Sammies walked in groups, talking and laughing. Labourers, technicians and scholars, heading to and from the camp on the edge of the excavated zone. The occasional patrol passed by, barely alert.

Silo noted that there wasn't a single Dak or Murthian to be seen. This place was so secret that not even slaves could know about it. Anywhere else, Murthians would have been doing all the labour while the Daks did the overseeing, administration and everything else. The Sammies would only be there to call the shots. But here, they had *sha'awei* to do all the work – brown-eyed Samarlans from the common caste – and they were being bossed around by the golden-eyed *yansi* nobles. He felt a certain bitter satisfaction at the thought of them getting their hands dirty for once.

Bitter, but not angry. The sight of Fal bleeding out in the arms of his wife had been the end of his youthful rage. Oh, he still hated the Sammies, alright; but after so long away, the lust to kill had faded. There was no satisfaction in it. Coming back to Samarla had briefly reignited the passion, but it hadn't lasted.

He'd kill them if there was a need, just like he'd kill anyone else. But he didn't crave it like he used to.

Besides, he had responsibilities now. *Keep 'em safe for me*, the Cap'n had said.

If I can, Cap'n. If I can.

There was a rustle in the leaves as Malvery shifted his bulk. 'That power station is very pretty and all,' he said. 'But how are we gonna get to it? And what do we do when we're there?'

'Regardin' the second question,' said Samandra Bree, 'I think my partner's got a plan.'

Silo looked over his shoulder at Grudge. The huge Century Knight was hunkered in the shadows, eyes glittering amid a shaggy mass of black hair and beard. He brought out a small satchel from beneath a mass of ammo belts and pulled the flap open. 'Dynamite,' he rumbled.

'Colden here don't go anywhere without his dynamite,' said Samandra.

'It's good stuff,' said Grudge. 'Stable. You could shoot it 'n' it probably wouldn't blow.'

Silo looked in the bag. There were about eight sticks in there. Enough to make a big hole in pretty much anything.

'So here's what I reckon,' said Samandra. 'We get in there. We find somethin' that looks like it shouldn't be blown up. And we blow it up.'

'That's the best the Century Knights have got?' Ashua asked. 'I gotta confess, I'm a little disappointed. After all I heard about you lot in the broadsheets, I expected some kind of fiendishly clever strategy. *Blow it up?* That sounds like something the Cap'n would come up with.'

'Sometimes the old plans are the best plans,' said Samandra, with a charmingly venomous smile. 'Listen, there's Knights that could sneak in and out of there and blow up that power station so quiet the Sammies wouldn't notice for a week. But you got us instead. And no one's gettin' out of here with that thing still runnin'.' She peered through the foliage. 'Right now, we got the advantage of surprise, and the fact that Grudge has a damn great autocannon. We got your golem, and I ain't a bad shot myself.'

'Ain't no way we runnin' up three o' them great big ramps with Sammies firin' down on us,' said Silo. 'Cap'n wants me to bring some crew back alive.'

'Aye,' said Malvery. 'Pinn's been shot enough lately, I reckon.'

'So what's the plan, Mr First Mate?' said Pinn, with a challenge in his voice that said he was faintly jealous of Silo's appointment.

Silo looked out of the undergrowth at the alien streets and avenues, bone-white in the lamplit twilight. His gaze fell on the colossal earth-moving machines, abandoned after the day's excavation.

'Ashua,' he said. 'You ever steal a vehicle?'

'I grew up in the Rabban slums,' she said. 'I can steal anything.'

'In that case,' said Silo, sitting back and looking at the men and women under his command. 'I got an idea.'

The lake was a sullen red, a mirror to the last light of the day. The rising moon swam in it, a perfect orb.

Crake stared across the water. The birds had stilled now, and the insects were subdued. The foliage that choked the shore rustled softly in a warm breeze carried from the desert. It was quiet enough to hear the faint voices of the Samarlans, further along the lakeshore and upslope.

He felt the hand of history on his shoulder. Spit and blood, that he should be here and see this! An Azryx city! And there was no doubt that it *was* Azryx, or whatever the true name of the race was that Professor

Malstrom had been blindly groping for. He and Jez had talked of Malstrom's theories from time to time. He'd scoffed at them; Jez had pitied the Professor for being so obsessed and so wrong.

But Malstrom hadn't been wrong. He'd just been looking in the wrong place.

The architecture and materials put this far beyond the reach of ancient Samarlans. These people had been here long before any currently known civilisation had ever existed. These people had practised daemonism to a higher art than the best practitioners of today. The craft that he'd devoted his life to was not new, it was a rediscovery of the work of their betters. That thought made him feel dwindlingly small.

The building that Ugrik had led them to was down by the shore, beyond the encircling wall that divided the inner city from the outer. It was possible to make out the shape of the place, rather like a ball squashed from above, with four thin spikes set around it in a square. The Yort was searching through the dense mass of trees and vines that surrounded it, muttering to himself. He'd found a way in before, he said. Somewhere around here.

The buildings near the shore had an elegance and delicacy far beyond the outer buildings, which tended more towards blocks of dwellings and huge structures like the power station. Just being here made Crake's mind race. The scholar in him was overwhelmed by a wealth of input. He'd decided that the inner city surrounding the lake was for the upper class, and the outer city was where the workers lived, and where factories and other essential buildings were constructed. He noted that the city's only visible landing pad was in the outer city too.

But there had been gates in the wall to shut people out. Maybe the Azryx kept slaves like the Samarlans did? Maybe there was a strict divide between rich and poor? Or maybe… maybe it was something entirely beyond his experience.

No. Strange as this place was, it was a place built for humans, by humans. He had to think of them as such.

But where had they gone? And how had they disappeared so utterly, undiscovered until now?

He stared across the lake, and amid the wonderment he felt a growing fear of what the night might bring.

'It occurs to me we should have made a little more haste and spent a little less time messing around,' he said. Nerves were making him irritable.

Frey, who was standing beside him, took out his pocket watch and checked it. 'That fat Sammie sorcerer said I had until full dark,' he said. 'I make it at least an hour. And Ugrik said he took the relic from right in that building.' He clicked the pocket watch shut. 'Plenty of time.'

Plenty of time? Crake marvelled at how his friend could be so casual. Crake was the kind of man who turned up a quarter of an hour early for appointments, in case something unforeseen occurred on the way. He'd often been mystified by his crewmates' attitude in the face of danger. It was Crake's opinion that intelligent men *should* be terrified when faced with a predicament like this. Anyone who wasn't had simply failed to understand the situation.

But then, that would make Harkins the smartest man on the *Ketty Jay*, so he supposed his theory wasn't as clever as it sounded at first.

Be honest, Grayther. You're scared because you don't want to face the daemon.

That was the truth of it. All his plans and formulae made fine theories, but he was far from ready to put them into practice. He needed more time, to test and test again. This seat-of-the-pants approach scared him witless.

He remembered how he'd dreamed of pioneering a new kind of field daemonism, something no one else had successfully explored. How boastful and hollow that all seemed, now he came to it. The last time he'd been so arrogant, it had ended in tragedy. It had ended in Bess.

His eyes went to the excavated zone, the bald patch in the jungle where the bones of the city had been laid bare. Bess was there, and Samandra with her. He wasn't sure which one caused him the greater shame.

Whatever the Cap'n said, he didn't think Samandra would ever forgive him for what he'd done, and nor should she. But she could handle herself, at least. Bess was a different matter. He should never have let her go off with the others. He saw the sense in it – Bess would do no good here, and the Cap'n needed him – but it still left him worried and guilty. He should be there to watch out for her, but more importantly, he should be there to *control* her. She was always a little erratic, and without him to keep her in check, he was afraid of what she might do. He was the only one she really listened to.

He wished they'd left her on the *Ketty Jay* with Harkins and Jez. But it was too late for all that now.

'Found it!' Ugrik said. He began pulling vines aside. 'This is the way in.'

'See?' said Frey to Crake, as they picked up their heavy packs full of equipment and made their way towards the Yort. 'Still got an hour.'

'I wonder if you've considered that daemons may not practise such precise timekeeping as your pocket watch?' Crake inquired. 'Them being pan-dimensional entities from beyond infinity, and all that?'

Frey became worried all of a sudden. 'But the sorcerer said—'

'The sorcerer was off his face on hookroot bark,' Crake reminded him.

'Oh,' he said. 'Right.' He quickened his step. 'Best get moving then, eh?'

Crake felt a small, malicious pleasure at infecting the Cap'n with his sense of urgency. He followed Ugrik and Frey through the mass of vines, and into the Azryx building.

They came in through what must have been a window. The doorway was hopelessly choked with tree roots. Crake stared around in wonderment as he climbed down into the room. Seeds and weeds had tunnelled into it here and there, and it was cracked in places, and everything was covered in dust. But despite that, it wouldn't have been out of place in the Archduke's palace.

It was light in here, illuminated with a soft and restful glow that seemed to emanate from all around. The exterior had been the same skeletal off-white colour as the rest of the city, but inside, the walls and ceiling retained a blush of pink. The ceiling was scalloped like the inside of a clam shell. Everything flowed into everything else, with no joins or hard edges, and there was an organic quality to the place, as if it had been grown rather than made. Any furniture had long since decayed into nothingness, but there was a semicircular barrier just inside the front door, made of the same stuff as the walls and floor.

Crake considered the barrier for a moment, wondering what it could be for. Then he realised. It reminded him of nothing more than a reception desk in a foyer.

Yes! Yes, that was what it was! This place was a foyer, he decided. The thought made him dizzy. He felt a connection across ten thousand years, the reality of the people that had once lived here.

To think I might have missed this. To think I might have barricaded myself in a sanctum, and never known this moment.

Ugrik led the way down a corridor that went off to one side. A corridor, or perhaps a tunnel, since it had no corners and it curved as it progressed. He saw a doorway to their right, a smooth oval gap in the pinkish surface, and peered inside. Beyond was a small room with eight beds in two rows. Their frames, made of the same curious ceramic as the city, had survived the millennia. They had a strange, crablike look to them. The beds and their occupants had disappeared, but there were still the remains of ancient devices in there. They were little more than hollow boxes that stood on short poles, but whatever metal they were made of had survived the millennia with only a small amount of corrosion.

'Hey!' called Frey, from up the corridor. Crake realised he'd been lingering in the doorway. 'Come on, Crake. It was you who wanted to hurry.' He said it in a tone which suggested it was Frey who wanted to hurry now.

Crake shouldered his pack and jogged to catch up. The weight of his equipment was making his back ache. Not for the first time, he cursed the lack of portability that went with his chosen profession.

'Did you see those beds?' he asked.

'I saw 'em last time I was here,' Ugrik said.

'What is this place?'

Ugrik sniffed and wiped his nose with the back of his hand. Crake was amazed his nose worked at all with that great big ring in it. 'Hospital,' he said. 'There's more wards like that about, 'n' operating theatres over the other side.'

'This place was a hospital?'

'Aye.'

Crake experienced another unsettling moment. Being here, he felt strangely close to these people. *They lived and died so long ago, yet they seem so like us.*

The corridor opened out into a larger chamber, bigger than the foyer, with two balconied galleries running along either side. Along the length of the chamber were twelve containers in three rows of four. They were white ceramic boxes inside cradles of some metal that looked like polished brass. Each was a little over two metres in length and half as wide.

There was an eerie feel to the chamber. Time had been less kind to it than the foyer. There was rubble on the floor and grass had taken root in the corners. Dust lay thick all around. Though there was the same soft light here as elsewhere, it only seemed to emphasise the desolation and emptiness.

And those boxes looked unsettlingly like tombs.

Ugrik and Frey seemed to feel none of his unease, however. They headed for the far end of the room, where there was a curving stairway that seemed to have melted out of the wall, leading up to one of the galleries. Crake followed more slowly. There was something out of place here, something he couldn't put his finger on.

The boxes had an internal glow all their own. He studied them as he walked between them. Their walls were thin, and he could see the faintest of shadows through them. As if something was inside.

Then he realised what had been nagging at him, and he stopped still.

'Crake?' Frey called. 'Can you stop dragging your arse, please?'

Crake ignored him. He put his hands on top of one of the boxes, feeling around for a seam.

'Oi! What are you fiddling with?'

'There's no dust on 'em, Cap'n.'

'What?'

'These boxes. There's dust everywhere else, but not here.'

'So?'

He found what he was looking for, and hauled. 'Well, Cap'n,' he said. 'Who's been dusting them?'

The top of the box came open. It rose up and slid to one side and tilted out of the way with a silent mechanical movement. Frey looked inside. His eyes widened.

'What is it, Crake?' Frey called, seeing the expression on his face.

'Spit and blood,' he said. 'There are still *people* in these things!'

The ceramic walls of the power station had resisted nature's best efforts to destroy them for thousands of years. It took Ashua less than a second to do the job with a dump truck.

Bullets pinged off the metal skin of the massive vehicle as she climbed dizzily out of the cab. Her neck and back were numb from the whiplash. Fallen rubble had crashed down onto the truck's mangled muzzle and shattered the windscreen. She heard the others returning fire on the Sammies from the shelter of the dump box behind her.

They were in. That was the important thing. They were in.

The Sammies had been slow to react to the sight of a dump truck clumsily thundering through the streets. Even when it went rolling up the ramps between the platforms that led up to the power station, they hadn't suspected the hand of foreigners. Maybe they were too confident in the belief that this place couldn't be found. Either way, she'd made it to the second platform before anyone thought to shoot at them. But her passengers were hidden and protected, and Ashua was a hard target inside the cab, so she kept on going.

It was only when they got to the top that she realised their predicament. There were twenty Sammies up there, maybe thirty, that they hadn't been able to see from below. They had a machine gun, and they were forewarned.

It seemed the guarding of the power station was a serious matter, even when they thought the city couldn't be found. Getting out and knocking on the door wasn't going to be an option.

But the monster vehicle she was driving was the height of three men and weighed several dozen tonnes. Its wheels alone were three metres high: there were railed stairs on the front of it just so you could get to the cab. The cab itself was set back from the muzzle, well protected, and overhung by the dump box. And she reckoned the wall of the power station couldn't be *that* thick.

The sheer strength of the vehicle made her feel invincible. So she put her foot down, and strapped herself in.

With their black skin, black hair and black uniforms, the Sammies looked like shadows made flesh. They certainly melted away like shadows when they saw the dump truck lumbering towards them. The machine gun punched bullets across the body of the vehicle, but the tiny cab was sheltered by the enormous engine casing in the front. She yelled out a warning to the others in the back, but she wasn't sure if they heard it over the bellow of the vehicle.

She braked just before they hit the power station, warned by an instinct for self-preservation. Her instincts were good. The jolt of impact wasn't violent enough to send her flying into the dash, but it was hard enough to crack the thin Azryx ceramic. Instead of ploughing hard into the building, the dump truck only shoved its muzzle through the outer wall, then coughed to a stop.

When she got out, everyone was shouting. She blinked dust from her eyes and looked back along the flank of the vehicle. The machine gun emplacement was getting smashed to pieces by Grudge's autocannon. Samandra Bree slipped lightly down the side of the truck, dropping onto one of the wheels and then to the ground. She swung out her shotguns and started blasting as the Sammie guards came running at them from the side.

Ashua couldn't help taking a moment to marvel. There was something magnetic about the sight of a Century Knight in action. This wasn't the scrappy, hectic gunfighting she'd seen on the street, or the sterile, regimented form of the soldier. Nothing was random, and everything was fluid. Samandra was always moving, but she always knew where she was moving to. There was a lever-action shotgun in each hand. Between each shot, she spun the shotgun fast as an eyeblink, chambering a new round as she did so. Every time she pulled the trigger, Sammics at impossible range went down.

These were the Century Knights she'd heard so much about, the heroes she'd idolised as a child. These were the men and women who let nothing stand in their way.

'Get inside! We'll take care o' these fellers!' Samandra called over the booming of Grudge's autocannon. The others were already clambering over the front of the dump truck, picking their way through the rubble and down the smashed front steps into the power station. Ashua joined them.

She found herself in a cavernous corridor. It was lit by some unknown source, but the faded hue of the walls was dark and vaguely menacing. A thin ridge followed the curve of the ceiling like a spine, and exquisitely fashioned ribs ran its length. There were small signs of decay, cracks in places and bits broken off here and there, but it still retained a louring grandeur.

Oh, Maddeus, she thought. *Gloomy and elegant. You'd have loved this place.*

Bess leaped off the muzzle of the dump truck and crashed to the ground in front of her, making her jump. Malvery slapped her on the back.

'No time for daydreaming, eh?' he said cheerily.

'It's alright for you,' she said, rolling her neck. 'You were in the *back* of the truck.'

'Ah, you're a tough little thing. You'll live,' he said, and then strode off to help Pinn, who was struggling his way down the front of the vehicle with only one working arm.

She'd have thought it condescending from anyone but Malvery. But she didn't like to be snappy when the doctor was around. In fact, his bluff, comradely manner made her feel quite good about herself. He inspired an unfamiliar emotion in her. Trust. He just seemed, well… *decent*, somehow. And Ashua couldn't remember that last time she'd thought that about anyone. Not even Maddeus.

A smile touched the corner of her mouth. Maybe Maddeus had the right idea after all, forcing her in with this lot. Maybe he'd been looking for someone to hand her off to for a long time, ever since he knew he was dying. She wondered how much he'd already known about the crew of the *Ketty Jay* when she came to him with the news that they were working together. She wondered, in fact, who had started the chain of whispers that led Frey to her in the first place.

Maddeus wasn't a decent man. But he looked out for her. He always had.

She put thoughts of her erstwhile guardian from her mind, before they could threaten her. Night was the time for those thoughts, when she was alone in her nook in the hold, and the black sadness came for her. For now, she would only permit herself the hard, sharp thoughts of a survivor.

The others were grouping up now, and together they hurried further into the building, with Bess leading the way.

Ashua flexed her hand on the grip of her pistol and followed. This place unsettled her. She'd spent her life in the bomb-torn ruins of Rabban, and later in the close, dusty streets of Shasiith. She'd never seen anything like this, and it made her feel threatened.

But she'd deal with it. The way she dealt with that golem, and the fact that Jez had turned into a daemon right in front of her eyes. Because that was how she lived. She took the world as she found it. She didn't expect a thing and she didn't give a whole lot back. What was, was, and that was pretty much all there was to it.

The corridor bent ahead of them, and the golem disappeared. Ashua hung back, keeping her eyes peeled for soldiers. She heard shouts and gunfire, and Bess roaring, and then a wet rending sound. A Sammie screamed briefly for his mother.

By the time Ashua came round the curve of the corridor, the screaming had stopped and the floor was bloody. Bess was chasing a couple of guards, who were fleeing for their lives. Pinn kicked someone's detached arm out of his path.

They came to a junction where three corridors gathered in, their curves flowing into one another as if they were liquid frozen in place. Bess was waiting for them, the guards having escaped her. Bree and Grudge caught them up there, Samandra reloading as she came.

'They'll keep their heads down for a little while,' said Samandra, thumbing over her shoulder to indicate the way they'd come. Grudge was backing up the corridor behind her, his autocannon slung low on his hip. 'Won't be long in followin' us, though. We'll have to fight our way out like we fought our way in. And they'll be waitin' out there in numbers, you can bet on that.'

'Bess,' said Silo. 'How tough you think these walls are?'

Bess put her fist through one.

'Reckon we can make our own exit when the time comes,' said Silo.

'Colden!' Samandra called to her hulking partner. She pointed at the hole in the wall. 'Now why can't you do that?'

'Ain't strong enough, I guess,' came the humourless reply.

Samandra winked at Silo. 'Colden. He's a real card. Keeps me in stitches.'

Silo showed his customary lack of reaction.

'Apparently you Murthians ain't exactly a laugh a minute yourselves,' Samandra commented.

'Ain't much about our situation that's funny,' Silo replied.

Ashua was used to Silo's inscrutable manner by now. At first she thought he was arrogant in his silence, a haughty freed slave aping the style of the Sammie nobles. Later, she wondered if he was just dumb. But she'd noticed the quiet respect the others gave him, and she'd seen the way they all accepted his command without question. Even Crake, who was the smartest man on the crew in her opinion. So maybe there was more to Silo than he showed.

They came across a few more Sammies as they made their way deeper into the power station. Not all were guards; some were technicians, or perhaps scholars of some kind. They let those ones go, but nobody who was armed escaped Samandra's shotguns. She was almost casual about the way she took them out. Ashua admired her callousness. There was no room for sentiment in their world.

There weren't many Sammies on the inside, and the intruders kept up such a rapid pace that nobody had time to organise against them. The corridors curved and branched, rarely straight and rarely displaying a sharp angle, running like veins through the building.

The rooms they saw had all been cleared of furniture and debris, but what was left was fascinating enough. There was a long chamber with formations like stalactites hanging down from the ceiling, black and glittering, made up of millions of tiny cuboids that lit up in curiously organised ripples. There was a room of many platforms, a three-dimensional maze of smooth dark ceramic, and a room full of sunken trenches that twinkled with blinking lights.

Then Samandra, who had been scouting ahead, came hurrying back down the corridor. She beckoned to them, a strange smile on her face.

'Ladies and gentlemen,' she said. 'You *gotta* see this!'

FORTY-TWO

❖

THE DREADFUL ENGINE—OBLONGS—BESS MEETS THE LOCALS—THE BRIDGE

Ain't right, thought Silo. *Ain't right at all.*

The room that Samandra had led them to was no more remarkable than any other he'd seen in this place. But there was a large elliptical hole in the far wall, where once there might have been a window. The raucous noise of machinery came from beyond. And it was through that window that they saw the thing which had got Samandra so excited.

They looked out over a chamber of breathtaking size. It must have spanned the whole width of the power station's central building, because it was possible to see the massive flanks of the hourglass structures at either end. The sloped sides of their lower halves swirled with gas and lightning, and every few seconds the vast rotating arms that stirred them went swooping by with a low rumble.

The near side of the chamber was taken up with dozens of black oblongs, standing upright and arranged in staggered rows. They were five metres on their longest side. Slow lightning writhed beneath their surfaces.

Beyond them, the floor suddenly dropped away, and a narrow bridge reached over a wide trench to a small semicircular platform. There, Silo could see what looked like a bank of panels and controls. They were dwarfed by the machine that loomed over them, as if they were the keyboard to some monstrous pipe organ. It was the machine that drew his eye and appalled him. A dreadful engine, unlike anything he'd ever seen before.

It was a mass of thrashing movement. Pistons pumped in and out, brass arms rotated, gears clanked and shifted. In amid the more familiar elements were stranger ones. Cylinders of bottled lightning, flickering inside coloured gas. Rows of spikes that tilted rapidly back and forth in sequence, and shot sparks when they came near the conducting rods that stood opposite. Globes that crackled with energy. Fields of tiny connections which shivered and switched back and forth.

The metal parts he could understand. The lightning fascinated him. But that wasn't the problem.

The damned thing had *muscles*.

At first he couldn't be sure of what he was looking at. It was only as he watched them stretch and flex that he recognised them by their movement. They were muscles, giant muscles sewn into the machinery, bulging and loosening with the tug and thrust of the parts around them. Taut diaphragms stretched in the spaces between the metal. Tendons pulled. The fleshy parts were a deep red-black, and glistened with lubrication.

Pinn watched the muscles pumping, an expression of utter disgust on his face. Eventually, he gave his verdict. 'That is bloody horrible.'

'If there was anythin' needed blowin' up in this whole city, I reckon it's that,' said Malvery.

Samandra pointed down at the bridge, and the small semi-circular platform at the other side. 'There,' she said.

Silo grunted his agreement. 'Move out!' He ushered them towards an oval doorway at the side of the room.

The doorway led to a gallery overlooking the engine chamber, and from there they found steps leading to the chamber floor. The chamber seemed even larger from down here. The vast ceiling had the same dark, supple grandeur of the corridors they'd passed through. He could appreciate the size of the hourglass structures now: their brass-and-bone shells towered to either side of the great machine. The whole place was like a temple, and it might have been wondrous, if not for the repulsively organic engine throbbing and churning at its heart.

Rows of black oblongs stood between them and the bridge. The rows were set irregularly, so they would have to pick their way through. Pinn, who had been one of the first down the steps, was staring into one of the oblongs, watching the progress of the blue lightning as it moved slowly across the darkness.

'What are they?' Pinn asked.

'Batteries,' said Silo. 'Best guess, anyway.'

'Then what are *they*?' Malvery asked. The doctor had turned around and was looking behind them. The wall to either side of the stairs was covered with dozens of strange bulges. They were bulbous at one end and thinned to a point, almost two metres end to end. They looked like seed pods, except that there was machinery integrated into the leathery white exteriors, a framework of metal with many small dials and gauges set into it.

Before anyone could advance an opinion, they heard shouts from overhead. Sammies, somewhere out of sight. Reinforcements.

'Don't touch nothin',' said Silo, and they moved on into the forest of oblongs. This whole damn place set him on edge. The sight of that engine… It was against nature, against Mother. Metal and flesh, fused. Was it *alive* in some way?

He spat. Didn't want to think about the possibilities. What kind of people built a thing like that?

As they moved further into the rows, they saw Sammies emerging onto the gallery above them. One of them aimed his rifle, but another man knocked the barrel aside angrily. Silo couldn't hear them well enough to make out the words, but it seemed to be a heated discussion.

Then, nothing. Nobody fired. Nobody made any move to descend the stairs and pursue.

Silo didn't like that one bit.

'Why aren't they following?' Pinn asked.

Silo saw something move out of the corner of his eye, further down the row. He spun towards it; but whatever it was, it had moved out of sight. After a moment, he wondered if there had been anything there at all.

'Keep goin,' he said, his voice low and wary. He kept staring at the spot where he'd seen the movement, but he saw nothing more. After a moment, he took his own advice.

Better to say nothing. He was supposed to be the leader here. Spooking the troops to no good end would only make them doubt him.

They moved through the oblongs as if through an alien forest, staying close to the silent objects in order to keep out of the Sammies' line of fire. The guards didn't look inclined to shoot, but Silo felt threatened all the same. No one wanted to present their backs to the Sammie guns, so they slipped from cover to cover in awkward little runs.

Each oblong was spaced apart from the others, so it was possible to slip through the rows quite rapidly, but it also meant that it would be easy for something to get close to them without being spotted. They trod gingerly, careful not to touch the objects, until Pinn stumbled and bumped into one. When he didn't suffer any kind of terrible death, they relaxed a little. But only a little.

'Silo!' said Malvery suddenly, coming up on his shoulder. Silo turned. The doctor's face was serious, eyes hard behind his green-lensed glasses. 'Think I saw something.'

Silo nodded. He looked to his left and right. The Century Knights were prowling up on either side. Bess lumbered noisily past him, oblivious to the Sammies on the gallery. The others were spaced out more widely than he'd like. He opened his mouth to tell them to tighten up, when he heard the clank and scrape of sudden movement from Bess.

He found her looking off to one side, her metal body tensed. She turned this way and that, twisting her whole body because she had no neck. Her agitation was obvious. She'd seen something, or sensed it.

'Easy, Bess,' said Silo. Clutching his shotgun, he passed her and moved on to the next row. He looked to his left, and went still.

It was so strange that it took a moment for his senses to untangle it. His first reaction was instinctive repulsion. It looked like a giant white spider, the size of a man. But as it moved, he saw muscle and mechanisms, and a face of sorts, a rounded blank mask studded with a half-dozen lenses of various sizes. It was plated with something like chitin, but flesh flexed wetly at its joints.

The thing had climbed up the side of one of the black oblongs, a short way along the row. Two sets of spindly legs stood on the floor, a third gripped the oblong's sides, and its forelegs functioned like arms. Each of these arms split at the last joint into several thin appendages, which ended in drills, pincers, soldering irons and other devices that Silo couldn't easily identify.

An automaton? No. An animal? Not that, either. It was a bastard hybrid of meat and machine and other arts, something entirely unnatural, like that terrible engine which pumped and screeched nearby.

As Silo watched, the hybrid slid out a section of the oblong from near the top, where there had seemed to be no join at all. It was about the size of a dinner tray, and completely black. The hybrid began tapping at it with one of its appendages. Immediately, Silo noticed a change in the oblong itself. The movement of that lazy lightning had altered somehow, curling and rolling in a different manner to the way it had before.

He couldn't see what the thing was up to, but he recognised its purpose. Maintenance. This creature was a caretaker, looking after the power station, millennia after its makers had gone.

He trained his shotgun on it as it slid the tray closed. The appendages in its forelegs folded up and retracted and it climbed off the oblong and down to the floor. It appeared to notice him then, tilting its face towards him for the first time. The lenses in its mismatched eyes whirred as they focused in and out.

Then it came walking unhurriedly along the row towards him, moving with a repulsively arachnid gait.

Silo felt the urge to shoot it out of sheer horror, but he mastered himself. He backed up instead, keeping it in view, watching for any sudden moves. He'd only gone a few steps when he bumped into Bess, who was coming through the rows behind him. The golem swivelled, and suddenly froze, like a cat spotting a mouse. She'd seen what he had.

'Easy, Bess,' he said again. He glanced up at the Sammies on the gallery, then back at the approaching hybrid. No wonder they hadn't come down here. They were scared of these things.

The golem moved, a quick, uncertain jerk. She was alarmed and agitated, and that wasn't good. He wished Crake were here to calm her. Grudge appeared in the next row, autocannon trained on the hybrid; at the same moment, Samandra ghosted in behind it, her shotguns ready. The creature continued on its way, apparently unconcerned by the guns.

'Say the word,' said Samandra to Silo.

'Don't,' said Silo. 'It don't seem too hostile. Maybe best if we just get out of its w—'

He was interrupted by a roar from Bess. She pushed past him, shoving him roughly aside with the implacable strength of a bulldozer, and lunged forward.

'Bess!' he barked.

She skidded to a halt, directly in the path of the hybrid, her shoulders set in a challenge. The hybrid stopped and looked her up and down, eye-lenses whirring.

'What the spit *is* that thing?' Malvery asked, from over Silo's shoulder.

'Looks like something I caught off a whore one time,' Pinn quipped merrily.

Silo paid no attention. Pretty much everything that came out of Pinn's mouth could be safely ignored. Instead he focused on the golem.

'Bess?' he said, as if placating a wild dog. 'Leave that thing alone, Bess. It ain't harmin' us right now. Best not to mess with what we've yet to figure out. Let's just leave it to be about its business.'

There was a long moment of tension. Then the hybrid moved a leg.

Whether it was attempting to attack or just trying to get around the obstruction, they never knew. Bess was on a hair-trigger, and she reacted with violence, grabbing a forelimb in one huge hand and wrenching it off. The hybrid flailed, legs skidding on the floor as it fought to retreat, but Bess's bunched fist came down on its back like a hammer, flattening it to the floor, cracking its chitin plating.

'Bess! No!' Silo yelled. But it was no good. The golem was beyond his control. She raised a foot and stamped down on the hybrid's head like a child stamping on an insect. Its head split and shattered in a spray of glass and fluid.

When she raised her foot again, the hybrid was still. It lay in a pool of slowly spreading transparent liquid. A sharp, oily stink filled the air.

'Huh,' said Samandra, lowering her weapons. 'Seems your pet didn't take to the locals.'

Pinn chuckled. Silo didn't. He had the sense that something very bad had just occurred. He looked up at the Sammies on the gallery, and saw them retreating hastily from the chamber. There was a series of hissing sounds coming from that direction, beyond the obscuring rows of batteries. His engineer's instincts placed the sound immediately. The hiss of escaping air or gas, such as when a pressure valve was released. The sounds of many things opening.

Then he remembered the odd, podlike structures set into the wall under the gallery.

'Run,' he said quietly.

'Beg pardon?' Malvery asked.

'*Run!*' he cried, now overwhelmed by the certainty of impending doom. 'Make for the bridge! Go!'

They didn't question him, not even the Knights. The rare note of urgency in his voice propelled them. They took to their heels and raced towards the monstrous edifice at the heart of the chamber. Silo ran with them, dodging between the strange batteries with their slow blue lightning trapped within.

He could hear a noise growing behind him, a tide of rapid clicks and taps. He risked a glance over his shoulder, and his worst fears were confirmed.

The batteries prevented him from seeing all their pursuers, but some were clambering over the tops of the oblongs, leaping from one to another with insidious jerks. They moved like the spiders they resembled. Each was identical to the creature Bess had killed, except that their mismatched clusters of eyes glowed red. There was no question that these were hostile, and judging by the din of tapping feet, there were dozens of them on their way.

They broke free of the oblongs into an open space, ending in a deep trench not far ahead, and a narrow bridge crossing it. The gnashing, pounding engine of muscle and brass loomed before them. Silo didn't want to go that way – he knew they'd be trapped if they did – but it was the only defensible place he could see. At least the bridge would form a choke point that would negate their superior numbers. If they were caught out in the open, they were dead.

The Century Knights had reacted fastest to his warning, and they were the first to reach the bridge, just as the hybrids swarmed out of the rows of black oblongs. They took up defensive positions to either side and laid down suppressing fire for the *Ketty Jay*'s crew. Silo ran with his head down, bullets and autocannon shells raking through the air around him, and when he got to the bridge he turned and added his weapon to theirs.

There were already hybrid bodies littering the open space behind them. Grudge's autocannon smashed its targets, tearing them apart in a spray of transparent fluid. Samandra's shotguns were ineffective against the hybrid's chitinous plates, but she was aiming for the fleshy parts at the joints: the legs, knees and throat. Those she couldn't kill outright she crippled and maimed with astonishing accuracy.

Silo did what he could to help out as the others went running past him onto the bridge, but his shotgun was not made for long range, and the best he could do was stun the enemy. He realised that Samandra's shotguns must have been modified to carry extra ammo:

she already seemed to have fired too many times without reloading. But even she ran out soon enough, and in that moment, one of the hybrids got through.

It was Bess who'd been slowest to follow, and Bess who was caught. It leaped onto her back, gripping her with its lower legs. Its forelimbs split into an array of smaller arms, tipped with maintenance tools, and it began to drill and hack at her. She thrashed and roared, stumbling towards the bridge while trying to reach behind herself to get it off.

'Come on,' said Samandra to Silo. 'We're done here. Leave it to the heavy hitters.' She tugged him towards the bridge.

Silo resisted for a moment, reluctant to leave Bess to her plight, but in the end he went with her. She was right; they would do no good by staying. Their shotguns were empty and there was no time to reload.

They ran onto the bridge, and now Silo could see over the side. Below them was a deep, wide trench, like a dry moat surrounding the massive engine. Its walls were studded with tiny lights and panels of strange machinery. He reckoned these were the guts of the machine, a complex system of unfamiliar technology beyond anything he knew. Small holes ran all the way up the sides of the trench in a regular grid pattern, each as wide as a fist, but he couldn't imagine what manner of device might be plugged into one.

Grudge had backed on to the bridge ahead of Bess, who came staggering after, pawing at the creature that was trying to drill into her humped back. She caught hold of its leg and flung it away from her. It went spinning through the air and smashed against the side of the trench, falling brokenly to the floor. Bess turned around with a bubbling growl and planted herself; she was wide enough to block most of the bridge. Grudge moved up alongside her, his autocannon held at the ready.

The others had reached the small semicircular platform on the far side of the bridge, and taken cover behind the banks of panels there. Silo and Samandra joined them. The Century Knight began reloading her shotguns while Silo made a quick check on the people left in his care.

Nobody was hurt, but they all had the same grim look in their eyes. They knew what he knew. They couldn't get off this platform except by the bridge. There were still dozens of those damned Azryx horrors blocking their escape. Grudge's autocannon would run out eventually, and Bess's raw strength could only do so much.

He peered out from hiding. The hybrids had halted in their charge. They'd gathered at the end of the bridge, studying Bess and Grudge curiously, tilting their heads left and right. And he'd be damned if they didn't look like they were calculating, weighing up their opponents, considering tactics.

Silo knew what they were thinking. He was thinking the same.

There was no way out.

FORTY-THREE

TROPHIES—CRAKE, REFLECTED—THE VANDAL—
'LET'S GET THAT DAMNED CURSE OFF YOU.'

Crake looked down into the box. It was not a tomb, as he'd first thought. It was a tank full of transparent liquid that glowed with a sullen light from within. And lying there, submerged, was an Azryx.

The body floated inside a snaking cradle of wires and tubes. There was no question the man was dead. It was just that he looked like he'd been dead a week or two, instead of thousands of years. His eyes and cheeks were sunken, muscles withered, ribs starkly visible through the taut brown skin of his chest. The last wisps of black hair still floated around his head.

They were real, he thought. *They were really real.* Even being in this city, walking about inside their buildings, hadn't brought it home as hard as this. The sight of one of these ancient men in the flesh filled him with a sense of awe such as he'd not felt since he first grasped the possibilities of daemonism.

The man's mouth and nose were covered by a breather mask, and there was some kind of waste-removal system concealing his nether parts. Tubes ran from chattering devices in the corner of the tank and disappeared into major veins and arteries. Crake surmised that the liquid and the machines must have preserved him somehow, long past the point where he should have decayed. And he could guess at the reason for being in the tank, too.

The man was horrifically scarred. Not from wounds, but from some kind of pox. There were cratered sores all over his face, torso and limbs.

An idea struck him. He went to the next tank in the row and opened it, as he had the first. Inside was another body in a similar state. This one had been tall and brown-skinned, like the last, and was afflicted with the same disfiguring ailment.

What happened here?

'Crake!' Frey snapped. He was standing with Ugrik at the bottom of the stairs at the far end of the chamber. 'You can poke about to your heart's content afterwards, alright?'

'Yes, sorry, yes,' he muttered. He shouldered his pack and retreated from the tanks. His mind was awhirl. He was so bowled over by the magnitude of their discoveries that he'd almost forgotten why they were here in the first place.

After they'd seen to the Cap'n's little problem, Crake would come straight back here. He promised himself that. Sammies or no Sammies, he was going to have a damn good look around.

Ugrik led them up the curving stairway to one of the galleries that overlooked the chamber. They went through a door and further into the building, and then up another set of steps. The nature of the rooms changed. Crake had expected to see wards and theatres – things he associated with a hospital – but the upper level was laid out in a different style. He couldn't imagine a place like this crowded with patients and medical staff. It seemed more like some kind of grand dwelling, though it was hard to tell with the majority of the furniture turned to dust and creepers invading through the windows.

'You know, someone was looking after those bodies in the tanks,' he said, as they slogged through the corridors under the weight of all the equipment he'd brought. 'Those things didn't dust themselves.'

'I heard you the first time,' said Frey. 'If they show up, we'll shoot 'em. How's that?'

'About as diplomatic as I've come to expect,' Crake said.

They passed several more doorways, but Crake barely paid attention. His mind was on the pox-covered corpses in the tanks.

A plague? Was that what happened to the Azryx? Was that why they disappeared? But who's been caring for the patients all this time?

The corridor ended in a room which had a cavity in one wall that looked remarkably like a fireplace. Set into the pinkish, seashell-like surface above it was a large, teardrop-shaped piece of metal, thick with dust but perfectly intact. Frey came to a halt as he saw it. Except for its size, it was identical to the one on the inside of the lid of the relic case, with a stylised jackal at its centre.

'There are marks underneath it,' Crake observed. 'Looks like someone's wiped off the dust recently, too,' he added with some alarm.

'Aye,' said Ugrik. 'That was me, last time I was here. I was tryin' to read it.' He held up his hand to forestall the question on Crake's lips. 'I know Old Isilian. It ain't far off.'

'You can speak Old Isilian?' Crake asked, impressed. He'd assumed, given his appearance, that Ugrik was something of a brute and a dunce. It was hard for him to equate the idea of scholarly excellence with a ring through the nose and blue ink all over the face.

'I can *read* it,' the Yort corrected. 'Nobody can *speak* it. Ain't been spoken for thousands of years.'

'Yes, yes, of course. But Azryx writing is similar?'

'Aye.'

Crake was back in a state of academic excitement again. 'So it stands to reason that Old Isilian came from Azryx, and all the other languages after tha—'

'What does it *say*?' Frey interrupted impatiently. 'The writing on the jackal thing?' Frey eyed it uneasily, then added 'Actually, you can tell me on the way. Let's get moving.'

'Couldn't make out much of it,' said Ugrik, as he led them into the next room. 'I think it was the name o' the feller who lived here. And two words. *Warrior* and *scholar*, or near enough that it makes no difference. I reckon that thing is a family coat of arms, or whatever the Azryx had. So I'm thinkin' this warrior-scholar feller lived above the hospital, might have owned it or whatnot. Studied the patients, perhaps.'

'An aristocrat who *wasn't* a massive wimp?' Frey exclaimed. 'Bugger me.'

'Ow!' Crake said. 'My feelings!'

'Sorry. Forgot.'

Crake let it pass. When he thought about it, it was a fair comment anyway. 'It might explain the jackal, anyway,' he said. 'The one that's been after you, I mean.'

'How so?'

'Well, it's kind of like a calling card. So you know who cursed you. The daemon takes the shape of the family's coat of arms, with a few modifications based on whatever horrors it can dredge up from your psyche.'

Frey thought about that. 'One thing I don't get,' he said. 'Why have the damned thing turning up over and over again? Why not just have it kill me straight away and take the relic? That's what I'd do.'

'Because even the Azryx can't conjure a daemon that powerful out of nothing,' said Crake. He glanced at Ugrik, pleased for the chance to reassert intellectual superiority over the Yort. 'It can only maintain itself in our reality for a limited time. But each time it's appeared, it's lasted for longer, hasn't it? Given its nature, I suspect it draws energy from its victim's fear. It's been gathering strength. Tonight, it will be able to bring itself entirely into our reality, and it won't go away till its job is done. Unless the relic is returned to the place it was stolen from.'

'So it's win-win for the owner,' Frey said. 'Either they frighten the thief into bringing the relic back, or the daemon eventually kills them and *takes* it back.'

'Exactly,' said Crake. 'It's really rather clever, actually.'

'Yes,' said Frey flatly. 'Very clever.'

'We do have one thing in our favour, though. Previously, the daemon only appeared to one person at a time. Nobody else could see or sense it. But when it's fully manifested, it'll be as real as you or I, and we'll all be able to see it.'

'Yeah, but can we *kill* it?' Frey asked.

'Not by conventional means, I'm afraid. It's still a daemon. But at least you won't have to face it alone.'

'Reckon we won't need to worry about that for much longer, anyway,' said Ugrik. He shifted the relic to his left arm, pointed at a doorway with his right and said 'In there. That's where I found it.'

Crake felt his heart lift, and he saw the same reaction on the Cap'n's face. Could it be journey's end at last? They hurried inside.

The room beyond was darker than the rest of the building. The illumination from the walls and floor was choked by thick vines that coiled in through a great gash on the far side. They'd consumed half the room in a dense tangle, and their furthest tendrils reached almost to the doorway. The full moon glared in through the gap.

'That's it,' said Ugrik, pointing. 'Took it from there.'

In the centre of the room was a narrow pillar of what looked like coral. It bulged and branched, reaching out arms here and there, forming shelves and nooks and cradles. Most held only dust, but some objects were still intact. A black orb was cupped in an alcove, and there were the remains of mechanical devices, and some ceramic things that might have been sculpture, or awards of some kind. The jackal crest was set proudly into the pillar, made of the same iron-like metal as the one they'd seen earlier. Everything fitted so snugly into its niche that it was hard not to conclude that the pillar had been moulded specifically to their shapes.

Reaching horizontally out at waist height were two delicate branches of coral, curling up at the end to form corners. Behind the arms, the coral of the pillar sloped backwards at an angle. It only took a glance to know what should go there.

Frey looked to Ugrik for confirmation. 'Aye,' he said. 'It was in the case, and the case was open. Best put it back just the way I found it, I'd say.' Ugrik held out the black oblong case containing the relic. 'You ought to do it.'

Crake checked the sky through the break in the wall. It was a deep blue-velvet. 'It's not yet full dark,' he said, with relief in his voice. 'Despite your lax attitude to deadlines, Cap'n, you might actually have made it in time.'

They took off their bulky packs and put them aside. Frey put the relic case on the ground in front of the pillar and began feeling around its edge. 'That's good,' he muttered. 'Except it usually takes me quarter of an hour to find the thingummybob that opens it.'

Crake assumed he was exaggerating. He hoped so, anyway.

Ugrik hunkered down next to the Cap'n, offering useless advice and occasionally attempting to interfere until Frey slapped his hands away. Crake left them to it and let his eyes wander the room. Beneath the vines on the near side of the room, where they were not so dense, he could see more shelves and alcoves in the wall, with more objects hidden there. Nearby, he caught sight of a pedestal in the foliage, overturned by the growth of the plants.

Once more he found himself trying to understand his surroundings, to bring this dead culture to life and connect with it. Was this a trophy room of some kind?

He moved away from the others and began searching the thicker tangles of vines, looking for more clues.

There! he thought, peering into the gloom. *What's that? It looks like—*

Suddenly the shape made sense to him. A white, haggard face loomed out of the dark and he recoiled with a shout of alarm.

'What? What?' Frey had his pistol out and was casting around the room for danger.

Crake stared, his heart decelerating. The figure trapped in the vines didn't move. He began to feel foolish.

'It's nothing, Cap'n,' he said. 'I thought...' He decided he'd only dig himself a deeper hole if he explained. 'Never mind.'

Frey shook his head angrily and went back to the relic case. 'I'm wound up enough as it is, Crake. Yell like that, I'm liable to put a bullet in you.'

Crake wasn't listening to Frey's grumbles. He was peering through the vines again. There was no dead man in there, only a suit of some kind. A black body suit that seemed to be made of tiny scales. There were gloves hanging by its sides, and presumably boots down there somewhere. It must been standing on display once. Some kind of armour, perhaps, but thinner and more flexible than any he knew.

And of course the white, haggard face he saw had been his own, reflected in the blank, smooth faceplate of the helmet. Spit and blood, had he deteriorated so much that he startled *himself* now? These recent days had worn him down with sleeplessness and care. His beard, which he'd once thought pleasingly rugged, made him look like a hobo in conjunction with those baggy eyes and gaunt cheeks.

Grayther Crake, he told himself. *You need to smarten up.*

He studied the helmet more closely. It fitted over the whole head, sealing in the wearer. Tubes ran from the jawline over the back. While puzzling over its purpose, his attention drifted to the reflection in the faceplate. In the light from the doorway, he could see the Cap'n and Ugrik, still fiddling with the box.

'Wait...' the Cap'n was saying. 'Got it!'

A small movement made Crake shift his gaze minutely. His eyes widened.

Something was in the doorway, unnoticed by Ugrik or Cap'n. Something that was gliding silently into the room. A glint of tarnished metal.

He spun around with a yell, fumbling his pistol free of his belt.

'What is it *this* time?' Frey cried, then went pale as he saw that Crake was waving a gun in his direction. He and Ugrik lunged out of the way, more because they were afraid of Crake than through any awareness of the danger behind them.

He caught only the briefest impression of it. It floated in the air a half-metre off the ground. A ring of long, grasping arms surrounded a cylindrical torso topped with a flat round head, with two lenses of different sizes to function as eyes.

An automaton.

He fired wildly out of panic, blasting off all five chambers as quickly as he could pull the trigger. Bullets caromed off the automaton and ricocheted away. He might have closed his eyes after the first shot; he wasn't sure. What he *was* sure of was that the recoil knocked his aim all over the place, and it had been abysmal to begin with.

Frankly miraculous, then, that when he opened his eyes the Azryx thing was lying on the floor, with one of its eye-lenses smashed. Crake let out a disbelieving gasp.

'I hit it!' he said.

'You almost hit every bloody thing else as well!' said Frey, as he got to his feet from a cringing position. 'Including us!'

Ugrik cackled. 'Looks like he bagged himself an Azryx toy, though.'

'Exactly! I saved your lives!' Crake said, indignantly. He strode over to the fallen automaton, slightly miffed that the Cap'n wasn't more grateful.

Ugrik was already studying it. 'You sure it was goin' to hurt us?' He lifted up one of its arms. What had seemed a fearsome claw at first was actually rather delicate-looking.

'Well, I...' Crake began. He swallowed. 'Er.'

'I'm just forwardin' the possibility that you might have just destroyed a ten-thousand-year-old Azryx automato—'

'It was going to kill you!' Crake protested. 'It was pawing the air and stuff!' He pawed the air to demonstrate, in what he hoped was a sufficiently frightening manner.

'Aha!' Frey crowed. '*Now* who's the vandal? All that rubbish I smashed back at the Mentenforth institute wasn't half as old as *that*!'

In fact, now that it was lying inert, it didn't look very threatening at all. It began to sink in that this was, well, an *automaton*. A metal being capable of movement. Quite possibly it was the caretaker that had looked after the bodies in the tanks all this time, which would indicate some kind of complex mechanical thought. And that put it far above anything the best of Vardic scholars could even dream of right now.

'But... I...' Crake blustered, horrified by what he'd done. The thought that he might have shot the single greatest scientific discovery since aerium was refined made him nauseous. 'What do you mean, *rubbish*?' he demanded, in a feeble attempt to throw some kind of blame back on to Frey.

'Vandal,' Frey said with a smirk. He swept past Crake and knelt down next to the relic. The case had come open, and inside was the double-bladed weapon, resting in its wrought-metal cradle. Crake stared at it, stunned by this terrible turn of events. It lay there, unmarked and pristine, untouched by the calamity and tragedy it had brought. The cause of all their strife and labour. Spit and blood, he'd be glad to never see that thing again.

'Put it where it belongs,' he said. 'Let's get that damned curse off you and get on with our lives.'

'Right,' said Frey, scooping up the case. 'Where did you say it went again, Ugrik?'

The Yort got up and pointed. 'Right… er… there.' He trailed off.

'Oh, no,' Frey said quietly.

Something in the tone of his voice send a slow dread creeping into Crake's belly. All the Cap'n's cockiness was gone. What was left was fear.

Crake looked at the pillar. Where there had once been two arms reaching out to hold the relic case, now there was only one. The other was lying on the floor, in several pieces.

Smashed by a bullet.

Frey dropped to his knees and hung his head. It was as if all the strength and vigour had suddenly gone out of him, like air from a balloon. 'Of all the luck…' he muttered. 'Of all the shit-eating luck in the world…'

The sheer *defeat* in his voice terrified Crake. He was suddenly desperate to offer hope, desperate to make amends. Desperate not to be the one responsible.

He snatched up the relic case. 'No, look, maybe we can still…' He tried to fit it into its spot in the pillar. It wouldn't stay, so he knelt down. 'Maybe if we hold it there…' He struggled to jam it in somehow, but the whole arrangement was too delicate. With that arm gone, there was nothing they could do. 'If we had some glue…'

The silence from the others stopped him. He looked over his shoulder.

Frey had taken off his glove and was staring at his hand with dead eyes.

The black spot was still there.

FORTY-FOUR

CLOSE QUARTERS—PINN'S IDEA— SILO IS CUT OFF—LIGHTNING

'We gotta get out of here!' Pinn cried. Silo would have been the first to agree, if only he could see some way to do it.

Halfway across the bridge, Bess was struggling beneath two of the spider hybrids, who were drilling and hacking ineffectually in search of a weak spot. She wasn't in much danger from their attacks but, while she was occupied, others slipped by. The Century Knights had taken position behind her, at the edge of the platform where the *Ketty Jay*'s crew hid behind banks of mysterious mechanisms. Bree and Grudge mopped up the ones that got through, working in partnership, choosing their targets carefully and covering each other while they reloaded.

They were holding the enemy off for now. But it would only last as long as their bullets did.

Silo felt the pressure to act. Malvery, Pinn and Ashua were looking to him for a decision. He'd told the Cap'n he'd get them out safely. But how? They were trapped here, and breaking out would get them nowhere but dead. They'd be mobbed in the open.

He scanned his surroundings. There was little to offer hope. The semicircular platform was only about five metres deep, barely enough to cram them all in if Bess joined them. Panels ran around its curved edge, where those who weren't fighting the hybrids had taken shelter. At the back was a wall of controls, set into the base of the enormous engine of flesh and metal that thrashed the air above them, pumping and bellowing. Lights blinked and gauges trembled. He recognised bits of technology – a lever, a dial, simple things like that – but for the most part he had no idea what they did or how to operate them.

*Come on, Silo. The Cap'n trusted you. Think. You ain't losin'
another bunch o' people. Not these people.*

'Over the side!' he heard Samandra call to her partner. He saw
what she meant immediately. Some of the hybrids had given up
attempting to get past Bess. They were climbing down the walls into
the trench.

Suddenly Silo realised what the holes he'd observed earlier were
used for. They were made to fit the hybrid's spider legs, to allow
them access to the entire height and breadth of the wall and the
machinery there.

If they could climb into the trench, they could climb out of it again
on the far side. They could climb up onto the platform, behind Bess
and the Century Knights.

Any thought of defending their position disappeared. If there was
ever a time to act, it was now. And yet all ways led to death and failure.

Grudge, responding to Samandra's warning, swung his autocannon
over the side of the bridge and let fly. He obliterated two of the
creatures as they crawled towards the floor of the trench. His third
shot missed as its target jinked aside. It smashed into a panel of
machinery instead.

The reaction among the hybrids was uncanny. Just for an instant,
they all froze at once. Then they resumed their attack as if nothing
had happened.

But not all of them.

The hybrid that Grudge had missed stopped its climb down the
walls. Its forelegs split into an array of tools, and it began attending to
the damaged panel. A moment later it was joined by two more, their
nimble limbs busy as they cooperated.

And then Silo saw a chink of light in the darkness. The tiniest
glimmer of hope.

'Grudge!' he called. 'Give me the dynamite!' He ran out on to the
bridge. Grudge pulled the satchel from beneath his depleted ammo
belts and tossed it to him without looking.

'We gonna push forward!' he yelled at the Knights over the
rattle and boom of their guns. 'When I give the word, not before!
Everything you got! Get us back across this bridge!'

Samandra glanced over her shoulder at him, a look that was part
puzzlement, part suspicion. Deciding whether to trust him or not.

Deciding whether to accept his command.

'Meanwhile,' he said to Grudge. 'Don't shoot the *spiders*. Shoot the *machinery*!'

He didn't wait to see if the big man took up his suggestion. He was already running back to the platform. He crouched down by the back wall, at the base of the great engine. The others came over as he was digging the dynamite out of the satchel.

'Er, mate,' said Malvery. 'You do know that setting off that dynamite is liable to kill us all, don't you? There ain't much space on this platform.'

'We ain't gonna be here,' said Silo. He jerked a thumb towards the bridge. 'We goin' out that way. Gonna blow this damned thing on our way out.'

'Not with *those* fuses,' Ashua said, pointing at the stick in his hand.

Silo looked, and saw. He felt a fool for not having spotted it before she did. The dynamite was short-fused for throwing. Grudge didn't carry it around for demolition; he used them to blast enemies out of hiding.

He cursed inwardly. They'd get five seconds out of a fuse like that. Five seconds wasn't nearly enough time to get away from the concussion created by eight sticks of dynamite. Not with all those creatures in the way.

He wracked his brains, but nothing came to mind. There was no time for a new plan, not with the hybrids crawling into the trench, coming closer by the second. Just for a moment, he thought he'd seen a way out. But it had been a false hope after all.

All that was left was a charge. If they could get across the bridge, maybe they could use the dynamite to take out some of the enemy by throwing it among them. But he knew in his heart there were too many.

He was drawing breath to give the order when Pinn blurted: 'Flame-Slime!'

Malvery and Ashua exchanged a look. 'I could've sworn he just said "Flame-Slime",' said the doctor.

'Professor Pinn's Incredible Flame-Slime!' Pinn said, his chubby face alight with enthusiasm. He brandished a small tin from his pocket. 'You put some on the fuse, and…' He looked amazed that he'd even come up with the idea. 'It'll work!' he insisted. 'It'll actually work!'

Malvery was equally amazed. 'It actually will,' he said.

Silo took the tin and unscrewed the top. Inside was a transparent jelly. Yes, he saw how it could be done. If they stood it upright and only coated the tip, the fuse wouldn't light until the insulating jelly had burned through.

'How long?' he demanded of Pinn.

'Thirty to forty seconds,' said Pinn. 'I timed it,' he added proudly. 'Scientifically.'

'Silo!' yelled Samandra from the bridge. 'They're gettin' through! Whatever you're gonna do, do it fast!'

Thirty to forty seconds, and five for the fuse. It'd be enough.

'Get ready,' he said. 'We're fightin' our way out.'

They nodded, and he saw the determination on their faces. They had a chance, and they were going to take it. In that moment, he felt what the Cap'n must feel at times like this. Pride. They were a ragtag lot, no question, but no one could say they didn't have heart.

'Bess!' he shouted over the din of gunfire and the sound of the great engine. 'Clear us a path!'

The golem heard him, and this time she listened. It took Crake to restrain her, but anyone could spur her to violence. She roared and began bulling her way forward, scooping up the hybrids like a snowplough. The Century Knights moved up behind her, shooting any that spilled past her outstretched arms.

'Go!' he barked at the others. 'Help 'em out. Do what you can.'

They did as he told them. He took a slap of flame-slime and coated the end of a fuse in it. Then he put the stick of dynamite upright among the others, and rested the satchel against the wall. It wasn't the ideal setting for an explosive charge, but he had nowhere better and nothing to tamp it with. He just had to hope the mechanisms that operated the power station were as delicate as they were complex.

Ashua shouted from the bridge. 'They're climbing up the wall! Get out of there!'

He pulled a box of matches from his pocket. No time to finesse this, then. If the flame-slime didn't work as expected, they'd still be too close to the explosion when it went up. But if he left it any longer, the hybrids would be on him.

He struck the match and touched it to the fuse. Fire bloomed at the tip, but it didn't fizz as a fuse should. The flame-slime was burning, but the heat hadn't reached the black-powder core of the fuse.

'Silo!' Ashua screamed. He looked over his shoulder and saw the forelegs of a hybrid reaching over the top of the panels at the edge of the platform. Ashua began blasting at it from the bridge, but her pistol didn't slow it in the least.

Silo jumped to his feet, snatching up his shotgun from where it lay next to the bag of dynamite. As the hybrid's head came over the top of the panels, he unloaded point blank into its face. Glass sprayed him as its eye-clusters exploded, and it flew backwards and off into the trench.

Now he could see into the trench, he saw that Grudge had followed his advice. The wall of the trench was cratered with autocannon blasts. Around each crater were two or three of the hybrids, frantically repairing as best they could. Between them and the creatures already in the trench, the numbers at the end of the bridge had thinned.

Bess was shunting a tangled pile of hybrids along the bridge, driving them forward with her inexorable strength. She was almost at the far side now. The others were firing every which way, shooting at anything that moved.

All this he saw in an instant. And in that instant, a hybrid leaped up off the wall of the trench and landed on the bridge, cutting him off from the others.

Time decelerated. He chambered a new round as if in slow motion, glancing at the dynamite as he did so. The flame-slime hadn't burned through yet. How many seconds had passed? How many more to go?

The hybrid on the bridge shook out its forelegs. They split into a dozen smaller arms with tips that burned and sawed and cut. Bess might have been impervious to them, but he wasn't. His crew saw the danger, but they were too far up the bridge, almost at the other side now, following in Bess's chaotic wake.

He fired. The blast did little more than stun it. He stepped forward, cranked the lever of the shotgun, and fired again. One of its back limbs came off and went spinning away. Step, crank, fire. It staggered back against the edge of the bridge, limbs flailing spasmodically.

Step. Crank. Fire.

His last shot blew it off the side of the bridge, sending it tumbling to the floor of the trench. Already more were clambering onto the platform. Some moved towards him, but one of them went straight for the dynamite. He backed away onto the bridge. His way was clear now, but he was afraid of what that hybrid might do. If the dynamite didn't go off, they were all dead.

The hybrid tilted its head this way and that, its multiple eyelenses whirring, studying the satchel. As if dynamite were something it had never seen before, and it didn't know what to make of it.

The dynamite fizzed and the fuse sparked into life. The hybrid jerked back in surprise. Silo turned tail and ran.

Behind him, the hybrid picked up the lit stick of dynamite, raised it to its face, and tipped its head quizzically.

The explosion lifted him up and threw him forward, pushing the breath from his lungs. He flew through the air and crashed down onto the bridge, skidding and sliding with uncontrollable momentum, until he fetched up in a heap at the feet of his crewmen.

His head was filled with wool. His senses were deadened, his sinuses throbbed, and there was a high, piercing whistle that seemed to emanate from inside his skull. He felt strong arms on him, and Malvery pulled him blinking to his feet. The doctor was saying something – he could tell by the movement of his great white moustache – but he couldn't understand what. He wobbled, childlike in his confusion.

Then he was being pulled along. He stumbled to keep up. Guns were firing all around him, and huge arachnid shapes rushed past in a stampede. He watched, uncomprehending, as the horde of creatures flooded on to the bridge he'd just vacated. The things seemed to have no interest in attacking him or his companions. Instead they were rushing towards the shattered platform at the other end. There was an ascending whistle coming from that direction, as of pressure building and building.

Another explosion, bigger than the first, blasting pieces of flesh and chitin everywhere. The force of it shoved him back against Malvery. The doctor tripped, and they both went to the floor. Mangled and charred metal panels flipped through the air above them.

He was helped up a second time by other hands. By now his senses had reasserted themselves, and he could see the damage they'd wreaked. The platform was entirely gone, and half the bridge with it. All that was left was a large blackened gash at the base of the engine. Electricity sparked and sizzled within, and there was a distressing metallic whine coming from somewhere in the guts of the machine.

Those hybrids that hadn't been destroyed in the explosions swarmed over to it, blindly obsessed with its repair. As Silo had hoped, the invaders had been entirely forgotten.

'Yeah!' cried Pinn, fist pumping the air. 'Let's hear it for Professor Pinn's Incredible Flame-Slime! Artis Pinn, *inventor*!'

The sarcastic comment Malvery was preparing was cut off by a third explosion. This one came from off to the side, where the enormous flank of one of the hourglass structures sloped into the chamber. The blast shattered a section of the containing vessel. Coloured gas began to seep through the cracks, and electricity crawled across its surface.

'Er,' said Pinn.

Suddenly, a fork of lightning lashed out across the chamber, blasting the shattered section apart as it went. Where it hit, an explosion threw a bloom of flame into the air.

Silo and Malvery stood next to one another, momentarily still, mesmerised by the sight of what they'd done. Samandra stuck her head in between the two of them and laid her hands on their shoulders.

'Boys,' she said. 'I'm thinkin' we might want to be elsewhere. What say?'

'The lady's got a point,' Malvery said.

Samandra patted them both on the shoulders, then turned and ran like her heels were on fire.

FORTY-FIVE

HONESTY—A REASON TO LIVE—THE IRON JACKAL ARRIVES—THE CIRCLE—A STORM OF DAMNED VOICES

'Frey! Pay attention!'

Frey did his best to focus on what Crake was telling him.

'You press *here*, got it?' said Crake, showing him the thumb-stud on the device in his hand, as if it wasn't obvious.

'Got it,' he said. But he didn't get it. He couldn't wrap his head round the reality. Even when he'd been at his lowest ebb, he'd always secretly believed he could evade this confrontation. No matter the odds, in his heart he'd never thought it would come to this.

But full dark was almost upon them, and the Iron Jackal was coming.

Crake carried on wittering about his machines, using terms like 'interference fields' and 'resonance pathways' and so on. They stood in the chamber where they'd found those creepy tanks occupied by dead Azryx.

Tombs, Frey thought. *Appropriate.*

Frey and Ugrik were both wearing cumbersome backpacks, each comprising a bulky battery and one of Crake's machines, belted clumsily together. Ugrik had jammed the relic in there too, because he refused to leave it behind after all this trouble. In their hands they each held a thick, stumpy cylinder of metal tipped with a pinecone arrangement of small rods. Cables ran from the cylinders to the machines in their packs. Crake, with Silo's help, had jerry-rigged them together using the gear in his sanctum and a few extra parts. He called them 'harmonic arc generators'.

Frey didn't care what they were called. They were the only weapons they had. Daemons could be drawn into the world by use of frequency and vibration, and they could be sent out of it the same way. Crake claimed that his array of devices could 'disorient them with interference, restrain them by using resonance opposed to their base chords, or tear them apart in sonic flux,' at which point Frey had switched off entirely.

Crake kept on casting him guilty looks. He was in torment over the misplaced bullet that had put paid to any hope of lifting the curse. He'd apologised over and over until Frey told him to can it.

'You're not on my crew for your accuracy with a pistol, Crake,' he'd said. 'You're here 'cause you're a daemonist. So, I dunno… Daemonise, or something. Or we're all gonna get mortified.'

Even in the most abject depths of his shame, Crake had been unable to let that one pass. 'Er,' he said. 'Listen, Cap'n. Mortified doesn't mean killed.'

'It doesn't?'

'No. It means embarrassed. And mordant doesn't mean dead. It means, er, bitingly sarcastic.'

'Huh,' said Frey.

'And when Ashua keeps calling you a narcissist, it doesn't mean you're brave. It means you're in love with yourself.'

'Ah,' said Frey. 'That makes sense now, then.'

Crake had expected more of a reaction. 'Aren't you angry?'

'About what?'

'Well, because we were making fun of you.' He fought for a nice way to say it. 'Because you don't read very much.'

Frey was unable to see where the mockery was coming from. 'But I *don't* read very much,' he said. 'Barely at all, in fact.'

'Oh,' said Crake. 'Well, I'm glad you see it that way. I just thought you should know, that's all.' He'd coughed and looked awkward then. 'We should probably go get set up. We haven't got much time.'

Since then, Crake had been working frantically to prepare for the Iron Jackal's arrival. He'd chosen the largest chamber in the building for their stand, saying that they needed the space. He'd laid out a double circle of upright rods and small metal spheres, connected by cables to a metal box covered with dials and gauges that he called a resonator. In turn, the resonator was connected to a portable battery, and also to a smaller box which comprised only a single button.

'This is the trigger,' he'd said. 'Everything in the circle will be set up to go, but I'll need to hit this to turn it on.'

After he was done fussing with the dials, he wired up the equipment in the backpacks that Frey and Ugrik wore, and instructed them in its use. Frey was too distracted to listen to most of it, but he got the gist.

'Yeah, yeah. You hit it with your sonic thing. We point the rods at the daemon. Hold down the buttons. Daemon is paralysed.'

'These things eat up batteries, which is why you have to carry bigger ones,' Crake said. 'You'll get thirty seconds out of them at best. Don't waste it.'

Frey was deeply uneasy about the plan Crake had outlined. He didn't trust this daemonism stuff at all. In fact, he wasn't a big fan of invisible forces in general, although he supposed gravity was fairly useful, except when it made his aircraft crash. Still, this was Crake's show now, and Frey had to trust him.

'All this, I should add, is entirely theoretical,' Crake explained. 'There's no guarantee that it will work.'

'You just had to add a little disclaimer, didn't you?' Frey griped. 'Couldn't you just *pretend* you were confident? For my sake?'

'Sorry, Cap'n. I was brought up to be honest.'

'Well, there's your problem,' Frey replied. 'And I warned you about apologising.'

'Sorr—' He stopped when Frey gave him a dangerous glare. 'Yes, anyway, if all else fails, you've got the cutlass.'

Frey noticed how he avoided saying '*your*' cutlass. Crake never seemed to have stopped thinking of it as his. Frey wondered if the daemonist secretly regretted trading it for his passage on the *Ketty Jay* all that time ago.

He drew it from his belt. 'What good will that do?' he asked. 'I thought regular stuff didn't work on daemons.'

'That's the point. It's *not* "regular stuff". It's daemon-thralled, and a damn fine job I did of it, if I do say so myself. The best way to fight a daemon is with another daemon.'

'Why didn't you tell me that before?'

'I didn't want you getting any ideas about taking it on hand-to-hand.'

Frey turned the cutlass in his hand and made a few practice sweeps. Having a weapon he could see and touch, instead of all this harmonic resonance rubbish, made him feel much better.

The illumination from the chamber's walls and floor dimmed suddenly. All three of them looked up, alerted. Was it because of Silo's efforts in the power station? Or something else?

Frey felt a prickle of fear. The atmosphere was changing with the fading of the light. The eerie sense of decay in the room turned sinister as the darkness grew.

Crake pulled a handful of signal flares from a satchel on the ground. He struck them one by one and began tossing them in a loose ring, with the daemonist's circle at the centre. They were surrounded by a red glow, a restless hiss and the reek of burning phosphorus.

The temperature dropped as the glow from the walls died. The desert air turned chill. They stood among the preserving tanks inside a boundary of fizzing flares. Beyond that, the darkness was now total.

They stood back to back. Frey had his cutlass ready, Crake's metal cylinder in his off-hand. Ugrik carried a shotgun and the other cylinder. A burning flare lay at his feet, illuminating his bearded face from beneath. With the ornaments and ink-stripes on his face, he seemed every inch the murderous Yort barbarian of folk myth. Crake held a metal sphere, attached to a small belt battery, similar to the one Frey had used the last time he faced the Iron Jackal. This one, Crake assured them, would have a more dramatic effect.

In the bloody light of the signal flares, they looked like the damned.

He caught sight of the ring on his little finger, and Trinica came unbidden to his mind. *I doubt we'll meet again*, he heard her say. Maybe she'd been more right than she knew. Would she cry for him when she learned of his death, he wondered?

Who was he kidding? She'd never even know. If he died here, he'd disappear without a trace, swallowed up by the desert like the Azryx city that would become his tomb.

The sheer sense of loss overwhelmed him. To have almost had her again, and lost her… It was too much to bear. He was truly terrified then. Not of dying, but of what his death would mean.

It would mean he'd failed her. That he'd given up, left her as a cruel ghost of herself. She was still there, beneath: the true Trinica. She could be that person again. She could be happy, she could let herself be loved, he *knew* it.

But not if he died tonight.

He made a promise to himself then. If he survived to see the dawn, he'd search for her again. He'd go back to Vardia, and he'd find her, and he'd do whatever it took to make amends for the things he'd done. He swore it, a fierce, determined oath. If he survived.

Damn, Darian, he thought to himself. *Did that woman just become your reason to live?*

He'd never have admitted it to anyone, not even from the depths of the deepest mug of grog. But here, in the bleakness of the moment, that thought gave him strength.

He swivelled, raising his cutlass. Something had moved at the far reaches of the light.

'It's here,' he said.

'I know,' Crake said. His face was grim, eyes restlessly scanning. Ugrik was murmuring to himself.

Frey licked his lips nervously. His senses strained for a sign, the split-second warning that might mean the difference between life and death.

'*Don't you leave me here!*' screamed Rabby from beyond the light. The last despairing wail of Frey's doomed navigator as he was abandoned. Frey felt a cold hand brush down his back.

'Don't listen to it,' Crake told him. 'Don't pay attention to anything it does or says.'

Easier said than done, thought Frey. He shifted his feet, feeling vulnerable. He could sense the Iron Jackal out there somewhere. He was getting used to the paranoia and dread that came with the presence of daemons, but it didn't help much.

A trickle of sweat inched past his temple and down his stubbled cheek.

'What's it waitin' for?' Ugrik asked, but no one answered.

A low growl drifted out of the dark. A muzzled face slid into view, one half moist and glistening fur, the other dull metal. The shine of its mechanical eye was lost in the red glow of the flares, but its other eye was a black pit, and it fixed on Frey and filled him with horror.

'Bugger this!' said Ugrik. He raised his shotgun and fired one-handed. The blast echoed through the chamber, among the tanks of silent Azryx.

If he hit anything, they couldn't tell. The Iron Jackal had disappeared.

'Don't waste your ammunition,' said Crake. 'You can't hurt it with bullets.'

'Aye?' said Ugrik, chambering a new round. 'Well, I reckon I'll try anyway.'

Laughter fluttered around the chamber. A woman's laughter, the cold sound of Trinica at her most scornful. It was the final straw for Frey. Something snapped inside him: fear had finally driven him to rage.

'Come on, then, if you're coming!' he yelled. 'You think I'm scared of you, you ratty little mutt? Show yourself and I'll stuff those bayonet fingers of yours up your stinking puppy arse!'

Ugrik cackled at that. Crake just looked horrified, as if making the daemon mad would somehow make things worse. But when a few seconds had ticked by, and nothing happened, he relaxed a little.

'Well,' he said. '*That* didn't work.'

The Iron Jackal flew at Frey, leaping into the light, bladed claws spread wide, jaws gaping. Frey threw himself aside, but his heavy pack made him clumsy. He avoided the bayonets, but some part of the daemon slammed into the side of the pack and sent him spinning. He tumbled and crashed down onto his back, jarring his spine against the heavy equipment. The cylinder fell out of his hand and rolled away.

He tried to get up and found himself helpless, lying on the ground like an upturned turtle. The Iron Jackal was turning around for another attack, slouched and terrible in the gory glow. Panic burst in his brain. He scrabbled for the cylinder, which Crake had assured him was his best defence, and found only the cable that attached it to the equipment in his pack. He reeled it in, but even as he started he knew it was too late, because the Iron Jackal was already racing back towards him and—

The boom of Ugrik's shotgun made him shudder. The Iron Jackal was blasted away as if swatted aside by a giant hand. It skidded along the floor, out of range of the flares, and was gone.

Frey tipped over to his side and finally managed to get to his feet. Cutlass in one hand, cylinder in the other, he looked around wildly for the next attack.

Ugrik smirked at Crake. 'Can't hurt it, eh?'

'You *didn't* hurt it,' said Crake. He was fiddling anxiously with the orb in his hand.

'Where were *you*?' Frey snapped at him. 'You were supposed to *stop* that thing!'

'It doesn't *work*!' Crake said, frustrated. He thumbed the button on the orb in his hand.

'Check the wire on the battery pack,' Frey told him, remembering his own experience in Shasiith.

'The wire?' Crake looked down at the battery pack on his hip. 'Spit and blood! You're right! How did you know?'

'Wild guess.'

Crake began fiddling with it. 'Nearly there. Just hold it off for a few seconds.'

'*Hold it off?*' Frey cried, and at that moment it came again, jumping out of the darkness to land before him, hydraulic legs hissing with the impact. Frey felt his bowels turn to water as it loomed over him. It seemed to grow in the red light, swelling with each breath. Cables and mechanical tendons sewed through slick fur.

It swung a claw at him, and Frey's cutlass reacted, darting out to parry. Sparks flew as the blade met the bayonets and turned them aside. His cutlass cushioned him from the worst of the jolt, but it was still strong enough to make him stagger.

The Iron Jackal attacked again, slashing at him with long, sinewy arms, pressing forward. Frey's cutlass turned frantically this way and that, blocking again and again as the creature pounded at his defences. Each new blow struck more sparks, lighting up the snarling muzzle of the beast. Trinica's black eye glowered madly at him.

He saw Ugrik off to one side, trying to get an angle on the beast, but they were locked too tightly for the explorer to dare a shot. Frey wanted to yell at him to fire anyway, because he couldn't hold out, not against this inhuman savagery and strength. But he barely had time to draw breath.

Each time the Iron Jackal knocked his blade aside, the next parry was weaker. His arm was turning to rubber. Finally, the monster swept both hands at him together, a sheaf of bayonets, and the cutlass twisted out of his grip and went clattering to the floor.

Frey staggered, arm numbed by the impact. The daemon drew back a claw for the death-blow—

—and the air was filled with a high shriek, pitched just at the edge of Frey's hearing but painfully intense. The Iron Jackal shrieked with it. It stepped backwards, flailing at the air, then tripped on a root that had broken through the floor. It crashed against one of the Azryx tanks, spilling its contents in a flood of liquid and a tangle of cables and withered limbs. Frey stared in amazement as the Iron Jackal found its feet and stumbled away from the tank, moving as if drunk.

'The harmonic arc generators!' called Crake. He was holding aloft the orb in his hand. 'While it's disoriented!'

It took Frey a moment to work out what he meant. In the chaos of the fight, he'd almost forgotten the cylinder in his hand, with its pinecone arrangement of rods at the end. He thrust it towards the daemon.

'Not yet!' Crake shouted. 'Wait for Ugrik to get round the other side of it!'

The Yort was already going. Evidently, he'd been listening to the instructions that Frey hadn't been paying attention to.

'Ready?' Crake said, once they were on opposite sides of the beast. 'Now!'

They pressed their thumb-studs together. The pack on Frey's back hummed into life, and the Iron Jackal froze and screeched in agony. It tried to thrash, it howled and raged, but it had been straitjacketed, trapped in an invisible cage of frequencies.

Frey felt a desperate grin come to his lips. It was working! They were *hurting* the bastard!

How'd you like that, you pan-dimensional piece of shit?

'Move it over to the circle!' Crake instructed them. The high-pitched sound from the orb faded as the battery died. 'Quickly!'

Quickly. Frey remembered Crake's warning. They had thirty seconds, if that.

Staying on either side of the daemon, they moved towards the circle of rods and spheres. The Iron Jackal resisted; they had to haul against its strength. Frey's confidence wavered. Were Crake's devices strong enough to hold it? Conscious of the need for haste, he picked up the pace, hoping to drag the creature with him on its invisible tethers.

The tension on his arm slackened suddenly. The creature lunged at him. He had only time for the briefest flash of utter terror before it was arrested again, a moment before it struck. Its back arched and twisted, and it wailed, trapped once more.

'Idiots!' Crake shouted at them. 'One on each side, or it breaks the cage. Move *together*!'

Frey was drenched with sweat. Shocked, he did as he was told, keeping his eye on Ugrik rather than the beast. He should have listened the first time.

How many seconds left? Fifteen? Less? If the beast was released, he had no more weapons to fight it.

They sidestepped, pulling the Iron Jackal between them like two handlers wrangling a maddened bull. The daemon came with them, caught within the confines of its cage of sound. It seemed an impossibly fragile restraint for a creature like that, and yet it was working.

One step. Two. Three. Then they were at the edge of the circle. Surely that was fifteen seconds? It felt like ten minutes had passed. Crake had moved to crouch by the box with the trigger button, ready to activate the circle.

Frey frowned. Was the humming from his pack getting quieter?

'Now!' Crake said.

Frey and Ugrik stepped to either side of the circle in perfect sync. The Iron Jackal resisted them with all its might. Frey felt the force of it through his arm. But when he and Ugrik tugged together, it stepped clumsily forward. The instant it was inside the circle, Crake stabbed the button.

If they'd thought the Iron Jackal's unearthly screeches had been terrible before, they were nothing compared to this. The sound was like a sandstorm, flaying the senses. The daemon writhed and thrashed as if on fire, twisting and turning in the hideous red light from the flares. Frey and Ugrik stepped back, staring, the cylinders in their hand useless now and forgotten.

It had become indistinct at the edges, hazy like smoke. But seconds passed, and no more than that occurred. It was clearly suffering, but it was still there in the circle.

'What are you waiting for?' Frey demanded of Crake. 'Kill it!'

Crake's eyes were wide with fear as he fiddled with the dials on the machine. 'I can't! It's too strong! It was supposed to be torn apart in the flux!' The Iron Jackal howled anew at each change of the settings, but it was still holding together. 'The battery won't last much longer!'

The creature's gaze fixed on Frey then, as if it *knew*, as if to say: *I'm coming for you. As soon as this is over, I'm coming for you.*

No. He wouldn't let that thing win. He'd been to the edge too many times to give in to it now. He'd been through fear and rage, and now there was only blazing defiance.

He shucked his pack off his back and let it fall to the floor. Then he walked over to his cutlass, picked it up, and turned to face the daemon.

'This ends here,' he said grimly.

'Well, end it bloody fast, then!' Crake screamed.

He strode to the edge of the circle. The Iron Jackal saw him coming and bared its teeth. Either the circle was weakening or it had found new strength, because it was becoming solid again, mastering its pain. Frey drew back his cutlass, aiming the point between the armoured plates on its chest.

And suddenly there was no daemon in the circle any more.

The change happened as if in a dream, as if Trinica had been there all along. As if it had always been Trinica he'd been fighting. She stood in the centre of the circle, all in black, her white face red in the fading light. Darkness was gathering as the last of the flares died, but he could see that her black eyes shimmered with tears as she gazed at him with an expression of heartbreaking sorrow.

'Darian,' she whispered. 'Please.'

He hesitated. His mind told him it was a daemon, but his instincts rebelled. He knew that it was just trying to buy time for the battery that powered the circle to fail, but the thought of hurting Trinica, even an effigy like this, paralysed him.

But this wasn't her. This was the pirate queen that had taken her place. This was the mask, the shell, the cold nemesis that betrayed and shunned him.

'Wrong Trinica,' he said, and drove the cutlass into her heart with all the strength in his body.

The scream was like nothing he'd ever heard before, a sound that cut right through to the marrow of his being. It was a storm of damned voices, made up of tones and pitches that didn't belong in this world. A hurricane wind blasted out from the circle, scattering equipment and people, sending Frey tripping and tumbling away. The last of the flares flew into the dark and died.

And, in an instant, it was over.

Silence, and blackness. Then, slowly, the ambient glow from the seashell walls returned, lighting the room by degrees until they could see again.

They picked themselves up, dazed. Frey looked around the chamber, scarcely able to believe what had just occurred. He couldn't get Trinica's face out of his mind. That scream, the look of terror on her face, the feel of the blade shoving into her chest. Had he... Had he *really*...?

No. You killed a daemon. Nothing more.

Crake dusted himself down. 'And *that*, gentlemen, is a demonstration of field daemonism in action.' He motioned towards Frey. 'Your hand, Cap'n?'

Frey removed his glove. The skin beneath was pink and smooth, without the slightest hint of gangrenous corruption. He stared at it, then at Crake.

'You did it,' he whispered.

'*We* did it,' said Crake.

'Actually, I'm pretty sure it was mostly you.'

'I ain't *ever* seen anything like that!' Ugrik said. A toothy grin spread across his face and he cackled loudly. 'That was somethin'! That was definitely somethin'!'

Frey walked over to Crake. 'Thank you,' he said. 'I mean it.'

Crake held out a hand to shake. 'My pleasure, Cap—'

Frey grabbed Crake in a crushing hug, driving the breath from his lungs.

He was alive. All the fear and tension that had been dammed up inside him suddenly broke, and he was so overwhelmingly, completely *grateful*. The whole crew had backed him every step of the way, but Crake had stood alone as his last line of defence. He'd worked himself to the bone for Frey's sake, to save his Cap'n from the mess he'd got himself into. And in the end, he'd achieved what they both thought was impossible.

'You're a real friend, Crake,' Frey muttered. Then he felt slightly embarrassed, so he broke away and slapped the daemonist on shoulder with an appropriate amount of manly gusto. 'Not to mention a damn genius.'

'I am, aren't I?' Crake said. 'Can I have my cutlass back now?'

Frey's smile faltered. 'You want the cutlass back?'

'Just as a little thank-you. For saving your life and all.'

Frey fought to keep the good humour on his face. The cutlass was his most precious possession after the *Ketty Jay*. It had saved his life several times. And yet, how could he refuse the daemonist now? After what he'd done? The joy of the moment curdled in his guts, but he swallowed down the bile and nodded.

'Alright,' he said. It had fallen from his hand after he stabbed the daemon. He looked around for it, and spotted it lying nearby. 'Fair's fair, I suppose.' He went over and brought it back, then held it out to Crake.

Crake took it from him and swept it experimentally through the air a couple of times.

'It's a fine sword,' Frey said.

'It *is* a fine sword,' Crake agreed. Then he tossed it back to Frey, who caught it in the air. He beamed. 'I'm only joking, Cap'n. Just wanted to see if you'd do it.'

Frey gaped at him, aghast. 'You horrible son of a bitch!' he accused, but he stuck the cutlass back in his belt before Crake could change his mind.

This time it was Crake who embraced Frey. 'Glad you're still with us, Cap'n,' he said warmly. 'Wouldn't be the same without you.'

After a few moments, he felt a burly arm sliding round his back. They looked into Ugrik's grinning, bearded face. The Yort was hugging both of them.

'Er,' said Crake stiffly. 'What are you doing?'

'Just wanted a piece o' the love in this room.'

'Would you get off, please?'

They disengaged awkwardly with much shuffling and looking at their shoes.

'Right, then,' said Ugrik, looking round the empty chamber. 'Curse is gone. Now what?'

Frey felt a tremor through the soles of his feet. He frowned.

'Did you just feel that?' he asked. Crake shushed him. The daemonist had an intent expression on his face. He was listening.

'I can hear something from outside,' he muttered.

Frey listened. He could hear something too, but it was too faint to tell what it was. There was another tremor, like a distant earthquake. The sounds got a fraction louder, and he managed to place them at last.

'Are those *screams*?' asked Crake.

'Yep,' said Frey. 'Definitely screams.'

FORTY-SIX

❖

THE JUGGERNAUT—CONTACT—HEADING FOR
THE RENDEZVOUS—VINES—MAN DOWN

Samandra Bree had predicted that getting out of the power station would be much harder than getting in. She was wrong. There wasn't a Samarlan left in the building.

When they got outside, they saw why.

The gates had been left open and unguarded, black doors with a faint sheen of green like a beetle's carapace. The Century Knights went forward with Bess, cautious of an ambush. Silo heard Samandra let loose a deeply unladylike oath as he followed them out.

The upper platform on which the power station sat was deserted. Samarlan bodies lay here and there, remnants of the earlier firefight, but the living had abandoned this place.

The lake was at their back and the city spread out before them, rising up the bowl-shaped sides of the oasis. The slopes were speckled with the light of many windows, peeking through the dense foliage. The moon hung high overhead: full dark had come. Surrounding them was the excavated zone, where Azryx boulevards and plazas lay revealed. They could see men running there, and hear their shouts and hysterical shrieks.

The platform trembled beneath their feet. Silo looked up, and saw what had caused Samandra to swear. Further up the slope, just beyond the edge of the city, something was rising from beneath the ground, sloughing off soil and vines and trees. Something enormous.

The sheer size of it beggared belief. It was bigger than the power station that towered behind them. As it rose, it tore up the earth around it, sending a landslide of dirt through the foliage, which rolled over the city's outermost buildings and buried them.

At first he wondered if it was an incredible aircraft, or some kind of massive subterranean machine. But then its legs began to unfold, and it *shook* itself. A cloud of displaced earth cloaked it from sight, and clods rained down on the jungle canopy for kloms around.

But the cloud settled, and the upheaval ceased, and then it was revealed. The most colossal creature he'd ever laid eyes on.

'What in the name of the Allsoul's sacred bollock sweat is *that*?' said Pinn, ever one for a bit of creative blasphemy.

Nobody had an answer. In form, it was something like an ape, with large powerful forelegs and smaller hindquarters. But there the resemblance to any living animal ended. It was covered in interlocking plates of white armour, made of some material with the matte smoothness of eggshell. At the joints, where it was necessary to flex, it was possible to see the wet glitter of dark red muscle. Its face was like a gas mask, with that same disconcerting lack of expression. Two blank white eyes without brows or lids bulged above a short round tube of a mouth, like the turbine intake of an aircraft, forming a grotesque muzzle.

Silo stared in horrified awe. He recognised the same technology he'd seen in the custodians of the power station, the same unnatural fusion of organic and inorganic. But this was on such a scale as to make the hybrids seem like toys.

The Murthians had tales, told by the witch-sisters in the dreaming-house. Tales of the Tall Walkers, whom Mother had sent to cleanse the world of her first twisted brood that the Vards called Gargants. When these new monsters had destroyed the old, they died and left the world to the new generation, the humans.

But only the Murthians still kept the faith with Mother. Samarlans had a different version of history, and their own legends. Their versions of the Tall Walkers were malevolent, sent as punishment by their absent gods, and they had a different name. Silo could hear them screaming it in the streets below, but the word that came to him was Vardic.

Juggernaut.

'You think maybe we woke that thing up?' Ashua asked, her voice small.

Malvery put a hand on her shoulder. 'Welcome to the crew of the

Ketty Jay,' he said. 'You ain't a member till you've caused at least one major catastrophe.'

There was an explosion from deep in the bowels of the power station. Silo looked up at the hourglasses to either side. The lightning within was becoming frenzied, striking everywhere with rapid fury, pummelling at the walls of its prison. The sweeping arms that orbited around the inner edges had slipped out of sync and lost their rhythm.

The city lights wavered and went out.

Darkness came suddenly. The slopes turned black, as if a hundred thousand glowing eyes had all closed at the same time. All that remained were the clunky Samarlan lamps, running off their fuming generators, in the streets of the excavated quarter. All else was moonlight.

The Juggernaut slowly turned its massive head towards the city, towards the screams and the light. Its expressionless eyes regarded the scene, its mouth an idiot O. Then light began to gather in front of its face. A million sparkling particles ignited in the air around that turbine mouth, and were pulled inside, as if the creature were sucking in a huge breath. There was an ascending squeal as it drew in more and more of the bright motes that twinkled out of the dark.

It stopped. The twinkles faded. The squeal fell silent.

A heartbeat passed.

Then the Juggernaut fired.

The mouth wasn't a mouth. It was a cannon. A beam of scorching, seething white energy screeched forth, down into the buildings and streets where the Sammies ran. Where it touched, everything exploded. It raked the beam across the city, leaving billowing clouds of fire blossoming in its wake. The detonations were more than a klom away from where they stood outside the power station, but they felt the hot air on their faces, and the sight was enough to make them cry out and shield themselves instinctively.

It lasted no more than a few seconds. But those few seconds left a flaming scar of devastation across the width of the excavated zone and beyond. Leaves burned and buildings slumped into blackened alleys.

Pinn lowered the sling-wrapped arm he'd thrown up in front of his face. 'I *need* to get a gun like that,' he said reverently.

'Silo? Are you seeing this?'

Silo remembered the earcuff he was wearing. The Cap'n must have just put his on. Frey hated wearing it when he didn't need to; he found the background babble of other voices distracting. Of course it meant they could only talk when the Cap'n wanted to but, well, that was his way.

'I'm seeing it, Cap'n. You alright?'

'Never better. How are your lot?'

'They all in one piece so far. We oughta head for the Rattletraps, though.'

'Is that the Cap'n? Is he alive?' Pinn was asking. Silo, who was trying to listen, waved him away with a terse nod. It only occurred to him then that the Cap'n really *was* alive, that he must have overcome the curse.

The mantle of owner of the *Ketty Jay* and leader of her crew wouldn't pass to him after all, then. He'd been so focused on his task that he hadn't fully taken in the gravity of Frey's request. Now he found himself deeply relieved. Maybe he didn't want to be a slave any more, but he didn't want to fill the Cap'n's boots either. First mate would serve him just fine.

'Hey, everyone!' said a chirpy voice in his ear.

'Jez!' said the Cap'n. 'How was your coma?'

'Instructive,' she replied. 'Listen, you ought to know the *Ketty Jay*'s up and running again.'

'You fix her?'

'Nothing to do with me. Everything just came back at once.'

'Reckon whatever was suppressing the *Ketty Jay*'s systems died when the power did,' Silo said, then flinched as another explosion sounded from the building behind him.

'Are we gonna get moving anytime soon?' Samandra demanded, pointing towards the Juggernaut, which was lumbering down the slope towards the edge of the city.

Silo ignored her. 'Cap'n,' he said. 'Forget the Rattletraps. Ain't gonna have time to get to 'em. This power station ain't stable.'

'Jez, can the *Ketty Jay* fly?'

'Don't see why not.'

'We're gonna need a pickup,' said the Cap'n. 'Now.'

'On it,' said Jez. 'Where am I going?'

'Due east. Look for the landing pad, we'll meet you there. You ought to be able to see the city now the power's out.'

'City?'

'Long story. Get going. Oh, and Jez?'

'Cap'n?'

'Watch out. There's one awfully mean-looking bastard between you and us.'

The Cap'n's voice went silent as he took off his earcuff again. The others, having only been privy to Silo's voice in the conversation, looked at him expectantly. He pointed to where a landing pad sat on the edge of the excavated area, supported by a thin pillar that branched as it rose, giving it the appearance of a flat-topped, skeletal tree.

'That's where we're headed. Move!'

'At last!' said Samandra, who viewed plans as an unnecessary impediment to action.

They made their way down to street level. The Juggernaut was still visible upslope. It was some distance away, but not far enough for Silo's liking. As he watched, it reared up on its hind legs, and he saw that it had wide, spatulate feet with four armoured toes at ninety-degree intervals. It came down hard on a particularly large building, smashing in through the roof. The earth shook as it landed.

The Juggernaut was making its way towards the excavated zone, where the Samarlans were concentrated. Silo didn't know if it was attracted by the lights or Sammies, or if it was simply engaged in mindless destruction. Whatever its motive, it was perfectly willing to obliterate the city of its masters. Why would the Azryx – for it had to be Azryx in origin – build something like that?

Impossible to know. Maybe it had malfunctioned after millennia of inactivity. Maybe it was *supposed* to destroy the city, but had never been activated. Or maybe it recognised the people it was sent to annihilate, thousands of years ago.

None of it mattered now. The gulf of time was too great for guesswork. His only concern was getting them away from it.

A burst of gunfire shocked him. Two Sammie soldiers, caught between duty and self-preservation, had spotted them and opened fire. Samandra, who was in the lead, forward-rolled under their bullets and came up with both shotguns aimed. She fired them together, and the Sammies were blown backwards, minus their faces. Somehow, she managed to do it all without dislodging her tricorn hat.

She spun the shotguns, chambering a new round in each, and

looked over her shoulder. 'Better be careful,' she said. 'Ain't just that ugly feller we got to look out for.'

Silo didn't take them straight towards the landing pad. That would have meant crossing the entire expanse of the excavated zone. Instead he struck out for the edge, where it was bordered by foliage and there were no electric lights. That way he could avoid the majority of the Sammies, and hopefully the Juggernaut's attentions too.

They heard the sucking noise again, the squeal of power building, the dreadful pause before the devastation. This time it came close enough to terrify, lashing the streets nearby. They were forced to shelter as pieces of ceramic pelted them from the sky.

The Samarlans were still in disarray, but Silo could hear the sound of machine guns drifting up from distant streets as some of them attempted to fight back.

Just like Sammies, he thought. *Too wrapped up in ideas of nobility and codes of behaviour to save their own hides. Ought to be runnin' as far 'n' fast as they can. Ain't a weapon in this city can hurt somethin' that size.*

But he'd have bet they were under the highest orders to keep hold of this place, no matter what the cost. So hold it they would. It kept them occupied, at least.

Silo and the crew made good time, and only encountered a few soldiers on the way. The Century Knights took them out with no hesitation. Most of them didn't even have time to raise their guns.

The Juggernaut pounded onward, dragging a trail of destruction with it. Despite Silo's attempts to avoid the monster, it was getting closer. It may have been slow, but its stride was long, and it didn't trouble itself with following the streets. The ground shook as it barged buildings aside, blank gas-mask face turning this way and that as it scanned for targets.

A barrier of tangled greenery rose up before them as they reached the edge of the excavated zone. Silo would have liked to take them into the trees, where no one could see them, but one glance at the power station changed his mind. Smoke was fuming from its empty windows, and as he looked back, a section of the roof blew outward. One of the hourglasses had cracked near the top. Gas leaked out in a pastel cloud. Lightning flickered and roved around the damaged area.

The trees would be safer, but making their way through the

undergrowth would take three times as long. They couldn't afford the delay. Silo didn't know how Azryx technology worked, but that power station looked an awful lot like it intended to explode sometime soon. So he led them along the streets, staying close to the foliage and as far from the conflict as he could manage.

For a few minutes they lost sight of the Juggernaut. They hurried along narrow, curving ways between high buildings, where there were no Sammies. Though they were hidden from the monster's view, they could still hear it and feel its footsteps, nearer and nearer each time. There was nothing to do but keep going. Sometimes their way was blocked by encroaching trees and vines, or piles of banked earth, but for the most part they made progress towards their destination.

The foliage drove them on to a street which ascended sharply, becoming a ramp to a higher level. With no other option, they took it. It slipped between the shoulders of two close-set buildings and became a thin, graceful bridge that spanned a street choked with trees and undergrowth. Vines and creepers had made their way along its length, to clamber up the buildings on the far side.

They emerged onto the bridge, and there was the Juggernaut.

Silo's breath caught in his throat. It stood a few streets away, taller than the rooftops, near enough to hear the massive muscles creak as they stretched beneath its armoured plates. He was pinned like a mouse in sight of a cat, crushed into insignificance by its appalling size. Though he knew it to be Azryx in origin, he felt as if he were standing in the presence of some vast, incomprehensible god.

The Juggernaut hadn't seen them. Its attention was elsewhere. The ascending shriek had begun again, and bright motes were being sucked out of the air, warning of an imminent blast from its cannon.

'Go! While it ain't lookin'!' Samandra urged the group. She ushered them past her, onto the bridge, her eyes never leaving the beast.

Bess led the way, with Malvery, Pinn and Ashua close behind her. Silo and the Century Knights brought up the rear.

The shriek reached its apex. There was a taut moment of anticipation. Then the beam blasted forth with a scream of expelled energy, devastating everything it touched. The Juggernaut swept its head left to right, raking the beam in a wide arc through the streets in front of it.

Swinging towards them.

Silo saw it coming an instant before it happened, but far too late to do anything about it. There was an instant of blinding light, and a terrible sound like the fury of Mother herself. Then the bridge behind him exploded.

A wave of heat and force made him stagger. The world tipped. The ground shifted beneath him, and was suddenly gone. He threw himself forward, clinging to something, *anything* that would save him. His chest smacked against the surface of the bridge, now tilted almost vertical. He slipped and scrabbled, pulled down by invisible hands. Then his fingers found an edge and locked there.

Behind and below him was empty space. The bridge was a ruin, ripped through the middle. The sides of the tear drooped downwards in broken sections, attached to the main structure by thick cables of a tough, rubbery material that ran through the ceramic.

Silo lay flat against a dangling piece of the bridge's floor. He got his other hand up to the edge and hung there. Ten metres below him was a moon-grey mass of treetops, vines and rubble.

Up on the bridge, the others were shouting over one another. He heard Malvery and Pinn calling out names and arguing, and Samandra was swearing repeatedly through gritted teeth.

To his right, he heard the Juggernaut lumbering away. It hadn't even noticed his plight. They were insects to it.

His fingers were already beginning to burn. He pawed for a toehold, but the surface was frustratingly smooth. Looking around, he saw a thick cluster of vines to his left, straggling down from the sundered bridge. Too far, perhaps. He tried to reach them anyway. He took his left hand from the ledge and stretched, but his right hand immediately began to seize up and he lurched back to prevent himself from falling.

'Hey!' he shouted. 'Hey!'

Ashua's face appeared above him, face shadowed against the moon. 'Silo's down here!' she called. She scanned the terrain beneath her, a crazed ladder of cracked ceramic and strings of rubbery Azryx substrate. He was only a few metres below her, but it was too far for her to reach without climbing down herself.

In that moment, he froze her image like a ferrotype. His mind, suspecting the end, was eager to drink in every detail before his extinction. He saw her quick, wary eyes, the delicate tattoo on the left side of her face, her lean, spare frame to match her lean, spare existence. She was an opportunist, a scavenger, a survivor. Merciless and unemotional, because that was what she had to be. Whatever her true motives for joining the *Ketty Jay*, they were certainly selfish. The crew were useful to her, nothing more.

She wouldn't help him. Not at the risk of her own life. She wasn't crew.

If it had been Jez there, or Frey, they might have come down to save him. But Pinn was wounded, and Malvery too hefty. The Century Knights might have tried, but the noises coming from Samandra sounded like someone suppressing a scream, and he'd heard nothing of Colden Grudge.

His fingers began to shake. His tendons were on fire. He was going to fall. It might not kill him, but it would probably break him enough to make no difference.

Ashua's eyes shone, hard in the shadow. Then she shook her head and gave a tut of disgust. 'Shit,' she muttered. And she slipped over the side and went climbing down towards him.

She was from Rabban, a city of rubble, and she negotiated the shattered face of the broken bridge with ease. When she was low enough, she found a good foothold, hooked one hand into a crack and reached down with the other.

Silo didn't question his fortune. He reached up with his right hand and grabbed on to hers. She hauled, thin arms straining. He added what strength he could, but he didn't have enough left. He tried again for a toehold and failed.

'You're too heavy,' she said.

Malvery and Pinn had appeared at the lip of the bridge. Gunfire rattled in the distance. 'Hang on!' said Malvery. 'I'll find something to throw down!'

But there wasn't time for that. Ashua was willing, but she didn't have the muscle to lift him, and he was weakening fast. If she didn't let him go, he'd pull her off with him. And besides, what would Malvery find up there? Vines?

Vines!

'Swing me!' he said. He looked to his left. Ashua saw the bundle of vines, just out of his reach. She nodded, her jaw tight with the effort of holding him.

'Back and forth, alright?' she said.

'Ready.'

'Go.'

He let go with his left hand and grabbed on to her wrist, putting his whole weight on her dangling arm. At the same time he pushed himself away from the vines with his feet, swinging out like a pendulum, then back again. He heard Ashua cry out with the effort of holding him up, and then he felt her jerk and she shrieked and her grip came loose. He let go, flailing through the air for the briefest of instants—

—and his hands clamped firmly to the body of a thick vine. He crashed into the bundle, scrabbled for an instant, and then his feet found a loop and he pressed on it, taking the weight from his arms and hands. Relief flooded through him. He clutched himself to the vines, enveloped by their sharp green scent.

Ain't dead yet.

He looked over at Ashua. Her arm was dangling by her side, the other still hooked in a crack. Above her, Pinn was lying on his belly, reaching down.

'Doc!' Pinn called. 'Quit messing about. Get back here and help!'

She let Pinn pull her up, and once Silo saw she was safe, he began his own climb. Malvery appeared at the top in time to lend his arm.

Silo wasted no time on recovery. He was assessing the situation the moment he had his feet under him. The crew was all safe, thankfully. Bess sat on her arse against the side of the bridge, looking as bewildered as a faceless metal golem could. Samandra was sitting as well, in the midst of several slabs of rubble. Her teeth were clenched in agony and one leg was stretched out straight in front of her. The foot of her boot was twisted at an unnatural angle.

'Where's Grudge?' Silo asked.

Malvery looked about as if it had only just occurred to him. 'Dunno,' he said. ''Scuse me, I gotta see to Ashua.'

Silo followed. Ashua had collapsed to her knees, holding her shoulder. Her face had gone a darker red than her hair. Malvery took one look at her and said 'You popped the socket.'

'Yeah,' she said, between deep breaths. 'You gonna pop it back?'

'Have to,' he said apologetically. 'I ain't joking. This'll hurt.'

'You think?' said Ashua, with a sarcastic and slightly hysterical laugh. Then she sobered. 'Do it.'

He told her to lie back, and she did so. He put his boot on her chest and lifted her arm so it stood out straight. She screwed her mouth shut, trying not to make a sound.

'On five,' he said. 'One... *two*!'

There was an audible crunch of cartilage as he pulled on the straight arm. She made a small whimpering noise in the back of her throat, then let out a long gasp.

'Better?' Malvery asked.

'Shit, yes,' said Ashua, with transcendent joy in her eyes.

Malvery snapped his fingers at Pinn. 'Come here. I need that sling.'

'It's *my* sling!' Pinn whined.

'You're wearing a sling 'cause you shot yourself like an idiot. She just saved Silo's life. See the difference?'

'No,' Pinn said stubbornly, but he let Malvery undo the sling anyway.

Ashua sat up, massaging her shoulder tenderly. Her eyes met Silo's. He gave her a grave nod of thanks. He'd misjudged her, it seemed. He didn't do that often.

'Colden!' Samandra cried. He looked up and saw the Century Knight trying to get to her feet.

'Hey! Stay down!' Malvery barked at her. 'I'll get to you in a sec. That ankle's broken.'

She ignored him. 'Where's Colden?'

Silo went to the break in the bridge and looked over. Colden had been behind him when the bridge went. He wasn't there now. He felt a detached sort of regret, but he was more concerned with his own people.

The Juggernaut was moving away from them, but the ground still shook with its footsteps. Silo heard a crunch behind him, and saw a new crack appear in the floor.

'This place ain't safe,' he said. 'Everybody off the bridge.'

Pinn helped Ashua up, muttering jealously about her new sling. Silo went to Samandra, after checking that Bess was doing what she was told. Malvery followed him.

'Colden!' Samandra cried. The desperation was plain on her face. 'Colden! Answer me, damn it!'

'He gone,' said Silo.

'He's down there somewhere! We need to go back! Find a way down!'

Silo was impassive. 'I ain't riskin' my people. He ain't one of us. Nor are you.'

'Then *I'll* go!'

'You ain't in no state to save anyone. And this bridge could be comin' down any moment.'

He put his arm under her to take her weight, but she fought him. 'Colden!' she called over his shoulder.

'I'll go,' said Malvery.

'He ain't one of us,' Silo said again, firmly.

But Malvery had that look on his face, a look that Silo knew well. Like a man who just had to do a thing.

Samandra gazed at the doctor with feverish hope. 'Please!'

'I'll go,' said Malvery again, hefting his shotgun.

Silo knew there was no more to be said. He wouldn't order the man. Malvery wouldn't obey if he did. There was only so much responsibility you could take for another man's life; after that, it was all down to them.

'We'll wait for you at the pad, long as we can,' he said.

'See you there,' said Malvery, and headed off.

Silo lifted Samandra's weight again, more roughly than he needed to. He was suddenly angry with her. For getting injured, for asking Malvery to save her companion, for putting one of the crew in danger.

'Satisfied now, Miss Bree?' he said. 'Now get movin', or you gonna end up down there with your partner if this bridge goes.'

For once, Samandra Bree had no comeback. She leaned on him and hopped alongside, white-faced and silent.

FORTY-SEVEN

A LONG WALK—FOREIGN OBJECT—THE BOULEVARD—MALVERY VERSUS THE CREW

Malvery huffed and puffed as he scrambled down an incline of vines and rubble. It had taken him longer than he'd thought to find a way back to the street under the bridge. While he'd been following Silo, he hadn't paid attention to how complex and strange these Azryx paths were. He was already wondering if he'd be able to find his way back.

Not too far away, there was a huge explosion from the power station, loud in the night. He cast a worried glance at it and hurried onward.

If Colden hadn't been obliterated in the blast – which, to be honest, he probably *had* – then he'd have fallen into the foliage beneath the bridge. It was a long way down, but branches and vines made for a better landing than most surfaces. While there was a chance, Malvery had to look.

He had no special love for the man. In fact, he barely knew him, and Grudge had been an enemy as often as an ally. But that didn't matter. There was a rightness to what he was doing, a certainty of purpose that propelled him forward. That man was a Century Knight, one of the Archduke's loyal elite. The cream of Vardic warriors. And he was damned if he'd leave a soldier of his country behind.

He stopped to catch his breath. If only he didn't drink quite so bloody much. If only he'd stayed in shape. But all those soft years in Thesk had made him sluggardly, and in the years that followed he'd been more interested in booze than exercise.

Well, he might have the body of a fat bastard, but he had the heart of a young man. A young man who'd gone to war for his country once. A young man who'd been betrayed by the old man that succeeded him.

Angered by that thought, he stormed on, calling Colden's name. A Sammie soldier burst out of the undergrowth, attracted by the noise, waving his rifle. He was a young man too, and he seemed startled to find an overweight Vard with a flowing white moustache and round, green-lensed glasses perched on his nose. Maybe he'd never seen one before. His hesitation meant he never got a chance to see one again.

Malvery cranked a new round into his shotgun and walked on. The bridge was almost overhead now. Despite Silo's misgivings, it hadn't collapsed yet. The Juggernaut was still somewhere nearby, ripping up the city. Malvery did his best to ignore it.

Out on the battlefield, you couldn't think about all the dangers around you. If you did, you'd be paralysed. Every man knew they might be hit by a shell or nailed by a sniper at any moment, and they'd never see it coming. It didn't matter how careful you were, or how highly trained. It was blind bloody chance. You just had to get on with it.

He found Grudge at the foot of a tree, barely suspended in a cradle of vines, a dark shape in the moon-shadows. There were broken branches all around him, and his autocannon lay nearby. Malvery put fingers to his throat and felt for a pulse.

'Blimey,' he said.

He checked him over for broken bones, but all he found was a lump on his head the size of an egg, buried beneath his shaggy hair. He tilted Grudge's head towards the silvery light and peeled back the eyelids, looking for blood in the whites. Then he slapped him a couple of times to see if it would get any reaction.

Head trauma. Possible skull fracture. He might wake up in a minute, or never. Maybe he's already dead, but his heart and lungs ain't worked it out yet.

'Let's get you out of all that armour, then,' he said. ''Cause you can bet your arse I ain't carryin' you in that.'

Armour or no armour, he hadn't gone far before he realised exactly how heavy a man who stood over two metres tall could be. Malvery had always been strong, with a bulk that belied the delicacy of his profession, but he suspected that he'd overestimated himself this time. He'd been taken with visions of pulling a Century Knight's fat out of the fire, just like he'd done with those soldiers in the First Aerium War. Belatedly he remembered that he'd been in his prime back then, fit from Army training, and those men he'd saved had all been a good sight smaller than Grudge.

His legs burned. His back ached. He'd barely gone a hundred metres. *Gonna be a long walk.*

There was no point backtracking; he'd never catch up with Silo. He decided to make his own way.

The streets were confusing, always curving, sloping, splitting into different levels. The Azryx seemed frustratingly fond of dead ends. Malvery kept having to readjust his heading, navigating by glimpses of the landing pad between the buildings. The Juggernaut was still nearby, but thankfully its attention seemed to be focused in another direction. The sound of collapsing walls was an almost constant background noise, and Malvery tensed every time he heard the steadily climbing squeal that heralded another blast from the cannon. Gunfire floated up from the streets as the Sammies fought back.

He put his head down and kept going. All he could do was put one foot in front of the other and hope no one – *nothing* – noticed him.

After a short time, which seemed like an age, he found himself standing on the edge of an enormous plaza. He knew this place; he'd seen it earlier. It was the Samarlan base camp, where dozens of tents had been set up as barracks, command centres and the like. The hub of the Sammies' operation.

Where there had once been orderly rows of tents, now there were only smoking rags, flapping in the rising thermals. The burnt-pork stink of cooked human flesh was thick in the air. The debris of a military encampment was everywhere: blackened stoves, melted weaponry, scorched foot lockers. To either side of the plaza was a trench of rubble that cut through the surrounding buildings, marking the path of the Juggernaut's beam.

Malvery stared for a moment, rocked by the raw power of the thing.

The author of the devastation was lumbering across his path, several streets away, searching for new targets. Its smooth white armour sparked now and then as bullets bounced off it. Beyond it, a short way upslope, was the landing pad, rising like some ancient tree above the city.

He deliberated a moment, catching his breath, then struck out across the plaza. To go around would be a detour he wasn't sure he could manage. He was hot and damp and red-faced, every muscle hurt, and he didn't know how much he had left in his legs. It frightened him to be so exposed with that thing nearby, but there it was. No help for it.

He just had to hope the damned thing didn't look his way.

He staggered on through the wreckage of the camp. The smell of burnt bodies seeped its way down the back of his throat. They lay bundled up among the tatters of the tents, curled in on themselves or clawing grotesquely at the sky. There must have been a lot of Sammies here when it got hit.

The carnage didn't much bother him. He'd seen enough bodies in his time as a medic. After a while they became like dead trees or blasted vehicles: just another part of the battlefield scenery.

He was most of the way across the plaza when he saw something he recognised. Something that shouldn't have been there. He came to an unsteady halt.

It was the shape of it that caught his eye. A cluster of straight lines and regular circles amid a landscape of bent and broken things. A bright emblem of gold, glinting in the light of a nearby fire. It was set into a small metal box lying amid a scattering of curled papers that skidded and rolled in the updrafts from the baked surface of the plaza. He glanced up at the Juggernaut, which had turned away from him.

'Sorry, mate,' he said to the man on his back. 'Gonna have to put you down a minute.'

He let Grudge slide off his back and laid him on the ground as gently as he could. After a quick moment to examine his patient, who still showed no signs of waking, he walked painfully over to the box. He winced as he bent down to pick it up.

It was still hot to the touch, and the gold of the emblem had melted slightly. It was a document case, often used to protect and secure precious letters and files in transit. He tried to open it, but it was locked. He turned it around, looking for clues, but there was nothing to be seen but the emblem. Six circles, joined by interlocking lines. It was something every Vard grew up seeing in the towns and cities of their homeland, and tattooed on the foreheads of the faithful.

The Cipher. The symbol of the Awakeners.

But what's it doing here?

He stared at the emblem, and felt a cold certainty that the answer

462

to that question would open doors he might never be able to shut. But before he could consider it further, he heard the sharp crack of a rifle, and a bullet splintered a nearby tent pole.

He looked up and saw two soldiers on the far side of the plaza. One of them was just raising his rifle; the other was aiming again.

He swore under his breath and ran back to Grudge – though it was more of an agonised jog – taking the document case with him. He hauled Grudge across his back in a fireman's carry, gritted his teeth and tried to stand.

The strain was incredible. Picking him up a second time was twice as hard as the first. His muscles were already fatigued, his back ached, and he'd be damned lucky if he got out of this without a slipped disc and a double hernia. But still he lifted, driven by a strength he didn't know he possessed, and somehow he found his feet.

'You,' he puffed, 'are one dead weight son of a bitch.'

He set off as fast as his legs could carry them, the document case clutched in one hand. The Sammies were shouting behind him and more bullets whined through the air, but they'd have to be better shots than that to hit him at such a distance.

Of course, they wouldn't need to be such good shots once they caught him up.

He couldn't let himself worry about it. Couldn't even look behind with Grudge draped across his shoulders like a fallen bear. All he could do was stumble towards the edge of the plaza.

It didn't even occur to him to leave Grudge behind.

Beyond, the streets resumed, winding ways bordered by white ceramic dwellings that flowed into each other like blown glass. He blinked sweat from his eyes. He felt like he was at the limit of his strength. He'd felt like that for a while now. Yet somehow momentum carried him on, even though his legs trembled and his neck hurt and his spine felt like it was being crushed. Any minute now, he'd be shot, but there was no help for that. All he could do was prolong the moment as much as he could.

Ahead, the rattle of a machine gun. A building fell in an avalanche of rubble nearby. The Juggernaut was close. He caught sight of it through a gap in the buildings. The curved alley he'd chosen was taking him right towards it.

No help for that, either.

At the end of the alley he halted. A wide boulevard lay in front of him like a still river in the yellow glow of the electric lights. On the far side, more alleys.

It sounded like he was almost on top of the machine gun, so he peered out. To the left, in the middle of the boulevard, a dozen Sammies had set up behind a barricade of fallen debris. To the right was the Juggernaut, turning into the street, dragging a slithering slope of rubble with it. The machine gun kept up a hail of bullets, shredding the air along the boulevard, as the creature swung its head towards them.

Malvery turned about, swinging Grudge's weight with him. He could hear the soldiers coming up behind him. He swung back and stared across the width of the boulevard. The space between was busy with invisible agents of death. From the Juggernaut, he heard the now familiar squeal of gathering power.

No help for it, he thought, and he wondered how a man who was once so in control of his own life had become a man accustomed to having no choice.

Then he ran out onto the boulevard.

He looked neither left nor right. His brow furrowed, he stared only at his destination, as if by force of will and concentration he could deny the bullets that whined past them. He ignored the surprised shouts of the soldiers behind the barricade; he closed his ears to the rising sound of the Juggernaut's cannon. He forged doggedly onward, fast as he was able, and that was all.

Seconds passed. Impossible seconds, as he hurried across the boulevard. Then the Juggernaut's squeal fell silent, and there was only the clatter of the machine gun.

He surged forward, forcing one last effort from his legs. His balance failed him and he tripped, but Grudge's weight on his back bore him onward, and he stumbled into the shelter of an alley. He twisted as he fell, and the Century Knight came off his shoulders. They fell in a heap with Malvery on his side. He looked back in time to see his pursuers rushing headlong out of the alley he'd come from. Then the Juggernaut unleashed its beam down the length of the boulevard, and all was screaming whiteness.

Malvery threw his hands over his head as the boulevard detonated. Flame boiled up in the mouth of the alley. A wall of baking air blasted both him and Grudge, sending them sliding away. Chunks of ceramic rained down, falling to the ground around them with solid, bone-breaking thumps.

Then, quiet.

Malvery raised his head. His glasses fell off his nose and cracked on the ground. His skin burned, his lungs and throat felt scorched, and he was weak with shock and fatigue.

'Damn,' he croaked in amazement.

Slowly, painfully, he climbed to his feet. He shuffled over to Grudge. The Century Knight was still unconscious, but otherwise unhurt.

Malvery would have dearly liked to lie down and sleep right there. Instead, he hauled Grudge into a sitting position, put him over his shoulders, and stood up.

The landing pad was close now. It didn't feel like he could possibly make it. But he was going to try anyway.

There was no help for it.

'There she is!' said Crake, pointing up into the starry sky.

And there she was, coming in over their heads: the *Ketty Jay*, slipping through the moonlight towards the landing pad.

Frey hefted his pack and allowed himself a private smile. She was coming in with no lights and her thrusters on minimum. Jez might have been out of it ever since Gagriisk but she still understood the need for stealth without having to be told. He could kiss that woman sometimes, assuming she wouldn't mutate into some bowel-loosening horror and tear out his kidneys.

The Juggernaut hadn't seen her. It was marauding away in a different direction with the landing pad to its rear. There had been a minute or two when it had come uncomfortably close, and Frey had half-expected it to destroy the treelike structure out of spite. But it seemed more interested in attacking people than indiscriminate destruction, and the landing-pad had been deserted then.

He wondered if it would take more of an interest if it saw an aircraft there, and hoped he wouldn't have to find out.

Ugrik was jogging along beside them, his pack troubling him not one bit. Crake was unencumbered. They'd been forced to leave some of his equipment behind for the sake of speed, since they didn't have time to pack it up. Crake had protested furiously until Frey promised to replace whatever was lost. Between that and a new Firecrow, it would wipe out all the gains he'd made from betting on Harkins in Crickslint's race, but Frey would have promised him anything to get him moving.

They made good speed and were panting by the time they reached the base of the landing pad. There had been a certain amount of backtracking to negotiate the demolished streets, but Frey counted them fortunate to have made it the whole way without coming across a live Sammie. Still, he reckoned with all the bad luck that had come his way lately, he was owed a bit of the other kind.

'How do we get up there?' asked Crake, who was annoyingly spry. Ugrik had barely broken a sweat, either. It was only Frey who seemed to be suffering, which was frankly a bit unfair.

He looked up the shaft of the structure to where it split out in white branches to support the flat top. 'Isn't there an elevator?' he asked plaintively.

'Power's out,' said Ugrik. 'Bet there are stairs, though.'

There were. By the time they reached the top, Frey was starting to wonder if it would have been preferable to have died at the hands of the Iron Jackal.

They emerged on to the landing pad to find the *Ketty Jay* idling there with her cargo ramp open. The sweet, wonderful *Ketty Jay*. And the rest of the crew were already here! He saw Bess disappearing inside, and Silo was ushering Pinn and Ashua after her. Between them they carried Samandra Bree, who was hopping on one foot.

Silo spotted him and hurried across. Frey was doubled over, sweaty and parched.

'You ought to wear your damn earcuff every so often, Cap'n,' Silo snapped. 'Had no idea where you got to.'

'Yeah. Uh... sorry,' said Frey, who was a bit surprised to be spoken to that way. Then Silo hugged him, and Frey hugged him back.

Crake's gaze had drifted to the *Ketty Jay*. 'I might just go and... Er...' he said, walking off.

Frey stopped him. He shucked off his pack and shoved it into Crake's arms. 'Here. You can carry it the rest of the way,' he said. 'Now go see your bloody sweetheart.'

Ugrik cackled and followed Crake into the *Ketty Jay*, having a conversation with himself as he went.

Frey rolled his neck and massaged his aching shoulders. 'Everyone alright?' he asked.

Silo's eyes flickered downward for an instant. 'Not everyone. Grudge went missin'. The doc went off after him.'

Frey stared at him. *And you let him?*

'Only so much you can do when a man's determined, Cap'n,' Silo said.

He suppressed the urge to anger. Silo was right; there were plenty of times when he'd failed to stop his crew doing something daft. This wasn't the military. And if he chewed out Silo, he'd be undermining the authority he'd given him as first mate.

'Alright, well, it's done,' he said neutrally. He looked out from the edge of the landing pad. From up here the bowl of the oasis sloped away from them, and he could see the whole of the city. Most of it was in darkness and concealed by the trees, but there were still electric lights in the excavation zone, showing up swathes of ruination left by the Juggernaut. The night was lit up by a fresh string of explosions as the creature unleashed its beam again.

Silo touched his ear as if listening. 'Yeah, he here, Jez. Still not wearing his earcuff, though.'

Frey took the hint and dug it from his pocket. 'I'm here, Jez. What's up?'

'What's *up*?' she cried. 'Have you *seen* that thing? Can we get out of here yet?'

Frey's face became hard. It could only be a matter of time before the Juggernaut spotted them. And if it chose to fire that terrible beam their way, they'd never have time to take off before the landing pad collapsed.

Silo had the same thought. 'What you wanna do, Cap'n?'

What *did* he want to do? The brief hours of freedom he'd felt in the desert were long gone now. The burden of captaincy was on him again. The doc could well be dead. Waiting for him might easily doom them all. But abandoning Malvery? Could he really do that, even for the sake of the others?

No. If there was one thing this whole sorry mess had taught him, it was that they were meant to stick together. His crew had followed him here, even after he tried to leave them behind. He couldn't repay that loyalty by betraying the doc.

'We wait,' he said. 'And hope to damnation that thing doesn't spot us.'

As if it had heard him, the Juggernaut turned its face towards them.

'Cap'n?' said Silo. 'Think it just did.'

Frey felt a pit open in the bottom of his stomach as he felt its blank, dreadful regard. There was the eye that he'd seen buried beneath the foliage when he'd first arrived with Ugrik. He'd thought it was a statue then; but it was something much, much worse.

'Hate to say this,' said Jez, 'but we really gotta go.'

'Not yet,' said Frey. 'Fill the aerium tanks so she's right on the edge of floating. Keep the thrusters hot and—'

'I'm doing that already!' she interrupted. 'It's coming this way!'

There was no mistaking its interest now. It was moving closer with slow, deliberate strides.

'Anyone notice how long it takes between cannon blasts?' Frey asked.

'Huh?' said Jez.

'Well, it could level this place with that beam, but I haven't seen it fire twice in a row without a pause, and the beam never lasts. I think it needs time to charge.'

'I haven't been here long,' said Jez. 'A few minutes, maybe. But it's fired twice in that time.'

Frey chewed his lip. *Damn it. Damn it.*

'We can move off and circle,' Jez suggested. 'We could come back.'

Frey's gaze went to the power station. The hourglasses to either side were heavily cracked now. Lightning flickered over the whole building, and it was surrounded by a cloud of pallid gas that glowed with bruised colours.

If they took off, they wouldn't be coming back. He knew that, even if Jez didn't. He had as much responsibility for everyone else on board as he did for Malvery, and he had to get them safe.

Frey was a man accustomed to riding his luck. But this time, the stakes were so, so high.

'Cap'n, we got to go,' said Silo, his voice low and hard.

'Not yet!' he replied stubbornly.

'He ain't comin'.'

Frey bit back a retort. Whatever he said would sound childish. He knew the doc wasn't coming. He just wanted to believe that he would.

The Juggernaut stamped onward, crushing the rubble of the shattered city beneath its feet. Its blank face was a mask of dispassionate brutality. How could Frey stand up to that?

They had to go. Waiting longer would be suicide. Frey opened his mouth to say it, but other words appeared in their place.

'*Will someone bloody help me?*'

If Frey had believed in any kind of god, he'd have fallen to his knees and thanked them then. But damned if that wasn't *Malvery's* tortured bellowing.

The doctor appeared at the top of the stairs, rising step by clumping step, with Colden Grudge slung across his back. His face and pate were bright red, giving him the appearance of a tomato with a moustache. He took one last step, tipped the Century Knight off his back and collapsed.

Frey and Silo ran to them. Malvery was wheezing so hard that Frey seriously thought he was having an attack of something. 'Stairs…' he whispered, with a noise like a deflating tyre.

There was no time for sympathy. Silo picked up Grudge and Frey dragged Malvery to his feet. 'The box…' Malvery gasped, pointing down at a small metal box the size of a book that he'd dropped when he fell. Frey picked it up without really looking at it, and then they carried their casualties as fast as they could towards the cargo hold.

A shrill sound drifted through the night. An ascending squeal. In the distance, the Juggernaut was powering up.

They were met at the cargo ramp by Ashua, who had left Samandra with Pinn, and by Crake, who had evidently thought better of facing her right now. 'Move it, Jez!' Frey yelled as soon as his feet touched the ramp. 'Move it *now!*'

The *Ketty Jay* lurched forward, screeching on its skids. The thrusters kicked in before the aerium lift could get it off the ground. Frey shoved Malvery into the waiting arms of Ashua and Crake; the three of them staggered into the hold and fell flat. Silo, unbalanced by the sudden movement of the aircraft, dumped Grudge to the ground and then fell over as well. Frey tottered and clutched one of the ramp's hydraulic struts to stabilise himself.

The floor tipped as the *Ketty Jay* rose, pushed forward and banked all at the same time. The inert bulk of Colden Grudge slid up against one wall and stayed there. Silo got his arm through one of the restraining straps they'd used for the Rattletraps. Ashua and Crake were pulling the gasping doctor to safety as best they could.

Beyond the ramp, the world tilted and swayed. The landing pad disappeared behind them, swinging out of view. Suddenly Frey was standing on the edge of a dizzying drop.

He couldn't reach the lever to close the ramp. Jez could have closed it from the cockpit, but he didn't want to distract her. And besides, despite the danger, he didn't *want* it closed. There was something unbearable about the thought of shutting himself in and waiting in the gloom to be destroyed. If they were going to die, he'd rather see it coming, and end it with his eyes open.

The Juggernaut slid into view, behind and beneath them. Frey couldn't hear it over the roar of the thrusters, but he could see the sparkling aura around its tube of a mouth as it sucked in that deadly energy.

He could see when the lights went out.

'Jez!' he cried. 'Now!'

The *Ketty Jay* banked hard, and Frey's sight was filled with the blinding white of the beam weapon. It scorched past aft of them, missing them by mere metres. He clung on for his life as the *Ketty Jay* accelerated and climbed. As the dazzle faded from his vision he saw the excavated zone spreading out below him, and the dark city beyond it. The Juggernaut scraped the night sky with its beam, chasing after them like a searchlight, but the *Ketty Jay* was too fast and the creature couldn't sustain it for more than a few seconds. As suddenly as it came, the beam was gone, and they were out of the Juggernaut's reach.

The wind rushed around him, flapping his hair against his face as the buildings dwindled. He saw that one of the hourglass towers of the power station was collapsing, tumbling in slow motion. Lightning forked out from it in great crooked fingers, darting across the oasis, a wild barrage striking everywhere. He sensed what was coming, and braced himself.

A few more seconds. Just a few more seconds.

And now he could see the whole of the oasis, the excavated zone a patch of light and flame in the dark, and all of it surrounded by the endless moonlit desert.

That was the last he saw of the city before the power station exploded.

The detonation was silent. There was no shockwave, no debris flying this way and that. A great blue sphere of lightning swelled up from a single point to encompass the whole of the oasis, sending fizzing arcs writhing across the desert in all directions. It dissipated as it expanded, fading faster the larger it grew, until its outer edge was only an afterimage burned on Frey's retinas.

It was a peaceful, deadly obliteration.

When the lightning had reduced to crawling sparks, all that was left was a blackened crater in the desert. The oasis and everything in it had entirely disintegrated.

Sensing that the danger had passed, Jez eased off on the thrusters, and the wind calmed a little as they slowed to cruising speed. Frey gazed down at the crater, and he was taken with a huge sense of calm. It was over. It was finally over.

Crake stumbled across the hold and joined him, hanging on to another hydraulic strut. He, too, stared down into the crater, but there were tears glittering in his eyes.

'Did we just destroy a ten-thousand-year-old Azryx city?' he asked, with a wobble in his voice.

'Yeah,' said Frey proudly. 'I think we just did.'

FORTY-EIGHT

━━━❖━━━

OFF THE HOOK—SAMANDRA AND CRAKE— PATRIOT'S CHOICE—LIMBO

The moon looked down on them from a sky full of stars, benevolent now. It washed the desert with a serene light. Frey stood on the softly whispering sand, Silo by his side, and let his eyes roam the maze of cracks on its surface, the great dark rift that crossed it aslant like a wound.

The *Ketty Jay* was behind him, her tail towards him, cargo ramp open. Nearby was the Tabington Wrath that the Century Knights had arrived in, a state of the art heavy fighter craft that didn't look quite so impressive when it was half buried in a dune. Between them, his crew had built a campfire and lit it with the remainder of Professor Pinn's Incredible Flame-Slime. Malvery, Pinn and Ashua were singing lustily, passing a bottle, already drunk off their arses. Ashua and Malvery were leaning on each other like old comrades. Crake sat with them, taking a sullen swig now and then, sunk in gloom. He'd taken the annihilation of the Azryx city rather hard.

It probably wasn't the wisest thing to do to light a fire out here where it could be seen for kloms in any direction, but he reckoned they deserved to blow off steam. The Sammie patrols surely knew to stay well clear of this place in case they dropped out of the air. Besides, if they hadn't seen the city go up, they certainly wouldn't spot a little fire.

As to the others: Jez was nowhere to be found, Harkins was in the infirmary recovering from a mysterious knock to the head, Bess had gone to sleep in the sanctum, and Ugrik was wandering about arguing with himself. They were all safe and more or less alive. Relief soaked into him slowly, easing his tired body and tired mind. If just one of his crew had died on his behalf, he'd have been a lesser man for it. He was glad to have avoided that grief.

'You did good, Silo,' he said.

'You too, Cap'n.'

Samandra came hobbling over, using a rifle as a makeshift crutch. Malvery had set and splinted her ankle, and she carried that foot gingerly, wincing with the pain.

'Think we're about ready to go,' she said. 'Long as I don't try anything clever, I reckon I can still fly her with a broken paw.'

'How's Grudge?'

'He's awake. Bit embarrassed at what happened. Lost a few brain cells, but he won't miss 'em.' She gave Silo an unfriendly stare. 'I got your doc to thank that he's here at all.'

'So I'd say this kind of cancels out that whole incident at the Mentenforth Institute, wouldn't you? I mean, it's only you and Grudge that know it was us that trashed the place, and we *did* lead you to some highly important military secrets which were—'

'Yeah, yeah,' said Samandra. 'You're off the hook. *Again.* Besides, I guess that relic we were chasin' got destroyed along with everythin' else, right?'

Ugrik, who was passing within earshot, cackled to himself.

'Yes,' said Frey, grave and earnest. 'Yes, it did.'

Samandra touched the brim of her hat. 'Well then, I guess this is it. I got a whole storm of shit to deal with back home. Least, I will when the Archduke hears about what went down here.'

'You'll keep my name out of it, though?'

'If you like. And there I was thinkin' you enjoyed all that newfound fame o' yours.'

Frey wrinkled his nose. 'Fame isn't really for the likes of me. Think I'd rather just be quietly rich.'

'Yeah, well, good luck with that,' said Samandra, turning to go.

'Hey, wait. You're not done yet,' said Frey. He raised his voice and waved at the campfire. 'Crake! Get over here!'

'Oh, for rot's sake…' Samandra began, but Frey held up his hand.

'You, stay. We've just done a damn great service for our country, not to mention saving your partner's life, so the least you can do is—'

'You ain't no patriot, Frey! You were out to save your own pretty arse!'

'And you were out to kill it. Look where we ended up. Ah, Crake!' he said, as Crake approached in a nervous hurry.

'Miss Bree,' said Crake, with a charming note of terror in his voice.

'Mr Crake, of the golden tooth,' said Bree poisonously. 'I do believe we've met.' Crake's face collapsed.

'Now, now, fellers,' said Frey. 'This won't do. I pride myself as someone with a little experience of the delicate business between a man and woman. Let me give you a few plain truths so you can stop bloody well dancing round each other.'

Crake looked horrified. 'Frey, don't!'

Frey ignored him. 'This man,' he said, thrusting a finger at Crake, 'is the bravest man I ever knew. Not a few hours past he took on a daemon which made that thing which smashed up the city look like an enormous pansy. He's a loyal friend, loyal as you are to the Archduke no doubt, and what he did to you he did to save my life. Just like you'd kill any one of us to save your Archduke's life. Isn't that right?'

'Damn straight,' Samandra said, glaring at them all.

'So quit this wounded pride bullshit, Samandra. You know what duty means. It means doing stuff you don't always want to. Now I know for a fact that this feller is crazy over you—'

'Frey!' Crake nearly screamed.

'—and I know damn well you got a flame for him too, so will you both just be adults, kiss and make up?'

Crake, who had been staring aghast at Frey, now switched his gaze to Samandra to see what her reaction was to all this. She was looking at him thoughtfully, searching his face. Finally she sighed.

'Can you hold this?' she asked Frey, handing him the rifle she was using as a crutch. She hopped forward a step and put her hand on Crake's shoulder to steady herself. 'Why don't you go ahead and hold me by the waist, Crake? I'm a bit uncertain on my feet.'

Crake looked like he barely dared to touch her, but he put his hands on her waist as instructed, wearing an expression of bewildered hope.

'Just let me get my balance here,' said Samandra, tottering. 'There,' she said. Then she unleashed an uppercut to Crake's jaw that lifted him into the air and dumped him on the sand, out cold.

Frey gaped at her as she hopped back and reclaimed her crutch. 'Thanks,' she said. 'When he wakes up, tell him he can call on me.

He knows where to reach me, though I daresay I'll be fairly busy for a while.'

'Uh,' said Frey, looking at the unconscious daemonist. 'Alright. I'll do that.'

'Good seein' you again, Captain Frey,' she said with a wink. She nodded at Silo with markedly less affection and then made her faltering way back towards her aircraft.

'Smoothly done, Cap'n,' said Silo.

'You can't say I don't know women,' Frey said, gleefully ignoring the sarcasm.

Pinn and Ashua were rolling around laughing by the fire as Malvery wandered over, swaying slightly. He looked strange without his omnipresent glasses perched on his blobby nose. 'Anything I can do?' he asked, eyeing Crake, who was beginning to stir.

'Give him a hit of grog. He'll be fine.'

'Right-o,' said Malvery. 'Hey, Cap'n. Can I have a word in a minute?'

'Course.'

'Just let me deal with this feller first.' Malvery took Crake by the arms and began to drag him away, the daemonist slurring nonsense as he went.

Frey watched them go. A cool desert breeze skated across the grey dunes. 'Poor Malvery,' he said. 'Dunno how he's going to take it when I kick Ashua off.'

Silo turned his head and gave him a flat look.

'Well, she can't stay,' said Frey. 'I'll drop her wherever she needs to go, but I can't have her on board.'

The rest didn't need to be explained. The fact that he was attracted to her, however improbably, was enough to guarantee a messy ending if they were around each other for long enough. Frey had learned through bitter experience that liaisons with the crew were a bad idea, but he didn't trust himself in the face of temptation.

'You made her a deal,' said Silo.

Frey rasped. 'A deal doesn't mean anything if it's made under duress. We needed those supplies. Your people did.'

'Ain't right, Cap'n.'

'Since when did you care? She's not crew.'

'She saved my life, I reckon. Didn't have to do nothin', but she did. Look at her with the Doc. Crake likes her too, I see that. She wants to be here, an' I say she's earned her place.'

Frey shook his head. 'Can't, Silo. You know how I am. We've got a good balance here. She'll ruin it.'

'You want me as first mate, she stays.'

Frey turned to him in surprise. 'You learned to throw your weight around fast enough, didn't you?'

'She got value, Cap'n. And the whole crew heard you make that deal.'

Frey rubbed the back of his neck with his hand and spat. That was true. Breaking a business deal with a stranger was no problem, but that girl had insinuated herself too much already. If the crew started to doubt his promises, it would all be over.

'Bollocks,' he said angrily.

'That the kind of "bollocks" a man say when he agree, or when he don't?'

'The first kind,' Frey replied, sulking. 'Damn, I'm gonna regret appointing you as my conscience.'

Silo chuckled. 'That what I am?' he asked. Then, seeing Malvery heading over, he slapped Frey on the back and slipped away into the *Ketty Jay*.

Frey was still cursing to himself when the doctor arrived, a small metal box in his hand. Frey recognised it as the one he'd been carrying earlier. This time, he saw the emblem on its side: the sigil of the Awakeners.

'Tell me you didn't find that in the city.'

'If I did, it'd be a lie,' said Malvery.

'You looked inside?'

Malvery showed him the broken lock.

'What's in there?'

'Orders. The kind for deliveries. Can't read the Samarlan, but they're printed in Vardic too.'

Frey felt a weary resignation creep over him. He'd had enough tonight. New revelations had lost their power to shock.

'The Awakeners are getting supplies from the Sammies?'

'Best I can make out, they've been getting supplies of *Azryx tech* from the Sammies.'

Frey did his best not to think of the implications. 'What you wanna do?' he asked.

Malvery was turning the box over and over in his big hands, studying it uncertainly. 'Thought I'd maybe give it to the Century Knights. What do you think?'

'It'll mean civil war.'

'And if I don't, and it turns out to be civil war anyway, the Archduke ain't gonna have any idea what the Awakeners have in store.'

'On the other hand,' said Frey, 'this whole squabble between the Archduke and the Awakeners might blow over.'

'Maybe,' said Malvery, though he sounded even less convinced than Frey was.

Frey regarded him for a time before he spoke. 'I'm not a man with a surplus of loyalty to my country, Doc. It's kicked me in the pods too many times for that. Seems to me this is the kind of decision a patriotic man should make.'

Malvery harrumphed and looked away with a furrowed brow. Then, as if reaching some kind of resolution, he gave a quick nod. He tucked the box under his arm, dug into his pocket and pulled out a medal. Frey stared at it as he pinned it to the breast of his sweat-stained shirt.

'Since when did you have a medal?'

'Had it a long time,' said Malvery. He straightened up and firmed his chin. 'Just didn't deserve to wear it till now.' He gave a smart military salute, arm held across his chest. 'Cap'n.'

Frey did his best approximation of a salute in return. 'Do what you have to, Doc.'

Malvery held his gaze a moment longer, then strode off towards the Century Knights' aircraft. Frey thought he walked lightly for a man carrying the future of his country.

'What now, Cap'n?' said a voice above him, making him jump. He looked about for the source, and found Jez. She was crouched on the *Ketty Jay*'s tail assembly, gazing out across the desert. The sight of her unsettled him. Sitting up there, poised as she was, she looked like something wild.

'Come down if you wanna talk to me, Jez,' he said, in an attempt to reassert himself after his fright. 'I'm not yelling at you up there.'

Jez dropped off the tail of the *Ketty Jay*, plummeted ten metres and landed beside him in the sand with a soft *poomph*.

Frey swallowed back an oath and looked around to make sure neither of the Century Knights were about. 'Can't you be a *bit* subtle?' he said. 'I'm doing my best not to let the whole world know you're half Mane.'

She regarded him with an amused light in her eyes. No, not just amused: her eyes were *literally* brighter than before, reflecting the moonlight like a wolf's.

'There's something different about you,' he said.

'Just the same old Jez,' she assured him with a grin. And maybe it was the way she smiled, or a trick of the shadows, but damn if her teeth didn't look *sharper* than before. Then she tilted her head slightly, and the shadows moved, and it was as if he'd never seen it. 'Well? We got a plan?'

'The plan is to get out of this desert, for a start,' he said. 'Get as far as we can tonight, hole up and hide from Sammie patrols, then back to Vardia when night falls again. I need to buy Crake some new gear and Harkins a new Firecrow and then...' He shrugged. 'We'll see what's what.'

'Sounds good,' she said. 'I'll get on it.' She took a few steps towards the cargo ramp, then stopped and looked back over her shoulder. 'For what it's worth, Cap'n. I'm sorry. About her.'

He gave her a wan smile. 'No need,' he said. 'I'm not done yet.'

She raised her eyebrows in disbelief. 'You don't stop, do you?' She half-turned back towards the *Ketty Jay*, and paused there. Frey saw moisture glittering in her eyes. 'She's lucky to have you, Cap'n,' she said. And then she walked away, before he could ask her what she meant by that.

He wandered a little way from the aircraft and the fire, kicking sand as he went. Behind him, he could hear Pinn and Ashua drunkenly taking the piss out of Crake for getting punched out by a woman. It brought a little smile to his lips.

Dark times lay ahead, there wasn't much doubt of that. But he'd seen dark times before, and he'd survived them. Back in those days, he'd faced the world alone. Not any more, he thought. Those days were gone.

His crew had been more than just a crew for good while now, but it had taken the events of the past few days to make him truly believe that. Maybe he'd just needed them to prove it to him. A lifetime of insecurity and impermanence had left him as a man who didn't come easily to trust.

But he was sure of them now. After everything they'd done for him, for no profit and at great risk to themselves, he could scarcely be otherwise.

The glue that held them together was equal parts necessity, friendship, habit and desperation. But it held them fast, and Frey was deeply grateful for it. The men and women of the *Ketty Jay* were the only family Frey had ever had. And just like a family, they were exasperating, hilarious, fractious, affectionate, demanding, self-sacrificing, and he couldn't get rid of them if he tried.

He looked up at the moon, and felt as if he was teetering on the edge of something. Change was coming. Soon it would be time for the heroes to stand up and be counted.

Well, let them. Frey had his own concerns. He had a crew that had just swelled by one, and they'd be looking to him to steer them through the chaos ahead. That was his task. That and something else.

He looked at the silver ring on his finger.

He'd made a vow. A promise of atonement. And he meant to keep it.

He'd gone some way from the *Ketty Jay* now, and the immense quiet of the desert surrounded him. Here was limbo, a pause in the world. He was nowhere, and that suited him fine.

There was a feeling that had been growing inside him, for how long he didn't know. He wasn't sure what it was, but he'd had his suspicions from the start. Now he needed to name it, to try it on his tongue to see if tasted false. He didn't dare do it in front of anyone else, so he said it to the moon instead.

'I love her.'

He stood there a long while, letting the sound of it run through him. Finally, he nodded to himself.

'Right,' he said. 'There it is.'

Then he turned and walked back to the *Ketty Jay*, and his friends, and whatever would come after.

ABOUT THE AUTHOR

Chris Wooding grew up in a small town in Leicestershire, where not much of anything happened. So he started to write novels. He has written sixteen books, which have been translated into twenty languages. He is the author of the *Broken Sky* series, which has sold over 200,000 copies in the US alone, and *The Haunting of Alaizabel Cray*, which won the Silver Smarties award.

Chris has travelled extensively round the world, having backpacked all over Europe and North America, Scandinavia, South East Asia, Japan and South Africa. He also lived in Madrid for a time. When he wasn't travelling on his own, he spent his twenties touring with bands and seeing the UK and Europe from the back of a van. He now lives in London.